A KENNI LOWRY C(

BOOKS

DIGGIN' UP DIRT
BLOWIN' UP A MURDER
HEAVENS TO BRIBERY

TONYA
KAPPES
.COM

Southern Hospitality
with a Smidgen
of Homicide

BY
TONYA KAPPES

TONYA KAPPES
WEEKLY NEWSLETTER

Want a behind-the-scenes journey of me as a writer?
The ups and downs, new deals, book sales, giveaways and more? I share it all! Join the exclusive Southern Sleuths private group today! Go to www.patreon.com/Tonyakappesbooks

As a special thank you for joining, you'll get an exclusive copy of my crossover short story, *A CHARMING BLEND.* Go to Tonyakappes.com and click on subscribe at the top of the home page.

DIGGIN' UP DIRT

A KENNI LOWRY MYSTERY BOOK 7

CHAPTER ONE

"That youngin' is meaner than a rattlesnake. Givin' Woody's boy and Woody a fit all these years and the state pen let him out on good behavior." Mama elbowed me in the back of the Cottonwood Funeral Home. She nodded towards Woody's grandson, Rich Moss. "Done gone and put his daddy in the grave. Wouldn't doubt it if he put Woody there too."

"Mama," I scolded her, though I had heard that Lenora and Woody's only child had died of alcoholism years ago. "Don't be speaking like that in front of the dead," I warned and looked around to make sure no one else heard her. "Don't be throwing that bad juju on me." Chills ran up my spine and down my arms. "See what you did?" I lifted my prickly arm up to her face.

"Don't be looking at me in that tone." Mama's right brow rose, in her forewarned you're-never-too-old-for-a-scolding Mama way.

"Ah oh." Myrna Savage, owner of Petal Pushers Florist, scurried past with an open heart-shaped mold of white roses and white carnations. You know, one of them that's laid at the gravesite. "Someone is walking on someone's grave." Her brows lifted when she noticed me rubbing the goose-bumps away.

"Hhhmmmm," Mama's lips pinched, her nose curled. "Who sent those?"

"Lulu McClain." Myrna shrugged and headed straight up the middle row where Woody Moss laid in corpse, a polite, Southern way of saying "dead". "Vivian, you sure are slacking."

Mama watched in jealous silence as Myrna shimmied past the mourners and placed Lulu's wreath at the foot of Woody's casket.

"Which one did you send?" I asked, knowing the bigger the flower arrangement, the higher up in the social ladder you'd be that week.

"It doesn't matter," she quipped. "Where is your father? I'd like to get a seat up in the front before Preacher Bing starts the service."

"I'm sure he'll be here soon." I sucked in a deep breath and wondered the exact same thing about Finn Vincent, my boyfriend.

The sound of curtains opening just behind the casket caught my and Mama's attention.

"Well if I ain't seen it all," Mama gasped.

"What on earth is it?" I asked about the big window behind the curtains, which had a car pulled up to it looking right at Woody Moss.

"Max Bogus has gone on and put a drive-up window in the funeral home." A look of disgust drew across her face. "Next thing you know, he'll have the corpse sitting up, arm attached to a string like a puppet and waving somehow."

I wasn't sure whether to laugh or groan. It was the strangest thing I'd ever seen, especially when a bus from the Cottonwood Acres Rehabilitation Center pulled up and flung open the van door. The rehab center was more than just for therapies, it also had a small emergency room on one side. We didn't have a hospital in Cottonwood and Dr. Camille Shively wasn't open 24/7. We needed something for quick emergencies so that we don't have to drive forty-five minutes to Clay's Ferry or a bigger city close to Cottonwood.

"Well, I'll be damned," Mama spat with disbelief.

"Now, Mama." I patted her arm to get her to calm down. "Woody died in the rehab center and probably made some new, elderly friends that wanted to pay their respects."

It was like a train wreck. Mama and me couldn't stop gawking at the blue-hairs, the elderly, as they took a gander at Woody in his casket through the window.

"I'm telling you right now, hand to God," Mama said and flung her hand up in the air, "If you let them do that to me, I swear I'll haunt you the rest of your life."

"Just like Poppa?" I asked.

"Huh?" She jerked around and looked at me.

"Joking," I said, a flat out lie.

My Poppa, Mama's dad and retired sheriff of Cottonwood, hadn't necessarily been haunting me, but since I took over as sheriff, Poppa was my guardian angel deputy from the great beyond. Poppa only showed up when there were murders in Cottonwood and I was happy to report he wasn't here today so that meant not only that Woody wasn't murdered, but no one else in Cottonwood was either and all was well in our little town.

"If you'll excuse me, I'd like to go give my condolences to the family," I finished my sentence and wanted to get away before Mama realized what I'd said and questioned me further.

No one knew about me having the ability to see and visit with Poppa except Duke. Duke was my hound dog and I was sure he wasn't going to say anything to anyone.

Mama didn't say a word, so either she was still stewing over the fact that Lulu McLain was about to replace her on the top rung of the social status or that Daddy was late. Mama didn't like to be late and that rule included Daddy, who she claimed was a direct reflection on her as well.

I didn't want my relationship with Finn to be like that, so I took a deep breath and knew he'd get there when he could make it. After all, he was holding down the sheriff's department while I'd taken the time to come here early and shake a few hands.

As the sheriff of Cottonwood, I had to attend every funeral, birth, baptism, and whatever else appealed to a family. It was, after all, those times that the good citizens of Cottonwood would remember when it was time for me to run for re-election in a couple of years. Little did I realize that my saturated childhood of "yes, ma'ams" and "no, sirs" along with the bit of Jesus that Mama beat into my head would all come in handy when running for an election around here.

Or maybe it was all the lessons, Lordy the lessons—piano lessons, tap lessons, modeling lessons, clogging lessons and handwriting lessons to mention a few—that added to the lunacy of my life that made me want to follow in the footsteps of my Poppa and not become a debutant, which was the very thing Mama was trying to make out of me by doing all them darned lessons.

The funeral home was packed, which made sense because funerals, weddings, and births were a big deal around these Kentucky parts. Woody Moss's funeral would be front page news on the Cottonwood Chronicle and talk of the town down at Ben's Diner. That's just how it was.

"Hi, do." I nodded and shook hands as I weaved in and out of the crowd, making my way back to the room where Woody's family had gathered.

Even though I knew some of them people didn't vote for me, I always remembered what Poppa would say to me during his election years – "Don't cost a nickel to be polite."

Having good manners and giving social grace was just a way of life around here. I was sure that was why there were so many people at funerals whether you knew them or not.

There was a line of folks giving their condolences and telling stories they had with Woody. I couldn't offer any of those. He was an elderly man I really didn't know other than when I talked with him about my Poppa's reign as sheriff. Everyone loved Poppa. I made my way to the back of the family room and stood in line with my hands folded in front of me.

"I told you I did the best I could." I couldn't help but overhear a young woman with shoulder length blonde hair, fair skin, and the brightest of red lipstick on her lips talking to the man Mama pointed out as Woody's grandson, Rich.

"If I find out that your best wasn't good enough, they'll be hell to pay," Rich said to her through gritted teeth as she jerked her arm out of his grip.

"Is everything okay here?" Not that I wanted to butt my head into someone's business, but if I noticed it was a little more physical than an average conversation, I'd stick my nose into it.

"What's it to you?" Rich snarled.

"I might not have my plain brown uniform on," I pulled back the blue blazer I was wearing and exposed my five-point star sheriff's pin clipped to the waist of my blue skirt. "But I'm Sheriff Kenni Lowry and I sure hope nothing is going to get ugly while we are all paying our respects for you grandfather." I took it a step further. "Especially since I understand you

6

were let out of prison early for good behavior. What I just heard didn't sound like good behavior."

"I'm fine." The girl shook her head and turned, going back out of the room.

"Is she fine?" I didn't take my eyes off of Rich Moss.

He stood about five feet nine. Thick as a tree trunk and the blackest eyes I'd ever seen. He had olive skin and a five o'clock black shadow that seemed to be going on ten o'clock but wasn't yet a full beard. He was shiny bald on top and had a tattoo that went from ear to ear around the back of his head.

"She walked out without a limp, didn't she?" His cold words were like an ice cube dripping along my spine.

"I don't expect to have any trouble out of you while you're in town, right." It wasn't a real question. It was a threat, so he'd know that type of activity wasn't welcomed here.

"Yes. Sheriff woman." His lips curled up at the edges with a hint of laughter in his voice.

"Sheriff Lowry," I corrected him and turned around when I felt someone come up behind me.

"There you are," Finn said and smiled. "I saw Vivian and she's not in a good mood. She's trying to get Myrna to go back to Petal Pushers and make a bigger flower arrangement." He laughed and suddenly stopped when he noticed I'd not tried to grin. "What's wrong?"

"I'd like you to meet," I started to introduce him to Rich Moss, but Rich was gone. "Never mind." I shook my head and glanced around the room, not seeing him anywhere. "Did you get your parents settled?"

"You are going to have to brace yourself," Finn warned with a slight smile, guiding me out of the room. "They drove their RV and parked it right in front of Mrs. Brown's house."

"Oh no," I groaned, looking up at my six-foot-tall boyfriend, and knowing that she would be calling as soon as she saw it.

Mrs. Brown was the neighbor between my house and Finn's house.

"I already went to see her and told her they'd only be here for a few days so they can meet you." He melted my heart right there in the funeral home. His big brown eyes had a spark in them like a little boy that'd gotten exactly what he'd wanted.

Finn had wanted to me to meet his parents, who lived in Chicago, for a year or so now. We'd even made huge plans to be there over Christmas until the biggest blizzard to ever hit Kentucky blew in the day we were supposed to board the plane. Now, Mama was thrilled to death that it'd snowed to high-heaven because that meant we were stuck with her for Christmas.

"Where are they now?" I asked about his parents and pointed to a couple of seats near the front of the casket.

"They are at my house visiting with Cosmo." He put his arm around me. Cosmo was a cat that'd he'd taken in after the owner had gone to jail when we'd arrested her for murder. See, he had a huge heart and I loved him for that. "Really, waiting until they meet you tonight."

"I hope Mama acts her best." The thought of Mama hosting Finn's parents made me anxious.

I pointed to the empty seats next to us since Preacher Bing had taken his spot at the podium. I'd have to give my condolences to Woody's family a little later.

After the funeral, I made a quick exit out of the funeral home and let Finn do the repass, the after-funeral home festivities.

Howllll, howwwwwl.

Duke was happy to see me when I'd gotten back into the old Jeep Wagoneer after the funeral. Rarely did I ever go anywhere without him. He was known as my deputy dog. He'd even been given an award for actually taking a bullet for me once.

"I know, Duke," I confirmed how good the fresh air felt and smelt with the wind whipping in through the windows. Not to mention how good it felt to get the stink off of me from all the flowers at the funeral home.

There was no way to describe just how much I hated the smell of flowers at a funeral home, so much so that I'd changed my will to include no flowers at my own funeral. They reminded me of death. My Poppa's funeral was filled with flowers and that was a horrible time for me. The memory was still unsettling.

Duke's long bloodhound ears flopped in delight outside the window. His tail, that I was sure had a string to his heart, wagged in delight. There was nothing like when summer was right around the corner in Cottonwood.

"What a day for a funeral." The sun was hanging bright in the early afternoon. The only real thing I had to do was meet my friends at my house so they could help get me all prettied up to meet Finn's parents. That wasn't until late this afternoon.

Before I could turn the Wagoneer north of town after I'd pulled left on Main Street, Mama was calling.

"Before you start lecturing me," I answered the phone because I knew she was mad that I'd sent Finn to the repass after the funeral instead of me. "I have to get all gussied up for tonight when you meet Finn's family."

That would get her attention.

"You know I love when you actually dress in something pretty, but you've got to get over to Woody Moss's house," there was a bit of panic in her voice. "His house has been ransacked. Like someone has broken in and stolen stuff."

"Be there in a minute." I tried to tell her.

"You know, I bet that Rich did it. He was in jail. And I bet he'd steal a wreath off his Meemaw's grave." Mama had decided to throw her two cents in.

"Mama, I'm on my way." I clicked off the phone instead of listening to her theories, though they probably weren't too far-fetched. But there was no way I was going to tell her that.

I jerked the wheel to turn the Wagoneer around, all while grabbing the old-time beacon siren from under my seat and licking the suction cup before smacking it on the roof.

Rowl, rowl, Duke howled along with the siren. One of his all-time favorite things to do.

"Hold on, buddy," I warned and pushed the pedal to ground. "Who on earth would target the house of a dead man?" I'd heard of criminals perusing the newspaper to see who was dead and break into their house, but not on the day of the funeral.

"Rich Moss."

I was certain.

CHAPTER TWO

F inn had everyone out of the house, including Mama, who I could tell was already giving him fits. Her head was bobbing and weaving, trying to look around Lenora Moss's clothesline which Finn had used to make a makeshift police line, while he talked to Lenora herself.

I reached out the window and took the siren off the top of the roof and flipped the side switch off before I stuck it back under my seat. Duke jumped across the seat, ready to bolt out my door.

"Not now, buddy." I put my forearm up, reaching over to the seat to grab my bag off the floorboard. "I'm sorry," I said in a sad voice and gave him a good scratch behind his floppy ears. "I'll just be a few minutes and then we can get you to the station.

No matter how much I tried not to make eye contact with Mama, it didn't prevent her from high-tailing it over to me along with the Henny Hens following closely behind her—the endearing name I'd given Lulu McClain, Viola White, Ruby Smith and Camille Shively. All of Mama's closest friends and all of different ages and stages in life, bonded by the gift of gab and gossip.

"Kenni, now we've got food in the oven that's got to feed all these people who have come to pay their respects to Woody Moss." Mama nodded while the Henny Hens did the sign of the cross, which made no sense because none of them are Catholic. "Now, look at Lenora over there. Do you think she's in any shape or form to be dealing with this right now?"

Without a word, because I had to choose them carefully when I talked to her, I glanced over her shoulder to look at Lenora. It was a combination of worry and sadness that I saw on her face. She probably didn't care two-bits about people coming to the repass. From what I'd heard at my weekly girl's night out Euchre game, Lenora had spent many sleepless nights watching over Woody and the infection in his knee after his knee replacement. I'd also heard it got into his blood stream, which ultimately lead to where we were today. His funeral.

"Where are you going?" Mama asked when I took a few steps past her.

"Mama," I jerked around. "I'm going to talk to Lenora, that's what I'm going to do."

"Well," Mama gasped. "I'll never understand that girl," she told her friends. "I gave her life and everything she ever wanted. And that's the respect I get."

The Henny Hens all nodded in agreement, which only gave fuel to her fire.

"I hope you have ten youngin's like you one day," she hollered after me.

She exhausted me. But wait. . .I knew there was more.

"You're gonna wish you were nicer to me when I'm dead and gone."

There it was.

I swear Mama took a class in how to make your daughter feel guilty and she was driving the train to Guiltville, if there were such a place.

"Hi, Lenora." I looked between her and Finn. "I'm sorry you're having to deal with this."

"Thank you, Kenni." She nodded, her eyes red around the edges. "Can you just please tell everyone they can leave? Finn said this could take a few hours to fingerprint." The corners of her mouth dipped into a deep frown. "Why would someone do this?"

"I'm not sure" were the only words of reassurance I could offer. "I'm going to go inside and turn off the oven. Mama said they'd had stuff in the oven."

"Yes. She and the girls have been so kind. They left the funeral right before they put his casket in the hearse to go to the cemetery to get things

11

started." She sighed. "I told your mama and them to go in through the back door since it leads right inside the kitchen. It wasn't until Lulu's water dropped that she noticed the rest of the house and told your mama."

I tried not to laugh at the look on Finn's face when Lenora said Lulu's water dropped.

"Bathroom," I said to him. "Lulu had to go to the bathroom."

"Huh." He looked like he was still confused but continued to write. He looked up at me. "Can I speak to you for a second?" He nodded to take a few steps to the side, out of Lenora's earshot.

"Sure. Lenora, are any of your family members here?" I took a quick look around and noticed Rich wasn't here, but the girl he'd talked to was.

"Not unless we have more kin than I know. Rich is the only kin and he'll be back shortly." She looked over the crowd and I did too.

Ben Harrison, owner of Ben's Diner, had been stopped by Mama and appeared to be taking in everything she was saying. When he caught my attention, I could see the amusement on his face. He gave me the finger gesture to come over there.

"Finn and I are going to go in and clear the scene. I'll make the announcement that we aren't going to have the repass and you appreciate all of their support." I patted her on the back.

I stepped up on the porch and clapped my hands several times before the murmurs stopped.

"I'm sorry to inform you, but in light of what's taken place here today, Lenora is honored and blessed to have you all as friends and neighbors, but will be cancelling the repass," I spoke loud enough for everyone to hear.

"Sheriff?" Ben Harrison yelled even louder. Ben actually looked nice in his suit, making him barely recognizable without his usual flannel shirt, jeans, and baseball cap on backwards. "If Lenora doesn't mind, I'd like to offer to have the repass moved to the diner where all the food will be on the house."

Ben Harrison was such a stand-up guy and if he weren't my best friend since grade school, I might've had a big crush on him, but he was dating my girl-best friend, Jolee Fischer, and I couldn't be happier for them.

I glanced over at Lenora and she nodded with a grateful grin on her face.

"Okay," I nodded, "Y'all heard Ben."

The mourners clapped and all shook Ben's hand before they got into their cars or started walking down to the diner, which was only a street over on Main Street.

Mama still wasn't satisfied and by the determined looks on the Henny Hens, they felt the same. Only this time, Betty Murphy, my eighty something year old dispatch operator, had joined them.

"I'll head into the house to turn off the oven while you deal with that angry mob." Finn was talking about Mama. He kissed my forehead.

"Mama, who is that girl and boy over there?" Not that I truly needed to know, but it was the blonde I'd overheard Rich Moss giving all sorts of grief to at the funeral home.

"That boy is Sebastian Hughes." Ruby Smith took the liberty to answer the question, which wasn't unusual since her nose was literally stuck in everyone's business.

She owned Ruby's Antiques on Main Street, across the street from Ben's Diner. There wasn't a day that went by where Ruby wasn't showing up at someone's house, garage sale, or estate sale for a good piece to put in her shop. Ruby knew everyone in Cottonwood and who all was kin to who. Cottonwood had been growing and even as sheriff, I still didn't know everyone.

"He is one of them ambulance workers. His mama hails from Versailles. I don't know where the rest of his kin are. My grandmother grew up there with his grandmother and grandfather. From what I'd heard, his mama was married twice," Betty Murphy had taken over the conversation.

It wasn't enough just to tell what Sebastian did in Cottonwood, we had to learn the man's lineage.

"But I think his daddy was murdered across the river after a man shot him. Now don't quote me on that, but I was down at Tiny Tina's and I swear I heard Tina mention it. Then again, Tina had put that big blower over my curls and that thing blows right up in my ear." Betty pushed her glasses up on her nose.

"I recall that there was a sister too." Mama tapped her finger on her temples. "Billie…" she hesitated and snapped her fingers.

"Mmmhmmm," Ruby's lips snapped together while she ho-hummed.

"Billie Belle Short. She was married to Kenneth Asher before he died in that car wreck on the way to Clay's Ferry."

"Poor girl," Mama gasped.

"Don't you 'poor girl' Billie Belle. She blossomed like a Morning Glory soon after and married up again. If I remember correctly." Ruby added that last sentence to cover her tracks in case the big tale about this poor Sebastian was wrong. "That Billie Belle was so cheap the Dollar Tree wouldn't sell her."

The tale probably was wrong at some point in all of that and none of it I would remember.

"Here y'all are gossiping at a funeral," I couldn't help but to remind them.

"Honey, we ain't gossiping, we are discussing prayer concerns and right now, there's a lot of people right here that need that." Mama lifted her chin and looked around.

"To answer my original question, he's an EMT worker?" I asked, looking at Betty.

"Yes." Betty nodded. "And the girl, Avon Myers. She is a physical therapist at Cottonwood Acres Rehabilitation Center where Woody died."

"Isn't it strange to die in a rehab?" Mama asked. "Since Woody was there undergoing physical therapy for his hip replacement."

"Heart attack." Ruby nodded her head. All of them bowed their heads as if they were honoring a moment of silence. "Or infection or something. Either way. Sad."

That was how rumors got started. They had no clue how Woody had died, though I knew it was the infection from the knee replacement, but I didn't bother telling them. They'd get my words mixed up in there somewhere and end up having poor Woody die of cramps or something off the charts like that.

"Avon Myers?" I wanted to confirm in case I decided I wanted to ask her about Rick Moss's words to her at the funeral home.

"Yep. Her Meemaw and Peepaw live over on Sulphur Well..." Ruby started in on who Avon was kin to. "Not sure where her parents live."

I didn't bother to stick around to listen when I noticed Finn was standing at the Moss's front door. There were a pair of purple gloves on his hands and shoe covers on his feet with black dust powder around the edges.

"Did you find some fingerprints?" I asked and opened my bag where I had booties for my shoes and gloves.

"Lenora gave me a list of things that could be missing, but she's not sure. The only thing she said that was for sure was missing are the special cuff links from the jewelry box on her bedroom dresser." Finn waited until I got my shoes covered before he had me follow him into the house. "It's like they threw the cushions off the couch and a few things on the floor, but only really got the bedroom."

"Mama said things were ransacked." I glanced around the family room that was right inside the door.

"I'd say untidy is more like it. The kitchen wasn't touch." Finn said over his shoulder as we walked down the hall to the bedroom to see the most damage. "She and Wood slept in different bedrooms."

I walked in and all the contents of her dresser and the drawers were thrown all over the bed, which had the covers messed up and the mattresses all side-goggled. The jewelry box Finn had mentioned was tall with two doors. There were a couple of hooks to hang necklaces and two pullout drawers underneath for ring and earring storage. Most of the jewelry looked to be costume. The Mosses didn't have a lot of money. They were simple folks that kept to themselves.

I unzipped my bag and took out my camera.

"Here, I'll take the photos while you go talk to Lenora." Finn took the camera.

It was so great having a deputy that understood exactly what was needed without me having to tell him or needing to do all the work myself. He'd been like that since the first time I laid eyes on him.

When poor Doc Walton, Cottonwood's local doctor, had been murdered in his own home, my only deputy was retired and off on a vacation with his wife, leaving me a one woman show. I didn't mind, only the fact of the matter was that Doc Walton wasn't the only crime happening in Cottonwood. I had to call in a Kentucky State Reserve Officer from Frankfort.

Kentucky was made up of mostly counties, which meant we had more sheriff departments than police stations. Cottonwood is a county, and since we're a small community, it wasn't uncommon to have one deputy and one sheriff. In a time of need, as sheriff I was able to get help from the state reserve where they'd send me an officer to use on a case. That's when Finn Vincent walked into my life, did an amazing job, and filled not only the available deputy position but also my heart.

Like most women who guard their heart, I wasn't receptive to his Northern ways or all-business attitude since he was from Chicago, but I warmed up to him after a while and saw he was a good officer.

Here, he was clicking away and placing crime scene tags all over Lenora's room while I went down to ask her my own questions.

She was sitting at the old wooden kitchen table with a cup of coffee in front of her. There was a blank look on her face like she'd been kicked down a few times. I didn't blame her.

"Lenora, Finn said there's some cuff links missing." I sat down next to her and put a hand on her back. "Can you tell me about them and why someone might want them?"

"Not that Woody was flashy, but his grandparents had gone to New York City when he was a kid. They'd spent almost every penny they had taken with them and brought him back a pair of simple gold-knotted cuff links." She laughed with a soft look in her eyes. "Woody said that a young boy never wanted cuff links."

"I don't blame him," I agreed.

"He said that his grandparents were so proud of them when he put on his Sunday's finest that next weekend," she was referring to his church clothes. "He loved how happy he made his grandparents and took really good care of those links. He only wore them on special occasions. He loved telling that story to our boy and Rich." She grinned at the fond memory. "As we got up in age, we figured we'd better make a will and since we only have one boy, we knew he'd get them. Wally Lamb said we needed to get the value." She shook her head as she talked about the local lawyer. "He insisted we take them over to Hart's Insurance. Woody did. Come to find out," she drew back, her eyes grew big, "them little knotted cuff links were worth a pretty penny."

"Really? How much?" I listened really carefully because obviously someone knew they were worth something.

"One thousand and seven hundred dollars. Now, his grandparents didn't pay that much, but they knew they were worth something. That's why they told him not to get rid of them." She looked over her shoulder when Rich and another man walked into the back door of the kitchen from the outside. "Have you met our grandson, Rich?"

"Not in a formal way." Our eyes met, and we stared at each other for a second.

"He's a good boy." Her face lit up with pride, something only a grand-mother would say. It was the first time I'd truly seen her smile since I'd gotten here. It was my cue not to continue to question her in front of him, given his history and all.

"Finn and I will finish up here and let you have your house back." I stood up and patted her on the back. "Are you going to go over to Ben's Diner?" I asked about the repass that'd moved there.

"Yes. Rich is going to drive me over. I'm not sure I can walk that far right now." She glanced over at her shoulder at her grandson.

"Yep. We sure are." Rich smiled.

Something behind his grin told me not to trust him.

CHAPTER THREE

"What are you thinking?" Finn asked me once we got back to the sheriff's department, where I'd changed my clothes back into my brown, unflattering, sheriff's uniform.

It'd taken us a couple of hours to finish scouring the crime scene which was limited to Lenora's bedroom.

"I'm thinking Rich Moss is the burglar and I've got Scott Lee following him around town." I looked at the big white board where I had started putting the clues with cuff links as the header along with a photo of them that Lenora had given me that was in with the insurance estimate and another estimate from Ruby Smith.

"Lee's almost better than Duke," Finn joked and unscrewed the lid off the dog treat jar on his desk, flipping one in the air at Duke who was lying in his bed next to my desk.

Without missing a beat, Duke's snout flung up in the air, catching the treat.

Scott was sent to our department over Christmas break when Finn and I were supposed to take a much-needed vacation to his hometown in Chicago. That's when the snowstorm hit and we didn't get to go. Scott Lee stuck around and really helped us out. I'd been in front of the city council meeting a few times asking for more funding to add him to our department.

Since Cottonwood was growing, so was the crime and it was almost too much for me and Finn to get to all of it.

There was a meeting in a couple of days to announce the final decision and I hoped they'd do the right thing by letting us keep him on as a deputy.

"Apparently, Rich has been in jail for something and they let him out on good behavior to come to the funeral." It only made sense. There'd not been any other burglaries in town.

"Do you have a date of birth?" Finn headed over to his desk and sat down at his computer. "I can find him in the database."

"I don't, but I plan on going back over to see Lenora in the morning. I've got a bunch of questions to ask her and him." I tapped the board with the dry-erase marker. "Think about it. Rich just got out of jail. He has no money. Lenora said that Woody loved telling Rich the story. I overheard him practically threatening the physical therapist from the rehab center and then he disappeared from the funeral." I said. "That was probably around the break-in."

I walked over to my desk, unzipped my bag to get out my notebook where I'd made bullet points of Lenora's statement.

"There doesn't seem to be anymore items taken but those," I finished saying and put the notebook back on the desk, taking another look at the white board.

"You are very observant." Finn clicked away on the computer. "Richard Moss," he said, and the back light of the monitor twinkled in his eyes. "Write this down."

He leaned closer to his computer and I walked back over, picking up a marker. The printer started to run.

"Sheriff," Scott's voice came over the walkie-talkie strapped on to my shoulder of my uniform.

I pushed the button on the side of the walkie-talkie. When it beeped, I knew we were connected.

"Go ahead," I said.

"I just want to let you know that I've lost Rich and that guy he's with. I think they caught on to me." He clicked off.

"Okay. Stay put. I might have another place for you to go." I clicked back off, thinking about my next move with Rich.

"Ten four," he said back.

"I just printed his file and photo. Richard Moss theft charges include felonious assault." Assault with a deadly weapon. "Assault with intent to commit great bodily harm less than murder," he read as I wrote. "One was a pawn shop and another a jewelry store."

"A jewelry store and we have missing cuff links." I wrote down everything he was saying and took a few steps back from the white board.

"Jewelry and guns are number one items burglars look for when casing a home." Finn made a great point.

"We have the facts and the arrests that show Rich likes to knock off jewelry stores. It looks like we have a very good tie here. But probably not enough to get an arrest."

"It's enough for a warrant to find the cuff links." Finn's brows lifted. He was waiting for a signal for me to give him the okay to call the judge after hours to get the paperwork.

"Get it. I'll tell Scott to go pick it up and head over to Lenora's house to look around in Rich's stuff," Kenni said.

It was a first step to getting Rich back in jail where he belonged.

"While you do that, I'm going to head home and grab a quick shower before I meet you and your parents at my parents' house." My stomach flipped at the thought.

"They are going to love you," he looked up from the computer with a big grin on his face.

"Let's hope so." I sashayed over to Finn and gave him a kiss. "If not, we are in trouble."

"Why?" he asked and narrowed his eyes with a slight chin turn.

"There's no way it could ever work out if your parents didn't like me." My words made him laugh. "I'm serious, Finley."

"Finley?" He pushed back off his desk and folded his arms across his chest. "You are serious."

"I am." I leaned my hip on his desk. "My parents love you, but I'm a girl. It's the mamas of boys who seem to have the difficult time with the girlfriends. I could never date a man whose parents don't love me."

"You have nothing to worry about. What's not to love?" He grinned before he tipped his head to give me a kiss that told me everything was going to be okay.

The reassurance instantly made me feel so much better.

"I'm sure I'm just worried over nothing." The truth of the matter was that I had a weird feeling. My gut was generally right in the case of investigations and all things that came to run the sheriff's department. "I'll see you in a few." I patted my leg. "Let's go, Duke."

The sheriff's department was located in the back of Cowboy's Catfish, a restaurant located in downtown Cottonwood on Main Street. It might seem strange to some people that the department was located in a restaurant, but not in a small Kentucky town like Cottonwood. Our department, until recently, had consisted of Betty, Finn, and me. We had three desks and one cell. There wasn't need for much more, even though Deputy Scott Lee had recently been helping out and would hopefully soon be full-time.

The only problem having the department in the room behind Cowboy's was that my stomach always rumbled to life. Parking on Main Street instead of in the alley behind the department probably wasn't the best thing to do today since I'd been trying to hold off on eating until we had supper with our parents.

"I've got you something good to take home," Bartleby Fry, owner of Cowboy's Catfish, hollered out from the grill when Duke and I walked by. "I put it under the heat lamps."

He gestured to the brown to-go bag sitting on the ledge where he puts the finished plates for the waitstaff to take to the customers.

"You are the best." I probably shouldn't have taken it since I was having supper, but it would keep until tomorrow. Besides, I wasn't in the mood to tell Bartleby my plans. Not only would I never hear the end of it, the rest of the town would know before I'd even made it home. Gossip spread that fast around these parts.

"Don't you worry." He shook his spatula at Duke. "I've got a few things in there for you too."

Duke tossed his ears back, threw his nose up in the air and let out a howl.

"You're the best." I grabbed the bag on the way out the push-through door between the kitchen and the restaurant.

"Sheriff," Mayor Chance Ryland and Polly, his wife, greeted me from one of the windows next to the front door.

"Mayor." I nodded at him. "Polly."

"Kenni." Polly's pretty little button nose curled, and her blue eyes stared at Duke. "Must he go everywhere?"

"He must." I smiled. "Have a great night."

"Are you off for the day?" Chance pulled up the sleeve of his suit and looked at his watch. "Isn't it a bit early? I mean, you could be working on the Moss break-in."

"Don't you worry. Now that I've got Deputy Lee, he's taking a lot of the load off of me, so I can make sure the rest of Cottonwood is safe." I drummed my fingertips on their table and gripped the to-go bag.

"Isn't he temporary?" Polly asked and grinned, showing her big, white horse teeth. To this day I still think Beverly Houston, our local dentist, should be scolded for giving Polly those big veneers.

"Hopefully after this week's council meeting, he'll be hired on as full time." I gave the table one last tap. A hard tap. "I've got to get going."

"Sheriff," Chance stopped me. "I wouldn't count on the council approving your request."

One thing I didn't let people do was walk all over me. I was the first woman sheriff in Cottonwood and when I was first elected, all the men in the town tried to walk all over me, but I stood my ground. Mayor Ryland was the worst one. He was as cold as a cast iron commode. I was on a mission to warm that seat up.

"We haven't had the meeting yet," I reminded him and gave a good Baptist nod. "Have a good evening."

"You keep me up to date on the Moss break-in," he called after me as I pushed through the door.

CHAPTER FOUR

There was a crowd gathered around the big RV parked in front of Mrs. Brown's house.

I pulled the Wagoneer into my driveway and took a few minutes to watch as the neighbors gawked. It wasn't like they'd never seen a big RV, but we've never had one this nice parked on Free Row. And I couldn't help but wonder if they were trying to figure out how to steal the wheels.

Free Row was what I affectionately called Broadway Street, which is where I lived. The small ranch homes used to be very nice back in the day. I had fond memories of visiting and staying with my Poppa on this very street and in this very house when he was alive.

Since then and through changing times, Broadway had become home to lower income families that were on commodity cheese, and a few who cheated the system to get on welfare and food stamps when they didn't need it.

It was a well-known fact that my neighbors weren't on the higher social ladder nor did they care to climb it.

"Y'all go on and be on your way," I said and walked around the RV, trying to be as quiet as I could. I didn't want Finn's parents to see me in the ugly brown sheriff uniform that was clearly not made to fit a woman's body. It certainly wasn't how I wanted them to meet me. "I hope you are neighborly enough to Deputy Vincent's parents while they are visiting," I said, more a warning than a polite statement.

There were a few grumbles and mumbles, but they shuffled away.

I pulled my phone out of my back pocket and flipped through my contacts to call Finn.

"Miss me already?" he asked in his sultry Northern accent.

"Free Row is enthralled with your parent's RV," I said and ignored how he answered because it didn't seem right to talk that way when I was going to tell him about his parents.

"You mean how they've got them surrounded?" He laughed. "Mom already called. She said that she felt safer in Chicago."

"Good golly, are you serious?" I asked and unhooked the gate door leading to my backyard.

Duke took off like a lightning bolt to the far end of the fence to grab his tennis ball. He ran back, dropping it at my feet.

"They'll be fine. I told them to lock the door and we'd take care of it. I assured them they are harmless," he told me while I played fetch with Duke. "Did you see them?"

"No. I tried not to make too much noise because I want to look pretty and make a good first impression." I looked over my shoulder towards the gate when I heard the lock flip up. I waved in Katy Lee Hart and Tibbie Bell, two of my best friends who insisted they come over and get me all gussied up for the big family meeting. "Katy and Tibbie are here. I'll see you at Mama's soon."

"Don't be late." Finn was one for punctuality. He didn't like to be late for anything. "Remember, I love you and that's all the matters."

"I love you too," I clicked off and that weird feeling tugged at my gut.

"What's wrong?" Katy's brows furrowed as she looked me over.

She had several plastic dry-cleaning bags over her one arm. She shifted her hips to the side and put her hand in the crease of her thick waistline.

Tibbie was a little bit on the larger size but gorgeous. She had beautiful blonde hair that was parted to the side, falling down her back in loose curls. She was an event planner.

"Nothing's wrong." Tibbie's bright smile reached her hazel eyes with a sparkle. She pulled her long hair around one of her shoulders. "She's meeting her future in-laws. She's nervous."

"In-laws?" I asked and threw Duke's ball really far one last time before we went inside. "Aren't we rushing things?"

Not that I didn't want to get married, I was already married to my job, but it was that I didn't let myself think too much about the future. I took each day as it came.

"Nope." Tibbie walked into the kitchen door behind me and threw her purse on the kitchen table, pulling out a notebook. "Your mama's already got your wedding planner started."

Tibbie was an event planner and everything down to our weekly Euchre games were planned out.

"She even has the dresses you'd look great in." She flipped the page open to a hand-drawn bride that looked awful similar to me. The bride had the same honey blonde hair with golden highlights like mine and my green eyes. "That's one of my faves." Her shoulders drew up around her ears as her voice had escalated.

"Seriously. The more you feed Mama, the worse she gets. Just get me ready for tonight." I looked over the table where Katy had laid out the different outfits she'd pulled from her Shabby Trends collection. "Focus on tonight."

"Personally," Katy grabbed a long, elbow length, light brown sweater with a loose turtle neck and a darker brown pair of skinny jeans that looked more like slacks. "This is what I thought would go perfect with your hair color. Plus, these are slim fitting and give a little in case you have a little too much cake."

"Are you referring to my happy fat?" I questioned her.

"Well," Katy laughed, knowing that was what Mama had called my weight gain since I'd been dating Finn.

Happy fat. Whoever heard a such? Mama claimed we gained weight when we were happy because we'd enjoy food and drink more with the one we love. So what if Finn and I loved to eat good food and wash it down with a beer?

"The three-quarter length sleeves and turtle neck are perfect for the slightly chilly spring night weather." Tibbie made a good point. "And you better hurry up because I think I just heard the RV rev up."

The three of us jumped up and ran to the family room, which was in the front of my house. We stared in silence trying to get a good look at Finn's parents before the drove off.

"Did you get a look at them?" I asked.

"You've never seen a picture of them?" Tibbie asked.

"Never. I've met his sister and he has a picture of her in his wallet, but there's no other photos in his house." I shrugged and ran back into the kitchen, pulling off my uniform and tugging on the clothes.

Katy adjusted all the clothes, putting the seams in all the right places, while Tibbie put makeup on me. I'd never been one to fuss over my appearance. It was simple to throw my straight hair in a ponytail for work and to not wear makeup. Recently, I'd discovered the power of a good lip gloss and mascara for a quick fix when Finn started working at the department. Still...fully fixing my hair and putting on makeup everyday wasn't in my routine.

"You need a little pop of color for you lips." Tibbie rolled up the tube, exposing a darker shade of brown. "Here." She shoved a hand mirror in my face. "You look amazing."

"Maybe you should rethink your beauty routine every day." Katy peered around the mirror and smiled. "You really are gorgeous."

"Are you telling me that makeup makes me gorgeous?" I jutted the mirror towards them.

"You're naturally pretty, but the makeup is stunning." Tibbie took a step back and smiled at her masterpiece: me.

"I've got to go if I'm going to drive the back roads to beat Finn's parents." I pointed to Duke. "Can you please throw some kibble in his bowl and let him out one more time before you leave?" I grabbed my purse and flung it over my shoulder. "Jolee is going to stop by later and let him out on her Meals on Wheels route."

My true best friend was Jolee Fischer. She owned On the Run Food Truck and also used the truck to deliver meals to the elderly and shut-ins. Mrs. Brown, my neighbor, was a Meals on Wheels recipient. Duke loved

Jolee and she loved him. He'd much rather be in her food truck all day than sitting in the office, so he was used to her coming over.

Tibbie and Katy waved me off, shoving me out of the door.

Today was a good time to know all the back roads and short cuts to my childhood home.

There was a bit of relief when I turned into my parent's driveway and saw no sign of the Vincent's RV.

Mama was peering out of the living room window that was in the front of the house. When I waved, she drew the curtain shut as if she didn't see me. She was probably as nervous as I was.

Mama was the typical Southern woman who took pride in her house and all the things she had in it. There was no doubt in my mind she was going to pull out all the stops to impress Finn's parents.

I wouldn't even put it past her to have the Sweet Adelines, her local singing group, there to give a small concert. Thankfully, I didn't see any of their cars, but I still wouldn't count it out just yet since it was still pretty early in the night.

I walked up to the modest three-bedroom brick ranch and stood under the long-covered porch in the front, looking both ways down the street before I walked into the door.

"Hello," Mama chirped with delight. She gasped when she truly looked at me and clapped her hands together. "You do love me," she gushed and walked around the foyer with me in the middle taking a good long look at me.

"Not that I care what they think about my looks, but I didn't want you to look bad," I lied. I totally cared what they thought of me or I'd not told Finn how important it was for them to like me.

"Is that my baby?" Dad asked, walking into the foyer.

Unlike my mama, he walked over, towering over me, and gave me a hug.

"Don't she look beautiful?" Mama gushed with a squeal.

"She always looks beautiful." Dad's brown eyes squinted as the smile crossed his lips.

"She looks especially pretty with the makeup and hair fixed and new clothes." Mama had no idea when to just leave well enough alone. She had to beat it to death.

"Viv, she's always pretty." Dad knew that Mama could take anything a little too far. "Let's just have a good night."

"I was just sayin'," she snarled.

"Thank you, Mama." My brows rose in hopes my response would stop her. "Daddy, I see you've been to Tiny Tina's."

"Doesn't it look gooooood?" Mama had a way of drawing out her vowels with her Southern drawl. She racked the edges of Daddy's freshly dyed black hair that used to be a little more salt and pepper. Now there was no salt to be found. Not even a speck.

"It looks great." I laughed and jumped around when I heard the rumblings of the diesel RV. "How do I look?" I turned to Mama, my heart beating a million miles a minute.

"Oh dear," Mama's smile said it all. Everything she'd been waiting for all her life. Her daughter asking her for fashion advice. "You are nervous, child."

"How do I look?" I asked with an exhausted sigh.

"Amazing." She pinched a smile, drew her shoulders back and flung the door open in a big Southern and dramatic way. "Welcome." She drew her arms wide open.

Over her shoulder, my eyes caught Finn's and we smiled. I sucked in a deep breath knowing he was here and everything was well with the world. For now.

After Mama did her formal introductions and finally moved over for the Vincent's to enter the house, we made our way to the back deck where Mama had a bar set up with every sort of cocktail mix you'd think of.

Shelby and Clay Vincent.

Shelby had her hands folded down near her rounded belly. She wore a black mid-calf dress with small white polka dots and a pair of black loafers. Clay wore a button-down shirt, a pair of khakis, and a pair of brown loafers without socks. A very preppy thing to do and I was sure Mama was all over it, which made me think she was for sure going to have Daddy stop wearing socks by this time tomorrow.

Both Finn's parents had nice thick hair, both grey, which also told me Finn was going to be grey at some point in his older years. Not me. Mama didn't dare have a grey hair or she'd plucked them out one at a time. Still,

Finn's dad was definitely a silver fox and by the way Mrs. Vincent had a hold of his arm, she knew exactly what she had.

They looked like a Shelby and Clay and I gave them a sweet smile, hankering for that drink to help me get over my nerves. I could feel Shelby's eyes giving me the so this is what my son has been dating onceover. Not sure if it was a good look, since I'd not learned to read her but fully intended to do so tonight. Instead of pondering on it too long, I decided to leave well enough alone and try to engage in conversation best I could.

Clay had taken dad's advice and opted for a Kentucky bourbon and coke while Mrs. Vincent picked a red wine from one of Kentucky's up and coming vineyards. Mama took the time to explain to Mrs. Vincent how the limestone, which made the Kentucky bluegrass so famous, was also what made the grapes for wine in Kentucky so amazing. I wasn't quite sure if she was serious, but I believed her.

"How do you think it's going?" Finn cozied up next to me on the outside couch and asked the question I'd been wanting to ask him for the last ten minutes.

"I think they're getting along and Mama sure is acting her best." I looked deep into his eyes and smiled, wondering why on earth I'd been so nervous about this night. "How do you think they're going to feel when they see me outside of all this makeup and fancy clothes?"

"They're going to love you just like I love you." Finn's lips met mine and for a minute we were lost until Mama cried out.

"Children," she scolded. "We are still your parents. Where are your manners?"

"I think it's sweet." Mrs. Vincent said with a refreshing tone. "I love seeing my Finny so happy."

"Finny?" I drew back and laughed.

"Mom." Finn shot his mom a look.

"I know you told me not to say anything, but he's our little Finny." She winked. I instantly loved her.

She was nothing like Mama. She didn't try to fix his collar like Mama tried to fluff up the turtleneck on my sweater. When I got up, she tugged the edges of it down over the waist of my pants. Every time I slapped her hand and gave her a look.

"Thank you for calling him Finny in front of me, Mrs. Vincent." I couldn't stop from laughing. Finn had turned red and I'd never seen him in such a flutter.

"Shelby, dear. Call me Shelby." She winked and smiled. Her Northern accent caught her name.

"Supper is ready." Dad had been making steaks on the grill.

"Supper?" Shelby asked with a laugh.

My head snapped towards Mama. Mama's face reddened.

"Supper. Your food." Mama's tone took a nose dive and fast.

"Dinner, dear," Clay spoke up and tapped Shelby on the forearm.

"We call dinner, supper. Dinner is lunch to us. It's a Southern thing." My shoulders shrugged. A subtle gesture for Mama to not go off.

"Yes. It's Southern. Finn has really been taking to our ways." Mama repeated, her face softened. "Let's have dinner now."

Mama looked at me and I mouthed "thank you" so she'd know I'd noticed the extra mile she'd just taken to reel in her crazy.

"That was a close one," Finn whispered in my ear from behind after we'd followed our parents into the house. "I was afraid Viv was going to give Mom a lesson in Southernisms, though I did warn Mom how she could be."

"How she could be?" I flipped around. My brows furrowed when I noticed Preacher Bing had showed up. "What does that mean?"

"You know how your mom can be." His brows formed a V and I didn't like his tone. "Preacher Bing," Finn said after he looked up from our little chat. "What are you doing here?"

"Per Vivian's request, I've come to give the blessing over this fine union." Preacher Bing's large forehead crinkled when he smiled. His hair was thin and brown, just like the suit he had on.

My jaw dropped and so did Finn's. Mama looked between us.

"I'm sure your parents don't mind." Mama stood over the kitchen table where all the food had been laid out. "Preacher Bing." Mama called him over and did some quick introductions. "I do hope you'll stay for supper after the blessing."

"I'd love to," his deep voice started to escalate like it did at the Cottonwood Baptist Church right before he was going to ask the congregation to bow their heads to pray. "Shall we bow our heads?"

Then the shit hit the fan.

Mr. and Mrs. Vincent, like robots, drew their hands up to their heads to do the sign of the cross. Like real Catholics, not like Mama and her group of Henny Hens. Then my "ah-oh"

meter went off.

Preacher Bing started to say a prayer just as the Vincent's, along with Finn, started to say the Catholic food blessing.

"Dear Father, we ask that you..." Preacher Bing started.

"Bless us, O Lord, and these, Thy gifts, which we..." The Vincent's stopped.

Religion, I groaned. Why had I not even thought about religion?

"What's going on here?" Mama opened her eyes and looked around.

"We are Catholic," Shelby said, gesturing to Clay and Finn.

"We are Baptist," Mama said with a loud Southern, prideful voice. "And as for our house, we will let Preacher Bing say the blessing over this fine meal my husband and I prepared for you."

"I think that we will thank the Lord by the sign of the cross." Shelby did a very dramatic sign of the cross with very pinpointed pronunciation of her words. "Father. Son. Holy Spirit," she spat.

"If you think my daughter will ever become Catholic for a boy and his family," Mama started to say before she began to bounce on her toes. A hissy fit was bubbling up inside of her. "Then you have another thing coming, Finn Vincent!" Mama jabbed her pointer finger her way.

"If you think our grandchildren are going to be raised Baptist and have supper, you've got another thing coming, Kendrick Lowry!" Shelby screamed at me. "Let's go!" She grabbed Finn with one hand and Clay with the other, jerking them out of the kitchen and out of the house with a dramatic door slam.

I knew I should've listened to my gut.

"Mama, what's wrong with you? You made them feel as welcome as an outhouse breeze." I stomped out of the kitchen. "No one will ever marry me with a Mama like you!"

My exit was equally as dramatic as the Vincent's and my door slam was even louder. I'd done it plenty of times before and knew exactly how to do it right.

31

CHAPTER FIVE

There was no sign of the RV on Free Row when I got home. Finn's Dodge Charger wasn't even in his driveway. I'd spent all night tossing and turning in the bed, listening for any sounds of cars coming down the street, while trying to tame the catfish supper Bartleby Fry had sent home that hadn't set well in my belly. Who knew what time I'd finally fallen asleep.

It was a call on my phone that woke me up. Figuring it was Mama, since she'd had all night to think about her ridiculous behavior, I took my time to reach across my bed and get the phone off the bedside table.

"Hi, Toots," I answered knowing it was weird that Toot's Buford would call me so early and on my cell. "Are you okay?"

"I'm fine, but I found something strange when I pulled into work." She worked as a cashier at the local Piggly Wiggly grocery store.

"What's that?" I asked and patted Duke, who was still snoring next to me in the bed. I sat up at the edge of my bed and patted him awake.

He crawled his front legs to the edge of the bed and slid them off until they hit the floor where he pulled himself into a big long stretch before dragging his back legs off the bed.

"I pulled in and there's an RV with tags from Illinois in the parking lot. I think someone is living in it and parked it at the Piggly Wiggly," she started to describe it as I walked down the hallway. "Now, Kenni. They can't be goin' and parkin' in the Piggly."

I let her ramble on knowing it was Finn's parents, though I wasn't going to mention it to her.

"It's not unusual for RV's to pull off when the drivers are tired at night. I know that Walmart lets them do it in their parking lot, but I'll be sure to check it out," I told her and opened the back door to let Duke rush out into the backyard to do his business.

There was a bouquet of daisies, a cup of coffee from Ben's and a note on the porch table.

"Do you think they're here to rob me? I mean, I'm the only one opening up this mornin'." Her voice cracked.

"No. I'm sure you're fine. In fact," I probably shouldn't have told her because it'd be all over town that Finn's parents had moved their RV to the grocery store parking lot.

But after seeing the little love note Finn had left me this morning, I knew I needed to make things right with his parents.

"Don't worry. It's only Finn's parents. I told them to park it there for the night. Do you mind taking them a few delicious donuts from your bakery and some hot coffee after you get settled in?"

Piggly Wiggly might be a grocery store, but they did have a great in-house bakery, and it made me wonder if the Sweet Shop had hurt their business.

"Why, I love that," Toot's tone picked up and she sounded more at ease. "I'd love to. I'll be sure to keep an eye out and when I notice them shades go up, I'll hurry out there."

"Thanks, Toots. I owe ya." I hung up the phone knowing I'd regret saying that to her one day. Though it was just an expression on my part, but knowing Toots, she'd cash on in the favor owed.

While Duke ran around and sniffed out all the new smells since last night, I sat down in the chair and took a sip of coffee while I read the note. Finn had written that we weren't our parents and we were the ones to make the decision about what religion we'd be when the time came. There were a few I love yous and even some x's and o's to end that gave me a big smile.

It was his day to do the early shift of driving around town and making sure all was right with Cottonwood before the day got started. Since Scott had joined us, we made it a point to meet at the department every morning around eight a.m. for a quick briefing of the day.

The bouquet of daisies, my favorite flower, looked beautiful in the middle of my kitchen table. I stood there with a hip leaned up against my counter staring at them while Duke ate his morning kibble.

I didn't waste too much time basking in the joy the flowers gave me before I got ready for work in the usual brown sheriff's outfit and filled a bag with a sweatshirt and jeans for my weekly girl's night out Euchre game. It was my night to close the department down, which left me no room to come home and change. If I had any sense, I'd not go tonight since I knew that everyone in town had probably heard about Finn's parents being Catholic before the stroke of midnight.

I could just see it now: Mama stomping around the house fussing at Daddy, who was ignoring her and not responding, which made her have to pick up the phone and call everyone on her speed dial.

"You ready?" I walked down the hall and into the kitchen with my bag of clothes in my grip. I took my phone off the charger and slipped it into my back pocket.

Duke jumped to his feet and rushed to the back door, thumping his wagging tail against the bottom kitchen cabinets in anticipation of getting a car ride. One of his favorite activities.

I'd just stopped at the stop sign at the end of the street and rolled down my window and Duke's window when my phone rang.

"Finn," I said his name with a big smile. "Good morning," I answered. "I was just on my way to our eight a.m. morning meeting. Don't want to be late."

"Sheriff," He only called me that when there was an emergency.

"What's wrong?" My heart fell to my feet. Had something happened with his parents?

"There's been a body found in Rock Fence Park." His words stopped my heart. "I'm not sure who she is, but I have to tell you that your Mama and her walking group found her."

He meant the Henny Hens.

"I'm on my way." I threw the phone down, grabbed the siren, licked the

34

suction cup and threw the beacon up on top of the roof, jerking the wheel left onto Main Street.

"Goin' to be diggin' up dirt on this one," the soft whisper came from the back of the Wagoneer.

My eyes slid to the rearview mirror, but my brain already told me who I was going to see before I looked.

"Poppa," I gasped knowing the only time the ghost of my Poppa, Elmer Sims, showed up, it meant one thing.

There was a murder in Cottonwood and a killer was on the loose.

"Are you here because..." I gulped, gripping the wheel to keep the tires on the road. "The dead body isn't just dead...it's..." I gulped. "Murdered," I muttered.

Duke jumped into the back seat and took his happy place next to Poppa.

"I've missed you, boy." Poppa patted Duke.

Duke's tail wagged with excitement. I'd always heard children and dogs could see ghosts, but never truly believed it until Poppa appeared and proved Duke could see him.

Duke and I were the only ones who knew about Poppa. There'd been a few times that I'd been caught talking to him but was good at acting as if I were talking to myself. The fact that Finn and I were getting closer than just dating, I'd toyed with the idea of letting him know about Poppa's ghost–that Poppa only showed up when there was a murder in Cottonwood, which made him my Deputy ghost.

Up until a few years ago, there'd never been crime on my watch as sheriff. It wasn't until there were two crimes in our small town that Poppa had shown up. All the ideas that there wasn't crime in Cottonwood due to my amazing job as sheriff had been flattened after Poppa informed me that he'd been running around town in ghost form scaring off any would-be criminals.

Apparently, a ghost couldn't be in two places at once, even if he did ghost from one crime to another.

"I have a sneaky feeling it's going to be covered and you're gonna be diggin' for days to solve this one." His eyes were sharp and assessing.

Poppa took his wrinkly hand off Duke and rubbed over his comb-over. He adjusted the collar of his brown sheriff's uniform and neatly tucked in the edges of his shirt into his brown pants. He lifted the flap of the pocket on the front of his shirt.

"You lookin' for this?" I held the wheel with one hand and picked up his sheriff's pin out of the beanbag coffee holder that was draped over the hump on the floorboard between the driver's side and passenger's side.

"I forgot." He winked.

"I don't think you forgot. I think you wanted to remind me to put it on." I palmed it and moved my hand back to the steering wheel as I took a left at the light off of Main Street to turn onto Oak Street, where Rock Fence Park was located.

"Oh, Kenni bug," he referred to me by my nickname he'd given me as a young child, "I'm so proud of you."

The siren echoed in the air that filled the park, causing all the citizens who'd already gathered there to turn around.

"Here comes trouble." Poppa laughed, referring to Mama, before he ghosted out of the car.

"Come on, Duke." I got out of the car after I put Poppa's pin on my shirt and opened the back door to let him out and get my bag. "Not now, Mama," I warned her before her opened mouth could vocalize.

Her pink silky track suit swooshed with each step she took as she got closer to me. She pushed the matching headband a little further up on her forehead. Leave it to Mama to be dressed for the occasion as she did every event in her life.

"But, Kendrick, we have to talk about this religion issue," she said through gritted teeth. It was like I was staring into a mirror, all the way down to our green eyes. Only Mama had a few more wrinkles around her eyes. I would never dare to point them out in fear she'd be down at the plastic surgeon in two shakes of a lamb's tail.

"Excuse me, Darlin'." She drew back and sucked in a breath to keep going. "This is going to make a mockery of your relationship and your position here in Cottonwood."

"Woooweee." Poppa stood grinning. "Glad to see some things never change."

He was referring to the volatile relationship between his granddaughter and daughter.

"You've gone done put a giddy up in her hitch this mornin'." Poppa was entertained easily. "She looks like she'd 'bout give you nine kinds of hell."

"I said not now, Mama. Apparently, you found a body and I need to do my job now. I'll talk to you in a minute." I shoved past her, ignoring Poppa, and glanced around to see where Duke had gone.

Duke had darted off to where Finn was standing near a tree at the front of the small hiking trail located past the playground. Not even a child could get lost on this hiking trail. It was there just like the swings. For fun.

Finn had already strung police tape across the play swings, through the jungle gym, around the large slide, and knotted it off at the teeter-totter.

"Do you have any idea who the victim is?" Edna Easterly yelled at me when I walked past the crowd with her hand stuck way out holding her tape recorder.

All the Henny Hens, like little puppets, slightly turned their heads, leaning an ear closer to get the scoop.

Edna was the editor for the Cottonwood Chronicle, our local newspaper. This would be a big scoop for her since most of the stories in the Chronicle were about births and other non-news issues.

Edna's outfit told me she was going to be out of her office today to investigate this story. Her fisherman vest was equipped as a traveling office where she kept her much needed supplies in the many pockets it had to offer.

The feather she'd hot glued on the brown fedora waved in the early morning wind, making it hard to read the notecard, also glued on the hat, where she'd scribbled the word "Reporter" on it.

For a second, I wondered how all of these people knew, not that I didn't put it past Mama and the Henny Hens to have called everyone, but when I noticed Max Bogus had pulled up behind the Wagoneer, I knew Finn had called Betty Murphy at the department where she dispatched the county coroner, Max Bogus.

Everyone in Cottonwood had invested in a police scanner. After all, no one wanted to be left behind on what was going on in our small town.

"What do we have?" I asked Finn, putting the personal issue we'd had last night on the back burner.

Our job and our commitment to Cottonwood had to take precedent over the personal life issues we were having at the moment.

"You okay?" Finn's eyes had a sheen of purpose.

"I'm fine. I guess we have another killer to find." I shook my head and walked over to the tree line where Finn had placed a couple crime scene numbers.

"Killer?" He questioned. "I've not even taken a good look at the body. I simply felt for a pulse and checked for a heartbeat."

"Definitely a murder. Definitely a killer," Poppa stood over the body. Duke wiggled at his side. "Go on, tell that Northerner it's a murder."

"Duke," I called. "Get over here." He trotted over giving me some time to think real fast on how to answer Finn's question. It was these types of subtle things about Poppa's ghost that I let slip, making Finn stop and question my every thought. "Then what? Hiking and had a heart attack?"

I knew my tone was a little snottier than normal.

"I'm sorry. Not enough coffee in the morning for a call like this." I offered one of those "sorry" smiles before I bent down over the body.

Finn walked away and greeted Max a few feet back from me.

The body was lying face down, wearing a black hooded sweatshirt, and what looked to be a blue pair of scrub pants that a doctor would wear. I had no clue if the victim was a male or female, until I turned the body over.

The small puddle of blood in the middle of the back didn't go unnoticed and from an initial look, it appeared to be a bullet wound.

After I carefully turned the body over, I instantly recognized the fair skinned young woman underneath the hoodie. Avon Meyers. The young woman I'd seen talking to Rich Moss at the funeral home.

More like the woman Rich Moss was threatening.

"Bullet wound right through the ticker," Poppa pointed out. He danced a little jig and clapped his hands. "Whoooweeee, Kenni bug. It looks like we are back on the case again. Me and you." He rubbed his hands together. "We can play our little game."

I stayed with Poppa a lot more than I stayed at home with my parents. Mama actually blamed Poppa for ruining me by brain washing me into becoming a police officer and not fulfilling my destiny in becoming the president of the Junior League and chairwoman of many clubs. When I went to college to get my four-year degree in law enforcement, it nearly put Mama in the bed with a nervous breakdown.

She thought it was cute when I told her I was going to run for Cottonwood sheriff, an elected four-year term. She had made all sort of bedazzled signs and used pink paint, puff paint mind you, as if it were a joke.

When I won, she took to the bed once again.

Eventually, she got over it and during the last election, where I had to be reelected, she took it personally if someone didn't put a "Vote For Kenni Lowry" sign in their yard.

"Poppa, I'm going to have to limit my conversations with you," I said under my breath. "Finn and I are getting a lot more serious. Mama practically has my wedding dress picked out."

I unzipped my bag and took out my camera to get some up-close photos of Ava's body, trying to make it appear as if I was doing my job instead of trying to sort out all the jumble in my head. The thought of Finn's parents and the messed-up supper party last night shouldn't be taking up my thoughts. Poor Ava should be and the fact that I knew she was killed didn't help matters since I couldn't just say to everyone that I knew she was murdered because Poppa was here.

We Southerners might wear our crazy like a banner and parade it down Main Street, but we aren't the "seeing the dead" kinda crazy. That was the stuff that got a person put in a room in the looney bin.

"What do you mean?" Poppa stomped a foot. "We are the best duo with our little back and forth game of 'what if this happened'. We've solved many crimes that way. Why not now?"

He was right. As a child, Poppa would give me scenarios of the crimes he was working on and we would sit at his kitchen table for hours asking each other "what if this happened" to formulate how the crime had happened and who had done it. Granted, most of them didn't involve murder, but it was still like putting together a puzzle and we were good at it.

"I'm in love with Finn and I'm not sure how he's going to take it if he found out that I'm relying on my Poppa's ghost as my deputy more than I am relying on him," I muttered and snapped the camera at the same time.

"Well if this don't beat the band." Poppa did a little more stomping. "You tellin' me that this Yankee had more influence over you than the actual man who gave you the spirit and drive in your soul to be a sheriff?"

"What do we have here, Sheriff?" Max Bogus walked up with his clipboard in his hand. His pen at the ready.

"We have Avon Meyers, a physical therapist at the Cottonwood Acres Rehab." I waited for him to finish filling out the top of his paperwork before I continued.

Finn and I were already like a well-oiled machine. He took the camera from me and continued to take pictures of the victim while I filled in Max on what I found.

"It appears the victim has a gunshot wound to the chest here." I took my pen from my shirt pocket and used the tip to point to the wound. "Before I flipped her over, there was an exit wound that appeared to be a straight line from here. There doesn't appear to be any other types of wounds or bruising externally."

"Or vice versa," Max corrected me. He'd know best. This was his area of expertise.

Out of the corner of my eye, I could see Poppa assessing Finn as if he'd not already formed an opinion of him. Poppa stuck to Finn like Edna Easterly's feather was glued to her fedora.

"What was Mama's account?" I asked Finn while Max did his initial assessment and took his photos of Ava before he'd go retrieve the church cart to wheel her off into the hearse.

I turned my back towards Poppa, shifting every time he tried to get into my line of vision before he disappeared. Duke yelped and barked. Finn put his hand out to pat him, satisfying him for the moment.

"I was out doing the rounds when Betty called saying Viv had called in a body on the hiking trail. When I got here and asked her what happened, she told me that she wanted to talk directly to the sheriff." The lines in his forehead creased as his brows rose.

"She said that?" I asked.

"Yep. She's not talking to me. She's still sore from last night." What he said should've alarmed me, but knowing it was coming from Mama, it didn't surprise me one bit.

"The supper?" Max looked over his clipboard at us.

"You already heard?" I shouldn't've been surprised.

"Heard?" Max laughed. "When Vivian Lowry gets hotter than donut grease, everyone hears."

"She'll get over this like she has every other time I've disappointed her." I looked at Finn to give him reassurance.

Mama's arms flew up in the air and flailed them about her head when she caught me looking.

"I guess I better question her before she opens her big mouth to her friends." I brushed my hand down Finn's arm and gave him a little squeeze before I walked back towards the crowd.

There was a murmur coming from them when I started walking that way that died down to a blanket of silence as they anticipated what I was going to do. I was keenly aware all eyes were on me and knew they assumed I was going to make a statement.

"Vivian Lowry," I stated Mama's name. "Can I please see you over by my car?"

"I'm your mama. Why so formal?" She questioned me.

"We can either go by the car or go down to the station." It was a statement that caught her off guard.

"This must be official business," she told Lulu McClain who was standing next to her. "Save my spot."

Lulu's head nodded in agreement.

"Who is it?" asked Mama on our way over to the Wagoneer as if she wanted to gossip.

I took out my small notebook from the pocket of my shirt and clicked the pen.

"Over here please." I used my polite words to maneuver her to the back of the Jeep that shielded us from the crowd. "Why on Earth didn't you answer Finn's questions when he got here?"

She stood ramrod straight, lips pressed together, her beady little eyes staring at me.

"Don't you know that you could be arrested for that? You could be in the jail cell right now, forced to smell fried catfish." I knew she gagged at the smell. Mama was all about Southern home cooking, but fried catfish wasn't her specialty.

"I'm mad, that's why." She folded her arms in front of her.

"You can be mad at us, but you can't hold back on an investigation, Mama. They are two separate issues." I couldn't tell if she understood me and how important to the case it was that she'd answered Finn's questions.

"It didn't bother a thing," she protested.

"Did you see anyone leaving the trail? Did you see anyone leaving the park? Who was at the park when you discovered the body?" I continued to ask questions that I could see were making her head swim. "Who was walking with you? Did you hear a gunshot?"

"Gunshot? Was this a murder?" Mama gasped.

"What if it was? What if the poor girl," I started to say but she interrupted me yet again.

"It's a girl?" Mama gasped again.

"Mama, focus. I'm trying to tell you why you should've answered Finn's questions instead of playing this role of getting back at him for being Catholic. There is a dead body over there and if it is a homicide, and you seen someone walking away, then you could've just let the killer free."

Mama's lips formed a dramatic "O" as her eyes bulged out of her head.

"My." She drew her hands up to her chest, laying them flat on her track suit. "I never thought about that."

"Mama, you never think about your consequences when the agenda doesn't suit you." It was harsh to say, but I was speaking as the sheriff, not as her daughter. "This is the type of thing that citizens will remember and not reelect me for some time."

"Don't you dare say that," she scoffed. "You are the best sheriff there ever was."

"Including Poppa?" I joked. "Seriously, can you answer some questions for me?"

"Yes. I will." She drew her shoulders back, her chin lifted. "I'm ready."

"How did your friends know about this?" I glanced over at all the Henny Hens, staring at me and Mama.

"I need emotional support, Kendrick." She sighed along with her dramatic hand wave.

"What time did you get to the park this morning?" I asked, letting the emotional support comment go.

"It was around seven thirty. I know it was because Lulu was late. I looked at my watch." She uncovered her watch with the sleeve of her light jacket and showed me the watch.

"Did you and Lulu hike the trail or just walk around the park?" I asked.

"We did both. We walked around the perimeter of the park first because Lulu has this thingy she wears around her wrist that tells her how many steps she's taken. She insists she needs at least ten thousand steps a day." Mama rolled her eyes while she unzipped her fanny pack. "It just made me tired thinking of it."

"Focus, Mama." I looked down at my notebook and wrote down her words about doing the perimeter first. "Do you have any idea what time it was that you went on the trail?"

"Heavens no. We were too busy looking at that thingy around her wrist," she said. "Here, put some of this on." She'd pulled some lipstick out of her fanny pack and rolled it up.

"When did you notice the body?" I asked, pushing her hand out of my face.

"Edna is taking photos and you need to look a little presentable." She tried to smear the lipstick on my lips before I jerked away and gave her the death look. "Fine," she snarled, rolling it down and putting it back.

"Please, Mama, answer my questions." Then it occurred to me to use the guilt on her that she used on me. "What if that was me? Wouldn't you want the sheriff to interview the person who found me?"

"We found her when we was walking out." Her head tilted to the right as though she were contemplating it. "Yes. It was when we were walking out because we'd not paid much attention to where we'd kept walking to since we were looking at her steps. We ended up catching the other side of the trail to bring us back here after we looked up and saw we were walking on the town branch."

Like Free Row was an affectionate name for Broadway Street, Town Branch was what we called North Second Street. There was a small creek, in the south we call it a branch, that runs right alongside of North Second Street. All the houses have little concrete bridges from the street to their driveway in order to go over the branch.

"You mean to tell me you walked over there to North Second Street and didn't even notice?" I thought it was weird they didn't notice they'd left the park, though in her favor, North Second was the street that Rock Fence Park butted up to closest to the trail.

"I guess we didn't." She shook her head. "But Lulu wasn't with me."

"Where did she go?" I asked.

"When we made it shy of the park, she said that she didn't get enough steps and was going to track back to North Second and take the sidewalk around to her car. That's when I saw that body. I let out a big ole scream and took off running. It was Lulu who heard me and ran towards me." Mama was talking so fast, I was having a hard time writing it all down. "She said I looked like a ghost. I told her that I found that body, but the reason I looked so bad was because them people had the silly notion that my daughter," she emphasized my, "was going to become Catholic. That's why I was so pale from no sleep." Mama shook her head. "Lulu said they had some nerve and I agree." Mama patted me on the arm. "I'm so sorry you and Finn won't be working out, but I've heard that Nick Lyman is newly single."

"Nick Lyman?" I groaned. "Mama, me and Finn are just fine. Nick Lyman and I are no match."

"Just because he's a plumber..."

I put my hand up.

"It has nothing to do with him being a plumber," I assured her. "I'm in love with Finn and we will figure this out. Alone," I stated just as she opened her mouth to protest.

She snapped her mouth shut.

"Back to my questions." I tried to keep Mama's attention as Max Bogus had walked by to retrieve the church cart from the back of the hearse. The sound of him clicking the wheels in place made her flinch. "Did you see anyone at the park?"

"Kenni, there are tons of people at the park in the morning." Mama turned to look at Max as the wheels of the gurney squeaked while he pushed it.

"Anyone you recognized?" I asked.

Mama bit the edge of her lip and closed one eye like she was thinking real hard.

"Can't say so." She didn't seem so sure. "Can I think on it and get back to you?"

"That'd be great. In fact, I'll need you to come down to the station and sign off on your account of what happened after Betty writes it up." I flipped the notebook shut.

Mama had lost all interest in anything I had to say while Max made his way over to the body. She was too busy making sure that she didn't miss anything. I was all too happy to have her come to the department. It wasn't unusual for a witness to not remember everything until a few hours or even days after the incident. They were in shock whether they realized it or not and sometimes their memory blocks things out.

It was hard for me to think there were people at the park and Mama didn't know a single one when she knew everyone.

"Mama, this is an ongoing investigation. Do I need to remind you that you can't talk to anyone about the case?" I asked, though she really didn't have any information.

"Oh yes." Her chin moved up and down in dramatic fashion. A sure sign she was lying.

"Because if you do and the body was murdered, you could give pertinent information that would let the killer off if they knew you were blabbing." I put the notebook back in my pocket.

"Blabbing? You think I blab?" She snarled.

"Mama, I'll see you either at the station or at Tibbie's." I looked towards North Second Street where Tibbie lived off the town branch.

If there were a gunshot, wouldn't someone have heard it and reported it?

CHAPTER SIX

"Where are you going? I thought we could head over to Ben's for a cup of coffee before we went back to the office to start putting together the case file." Finn stood next to the hearse where Max had just loaded up Avon's body. "Deputy Lee is finishing up scouring the trail and once he's done, we can come back and recheck to make sure."

"I'm going to walk along the trail and finish up over on North Second Street. I want to check if any of the residents heard a gunshot." The one thing Max did say about the shot was that Avon had been looking at the shooter. I could only imagine how she felt or even what she'd said. "I'd like you to get all the information you can on Avon. Where she lives. Look into her job. Her friends and family," my voice trailing off.

"Do you want me to go?" Finn knew telling the family was always my hardest part of the job.

"No." I shook my head. "If you get me their address, I'll stop by." I gnawed on my to-do list. "If a shot rang out in the city limits, someone had to have heard it."

"Unless there was a silencer on it" He shrugged one shoulder.

"Maybe in Chicago people use silencers, but in Cottonwood, they take pride in their gunshots." We were a big hunting town and even had our own

46

hunting club that did a lot of good for the community. "I'll also walk on down to the rehab since it's down the Town Branch on the left."

"Sheriff!" Scott stood in front of the police line and waved me over.

"You go on and get the paper trail started. I'll let you know if he's found something and be there soon." I just wasn't quite ready to be alone, though Ben's Diner would be buzzing about the murder.

Even though Finn and I knew we'd get past this little hiccup in the relationship department, I couldn't help but think this was a big deal if we did get married. I'd never thought I'd get married in any other church besides Cottonwood Baptist. I'd always imagined my kids doing the big Easter Egg hunt and even participating in the Christmas Eve Pageant put on by the children in the church while I sat in the front row with a camera and pride in my heart.

"Alright. I'll have you a cup of coffee waiting." He smiled. "Do you want me to take Duke?"

"That'd be great." I whistled and Duke came running over.

"Let's go, Duke." Finn walked away and Duke was right by his side.

I waited there until he drove off. Poppa must've thought it was his time to reappear.

"Thank goodness you got him out of here." He stood with his arms crossed. "Let's go see what this feller knows." He nodded towards Scott, who was still standing at the police tape with something dangling from his hand.

As much as I wanted to yell at Poppa and tell him to leave because I just wasn't strong enough to tell Finn that I see my ghost Poppa, it felt so good to have him here with me. He was my rock when he was living and the day he died, I thought my world was over. Little did I know that years later I'd find out he'd been my guardian angel.

No matter how much I tried to convince myself otherwise, Poppa and I did have a better working relationship and we did understand each other better than me and Finn. Finn had gotten better over the last couple of years picking up on my little idiosyncrasies, but we still weren't as fluid as me and Poppa. We could practically see into what each other was thinking.

I'd thought about my situation a lot. What would happen if I told someone about Poppa? Would it make Poppa disappear forever? I wasn't ready for him to leave me again. What if I did tell Finn about Poppa? Would he think I was crazy and leave me? I wasn't ready for that either.

As I saw it, it was a no-win situation on my part. My future with Finn had now been questioned and keeping Poppa a secret, for now, was my best option.

"Fine. I need you to help me," I whispered to Poppa as he ghosted past me.

"Yipppee!" He screamed. "Now you've come to your senses."

"What do you have there?" I asked Deputy Lee and noticed it appeared to be a purse.

"It's Avon Meyers purse. It looks like this could be a robbery. I found the purse about thirty feet into the woods." He turned around to show me there were some gloves in his back pocket.

I tugged them out and put them on my hands, taking a look inside of the purse while he held it for me.

"There's a wallet about ten feet from the purse. I used your camera to take photos before I picked it up and placed markers there too for you to look at." Deputy Lee was thorough. He was a good addition to our department and that had to be a plus when it came to the decision of the city council.

"You're doing good work," I complimented Scott and walked around to look at the markers. "I want you to be sure that you package up all this evidence and write a thorough report. Lock this purse up in the evidence vault at the office. Have it on my desk by tonight so I can go through it and have it ready to present at the city council meeting tomorrow."

"Do you think they're not going to approve the new position? I mean, if I weren't here now, Deputy Vincent couldn't be looking into the victim's history. You'd not be able to oversee the entire operation."

"You and I know that, but the budget doesn't know that. Plus, Mayor Ryland has his own agenda and he likes to run a tight budget. He might give a little pushback, but if we make a good case for ourselves and this here is a start, we might have a good shot."

"No stone unturned," Poppa reminded me of his catch phrase as he ghosted himself next to Scott. "I like this guy."

"No stone unturned," I repeated.

"Yes, Sheriff." Scott nodded.

"I also want you to go around to the pawn shops and continue to look for the cuff links stolen during the burglary at the Moss house." That crime couldn't be put on the back burner because of this murder. Though a dead girl did take precedence over the burglary. "Can you please process her car after Sean Graves tows it to the tow lot?"

I wasn't sure which car belonged to Avon, but I knew her parents would know.

"Okay. I will," he confirmed before I headed back to clearing the park.

The sun was starting to pop up and for a late spring, early summer morning, and I could tell it was going to be unseasonably hot. The humidity had already picked up and I'd already started to sweat a smidgen. Something I really didn't like to do.

The hiking trail wasn't all that terribly long or hard to travel. It was just in the local park where children loved to romp and roam. The park was surrounded on all four sides by either a street, a subdivision or a business. Someone had to'd seen something, I didn't care what hour Max Bogus was going to put her time of death.

The sunlight found its way through the branches of the trees, filtering down on the man-made path. There were a few squirrels along the way, but that was about all the creatures you'd see in Rock Fence Park. Still, with the death looming over my head, any crackling noise made goosebumps crawl along my neck and clutch my bag with a tighter grip.

I ended up following the trail that Mama said Lulu McClain had taken, which was on the side of the Town Branch. When I looked left across the street, I could see Tibbie's house.

"If I were going to rob someone in the park, I'd pick the least visible place to get out of there and I think North Second Street would be it." I pointed to the end of the trail where I'd walked from and dragged my finger to where we were standing. "There's a lot of space here to just pretend to be walking down the street."

"I think it'd depend on the time." Poppa was really good at establishing a time frame for all the crimes he'd solved. "If it was before midnight, the killer could've easily come from the back of the park, robbed and killed her, then took off through the front of the park since it isn't lit up."

"Another one of Mayor Ryland's awful decisions." I made a mental note to bring that up at the council meeting.

Parents had come to the meeting a year ago and asked to have lights put up at the park. He insisted that the park was only for daylight hours, when in reality, he'd just wanted to use that money for something else.

I unzipped my bag and took out my camera. Rotating at all different angles, I took photos of the park.

"If the killer ran through here in the middle of the night, no one might've seen them." Poppa's eyes lowered as he followed a path with his eyes. "I really don't think they would've gone Oak Street, seeing cars were probably traveling through there all night."

"Then you have South Second." I ran my finger in the air behind the park and parallel to where we were currently standing. "I'm just afraid the killer ran out unseen."

"We've got a lot of things we need to get to." Poppa smiled. "I love this."

"I know you do. So do I, but I also have to live my breathing life and that means Finn right now." I gulped back the lump forming in my throat. "I'm not sure how I'm going to fix the situation with Mama and Mrs. Vincent."

We walked out of the parking lot and headed back down towards the park, stopping at the foot of the trail.

"Your mama has always had a plan for you in her head. She finally accepted you as a sheriff and knows you're good at it." He talked while I snapped more photos. When a car drove by, I made sure I didn't open my mouth since it would appear as if I were talking to myself. "Then the little hiccup you and Finn had to get through over Christmas when you were going to spend the holiday with his family."

"That made her go nuts." I could laugh at it now, but when Mama first heard of my plans to go to Chicago for Christmas, she flat out pulled a crazy.

I swear she had a direct line to God because she prayed for the blizzard that'd been predicted, knowing the history of the weather forecasted on the news was never right. Of course, the day Finn and I were going to fly out of the Bluegrass Airport for Chicago, the biggest blizzard on record hit Kentucky and grounded every flight and bus for two weeks. We were stuck, and Mama was as happy as a fuzzy peach.

"You know, Viv, she loves her religion. And her mama and I made sure Viv grew up in the church learning the good word. And she did that for you too." Poppa gave me a square look. "She might have her heels dug in on this one. She's pretty firm on her beliefs."

"I'm not saying she's not right, but does she have to worry about that now? Finn and I are just dating. It's not like he's asked me to marry him or nothing." I glanced around and realized I'd taken photos from every angle possible.

More than likely, I was snapping away to continue my conversation with Poppa. If anyone knew Mama well, it was him.

"I'm not saying you are going to marry him, but it's something you need to think about because if that boy is wanting to ask for your hand in marriage, you better know where y'all stand on issues like religion, children, where you're going to live." Poppa's words were wise, but I knew I'd always live in Cottonwood.

My phone rang and I pulled it out of my pocket.

"It's Finn." I wiggled the screen towards Poppa. "Hey," I answered. "Listen, do you see yourself living in Cottonwood all your life?"

He surprised me with a little laugh.

"I don't think I want to stay a deputy for the rest of my life. I'd like to move up to sheriff or something bigger." He caught me off guard.

"You're going to run against me?" My heart took a dip down into my toes.

"No. There are other sheriff's departments. Maybe back home." He hesitated. "Listen, I called to give you Avon's parent's address. It's actually on North Second Street. I didn't call to discuss our future."

"Do we have a future if you don't want to live in Cottonwood?" I was a little angry at Finn and annoyed at Poppa that he'd actually put this in my head.

"Kenni, honey, I know this murder is stressful, but can we just do our job today and maybe talk about this tonight?" He questioned, making a lot of sense in the professional department.

"Of course." I stopped myself from anymore nonsense about our personal life. It was one thing that we'd discussed before we let the cat out of the bag, so to speak, to the public about us dating.

51

I insisted that our personal life didn't interfere with our professional life and here I was doing it.

"Just text me their address and I'll keep you posted after I talk to them." I clicked off the phone and turned to give Poppa my speech about how I couldn't discuss anything but the case with him.

But he was gone.

How convenient.

CHAPTER SEVEN

Avon Meyer's parents lived on Stratton Avenue, a few blocks going away from the park. It wasn't too much further down where the Cottonwood Acres Rehabilitation was located.

The walk down the street to Avon's parents' house, even though the humidity had picked up, was much needed to clear my head from the conversation Poppa and I were having about Finn and getting my head back into my job.

The house number Finn had texted me, left me standing in front of a white picket fence. Quickly I scanned down the stats Finn had uncovered. Avon was a graduate of a state college with a physical therapy degree, Cottonwood Acres Rehabilitation Center was her first job, only child, age thirty-three, not married and lived alone in a house on Hickory Hill.

With my hand on the gate, I took a second to notice the clapboard house with the two dormer windows in the front. I imagined Avon playing on the covered front porch and even looking out of one of the windows as a child. The news that was about to come out of my mouth was unimaginable, and the woman who opened the front door after I knocked, staring at me, knew something was wrong.

The screen door creaked when she opened it and stepped out onto the porch, a cup of coffee in her hand. Something I was in much need of at this moment.

"Sheriff, what's wrong?" She was about fifty years old. She had on a pair of jeans and a "Kentucky Y'all" tee shirt. "Wesley, get out here. The sheriff is here," she called over her right shoulder, keeping her eyes on me.

"Mrs. Meyers?" I questioned to make sure I had the right house, though Finn had texted me Carey and Wesley Meyers, which matched with the name of the husband that she'd called to come out. "Carey Meyers?"

"It's Avon, isn't it. She's done something to Mrs. Brumfield. I know it. I knew it." The coffee was spilling over the edges of her mug. "I told Wesley that he needed to step in and do something, but he swore up and down that Avon had to be an adult and learn to get along with everyone."

"What's all the fussin' about?" A man, I assumed to be Wesley, came to the door, shirtless, gut hanging over his jeans and barefooted. His eyes traveled down their front walk and fixed on me standing at the gate. "Sheriff."

"Wesley Meyers? Avon Meyers's father?" I tried him since Carey hadn't responded.

"I told you." Carey spat at her husband.

"Shh." He opened the screen door, putting a hand out for his wife to be quiet. "Let the sheriff say her piece."

I took that as an okay to enter and let myself in the gate and walked up to the porch.

"Can we go inside to talk?" I questioned when I heard someone next door to them clear their throat.

"Would you like a cup of coffee?" Carey waved me up to the porch and Wesley held the door for us to walk inside.

"I'm good. Can we sit?" I gestured to the small couch in the room we were standing in.

"Yes. Sure." She nodded. "You're making me nervous. I think I'll stand."

"I think you'll want to sit." I'd made this mistake before, where I'd let a parent stand while I gave them the same awful news about the death of a child and when they fainted, they had to go to the hospital for a concussion.

"Wesley?" Carey seemed to understand the severity of why I was there. The scared look in her eyes searched her husband's face for a quick answer.

"I'm sorry to inform you, but your daughter Avon was found deceased in the park this morning by a walker." I bent my head down so I didn't have to see the scene that started to play out before me.

The coffee cup slipped from Carey's fingers, shattering on their hardwood floor and splattering coffee around the room.

"Sheriff, how? How did my girl die?" Wesley held his wife close to his chest, tears streaming down his face. "She's so young and I'm sure she's fit. She wasn't sick."

"She has a gunshot wound to her chest." My words were like a bullet to their heart and it killed me a little inside each time I had to tell a parent. There was nothing normal about this situation.

Carey gasped as sobs, uncontrollable sobs, escaped her.

"We believe that she was robbed at gunpoint and the robber shot her." There was no other explanation I had at this time. "Though it could change since we are just a few hours into the investigation."

"Do you have anyone in custody?" Wesley had eased Carey down onto the couch. He held her close.

"We are working on fingerprints and hoping to have someone by the end of the day." That was pushing it, but it gave me a few hours for them to let the information sink in about their daughter.

"Can I see her?" Carey looked up. Her eyes had already grown red around the rims.

"You can. Max Bogus has her down at the morgue doing an initial autopsy on her. We will need to you come down to identify her, but you won't be able to touch her until we make sure there's no DNA from the killer or evidence on her person." I put the bag on the ground and took out my notepad from my shirt pocket. "I know this is a lot to take in, but you said something about Mrs. Brumfield. Do you mean Lita Brumfield?"

Lita was an elderly woman in the community that pretty much kept to herself. She'd been on a few committees with Mama when I was a child but had really become quite the recluse as she'd gotten older. She was one of Jolee's Meals on Wheels customers and I remember Jolee saying how Lita made her leave the food in the old tin milk carrier that sat outside of her door on Hickory Hill. Not that Lita killed Avon, but no stone unturned.

"Our Avon is a good girl. She went to college and ended up a physical therapist. She got her a good job over yonder at the rehabilitation center.

She'd stop by every morning for a cup of coffee and when she didn't show up today, I figured she was running late since she and Lita had that run in last night." Carey continued to look down at her fingers that were shaking in her lap.

I walked over and sat down next to her on the couch, ignoring Wesley as he paced back and forth. The grieving process for men and women were so different. She needed to be comforted while he needed to work out some anger in his head. As the sheriff, I should remain as professional as I could, but I always felt a need to comfort and it was the Southern gal in me that my Mama raised that made me reach over and put a gentle but firm hand on Carey's. She looked up at me. Her nose flared, her head shook back and forth.

"What happened last night with Mrs. Brumfield?" I asked.

"She's always hated that we bought and gave Avon the house for her graduation present. We wanted Avon to live here in Cottonwood and she's accumulated so much debt from college, we wanted her to have a good start in her career. Wesley had talked to the owners who said that Lita was interested because she was getting older and wanted her son and his family to move there so they could take care of her. We don't have anything against Lita and her family, but we had to look out for our family. Our Avon." She wiped her eyes on the sleeve of her tee shirt. "Lita has given Avon a fit ever since she moved in. Ask Deputy Vincent about it. He stops by there at least once a month on a complaint."

"I will." I wondered why Finn hadn't mentioned that. "What sort of things did Avon do to warrant Mrs. Brumfield to make a complaint?"

It was interesting the dynamics—Carey referred to Mrs. Brumfield as Lita and I referred to her by a proper name.

"Avon parked on the street once and you're not allowed to do that overnight. Then Avon would have friends over and if they went a minute past midnight, she'd call on them," she said.

I made sure I wrote everything down. It wasn't something I recalled Betty Murphy reporting to me in the morning meetings, so I'd have to check with Clay's Ferry dispatch. Since we were a small town, we didn't have dispatch twenty-four-seven, so we shared it with Clay's Ferry. There wouldn't be a report, nor would their dispatch let us know of a disturbance if it was resolved and nothing had come of it. Which was probably the case.

"What kind of car did Avon drive? And color?" I asked. "I'm sure her car is in the parking lot and I'll need to get it processed after we get it towed using Graves Towing."

"It's a grey Ford Taurus. Nothing special." Wesley got up. "I've got the extra set of keys for it here. She made sure we kept a set just in case she locked herself out."

"I'm sorry, what were you saying about Lita?" I asked.

"Avon was very respectful to her, but last night when Avon had gotten home from a long day." Carey paused. "One of her favorite rehab patients had died and his funeral was yesterday."

"Woody Moss?" I questioned and was met with a confirming nod. "I saw your daughter there."

Another wave of sobs escaped her. I continued to rub her back. Wesley had found a seat in the chair where he'd buried his head in his hands.

"I'll go see Lita. But can you think of anyone else that Avon had an issue with?" I asked.

"I thought you said she was robbed," Wesley said through gritted teeth. His eyes filled with anger.

"We aren't sure, and I want to make sure we don't miss someone that could've possibly made it look like a robbery." I knew it was like pouring salt into the wound. "I hate to ask you all of these questions, but time is very important in a case like Avon's."

"She had been written up by her supervisor at work last week and she was upset about that." Carey sucked in a deep breath. "This just doesn't seem real." She blinked several times.

There was no need for me to ask the supervisor's name when I was going to go there anyways.

"Is there anyone I can call for you?" I asked wondering if they had anyone to come take care of them.

"No. I'll call our family." Wesley rubbed his hands together.

All of us jumped towards the door when a woman bolted through. She stood there looking at Carey in shock. The news must've already gotten around town that it was Avon Meyers who was found in the park and friends of the family were already coming to give their condolences.

The women grabbed each other like they were hanging on to a lifejacket, in fear of letting go. The horrible sounds of grief expelled from deep within both of them. Wesley found himself back in the position of the chair, seeking grief in his solicitudes.

"I'm going to leave now." I took out a business card and gave it to Carey. "I'll be in touch this afternoon."

She nodded.

Wesley jumped up from the seat and followed me out the screen door. My insides jarred as it slammed shut behind us.

"I'm gonna kill that old lady," he warned.

"Wesley, don't go over there." I put my hand up to his bare chest. "That's not a good idea and it's not going to solve anything."

"It'll solve a lot." His nostrils flared, anger spewed from his body.

"No. It won't. We don't know if Mrs. Brumfield had anything to do with it. But it would be helpful if you told me what happened between her and Avon last night." It was something Carey hadn't finished telling me.

"Avon loved to work in her little garden. There's a chain-link fence separating their back yards." He lifted his hand in the air and brushed it through his hair. "When Avon moved into the house, she planted an apple tree. She'd really nurtured that tree." There was a faint smile on his face. His eyes dipped. "She makes. . . made," he caught himself. He paused and choked back tears. "She made the best apple pies." His bottom lip curled under his front top teeth. "Anyways, that old bat had someone come and cut off the branches that were hanging over the fence into her yard. She couldn't even reach the branches. Avon had told her she was going to have them pruned back once the apples on those branches had fully grown in a couple of months. But that wasn't good enough for Lita. She made Avon's life a living hell there."

He looked out past the picket fence where people were pulling up to the curb in front of their house. All of them emerged with food in their arms. In a small town, after someone had died, the masses came in droves with food and drinks and anything else the grieving family needed. It was one of the great things that I loved about Cottonwood. In time of need, all the citizens put their differences aside and came together.

"We would tell Avon that old Lita couldn't live that much longer and to tough it out." His head jumped back as a bitter laugh escaped him. "Joke was on us."

He took a step off the porch, taking a handshake from a man as they exchanged sorrows.

"I'm going to let you do your investigation, but if it's not to my liking, I will go see Lita," He warned on my way out.

CHAPTER EIGHT

"Kenni Lowry, what are you doing slumming on the town branch?" Tibbie Bell was standing outside of her small brick, ranch-style house with a watering pail. "Oh no, something's wrong."

There was more than something wrong. I'd practically balled my eyes out walking down North Second Street to get back into the Wagoneer so I could collect myself. In between the tears, I'd texted Finn that I'd just left Avon's parents' house and Avon lives on Hickory Hill next to Lita Brumfield, leaving it up to him to grab the address and get over to the house to block off as a possible crime scene. When Tibbie had called out to me, I was texting Avon's car information to Sean Graves so he'd come out and tow Avon's car that was parked along the Town Branch.

"There was a girl found dead in the park this morning." I pointed across the street to Rock Fence Park. "Her parents live on Stratton Avenue and I just left their house."

"Oh, Sugar." Tibbie wrapped her arm around me. "I've got a fresh pot of coffee on. Come inside and have a cup."

I pulled my phone out of my back pocket and noticed it was only ten thirty in the morning when I felt like it was much later than that.

"I could use it." Noting that usually by this time I'd already have downed at least two pots of coffee.

"Do you know who did it?" she asked once we were in her house.

"No. Shot to the chest." I noticed as I followed her back to the kitchen, she'd already set up the table in the room off the right with the card tables we used for our weekly Euchre game.

She always hosted it because not only did she have the space, but she was single with no kids and loved ones to entertain. I was sure this was why she was so good at her job as the event planner.

"It looks like a robbery." I said and sat down on one of the bar stools butted up to her counter, waiting on her to pour the coffee.

"Looks like?" Her right brow rose as did the tone in her voice.

"Nothing is ever as it seems, is it?" I questioned and took the mug of coffee from her.

"Are we still talking about the robbery or you?" She was a smart cookie. "We aren't good friends for nothing." She winked over top of her cup as she took a sip.

"You're right. Last night was a disaster." I might as well change the subject since I really couldn't talk about the Avon's case. "We didn't even make it to the table before they stormed out."

"What happened?" Tibbie had already gotten ready for her day. Her long brown hair was neatly parted down the middle and pulled up in a messy top knot in a very stylish way. The taupe eye color really made her hazel eyes pop. She was always so good at putting on makeup and I hardly wore any. She had a bell sleeved chiffon shirt tucked into a flowing skirt with a huge belt around her waist. Though she was a bigger figure, she dressed to the nines and looked amazing.

"Mama had asked Preacher Bing to come bless the food. Finn apparently is Catholic. Though he's been going to the Cottonwood Baptist Church with me on Sundays," I mentioned.

"When you go," Tibbie corrected me. "Which isn't often."

"At least I go." I had to find something good about this conversation. "Anyways, when Mama realized this, she had a conniption and informed them that I'd never be Catholic and in turn Shelby said her grandchildren would never be raised Baptist."

"Those are fighting words. Your mama is Baptist to the core." Tibbie didn't tell me nothing I didn't already know. "What did Finn say?"

"He left with them. They didn't even park the RV in front of Mrs. Brown's house. I'd gotten a call from Toots Buford this morning about an RV parked at the Piggly Wiggly. I assumed it was them." I took a sip. "Poppa made a good point."

"Poppa?" Tibbie had a half-cocked grin on her face. "You went to the cemetery about this already?"

"Umm..." I gulped down more coffee. "Yeah. You know me. When I need advice, I go to Poppa's grave and talk it out."

Good recovery, I thought to myself.

"What did Poppa whisper?" Tibbie gave a quiet snort in the back of her throat.

"I just had a feeling that I should ask Finn now about how he sees his future. Where he will live," I started to tell her.

She interrupted, "...in Cottonwood, of course."

"I thought so too, but when I asked him, he said that he didn't want to be a deputy all of his life, which means I'm either going to not be sheriff here or he move." My words met a dead silence between me and Tibbie. "What am I going to do?"

"You aren't engaged. Maybe you can tough it out until this investigation is over and then you two have a come to Jesus meeting about your future." Tibbie sighed.

Wesley Meyers told Avon to tough it out. What if I'm toughing it out with Finn when he really doesn't feel the same way I do? Like Avon, was wasting my life away only to come up dead from heartbreak in the end?

"Our future? Our future requires someone moving to advance in their career. I'm happy staying here in Cottonwood along with my family and friends while serving as sheriff. What man wants to have a wife as his boss, plus he went to school to train to move up the ladder not stay a deputy." I wasn't sure if I was trying to sell her the idea that Finn had a valid point or I was starting to train my heart to expect a blow when Finn did leave to pursue other job opportunities.

"I think you're putting the cart before the horse. Taking the deputy job was obviously a step down from being a Kentucky State Ranger." Her assumption was something I'd never even thought of.

At the time, I just needed a warm body to keep at the department while I investigated the death of Doc Walton. Little did I realize how valuable he was.

There was a moment of silence between us as I pondered what she said.

"Maybe he stayed as long as he has because he's truly in love with you." Leave it to Tibbie to always be the romantic. Out of the four of our friends, she was always the one who made us go to a romantic movie night over in Luke Jones's basement that was converted into the town's movie theater.

"Or he was willing to stick it out since it was an election year." I took another sip and decided to take the glass half empty approach to the subject matter.

"What are you talking about?" Tibbie's lip curled up as if she disapproved of what I'd said.

"Maybe he was sticking it out," there was that phrase again, "to see if I was going to be re-elected. If so, he could take on more responsibility by dating me because I'm a sucker and the town would see that he was in charge but that my name was on the door."

"Are you saying that Finley Vincent took the case with Doc Walton to come to Cottonwood because you are a girl sheriff?" Tibbie's jaw dropped in disbelief.

"Tibbie Bell, you need to come out of all the fairy tales of event planning that you do to realize some people will do anything in politics to get ahead." I sucked in a deep breath. "Especially in Cottonwood."

"Thank you very much, but I love living my fairy tale world of event planning because I make people's dreams come true." She grabbed the glass coffee carafe and refilled her cup. She held it up towards me, asking if I wanted more.

"No thanks." I took the last drink from my mug and stood up from the table. I walked over and put the empty cup in her sink. "I've spent too much time here already. I've got a killer on the loose and I have a feeling this one isn't going to be as easy to solve on my own."

"What are you talking about?" She asked. "You've got more help now than you did a few years ago."

"I'm thinking it's high time that Finn took a little more of a back seat and let me do the full investigation." It wasn't something I wanted to do, but I knew how the citizens of Cottonwood were. One minute they were your greatest contributor to your campaign fund. It only took one little thing to make them want you voted out. Of course, they'd claim it wasn't personal and for the good of the town, but I would take it mighty personal if I was doing a good job and by goodness, I was going to make sure they knew I was doing my job.

"That's right, Kenni bug." Poppa trotted alongside me on the sidewalk after I left Tibbie's house. "You stick with your old Poppa-sa and we'll keep the duo alive."

"Poppa-sa," I whispered with a new gitty-up on my go.

I couldn't help but laugh as I turned at the corner to walk up Oak Street where I'd parked the Jeep at the front of Rock Fence Park.

"Poppa-sa ain't too stupid." He winked and tapped his temple with his thick finger.

I couldn't help but feel a little better like I did when I was a kid or even up until the day he died. I'd go to him with either an issue with Mama or something in my struggling days at the police academy. He'd always give me sound advice and follow it up with Poppa-sa ain't too stupid.

Somehow, hearing him say those silly words always made me feel better and fixed a lot of things. I sure hoped it was going to fix what was going on not only with bringing a murderer to justice, but the struggle going on deep within my heart.

CHAPTER NINE

Before I whipped the Jeep around on Oak Street to turn right on Main Street to head south of town to Hickory Hill, Avon's house, I looked at my phone where Finn had sent a text back saying he was on his way to the house.

"Where did you go?" I asked Poppa under my breath since I didn't want anyone seeing me talking to myself.

"I went to check out Cottonwood Acres Rehabilitation." He sat next to me, like right next to me. It was something he'd always done.

Even when Mama or Daddy would pick him up or ride somewhere together, Poppa sat right in the middle of the front seat, right next to the driver. Now, as a ghost, he did it, but when Finn was in the car, Poppa was good at sitting in the backseat tormenting Finn by blowing on his neck or tweaking his ear lobe. Anything to make Finn uncomfortable.

"I know you're thinking Rich Moss did it, but you've got to think why? What was his motive?" Poppa had started to investigate a suspect before I'd even cleared all the scenes.

"I want to go to her house and check out any emails from her computer, her phone records or even a calendar." I gripped the wheel when my stomach growled as we passed Ben's Diner on Main Street, realizing I'd yet to have any food and was starving. "I'd like to question Rick about what I'd overheard him say to Avon as well as what her parents told me about her neighborly dispute with Lita Brumfield."

"I've known old Lita all my life and she's always been a lot of bark with no bite. She's a simple woman. There's no way on God's green earth that Lita shot that girl." Poppa wasn't going to hear of it.

This was one way he did his investigations. On the principal of someone's morals, not the evidence.

"You know how I feel about evidence. It can be skewed to make it look like someone else did it. Maybe the killer knew about the fight between Lita and Avon. It'd be easy to pin it on her," Poppa said.

"Like you say, no stone unturned." The Wagoneer rattled when I slowed it down to take a right off Main Street onto Hickory Hill Road. "Rich is the most likely suspect. What if she overheard a conversation with him at the rehab center with Woody where he wasn't getting the cuff links?"

"That doesn't make sense either." Poppa slapped his leg. "When I went to the rehab center, there was word that Avon had been killed and that's why she wasn't at work."

"Really?" I took the street slow since I'd turned up into the neighborhood and a lot of children were already out and about since their summer break had started.

"Yep. They said that they thought it was weird how she took such good care of Woody Moss and he ended up dying anyways. Plus, they also mentioned Wally Lamb and how he was taking the news of her death."

"What does he have to do with it?" I pulled up in front of the orange brick ranch and glanced around the neighborhood before I turned off the Jeep.

"I guess you're just going to have to ask him." Poppa gave a shrug. "But I'll keep my ears peeled."

"You just float around and see what you hear around town too." I smiled at him. "It's good to have a ghost deputy." I smiled and shoved the gearshift into park as soon as he ghosted away.

I jerked around with my fists up ready to punch someone out when someone opened my driver's door. That someone being Finn.

"Whoa." He put his hands up to shield being knocked in the face.

"Sorry about that." I sighed and reached over the seat to grab my bag. "I was lost in my thoughts."

"I noticed you were talking to yourself again." His deep voice was smooth and soothing. It was one of the things I loved about him. It made me feel safe and he knew it. Was this his ploy?

"Listen, we have to have a very serious talk." I got out of the Jeep and tried to contain the pitter-patter of my heart as soon as I smelled his cologne.

"I agree." He took a few steps back to give me space to step away from the Jeep. "My mom would like to meet you for lunch or afternoon tea today. I think it's a great idea and I can cover what we need to do with the investigation for an hour or so."

"I want to talk to you, not your mom." I headed towards the front door of Avon's house and slid a glance over to Lita's, where she was standing on her front porch with her hands planted on her hips, her eyes narrowed. "I'm not doing anything other than investigating this murder. So if she wants to discuss what happened last night, she's going to have to wait."

"They are leaving town in a day." His legs took extra-long steps to keep up with my pace. "You're mad."

"I'm working." I nodded over at Lita before I let myself into Avon's house.

"There's something wrong with you." Finn put a hand on my arm once we were inside of Avon's house.

"This isn't appropriate." I jerked my arm away, the bag swung violently in my grips. "We are on a crime scene. Our personal life comes second. That was always the rule. When did you decide the rules we set were no longer in play?"

"Fine." He rolled his shoulders back, parted his legs, and took out his notebook from his pocket. "Sheriff, Avon Meyers, a thirty-two-year-old single woman, who was a physical therapist employed by Cottonwood Acres Rehabilitation Center on North Second Street. She's had several run-ins with her neighbor Lita Brumfield."

"Speaking of these run-ins, why haven't you told me about them?" I asked, getting ready to put him in his place. "Apparently, there's been a lot."

"I have no idea." A scowl drew across his face. "Are you accusing me of something that I have no idea I'm battling? Or are you taking out on me what happened last night because I thought we talked about this earlier."

"According to Avon's mama, she said that Avon and Lita had this ongoing feud over anything as simple as a tree branch over the fence line. She said the law had been called several times. I'd not heard anything about it. I'm betting that you've been on all the calls." I stopped to give him an opportunity to respond.

"Thank God you aren't a betting woman, Sheriff, because you're dead wrong." He looked down at his notes. "I guess you'll need to look into those claims." He began to rattle off the rest of his notes about what he'd uncovered about Avon's personal life that I'd asked him to do earlier.

There wasn't anything in there alarming. She was single, worked every day, and looked to lead a simple life as a Cottonwood citizen.

We both looked back towards the door where someone had knocked. There was a shadow of a person standing there with their hands up around their eyes like they were trying to see in.

Finn opened the door. There stood Lita Brumfield.

"Mrs. Brumfield," I greeted her and walked over so she didn't come in. "I'm Sheriff Lowry."

"I know who you are, and I figured she'd called you about the apple tree." Mrs. Brumfield lifted her chin and drew her eyes down her nose to get a good look at me. "I figured I'd come on over and tell my side of the story so you don't have to make a trip across the lawn."

I stepped outside on the porch and shut the door behind me.

"I was going to stop by and see you." I took out my notebook. "Why don't you give me your account of last night's events."

"It's no secret I wanted to buy this house for my boy and his family. I'm getting up` in age and I don't want to go to no nursing home. I want to stay right here on Hickory Hill in my house. So when Avon's daddy overbid me on the sale of the house, me on limited income and all, I must say that I got a little bitter." The wrinkles around her eyes deepened. "I've made sure that I kept a close eye on her and the laws of this town. I know that she loved her apple tree. But I warned her that if it ever got along my fence line, I'd have it cut back. That's exactly what I did. I didn't go back on my word and I told her near as much a week ago when I saw it was already dangling over into my yard."

"To my understanding, she wanted to pick the apples first. So you couldn't wait until she did that?" I asked, wondering why a little old woman would be so cruel.

"I told her a week ago. She should've kept her eyes on it because those apples started falling a couple of days ago into my yard, sending the squirrels into a frenzy," she spat, her hands trembling at her side. "Now, by the law, I had every right to get those branches cut back."

"I understand that and yes you do, but by civility, we sometimes let things slip. Even a few apples." I couldn't help but think that Lita Brumfield was that neighbor that everyone didn't like, and she used the law to her advantage rather than doing the morally right thing of turning the other cheek when it really wasn't life or death.

"If you let a few apples go here and there, she'd take the whole garden." Lita tried to give me the analogy of give an inch take a mile kind of thing, but she really fell short.

"Can I ask you a personal question?" I couldn't help but notice her shaking hands.

"Yes, you may." She nodded.

"Why are your hands shaking? Do I make you nervous? Is there something you need to tell me?" I asked.

"No, you don't make me nervous." She adjusted her posture to stand as tall as she could. "I'm just fine."

"Can you tell me where you were this morning?" I asked.

"I was sittin' in my house watching the news. How's that any of your business?" she asked. "If you're going to give me a lecture on morality and being a good neighbor, you can save it. I'm planning on going to that town council meeting tomorrow night and bringing up this neighbor, as well as their apple tree issues."

"I'm assuming the town gossip hasn't caught up with you yet." I knew Jolee kept her up on the latest. Jolee loved talking about how all the women who received the Meals On Wheels loved to get her take on the town news while them men just took the food and shut the door in her face.

"I don't gossip. It's a sin. Preacher Bing says so." She swiveled her face over my shoulder when Finn walked out.

"Then you don't know that Avon Meyers's body was found in Rock Fence Park." My words drained the color of her face.

Finn noticed it too and gave her an arm to lean on.

"Mrs. Brumfield," I said her name to get her to blink her eyes. "Did you know Avon was murdered?"

"Oh my stars." She lifted her wrinkly hand to her head and shook as she tried to scratch her eyebrow. Her jaw dropped open. "I had no idea. She was full of life when she beat on my back door after she'd noticed I'd had the limbs cut back." Her voice was softer and held a twinge of disbelief.

"For someone who didn't like her neighbor too well, you seemed to be a little shocked," I said.

"Sheriff, I'm sorry but when anyone dies, it's a tragedy, especially if she was murdered." There was a sadness in her eyes that wasn't there when she was previously talking about Avon. "Are you saying that you think I had anything to do with it?"

"Did you?" I asked. "I mean, you didn't want her moving in and since she has, you've spent a lot of time making sure she'd kept with the laws."

"I think you'd know the full story if you'd showed up when I called the law, but apparently, Cottonwood Sheriff's Department shuts down exactly at five or six p.m. and you let the Clay's Ferry's Sheriff's Department take over, which seems to me that you don't want to keep the hours it takes to be sheriff in Cottonwood and maybe that needs to be brought up tomorrow night."

"Ma'am, we are just trying to get to the bottom of what might've happened to Ms. Meyers." Finn stepped between me and Lita. "Do you drive?"

"No, sir." She gave me one last hard look before she shifted her gaze to Finn. "My son takes me to places I need to go. Or that sweet Jolee Fischer takes me places."

"What's your son's name?" I asked.

"Herb," she said. "Why you ask?"

"I'm just doing my job." Because I'm going to check Herb out, but she didn't need to know that. "Do you think you can come down to the department and give a statement about the turmoil between you and Ms. Meyer or anything you might've seen as a neighbor?"

He had a way about his interrogation that made women putty in his hands.

"I'll call him as soon as I get home and let you know." She nodded.

"Here you go." Finn took a business card out of his pocket and handed it to her. "Here's our number, though I know you have it," he grinned and she gave a slight smile, "if you can remember anything strange or odd, please give me a call."

She pinched a look my way with a straight face, taking the card from Finn.

"Does that sound good?" He asked, bringing her focus back to him.

"It sure will do." She turned to walk down the porch, grabbing the railing with a shaky hand.

We stood there and watched her walk down the front walk leading to the sidewalk before we spoke a word.

"What was that?" Finn muttered.

"It was real sheriff's work." I stood firm.

"You're the one who always yells about being nice and kind. That people in Cottonwood will remember during election time." He huffed.

"That's what you want. You want people to remember just how sweet you are and how I'm the bad sheriff when election time comes so you can take my job." I bit back the real possibility that Finn only wanted my job and not me.

"What are you talking about?" His eyes rounded like this was the first time he'd really honestly thought about the tension this could have on our relationship. "This religion thing has really messed you up."

"I'm not talking about his right here." I headed back into the house, he followed me. "Why do we even care about the religion thing when you want to be a sheriff?"

"Because it's important to know where we stand on it as a couple. What does being a sheriff have to do with it?" He asked, urgency in his voice.

"We both can't be sheriff in Cottonwood." I informed him, proving that I was on to his little scheme.

"Are you kidding me?" He asked with a snarky scowl, lifting his hand, running it through his hair as he paced back and forth in Avon Meyers's front room.

Like the rest of her house, it was nice and tidy. Instead of fussing with Finn, I headed into the kitchen to look around. He continued to talk while I looked through the cabinets and refrigerator. I noticed a laptop open on her kitchen table. When I sat down, the computer screen popped awake.

"We need to take this with us." I closed the laptop and put it on the edge of the table along with my bag so I wouldn't forget it.

I headed over to the refrigerator. Finn was still going through the cabinets.

"I don't want to be sheriff of Cottonwood. I'm more than happy being the deputy, but I can be a sheriff somewhere else. You can be sheriff here. But for right now," he paused, stopping next to the open refrigerator door where I had stuck my head in. He touched me, I turned around. Looking down, he ran a hand down each one of my arms and clasped our fingers. "I'm perfectly happy with us. I'm more than happy being next to you while you take the lead. I'm proud of you. I don't have some big ego that needs to be the man of the relationship."

There was a chill from his touch, or maybe it was the cold draft of the refrigerator door still open, but I still liked how he was holding my hands.

"So, you aren't trying to. . ." I gulped, stopping myself from the silly accusations I'd made in my head and realized they were just in my head. "I'm sorry. When I heard you say something about not wanting to be a deputy all your career and then Avon's parents told me about all the calls Lita had made to the sheriff's department, my mind went wild with all sorts of ideas about you wanting my job."

"No. I don't want your job. But you do have to think about what I said about not being a deputy all my life." He pulled me close to him. "Would you want to be a deputy all your life?" There was a silent pause because he knew I really didn't have to answer that question to know the truth. "On a side note, we do need to think about what Mrs. Brumfield said about adding night hours to our department, even if the town council doesn't approve Deputy Lee for a full-time position."

I was ashamed of myself and he was right. We did need to serve the citizens of Cottonwood a little better with longer hours.

"We will be sure to bring it up tomorrow night. It still doesn't leave the fact that we've got a murder on our hands to solve," I reminded him and looked back into the frig. "Nor does Mrs. Brumfield seem any less a suspect."

"I never said she wasn't a suspect. Even with shaking hands." He took the words right out of my mouth.

"I wonder what's wrong with her? I'll see Jolee at Euchre tonight. I'll be sure to question her." I took out my notepad, flipping it open. I made a few notes about Avon's house been tidy and the fact her food choices were all healthy. From the looks of her body, she appeared to be in good physical health. "It also doesn't mean that Lita didn't hire someone to kill her."

"She really made it clear she didn't want to go to a nursing home and if something is wrong with her health, then she could be really desperate for this house to come on the market." There was an insinuation that if Avon's house did go back up for sale, Lita'd snatch it at any cost.

But murder?

I tugged the walkie talkie strapped onto my shirt's shoulder and pushed the button.

"Betty?" I called for her. It was the best and fastest way I could communicate with her.

"Yes, Kenni," she answered back.

"I need you to pull background checks on Lita Brumfield and Herb Brumfield."

"Lita and Herb Brumfield. Got it." The beep, meaning she'd clicked off, echoed into Avon's house. I reached down and unzipped my bag, plucking out a couple of pairs of gloves. "Let's look for clues around here."

"Sounds good." Finn snapped the gloves in place. "You go that way and I'll go this way. Unless, you have a better idea."

He caught himself giving me an order when it should've been the other way around.

"Stop it. We work well together. I think I can let you lead on this one." I gave him a reassuring smile.

"Kenni bug," Poppa voice echoed from the direction where Finn was going to go look around. "Come in here!"

73

"On second thought," I cringed at what I was about to do since I'd tried to convince him I'd let him take the lead. "Why don't you go that way."

"Yes, ma'am." Finn gave a thin smile and headed in that direction while I hightailed it down the hall until I found Poppa in what appeared to be Avon's office.

"Check out her files." Poppa stood near an old metal filing cabinet.

I wrapped my hand around the handle and pushed the button to the right to release the automatic lock on the drawer. The wheels squeaked when I pulled the drawer open. The files weren't alphabetized but were named. There was one for taxes, student loans, house bills, and CAT.

"Take out the CAT one," Poppa instructed me.

"Okay." I took it out and laid it open flat on her desk. I flipped on the small desk light so I could see better.

This was the time I loved having Poppa as a ghost deputy. He led me right to where I needed to be without going through the hassle of finding things. He didn't cover everything all the time, but he did hit a lot of things on the head. This was one of those times.

"Finn!" I hollered when I noticed there were several write ups from Avon's nurse manager.

When I heard Finn's footsteps stop at the door, I took hold of the file and held it up.

"Apparently, Avon wasn't the model citizen her parents lead me to believe. She has several write ups at work from her nurse manager. Someone by the name of Reagan Quinlan." I held out the file for him to take a look.

"It seems like Avon didn't play by the rules there either." He glanced up at me after he'd read a couple of the charges against her. "Taking a patient out to lunch? When I had rotator cuff surgery, my physical therapist never took me to lunch."

"You had rotator cuff surgery?" I asked.

"No big deal." He shrugged off what seemed like something I should know.

I let it go, but realized we had a lot more to learn about each other than just a religion.

"Rich Moss, Lita Brumfield and now this Reagan Quinlan." I named off the three people that I needed to question about their relationship with our victim. "It looks like we've got a few people to look into."

The rest of the house didn't produce anything that stood out as evidence, but we made sure we took the next couple of hours to comb through everything.

"I'm going to give the Meyers a call and let them know we haven't cleared the house." I pulled my phone from my back pocket. "I'd like to come back with fresh eyes tomorrow or even have Deputy Lee come in."

It wasn't unusual for us to keep a scene a few days, even though it technically wasn't a crime scene.

As I was making my call, Finn's phone rang.

"It's my mom. I need to tell her. . ." he started to say that he needed to tell her I wasn't willing to meet her for lunch, but I was starving and needed to eat anyways.

"Tell her to meet me at Ben's in ten minutes." My words put a smile on his face. I turned the corner to get some privacy while I spoke to Wesley after he answered. "Wesley, this is Sheriff Lowry, I wanted to let you know that I've got some solid people to talk to in the case of Avon. And that we don't want anyone to come into the house as we are treating it like a crime scene."

"Thank you, Sheriff." His voice was low. "We are getting ready to go to the morgue to claim her body. Please keep us up on any details."

"Don't worry. We will keep you posted the entire time until we have whoever did this to Avon in jail." It was a promise I had made and one I was going to keep. No matter what.

CHAPTER TEN

Ben's Diner was in walking distance on Main Street from the department. I'd decided to hoof it down there after I parked the Jeep in the alley behind Cowboy's Catfish. I needed to get my blood flowing and mind cleared of Avon's murder and the Moss's break-in.

There were so many conversations I'd had in my head and things I wanted to say to Shelby but wasn't sure how she was going to take it. After all, if she did bring up the whole religion thing, at no cost was I about to convert to Catholicism.

Through the large diner windows, I could see it was still busy from the lunch crowd, unusual for the time of day since we were past lunch. Someone pushed their way out of the door, without even recognizing I was standing there because they were too busy on their cell phone. I caught the closing door with the heel of my shoe, caught the handle and pulled it open.

The bell over the door signaled my arrival and the smell of delicious cornbread and brown beans made my stomach growl and mouth water.

Ben Harrison stood behind the counter with his normal dress attire of a plaid shirt, jeans, and a dishtowel flung over his left shoulder. We caught eyes and I watched as he looked towards his left where Shelby was waiting. He gave a slight head nod with a grin that told me what had happened between mine and Finn's family had already made the gossip rounds.

I zigzagged through the crowd trying not to make eye contact with anyone. That didn't last long.

Luke and Vita Jones were in the booth behind Mrs. Vincent. Their fidgeting as I got closer was a sure sign they were going to ask me a whole mess of questions. I prided myself on reading body language, since I was the top student in that particular class, and I knew Luke and Vita Jones were hankering to question me about something.

"Hello, dear," Shelby stood up. She fussed with her hands before she dropped them to her stomach.

"Hi," I said, taking a step closer to hug her. Not that she and I had that type of relationship, but Finn and I sure did. She meant a lot to Finn, so I had to try my best. "Sorry about my appearance, but I don't get all gussied up for work."

"Gussied up." She patted me with a pinched look on her face. "Charming."

No, no, no, the words begged my mind when I saw Vita jump up out of the booth and mosey my way.

"Hi do, Kenni." Vita stuck her hand out towards Mrs. Vincent. "You must be Deputy Finn's mama. I'm Vita Jones and this here is my husband, Luke." She put her hand out behind her gesturing to Luke, who at this time had turned completely around in the booth and hunched on his knees.

"Ma'am." Luke took off his John Deere hat. "I hope you ladies come to the theater and enjoy tonight's viewing of Calamity Jane. It's a real humdinger, especially since Kenni here is Cottonwood's own Calamity Jane."

I wasn't sure if that was a compliment or a not. I certainly didn't think I was a salon owner who woo'ed Wild Bill or was Luke trying to make a comparison between me and Finn. With his comment left to hang there, I turned back to Vita.

"I have my Euchre night tonight. I'm sure you'll draw a crowd." My brows rose as I sucked in a deep breath.

"Euchre." Mrs. Vincent's hand tapped the table. "I'm in. I love me a good Euchre game."

"You can't." Vita's nose curled. "They've already got set partners. I've been trying to be invited for years."

"Then you can be my partner." Shelby had totally invited herself and Vita.

"That sounds like a swell idea. I mean, Vita could take Kenni's place since I'm sure you're working on the murder case and all." Luke had readjusted himself. He sat in the seat with his arm up on the back of the booth, turned around.

"Murder investigation?" Mrs. Vincent's mouth dropped, her eyes nearly popped out of her head with shock. "Cottonwood?"

"Why yes, ma'am. Cottonwood's had a few of 'em." Luke nodded.

"They've all been isolated incidents as I'm sure this one is. Now, if you two don't mind, we'd like to order." I threw my hand up in the air for Ben's attention.

"Honey, I don't know what I want." Mrs. Vincent's tone told me I was being rude.

"Here." I plucked the paper menu from in between the salt and pepper shaker. "I suggest the beans and cornbread."

"I'll see you tonight." Vita shimmied her shoulders. "I'm sure you'll go with Kenni." She wiggled her fingers in the air. "See you at Tibbie's."

"That was so kind of her." Mrs. Vincent's eyes scanned down the menu. My silence must've made her look up. "Oh dear, was I not to invite her?"

"It's just that our Euchre games are. . .um. . ." The words all of the sudden left my brain. "It's fine."

There were a chorus of greetings filling the front of the diner. Shelby and I turned to the door. My stomach dropped when I saw it was Mama and her Sweet Adeline group. My presence didn't go unnoticed. Our eyes met before she glared at Mrs. Vincent.

Mama touched her sleek, brown hair with her white gloved hands. It was a polished coif, a sure sign that she'd be going out. She whispered something to Viola White and fluttered a finger towards the counter. Viola motioned for the others to follow her where they took the open stools butted up to the counter.

Mama's purse dangled from the crook of her arm and swung to and fro as she made her way over to our booth.

"Here's a couple of waters." Ben made it before Mama. He pulled the pen from behind his ear and tugged the ordering pad out of his back pocket. "What'll y'all have?"

"I see we are having some lunch." Mama peered behind him before she took a step in front and scooted Ben to the side.

"We'll have the cornbread and beans." Shelby tucked the menu back between the salt and pepper shaker. "I'd ask you to join us, Vivian, but I see you're with your friends."

"The Sweet Adelines. We are the local singing group. We are very good." Mama plucked the gloves off, one finger at a time.

I rolled my eyes because her dramatic flair was as subtle as a choo-choo train blowing its whistle.

"I'm sure you carry a fine tune." Shelby brought the glass of water up to her lips and took a drink.

"Well, Kendrick." Mama's nostrils flared as she tried to keep her composure. "I'll be seeing you later tonight."

"Me too. I love a good competitive game of Euchre." Mrs. Vincent's lips curled into what I'd call a getting-even smile because she knew she had Mama in a little pickle.

Not only was I sitting there eating with her, but now she was going to our weekly Euchre game, which would have been Mama's chance to let everyone know about the whole supper fiasco.

"Well," Mama gasped. "You've got to have a partner."

I gripped the edges of the vinyl booth just waiting for Mama's reaction when I saw Shelby open her mouth.

"Lucky for me, I've got Vita," Shelby looked as me and asked, "Vita, correct?"

I gulped and nodded.

"Vita is free tonight. I believe she runs a movie theater in town." Shelby fluttered her hands. "Anyways, we are looking forward to it."

"Kendrick," Mama said my name with gritted teeth behind her smile. "I'd like to see you outside."

"Excuse me." I got up and grabbed a piece of the warm plate of cornbread Ben had reached around me to put on the table.

Mama's heels were clicking so hard on the black and white old tile of the floor, I swear I thought she was going to break one. Ben had just spent a lot of money and hours redoing the diner after it'd been showcased on the Culinary Channel's Southern Home Cookin' Show.

He really had Mama to thank for all the exposure and pick up in customers who had come far and wide to visit the diner. She'd won a local cooking contest and somehow someone in the culinary industry got wind of it. They featured her and her chicken pot pie on the show. Her head had been twice the size of Cottonwood. It took a few months for it to deflate, but she deserved it. She was a good cook.

"What do you think you are doing?" Mama grabbed me by the elbow.

I cringed at the pinch.

"I'm a grown woman and can eat with whoever I please." I jerked away. "Stop treating me like this in public."

"I don't care who you eat with, but I do care that you invited her into our private group. Vita. Vita Jones?" Mama's jaw dropped. "You know that Camille Shively and Vita don't get along."

"I think Camille Shively is adult enough to put aside whatever feelings she has for Vita Jones." I referred to the town's doctor as I shoved the cornbread in my mouth.

Apparently, Vita had sent Luke to her. Luke went home and commented how pretty Camille was and Vita made an unfounded claim that she'd made a pass at Luke. A far cry from the truth, I'd bet my whole career on it.

There was a hurt in Mama's eyes. More of a betrayal than hurt, but to me, it was all still hurt.

"Listen." I inched out of the way of the door that someone was trying to get through, dragging Mama with me. "You're my mama. Things might not've gone exactly how you and I saw it. But she loves her son just as much as you love me." I lifted up my left hand. "Do you see a ring on this finger from White's Jewelry? Did Viola White tell you that Finn came in to get an engagement ring? Or even better, did Finn ask you and Daddy if he could marry me?"

My head started spinning. Was he going to do the right thing when the time came and ask my daddy for my hand in marriage? Had he gotten Southern enough since he'd been in Cottonwood to know he was supposed to do that?

"No, Viola has not and he's not." Mama's chin lifted with a little more spirit in her eyes.

"Then you don't have to worry about me taking a kneel in any Catholic church. Why can't you just enjoy his family while they are here. They want to like me as much as you love me and you're making that difficult." It was a reality that I knew she needed to hear. "I love that you're a big Southern mama and I hope to be just like you one day."

"If that's the case," she muttered and snapped open the top of her purse, "you can start by putting on some lipstick. You look like that dead girl I found." She rolled up the brightest red lipstick and handed it out to me.

"You just won't do." I laughed and applied the glossy red to make her happy.

"Speak of the devil." Mama's head tilted around me. "If it ain't Wally Lamb."

"We weren't talking about Wally Lamb." Or had I totally missed some sort of conversation Mama had but too caught up in making things right with Shelby that I didn't hear her.

"No, but I was going to ask you about him and that girl." Her gaze shifted as she followed him getting closer to us. "Mrs. Kim said that her daughter, Gina Kim, told her that Wally and Avon come into Kim's Buffet. They shared a moogoo gipain."

"Is that right?" I knew I'd heard some rumblings about it earlier but figured nothing of it. "Wally," I greeted him just as he stopped shy of us.

"Just the sheriff I wanted to see." Wally's face was different today. He still had on his cheap two-piece brown suit and his blond hair was slicked back with gel, the new way he'd been wearing it. The brown leather shoes were shinier than his hair. "We need to converse."

"Is that your way of asking to talk to me? Because I need to talk to you, but I'm currently having lunch with Finn's mama." I pointed back into the diner where I'd left her.

"Now. Right now." He nodded his head.

"What's this about, Wally?" Mama stuck her nose in it.

"Mrs. Mother Sheriff, I think it's none of your business." He gave Mama a hard stare that told her to butt out.

"Wally Lamb, you outta be ashamed of how you treat the elderly. I bet your mama won't like it when I tell her at bell choir just how much you acted up today." Mama didn't mind scolding someone for bad manners, no matter their age. "Kendrick, I'll see you at Euchre." She patted my hand. "You go on now and I'll take care of Shelby, though she really shouldn't have that name. It's a disgrace. The Catholic thing and now Shelby."

"What on earth are you talking about now?" I felt my blood pressure rising. What on Earth had she found fault in her this time?

"Shelby was a beloved character, Southern mind you, in Steel Magnolias. She has tainted that name forever." Mama lifted the back of her hand to her forehead as if she were about to faint at the idea.

My right brow lifted in disbelief.

"Wally, give me a second to say goodbye to her." I held up a finger and pulled the door of the diner open.

Mama headed in before me with a little more sashay in her walk. My little talk to her must've done some good because her attitude was much better than it had been a few minutes before.

"Mrs. Vincent." My mouth watered when I saw the bowl of beans had been delivered. "I'm sorry but I've got to go. I need to talk to someone about the case." I grabbed my bowl of beans and looked over the heads of the crowd to find Ben.

All I had to do was hold it up in the air and he hurried over with a to go bowl and box that I was sure was filled with cornbread.

"Don't you worry." Mama sat down where I'd been sitting. "We've got a little business of our own to discuss. We'll be just fine, Kendrick." Mama gave a sweet smile that kinda scared me. "Isn't that right?" The smile never faltered as she looked over at Mrs. Vincent.

"Yes. We'll see you tonight at Euchre." Shelby took the napkin from her lap and dotted the corners of her mouth.

CHAPTER ELEVEN

I hated leaving Shelby alone with Mama. Ben told me he'd keep an eye and ear on them after he'd handed me my to go boxes. The issues between the mothers was going to have to work itself out one way or the other.

Wally Lamb was standing outside of the diner waiting on me.

"I hope you got an extra bowl for me." Wally winked, something his old self would do.

"I didn't." My words were going to be straight forward because Wally had a knack for switching things around on me. "I've got two things to discuss with you."

The sun was beating down and the temperatures were getting into those hot late summer afternoons where you just didn't feel like doing anything but sippin' on some cold, fresh, and sugary iced tea.

"I'm probably going to be discussing the same with you." He walked down the sidewalk next to me.

"Avon Meyers," I said.

He said at the exact same time, "Woody Moss's cuff links."

I stopped, and he stopped. We looked at each other.

"How did you know about Avon and me?" His eyes narrowed.

"You don't know that she was killed this morning? Someone found her

83

in the park." How had this type of gossip not gotten ahead of the police announcement? A rarity in Cottonwood.

"Where?" He asked with a stiff upper lip.

"Rock Fence Park. Was there something going on between the two of you?" I asked.

"Nothing personal." He looked at his watch. "I have, had, a meeting with her around five tonight to discuss something she said she'd uncovered and needed help with."

"What was it?" Did Wally have a clue as to why someone had killed Avon Meyers?

"I don't know. She called me and we had lunch at Kim's Buffet. She asked all sorts of questions about what if she knew there was a crime about to be committed. If they got caught and she was named that she knew about it, would she get in trouble." He followed me around the corner of the building of Cowboy's Catfish.

Bartleby Fry probably wouldn't've been happy if he'd seen me walk in with a Ben's Diner bag.

"I told her that it could be considered aiding and abetting, depending on the severity of the crime." He walked into me when we rounded the corner to walk down the alley.

"She didn't tell you anything about it? Or anyone involved?" I questioned and opened the door to the department.

"She said that she'd get back to me after she thought about it." He reached over my head and grabbed the door, holding it for me.

It took a second for my eyes to adjust from the bright sun to the dim lights inside. Betty Murphy was sitting at her desk and Finn was standing next to one of two white boards with a dry-erase marker in his hand. Deputy Lee wasn't there.

"What's going on?" Finn was taken by surprise after he noticed the bag I was holding.

"Wally Lamb wanted to talk to me." I set the bag on the top of my desk and opened it.

Duke was fast asleep in his dog bed next to my desk. His snoring made me smile. I was tired too and a bit jealous he was getting in some much-needed rest.

Ben had scribbled a note that he'd put three bowls of beans for the group at the department, meaning me, Betty, and Finn, and taped it to a bowl along with plenty of cornbread. "I'm thinking we were going to talk about the cuff links and Avon Meyers."

"I don't know a thing about her." His eyes were fixed on the containers I was taking out of the bag. "Like I said, we were going to meet tonight because she saw me at the funeral home and told me that she wanted to meet with me today at five when she got off work."

I handed out the food and gave Wally my bowl of beans since I'd lost my appetite. I traded Finn the dry-erase marker for his bowl of beans. He'd already put the header on the boards. One was labeled Moss Burglary and the other white board was labeled Avon Meyers Murder.

"Hasn't he got it all together?" Poppa had ghosted himself between the boards, looking at them. Duke jumped up out of his deep slumber to rush over to the ghost.

Poppa had actually given Duke to me as a present one year. Duke and Poppa had a special bond.

"What's wrong with him?" Wally asked when he noticed Duke jumping up, wagging his tail and settle down a few times when Poppa patted him, only to go right back to jumping on his hind legs to get Poppa to continue to rub.

"He does this every few months." Finn shrugged a shoulder and reached over to the edge of his desk to grab one of Duke's treats from the jar. "Here, buddy!" Finn gave a little whistle.

"My big Duke, boy." Poppa made sure he kept Duke's attention with kisses and rubs so Duke wouldn't fall for Finn's tactics. "Who's Poppa's big furry boy?"

I gave a hard eye roll.

"He's a dog. Who knows what they think," I said to Wally and focused my attention to the white board with Avon's name. "She knew something?"

"She said she needed legal advice about if she knew something was happening illegally and if she'd get in trouble if she didn't report it." He put his hands in the air. "When I heard she was killed, a red flag went up."

Wally grabbed one of the chairs in front of my desk and dragged it over to the edge of Finn's desk where they opened the takeout food.

85

"It certainly should. If she knew something illegal was going on, the person obviously wanted her silenced." I wrote down on the board how Avon got in contact with Wally Lamb.

Finn had started eating his food and flipped through his notepad.

"No better way to silence someone than kill them," Poppa said. "Kenni Bug, I think a great place to start is the rehab center where she worked since she was there all the time."

"We need to go to the Cottonwood Acres Rehabilitation Center since she was there all the time." Finn looked up from his notebook. He took out some envelopes from her file. "Here are some paystubs. She worked a lot of overtime and PRN. Maybe she knew something going on there."

Finn's words were almost identical to what Poppa had said. Mine and Poppa's jaw dropped at the same time.

"Can you see me, boy?" Poppa ghosted next Finn, wildly clapping his hands in Finn's face. "Don't you be ignoring me, boy."

"Umm." I tried to shake Poppa off Finn, but he was like a hound dog on a coon.

"Can you hear me?" Poppa started to whistle, Duke started to howl and I couldn't hold in my laughter.

"What is going on around here?" Wally Lamb's face contorted. "You've lost your mind, Kendrick Lowry."

"I did that a long time ago." I joked and got my composure together. "Like Finn said, maybe Avon knew something about the rehab center."

"I said that." Poppa pointed to himself. "I did." He ghosted away.

"Like insurance fraud. Or even elderly abuse," Betty chimed up.

"Elderly abuse?" I questioned her, happy to have Poppa gone so I could concentrate.

"Yes. I've heard so many terrible stories about how those places treat their elderly clients. Especially the Alzheimer's patients because they don't remember how they got a bruise when someone beats them." Her words formed images in my head that made me so sad.

"I wonder if that's why Lita wanted someone to take care of her at her house and wanted her son to move in." I wrote down Lita's name under Avon's name.

"Lita Brumfield?" Wally asked.

"She and Avon had a very volatile neighborly relationship." I put dots under Lita's name so I could go back and fill in what she'd told me earlier. I wasn't finished with interviewing her.

Betty was sitting at her desk. She was watching everyone speak and taking it all in.

"Betty, are you dictating all of this for Avon's file?" It was part of her job to take the notes and update the computer files so we could easily access those.

Since Finn had become a deputy, he'd tried so hard to bring us up to modern technology. The new computer system had made it so we could tap into the larger, universal databases, which was nice. But when it came to cell phones and computers in the cars, Betty and I put our feet down. We liked our walkie-talkies. They were easy to use and easy to charge. If we needed something quick, it was on the walkie-talkie so everyone in the department was informed. If I needed to talk to one of them about a certain subject that didn't need to involve everyone, then I used the cell phone to call.

"Got it." Betty twirled around in her chair. She put her hand on the computer mouse and shook it back and forth a few times before her computer buzzed to life.

"Tell me when you're caught up," I said to her and took the time to let the boys eat and for me to finish writing on Avon's board. "According to the paperwork we found at her house, she had been written up a few times and we need to talk to the nurse manager about that while we are there.

Under Lita's name, I made bullet points about how she'd complained about Avon and made a note to get the transcripts from the Clay's Ferry sheriff's department dispatch services. I also put that in my notebook so I wouldn't forget. I had to drop off Avon's purse to Tom Geary's crime scene lab that I used, which was located just on the outskirts of Clay's Ferry. It'd be easy to just drop that off for fingerprints and head straight into Clay's Ferry while I'd be in the area.

Unfortunately, daylight and time was running out today. These were some things that would have to wait until tomorrow or the next day.

"You can't do it all in one day." Poppa had come back. "I can read you like a book, Kenni bug. His eyes shifted to Finn. He shook his head with a disappointed frown.

Finn was gobbling up the beans and cornbread talking to Wally about the upcoming high school football season. It was a big deal around here. Cottonwood lived for their high school sports. The football team had done really well the last few years and won state, making the games the biggest Friday night activity during the fall and winter months.

I turned back to the white board and continued to write under Lita Brumfield's name. I even began to write questions, so Poppa could see since we couldn't play our

"back and forth what if" game right now because everyone was here.

Does Lita know anything about elderly abuse at the rehab center? I wrote, following up with more questions. Did Avon know about elderly abuse or other illegal activities? Is this why the nurse manager was trying so hard to write her up? Avon appeared to have been written up for silly things like being a minute late, eating lunch at her work station, wearing non-slip shoes while doing PT with the clients. Though I did understand it was probably crossing the line when she took a patient out to lunch, but who was the patient? Was it Woody Moss?

That made me write Rich Moss on the white board.

"Rich Moss?" Wally took the napkin and wiped off his mouth. "What's that guy got to do with anything?"

"When I was at Woody's funeral, I overheard him threatening Avon. It was odd. I have a plan to go over there tonight on my way to Euchre since their house is right there." I tapped the marker on his name.

"You know, Woody came to me and asked me to defend the kid." Wally looked up to ceiling and rolled his eyes. "He was on the video camera smashing in the glass cases of the jewelry store. He even looked at the camera and smiled." He leaned back in his chair and put his hands on his full stomach. "I told Woody there was no way I was touching that case."

"If Woody was so good to him, why would Rich want to burglarize the house?" Finn asked a good question and looked at the other white board.

"These are two separate crimes, right?" Wally looked between me and Finn, the lines on his forehead deepened.

"Yes, but it seems like Rich has ties to both." I wrote Rich's name down under Moss Burglary. "Were you Woody's lawyer? Is that why he came to you about Rich?"

There was a loyalty with Southerners that ran as deep as blood. Once they found a doctor, they stuck with that doctor. Same went for hairdresser, church, clubs and friendships. They might have disputes among themselves, but when it came to a time of crisis, loyalty ran deep.

"I was. In fact, after that boy was tried and sent to jail, Woody had me change his will." Wally nodded. "Had me take him completely out. Now with the state law, I even had to put the clause in there that said Mr. Moss had specifically taken Rich out of the will with sound mind."

"Really?" I bit the inside of my jaw. "He didn't so happen to be giving Rich those cuff links, did he?" That gave Rich full motive to take those cuff links.

"You know about those, huh?" Wally sat up, taking interest.

"Those were the only things missing from the burglary that Mrs. Moss could tell." I finished writing down how Woody had his will changed. "Can I get the dates of the will change?"

Wally let out a long sigh like he was thinking about it.

"It's easier if you sign off on the paperwork than making me go through a judge for a warrant." I reminded him that no matter what, I'd get the judge to make him turn those over.

"I don't see why not but let me make sure with Mrs. Moss first." He wasn't about to give up a client. The Moss family was loyal to him. Like I said, blood or not, loyalty ran deep around here and he was just as loyal to them.

"Sheriff's department," Betty grabbed up the phone. Her round eyes caught mine. "Yes, Mr. Mayor, she's right here. Hold on." She held up two fingers to let me know he was on line two.

"Hello, Chance," I answered the phone and put the lid back on the dry-erase marker. I sat on the edge of my desk with the phone cradled between my shoulder and ear and continued to look over the white boards. "We are just having a little pow-wow to go over both investigations," I answered his question on how far along we were into both crimes. "I'll have an update for both of them and some leads before I come to the town council meeting."

"He's always on you," Finn said after I'd hung up the phone with the mayor.

"Yeah, but even with his flaws, he still asked Polly Parker's dad for her hand in marriage," I let out a long sigh like that really meant something to me, since I was fishing for an answer to my earlier questions of Finn's actions when it comes to marriage.

"That was a random thing to say," Wally scoffed with a laugh, elbowing Finn's upper arm as he got up to throw away his empty food containers.

"Chivalry isn't dead on everyone." I didn't bother trying to go into more detail because being subtle wasn't a strong suit of mine and if Finn didn't catch on to what I was saying now then he wasn't going to.

"It's five o'clock," Betty reminded me it was time for her to go home. She didn't work a minute after. "Is this all?"

"You can go on. We won't be able to solve this in a day." I looked over at Poppa. He was sitting in my chair with his legs propped up on the desk, a glow exuded from the smile on his face. He loved when I quoted him. "In the morning, I'll be running around to look into various leads, so if you need me, just call my cell. Or if it's important, you know how to use the walkie-talkies."

"What are you going to have me do?" Finn asked, cleaning up his empty food containers. Since I'd voiced my opinion to him earlier about the roles in our jobs, he seemed to be more accommodating to asking me what I needed of him.

"Since you and Wally are so chummy," I gestured between them, "I'd like you to go to his office and get a copy of the dates of the will change and even look into Rich's jail time. If he got off on good behavior, how? What did he do?"

I knew it was menial work that needed to be done, but it kept him out of the way of my investigation since I still wasn't so sure about his loyalty to me as the sheriff. I could definitely say he was loyal as a boyfriend, but not so much in the area of our job.

Finn wasn't born and bred Southern or Baptist. There was some doubt in the back of my head that made me want to discover the truth before we did take our relationship further than it'd already gone.

"I'll be in my office tomorrow around 9 a.m." Wally's voice carried from across the room where he walked into the bathroom and shut the door behind him.

Betty put her pocketbook back on her desk and took off her coat. She sat down at her desk. I looked at her and put the lid back on the dry-erase marker.

"I forgot, I've got something I can finish real quick." She busied herself by shuffling a few papers and sticking some loose pencils in her pencil cup.

"We have to get to our Euchre game." I referred to me and Betty, putting the dry-erase marker down and walked over to my desk to gather all my things, putting them in my bag.

Even though I left the office, the crimes were going to be in the fore front of my head. There were many times I'd sit at my kitchen table and have everything spread out like a jigsaw puzzle. Sometimes my brain worked best when the evidence was in front of me and I could see if any of it fit together.

"Don't forget the purse," Finn reminded and walked over to the small safe where he checked to make sure it was locked.

"I'll come here in the morning and grab it before I head out of town." There was no way I was going to take it home with me and risk the accusations of any sort of contamination.

"Sheriff?" A male voice cut through the air after the door opened. We turned to see who it was.

"Yes?" I instantly recognized the man. It was the man Avon was talking to at the Moss's house after Woody' funeral. He had the same light brown hair that was a little longer in the back, making it curl up around the edges of his neck line. He had thick brows and tan skin. He wore a blue shirt with an EMT logo I'd recognized from the fire department's ambulance service that the town council had approved to work side jobs. His biceps told me he worked out often.

"Sebastian Hughes, is it?" I asked, dropping the bag back on the floor next to my desk.

Duke sensed we weren't leaving because he let out a groan and went to lay back down on his bed. Poppa wasn't anywhere to be seen.

"How do you know my name?" He asked with a curious look on his face.

"You were at Woody Moss's house after the funeral." I watched his eyes scan over my shoulder and look at Avon's white board before he slammed his eye lids shut like he didn't want to see it.

"I also know that you were talking to Avon Meyers. Is that why you're here?" I had already written in my notebook to be sure to see him about their relationship.

Without me saying anything, Finn got up and rotated both boards around so they weren't visible to the public. We didn't know Sebastian. Maybe he knew something, maybe he even knew who did it, and we didn't want any information we had leaking out.

"That's why I'm here," he said.

It looked like I was going to be late to Euchre. And so was Betty Murphy. She leaned in, peeling an ear to pick up any juicy tidbits. Her curiosity was one of her greatest vices.

"Can I get you something to drink?" I asked him. He shook his head. "Then why don't you have a seat." I turned my chin over my left shoulder. "Betty, please dictate."

While we all got a little more comfortable, Wally exited the bathroom drying his hands with a paper towel. He looked up with a bit of a surprise on his face when he noticed the young man at my desk and everyone was back to business.

"I'll see you tomorrow." Was Finn's polite way of telling Wally goodbye. Plus, Finn holding the door open wasn't exactly a subtle gesture.

"I'll have everything ready." Wally gave everyone one last look before he left.

I'd seen him do this before in legal situations. Wally would make a mental note of everyone and everything going on in a room. When he left the room, he'd quickly jot down everything he could remember. It was a defense he liked to use in court with his clients. Details, details, and more details. He confused the jury more than clarified for them. He used all of the details to his advantage to prove that there still might be reasonable doubt that his client is innocent.

The top drawer of my desk held the mini-tape recorder. I opened the drawer and put a new tape in before I hit the record button, placing it at the edge of my desk.

"Please state your name and the date." I began taking notes and could hear Betty typing as he answered my questions. There was nothing I wanted to miss. It was actually the first person who'd come forward that wanted to talk about it. Generally I had to hunt people down.

"Why are you here today?" I asked.

"I wanted to come by and tell you something I'd seen because I think it has to do with Avon's murder." His brows furrowed.

"What is that?" I asked.

Betty's chair creaked. I could imagine her really leaning forward to hear well. Not for the sake of the job, but for the gossip, which she would need to be reminded was all confidential.

"I worked with Avon. Not really worked with her, but I work as an EMT for Cottonwood and the rehab center. So we would see each other from time to time." He leaned forward, placing his elbows on his thighs, his hands clasped in front of him. "She had been going on some dates with this guy. She told me he liked nature and outdoor things. I had to work the early shift one morning. We had a kid from the high school football team brought in to the rehab for a quick x-ray because he tore his ACL."

"Which kid?" Finn asked.

I shot him a glare.

"Sorry. It's just they are supposed to be good again this year and if he's a big asset to the team, it could change it all." Finn shrugged.

"You two can talk about that in a minute." I turned back to Sebastian. "You transported the kid to the rehab. Go on."

It wasn't unusual for the rehab to have an EMT squad run since it was a huge facility that did take emergencies on most orthopedics and did the surgeries there. Even the overnight beds, where Woody had stayed, wasn't uncommon so they could get the physical therapy they needed.

"She wasn't there yet. Which was really unusual. She would typically be there early drinking coffee and eating some pastries from the Sweet Shop."

I wrote down the Sweet Shop on my list of stops for the case in my notebook.

"When I finished the paperwork from the kid, I asked Reagan where Avon was." He stopped when I held up a hand.

"Reagan Quinlan, the nurse manager?" I asked to clarify since I already had her listed as a suspect.

"I don't know her last name but she's the manager," he confirmed. "She said that she didn't care because this was Avon's third write up which meant she was fired."

A pin-drop silence fell across the room as his words crawled out of his mouth.

"Reagan told you this?" I confirmed. It was a bit odd for a professional manager to react in such a way.

"Yes." He nodded.

"You know that I'm going to need to confirm this with her." I let him know up front in case he was unaware that that was how investigations went.

"If it brings Avon's killer to justice, I'm fine with it. Avon is..." he looked down at his hands, "was a very good person. She was honest, kind, and caring not only to her patients but all the people she worked with."

"Other than Reagan," Betty's sarcasm was apparent in her voice.

"Yeah. They had a really bad relationship. It seemed like all of Avon's relationships were strained and I wasn't sure why." He let out a grunt noise that made me believe he was going to say something else but stopped himself.

"How well did you know Avon Meyers?" I asked.

"Just working with her. That's all, but she was easy to talk to and get to know. I hate that someone did this to her." He straightened himself up in the chair.

"Is there anything else you wanted to tell me?" I asked, not forgetting the pause he'd had a few seconds ago.

"No." He shook his head. "I just don't know of anyone who didn't like her other than her manager. That to me is a likely suspect and I told her parents that when I went over there to give my condolences. They are the ones who told me to come tell you what I saw at work and what I'd heard."

"What do you mean by what you saw?" I asked.

"Just the way Reagan groaned when Avon walked into her line of vision. The scowl on her face like she couldn't stand the sight of her. It was really odd." He was looking off into the distance as if he were playing the images in his mind. "But that's all I know. I hope this won't hurt my job because I need it, but I just had to come forward."

"I appreciate you coming in tonight." I put the pen down and sat back in my chair, folding my hands over my stomach. "I'll be sure to follow up on all this. But in the meantime, if you remember anything else, please come back.

You did the right thing. Any information, no matter how small or big, is always information that can lead to an arrest."

"Yeah, man." Finn got out of his chair. "Like you, her parents and we want this to be brought to a quick close. Avon deserves that. You did the right thing."

Finn put his hand on Sebastian's shoulder and they shook hands with the free hand. Finn guided him out the door. I overheard him say, "Tell me about that kid you brought in."

Betty and I looked at each other.

"Men." She shook her head. "Let's get to Euchre. Better late than never."

"I'm afraid I'm going to be a little later." My eyes narrowed on the back sides of the Moss's burglary white board. As though I had x-ray vision, I could see one bold name.

I know what Sebastian had said about Avon's relationship with the nurse manager, but there were two crimes in Cottonwood less than twenty-four hours apart and only one common denominator.

Rich Moss.

CHAPTER TWELVE

The days were getting longer, which made it feel like it was earlier than it really was. The burnt orange sun was touching the tops of the trees and the shadows of the last bit of rays splayed across the pavement in front of the Jeep as I made my way over to see Lenora Moss.

Technically, I didn't want to see her, I wanted to see if she'd let me go through Rich's things. Or better yet, talk to Rich myself since I'd yet to tell him that I wanted to interview him. My plan was to see what he was willing to admit to and compare notes after I'd gone to the sheriff's department in Clay's Ferry in the morning.

The clothesline on the side of Lenora's house had freshly cleaned linens secured with wooden clothes pins. The pieces swayed back and forth as the light breeze circled around them. There was a certain fresh smell to line dried clothes and no matter how hard a detergent company tried, they'd never get that smell. It was so strong, the clean scent floated through the open windows of the Wagoneer when I put it in park at the front of the curb nearest to that side of the house.

There didn't seem to be any other cars besides Lenora's tucked into the carport that was attached to the small house. There was a light on in the window in the front of the house. If I recalled correctly, it was where the family room was located, but we'd spent most of our time in the bedroom where the burglary had taken place.

"You stay here," I instructed Duke.

He groaned, leaning his body against the passenger seat, and resting his chin on the sill of the open window.

Once I got up to the front door, I glanced back at him. His eyes were closed, and the last bit of the day's sunshine was beating down on his snout. He loved resting in the sun.

The doorbell was lit up on the side of the door. When I pushed it, I heard a faint ding-dong on the other side of the door followed up by some footsteps. When the footsteps stopped, I took a step back from the door to let Lenora see it was me when she peeled the curtain back from the window and peered out.

"Sheriff, come on in." She'd opened the door and extended her arm to open the screen door as far as she could.

"I didn't catch you at a bad time, did I?" I asked.

"No, no." The dark circles under her eyes told me she was just being polite. "I'm in here trying to figure out these bills. Woody did all the payments and I'm not even sure how much is in our checking account or anything." She waved me in.

When I took a step inside, I noticed her body tensed as she glanced around before stepping back inside of the house.

"I'm hoping you found the cuff links because we sure could use the money." The edges of her eyes dipped with concern. The TV was playing the local news in the corner of the room, but the sound was down. All sorts of papers were spread across the coffee-table and a few had fallen on the floor. There was a calculator next to a pad of paper with some sort of math scribbled on it.

"I'm sorry. I have Deputy Lee checking out all the pawn shops around here and surrounding counties. It would be helpful if you had a photo of Woody wearing them to take with me," I suggested.

"I'm not sure I have anything, but I'll go check." She took off towards the hallway but turned back around. "Don't mind all that. Just sit down and make yourself at home."

Though Lenora had said something about the checkbook and their finances, plus the fact that it wasn't my business, I still couldn't keep myself from looking. It wasn't nosey if the papers were right there in front of me.

I leaned over the table and noticed court records without even trying to figure out what they were. I was very familiar with them, only it had a Clay's Ferry seal on top. The name typed on the papers was "Rich Moss."

It was his early release paperwork. Next to that was the piece of paper where Lenora'd done a little math. After it was all totaled up, she'd put a big circle around "twenty thousand." Was that dollars? Did they owe that much, and she was trying to figure out how to pay it? Or was that what she had in the bank? Why was Rich's paperwork lumped into her financial paperwork?

The tip-top of the Cottonwood First National's letterhead, our local bank, was peeking out from another stack of papers. I barely slid it out to see if I could see what it was. Maybe their statement or their house payment. There was a big red stamp on the top right corner that said it was paid in full.

I looked around and kept my ears and eyes open so I could hear or see if Lenora was coming back before I pulled the bank statement out from under the stack to get a good look at it.

It was a mortgage pay off on their house from two years ago. It seemed like Woody had left Lenora a paid-off house, which was pretty great. So why all the paperwork and what did the twenty thousand mean?

The shuffling of feet on carpet was coming closer. I stuffed the paper back under the stack and quickly sat down in a chair next to the couch.

"I couldn't find one, but I'll be sure to keep looking." She shook her head. "I don't know where my manners are, but would you like a cup of coffee?"

"No thank you, I'm good." I watched her ease back down into the couch with that same worried look on her face.

"Lenora, are you in financial trouble?" Her body language shifted to stiff. "I hate to ask, but you said that 'we could use the money'. Who is 'we'?"

"Me. I mean," she hesitated and reached over to the paperwork, flipping some of the papers over. "I don't work and I need to know my money."

I could tell she wasn't going to tell me anything.

"I came here to ask you more about the burglary. Specifically, about your grandson Rich." There was an audible inhale through her nose when I said his name. More a sound of frustration than regular breathing. "I understand he was let out of jail on good behavior for a theft crime."

"You think he stole Woody's cuff links?" Her brows lifted in the air. "He didn't."

"It was my understanding that Woody had changed his will and had taken Rich out of it." I paused to see if she was going to say anything.

It was the pregnant pause tactic that we were taught in the police academy to use when we wanted to get information out of someone. Just a few seconds without talking when questioning someone made them uncomfortable and forced them to say things.

In Lenora's case, it wasn't working. She sat tight lipped, hands rested in her lap. Cool as a cucumber.

"When I was at Woody's funeral, I couldn't help but overhear Rich threatening a young woman." My words caused her to look up at me. "That young woman was Avon Meyers, Woody's physical therapist."

Lenora's eyes grew big. Her throat moved up and down as though she was swallowing words back.

"Avon Meyers was killed this morning. She was found at Rock Fence Park with a gunshot wound." Without actually coming out and accusing Rich, I danced around the fact that he had a connection to both crimes. "In my line of duty, when there are a couple of crimes committed around the same time as each other, and someone is linked to both, I have to take a serious look at that person." I eased up on the edge of the chair. I wanted her to hear me loud and clear. "I'm not saying Rich did anything wrong. I'm saying that it is odd that I had seen him at the funeral home arguing with a young woman. He leaves the funeral home before it's over. We come back here and your husband's expensive cuff links that were willed to Rich had been stolen—the only thing stolen."

Her body language told me she was uncomfortable with where this was going. Her mouth continued to swallow and her eyes shifted around the room. Her toes barely tapped the floor.

"The young lady he argued with just so happened to turn up dead. Is this all a coincidence? Maybe. But in my line of work, that's rare." My voice turned soft and caring, "I came here in hopes you'd let me look into his things since he's staying with you."

"He's gone." Her words were to the point.

"What do you mean by gone?" I asked.

"He's left town already." She wrung her hands in front of her.

"Where did he go?" I asked her.

"I don't know. But I do know that he didn't kill that girl." She didn't quiver when she said that. "He was with me all night until this morning."

"What time did he leave you this morning?" I wanted to check the time with the timeline Max Bogus came up with, which reminded me that I'd yet to hear from him with that information.

"He left around four thirty." She stood up. "If you don't mind, I'm tired. Please let me know when you find the cuff links."

This was my cue that she was done.

"Lenora, please, let me know if you remember anything about Avon's interaction with Rich at the Cottonwood Acres Rehabilitation Center. I'm trying to help her family cope with their loss like your loss. I'm doing everything I can to find Woody's cuff links." My words were only words to her, but I meant all of them.

"Don't worry about the mule going blind, Kenni Bug." Poppa gave a good hard stare at Lenora. "Just load the wagon." He repeated, "just load the wagon."

In Poppa speak, he was telling me not to worry about what Lenora was keeping from me. Collect the clues and they'd all fall into place. That was exactly what I was going to do. Load the wagon.

CHAPTER THIRTEEN

My eyes focused on the spot in Rock Fence Park where Avon was found as I drove past, very slowly, on my way to Tibbie's house. The thought crossed my mind that at this time yesterday, the likeable, vibrant girl full of life and adored by many was living her life, only to be killed less than ten hours later.

The first forty-eight hours of a homicide was crucial to finding the killer. In an elected position like sheriff, it was very important in a small town like Cottonwood to get the crime solved and killer brought to justice if I wanted to be reelected. Learning the timeline of her death was crucial.

Here, people were connected to each other on various levels. Someone had to know Reagan Quinlan well enough to know why she didn't like one of her physical therapists. I needed to find out more about her.

That was something I was definitely planning to do in the morning. I pulled the Wagoneer in front of Tibbie's house on the Town Branch and could see in the windows that everyone was still gathered in the room on the left, which was were Tibbie kept the food.

The room on the right where the Euchre tables were set up was empty. Surely they weren't waiting on me. There was always an extra person there in case someone didn't show or was late. Then I remembered Shelby and Clay and maybe that'd thrown them for a loop.

Before I went in, I let Duke run around as he was determined to sniff every blade of grass and smell all the bushes, while I made a quick call to Max.

"Good evening, Kenni," Max greeted me as soon as he answered the phone.

"Hey, I was about to go into my Euchre game and I wanted to touch base and see if you've got a time of death." I gave a little whistle when Duke crossed into the neighbor's yard. He darted back towards me.

"I'm putting the time of death between seven and eight a.m. She appeared to be ready for work in her scrubs. It appeared she'd just eaten donuts because her stomach had yet to digest and there was still some in her mouth like she'd been chewing."

"Do you think she was having a conversation with someone and eating then they killed her?" I valued Max's opinion.

"I don't know if she was having a conversation, but she was eating when she was killed. I'm about to quit for the night, but you can stop by tomorrow afternoon to pick up a copy of the report. I'll probably have it all wrapped up by lunch. Also, her parents came by to identify her." I was glad to hear him say they'd come. "They want the body as quickly as possible for a funeral. They want to cremate her."

"Did you tell them that we can't release the body until the investigation is over?" I asked.

"No. I'm not the sheriff." He was right. It was my job to make sure they knew that. "I told them you'd be in touch with them after I got the autopsy report to you."

"Just another thing to add to my long list," I moaned under my breath. "I'll be by tomorrow after lunch."

We said our goodbyes and I quickly texted Finn and Scott the time of estimated death. Scott texted back that he'd stopped by all the surrounding pawn shops and didn't have any leads on the cuff links.

Tibbie's front door flew open. She stood there with her hand planted on her hip and a death stare. Duke's ears perked up and he bolted towards her. Her facial features softened when the big lug hopped around her in delight.

"He makes everyone happy," I called over to her and grabbed my street clothes from the back of the Wagoneer. "I guess you've not started the game."

"I think your mama has thrown everyone for a loop. She is introducing Finn's mom to everyone and talking about how they love the idea of the two families coming together. From what you told me this morning, Viv has taken a complete opposite attitude." Tibbie turned her head and looked into her house.

I peeked around her where Mama and Shelby were laughing and enjoying being the center of attention as all the Euchre ladies had gathered around them in a big circle.

"Your wedding is going to be bigger than any event around here." Tibbie laughed.

"What?" My jaw dropped.

"Babies." Tibbie's hands lifted into the air. "Can you imagine what all five of your children are going to look like? They'll be models." Tibbie winked.

"Are you telling me that these two have become sudden friends?" I wondered what happened to this whole religion fight.

"Friends? They are more than that. Like sisters." Tibbie's nose curled. There was some shuffling behind her.

"Are you engaged and we didn't know about it?" Jolee Fischer popped her head around Tibbie's shoulder. "Because I'm gonna be all sorts of mad if that's the case."

"Does it look like it?" I held my ring-less finger in the air and looked through the door at Mama.

Our eyes caught. She pinched a smile. Her brows lifted up and down in delight like I'd be pleased with the newfound friend and attitude she'd adopted. She went back to holding court, as we called keeping the attention, with all the gals.

"You need a cocktail." Tibbie rushed away leaving me with Jolee standing at the door.

"You comin' in?" My best friend asked me. The freckles across her nose grew bigger as the smile on her lips reached her green eyes.

"Come out here for a minute." I gave a quick head nod. "I need to ask you something about Lita Brumfield."

"What about her?" Jolee had her blonde hair parted in the middle and dangled down in two pigtails.

"Her neighbor was killed this morning in the park." I pointed to Rock Fence Park across the street from Tibbie's house.

"That was her neighbor?" Jolee gasped. "Wow. I had no idea. I heard about that but didn't know her."

Even though Cottonwood was a small town, it'd been growing from farmers selling off their land to developers. There'd been a lot more neighborhoods being built in the county part of Cottonwood.

"You don't think Lita did it, do you?" She almost laughed in my face. "She can barely write her name, much less kill someone."

"She and Avon had a very rocky relationship. According to Avon's parents," I knew this was an active investigation, but I needed the inside information Jolee was privy to, "Lita and Avon had a run-in about the apple tree hanging over Avon's chain-link fence onto Lita's property."

"Lita keeps a very clean house and yard," Jolee said. "She pays someone to come do it since she was diagnosed with Parkinson's."

"She has Parkinson's?" My mind rolled back to Lita's shaking hands and when she grabbed the railing on Avon's porch to go down the steps.

"I thought you talked to her. You didn't notice it?" She asked.

"I noticed it, but I thought maybe she was nervous about talking to me." I tapped the five-point star sheriff's badge on my shirt.

"Because you're so scary?" Jolee joked. "Seriously, though. You might know her as the nosey old lady who calls on the young neighbor all the time, but if you ask anyone at the Cottonwood Acres Rehabilitation Center, they all love her. She's not got a mean bone in her body."

"Wait. She goes to the rehab?" This was just another tie to the victim.

"Yeah. She goes for the Parkinson's at least a couple of times a week." Jolee patted her chest. "I take her sometimes."

My stomach lurched. This was a sure sign I had to get to the rehab center tomorrow. Not only to question Reagan Quinlan, but to find out if Avon had any part of Lita's physical therapy.

There seemed to be a lot of hidden things at the rehab that needed to come to the light.

"What is that look?" Jolee's eyes narrowed.

"It looks like I'm about to sweep right out under the rug at the rehab." Just like with our homes and personal lives, Southern businesses loved to keep their secrets swept under the rug and it was high time I discovered the ones Avon knew.

My mind wandered back to Wally Lamb. What on Earth did she know that was illegal? I couldn't help but think that the fact Avon was at work all the time, according to her timesheet we'd found at her house, and this big secret she was keeping were tied together.

Something in my gut told me.

"Are you getting in here?" Mama brought me out of my head and had replaced Jolee at the entrance of Tibbie's house.

Duke heard Mama's voice and ran over to her. He was the only dog she loved. He made sure of it.

"Look at my granddog," she gushed over him. His tail slammed against the brick of Tibbie's house with each excited word Mama poured over him. "Now, we just need some two-legged grandchildren before I die," Mama's tone turned sour.

She looked down at my hands. I cupped them behind my back.

"Did you not bring anything?" Her eyes grew scary big. "Kenni, your soon to be mother-in-law needs to know how things work around here and you know better than this."

My mama was referring to Southern charm, something that was taught at a very young age and meant bringing a dish of some sort to the host when you went to their house. No matter if you were stopping by for a quick visit or coming to Euchre.

"I'm embarrassed," she spat. "You know you can't show up empty-handed even if both your hands are amputated."

My mama was so politically incorrect, it was awful.

"How are you ever going to teach my grandchildren Southern charm if you don't have any yourself?" She appeared to have given up on me and went straight to my offspring. "I taught you politeness, table manners, kindness, but where's the grace?"

Around here, we were taught at an early age that you needed four things to have Southern charm as a true Southern gal. Those were table manners, politeness, kindness, and the one Mama said I was lacking, social grace.

"Enough, Mama," I said with an exhausted sigh. "How's things going with Shelby?"

"Not as good as your daddy and Clay." Mama took me by the arm and dragged me into the house. "Your daddy took him down to the Hunt Club's retreat on the river."

"He did?" I drew back and looked at her. I was completely surprised. "That's strange for Daddy."

"Clay said that he'd like to see what a real hunting club in Kentucky looked like, so he called up Sean Graves. You know," she said and patted my hand as we walked into the food room off to the left. "Your daddy has been spending a lot of time with Sean since Leighann's death. I've been trying to help Jilly in her grief." Another little tidbit I didn't know about. "Plus, your daddy and I have a wonderful marriage, so we knew we could help Sean be a better husband."

Sean and Jilly Graves had a rocky marriage. He was a bit gruff and sometimes knocked her and their daughter, Leighann, around. Unfortunately, Leighann had been brutally murdered. I should've been by to check on them more, but apparently, my parents had been filling in for that job.

"I still can't believe Daddy is down at the hunt club's retreat." Finn and I had been to that cabin a few times. It wasn't what my daddy was used to. I mean, there was no running water or bathroom. From the impression of Finn's dad, Clay, I wasn't sure he was cut out for the hunt club life either.

"It's just a couple of nights." Mama dropped my hand. "Kenni, where are your manners? Did you say hello to Shelby?"

"Hi. I'm sorry I had to cut lunch short." I apologized and ignored how Mama had thrown my manners under the bus when I'd yet to have time to even look around the room. "But, I see that you and Mama are enjoying yourselves."

Shelby was sitting in the middle of the room with the Henny Hens circled around her in seats that were supposed to be around the Euchre tables set up in the other room.

"We are. I'm having fun getting to know your mother's friends." She spoke so formal, all the women swooned over it as if she were just so sophisticated.

"Can I get you a drink?" I gestured to the punch bowl where Jolee and Katy Hart were manning the ladle. "I'm thirsty."

"I'm good." She looked down at the cup she was holding. "I've never seen ice cream in punch."

I was unable to decipher if she actually liked the punch that was a staple at all events and gatherings in Cottonwood, or if she didn't like it.

I was going with the first assumption that she liked it. Who didn't like punch? Who didn't like napoleon ice cream? The two together were amazing and if you were lucky enough to get a chunk of the ice cream in your cup, it was a bonus.

"I want some ice cream in mine." I instructed my girlfriends and headed around the table to scoop my own into a cup. If I did the ladle just right, I was able to use the edge to carve out some ice cream from the ice cream block. "Why aren't we playing Euchre?"

"All because of you." Katy Lee Hart's brows lifted. She tossed her long blonde hair around one shoulder making me so jealous of the loose curls springing into place and laying naturally against her.

"Me?" I smiled while I scooped out a big side of the orange ice cream, my favorite.

"No one wants to play because Deputy Finley Vincent's mother is here." She fluttered her eyes and fanned her hand in front of her face. "Makes me sick." She snarled before she started to laugh.

Finn was the talk of the town when he first came to Cottonwood. It wasn't a secret that every single, and not just single as in available, girl in town swooned over him. We'd never had the likes of him around here. It just so happened that I, a no makeup and no fuss kinda gal, was his type.

"Good, because I've got to talk to you." I knew it wasn't the right place to ask about the insurance policy on the cuff links, but I had to take the opportunity when I got it.

"About. . ." She hesitated. "What?"

"Let's go in here." I gestured towards the room with the Euchre tables.

Katy Lee walked in ahead of me while I took my time to peruse the food tables. It was the best night of the week. All the older women in the Euchre group took the opportunity to bake and cook their very best or even try out a new recipe on Euchre night. It was a big deal around these parts to be amazing in the kitchen and these ladies brought it out tonight.

I took a spoonful of homemade potato salad made with real mayonnaise, along with some homemade BBQ pulled pork, that I was sure Myrna Savage had brought from her farm and spooned it on Mama's homemade biscuits. The dessert table was on the other side of the room and I didn't want to risk getting caught up in another conversation, so this plate was going to have to hold me over until I finished talking to Katy Lee.

"Is this store bought?" Viola White snarled at the box of donuts in the Piggly Wiggly box. "Who brought these store-bought donuts to Euchre? The nerve."

Donuts? Euchre? Piggly Wiggly? I sucked in a deep breath knowing those were from Shelby. Probably the same ones I'd asked Toots Buford to take out to them.

"Shhh..." Tibbie held up a finger to her lips. "Shelby Vincent brought it."

"I guess she didn't know better." Viola's brows rose. "She ain't a bit Southern."

"Or Baptist," Tibbie whispered back. "They're Catholic."

It took everything I had not to turn around to give them both a piece of my mind. She was a guest, re-gifted donuts or not. Store bought or homemade.

"Did you know that Finn was Catholic?" Katy Lee's eyes grew big when she asked the question with a jaw drop. "I mean, your Mama," she gasped, "it was the first thing she said when she got here. I swear she ran into the house, leaving his poor mama outside to tell us that." Katy Lee laughed as though she remembered something. "After she told us, she put her finger up to her mouth and told us not to tell. But when I've seen her without Finn's mama at her side, she's letting everyone know."

There was a lot in that long-winded question Katy Lee had started out with, but I figured it was just best to address the question only.

"Yes. Finn is Catholic. Right now, I don't have the time to tell you what happened when Mama found out last night." My lips stretched across my lips, my teeth clinched in an eeck way.

"We have to have coffee this week. Have to." Katy Lee could barely contain herself. "All of your stories about Viv crack me up and make my week."

"I'm glad someone gets pleasure from my pain." I joked. It was good to be around my friends, though Mama was clearly on a mission to let the entire town in on the big Catholic conspiracy she felt the Vincent's were playing on me.

I knew my time with Katy Lee was limited. If what she told me was right about Mama flapping her jaws, it was only a matter of time before the others snuck around to question me about it.

"I need to know about the insurance policy on the cuff links Woody Moss took out with Hart Insurance." Out of the corner of my eye, I could see some of the women getting up from around Shelby. "Those were the only things taken from the Moss house during the robbery."

"I didn't even know they had a policy with us. It was probably a long time ago when we were kids." Katy Lee had started working for her dad when we had graduated from high school.

After that, she went on to get her licenses and now runs the business fulltime. Her father does come in time to time, but she was mainly in charge.

"You mean, Lenora hasn't come down to see for herself?" Not that a day was a long time, but when I saw those papers on her coffee table, I really did assume that figure of $20,000 might've been the tag on those cuff links.

"No. I've not gotten a call or a visit from Lenora and I've been in the office the past couple of days." She shrugged, and we were surrounded before we knew it. "I'll look tomorrow and talk to Dad. Let me give you a call back on that."

"On what?" Viola White, the owner of White's Jewelry and a Henny Hen, stood over us like a hawk rather than a hen. Her claws were out for a bit of gossip. "What you want with Lenora?"

"Kenni wants to know about some policy on cuff links stolen from Woody's house." Katy Lee looked at me. My jaw was dropped. "Oh, was I not supposed to say anything? Because you didn't say it was between me and you."

"It's fine," I sighed. It was already out there. It wasn't like people couldn't go down to the station to get a police report. "The only item stolen from Lenora Moss's house was a pair of cuff links worth some money."

"Who told you that?" Viola's nose curled. Her short grey hair had freshly been cut with jagged edges around her face. She wore a big, thick pair of rimmed glasses that was probably from her sixties wardrobe. Though she stood five foot four inches tall, she was mighty in spirit, gossip and in money.

Viola was the wealthiest woman in Cottonwood but dressed in the strangest of outfits and God-awful jewelry. She could be wearing some fancy diamond necklace, that would be too tame for her, instead, she had on a lime green golf ball sized ball necklace that was tight around her neck. The big lime green stone ring was probably worth something. To me, it looked like it'd come out of the dime machine for children down at the Piggly Wiggly.

"What are you carrying on about?" Toots Buford made her way into the room. Her...um...girls were flipping and flopping and nearly spilling out of her top, making me wonder if she forgot it was Euchre night and not boys poker night where she was rumored to turn up a time or two.

That all was neither here nor there, though, because Viola had something to say about Lenora.

"Vivian, get in here. You won't believe what Lenora Moss told your girl." Vivian held her hand up when I was about to protest.

I wasn't going to divulge any more than I had. Though curiosity was one of my greatest vices and if they did know something, it would be to my advantage.

"What in the world are you gandering on about? It better be good." Mama sashayed into the room like she was Vivian Lee instead of Vivian Lowry.

"Are you a doubting Thomas?" Vivian glared. "I've got something good. Lenora is an even bigger tale teller than Woody."

"Or she's taking over her husband's place in society." Ruby Smith had to put in her two cents all the way from the other conversation she was in, in another room. She was talented in this gossip department. I'd seen it firsthand. A true gift.

Ruby Smith could be talking in one conversation but listening to another in a different group of people. I'd heard the skill was an envy of many Henny Hens.

"Kenni?" Mama asked. "Tell us."

I knew better than to let them in on any investigation, but I was also smart enough to know that if I give them just a smidgen of information, they'd talk the lipstick right off their lips.

It was these types of conversations that Poppa taught me to weed through the gossip to get through to the truth.

"It's nothing like Viola or Ruby are making it out to be." My response to Mama was crisp and to the point. The only way she'd get it in her little head.

"Lenora said that cuff links were the only thing stolen during the robbery. Cuff links."

"Did you say cuff links?" Ruby's voice carried from the other room. She came into the Euchre game room and her bright orange lipstick looked like a blinking light while she talked. "Don't tell me they look like knots? Gold knots?"

"You've seen them?" I asked, jumping around to face her, but having to look up since she was five foot nine inches tall. A wee-bit taller than me.

"Seen them." She scoffed and dug her nails in the edges of her short red hair, raking the hair forward. "He tried to sell them to me years ago. It was the first time we realized he told lies."

"Now, now." Viola tsk-ed. "We didn't say he lied. We said he told heavy tales."

"Honey, no matter what you say or do. You can slip lipstick on a pig, but underneath it's still a pig." Mama shifted her head towards the floor and looked down with a pinched look on her face as she brought a shrugged shoulder to almost meet her chin. "Woody Moss had a way of telling part truth and part exaggeration."

At least Mama gave the dead man some credit.

"Anytime he told a story, you'd need to cut it in half. If he said he'd eaten two big steaks out at the Cattleman's Association fundraiser at the fairgrounds, that meant he ate one," Mama said.

"You've seen the cuff links?" I shifted back to Ruby.

"I told you that he came in the shop trying to get me to buy them after he'd gone to see Viola about her buying them. They came clear from New York City, he'd said," Ruby's drawn-on brows winged up.

"That meant that they come from the Dime Store in Gatlinburg, Tennessee," Viola grunted. "He said they were worth a lot of money when he came to the jewelry store. I told him that he must think I was a foolish woman, and didn't he know that women love jewelry, especially as a woman that owned the only jewelry store in Cottonwood."

"It's costume jewelry. That's what they were." Ruby gave a firm nod.

"Not worth more than a hill of beans." Mama looked at her friends. All three Heney Hens looked like three bobble heads and in sync. Nodding and looking and then rolled in a fit of laughter.

"Now she's gone and tried to tell Kenni the same exact thing." They continued to carry on.

My smile had faded and lost its luster by the time they'd told a few more stories that pretty much confirmed that Moss had liked tall tales. Harmless as they were, did Lenora really not know they were fake? Was there an insurance policy on them?

"Don't worry." Katy Lee had leaned real far over. The Heney Hens couldn't hear us because they were still too wrapped up in their own hooting and hollering to notice. "I'll check to be sure there's not another pair of cuff links that are worth something that has a policy on it."

There was a bit of relief. Something I could chew on and give to Lenora about the price.

CHAPTER FOURTEEN

By the time Mama and the rest of the women had settled down and started talking like they'd all had some sense, I was happy to say that they hadn't run Shelby off. She ended up staying and playing a few hands of Euchre after she'd caught on.

I had to say that she was even good at it.

Though at times, I could see there was a helpless look in her eyes. I wondered if behind them, she was wondering how on Earth Finn could love a small town like Cottonwood.

With every hand of euchre dealt, my heart raced and I was so pumped up from all the stories, I'd gotten a burst of energy, that when I left Tibbie's, I knew it needed to be put to good use. . .investigating.

"It's 'bout time you left." Poppa had ghosted into the front seat of the Wagoneer, forcing Duke to jump to the back.

He was happy about it with a wagging tale and his head hung over the front seat. The behind the ear rubs from Poppa didn't hurt either.

"I wondered where you were." I gave a side look to him and didn't bother hiding myself talking. It was dark outside, and I was sure no one could see me. "Tonight I got some tips on the cuff links stolen from the Moss burglary."

I'd be curious to hear Poppa's thoughts on it, so I quickly told him what

Viola and Ruby had disclosed about him approaching both of them with similar, if not the same cuff links.

"Do you think he never told Lenora the truth?" I asked Poppa.

"I've known Woody all my life." Poor Poppa went to the afterlife way too fast. He should be enjoying himself, riding around in this Wagoneer meeting up with his buds for some early morning coffee or even taking the old Jeep to the lake filled with a chest of ice-cold brew and his fishing poles.

Sadly, that wasn't the case. A heart attack took him away from me and death of others brought him back to me. As much as I wanted to solve Avon's murder, in the back of my head was the little tickle that the longer I took, the more time I had with Poppa. These were the things that I should be discussing with Finn, not whether we are going to be Baptist or Catholic.

"Did you hear me?" Poppa's ghost hand waved in front of my face, leaving some lingering fog.

"I'm sorry. What did you say?" I pulled the Wagoneer right on Main Street from Oak Street heading south.

"I was saying that Woody was a good storyteller. He might've lied about the value of the cuff links. But you said Katy Lee was going to check to see if there was a policy, so we just wait for that piece of the puzzle." He let out a long sigh. "When are you going to learn patience is a key. Just breathe. Both of these crimes will be solved in no time."

"I've done what you said about keeping my ears open and trying to pick out the pieces of gossip that might have some truth, but all I'm getting about the cuff links are that they are fake. Which makes me wonder if the burglar knew that." My thoughts shifted back to Rich, which then shifted to Avon. "I still can't unlink Rich from both crimes."

"It might be two crimes with one person. The killer and the burglar are the same." Poppa made a good point. "Maybe Avon knew he was bad and somehow knew he was going to steal. I don't know, I'm grasping here."

Our little game had begun.

"What if she overheard him arguing with Woody at the rehab center about him being cut from the will." I threw that out there, though I wasn't sure how or why Woody would tell him.

"Was Rich at the rehab center when Woody was alive? I thought he was released on good behavior for the funeral." I jerked the wheel right, making a hard turn onto Maple Street before taking another quick right and pulling down the alley behind the department.

"I guess we are going to the office." Poppa's face lit up. He rubbed his hands together. "Wee-doggy, Duke!" Duke jumped up and hung his head back over the front seat. "We've got our Kenni-bug back to ourselves."

"Don't be going silly." I smiled and winked after I put the Jeep into park. "We've got to go in here and look through Avon's purse. Get a good timeline to where she was before she was in the park."

"Sounds perfect to me." Poppa didn't wait for me to gather my bag and get Duke out before he floated into the building. Duke shot out of the back door when I opened it.

"Here, Duke," I called for Duke, juggling my bag and trying to look for him while fumbling getting the key into the lock of the door to the department.

Duke's nails got louder and louder, signaling he was coming like I'd called.

"Good, boy." He ran to my side just as the key slid into the door handle. "Let's get in here and get a treat." I turned the knob and pushed the door with my foot.

Duke headed on inside, I dropped my bag inside of the door and ran my hand up along the wall to flip the light switch. I shut the door behind me and let my shoulders fall as I took a deep breath and let it out in one long, enjoyable sigh.

"This place is a close second to home." I smiled at Poppa. He'd already taken his seat in my chair, which used to be his chair, with his feet propped up on the desk.

"It should be." He clasped his hand behind his head and lounged back. "You spent many days and nights here with me while your daddy worked and your mama did all those fancy clubs."

"I couldn't imagine where I'd be or who I'd be in life if it weren't for you." Without looking at him and at risk of crying, I took the lid off the dog treats on Finn's desk and flipped Duke a treat. "Especially on this case."

I walked over to the vault and bent down, rolling the combination between my fingers as I plugged in the code to open it.

"What do you have in mind tonight?" Poppa asked, still taking the moment to enjoy his old seat.

"I want to look into Avon's purse and wallet to see if anything is missing before I take it to Tom Geary's lab in the morning on my way to Clay's Ferry." It was perfect timing to drop it off and that's the way I liked to do things.

Orderly.

Most days, I'd planned my day out to make sure the stops I needed to make during the week were in the same area. It was probably the penny pincher in me since the Wagoneer was a gas hog and I used my own money to fill it up instead of the department money.

I tried to skimp on silly things like gas when we could use that money towards something like paying a new deputy. Which reminded me of the upcoming town council meeting.

"I've got to get my speech ready about hiring Scott to give to the town council tomorrow night. It sure would be good if I could get a solid lead and not just something as silly as fake cuff links." I pulled the evidence bag out of the vault and walked over to my desk where I plucked a pair of gloves from the box.

"He's doing a fine job at taking orders and following protocol." Poppa didn't need to point that out, but it would be good to put in my speech about how thorough and reliable he was.

"Let's see what we got here." I carefully removed the purse from its evidence bag and opened it. There was a bag from the Sweet Shop wadded up in it. It was pink with black lines and bright yellow writing with a donut logo. "Max told me on the phone that there were still some remnants of something sweet like a donut in her esophagus and the stomach. She'd been eating or was eating at the time of the death. Chocolate too."

There was some icing on the inside of the bag that was left behind from where she'd taken it out.

"I'm going to have to go to the Sweet Shop to see if she had stopped there that morning and if she was alone."

Poppa blurted out in laughter.

"Tough job, Kiddo." He licked his lips. "I sure do wish there was something like that when I was alive." He patted his belly.

"If it's any consolation, we can go together in the morning. I've yet to go, but Daddy loves it." I put the Sweet Shop bag aside and started to take out the rest of the contents, which didn't make me think anything was off. But I also didn't find anything else that most women might carry in a purse.

Me? I rarely carried anything but my sheriff's bag.

I walked over to the dry-erase board and turned it around from where we'd moved it earlier. Underneath Avon's name, I wrote the contents of her purse and noted how I was going to the Sweet Shop to check out Avon's visit. I also documented the contents on the evidence sheet before I put the purse back into the bag.

"Now to the wallet." It was a brown wallet with a zipper around the entire thing.

After unzipping it, I laid it flat open on the evidence bag. On the right side, there were pockets for credit cards. Only two contained cards. One was from Cottonwood First National, a debit card. The second was her driver's license. The middle of the wallet was a zipper area for change. When I flipped that to the right side, the left side had two long pockets one behind the other. One was empty, but the other had one hundred dollars in twenties.

"If this was a robbery, she got robbed and killed by a stupid one." I noted the cash wasn't taken on the evidence sheet and then proceeded to fill out the white board with the contents of the wallet.

"This is looking less and less like a robbery." Poppa had ghosted himself next to me at the white board. "Did she exercise in the park in the morning before work while eating a donut? I doubt it. She seemed to be in good physical health from the look of her, the stats Finn had found and the looks of her photo on her license."

"She was in good health from what her parents had said. But they couldn't discount she had two known women who didn't like her. Lita Brumfied." I circled Lita's name a few times. "And Reagan Quinlan." I circled her name a few times.

"You've talked to Lita." Poppa pointed to her.

"She's got Parkinson's." I'd just remembered what Jolee had told me about that. "I need to write that down."

I went back and forth from the white board to the written file we kept and noted everything.

"It was one bullet." Poppa's fat finger lifted in the air. "By the look of Lita's shaking, she's in the later stages of the disease, which makes me think she's a less likely suspect. Besides, is she even driving anymore? How did she get to the park? How did she steady her hand enough to shoot one shot, kill the girl and walk out of there without someone seeing her?"

"Gosh, I missed you." I wanted so desperately to put my arms around him, but I knew it wasn't possible.

CHAPTER FIFTEEN

I reached over to punch the alarm on my clock. There was no way it was already morning.

"Ugh," I groaned and went to roll over, catching myself before I hit the hard-cold tile floor of the jail cell. The sound of my phone ringing was actually what I'd mistaken for the sound of my alarm.

I stumbled out of the cell to retrieve the phone off my desk and remembered I'd been talking to Poppa and playing our "what if" game before I'd decided to lay on the cot in the cell for a few minutes. I must've fallen asleep. Duke was snoring in his bed next to my desk.

"Mama," I gasped when I saw her name on my phone and that it was one a.m. "Mama, you okay?"

Vivian Lowry loved her beauty sleep. There was no way she was up this early unless something was severely wrong.

"Kenni, get over to the Cottonwood Acres. Shelby Vincent has had a heart attack." Her words woke me up better than the black coffee from Ben's Diner.

It took a second for me to process what she was saying.

"Did you hear me?" Mama screamed into the phone. "Where are you?"

"I'm..." I gulped, blinking my eyes a few times. "I'm on my way." I ended the call and pushed the phone into my back pocket. "Let's go, Duke."

I grabbed the keys off my desk and my bag. Duke hurried out of the door and ran over to the dumpster to do his business while I turned the lights off, locked the door, and ran to the Jeep.

A good thing about it being one in the morning, there was no traffic. Literally, all the shops and restaurants were closed by nine o'clock in the evening, though some stayed open until ten, but that was rare. Though I don't always take advantage of my authority as sheriff, I did drive the back-roads to get to Cottonwood Acres by taking a right out of the alley behind the department and a quick right onto First Street.

Duke jumped between the front and back seats, as though he was nervous and knew something was wrong. He was a very smart dog and my actions were probably causing his behavior.

"It's okay, Duke." I tried to calm him down, but in reality, was telling myself it was okay. "Finn's mama is going to be okay."

The tires squealed when I took a right on Oak Street. Rock Fence Park was on my left and I couldn't help but notice how dark it was. The town council really did need to rethink their issue with not putting a light in there. It's a safety measure and I needed to bring that up at the meeting too.

I took a left on the Town Branch and zoomed past Tibbie's, passing Stratton Avenue where I couldn't help but noticed there were some lights on at Avon Meyer's parents' house. My heart tugged. I felt so bad that Avon's killer hadn't been brought to justice yet.

There was an ambulance parked up against the emergency room sign in front of the Cottonwood Acres Rehabilitation Center. I pulled right up alongside the entrance and threw the Wagoneer in park. I rolled down all the windows for Duke and left him in the Wagoneer until I could figure out what was going on.

"Sheriff," Sebastian was pushing the ambulance gurney out of the automatic sliding doors. "I think your mother-in-law is going to be okay."

"Mother-in-law?" I asked.

"Shelby Vincent, your mom said she was your mother-in-law. Well," he smiled, and I knew he'd been told a tale by Mama. "She said, 'You better save her life because this is the sheriff's mother-in-law and I'm her mama. You understand me?'"

Sounded like Mama.

"What happened?" I was trying to process what was happening. I needed the facts.

I followed him behind the ambulance where he had opened the double doors and pushed the gurney back into the ambulance.

"We got a call from your mom. They were at her house." He gestured for me to follow him back inside. "She showed the classic signs of a heart attack. I gave her a nitroglycerin tab under her tongue and got her in the ambulance."

"Kendrick." Mama had a look of relief on her face. "Where were you? Finn and I have been looking all over for you."

I pulled my phone out and looked at the calls. I'd missed several calls and text messages from both of them. I put the phone back into my pocket.

"I'm sorry. I was at the office working on the Meyer's case and I fell asleep there." Generally, I wasn't a heavy sleeper, but with the stress of two crimes, I couldn't dismiss the fact that the stress had probably caught up to my body.

"What about my RV?" Shelby's voice carried out into the hallway from behind the thinly closed curtain. "Your father isn't there to keep an eye on it and I just don't trust them people on 'Free Row', as you call it."

"Sheriff, I'm taking care of your mother-in-law." A woman in blue scrubs came up to me with a clipboard in her grasp. "Can you fill out some forms for me?"

My eyes scanned down the badge clipped on her shirt pocket. Reagan Quinlan, Nurse Manager was in bold black letters with a small photo next to it.

"I'm sorry." I had to correct the misleading information Mama had given them. "Shelby Vincent isn't my mother-in-law."

"Yet." Mama had to throw in her opinion. "They are going to be."

"Mama, please." I held a hand up to her to be quiet. "Why don't you go get in touch with Daddy, so Shelby's husband can get here by morning to be with her?" I brushed my hand for her to scurry off somewhere other than here so I could get the information from Reagan.

"My Deputy Finn Vincent is her son and we are together." I tried to put the fact aside that this was the Reagan I needed to interview about Avon and why she had such a beef with the girl. I had to put Finn and his mother first at this moment. "Is he here?"

"Listen, I'm going to get out of here." Sebastian pointed towards the exit.

"Wait!" Mama called out to him. "Kenni, he saved Shelby's life." Mama patted me on the arm.

"Ma'am, it's my job. I'm just happy to have helped." He smiled. He gave us a goodbye nod and headed back to his ambulance.

"Kenni, don't you have any nice Southern friends to set him up with?" She asked.

"Oh, Mama. Not now." I turned to Reagan, "I'm sorry, did you say if Finn was here?"

"He is in there with his mother. I was going fill you in on the situation, but now that it's come to light that you aren't the daughter-in-law," she said with lowered eyelids and a glance over my shoulder at Mama, "then I can't tell you unless they put you on the HIPAA form."

"No problem." I shook my head and followed her over to the curtain where she peeled it back enough for us to peek in.

"Kenni, dear. Please tell Finley I'm fine." Shelby didn't look fine. She was a little gray and didn't look fine. Far from it.

Finn nodded his head, gesturing me to meet him outside of the curtained emergency room.

"Where have you been?" His sad eyes searched my face. "I ran to your house and beat on your door even though I didn't see your car. I called your phone."

I curled my arms around him and pulled him into me, giving him a big hug.

"Oh, Kenni." He melted.

"I'm sorry," I whispered into his ear. "After Euchre I was wide awake and decided to head to the department to look over the evidence. I fell asleep on the cot in the cell."

He continued to hug me back.

"Did you say Reagan Quinlan is your mom's nurse?" I took the opportunity while I was consoling him to ask him since no one would hear me.

"Kenni." He pulled away from me and took a step back. The look of disgust went from his chin to his hairline. "My mom has had signs of a heart attack. The last thing on my mind is who is taking care of her as long as she's getting taken care of."

He darted back to the curtain and swung it open.

"What's going on?" Mama hurried over with a few cups of coffee stacked in her hands.

"Nothing. He's stressed." This wasn't the place to even act like something might be wrong because Mama would spend the next hours trying to fix it. "Let me help you."

I took a couple of cups of coffee she'd stacked and tried to balance.

"I'm fine," Shelby continued to try and convince Finn and Reagan when we walked in. "Tell them, Viv. We were laughing. Having a couple of glasses of wine. Talking about the kids."

I couldn't help but smile when she said "kids". Finn and I were far from kids, but not in our parent's eyes.

"Mrs. Vincent, can these ladies be in here? They aren't on your HIPAA form." Reagan pulled the form from the clipboard she'd been carrying around.

"Yes. Add them. Vivian and Kenni Lowry." She nodded. "Now, please can I get out of here? I've left my RV alone on the seedy side of town."

"Seedy side of town? Come on, Mom. It's Broadway not downtown Chicago." He reminded her of where she lived. "Besides, it's parked between my house and Kenni's. If someone was to hurt the RV, they'd be pretty darn brave."

I took my phone out of my pocket and texted my dad to make sure he and Clay knew what was going on and to come back as quickly as possible.

"We are going to have to do a heart catherization test, Mrs. Vincent." Reagan was reading off the chart. "They want to make sure you don't have any blockages that need to be taken care of, so we are going to admit you tonight and do the test in the morning."

"What about my husband?" Shelby's head darted around with a stark fear in her eyes. "I can't agree to anything unless my husband is here."

"Don't worry. Mama got ahold of daddy's cell and I can run down there to get them if I need to. I know exactly where they are." I wanted her to feel safe. She was so scared, I could see her hands shaking and it broke my heart. "Why don't we leave and come back in the morning before your test."

"That sounds great." Mama agreed.

I looked up at Finn and mouthed that I was sorry. I knew it was insensitive, but I'd not realized how serious his mom was. Regardless, there was still a dead girl and her possible killer was standing over his mom. That alone scared me.

My phone chirped a text.

"It's Dad. He and Clay are on their way back." It was a relief to see the stress melt away from Shelby's face when I told her the news. "They will be about an hour or so."

"Good." She turned her attention to Reagan. "After my husband gets here, we can discuss this test or whether we need to go home to our regular doctor."

"I assure you, ma'am, that our doctors here are well qualified to do the test. If you need surgery, we'd have to transport you to a bigger hospital." Reagan did seem to be knowledgeable and she was very professional. "I'll be on the lookout for your husband."

"You'll be here all night?" Shelby asked her. "You've been such a doll. I'm not sure how you calmed me down, but you did."

"I'll be here all night and some tomorrow. I'm short a few nurses, don't worry. I'm the nurse manager, so you're in good hands." Reagan smiled, laid the clipboard on the tray table and skirted out the curtain.

Mama started to hand Finn a coffee, so I took the opportunity to go out and find Reagan. I found her at the nurse's station where she'd already taken a seat at a desk and was staring at a computer.

"Reagan Quinlan, right?" I asked.

She looked up from her typing and smiled.

"Yes. Is there something I can help you with? I can't tell you if she's going to need more treatment until the catherization results." She was all business. "I've put in the orders and we don't do a lot of those here, so she'll go first thing in the morning."

"Actually, I wanted to talk to you about Avon Meyers," I said and noticed the shadow pass over her face, darkening her features.

"I understand she was killed, but I don't know what that has to do with me." She went back to clicking on the computer keyboard.

"I understand she worked for you and she'd been written up a few times. I have to explore all the possibilities as to why someone would want to kill her. Did she have a disgruntled client? Did she have enemies here at the hospital?" I asked.

"I'd heard from somewhere that she was robbed. That sounds like the wrong place at the wrong time to me." She hit a button really hard before she shoved her chair back from the desk. "If you'll excuse me, like I said I'm a little shorthanded and I've got to check on more patients." She jerked a file from the desk top and held it close to her chest.

"Actually, I will need to interview you." I flipped open the pocket of my shirt and handed her one of my cards. "I'm sure you know the sheriff's office is located in the back of Cowboy's Catfish, but here's my card just in case. What time do you get off tomorrow?"

"I'm going straight to bed when I get home." She wasn't budging. She looked at her watch. "Which is in about two hours."

"I can come to your house." I wasn't letting her off the hook that easy. "In the morning when you wake up," I clarified.

"Fine." She squirmed uncomfortably.

I added that to the things I needed to do tomorrow. Go into Clay's Ferry to get the reports from their dispatch that Lita Brumfield had filed, drop the evidence off to Geary, stop by the morgue to see Max, and touch base with all the deputies.

"What if you come back here tomorrow around supper time? I'm working the late shift again." She hugged the folder tighter as her arms wrapped around her.

"That'd be great. I'm also going to need to see your copies of the write-ups against Avon as well as the other employees she came in contact with and her patients." I knew I was probably overstepping my boundaries since I didn't have a warrant and by the look on her face, I added, "I'll have a warrant for you to obtain all of her files and records."

She didn't even bother telling me goodbye. I watched her hurry down the hall, opposite of me. Her body language told me that she loathed Avon

Meyers with a passion and that would be enough motive to kill someone. What on Earth did Avon do to her?

"We need a bed!" Sebastian rushed through the double electronic doors with another person on the gurney. "In A-fib!" He hollered, nearly missing me when I jumped aside.

"Lita Brumfield?" I gasped when I noticed it was her under the air mask and blankets.

"Yes." A tall man, who looked to be in his forties, was running alongside her, but was forced to stop once Sebastian had continued to push through Authorized Access Only doors.

"Move it!" Reagan came out of nowhere, pushing a pedal cart through the doors. Reagan and the man looked at each other. There was something between them when their eyes met, but I wasn't so sure what that was.

"Oh no. Oh no." The man cried out and paced back and forth in front of the emergency doors where they'd taken Lita.

He put his hands out just as Reagan and the cart disappeared.

"Can I offer you some support?" I asked the man. "I know I'm the sheriff, but I've spent my whole life listening to people."

"That's my mom." He pointed. "I can't. . .I mean, she already has Parkinson's." He abruptly stopped talking. "You," he gasped with a look of distain replacing the one of stress. "You're that woman sheriff that's been harassing my mom." He jabbed his finger at me. "She's in here because of you and your loose accusations."

Herb Brumfield. He had my full attention.

The emergency room doors flew open.

"You can see your mom now." Reagan held her hand out to the man. He took it but still had his eyes fixed on me.

I stood there watching the swinging doors go back and forth in opposite directions wondering if the two of them knew each other and dismissed the fact he felt I'd put his mom in the hospital. There wasn't anything I said to her that would make her sick. Surely, he knew her neighbor was dead, and I had to follow up on leads that his mom had complained and filed multiple reports on her.

When the doors finally came together and stopped, I knew I wasn't going to get any real answers out of anyone in here tonight. No one was thinking clearly, and even I had head fog. The crime certainly wasn't going to be solved in these late hours.

It was best that I get home and get some sleep. I had a big day tomorrow and getting the warrant for all the paperwork I was going to need to get some answers out of Reagan Quinlan had jumped to the top of the list.

CHAPTER SIXTEEN

"I'm going to need a full warrant," I told the judge's secretary while I stood in front of the coffeepot to wait for my coffee to finish the brew cycle.

I'd slept on and off, a few minutes here and there after I'd gotten home from the hospital. Duke was even still in the bed.

"Yes. For all of the records for Avon Meyers." I grabbed my thermal coffee mug from the cabinet and got confirmation that the judge's secretary would have the warrant ready for Scott to pick it up for me since I'd make sure Finn wasn't doing a dang thing today.

After she and I hung up, I called my neighbor, Mrs. Brown. She was always happy to help out with Duke when I needed her to.

"When are they going to move that big RV from in front of my house?" she asked. "They were so nosey last night that it woke me up. I had a hard time falling back to sleep."

"Last night?" I questioned.

"Yes. Well, technically, you'd say it was wee-early morning, but it was around four-ish." At first, I thought her recollection was off, but then I remembered that it was probably Clay.

"I'm sure they didn't mean to." I made a mental note to check in with Mama and see what else had transpired after I'd left the hospital. "Finn's mom might've had a heart attack last night. She was sent to the emergency room for some testing and I'm sure it was Mr. Vincent coming back to the RV to get some things. You know men," I joked. "They can't be quiet for nothing."

"Oh my stars, honey child," Mrs. Brown gasped on the other end of the phone. "She'll have to be put on the prayer chains, ASAP." I heard some shuffling on the other end of the phone. I knew for sure, because I'd seen it with my own eyes, she was getting her little black book with the prayer chain phone numbers. I guess you could call it the little black book of gossip. "I'll be over to get Duke. Don't you worry that pretty little head of yours."

The phone went dead. It was a relief to know that Duke wasn't going to be left here alone all day. I also knew that it was Mrs. Brown's day for Jolee to drop off her Meals on Wheels, which meant that Duke would be going to Jolee for the afternoon. Still, I texted a quick message to Jolee to let her know that Duke would be at Mrs. Brown's, knowing she'd be up getting the On The Run Food Truck ready for the breakfast crew where ever she was parking it that morning.

The sunrise over Cottonwood wasn't even peeking through until after six a.m., so this early morning I was going to have to put on my headlights for at least an hour and pray all the way into Clay's Ferry on those windy roads that I didn't hit a deer. It was birthing season and it was all woods between Cottonwood and Clay's Ferry.

My thermal cup was nestled in the bean bag coffee holder, which used to be my Poppa's, that laid across the hump between the driver's side and passenger's side floorboard. My bag was in the back. The only thing I needed to do was to stop real fast at the department to grab the evidence for the lab and head on out of town.

Heading north on Main Street, I passed Ben's Diner. The warm glow of the lights made me miss my morning routine I had to abandon while I was going to be investigating the robbery and the murder. I loved doing my rounds in and around Cottonwood before ending up at a corner table at Ben's where I enjoyed biscuits and gravy. If I was going there today, I'd have him add the chocolate drizzle on top. A sure sign that stress was tickling my nerves.

That's when I remembered the Sweet Shop and how I'd planned to go there first thing. It would be open, or at least they'd be there baking. Before I knew it, I'd whipped the Jeep around and headed straight toward the Sweet Shop on the north side of town near Lulu's Boutique.

Just as I hoped, the sign was flipped to open on the door of the small white cottage house that'd been turned into the Sweet Shop. There were two cars in the lot and I pulled into the spot between them. I grabbed a photo of Avon Meyers from the file and stuck it in my back pocket.

There was a round sidewalk in the front of the shop with a patch of grass in the middle. The small wooden sign mentioned something about dogs and picking up their business. There were small bushes planted around the perimeter of the grass circle with doggie bag stations between some and water bowls between others.

"Good morning," I called to the woman who looked up from behind the counter.

"Hi, there, Sheriff." A woman in her thirties looked up with a smile on her face. Her hair was tugged up into a hair net. She plucked it off and a massive amount of blonde hair with dark lowlights fell around her shoulders. "I think your dad comes in here a lot."

"I think you're right." I stepped up to the glass counter. My stomach gurgled. "I can see why."

There were rows and rows of donuts.

"It can be overwhelming. We have several types of donuts." She went down the line and pointed them out. "Glazed Twists, Long John, Frosted Chocolate, Coconut, Maple Bacon, Jelly, Devil's Food, Bear Claw, Crumb Cake, Strawberry, Blueberry Cake, Wonut, Baked, Sugar, Frosted Cream, Glazed, Buttermilk, Boston Cream." She came to the end of that counter and moved to the next. "Maple Bar, Spud Nut, Apple Fritter, Cinnamon Twist, French Cruller, Frosted Vanilla, Croissant Donut, Sugar, and Donut Holes."

"Oh my, they all look good." This was harder than I thought it was going to be. "Maybe you can help me though."

"Sure. What is your normal favorite?" She leaned her hip up against the counter. There was some noise coming from the back of the bakery. She noticed me looking past her and said, "That's one of my bakers. This is just the start of what we have out. I don't think you need to know what she's baking back there because you already look overwhelmed. But your father's favorite is the Maple Bacon."

Her fingernail tapped the glass and I peeked at the long donut with maple glaze slathered along it with bacon crumbles on top. Not just any bacon crumbles. Crispy bacon crumbles. Delicious.

"I bet he does." I nodded. "He loves bacon and so do I. Perfect choice. I'll take two."

Tom Geary had popped into my head and I knew he'd love one too.

"Do you want a coffee?" She asked with her back to me. She turned around to get my answer and had one of those black bags like Avon had in her purse.

"No. I have a coffee from home in the car. I have to be honest though, I also came in here to ask you about Avon Meyers." I pulled the photo out of my pocket and handed it to her. "She was in here yesterday morning, I think."

"She was. Did she come and complain about the shop?" She asked.

"I'm sorry, I didn't catch your name." In fact, she had never mentioned her name.

"Raven Birch." She ran her hands down her apron with the same logo as the bags and walked around the counter to shake my hand.

"Raven, I'm Kenni. It's nice to meet you but I have some unfortunate news." I put the photo back into my pocket because she'd already confirmed Avon was in there that morning, which would help me get that timeline started. "Avon was killed in the Rock Fence Park yesterday morning after she left here."

Raven's mouth dropped, in obvious shock at the news.

"Do you recall if anyone was with her?" I asked.

"No. She came in a few times. She'd buy several bags of donuts." Raven continued to blink her eyes like she was trying to get her brain to wrap around the news. "She was very nice, and she loved her job."

"You talked to her a lot?" I asked wondering how Raven knew Avon loved her job when she had a boss writing her up all the time. Raven walked back behind the counter and put my donuts in the bag.

"Not really. Just when people come in and buy in bulk, I always ask if it's for their children or work. She said that she had patients that loved donuts and she'd use them as bribes." Raven smiled as though it was a fond memory. "Can you imagine your physical therapist trying to get you to bend your knee after a replacement and dangling a donut in your face?"

"We are all children at heart." It was a cute story and showed just how much Avon cared for her patients.

"Do you have the killer in custody?" Her eyes dipped at the edges, her smile had fallen away.

"No. But I think they were talking over donuts and walking. She had your to-go bag in her purse with some remnants of chocolate icing. What made me think there were more than one donut was how the rings of icing were in separate spots inside of the bag." I couldn't wait until I got the report from Max. I'd have a lot more information about Avon's body and contents to add to the report.

"She bought three chocolate glazed donuts. I just can't believe it." Raven and I both turned around when the bell over the door dinged. She handed me the bag over top the counter and waved at the customer coming into the shop.

"Do you recall the time?" I asked.

"Actually." She grabbed a fistful of receipts from underneath the counter. "I keep a detailed log of what is sold and what didn't sell by writing down everyone's order after they leave. I put the time on them because some donuts are more popular in the morning than others. Like the Bear Claws. Those are very popular with the afternoon crowd for an after-supper dessert, while the Cinnamon Twist is the most popular in the morning with coffee." She didn't really need to tell me particulars of why or how she ran her business, but it was better than just standing there while she went through a handful of receipts. "And I put them in order." A big smile crossed her face. "Seven fifteen a.m." She held out the receipt.

"Do you mind if I get a picture of that with my phone?" I asked.

"Not at all." She slapped the receipt on the counter. I took my phone out from my back pocket and snapped a couple quick photos.

"I'm sorry we had to meet this way. I love your shop," I said and moved a little to the right to make room for the other customer to look at the glass bakery counter.

"If there's anything else you need, or I remember anything she ever said that might be important, I'll call you," she said.

"Great." I took some money out of my pocket and a card out of my sheriff's shirt and handed them to her. "Keep the change for when my dad comes in today."

CHAPTER SEVENTEEN

The moans that escaped my mouth while I was eating the maple bacon donut was not normal. No wonder my dad loved them. I couldn't believe I had waited so long to try them.

I sat in the Wagoneer with the full intention of actually writing down everything Raven had told me about what she'd learned about Avon while she was a customer. It wasn't anything different than what Sebastian had said about her personality that he'd seen as she worked. I would be interviewing a few members of the staff and also some of the therapists in addition to my interview with Reagan, while I was at Cottonwood Acres Rehab.

I went to reach for my notebook in the pocket of my shirt and realized there was gooey maple glaze smothered on my fingertips. Naturally, I put it in my mouth and licked off every single bit of it, giving me one more good groan of delight. These just might replace my chocolate drizzle and country gravy biscuits from Ben's. I'd never tell him that though.

I quickly wrote down that Avon had purchased three donuts on the day she died. Did she eat all three? It was something I could ask Max Bogus when I stopped by to get the autopsy report. This could determine if she'd eaten all of them or had the intention of giving a couple away. It would help determine what might've been in Avon's head. Was she meeting someone and took donuts to them as a good gesture? If that was the case, who did she meet? Was that my killer?

I looked back through my notebook to where I'd gone to Avon's house with Finn. Based on how my notes stated that her kitchen had healthy food and the fact that she had a healthy physical appearance, I'd bet that she didn't eat all three donuts. But only Max would for sure be able to tell me that.

By the time I'd finished writing down what Raven had told me, there was already a line out of the Sweet Shop's door. Who knew how well they would have taken off in Cottonwood. I was glad. This only added to my plea in hiring a second deputy. With growth of the economy, came more people and citizens. That was a good argument about how that alone would make the crime rate statistics go up.

The curvy roads leading to Clay's Ferry were empty. The trees had grown into a canopy overtop the road and filtered out any sort of the new day's sun. My mind was filled with many things and darted from thought to thought. It was too early for me to call Finn and check on his mom. It was definitely too early for me to call Mama.

"What's on our plate today?" Poppa suddenly appeared after I pulled into the parking lot of the lab.

"Good morning," I greeted him and pushing the gear shift into park, noticed that Tom Geary wasn't there yet. I'd have to save his donut for later. "It's been a busy day. Finn's mom had a heart attack."

"Is she okay?" Poppa asked with furrowed brows.

"She was talking last night, but her nurse was Reagan Quinlan. She gave me a gut tug, so I think we've got something with her. We will find more out when I go talk to her later today." I reached around the seat and grabbed the evidence bags with Avon's purse and wallet.

"Did you tell Finn the theories we came up with?" He asked.

"No. He was more preoccupied with his mom and when I did point out to him that Reagan was a person of interest, he got kinda mad and said his mom was top priority." I didn't blame him. I woulda been the same way. "So, it looks like today, me and you are on our own."

"The way I like it." Poppa's brows wiggled up and down in a dance.

"I'll be right back. Tom isn't here this early and I'm going to put it in the metal slot next to the door." Since Tom was a one-man operation, he couldn't be there all the time so there was a metal slot on the door that you could slide the evidence into. It led to a vault that only he could get into. It was convenient, and I'd never had any problem when dropping things off.

When I got back into the Wagoneer, Poppa was sitting there with a blank look on his face peering out the windshield.

"What are you thinking?" I asked.

"Do you really think these are two separate crimes?" He asked.

"I've gone over that a million times. Is it a coincidence that I caught Rich and Avon arguing? I've got a feeling it's not. I can't help but wonder if maybe it was Rich she knew something about and that's why we're going to see Sheriff Davis in Clay's Ferry." I pulled out of the parking lot and headed right into Clay's Ferry.

The sheriff's department was much bigger than ours and was its own building in the town's precinct district. The area included their courthouse, their department, and their jail. I was jealous that they had an elected jailer position.

"Are you going?" I asked Poppa and pulled into the parking lot closest to the sheriff's department. "I've got to go to the dispatch and grab the transcript they have on Lita Brumfield and Avon Meyers before I go see Sheriff Davis about Rich's early release from jail."

"I might take a gander around." He ghosted out of the car and I got out. I left my bag in there since I wasn't going to need it.

"Try to find out something good." I laughed and knew that there probably wasn't much he could find out since all of our suspects were back in Cottonwood.

The hours of operation open for public was six thirty a.m. until five p.m. with night shift hours for the dispatch and limited deputies on staff. This was something I needed to bring up at the town council. Then I wouldn't have to come here to get transcripts for my town.

"Sheriff, what brings you over here?" I recognized Wilma Gerhding's voice from when I'd called here before.

"You're Wilma." I offered a smile and walked up to the chest-high counter, placing my elbows on it.

"The one and only." She stood up from her chair. She was only about five-foot-tall, petite figure, and short curly red hair that reminded me of an older version of Annie from the movie Annie. There was a pair of glasses hanging down her chest from a chain around her neck. "What can I do you for?"

"We've got a murder investigation." I started to say.

"I heard. Anytime there's a murder, we hear about it." Her face remained facing forward, but her eyes shifted left and right before she leaned over the counter. "With what's going on around here, we have to talk about other counties to keep us feeling better."

"What's going on?" I'd been so involved with the cases, that I'd not heard whatever news she was talking about.

"I can't believe you haven't heard about the FBI putting Sheriff Davis on permanent leave." There was an element of surprise in her tone as if she'd just heard the news too.

"You're kidding me?" Immediately, my judge-y side made me think he was guilty of whatever it was.

"Not a bit. He was helping out a drug lord." She shrugged. "I've heard that it did have something to do with that guy from your town." She snapped her fingers. "Fiddle faddle. I can't remember his name." She held up a finger and turned on the balls of her feet.

She picked up the phone and pushed a bunch of numbers. She curled her small hand around the receiver and whispered into it before she hung it back up.

"Rich Moss."

"My Rich Moss?" Things had just become very interesting.

"Mmmhmmm. I don't know what he had to do with Rich Moss, but I hear it ain't good. He even let him go on good behavior." She wagged her finger. "That was a no-no. Last night the prosecutor put a warrant out for the judge to sign this morning when he gets in to put Rich Moss back behind bars."

My stomach lurched.

"I'm assuming you aren't here for that." Her eyes snapped.

"No, but that's good information. I'm here to see about getting the transcripts from my area from a call from Lita Brumfield. The young woman murdered has history with Mrs. Brumfield calling dispatch after hours. They've had neighborly disputes for a year or so and a lot of calls."

"Lita." When she said Lita's name, she dragged it out while typing. I watched her eyes scan the screen. "We've got a separate input for Cottonwood and she's called a ton." Her tongue outlined her lips and her fingers continued to tap on the keyboard. "Print."

The printer behind her started to spit out paper into the tray. She reached around and grabbed them.

"Here you go." She laid them on the counter. "It looks like she's called at least once a month." Her finger drew down the date column. "Pretty silly stuff too." She tapped the header under causation and laughed. "She claimed the young girl's car was an inch over the property line in front of the house." She shook her head in disbelief.

"You have no idea." My eyes glazed over the paper. I'd take much more time when I got back to the office to go over them.

"Kenni, bug." Poppa appeared in the doorway leading out to the hall that connected to the courthouse. He sounded out of breath. "You've got to come here fast."

"Thank you so much. And it was nice to put a name to the face." I smiled. "You've been so kind over the past few years and I truly do appreciate it."

"No problem." She went back to her chair.

"Come on!" Poppa screamed at me. "Look."

I followed his arm down to his pointed finger and in the distance, I saw a man in street clothes who looked like Finn.

There must've been a strange look on my face because Poppa confirmed what I was thinking.

"Yep. That's your deputy with the city commissioner." Poppa nodded.

I gulped and watched them disappear into an office. Finn didn't see me. My phone chirped a text from my back pocket. I grabbed it. Anything to get my mind off what I'd just seen. It was Katy Lee Hart. She asked me to call her when I had time. She'd gotten some information about the cuff links and their value for me.

Instead of heading down to the commissioner's office, I trotted back to get some information from Wilma.

"You're back." Wilma grinned.

"Wilma, did you say the sheriff's position is open?" I asked.

"Mmmhmmm," Her chin lifted up and then down in a dramatic way. "The commissioner is interviewing candidates all day today. Some big wig from the Kentucky State Reserve is in there now. They're really impressed with his resume."

Her words were like a sword stabbing my heart. Had Finn really come to interview for the job and not tell me about it?

I tapped the counter with a couple quick pats.

"Thanks, I'll be sure to keep my eyes peeled and send any candidates your way." There was a smile on my face that covered up the heart breaking in my chest.

The more I thought about what I'd seen, the angrier I got.

"How could he?" I beat the steering wheel with the palm of my hand, taking the curves back into Cottonwood with a heavier foot than I should. "I was even going to see the sheriff about Rich, but not now."

"Kenni bug, slow down." Poppa had his hand curled around the door handle. His ghost knuckles were whiter than usual. "You've got to settle down before you see him. Your head has to be on straight. We've got a big day ahead." He repeated what I'd told him earlier. "What are your thoughts?"

"My thoughts?" I snorted. "They are jumbled. Why on Earth wouldn't Finn tell me anything about Clay's Ferry? What else do I not know about him?"

I had some doubt in how well I really did know Finn and I didn't like having doubt in my head.

"Kenni bug," Poppa's tone had turned a bit condescending.

"What?" I spat, "You mean to tell me that all of the sudden you're going to take his side and stick up for him?'

"Not what I was going to say, but you've got to take care of you. You can't be worrying about him. You need to make sure your head is in the game. You need to be in tip top shape for interviewing Reagan, going back to talk to Lita about her boy. Go to the rehab to visit Shelby with a smile on your face and act as if you don't know a thing about Finn with the Clay's Ferry commissioner."

"How can you say that?" I asked, relieved that we had just driven over the Cottonwood town line.

"Because you have to be elected again. Everything you do will always be under a microscope. You can't worry about what he's out there doing." I both loved and hated when Poppa made sense and brought me back to reality.

I let what he said hang in the air between us as we continued our trip back into town. As we headed south on Main Street, I knew that I wanted to go the rehab center to check on Shelby and Lita Brumfield before I continued with the investigation I'd planned for today.

CHAPTER EIGHTEEN

"Good morning," Shelby greeted me when I peeled the emergency room curtain back.

She was sitting up in the bed with Clay by her side. Both of them had big black circles under their eyes.

"Have you talked to Finley?" she asked with a worried mom look on her face. "He left here last night when Clay got here, but we haven't heard from him this morning."

"It's still early," Clay said. "I told him to get some sleep because he mentioned you gave him the day off."

"I'm sure he's sleeping through his phone calls if you've called or texted him." It took everything I had in me to hold my tongue.

If I even let one little thing slip out, I wasn't sure I was going to be able to reel it back in. Until I talked to him and heard what on Earth he had to say about being there, which couldn't be about any of the cases because he'd have to go through me to go investigate outside of county lines, then I was going to try to just keep my mouth shut.

"I think they are going to let me go home." She let out a long deep sigh. "Not that they've not taken good care of me. They have. I just want to go home for any procedure if anything needs to happen."

"I told you not to stress out. We will cross that bridge when we come to it." Clay continued to assure her to just rest.

"Can I get you anything before I go?" I asked.

"You're already leaving?" Shelby asked. "I mean, you just got here."

"Dear, she's got a town to take care of." Clay looked at me with understanding in his eyes.

"I've got to go see another patient, but I'll pop my head back in before I leave and see if you need anything by then." I would've offered to bring them a coffee, but I wasn't sure what she could and couldn't eat.

Since there was no real healthcare plan in her immediate future, I'd go check on Lita and see what was going on with her.

I stopped at the circular nurse's station in the middle of the emergency room. There were a few nurses gathered around each other with different patient charts like they were giving instructions. It was shortly after eight thirty a.m., right at their shift change. A bad time for me to be asking questions.

My phone rang, and I pulled it out of my pocket.

"Good morning, Max," I answered and walked through the emergency double doors for a little more privacy.

"Good morning. I wanted to let you know first thing that I've got the autopsy report completed if you want to come by and take a look at the body while I go over it before I release her to the family." He was so good at pointing things out and explaining everything so I could completely understand and make an iron clad case.

"That's great. Do you have time now?" I asked. "I'm at Cottonwood Acres so I can pop on over."

"Sounds good," he confirmed. "I'll see you in a bit."

Instead of going in to say goodbye to Shelby or even try to check on Lita, I'd decided to head on over to get the autopsy report. Besides, I'd be coming back at lunch to meet with Reagan, maybe there would be updates with both of them by then.

I didn't understand why it took so long for tests to be scheduled and ran when there was an emergency. It was one of life's greatest mysteries when it came to healthcare. But in this instance, it was to my favor.

Poppa was waiting in the Wagoneer when I got back in.

"That place gives me the hivvies." His shoulders shimmied.

"If this place gives them to you, then get ready because we are going to see Max." I couldn't help but smile and play the conversation we were about to have when we pulled up in front of the Cottonwood Funeral Home.

It was one of those times where Poppa loved to reminisce. In this case, I wasn't sure if he forgot he always told me this story, or if he just wanted to keep up the fond memory of how our deceased family members were always laid out in the front window of the front room of the two-story red brick home that'd been remodeled into a funeral home.

"You see that window right there." He pointed to the large window in the front of the house.

"Mmmhmmm." I ho-hummed on autopilot like I always did when he told this one.

"That's where all the Sims laid corpse." He nodded with pride. "You know that your mama will lay corpse there one day and I hope you do too."

I nodded.

"How did your visit with Shelby go?" Poppa asked.

"She was waiting on the test to be done or doctor to come in or something." I really didn't know. "When she asked me if I'd talked to Finn, I had to get out of there in fear I'd tell her something that wasn't so nice about him. Like his betrayal."

"Maybe Max can shed some new insight on the case so we can leverage that at the town council meeting." Poppa had his eye on the prize of getting the additions of another deputy to the department. "Especially if Finn is going to take that open sheriff's job in Clay's Ferry. You're gonna need a deputy."

"Rub salt in the wound, Poppa." I got out of the Jeep and jammed the keys in my pocket before I grabbed my bag from the back.

"What if I don't get elected and move to Clay's Ferry with Finn," I teased and walked up the front steps of the funeral home.

"Don't be talking out of your head now." He ghosted into the funeral home.

Stepping inside, goosebumps crawled up my legs, across my torso, and down my arms, leaving me with the feeling I'd just stepped over someone's grave. It was the same weird feeling I'd always had when I came here.

Since Max was the county coroner and owner of the only funeral home in Cottonwood, he'd made the coroner's office in the basement where he'd had some state grant money and the latest equipment needed to do both jobs. It appeared as though no bodies were in the rooms for layouts, which was probably how Max had gotten Avon Meyer's autopsy finished so quickly.

"Hi, do, Kenni." Tina Bower, owner of Tiny Tina's salon, was standing in the doorway of the elevator with her hair tugged up in a top-knot. "You going down?"

"I am." I stepped inside as she held the door for me. "What on Earth are you doing here so early?"

"I've got me a client to fix up." Her words left a yucky taste in my mouth. "Avon Meyers's mama called me a little bit ago. Said her daughter was going to be laid to rest in a couple of days and wanted me to do her hair and makeup." She patted the bag hanging off her shoulder.

"I hope you don't use the same brushes and stuff on me." I shivered at the thought.

"I clean them." She snorted with a giggle, pushing the down button when the doors closed. "Besides, I guess this means you found the killer?"

"Not yet, but I'm here to release her body, so don't you lay any of your acrylic fingernails on her until I sign off on those papers," I warned her right as the doors opened back up.

The cold temperature of the basement curled around us. Max kept it this cold since it was literally the morgue and bodies needed to be preserved even though he had those pull-out drawers the corpse laid on in the big refrigerator.

"Two of my favorite ladies," Max joked and stood over Avon. He had on his white lab coat and scribbled something on a paper attached to the clipboard in his hands. "Carey Meyers just called and told me you'd be here shortly, that you'd just stopped by to get Avon's dress for her layout."

Tina opened the big bag and pulled out a long flowery dress that was perfect for a beautiful summer day. The sad thought that Avon wore that dress while she was so alive and now it was going to send her out to her death entered my mind.

"I'll get the dress ready while you two do your business." Tina also pulled out a pair of scissors and headed into Max's office to get started on Avon's clothes being used to get her ready for the layout.

Tina once explained to me how bodies stiffened up too fast to really dress them for funeral lay outs, so they had to cut their clothes to make them look like they fit.

Max turned after Tina shut the door between the morgue and his office.

"She was shot at close range from the back with a Ruger SP101." Max showed me the paperwork with the body outline on it. He pointed to the points of access. "The killer kept it simple with no hollow points or straight lead. It was a shoot copper jacketed .38's. Which makes me think the killer might be a woman."

"Because the gun with lighter grain bullets will kick back less and heavier grain bullets like a .158 will result in heavier felt recoil, making it not hurt as much?" I asked to prove his point and glanced at Avon's body on the metal table.

"Yeah. Plus, the Ruger SP101 fits in the palm of a woman's hand perfectly." He put one hand in the shape of a gun and placed it in his other. "Small space between Avon and her killer like Avon was walking ahead, talking and eating something with yeast. Not worried about the person being behind her."

"What were the contents of her stomach?" I asked. "She'd gone to the Sweet Shop the morning she was killed."

"Then I can say the yeast was a donut." He wrote down on the paper.

"A donut or many donuts?" I asked.

"She only had eaten one donut. She was eating at the time she was shot which makes me think she knew the suspect and didn't think they were going to kill her. Also," he continued and picked up the long silver pointer. He pointed to her fingertip on her right-hand pointer finger. "She was licking some of the icing off her finger at the time of impact of the bullet."

"How on Earth did you determine that?" I was in awe at his skills.

"The streak on the finger from where it was in her mouth, is the same streak on her tongue. She was eating the donut, licking her finger, the suspect was walking behind her and shot her in the back at close range, hitting the heart directly, which caused sudden death." He was as matter-of-fact as you could get.

"She did buy three donuts according to Raven the owner of Sweet Shop. I wonder who she was meeting?" Lita Brumfield, Rich Moss, or Reagan Quinlan, I repeated their names in my head.

"You've not found the gun?" He asked, handing me the clipboard.

"No. I'm hoping to see some warrants on my desk when I head back to the office." I found the big black "X" where he marked for me to sign off on it. "Avon's funeral?"

"Her parents reserved the front room for tomorrow. It's going to be an hour lay out before a quick funeral from Preacher Bing."

"Tomorrow? Isn't that quick?" I asked.

"I think they know she's not coming back. Some people just want to get it over with." Max sighed. "People grieve differently."

I walked over to the office and peeked in the glass window of the door.

"Tina, she's all yours." I pointed to Avon and gave her body one last look. "I'm going to find out who did this to you," I whispered.

It was a promise I made to her parents and a promise I was making to her.

CHAPTER NINETEEN

When I got back into the Wagoneer, I pulled my notebook out of my pocket and reread what I'd written down. The autopsy file laid open on my passenger seat and as I went over my notes, I continued to look at the notes Max had taken.

The more I thought about it, the more I was confident Avon knew her assailant. There was a tickle in the back of my head that said I was missing something. If only I knew what that something was.

I started going through the notebook where I'd written all the information about Rich Moss. I flipped a few pages over to where I'd dropped by to see Lenora. Cottonwood First National was written down with a big circle around it. The paper I'd seen on the coffee-table and all the other financial papers she'd had on top of it, told me she'd had some business at the bank.

That wouldn't be uncommon because Woody had died, but Lenora'd not gotten the death certificate this week, which made me wonder if she'd had her account put on hold. That did happen when there was a death in some cases, but what expenses did she need? The bank form was the payoff of their mortgage. What was the calculation of the $20,000?

Before I went back to the office to fill in the whiteboard and see if any of the pieces were starting to fit together, I decided to head to the Cottonwood

First National, the only bank in Cottonwood that Lenora's mortgage could have been through.

Not sure if Vernon Bishop was going to be able to tell me anything without a warrant, but he owed me a favor. I'd gotten Mama to give his wife, Lynn, a position in the Cottonwood Baptist elite bell choir. Not only that, but it helped get Lynn out of the house and get some rest away from their three youngin's. Vernon had mentioned a few times how it'd helped she was getting out of the house more.

Now was the time for me to remind him of that. It wasn't illegal, just a little immoral.

The parking lot was empty, which was to be expected since I arrived right as they'd opened. The teller line was along the back wall and the offices were in the front behind glass walls. There was literally no privacy for Vernon Bishop, so when our eyes caught, he couldn't run from me.

He waved me in and stood up.

He wore a nice three-piece black pinstriped suit. His hair, which was prematurely gray, was neatly combed to the side with the perfect amount of gel. His cologne was a nice touch. He was much younger than he looked, fifteen years older than me to be exact.

"How're Lynn and the kids?" I went ahead and used my ammunition and didn't beat around the bush.

"They are great. Though, she's got her hands full for the summer without school." He laughed.

"Mama told me they were already getting ready for this year's Christmas Cantata." I shook my head.

"It's the pride of Cottonwood and Lynn loves it." He smiled. "What's going on with you this early?"

"Well, I've been investigating Lenora Moss's break-in during Woody's funeral." I pulled out my notebook to make it look as if Lenora told me the information, though I'd seen it with my own eyes through my being nosey and all.

"I heard about that," he tsked. "I told Lynn the Cottonwood Chronicle needed to stop posting the funerals in the paper. It gives petty thieves all sorts of information. Edna Easterly might's well just post an open invitation."

"Lenora had paid off her mortgage and she'd mentioned she needed some extra cash. Did she come in here and ask about that?" I acted as though I was reading out of my notebook and made it sound as if I was checking a fact.

"She came in." He walked around his desk, gestured me to sit and closed his office door.

There was some mumbling coming from the teller line and since the bank was so open and the walls were glass, the room echoed even a whisper.

"Kenni bug, look." Poppa's ghost was on the other side of the glass office. His hand pointed.

I looked past him out the office and standing at one of the teller windows was Reagan Quinlan and Herb Brumfield.

"This is getting good." Poppa did a little two-step and swept up to the teller line.

Unfortunately, Vernon had shut his door, which meant I couldn't hear what they were doing, but Poppa was there with his big ears open. This was when it was good to have a ghost as a deputy. If only he could be a permanent ghost deputy now that I knew what Finn was up to.

"What happened when she came in?" I fidgeted in my seat. The murder of Avon Meyers was more important than figuring out what Lenora needed the money for at the moment, though I still think Rich knew more.

"She wanted to see if she could take out a home equity line for $20,000." He sat down on the edge of his seat. He leaned a little forward, trying to peer in my notebook.

"Did she say what for?" I pulled the notebook closer to my chest.

"She said she wasn't sure if she needed it but wanted to know how fast she could get it." His chin slightly turned to the side, his eyes narrowed. "I'm sure she told you all this in that little notebook of yours."

"I have to follow up on all the information." There was no lie there. "Time?"

"She said that she wasn't sure when or if she was going to need it. Since the house was in her name only, there was no hold on it, and I don't need a death certificate to give her a second mortgage." His hands moved around as he talked with them and many shoulders shrugged. "I told her it could be pretty immediate since it was just her."

149

"She never said what she needed it for?" I asked, pulling the notebook away and pretending to read it.

"Most the time when people need money quick after a death, it's usually to cover funeral expenses. I'm not sure how much Max charged for the funeral, but I do know they can cost well into the thousands." He made a good point. "She was still in shock about his passing, so I didn't think what she was saying made much sense. I'll check in on her in a couple of weeks if I've not heard from her just to be sure she's doing good."

"That's all." I stood up and turned around. I wanted Reagan Quinlan to see me. But they were gone.

"Is that it?" He asked.

"Did you see the couple that was just in here?" I asked.

"The Brumfield's?" He nodded. "Yeah."

"Brumfield's?" I asked and tucked this bit of information in the corner of my brain.

"Reagan and Herb Brumfield. I guess it's Reagan Quinlan now." He clasped his hands together. "Talk about someone in shock. Reagan couldn't believe it."

"Believe what?" This was getting more and more interesting as the day'd gone, making everything Max said about the killer was probably a woman even more plausible, if it were Reagan that murdered Avon.

"How she caught him cheating on her. She was devastated. From what I understood, she worked her butt off at the rehab center to make a better life for themselves. Then she got the demotion due to not having continued her education in time or something." His brows lifted. "I guess something younger and better came long."

"They are married?" I gulped.

"Were." He shook his finger as if he remembered something. "I think he cheated on her with someone she worked with."

"Avon Meyers," Poppa gasped, ghosting himself behind Vernon.

CHAPTER TWENTY

Myrna Savage was dangling off a ladder as she was trying to hang the new seasonal flower baskets from the dowel-rod on one of the carriage lights in front of White's Jewelers. The arrangements she'd made this year were filled with a bright yellow sunflower and different colored dahlias. The big, red balled dahlias were my favorite. The colors went perfect with the banners the Beautification Committee had approved at the last town council meeting.

They had "Welcome to Cottonwood" embroidered on the bottom with a photo of the white courthouse that stood out so boldly in the middle of town. I loved seeing how the drawing from the last meeting had actually come to life on the banners that were now hung on each carriage light and blowing in the breeze.

We waved at each other as I passed and passing White's made me remember to call Katy Lee about the insurance or if she'd even been able to dig anything up.

Instead of pulling around to the alley, I pulled into the open spot in front of Cowboy's Catfish. I needed an extra-large cup of coffee and Bartleby Fry made strong, I just needed to smell it to wake up.

"Can I get a coffee?" I asked the waitress behind the counter and dialed Katy Lee. "Hey there. I got your text."

"I was about to call you because I was shocked you didn't call me right back," she said.

"I was busy checking something out. I had to go to Clay's Ferry. I visited Shelby and then went to see Max." I rattled off all the stops I'd made. "What did you find out?"

I took the coffee from the waitress, mouthed "thank you", and took out a few dollars from my pocket and left them on the counter so she could swipe it up.

"I couldn't find anything here in the office, so I called Dad. He said that Woody Moss had come in years ago when you and I were kids. He recalled about the same story you told about relatives going to New York and getting him these big expensive cuff links." She started to laugh. "Here's the thing, they are fake. I mean Dad said that if you rubbed a finger across them, it'd leave a green streak on your finger like the fake rings we used to get out of dime machines."

"I was afraid of that." I groaned and walked into the department from the kitchen of Cowboy's.

Scott was standing next to Avon's dry-erase board and Betty was at her desk typing away on her computer.

"He said that Woody couldn't believe it. They are worth nothing of value. But Dad also said that Woody continued to brag about them, so the value to him was more personal than monetary."

"That's a good point." I never thought that Rich might have stolen them for their personal value and that's why they've not turned up in any pawn shops. He might want to keep them. It was definitely an assumption I should follow up on. "Thanks. I appreciate it."

We hung up the phone.

"What's the story?" I asked Scott, shifting my weight to one side and took sips of my coffee.

I was going to wait and tell them my big news about Reagan and her scorned marriage. I knew Avon had to be the other woman, this gave Reagan a clear motive to kill her.

"There wasn't anything in the car. Literally as clean as her house." He had written this down under Avon's name on the dry-erase board.

I looked at Avon's name on the board.

"According to Max Bogus," I said before Betty interrupted.

"Which reminds me," Betty held up a file. "Got the autopsy right here in the file. I see where you signed off on it when you went to see Max."

"Thank you, Betty." I gave her a two-finger captain's salute. "Avon had gone to the Sweet Shop." I gestured for Scott to write that down, then took another drink of the coffee.

There was time for a few sips as he began to fill in the timeline.

"The night before she had been a victim of Lita Brumfield's endless calls to Clay's Ferry dispatch." The last thing I wanted to do was to stop drinking my coffee, but I had to put it down to open my bag and take out the papers. "The papers here state that an officer came by to take a report placed by Lita."

"But I thought Avon was the one who was victimized by Lita cutting off the apple tree branches." Scott pointed to Lita's name.

"Avon didn't call. It was a verbal fight that broke out between the two of them that got Lita to call. Also, the officer asked Avon if she wanted to press charges against Lita and she refused." My eyes scanned down the page. "It was at nine thirty p.m., and according to her time sheets we found in her office at her home she had to work until nine p.m."

Scott wrote down the times and the incidents on the timeline.

"Go on and leave the hours between ten p.m. and seven a.m." That time period I assumed Avon was safe and asleep. "At seven-fifteen a.m. Avon was in the Sweet Shop where she bought three donuts."

Scott continued to write.

"Golly gee," Betty bemoaned. "You've got this gal tracked down to the minute."

"That's the sign of a good sheriff, right there." Poppa appeared. He did a little jig and pumped his arms up and down between his legs. He was never a great dancer, but he was entertaining, forcing me to look down and not let Betty see me smiling.

"Go on and tell them about the food in her stomach with that finger lick and all." Poppa patted his stomach and then licked his finger as though he were acting it out. "The affair."

"Max's time of death was between seven and eight a.m. This means that she left the Sweet Shop and it only took her ten minutes at the most to get across town, park her car, and walk into Rock Fence Park path in the back." I continued to picture her doing these things in my head.

"You think she was meeting someone and that's who killed her?" Scott dropped his hand to his side.

I picked up the cup and held it between both hands to ward off the chill crawling over me.

"You're right." Poppa nodded at me. "What your thinking is right."

"Betty." I shot my gaze to her. "Did you get those background checks back yet?"

"Not yet, but I'll let you know." She tapped on the computer and scanned the screen. "Nothing," she confirmed.

"I've got some news that's going to change all this." My hand circled the board. "Reagan and Herb Brumfield were married. According to Vernon Baxter, Herb cheated on Reagan with someone from her work. He didn't know it was Avon, and I don't either, but I've got a good hunch it was. Also, he told me that Reagan had recently found out she was losing her position as the nurse manager because she let the continued education classes pass by without doing them."

"Shut your mouth!" Betty's jaw dropped. "This is exactly why she killed that poor girl."

"That also gives Lita more motive to be even meaner to Avon. Or worse," Scott made a great point.

"I'm thinking Avon met with Reagan in the park. Avon was walking and talking while Reagan walked behind her. According to the autopsy, she'd only eaten one donut and the Sweet Shop donut bag in her purse was empty." I took another drink of coffee to give a pause, so my words could sink in. "She wasn't thinking she was going to die."

I proceeded to tell them about her licking her finger before whoever she was with had shot her in the back.

"Do you think Avon was up for the promotion that'd suddenly came available giving even more of a motive for Reagan to kill her?" Scott asked.

"I think it's a possibility worth exploring," I added and wrote down all the information on the white board.

"No weapon has been found," I said. "She was shot between seven thirty and eight a.m. and not been dead for long because according to Finn, Mama found her right after eight."

"How is Finn doing?" Betty's brows knitted together.

"He's a traitor!" Poppa herky-jerkied his way over to Betty's desk and slammed a hand down. If she'd been able to hear or see him, she'd have jumped out of her skin. "That's what he is!" Poppa stomped his right foot and darted his right arm up, jabbing the air with his finger for drama.

"I'm sure he's fine and with his mom. I did stop by there this morning. They're still deciding what to do," I sighed.

My phone rang, bringing me back to reality. It was Finn.

"Speak of the devil." I held my phone out to show them Finn's name on the screen.

"Yep. He's a devil," Poppa said.

"Hi, Finn," I said, but he'd already started talking. "Someone what?" I asked.

"Someone broke into my parent's RV last night. They took all the money they'd withdrawn for the trip and the place is torn up." He sounded mad more than anything and that scared me.

I'd never heard him sound so on edge.

"Someone broke into your parent's RV?" I asked to confirm.

"Yes. I'm going to go door to door down this street and get the sonofa..." He was spitting mad. I cut him off.

"Finn, do not do that," I instructed him. "That will solve nothing. Hang tight. We'll be right there." I grabbed my coffee and my bag. "Scott, we've got to go to Free Row. Betty, man the phones. Call us if you need us."

"Kenni bug," Poppa called my name. "Kenni bug."

The dispatch phone started to ring.

"Let's go." I gave Scott the big eyed "why on Earth are you lolly-gagging" look.

"Kendrick Lowry!"

"Sheriff!"

Poppa and Betty both were screaming my name.

"What?" I screamed towards Poppa in a frantic tone. I had to get to Finn. "What do you want?" I hurried towards him in a rage.

"I'm over here," Betty called in a calmer voice.

I looked like a complete fool yelling into the air facing the bathroom. I slowly turned around and took a deep breath, giving Betty my attention.

"I'm sorry. I'm trying to gather all the clues in my head." I tried the best to cover up my little burst of crazy, but by the look on Betty's scared face and Scott's silence, they weren't buying it.

"The phone call is Herb Brumfield, Lita's son." She held the phone to her chest. "Someone has broken into his mom's house and destroyed it."

The second phone line started to ring.

"That is why I was trying to get your attention." Poppa just wouldn't stop talking. "I'm afraid the killer and the burglars are the same. There's just some things you know as a ghost." He tapped his temple.

"We are sending someone now." Betty told Herb and clicked over. "Sheriff's department," she answered. "Mmmhmmm. I'll tell her."

"Who was that?" It was like waiting for the other shoe to drop. We'd not seen this much action on the phone since I'd been there.

"Lenora Moss. She'd like to see you." Betty shrugged.

"You go to Finn's and I'll go to the Brumfield house," Scott took the reins.

"Okay. I'll stop by there after I check out the RV." We agreed on a plan. "Betty, call Lenora back and tell her I'll be by a little later," I called and darted out the of the department door through Cowboy's.

156

CHAPTER TWENTY-ONE

"Poppa, you've got to stop talking to me when people are around." There was no way I could risk them thinking I was anymore cuckoo than they'd already thought. I gripped the steering wheel.

"But I had to tell you that these calls were coming in." He pounded his fist on the dashboard. "This whole ghost-deputy thing is new to us and I'm still trying to figure out what I can and can't do."

"The person committing these criminal acts works at the rehab, which makes me think you're right that it's Reagan." He put his hand up when I went to talk. "I know you've got this thing in your head that Rich Moss has done this, but that's what the criminal wants you to believe."

Since it wasn't a crime in progress, though if I didn't get to Free Row fast Finn might kill one of our criminal neighbors, I didn't put the siren on top of the roof.

The street zoomed by as my foot got heavier on the pedal. Not because I needed to go faster, but the thought that I was wrong was hard to take since Poppa was right, I'd pinned all this on Rich.

Why? Because I'd seen him have a conversation with the deceased.

"Go on. I'm listening." I put on my blinker to turn right on Broadway.

"Avon knew something about the rehab center and she was going to tell

Wally Lamb." He put up a finger. "Maybe Rich Moss also knew since he'd gone to see Woody in the rehab center." He held up two fingers. "Here is where you need to think outside of the box." He held up a third finger. "Woody Moss." He held up a fourth. "Lita Brumfield." He held up all five fingers. "Shelby Vincent."

"All of them were robbed." My jaw dropped. I'd never figured Reagan to be a burglar.

"Yep and they're all in the rehab staying the night. Someone at the rehab knows this and that's when they make their move. Reagan Quinlan. Only, somehow Avon found out and was going to spill the beans to Wally Lamb after she got off work that night."

"She knew Reagan and that's why she wasn't scared when they met even brought her a donut." I started to piece this puzzle together as Poppa laid out all the pieces.

"That's right." Poppa nodded.

"Only Reagan knew she was going to kill Avon and that's what she did." I turned down Broadway.

Poppa leaned back in the seat with his arms crossed over his chest. "Reagan Quinlan," he pondered her name.

"That's exactly who I'm thinking about and who has been connected to all three people." Then I suddenly remembered what Shelby had said about the RV. "Shelby made mention several times at the rehab center that she couldn't leave the RV alone. Reagan was in the room when she said it."

"It looks like we've got a good case against her. We just need a few solid details. You might be diggin' up some dirt, but you're gonna find them." He tapped his temple. "I know it."

I pulled into my driveway. The RV was parked in the street and the door to the RV wide open.

"Where is Rich Moss?" I still couldn't leave well enough alone. There was just something I couldn't quite put my finger on about him that didn't sit well with my soul.

"Why are you asking about him?" Finn's voice caught me off guard when he jerked opened my door. "Can't you just see that I need you?"

"Finn," I sucked in a deep breath. I could feel Poppa ghost away. "I was talking to myself. Working out clues on the investigation, which we need to talk about."

"I know you need me, but my mom is in the hospital. I came here to get her some clothes, and this happens." He threw his hands up in the air with frustration.

"You are a cop. You know that we have to treat this as a crime scene and I don't think anyone on Free Row did it." I grabbed my bag from the back seat and followed him as he stalked towards the RV. "If you can't look at it objectively, let me and Scott do it." I put my hand on his shoulder.

He held up a hand, shrugging off my touch. My hand fisted as I kept my anger from going off on him and telling him exactly what I thought of him going behind my back to apply for the Clay's Ferry sheriff's position.

"Get your tape recorder out. I'm doing this interview right now," his deep voice cutting through the silence. His jaw tensed, forming a shadow along his cheek.

It was what he wanted, so I did it. He knew the drill and knew the questions, so I didn't have to ask them.

"I got here fifteen minutes ago. I used my parents key to open the door to retrieve some clothing for my mom who is in the Cottonwood Acres Rehabilitation Center." I held the tape recorder up and listened while recording him. "When I got here, I noticed the RV was unkept which isn't like my mother. When I went back to the living area of the RV, I noticed the cushions on the couches and the linens on the bed had been ripped off and overturned."

His voice got a little shaky, but I refrained from touching him for comfort. All business.

"I called my dad because I thought maybe after he'd gotten back from the hunt club's retreat with your dad." He paused. His eyes opened like he was finally noticing me. Not sheriff me, but his girlfriend. "Shut that off." He waved the recorder away from him.

"Okay." I did as he'd asked and waited for him to make the next move. I was unsure of how to proceed. I'd never seen this side of him.

"I've got something to tell you. It's been eating at me all day and it's why I've not called." He ran his hands through his hair. "I know you gave me the day off, and I'm a jerk for not calling you."

"It's fine." All of the sudden I completely understood what he'd been saying about the difficulty of me being his boss and his girlfriend. A wave of forgiveness swept over me. I wanted him to be happy. He was a good man and a great cop. He deserved to be promoted. "You're under a lot of stress."

"Aside from Mom." He sucked in a deep breath and on the exhale, he said, "The sheriff in Clay's Ferry has been fired and when I went to Clay's Ferry to check out the reasons why they had let Rich Moss out of the state pen for good behavior, that's when I found out. It wasn't like I was going over there looking for a job. I was doing exactly what you'd asked me to do and I was just fine with that." He started to pace back and forth as he talked.

"Finn," I said trying to stop him and let him off the hook.

"Kenni, let me speak. I've got to get this off my chest." He continued to look down at the ground. "Rich Moss had made some good friends while he was in prison, so much so the FBI made him an informant on an insider drug ring. In exchange for his information, they gave him witness protection. In the meantime, anything having to do with him had to be changed. That meant the will Woody Moss had and when I went to pick up the information from Wally Lamb, it all matched. I've got it in my drawer at the department."

"I..." I started again.

"Please," he begged with his hands jutted out to me. "Let me finish."

"Fine." I put the tape recorder back in the bag that was sitting on the ground. I wrapped my arms around my body like a blanket of comfort. I knew what was coming and I truly wanted to be happy for him.

"Woody changed his will, so any trace of Rich would be erased because he really didn't understand the process. He was afraid for Rich's life. Rich kept this all a secret for months as he worked with the FBI. During this time is when Woody had the knee replacement and things went south with the infection of his body rejecting the replacement." This was all news to me and completely exonerated Rich Moss as a suspect. "The day of the funeral was when Rich was scheduled to go and give his last statement to the FBI. That's why he left the funeral early. They let him go to the funeral with a plain clothed agent. They left, and he gave his last bit of information before he was whisked off to the program. He's not the killer or the burglar because a FBI agent has been with him the entire time."

He stopped in his tracks, put one hand on each of my arms, guided me to the steps of the RV and sat me on the door jam. He bent down between my legs.

"Kenni, I swear to you that what I'm about to tell you never even crossed my mind until they called me last night." He pulled his lips together and let out a long breath through his nose. Whatever he wanted to tell me had been buried deep within him like he didn't want to let it out. "Late last night when the interim sheriff called me to give me the final details about Sheriff Davis funneling drugs throughout the Kentucky highways and out of state lines."

My mind swirled in all different directions in disbelief.

"They arrested him late last night, that's when they called me. Rich was the narc that helped put him behind bars. It was a big fish. Rich was all in only if he was given immunity and put into witness protection program. All of this went down late last night and that's why Lenora has been keeping her mouth shut." He held up a finger. He was really struggling with this and I let him. "The interim sheriff asked me to think about interviewing for the job. Of course, I brushed him off since you and I'd just talked about it. Then this thing happened to my mom, I was partly out of my mind when I called him back. I went there this morning and they called me this afternoon. I was on my way here to pick up mom's clothes and was hoping to catch you at home. If you weren't here, I was going to call and find you so I could tell you in person." His beautiful and strong brown eyes melted into the loving eyes I was used to seeing. He searched my face.

"Why did Lenora need the money?" I asked.

"That's what you heard after all that?" he looked at me in shock.

"No. I already knew about the sheriff's job. I was in Clay's Ferry this morning getting the dispatch paperwork between Lita and Avon when I saw you." A big smile formed on my face. "As long as it's not going to change us."

A sigh of relief escaped him and his face melted. He wrapped me into his big strong arms.

"Oh. My. God!" Mama squealed from my driveway next to her car. She had on her pink pill hat, pink pant suit, and pink satchel. A sure sign she'd been to a Sweet Adeline meeting. "We're having a wedding!"

"Wedding?" Poppa popped back in. "There better not be a wedding."

"There's not a wedding," I muttered with closed eyes trying to regain my composure.

"What is all this fuss about?" Mrs. Brown stood on her porch, her curlers still in her hair and her housedress still on.

"Grab the champagne! Finn has proposed!" Mama threw her hands in the air.

CHAPTER TWENTY-TWO

"Mama don't go and lose your mind," I insisted while I took photos of the burglary scene. I had finally gotten her and Mrs. Brown to settle down.

It was a little hard to get the photos with Mama shuffling around the RV with protective police slippers on her shoes and her phone right next to my eyes.

Finn had already taken some of his parent's prints off their coffee mugs and hair brushes for quick identification so when we did brush out the finger printing powder, we'd be able to see which ones weren't theirs.

"I've been saving all the wedding stuff on this new thing called Pinterest." Mama used her finger to scroll through the wedding board she'd created just for me.

"It's not new and . . ." My mind rolled back to Avon's computer. "Avon was on Pinterest."

"That dead girl?" Mama jerked back. "What on Earth does she have to do with your wedding?"

"Mama." I turned around. "Finn didn't propose. He's going to take the sheriff's position in Clay's Ferry."

"He's w...wh...what?" Mama never stutters. She was shaken to her core. Probably even more than me.

"The sheriff's position is open in Clay's Ferry. He went over to interview and they've offered him the job." I knew that would stop Mama from carrying on about any sort of wedding.

"He can't do that," she protested. "He lives here, and he serves Cottonwood. Did you tell him that?"

"No. He's a grown man that can make his own decisions," I said under my breath when I heard him in the living space near us. It wasn't my place to explain to Mama what was in Finn's head and I didn't want him to think I didn't support him.

Ultimately, I did think it would be very hard not to see him first thing in the morning and I sure was going to miss our afternoon rendezvous when we had the time.

"He needs help. He's obviously lost his mind." Mama's voice cracked. "I mean, stress with his own mama sick and all can do funny things."

"He's not stressed." I snapped a few more photos and continued to put fingerprinting powder over most of the things in the RV. It sure would help if I found Reagan's prints in here. "He is too good to be a deputy all his life."

"Then you be the deputy and he can be sheriff. That'd make us all happy." She never was able to give up a good jab.

"I'm not going to stop him. That's that." My voice was stern enough to get her attention.

She'd opened her mouth, shut it and then curled her lips together to keep from saying something.

"How's Shelby doing?" I asked. "I know you've already gone to see her."

I really didn't know. But I knew Mama. Her Southern hospitality would never let someone be in the hospital without her checking on them first thing, especially since it was Finn's mom.

"According to Lulu's contact, I heard they were going to let her go on home." She nodded.

"Not until I release this crime scene." I looked around.

"Crime scene?" Mama drew back.

"Why do you think I made you put booties on your feet?" I stood there looking at her in shock.

"I don't know." She willy-nilly waved her hand in the air. "I figured you and Finn were cleaning up after them. They are dirty people. You'd never know it by looking at her."

"Mama, they were robbed last night." My mind went right back to Reagan. "And so was Lita Brumfield."

"Were Herb and Reagan working things out? Did they kill Avon? What about Reagan's job? How would that help them? Then there were the break-ins. Were they working together?" Poppa ghosted in and started to ask me questions like I was just going to start playing our little "what if" game.

All great questions, but my lips were zipped.

My heart stopped. Poppa did make a lot of sense. Who all knew Herb was having an affair with Avon?

"Well, I better get out of here then." Mama scurried towards the door.

The day was getting much hotter than yesterday. A sure sign it was full blown summer. Even some of the neighborhood kids were riding their bikes up and down Free Row.

"Let me get this clear." Mama stopped shy of the door. "Finn didn't ask you to marry him, so I can't tell anyone what I saw."

"No, Mama." I wanted to make sure she heard me loud and clear. "Finn did not ask me to marry him."

"Then I'll see you at the town council meeting tonight." She switched her purse to the other arm, nestling it in the crook of her elbow before she left the RV.

"Any luck?" I asked Finn when he walked up behind me.

"Nope. None. It's like they had on gloves." Finn inhaled.

"Gloves as in medical gloves," Poppa gasped. "Reagan has access to those too."

"It looks more and more like Reagan's behind these and Avon's murder." When Finn gave me a strange look, I realized he had no idea what I'd uncovered at the bank from Vernon.

"You can bring her in on suspicion of murder," Finn said after I'd told him everything.

"I just might after I meet with her at the rehab here in a few." I looked at the time on my phone.

The day had gone by so fast and I still wasn't sure I was any closer to solving this murder. But I knew with all the information I'd gathered, I was on the right track.

"It would be perfect timing to get someone in custody not only before tonight, but before Avon's funeral tomorrow." I curled my lip under my teeth as I thought of the Meyers and wondered how they were doing.

"We need to talk about my departure." Finn put his warm, strong hand on my shoulder. "I need to give my resignation to you and tell the town council tonight."

All I could do was nod my head because the tears were filling my eyes.

"Are you going to be okay? If not, I won't take it." He had the puppy eyes going.

"How can I not let you fulfill your dreams? We'll be just fine," I told him even though my heart was breaking and I wasn't sure we would be. "Now." I got my act together. "Let's get this crime solved."

"I'll finish up here since it only appears they took the money. Then I'm heading over to see Mom. I think they're going to release her to go to her doctor. Dad said he can drive home faster than a plane ride." He was right.

Chicago was only about a five-hour trip from Cottonwood and I was sure Shelby would be more comfortable in the RV than an airplane.

"I love you, Kenni." He pulled me into his arms, bending his chin down to kiss me.

Right as I was getting back into the Wagoneer, leaving Finn to finish processing the scene and release it back to his parents, Scott called my cell phone.

"Sheriff, I've got an update on the Brumfield break-in," he informed me.

"Was anything of value taken?" I asked thinking that if Reagan and Herb were behind this, they would try and throw us off by making it appear as if his own mother's house had been broken into.

Some people might think that was far-fetched, but when people are desperate, they'll do just about anything to get the heat off of them.

"They took a TV and the police scanner."

"That's it?" I asked to make sure. "TV and police scanner?"

"Those are the two main things pawn shop owners have told me are big sellers right now. So I think this person is trying to collect as much money as they can." He continued, "Also the background check on Reagan came back. She does have a Ruger SP10. Its bullets are an exact match as the bullet that killed Avon."

"Go to the judge right now and get a warrant to search her house." This was the break we needed. There was enough circumstantial evidence to at least hold her until we did a sweep of her house, fingerprints and checked on her alibi. If she had one.

"How do we tie this to Herb?" I asked him and started up the Wagoneer, going towards Main Street. I wasn't convinced Reagan'd done this on her own. Especially after seeing her and Herb together at the bank. It was a little too suspicious to me.

"If he and Reagan did this, maybe they are trying to get out of town because she'd lost her job." I wondered how much time she had until it was taken, unless they gave her an extension now that Avon was gone.

If Avon was her replacement.

The images of Avon's lifeless body haunted me every time I passed Rock Fence Park. My heart ached, but it told me what I had to do. Bring Reagan in on suspicion of murder.

It was perfect timing too. Just as I was pulling into the parking lot of the Cottonwood Acre Rehab, Reagan Quinlan was getting out of her car.

"Scott, I've got to go. Reagan is pulling in to meet me and I'm going to bring her on in." I hit the gas to catch up to her before she even had a chance to step foot in the building. "Good work."

Reagan put her hands out in front of her like I was going to hit her.

"Are you crazy?" She smacked the hood of the Jeep. "You're nuts."

"Don't hit my car. This is an official sheriff's car and that's ground for arrest." I jerked my handcuffs off my utility belt.

"What do you think you're going to do with those?" She spat.

"Reagan Quinlan, I'm taking you in for questioning on the murder of Avon Meyers." I grabbed her by the arm and did a quick behind her back move, clipping the cuffs on her wrists.

I loved when that move went exactly like it was taught in class.

CHAPTER TWENTY-THREE

"I'm telling you I didn't kill her." Reagan was sitting in the chair in front of my desk.

I was in the process of fingerprinting her and she wasn't being very forthcoming.

"You're telling me that you don't hold malice towards Avon Meyers for stealing your husband away from you?" I asked.

Of course I had the tape recorder on the whole time.

"Ask her how Avon and Jerk Head met." Poppa ghosted himself in the seat next to her giving her the stare down.

"When did you find out about Avon and Herb?" I asked.

"He told me." Her shoulders relaxed and she sat back in the chair. "He said they met during an argument with Lita. Which Lita would argue with a butterfly." She expelled a quick laugh, shaking her head. "He was telling his mother he was going over there to talk her into selling so we could buy the house, when in reality, they were talking about how they were going to move him in and me out."

"Not only was he cheating on you with your employee, but she was also getting your job. The job which you let the classes slip that you needed to keep your management position." I watched her body language.

"Don't forget about the burglaries," Poppa chirped.

"It's true that I let the classes slip. I was going through my divorce. I wasn't in the right frame of mind and somehow, I thought I had until the end of the year. In reality, my year was summer-to-summer, not calendar." Her eyes filled with tears. One dropped out and down her cheek. "But I didn't kill her over it."

"Right." I winked at her. "Herb and you decided to get back together. You two have been robbing people who've come into the rehab, leaving their houses wide open."

"Elderly abuse," Betty muttered under her breath. "Seen it on one of them TV shows. It's a real thing."

"We did no such thing," Reagan insisted. "You're reaching now, Sheriff."

"Am I? Woody Moss, Lita Brumfield, Shelby Vincent's RV?" I held up three fingers. "All three were admitted while you were in charge and I was there when Shelby told you and Finn that she couldn't leave the RV open." I kept throwing questions at her as she sat there sobbing. "You only took things that could bring you instant money at a pawn shop."

"Admit it and let's just get this over with!" I planted my hands on the desk and leaned over. "Give Carey and Wesley Meyers the decency they deserve before they put their innocent daughter in the ground!"

"No! No!" She screamed back at me. "I didn't do this," she said through her tears.

"You didn't decide to meet her before work, where she knew that none of your write-ups could affect her since she was up for the job?" The meeting scenario I was accusing her of played in my head the way the evidence was laid out. "You needed her to help you. When she didn't agree to go along with her plan, you shot her. According to your background check, you own a gun. Where's the gun you killed Avon with?"

"I do own a gun, but I didn't kill her. Besides, it was stolen out of my car." She was almost convincing.

"How convenient." I pushed off my desk and straightened up. "What kind of gun?"

"It's a Ruger SP101." The muscle in her jaw spasmed.

"Did you have bullets in the car?" I asked.

"Yes. The ones the guy at the gun shop told me to get." Her vision narrowed, there was an edge of anger in her voice. ".38."

"Interesting." My temples began to throb by her attitude. "That's the exact same gun model and bullet that killed Avon Meyers. Your gun comes up missing? Stolen?"

"Yes. It was stolen from my car in the parking lot while I was at work." She smacked her hand on my desk. That was enough for the time being.

"How about you go in there and sit." I pointed to the cell. "Maybe you'll decide to tell me the truth after you've sat in there and thought about it. Trust me when I say that this cell is a spa compared to where you're going."

She stood up and walked into the cell without giving me any hassle. She plopped down on the cot watching me close the cell and turn the key.

"I'll stay here while you go to the town council meeting. Besides, I've got some paperwork to do." Betty knew that I needed her help. "I already told Scott to meet you there."

"You know about Finn?" I asked.

"He called after he said he told you and he wanted me to keep an eye on you." A lot of emotions were buried in Betty's words.

"Did he?" A smile dangled from my lips. It felt good knowing he'd actually taken the time to make sure I was okay.

"Mmmhmmm. Are you okay?" Betty asked. Her eyes shifted from me to Reagan, as though she weren't sure we should be talking about this.

"Yeah. Heck ya." I waved off any concern she might have. "I'm a Lowry." I winked.

"I want my one phone call now." Reagan had gotten up from the cot and wrapped her hands around two different bars, sticking her nose through them. "I've seen enough shows to know it's a thing. And you've not charged me, so what are you waiting on if you're so sure I'm the killer?"

She asked the very question I didn't want her to ask. I was waiting on all the information to be compiled, even Tom Geary's prints and the warrant to go through her house to find the murder weapon that she'd conveniently said had been stolen.

"Fine. Betty, can you take her the portable?" I asked Betty over my shoulder.

She turned her head, making sure we didn't hear her. I couldn't make out what she was saying in her mumbled whispers.

"Thank you. I should have a visitor shortly." She glared with her hand extended out between the bars with the phone in her grips. "Then you'll get my alibi."

"It's gonna have to wait because I've got a town council meeting to get to." I wasn't about to miss it. Not even for a murder investigation when I was pretty certain the killer was right here in front of me.

"But I've got rights!" She protested as I was heading out the door.

I wanted to tell her that her rights flew out the window when she pulled the trigger to kill Avon, but I had to stay above the emotional side of the job and keep my head on my shoulders. Sometimes that wasn't easy to do.

When I pulled up to Luke and Vita Jones's house, Jolee Fischer's On the Run Food Truck was pulled up to the curb, open for business.

"I've got a fresh pot of coffee brewing just for you," Jolee said when I opened the door to the food truck as she was serving up some good country ham and biscuits at the walk-up window.

"I need it," I groaned and then started to laugh when Duke had jumped up after hearing my voice.

He'd been laying in between Jolee's feet, snatching up every piece of food like a vacuum while she made the biscuits and cut the ham. His nose was covered with flour.

"You're so spoiled." I rubbed my hand on his head. He wagged his tail, danced around and darted around me, leaping around Luke's yard. "I better get him before Luke throws a fit. He doesn't like Duke peeing on his flower bed."

"I'll have Ben bring you a coffee and a biscuit when he gets here," she hollered as I shut the door.

A wooden podium stood where the movie screen was usually hanging, and Mayor Chance Ryland was banging the gavel against it, bringing the meeting to an order.

"Alright! Alright!" Mayor Ryland beat the wooden gavel. "Let's get this meeting started."

I looked around after I made my way up to the front of the room and took a seat in the front row in one of the folding metal chairs. Everyone was there. We gave each other a slight wave and the Baptist nod.

Shortly after the Mayor started to recite what was on the docket, Ben sat down in the seat next to me. He handed me my cup of coffee and a biscuit in a napkin.

"If you don't want the biscuit, I do," he whispered.

"Fine. Take it." My stomach was already in knots. I was about to tell all of Cottonwood about Finn's plans to leave and it wasn't going to be easy. He was probably more liked than I was.

"I'd like for Sebastian Hughes to come up and speak on behalf of the EMT service." Mayor Ryland got off the stage.

Polly Parker greeted Mayor Ryland on the far side of the front row with a big grin on her face and silently pretending to clap her hands like he had just given some outstanding speech. I still didn't get what she saw in him. He'd been her father's best friend and that just made it ickier to me. But she was happy and it was none of my business.

"The EMT service has had over eighty runs in the past couple of months." Sebastian rattled off numbers and statistics while I leaned back over to Ben.

"I should be at the diner in the morning after my rounds." I wiggled my brows.

"Our contract to work with businesses like the Cottonwood Acres Rehabilitation and transport the clients to and from their home is about to expire. I'm here on behalf of the EMT service, and since I'm the one off work tonight," Sebastian's words were met with laughter, "to ask for a year-long contract to be amended to the current contract since the service, which we've provided your town, has been greatly needed in and around Cottonwood." He pointed to me. "In fact, our very own Sheriff Lowry can attest to the fact that our EMT service has saved Deputy Vincent's own mother when she was having a heart attack."

A collective gasp spread through the crowd, making me realize that town gossip was still about Avon's murder. If it weren't for her, I would've fielded hundreds of calls about Finn's mom but I'd yet to have one.

"She can stand and tell you how valuable our service is." He caught me off guard but waved me up.

"Go on." Ben nudged me with his elbow.

I sat my coffee on the floor under my chair and trotted up to the podium.

"Yes. The EMT service has been vital to the community and also vital for the extra time and calls they've gotten from the rehab center." My eyes grazed the tops of everyone's head as I shifted my face back and forth addressing them for Sebastian. "Finn and I are eternally grateful for the fast service that was provided. Sebastian made the quick call to give her the attention she needed to save her life."

"That's all we need to hear." Doolittle Bowman took the liberty to stop the conversation. She was the town manager and she was ready to put it to a vote. "All in favor of extending the contract for the EMT runs for businesses and citizens, raise your hand."

She tapped her finger in the air as she counted the hands.

"You can put those down. All those who don't want to extend the contract put your hands up." She glanced around the room but no one had lifted their hand. "The EMT proposal has been extended." She looked at Sebastian and said, "You can go on and sit down, but Kenni, you can stay up here since your proposal is on the docket next."

"Well, as you know, the department doesn't have a nightly dispatch and we farm that out to the Clay's Ferry dispatch. I know it saves the town money to do it this way, but I can't help but think that Avon Meyers might be alive today if we'd had the service. Several times Lita Brumfield had filed complaints against her, forcing the Clay's Ferry sheriff's department to come to Cottonwood to figure out if charges were necessary." I stopped and looked around at all the faces staring at me to see if I could assess their thoughts.

"Are you saying that Ms. Lita Brumfield killed Avon Meyers?" Polly Parker Ryland's voice asked with a deep Southern drawl. "I mean, Kenni, aren't you grasping for straws? She's got Parkinson's Disease. She wouldn't hurt a fly."

"I never said that, I'm saying that I might've gotten to know Avon during these calls and maybe if she were having a disagreement with someone, she might've told me. That's all." My words were only met with Polly's eye roll. "Anyways, I was initially here to ask if we could keep Scott Lee on as a full-time deputy and extend the hours of the department."

There were some groans and uncomfortable shifting in the metal chairs.

"We already save money with the department being in the back of

Cowboy's Catfish." I wasn't about to ask for my own building like I'd done before because that was shot down fast. "But in light of certain things, my request has changed."

"What is that?" Chance stood up with his hand planted on his hips. He wasn't the type that liked to be blindsided. "This is my town and that's news to me. You work for me and the people."

He was always good at reminding me of that.

"Does this have to do with the sheriff's opening in Clay's Ferry?" He asked with a bird thin scowl on his lips.

"Deputy Vincent has been interviewed and taken the open sheriff's position in Clay's Ferry. He will be taking the position immediately, leaving me with Deputy Scott Lee to take his place. That's what I need to you approve. Scott's full-time employment with the sheriff's department." My words were met with a collective gasp.

There were murmurs that he'd left because we'd broken up, whispers of how the department wasn't going to be safe, and just a general all-around yucky feeling.

I slumped away from the podium and decided there was no more talking. I had to let this ride out because apparently, this took precedence over the fact there was a girl dead and we had someone out there burglarizing houses. Which was how a small town operated.

Needless to say, that whole messy issue abruptly ended the town council meeting in hiring Deputy Scott Lee as Cottonwood's newest employee, though he never showed up. They'd have some sort of ceremony for him at the Rock Fence Park after they'd gotten used to the fact he was replacing Finn.

By the time the meeting was over and Duke and I'd gotten home, I was exhausted. I slumped down in one of the chairs on my back porch. Duke ran around the yard doing his business.

"You up for company?" Finn Vincent let himself into the gate of my backyard. He had a six pack of beer in his hand and a bag of tortilla chips in the other—our favorite snacks.

"Only you." I swiveled the chair around to greet him.

Duke sprinted to the porch when he heard Finn. He had his old tennis ball in his mouth.

"I'm blaming Jolee for giving him food that's making him hyper." I laughed and watched Finn toss the ball to the very back left corner of the fence.

"I guess your mom and dad are gone?" I was sad that I didn't get to tell them goodbye.

"The test came back clear and they think she just had a bad case of heart burn. She couldn't wait to get out of here." He handed me a beer. "I'd love to tell people that my family is amazing, and we all get along, but the fact of the matter is that my family isn't like yours."

"You mean," I hesitated to find the right word. "Whacko?" I pulled the top of the chip bag open.

"Loving. Loyal. Accepting." He shook his head and took a swig of his beer. "Your mom and dad stopped by to see my mom. Your dad told me that they'd talked about the whole Catholic thing after the big fight the night of the supper. Your mom and dad agreed that no matter what happened, they'd stick by your decision about the religion."

"Did they?" I knew that Mama would eventually cave. She always did.

Duke ran up between us, dropping the ball at Finn's feet.

"Yeah. They love you so much. I can't say my mom would do the same." He took the ball and threw it another time. "I love them. They are my parents. But not every family is as picture perfect as yours."

"Mama is pretty picture perfect, literally." I laughed.

"I heard the meeting got a little crazy when they found out." He sat down in the chair next to mine. He popped off the top of two more beers.

I offered him the mouth of the open chip bag. We were like an old married couple already.

"I guess Scott is officially your deputy?" He asked and put his hand on my leg.

"He is." I tried to be happy and sound upbeat, but a tear fell from one eye, and no matter how many times I gulped and sighed, they kept coming.

"Kenni baby." He put the beer down and kneeled down in front of me, curling me into his arms. "Why are you so sad? This is a good thing. For me and you."

"I don't think so." I ugly cried into his neck.

"Remember when we started dating and you were so worried we'd get

175

sick of being around each other? You were so worried." He pulled back and his big strong hand wiped my cheek. "Look at us. Strong. Happy. Very happy."

"You're very happy?" I asked, searching his eyes for any hint of a lie, but they were truthful. He'd never been anything else.

"Very." He exaggerated with big head nod. "So much so that I'm not moving. I don't have to move. It's not in their laws that I have to live in the same county." He rubbed my head with his hand. "Free Row is stuck with me and Cosmo."

"Poor Cosmo." I felt better now that I knew he wasn't moving.

"I even get two days off a week since they've got a bigger department. I get my own office, so I can call you all day without anyone knowing." He leaned in, his lips warm against mine. "Honestly," he whispered, my eyes still closed, his breath warm on my lips, "if you don't want me to take the job, I won't. I love you."

"I could never ask you to do that. I love you too." I sealed it with a kiss.

CHAPTER TWENTY-FOUR

Avon's funeral was going to be at ten a.m.

Over the night there'd not been one call from Scott about Reagan and this morning Betty was going to go relieve him while I went to the funeral. Finn and I had made peace with the reality of our situation and we only knew that if we did end up getting married, we'd figure it out along the way.

Right now, I was happy that he was happy and Scott and I were going to work fine together.

I'd heard they were also going to have a graveside funeral at cemetery, where Poppa was buried.

I'd not seen Poppa since I'd put Reagan in jail and I wasn't sure how seeing his gravesite today was going to affect me. We didn't get to say goodbye this time like the other few times he's ghosted into my life.

Like Finn, my relationship with my ghost Poppa was something we had to figure out along the way. I hoped Avon's death wasn't the last I was going to see of him. Though I'd never wish anymore murders in Cottonwood. Still, no matter how many times Poppa came, there was never enough time to tell him goodbye.

My phone rang. I knew it had to be Mama. Anytime there was a big event, and trust me funerals were big events around here, she liked to call me and remind me that I was going to be seen as a lady. That was her way of telling me to put on makeup, tuck up my crazy, and add another layer of lipstick because a girl could never have on too much lipstick—according to Mama.

"Hello?" I picked up my phone, but it wasn't Mama, it was Scott.

"I'm sorry to bug you this morning since you're going to the funeral and all, but Reagan insists that you come over here and get her alibi. She has a lawyer stopping by this afternoon and she wants to go home."

There was some screaming in the background.

"Is that her?" I asked.

"Yes, ma'am." He sounded a little scared.

"She sounds like a screeching cat." I said with a smile.

"Ma'am, she's acting like a caged cat." Touché to Scott for slinging it right back. I liked that.

"I'll be there in a minute." It was part of the job and I'd have to text Finn and let him know that I'd meet him at the funeral.

If Finn was still with the department, I would've had him go with me and we would have left from there. This was my new normal.

"You stay here today." I tossed some kibble in Duke's bowl and made sure he had plenty of water. "It won't be a full day."

With Reagan behind bars, I could bring my work home and spread it out on the kitchen table so I could get it together in order of events for the prosecutor. It would be tricky without a confession, but I felt the evidence was enough, like the same gun and bullets, the affair between her husband and Avon, as well as the working relationship they had were all valid reasons for murder.

As the Wagoneer rattled down Free Row, I glanced over at the passenger seat where Poppa had sat this time yesterday. At a stop sign, I laid my hand on the seat. "Goodbye, Poppa. I love you."

Then I turned my thoughts back to Reagan.

I pulled down the alley and parked in my spot near the department door. It took a few minutes for my eyes to adjust from the bright sun to the inside of the office.

"Sheriff," Herb Brumfield caught me off guard, calling my name when I walked in the sheriff's department.

"Herb." My eyes darted between him, Scott, and Reagan. "How's your mom?"

"She's okay. Her doctors said it was a mild heart attack. But she'll be fine. I wanted to talk to you about Avon." He twiddled with his fingernails.

"Is that right?" My brows rose. "Fine. I've got a funeral to go to, so can we do this later?"

"I'd like to do this now." He kinda had me in a hard place since I was there to relieve Scott, it was my job to help him.

"Deputy Lee is here and he's able to do it." I walked over to Reagan. "I heard you wanted to see me."

"I want you to talk to him." She had one hand on her hip and jutted to the side. "He's my alibi."

I walked back over to my desk where I'd left my little notebook and flipped it to her statement.

"We were together." Herb hurried over, gesturing between him and her.

I shot her a look.

"Yes. We are getting back together." Reagan's words nearly knocked me off my heels. And I wasn't great at walking in them in the first place.

"Is this some sort of you two get married so the other can't testify against you in court scheme?" This was all sounding too good to me.

"No. Please. Here me out." Herb shook both hands in front of him, fingers spread apart. Very desperate.

"Then you won't mind me tape recording this statement." I stalked back over to my desk and flung the top drawer open to get out the tape recorder.

"It's true. Avon and I met when I would go over and talk to her about my mother. I know my mom can be a little much and one thing led to another." His face turned red as if he were remembering their little escapade that got her killed. I wasn't buying it. "I lost my job and my mom wanted me to move in next door because she's scared to death of going into a nursing home when she can no longer take care of herself as the disease progresses."

That I completely understood.

"After she found out about me and Avon, she said that she was going to make Avon's life a living hell. My own mother told Reagan before I could." He put his hand to his head. "I wasn't thinking. Avon's parents didn't know, they just knew my mom called the cops on her for everything. I put Reagan through hell. She forgot to go to her continuing education classes and lost her job over me."

"Avon took and took from you," I said to Reagan over his shoulder.

"I didn't care about her," she seethed.

"She took the house you wanted. She took your husband. She took your job. I get it." I threw my hands into the air. "Any woman would be at their wits end if this was them. But most of them wouldn't kill. That's where you messed up." I twisted around to Scott. "Tell us what you found in Reagan's house."

I was sure there was something there. Sure of it.

"Nothing. It turned up clean." He pointed to my desk. "The report is on the desk."

"Now that you don't have Avon to take care of you, you want Reagan back so you can mooch off of her. This is why you are here giving your alibi." I snapped my finger in the air. "But wait. Let me guess. Avon found out that you were cheating on her with your wife. Your ex-wife."

I added in the last part for good measure right as Betty Murphy came in for the day.

"I went to Avon that night after Mom had cut down the branches of her apple tree and told her that I still loved Reagan." He at least admitted to it.

Betty shrugged her coat off and sat down at her desk. Her eyes darted between all of us, taking it all in.

"Then you met her for breakfast before her shift and you rubbed it in her face. Right, Reagan? It was your turn to take from her. But it was her life you took." My words struck her hard.

She fell face down on the cot, burying her head in the flat pillow and sobbed.

"Our lawyer will be here this afternoon. And I expect an apology." Herb slammed the door on his way out of the department.

"Well, I expect the prosecutor will be bringing murder charges against you this afternoon," I said to Reagan and headed out the door myself.

The raid on Reagan's home, office, and car turned up nothing. I was hoping that he would have found the gun and he was pretty thorough.

CHAPTER TWENTY-FIVE

A breeze whistled through the trees in the cemetery. When I got there, I'd already missed the pallbearers taking the casket out of Max Bogus's hearse. Her parents must've bought the plots a long time ago because Avon was being buried in the old part of the cemetery up front where Poppa was buried. Only they probably bought it with the idea they'd be laying in it, not their daughter.

Finn greeted me with a smile when I walked up and mouthed asking if everything was okay. I gave a slight nod and tried not to smile too big when I saw him. Mama was staring at us from the other side of the gravesite and if I'd smiled too big, she'd think I was having a good time at a funeral. And who had a good time at a funeral?

Preacher Bing said a few kind words about Avon. He talked about how he wasn't surprised she went into the healthcare industry because she was always volunteering for the elderly.

Sebastian Hughes made his way over to me and stood on the opposite side of Finn.

"I didn't get a chance to thank you for talking on the behalf of the EMT service," he whispered low enough so only I heard him.

"My pleasure," I tried to whisper but my voice cracked when I saw Poppa sitting on top of his gravestone.

"Kenni?" Finn put his hand on me. "Are you okay? You're trembling."

I gulped and looked down at my hands. He was right.

"I'm fine," I choked out and looked up at Poppa.

He lifted his arm up in the air and pointed to his wrist. What was he trying to tell me? I squinted to see what he was mouthing.

I didn't have to know exactly what he was saying to understand him. Reagan Quinlan was not Avon Meyers's killer or he'd not be here.

Poppa's mouth contorted. Angrily, he jabbed the air in front of him with force. Jab after jab, pointing. I turned towards Sebastian, and Poppa clapped and pointed to his wrist.

Sebastian had his hand over his eyes to shield them from the sun. There was a dingy stain around the button holes of Sebastian's white dress shirt where cuff links should be.

"Kenni bug." Poppa ghosted next to us. "Don't move and don't look at me. There are a lot of eyes on you," Poppa warned. "Sebastian has rust marks on his shirt. The same type of stain I've seen many times when I wear cuff links that aren't real gold or silver."

"Finn," I didn't whisper this time. I wanted Sebastian to hear. "Before you go to Clay's Ferry this afternoon." I looked at Finn under furrowed brows so he knew to play along. "I wanted to tell you that money Lita Brumfield said was under her mattress. That $10,000." I nodded.

"Yeah. Did you go back and check that out?" He asked. His eye bore into me.

"No. But Herb is at the rehab staying with his mom and he said he went to check. It's still there, so the only thing the robber got was the TV and police scanner." I put my hand to my heart. "I'm so relieved and wanted you to know so you can put that in your report this afternoon to close your part of the case."

I gave him stabbing looks and clenched my jaw, trying to give a slight glance back to Sebastian on my other side without moving my head.

"You're pretty sure Reagan Quinlan killed Avon and committed the burglaries?" Finn was so good at reading me.

"Yes. The prosecutor is writing up the charges as we speak." I nodded. "But I've got to get to the office. You're taking her to the big cell in Clay's Ferry, right?"

"Yes. I'll see you in a few hours. Will you be at the station all afternoon?" He was closing the deal for me.

"I will." I curled up on my toes and kissed him before I turned to Sebastian, who was leaning towards me so hard he fumbled to stay upright. "My job never ends. I've got a bunch of paperwork to do. Thank you so much for all you do. Everyone is so grateful for your lifesaving techniques."

"Thank you, Sheriff." He smiled real big. "It's my civic duty."

"Yes. Yes, it is." I tried to be as discreet as I could while powerwalking back to the Wagoneer. I fisted my hands at my side so as to not swing them. The less attention I brought to myself, the better.

"Scott, it's Kenni." I was desperate to get to Lita's house. "I need you to listen to me very carefully. Reagan is not the killer. Sebastian Hughes, the EMT driver, is the killer and the burglar. I need you to get Herb to meet me at his mother's house. I have to get inside. I've planted a sting operation and I think Sebastian has taken the hook."

I reached over my back seat and grabbed my shotgun, dragging it up front as I took a left out of the cemetery straight to Lita's house on Hickory Hill.

"I know it's not good to leave Reagan in the cell while you leave, but you have to. I'm going to need back up."

"Yeeee little doggie!" Poppa appeared in the front seat, practically salivating over the gun. "I've not seen you use this little baby in a long time."

"Are you sure, Sheriff?" Scott questioned.

"Don't question me. Do it now." I threw the cell phone down and drove a little faster.

"How did you recognize that?" I asked Poppa. "If it weren't for you, I wouldn't have seen it. I thought you were gone."

"Something seemed off to me. So, while you interrogated Reagan, I hung around the rehab center and went over the clues. Who else was around that fit into the puzzle? None of the other nurses had much contact with Avon because Avon was doing PT. But Sebastian took a lot of Avon's clients to and from the rehab center because of the service contract with Cottonwood." Poppa was so good. "I didn't realize that he actually stays for the appointments. He's doing this with other therapists there too. It puts him in a position to get to know them."

"He did say that she was sweet and the donut thing." I beat the wheel with my hand. "And he brought in Lita Brumfield and Shelby Vincent. He was on the other side of the curtain when Shelby said she couldn't leave the RV alone." I shook my head and turned onto Hickory Hill.

I pulled down the street so he wouldn't risk seeing me if I did bait him about the fake money.

"I bet he broke into Reagan's car while it was in the parking lot and stole her gun. The exact same gun he used to kill Avon." Poppa's nose turned red at the tip as he talked and flailed his arms in the air. "We got him, Kenni bug. I know it."

I watched in the rearview mirror as I pulled down the street far away enough that if he pulled in front of Lita's house, he wouldn't be able to see me.

"What if he doesn't park this close?" Poppa asked. "Go park around the corner."

Poppa knew best. I did what he said and grabbed the shotgun. I jerked open the glove box and took out a handful of shotgun shells, burying them in my fist.

"I've never shot a gun in a dress before." I laughed looking at my deputy ghost. "I sure hope I don't have to today."

Herb pulled up with a frantic look on his face.

"What's going on, Sheriff?" He asked as he jumped out of his car. "Scott said to hurry."

"I need you to let me in your mother's house. We don't have much time." I quickly told him how I'd baited Sebastian and I needed his cooperation.

"Oh my God and I was bringing my mom home today." He ran his hand over his face. "You know, Avon was trying to tell me something about him, but it was when I was telling her about me getting back with Reagan. I wasn't listening to her." His nostrils flared as though he were trying to hold back a dam of emotions. "I could've saved her."

"No. No, you couldn't," I assured him because I needed him to have his head on straight. "I need you to leave after you let me in. You can go to the station and sit with Reagan because she's alone there. Don't try to get her out of the cell you won't be able to do it without me."

He nodded and blinked, as he fumbled getting the key off the keyring.

I'm not going to say that I was all calm, cool and collected. I was a mess. Finn was right. My hands were trembling and my heart was beating out of my chest. My temples began to throb as I tried to shake my head and clear my thoughts so I could be laser focused.

I'd quickly let myself in and locked the door behind me. With all the lights completely out, I hunkered down between Lita's mattress and side table. It seemed like forever until I heard some footsteps in the other room. I took a deep breath and let it out through my mouth in one long stream.

The footsteps stopped at Lita's bedroom door. The door made a long creaking sound as it slowly opened. I peeked over the mattress just enough to see it was Sebastian. He was looking around the room as though he were assessing it before he moved towards the bed.

His hand plunged under the bed. I brought the shotgun up under my armpit and slowly stood up, looking down the site.

"Sebastian Hughes, stop right there."

He jerked around. His face was blank.

"Put your hands up in the air," I instructed him. "I'm not afraid to shoot."

"I wondered if you were baiting me." He let out an evil laugh. "But $10,000 would've been enough to get out of here without getting caught."

"I know you burglarized Woody's house and took the cuff links. It took me a while, but I placed you at the scene of Lita's and Finn's parents RV. But I can't for the life of me figure out why you killed Avon Meyers." I took a step towards him.

He looked over his shoulder.

"I wouldn't run," I warned. "I'm a pretty good shot."

"I didn't kill her and you can't prove anything different." He put his hands down. "I'm going to walk out of here. You can kill me over the TV's, scanners, a little cash, and some fake cuff links, but you'll be featured on the news as a killer like the other cops on TV."

"I wouldn't kill you. Just get you somewhere where it hurts really bad, but not enough to keep you from going to prison." It was a great plan.

I kept my eye on him, trying to decide if I wanted to take another step forward. My ears were perked, waiting for Scott to get there.

"So you lied in your statement. I can add that on to your list of charges." I continued to talk to keep him engaged. "You said you hadn't seen Avon in a couple of days but you'd enjoyed a couple of donuts with her before you killed her."

"It was Reagan. She's the one who ate the chocolate donuts and killed Avon while she was licking her fingers. Unaware she was about to be killed," He'd just confessed and didn't know it.

"I never told you they were eating chocolate donuts and I sure didn't tell you Avon had been licking her fingers when you killed her." I made my words perfectly clear. "Sebastian Hughes, you are under arrest for murder in the first degree of Avon Meyers along with burglary and theft," I started to read him his rights, but he darted out the door like a jet.

"Hold it right there!" Scott stood at the end of Lita's hallway with his arms outstretched and his gun pointed directly at Sebastian's heart. "I believe the sheriff was talking to you."

A sigh of relief escaped me as I put down my shotgun and watched as Scott handcuffed Sebastian Hughes. Not only was it a relief that a murderer was brought to justice, but I knew Deputy Scott Lee and I were going to be just fine as the new duo in town.

CHAPTER TWENTY-SIX

"I'll have a Diet Coke and a large popcorn," I told Vita Jones as I stood in the doorway of her basement.

"I wondered if you were going to make it to Grease night and I see you have. Love the outfit." She pointed to the extra butter.

"Load it up. And a box of M&M's." There was just something about popcorn with M&M's sprinkled in.

"Kenni! Up here!" Jolee hollered. She, Tibbie, and Katy Lee were all turned around on the metal folding chairs and propped up on their knees. All of them had pink scarves tied around their necks, pink leather coats, black pants and flip flops.

"Enjoy the movie." Vita took my money in exchange for the goodies.

"Hello, Pink Ladies." I giggled and climbed over their knees to get to my seat.

We'd been seeing Grease in Luke Jones's basement every year since he'd started showing it. It was always in the summer, so when I was home from college, we still made it our thing.

"Luke's been trying to get the screen to pull down but it's not cooperating tonight." Jolee pointed and laughed at Luke grunting and pulling. The screen was for sure winning. "How're the new vibes at the office?"

"Good. Scott is pretty good. I mean, we've got a few things to work through, like him getting to know the town and roads better." I didn't tell Jolee, but the reason he was late getting to Lita's the night I'd set up Sebastian Hughes, was because he didn't know how to get to Hickory Hill.

He'd learned real fast that sometimes the roads in Cottonwood don't make it on to the GPS and he drove around frantically until he found it. Lucky for me that he did find it.

It was also good to know that Lita had a minor heart attack and was going to be okay. Shelby had a bad case of heartburn and not a heart attack. As for Herb and Reagan, they'd decided to give it another go, especially now that Avon's parents had sold Herb the house next to his mom's.

"What about Finn? Anything new with that?" She asked.

"He really likes the job. He loves the hustle and bustle of a bigger city." It was true. I ripped off the top of the M&M box and sprinkled them over the warm, buttery popcorn.

"He works a few days in a row but gets the weekends off." I grinned from ear-to-ear. "I like that."

"Isn't that going to change soon with the new hours the town council approved?" Jolee dug her hands into my popcorn, pulling out a fistful. She dropped a bunch of kernels, trying to stuff them in her mouth.

Luke Jones had given up. He got the ladder out of the closet and started to thumbtack up the old king bedsheet.

"And the religion thing?" Her brows furrowed.

"We've not discussed that. One thing at a time." The lights went out and I eased down into the metal chair, propping my feet on the one in front of me.

The sound of seagulls and the waves of the ocean beating against the rocks came through the speakers as Danny kissed Sandy under the sunset. I couldn't help but smile. Finn was my Danny. And he was the one I wanted no matter what city we lived in.

BLOWIN' UP A MURDER

A KENNI LOWRY MYSTERY BOOK 8

PREVIEW

The weather outside made the old barn rattle, and the chandelier in the back shake.

We all turned to watched the storm that'd finally rolled over top of the event. The curtains swept up, and the rain pelted through the open door.

Tibbie hurried to the back to pull the two barn doors shut.

Just as she tugged one last time to get the crack between them shut, a bolt of lightning flashed, illuminating the concrete party patio just outside the barn doors.

Shrill shrieks pierced the air inside the barn as the reality of the situation became clear. The spotlight shone on the body lying on the ground.

The waiter.

An umbrella sticking out of his chest.

"It sure has blown up a murder." A slight breeze carried the words to my ear of a voice I knew belonged to my poppa, Tug Lowry.

Who was also dead.

CHAPTER ONE

Oh Finn.

My heart twirled around just looking at him in the suit and out of his Clay's Ferry uniform. I'd seen him in that uniform a lot more often than regular clothes.

I never thought it was going to be a shock to see him in the new navy sheriff's getup since I was used to seeing him in the baby-poop-brown-almost-yellow sheriff's uniform we wore in Cottonwood.

We being me, Scott Lee, and Betty Murphy. I lump Betty in there only because she didn't participate in the uniform daily. She claimed the button-up shirt and pants were too stiff for her arthritis. I would've believed her if she'd worn some sort of easier outfit instead of jeans and a different buttoned cardigan every day. But who was keeping score?

It was one of those things Mama stuck in my head—obey your elders. That went for work as well, even if my elder was an employee.

"What?" Finn caught me looking at him. His freshly cut black hair was shorter than normal, which was fine by me because his big brown eyes became his best feature. His hand held mine, and both of them were resting on his thigh.

"You look handsome." I smiled since this was, like, the umpteenth time I'd told him since he picked me up for the wedding.

A wedding of two people I didn't know and had no clue who these people were. It was one of those invitations where all the government officials were invited, and since all was right in Cottonwood, Scott was at the department in case any calls came in. Scott got the job since it was Saturday and Betty did not work the weekends. I got all gussied up and dragged Finn with me.

He was sort of a buffer between me and Mama, who, by the way, was sitting next to me, sticking her long fingernail into my ribs and giving it a little twist.

"Aren't spring weddings so lovely?" Mama's nail dug a smidgen deeper.

"Stop," I warned with a head jerk her way.

"What?" Mama's Southern drawl came out as if she didn't know what she was doing. "I was talking to Lulu."

"You always have to worry about rain, and from what Edna Easterly posted into today's *Cottonwood Chronicles*, it's gonna come a gusher later on this afternoon." Lulu McClain's head was stuck up between me and Mama's shoulders. She had been seated behind us and scooted up to the edge of the bench, where she laid her forearms along the back of our pew so she and Mama could talk about wedding.

Lulu had short black hair and owned Lulu's Boutique, located on Main Street in downtown Cottonwood. She had very trendy items in the shop that catered to the South, horses, and the state of Kentucky.

By talk, I meant gossip, and they sure didn't care who heard them.

"That's why I think you need to have a summer wedding." Ruby Smith sat by Lulu and put her two cents' worth in, along with light touch on my shoulder. Her short red hairstyle was a staple for Ruby, as was her bright-orange lipstick. She, along with Mama and a few of their other friends in Cottonwood, were known as the Henny Hens, though really most of them were part of the Auxiliary Women's Club, where they'd met years ago.

"Tell her, Viv," Ruby followed up.

She encouraged my mama to keep playing the fantasy in her head that somehow Finn had popped the question, and he had not. He hadn't even mentioned the possibility of us getting married. Though his parents had come to Cottonwood to meet me and my family, and that didn't go over so well.

"Flowers are lovely in the summer. Myra was telling me the other day, when I went down to Petal Pushers to get a spring wreath for the front door, how peonies scream summer wedding with the billowing petals that give off a delightful scent." Mama's excitement was oozing out of her with the thought. "Did you know peonies come in several vibrant pink, yellow, and white hues that would go with any color of bridesmaid's dresses? Plus they are a larger bloom, so you really get more bang for your buck. That's what Myrna said."

"I can see it now." Ruby fanned her jewel-bedecked fingers out in front of her between us. Her arms were filled with bangles that were rattling with the hand swoops. "Gorgeous sunny day with those light pinks on each table in a round glass bowl filled just a little over half with water."

The Henny Hens didn't care what I had to say. They had Mama's back and agreed with her that I was getting older.

If I knew anything about hens, it was they were nosy. Mama and all her friends put their noses in everything. That included everything that was nothing about them. That did make my job a little harder at times, especially when it came to crimes in and around Cottonwood.

They'd hear something on the police scanner—every household had one —and be at the scene before I could get there. Since I was Mama's daughter, they felt they could not only get private police information from me but also tell me how to run the investigation.

"I think fall is lovely too." Mama's chin lifted as she kept her gaze forward before she shifted her eyes enough to take a gander at me and see if I was looking at her.

"And it would give us a few months to prepare." Lulu only made the situation worse.

"Mmmhmm," Mama sighed and looked ahead like I was engaged. "The church is so pretty in the fall too. Myrna did mention how rich and warm fall's most popular blooms can be." Mama gave a very satisfying sigh. "What she said made real sense too." Mama nodded. "She said no matter what the theme of the wedding—like rustic, chic, or classic—all those dramatic orange, red, yellow, purple, and even brown hues found in the fall are gorgeous."

"I'm thinking dahlias." Lulu patted my back. I didn't turn to look at her. "Don't you love the weather in the fall, Kenni?"

"I thought Finn was Cath-o-lick?" Ruby asked, as if the religion left a bad taste in her mouth.

"Do you ladies not see me sitting right here?" Finn dropped my hand and extended his arm over me and rested it around my shoulder, taking up the back of the pew and forcing Ruby and Lulu to scoot back into their seats.

"We are just talkin', Finn. You don't have to act all highfalutin now that you've got that big job in Clay's Ferry." Ruby's remarks to him garnered a few snickers.

"Myrna has done a real fine job with these arrangements, but everyone seems to get married in the spring. Only special weddings are in the fall." Mama had it set in her mind I was getting married in the fall.

Again I shot Mama a look.

"What, Kenni?" Mama put her hand on her chest like she was appalled at me even looking at her. "I didn't say it. Ruby did." She shimmied her shoulders.

The whole religion thing had been a sore topic of conversation, and one Finn and I had both skirted since our parents had had a huge disagreement over which church their grandchildren would attend. *Talk about putting the cart before the horse.*

Finn and I were nowhere near getting married, much less having children.

"Thank you," I whispered to Finn and looked over where I heard the side door in the front of the church open.

A man who I assumed was the groom walked out behind Preacher Bing and four other groomsmen. They had on long black tuxedos with tails and top hats.

"My oh my, they've gone all out." Mama leaned over and acted as if she only wanted me to hear, but the Henny Hens behind her moaned an "Mmhhmmm."

The traditional wedding song filtered over the speakers, signaling us to stand—a tradition we did as soon as the bride appeared to start her walk down the aisle.

I kept facing forward so I didn't have to fight to see the tip-top of the bride's veil over the crowd of people behind me. But the murmurs and gasps along with the clicks of cameras told me she was a sight to behold.

"Kenni."

I heard my name in a faint whisper. Behind Finn's shoulder was Polly Parker Ryland, the first lady of Cottonwood.

"Do you mind moving your head?" She jutted her phone at me, clearly wanting to get a shot of the bride.

I slumped down.

"Those are the family pearls. Antiques." Ruby had leaned forward and wiggled a finger at the bride when she walked past.

Ruby would know what was antique and what wasn't because she owned Ruby's Antiques on Main Street. Treasures to her, but whenever I went in there, it smelled old. That was what antiques were to me. Old.

"Are they?" Mama danced back and forth on her shoes to see around the people in front of us so she could try to get a glimpse of this family heirloom. "She's got too much lace on her face." I could leave it to Mama to find something wrong with the bride. Luckily, she did whisper that, so no one else heard.

Why did weddings always bring out the soft side of people? The entire ceremony, Finn held my hand, squeezing it during the sweet moments that didn't go unnoticed between the bride and groom. They had all the attention on them.

Not mine. I had assessed the church, locating the accessible exits, since some were blocked by candelabras filled to overflowing with wildflowers.

I'd been to church here a million times and knew the exits. It was by habit that I took in all the surroundings for the just-in-case-there's-an-emergency situation. While I did so, I couldn't help but notice one of the groomsmen stood a little further away than the rest and wasn't really included in the heckling some of them gave the groom, to which the bride was all smiles.

The groomsman who was all business had to have been a relative of the groom. After all, he was the one who had the rings in his pocket and seemed to give the groom more sincere, brotherly-love type of interactions during the ceremony.

After the bride and groom kissed and the final trumpet sent them down the aisle, Mama jumped to her feet.

"We've got to go to the reception. I heard it was to die for." Mama would have ridden on the bride's train if she could.

"You've got to wait until they release the pews one by one, Mama." I had to hold her back by keeping a fistful of the back of her dress in hand.

"Now, Kenni, don't be ridiculous. I know what good manners are, but I'm telling you, you might have to use the siren to bypass all the people going to this reception." She loved to think she was always within the law, but when it came time to use me for her good, she was willing to break it.

I gave her another look.

"I know you can't, but it sure would be nice if we got there and got a good seat. You never know." She plucked the white gloves out of her handbag and smacked me with them before she slipped them on her hands. "You might get some good pointers."

"Tibbie has already saved us a seat." I pointed at Mama, me, Finn, and the Henny Hens, which now included Viola White and Myrna Savage, all perched in the row behind us.

Tibbie Bell was one of my best friends, and she was an event planner. When she got the call about this job, we'd heard about it for over a year. Now the big day was here, and honestly I wasn't there with the hopes that the bride and groom would vote for me in the next election, though that was a real reason to come to these things around here. I was there to support Tibbie.

That was the way it was in Cottonwood.

Weddings were as big as having a baby. Having a baby was as big as a funeral. Funerals, well, those were social gatherings not to be missed, no matter how well you knew the deceased.

In Cottonwood those three events were always happening, which meant we were always together and pitched in whenever we could.

When I looked around while waiting for our turn to be let out of the pew, I saw a lot of the townsfolk there with big smiles on their faces, talking to one another, and being neighborly. As the sheriff, I loved seeing the community like that.

Cottonwood wasn't always rosy. I saw a few neighbors here socializing, but if I went to their houses, they'd be bickering back and forth about rose bushes a little over the property line or how someone let their paper sit in their driveway too long.

Not today. Today was a celebration of happiness and love.

"Here you go." The serious groomsman just so happened to be the one who let us out of the pew. "The bride is very environmentally friendly, so they're using bubbles to blow instead of rice to throw." He handed me a clear plastic bottle with bubble water in it.

"Isn't that clever?" Mama looked over her shoulder at me, tipped her chin down, and lifted her brows. "See? Something you can do."

"Keep walking," I told her.

The sunshine filtered through the doors at the back of the church that were spread wide open for us to gather outside.

"Looky there. Clouds." Lulu pointed off to the west where there were a few dark clouds in the sky. "Sunny one minute. Raining the next. That's the spring weather for you."

By the looks of the moving clouds, the rain was going to be coming rather fast.

"I sure hope they make it to the reception before then," Finn said and gestured to a white horse-drawn carriage that was open to the elements.

"Smile, you two love birds!" Edna Easterly held her camera up to her eyes.

I was a little taken aback at Edna's appearance. She wasn't dressed in her fishing vest with all the pockets that held all her journalist gadgets and her feathered fedora hat with the glued-on note card where she'd proudly written Reporter with a marker.

"A little closer, like you are in love." She gestured at us to get a little closer. "Look into the camera and smile!"

As soon as she clicked the shutter, a big bolt of lightning broke through the sky.

"That made me shiver." I shook a bit before the goose bumps crawled along my arms.

"Hmmm." Mama pinched me. "Someone's walking over your grave, Kenni."

199

CHAPTER TWO

I'd never bring to light what I was thinking after Mama said that to me. It was never good to hear someone tell you someone was walking over your grave. It was like a "bless your heart," only it wasn't the good kind of "bless your heart."

Mama didn't have to tell me anything that I wasn't already feeling. As sheriff, you get keen on your senses, and when something was off, then something was wrong.

Instead of dwelling on that weird and unusual feeling, I chalked it up to the weather and how I felt bad for the bride and groom having to hurry off in the carriage just to make it to the reception. It was being held out at the Cottonwood Barn and Farm, an old barn located in the country in Cotton-wood, and probably the only place big enough to accommodate so many guests. Because of its size, it'd been turned into a much-needed events center.

"Isn't it great?" Tibbie bounced with glee. She took in the barn with wide eyes like she'd just seen it for the first time.

Far from it. Tibbie had been talking about this events center for months and tried to get us out here to look at it. I held off after she'd told our group of gal pals about how this was the first wedding in the redone barn.

That was a big deal for her and her business.

"It's beautiful," I agreed, taking in the surroundings. "You know Mama is going to go crazy."

"I know. She'd already pulled me aside to ask about some of the service." Tibbie grinned and jerked up when one of the staff members of the venue called for her. "Don't forget to try the food! This is the first time I've used the caterer, and Venetta's been great!"

I'd noticed the name of the caterer earlier and grinned at the catchy title, That's A Toast.

Though it appeared Tibbie initially had planned for the supper portion of the reception to take place outside, it was nice how there was space indoors to easily move it.

There was a rustic, vintage feel that seemed to fit the couples and their guests. It would be hard not to fall in love with the charming, tranquil countryside that lay just outside of the barn.

"There's even guest houses on the property." Mama had found me. "Kenni," she gasped. "This would be perfect for out-of-town family."

"Who lives out of town?" I asked and grabbed a flute of champagne off the tray of the waiter passing by.

"You mean you wouldn't invite Finn's family?" She asked it like it was a good idea.

"Mama." I lifted the flute to my lips and took a nice swig before I said my piece. I lifted my hand in the air. "There's no ring on this finger. There's no plans for there to be a ring on this finger, so let's just drop it."

"You're right. There might be a better place to host a wedding reception by then." She pinched me, and in an instant she flipped a switch by wearing a huge open-mouthed smile and a wave. "Hi, Darlene!"

She didn't bother telling me goodbye as she darted off to talk to someone she recognized.

The back of the barn had the double doors open to take in the scenery. By the way the gray clouds were rolling in, I was sure it was already raining in downtown Cottonwood.

The sheer curtains hanging over the door and down each side waved a little as the breeze from the oncoming storm brushed past. The pink chandelier, dead center of the door and dangling from one of the cedar beams above, swayed some before the crystals made a light clinking noise.

On each side of the door were old bourbon barrels with boxes for cash presents, along with some cute signs that read Mr. and Mrs., and on the floor next to them were two umbrella stands with the bride and groom's names on them.

Nice touch, Tibbie, I thought.

Cheers filtered through the opposite end of the barn. I turned around. The groomsmen and bridesmaids were walking inside. Several of the bridesmaids had their bouquets raised above their heads, swirling them around in celebration of what the night was going to bring.

The DJ was playing Garth Brooks's "Friends in Low Places," which I found a little odd for a wedding since the song was about an ex showing up at the bride's wedding.

The best man was singing it so loud, he grabbed a shot glass off of the waiter's tray and raised it high in the air before he downed it.

The waiter shook his head and kept walking.

They'd be partying it up while I'd be long asleep. Not that I was old and didn't love a good time—very much the opposite—but I had to work a full shift in the morning, and there was nothing worse than sitting at my desk in the department.

The sheriff's department was located in the back of Cowboy's Catfish Restaurant, and smelling fried fish while nursing a hangover didn't mix with my stomach.

The song got cut off, and the DJ started another, much more appropriate, song.

I couldn't stop smiling when the DJ played a song and announced the names of the wedding party before he did the grand introduction of the bride and groom.

"Join me in welcoming Mr. and Mrs. Dickie Dee!" The DJ barely got it out as the guests erupted in cheers and woot woots.

My champagne glass was still full, so I gave a half-hearted clap then downed the rest of the flute before I set it down on one of the empty tray stations next to me.

Finn's eyes caught mine. He was leaving the hors d'oeuvres stand with a plate piled high. I lifted my chin with a smile to welcome him.

"These people went all out," Finn said and held up the snacks after he'd made it over to me.

"They did. I can't wait to see what kind of business Tibbie gets from this." Saying her name, I looked for her to check in to see what she was doing.

Over the crowd, I spotted the messy yet fashionable bun her long brown hair had been professionally styled in in a different part of the barn where there were very long tables and chairs.

The tables went along with the rustic feel, as they were made out of reclaimed barnwood. She'd kept the romantic feel by putting lacy runners down the middle of each table with lots of greenery, soft pink and cream roses, and gold-speckled candleholders nestled every few inches with a glowing candle inside.

Each seat had a place setting with a gold charger that held a cream plate with gold edging. Even the neatly and correctly placed silverware was far from silver. It was gold.

"Who are these people?" I asked Finn and took one of the cheese crackers off his plate. "Mmhhh." There was no denying this fancy cheese. "This is a long way from our spray cheese," I joked.

"No kidding. Maybe I can sneak some of these in my suit pocket." He wiggled his brows.

"Good idea." I took another one and laughed before I popped it into my mouth. I nudged him and gestured to the serious groomsman.

"What about him?" Finn asked.

"I wonder if he's the brother of the groom. He seems to want everything to go smooth." I noticed him looking at the table setting, moving a few things and showing Tibbie something.

Her messy bun flung up and down as she nodded her head in agreement to whatever he was saying.

"Excuse me for a minute," I told Finn when I saw Tibbie start from the top of one dinner table and rearrange a few things. "I'm going to help Tibbie."

"I'll go talk to Luke." Finn took his plate and walked over to some of the guests we did know.

The groomsman had passed by me and stopped where a few of the other groomsmen were throwing back a few shots of something.

"How are you doing with all this?" I heard one of them ask the serious groomsman.

"He got the sloppy seconds." His words seemed a bit off.

Sloppy seconds. I rolled my eyes so hard I saw my brain. What a jerk, I thought. Since he was a big baby, his ego had gotten bruised from whatever history the other guys were referring to.

"What can I do?" I asked Tibbie.

"Apparently, I put the salad fork and the shrimp fork in the wrong place." She looked relieved when I walked up. "Do you mind?"

"Nope. I'd love to help." I walked over to the other side of the table. "You do that side, and I'll do this side."

"I'll be so glad when this is over and tonight we will enjoy a late-night euchre game." Tibbie had organized a late-night game, and since we were all at the wedding, she thought we might as well continue the night with our weekly game.

We'd gotten the first table rearranged then started on the second one.

"Have you ever seen such?" Tibbie whispered over the table and held up the gold fork.

"Gold silverware?" I laughed at the oxymoron. "Is it real?"

"Oh," she scoffed. "Yes. This is old money. Kentucky old money. See that person over there?"

I glanced over my shoulder.

"Edna?" I asked. I thought Tibbie was referring to Edna Easterly, who was taking so many photos. Initially I thought the bride and groom had hired her for the wedding, but now that I saw the videographer and what appeared to be a real wedding photographer, I knew Edna was here to get photos for the society section of the *Cottonwood Chronicles.*

"No!" Tibbie chuckled. "The real people. Those people are from *Barnwood Brides.* That big magazine. If this wedding goes exactly like I planned it, they are going to do a spread in their magazine, and my name, my business, will go in."

She curled her lips in as if she didn't want to squeal out loud, letting her eyes bulge as if the excitement inside needed to find a place.

"Tibbie!" I was so excited for her. "That's amazing news."

"And all those girls up front there" —she pointed to the bridesmaids— "they are all engaged and took my card. Now you see why I've been talking about this event for so long."

"I know you're going to be so popular from this. Amazing." I was so proud of my friend.

The DJ had turned off the song as the string orchestra took over.

My eyes grew wide, and I slid them over the table at Tibbie in disbelief.

"They spared no expense for their daughter." She threw a sweet smile on when the mother of the bride walked past.

I recognized her from the wedding.

"Everything is looking lovely," she complimented Tibbie. "I can tell the magazine is very interested."

"I'm so glad. It's your gorgeous daughter who is the centerpiece." Tibbie was so good at brownnosing her clients.

Both of us hurried to get the gold forks properly placed, since the next thing on the program was the toast and the invite for everyone to take their seat.

Finn and I sat at a table in the far back along with the other government employees, which included Mayor Chance Ryland and his wife, Polly Parker Ryland.

"Have you ever seen the like, Kenni?" Polly Parker was in her element. She picked up the gold fork. "I was just telling Chance I've been looking at gold silverware for our home." Her perfectly lined pink pouty mouth contorted with envy, her nose curled as she looked at me. "Ain't that right, honey?"

"Mmhmm, dear." That was Mayor Ryland's standard answer.

"If she thinks he can afford that on his mayor salary, she's more distorted than that marriage of hers," Vita Jones said under her breath, nearly making me choke on my spit.

Vita was a hoot and a half. She was married to Luke Jones, who sat on the town council.

As soon as the toasts began, the thunder and lightning started outside.

The lights inside the venue were brought down to a glow and a spotlight placed on the bridal party table.

One by one the bridesmaids gave a sweet toast about the bride and how she was such a great friend. The spotlight followed each speaker.

Of course the groomsmen were much different. They gave the groom more of a roasting about his raucous past that included a few women along the way.

"Bradley!" The DJ called over the speaker when it was the best man's turn. The spotlight was focused on Bradley's empty seat.

The groomsmen started to smack the top of their table, chanting Bradley's name.

The weather outside made the old barn rattle, and the chandelier in the back shake.

We all turned to watched the storm that'd finally rolled over top of the event. The curtains swept up, and the rain pelted through the open door.

Tibbie hurried to the back to pull the two barn doors shut.

Just as she tugged one last time to get the crack between them shut, a bolt of lightning flashed, illuminating the concrete party patio just outside the barn doors.

Shrill shrieks pierced the air inside the barn as the reality of the situation became clear. The spotlight shone on the body lying on the ground.

The waiter.

An umbrella sticking out of his chest.

"It sure has blown up a murder." A slight breeze carried the words to my ear of a voice I knew belonged to my poppa, Tug. Who was dead.

CHAPTER THREE

"Excuse me, excuse me." I had gone up to grab the microphone from the DJ. "I'm Sheriff Kendrick Lowry. I'm going to need everyone to stay put."

Scott Lee hurried up to the DJ booth.

"Deputy, I need you to secure the barn and have anyone who might have been handling this reception and all the guests detained." I had barely finished my sentence before Scott hurried off with Tibbie Bell in his sights.

"What can I do?" Finn asked, even though he already knew what needed to happen.

"You can take yourself right on over to your table since you got fired." Poppa had appeared right up next to Finn.

I shifted my eyes slightly past Finn's shoulder so I could give Poppa the eye. I didn't need him whispering things that did not pertain to the issue at hand.

Murder.

I glanced around the room. Everyone was in shock as they were all trying to figure out exactly what was going on.

Max Bogus, the county coroner, was sitting at a table with Mayor Ryland, Polly, and the Joneses.

"Max Bogus." I gave him a nod, grateful everyone who needed to be here at the crime scene was already here. "Please and thank you very much."

Good manners never did go out of style, and even though this was a grave situation, it was still better to be polite.

He ran his napkin across his lips as he jumped up, knocking over a few water glasses as his thighs hit the edge of the table, causing Polly Parker Ryland to jump to her feet, only to take a tumble when her heels gave out.

"Polly!" Mayor Ryland was quick to his feet to help her up.

"Listen here." The bride ran over, all that crinoline on her fancy wedding dress crumpled up in the crook of her arm, her bouquet flailing around in front of her as she wagged it in my face. "I don't know what is going on here."

I pushed the bouquet away.

"This is my day. I don't know who that is, but it has to be moved. I'm not going to stand here and let you—" Her eyes searched around for something on me, maybe my badge.

"Sheriff Kendrick Lowry," I informed her.

"That body has to be moved." She let go of the dress and snapped her finger at the DJ. "Music! Now!"

"No." My head swiveled on my shoulders and I gave a stern warning to the DJ. "Don't you dare turn that music on. This is a crime scene, and we are going to need everyone to cooperate."

"No!" The bride got right back up into my face. "My guests are going to finish eating their supper, then we are going to dance and have cake, and I'm going on my honeymoon."

"I'm sorry, but that's not going to happen." I had to be straight with her.

"Daddy! Daddy!" she screamed, and before I could do anything, she whacked me over the head with the bouquet. "You are going to leave right now!"

"I guess that's one way to get the bouquet so you can get that daughter of yours hitched," I heard Viola White say.

"You are going to be put under arrest for assaulting a police officer if you don't stop!" I had my hands over my head to try to stop her from hitting me. "Is this how you want to spend your honeymoon night?"

"Do something, Daddy! You made me invite all of these government people, and now they are ruining my wedding." She whacked with every word.

It seemed like a long time, but in reality, it wasn't but about forty-five seconds before Finn had grabbed her around the waist and picked her up. But the flailing continued with all four limbs moving in a bicycle motion.

"Get. Your. Hands. Off. Me!" The bride's voice got angrier and louder the further away she got from me, as Finn carefully backed up with her flailing around like a fish out of water in his arms.

"I'm sorry about this." I put the microphone back up to my mouth and looked past everyone to the back where the body was lying. Max had used one of the white tablecloths to put over the deceased. "Tibbie, if you don't mind bringing up the lights."

The lights were still on low beam for the romantic ambiance, and there was not one bit of low light that was going to even give a hint of that emotion at this current time.

"I'm going to need everyone to stay at their table." I looked behind me when there was a bit of rustling at the wedding party table. Bradley, the groomsman, was shuffling behind all the chairs.

He had his palm tight against the black tuxedo jacket so it didn't hit anyone's head as he moved behind them to get to his seat.

"You might as well get comfortable, because this is going to take a while to take everyone's statements."

Finn had to take the bride out of the barn in order for her to stop throwing her hissy fit.

I put down the microphone and unplugged the DJ's cords in case the bride came back and decided to spin the tunes herself. I had to give it to her —a dead body didn't seem to bother her one bit, which was odd.

"I'll start with the wedding party," I told Scott after I'd finally made it over to him and the body. Max Bogus was doing his best to assess what had happened, even though we could clearly see the man had been stabbed with an umbrella.

Not just any umbrella.

The wedding umbrella.

Scott shook his head, and we went opposite ways. He took the table closest to the back of the barn where the party patio was located. If anyone had seen something, it had to be them.

"Hi there." My Southern accent filled the silence of the wedding party. Quiet whispers fluttered behind me. I started my introduction. "I'm Sheriff—"

"We know who you are. You ruined Jasmine and Dickie's wedding." Bradley snickered from his seat next to the groom.

The groom nudged him to hush.

Bradley covered his mouth with his hand, hiding his laughter.

"That one there is one to look out for." Poppa ghosted himself behind Bradley. "He's wet too. No umbrella."

"It's my understanding everyone in the bridal party got an umbrella with the happy couple's monogram." I smiled sweetly at the group. "Bradley, is it?"

The grin that had been on his face faded to a stern, sinister look.

"I recall that during the toast and before our friend was found dead, an umbrella stuck through his chest"—out of the corner of my eye I could see the sheer horror on the others' faces—"that you were missing. Didn't y'all here start to chant and even bang on the table?"

Slowly I slid my eyes down the table of the wedding party and made sure to make eye contact. Bradley was the only one who didn't have a look of fear on his face.

"I oughta wipe that smirk off of him right now, Kenni bug." Poppa never liked anyone to disrespect a person of the law, especially when it came to me. "Let me just do a little something like rattle his chair leg. That'll straighten him up."

As much as I'd have loved to see some fright put into Bradley's face, there was no time for ghost shenanigans.

I gave a slow shake to my head.

"You're no fun. Use me. Let me shake up this jerk." Poppa had not been like this when he was sheriff of Cottonwood, Kentucky. He was always by the book, but now that he was a ghost deputy, which was still hard for me to even swallow, he liked to use his invisibility to anyone but me and Duke, my dog, to my advantage, so we could get crimes solved.

This would be the eighth time I'd seen the ghost of my poppa, and that meant eight crimes.

I thought I was a true badass when it came to zero crime when I took over as sheriff of our small town, but in reality it was the ghost of my poppa who was scaring off any crime so I was safe.

Unfortunately even a ghost can't be in two places at once. When there was a murder and a break-in a few years ago, well, that's when I discovered I'd had a ghost deputy and didn't know it.

Too bad he only showed up when there was a crime, because I sure did miss him a lot. Another thing, I couldn't even really talk to him when he was here, or people would think I was crazy talking to myself.

The embarrassment I caused my mama today would be nothing compared to what rumors of me talking to myself would do to her. It'd send her straight to the loony bin.

"And by the look of your tuxedo jacket, it looks like you were out in the rain without the umbrella the bride and groom I'm sure paid a pretty penny for." The smirk faded from his face. He drummed his fingers along the top of the table. "Is there something you'd like to tell me?"

"Nope." He lifted those drumming fingers up, giving me a hand gesture. "I've got nothing to hide. I was outside smoking."

"In the rain?" I asked.

"I vape. It doesn't require a flame." His right brow lifted, a condescending look in his eyes.

"I've never liked a punk. You just need to take him on down to the jail cell and see if that suits him." Poppa had all sorts of illegal activities he wanted me to perform.

"Excuse me, Kenni," A hand touched my arm, and I turned around to find Preacher Bing slightly behind me. "Can I have a word with you?"

My mama's eyes pierced through the crowd and seared right through him.

"Your mama asked me to come over." He smiled and looked back where Mama's scowl had been replaced by her friendly smile.

It was something she did. She could give me the look at a moment's notice, and if someone glanced her way, she'd switch it off in a split second.

"She's wondering if there's any way you can do this differently."

"And just how can I do that? Pick up the dead body and move it to another location where it wasn't found and lose all this evidence?" I pulled back and smiled. "Now Preacher, you aren't asking me for the sake of embarrassing my mama to not find justice for that poor man who is lying underneath a tablecloth. After all, he has a mama, and I'm sure she'd love to see him alive at this moment."

"Yes. I'll go speak to Viv." He tugged his lips together.

"You be sure to put a little more in the collection plate this week too." I winked and sucked in a deep breath before I turned back around to look at Bradley. "I'm sorry about that. Mothers. I'm guessing you have one of those, right, Bradley?"

"Yeah." He snorted like I was an idiot. I didn't like anyone thinking I was an idiot.

"I'm sure she told you never to go outside in the rain because you can catch a cold." It was an old wives' tale, but at this moment he was all I had as a suspect. "I'd love to take you back to the sheriff's department for a friendly chat."

"Do I need a lawyer?" He suddenly seemed a bit anxious.

"Only if you did something wrong," I said, never once taking my eyes off him. Reading his body language was so important, but not looking at Poppa was a priority.

"I did nothing wrong," he insisted.

"Good then. Why don't we take it on down to the station." I knew by the noise behind me that Max Bogus had gotten ahold of someone down at the funeral home to send down a hearse and a church cart so they could take the body.

Reluctantly Bradley stood up and gave the groom a pat on the back, the good-ole-boy-style back smack, while I waited patiently for him to emerge from behind the table.

Not being in a rush had become a skill. Of course when I was just out of the academy and a crime happened, the first thing I wanted to do was jump on it. What I'd come to learn was slow and patient was a surefire way to get the killer or criminal. Wait them out.

I had no problem waiting Bradley out until he talked.

"I'm not going to be able to show my face again," Mama cried loud enough for me to hear as I ushered Bradley past her on our way out the barn door.

CHAPTER FOUR

"Deputy Lee." I started giving orders with the little time I had left. I needed to get a lot accomplished after he'd stuck Bradley in the back of his deputy truck. It wasn't like we could leave the scene just yet.

It was only the two of us in the department, and if either of us left, we'd never get through all the guests to start questioning them.

"I need you to get all the overhead lights pulled up, these floodlights on." I pointed to the lights on the outside of the barn when I noticed they were there. "These low-hanging clouds don't look like they're moving anytime soon."

I wasn't going to complain about how the rain had slowed to a spit. It wasn't like it was night—it was not. It was an afternoon wedding, but the day was filled with gray, almost black clouds that hung so low it made it feel like night.

"Kenni! Kenni!" Mama stood at the door, wagging one of the wedding umbrellas in the air. "Honey, you need to cover up. You might catch a cold!"

"I'm fine, Mama," I assured her. Scott laughed. "Nothing like an investigation with Mama around."

"You're lucky you've got a mama who cares." The tone in Scott's voice plucked a chord within me, making me wonder exactly what he'd meant. He headed back inside.

It wasn't like we knew each other all that well. When he came to work at the department, we'd pretty much kept it professional.

"Yoo-hoo! Kenni!" Mama yelled.

"Mama, I said I was fine. I'll be in soon," I assured her right before the floodlight clicked on. "You do me a big favor and don't you dare let anyone leave that barn!"

Mama's eyes grew real big. With confidence she gave a big nod, pinched her lips, and took the order very serious.

"That should give her something to do." I looked down at the concrete for any visible evidence. The waiter was wet, so he had to have been outside.

There were a few muddy footprints around the outdoor cigarette deposit stand next to the door.

"Don't let anyone out here," I told Scott when he came back outside. "I've got to go get my bag."

I slipped my heels off, not only because I could walk faster from here to the parking lot where Finn had parked the old Wagoneer, but the spikes on my shoes were sinking into the wet grass.

I could've taken the walkway to the parking lot, but my Jeep was clear to the other side, and it was faster to cut through the grass.

"What do you think we've got, Kenni bug?" Poppa's ghost was sitting in the back seat as if he were waiting for me.

"A dead body, an umbrella, and a cold, rainy afternoon." I looked at him and opened up the duffle bag I kept in the car with an extra set of clothes and shoes.

"Did you see anything?" I asked him as I unzipped the bag to get out the pair of tennis shoes before I wiggled my feet into the tied shoes and stomped them on the ground to get the heel of the shoes on.

"Too early to tell, but look around, very carefully. There's something out there. Some sort of clues. Everyone is a suspect." He didn't have any words of wisdom but the ones I already knew. "This is very early in the investigation. See what Max has to say and then go from there."

"I don't have to wait for Max to tell me this was a murder." The umbrella did that.

"Just like I said." Poppa's ghost started to evaporate. "Photos, videos, revenge."

215

"Revenge?" I asked just as he whispered away. "Where are you going? I need you. Aren't you my ghost deputy?"

"Ghost deputy?" Finn laughed. "You mean as in a ghost writer? I help you, but no one knows since we aren't on the same team anymore?"

"Yep." I turned around. "That's right. I need your help while you're here."

I turned back around and closed my eyes really hard, remembering just how careful I had to be when I talked to Poppa. People seeing me talking to Poppa, even if it was Finn, made me look crazy. I looked like I was talking to myself.

"Here." I grabbed a few of the evidence markers from the floorboard. "We need to make sure no one leaves until we get their name and phone numbers and see if they will either let us download their photos right now or send them to me."

"Sounds good." Finn's face changed from the loving boyfriend to the serious sheriff. "I'm more than happy to be your ghost deputy."

He took off while I leaned into the car a little further to grab my bag where I kept all the things necessary for a crime scene.

"I'd say, "Over my dead body will that boy take my job,' but I'm dead." Poppa reappeared.

"At least he didn't run off." I had to let my poppa know I didn't like him ghosting in and out without telling me what he was doing. "Where did you go?"

"I counted eleven umbrellas and twelve wedding party members. At first I wondered if some guests had gotten an umbrella as a souvenir, but now that I've done a little further investigating, I do believe they were only bought for the wedding party." Poppa looked up to the barn. "It was his seat that was missing the umbrella."

I looked back at Scott's truck. Bradley was watching me.

"Yeah. He knows more than he's saying." I tried to talk with my mouth closed so Bradley didn't see.

When I walked back to the barn, I had a tight grip on my bag and didn't dare look Bradley's way, though I could feel the burn of his stare.

I set my bag on top of the concrete on the party patio and unzipped it.

"Is there anything I can do?" a woman in her midfifties asked. Her shirt had her name embroidered on it.

216

Venetta.

"Venetta, are you in charge of catering?" I asked.

"I'm the owner of the company. I come to all the events." Her being here made it much easier for me than trying to track her down.

"Then I do need to talk to you." I took out two pairs of surgical booties and two pairs of gloves. I gave a set of gloves and booties to Scott. "Here."

Finn had already placed a couple of the evidence markers around the footprints and taken the camera out of my bag to snap a few photos.

"Anything you need." She gasped when Max Bogus passed by us, the church cart rattling with the weight of the body underneath an appropriate corpse cloth.

I slid Scott a look, and he sidled up to Venetta, taking her by the arm. He walked her over to one of the wrought-iron chairs and swept his hand across the seat to get the puddled water off.

"Kenni." Max Bogus stopped shy of me.

"Anything?" I asked in hopes there'd be some evidence on the body.

"I'm not so sure until I get some X-rays." That was a new one. Max had generally given me a few possible options.

"Kenni bug." Poppa stood next to the body. "I think the umbrella was shoved into him postmortem."

I gulped, trying not to even flinch. If that was this case, the murderer was someone very angry. A hate crime, if you will.

"Don't cut him open until you get the X-rays." I told him. "I want to make sure what his insides say before you break open his chest cavity."

"That's right, Kenni bug. Let the body tell you what happened." Poppa disappeared.

CHAPTER FIVE

T he old Wagoneer rattled to life after I let Bradley sit in the passenger seat and got the key into the ignition.

"I hope you don't mind dog hair." I could see the look on his face when he noticed Duke's hair was all over his black tuxedo jacket. "My deputy dog, Duke, rides shotgun."

"When I'm not here." Poppa appeared right in between me and Bradley with his body sitting on the edge of the bench seat in the back.

"What?" I asked Bradley. "Cat got your tongue? You were all willing to talk back at the reception."

I wanted to make sure he knew the sudden shift in his behavior had not gone unnoticed.

"I guess I'm not up to talking until my lawyer is present." Bradley played the lawyer card, which was fine with me.

"Alright then. I'll have Betty call your lawyer when we get to the department." I flipped on the radio to some pop music and tapped the wheel to the beat.

The radio screeched and squalled as Poppa switched the station.

"My car," Poppa proudly stated.

"What the?" Bradley jerked back, pushing up against the seat as far back away from the radio as he could get himself.

"What?" I played dumb, though it was a little enjoyable to see the man frightened.

"The radio just turned itself." He stuttered the words out.

"For heaven's sake, Bradley." I pished it. "This is an old Wagoneer, and things just happen. Sometimes the windows roll down on their own too." I flipped the windshield wipers on high.

The wind had whipped up, and the rain was coming down sideways.

About that time Poppa put his arm between the passenger seat and the door, slowly cranking the window down.

Bradley jerked to his left, pushing away from the door.

"Are you alright, Bradley?" I asked as if nothing were wrong. "You seem pretty jumpy. Maybe you should stop smoking those vape things. Can't be good for your health."

I let go of a long sigh and kept silent as we headed toward Main Street, which was just about fifteen minutes from the barn, so the drive wasn't too painful. Bradley didn't make a peep.

When we passed Lulu's Boutique on the right on our way into town, the On The Run food truck was parked up to the curb, and Jolee Fischer was in the window serving up something good. The rain didn't look like it kept people away.

My mind strayed from Bradley to Jolee. I wondered why she wasn't at the wedding. Or at least there to help Tibbie. The three of us were thick as thieves, and it never crossed my mind to ask. Instead my mind was too occupied by Mama and all the things her mind was percolating about any sort of wedding ideas she had for me. But I knew Jolee would be at euchre, so I'd ask her then.

My eyes shifted to the cemetery on the left when we passed, then they moved to the rearview, where Poppa still sat in his ghostly form.

"I can see what you're thinkin'." He tapped his thick finger to his temple. "You and me need to have a talk."

He was exactly right. I tried not to smile. After Poppa had died, I found visiting the cemetery to be rather comforting when I became sheriff and had to deal with the everyday hard knocks that came with the job, not only politically but also being a woman sheriff in a mostly male government in Cottonwood.

You can hear Mama now, telling me how it wasn't fittin' for a girl to be sheriff, but it was reputable to have a secretary job for the sheriff. I'd decided to skip all that a long time ago, and it was no different today.

I'd gotten used to disappointing Mama, and at this point in my life, it was almost enjoyable just to see what kind of rise I could get out of her.

Today was going to be the icing on the cupcakes.

She'd be gabbing about this wedding, not to mention the dead body, but the thought of me stopping the reception due to the crime scene and the bride physically assaulting me, well, I was sure I'd get a call from Daddy by the end of the night letting me know Mama had taken to the bed.

I turned the old Wagoneer down the alley where the department was located in the rear of Cowboy's Catfish, a local diner downtown. Now it might seem weird to some folks that the government would lease such a space from inside of a restaurant, and I'd agree if we weren't in Cottonwood. The town was just a blip on the map in the state of Kentucky, and well, there was really no crime to even need a big-time facility.

We had everything we needed. A one-room cell in the corner of the office and three desks—one for me, one for Scott, and one for Betty Murphy. Duke even had his own dog bed there, along with a jar of treats.

The closet was a great place to store any extra uniforms and where the printer was located along with the fax machine. Plus we had our very own food service from the other side of the door whenever we wanted it.

"Where are you taking me?" Bradley looked a little scared after I'd pulled up to the dumpster real tight.

"You'll see," I said and got out of the car to walk around and get him. I noticed Poppa was gone, and figured he'd already gone inside the department.

"I don't think this is right?" Bradley gave a little tug of his shoulders when he turned around to look at me as I kept a grip on his cuffs.

"Oh, it's right, alright." I jerked my hand to push him forward.

"What kind of town is this?" Bradley tried to wiggle. "Crazy people around here. There's a killer on the loose, and I didn't do it. Now you've got me cuffed and going into some back alley."

We stopped at the door. I put the key in and opened the lock, deliberately not saying anything.

"Uh-uh. I'm not going in there. I want my lawyer," he protested, the rain beating down a little heavier now.

With a little forceful coaxing, I got me and him through the door.

"I'm sorry. I rarely do my hair, and today was a special day." I tried to speak to him as kindly as I could. "Was a special day for Jasmine and Dickie Dee until you ruined it and my hair."

I gently guided him toward the cell in the far corner.

"Is this the department you so boldly said you were taking me to?" Bradley had that smirky grin on his face.

"Mmhmmm." Once in the cell, I uncuffed his hands and left, shutting the cell door and locking it behind me.

"Really? Am I on *Punk'd*?" He threw his hands in the air. "I get it. Jasmine and Dickie are getting me back for the bachelor party. Right? The waiter person isn't dead, but since I was outside smoking, they knew it would be a funny joke. Okay, take me back to the reception." His voice was loud, like he was trying to let anyone hear him.

"I thought you said you vaped."

"Smoke, vaped. All the same." He walked over to the bars and curled a hand around one. "Listen, this is a joke, right? Prank?"

"This is no joke." I sat down in my desk chair and took out the paperwork I needed for the crime scene investigation.

The door between Cowboy's Catfish and the department opened, and Bartleby Fry stuck his head around.

"Kenni, I heard what happened, and I figured you didn't get to eat, so I made up some fresh hush puppies and cod for you." He pushed the Styrofoam food container through the door.

"Hilarious!" Bradley smacked his hands together. "This is just like that old show with that crazy deputy and sheriff." He scratched his chin. "I can't think of it, but my granddad used to love it."

"*The Andy Griffith Show?*" Bradley asked.

"Yep! That! Come on, guys. The joke is on me. You got me." Bradley voice got louder with each word.

"Why are you yelling?" I asked and waved Bartleby to come on in.

"So the recording device can hear me." He snorted. "Where is it?"

"Shoowee, Kenni, you've got you one today." Bartleby's eyes grew. He shook his head and walked out of the department.

"What did that mean?" Bradley pointed to himself. "Is he talking about me or this?" He pointed around the department.

I sucked in a deep breath, about to go through the entire process again in hopes he'd hear me this time, but the door to the outside flung open, the rain rushed in, and so did Betty Murphy.

"I reckon we gonna be working late. I got word on the scanner about the big murder." Betty's voice quivered as she shook off the pellets of rain from her umbrella before she fully came in from the wet and now cold outside. "Oh dear."

Her blue eyes focused on Bradley.

"Goodness gracious. I knew something was going to happen when I saw the big thunder cloud rolling into town." She untied the small string underneath her chin that kept her rain bonnet in place. She tucked it down in her pocketbook in the crook of her arm.

"Are you from the local theater company? Because for your age, you play a good Aunt Bee. Wasn't that her name?" Bradley was digging a deeper and deeper hole.

Betty jerked up and looked at Bradley. I knew she was storing every single detail up in her brain so when she talked to her friends, she'd have all the details right.

Cottonwood wasn't a very big town. With the help of Betty Murphy, Mama, and her Henny Hens, not much remained private. Not even things that happened here in the sheriff's department.

"I heard your mama about died." Betty stopped at my desk on the way to her desk to see what was in the box.

"You can have it," I told her. "I'm not hungry."

"Really?" Bradley sounded exhausted. "Can we just stop the play pretending and get on it?"

"So you do want to give me your statement without your lawyer?" I asked.

"Wait." He hesitated with one hand pushed out in front of him, his fingers spread apart. "Is this for real? Like for real real?"

"What did you think this was?" Betty was old-school when it came to respecting your elders. It was something that was taken very seriously around here, and I could tell by the tone in her voice she'd not approved of how Bradley was treating the situation.

"He thinks this is some sort of prank the bride and groom have played on him." I could tell by his fidgeting the reality of where he was had started to sit in his bones.

His face stilled. His Adam's apple bobbled up and down as his eyes shifted around the room. He picked up the pace as he walked in the cell.

"You want me to call Clay's Ferry to pick him up?" Betty asked. "Just so you know, we are just a holding station for the big house. That's over in Clay's Ferry."

"Big house?" He hurried back to the bars. "This isn't a joke, is it?"

"Did Sheriff Lowry ever tell you it was a joke?" Betty popped one of the hush puppies in her mouth. "You better wise up. If I'm not mistaken, I believe you're about to be arrested for the murder of…"

"Gary Futch." I looked through the notes Scott had taken at the scene for me from the caterer who'd employed Mr. Futch.

He'd also noted his conversation with Venetta Stenner, the owner of That's A Toast, the catering company and Gary Futch's employer. According to Scott's notes, Venetta paid a flat fee of two hundred dollars per catering job, and that's what Gary would be paid at the end of the night. He'd worked a few of her jobs over the past six months. He was always on time, and she'd never had a problem with him. No known disagreements with any other catering events, and she didn't have any idea about his personal life. "Quiet and shy" was how she described him.

Interesting. Someone with such an exemplary work ethic and being shy as well as quiet normally didn't get an umbrella shoved into their body.

"So either you better start talking, or call your lawyer." Betty didn't even look at him when she told him his options. She'd moved on to the coleslaw.

"I want to talk to my lawyer." Bradley's lips buttoned up once again after he'd given Betty his lawyer's information.

"Are you sure? There's no one that's going to be more understanding to your situation than me at this moment." It was time for me to soften a smidgen. If I wanted to get him to talk, I was going to have to use honey and not vinegar. "Things happen."

"I want a cigarette." Bradley eyeballed me. "I need a smoke. Can I get one?"

I gave a slight lift of the chin to Betty. "I'll be right back." I grabbed my badge off the desk. "Keep an eye on him."

I got up and headed to the door between the department and Cowboy's Catfish. It wasn't too long ago when customers could smoke at the bar in the greasy spoon restaurant. There were a few grumbles from Bartleby's regulars, but the food and conversation with friends kept them coming back. Taking smoke breaks outside was fine for them.

"Order up!" Bartleby yelled and put a couple of plates of food in the pass-through window between the restaurant and the kitchen. "Kenni. You okay?"

"I'm good. Who out there smokes?" I stood in the hallway outside the door to Bartleby's kitchen.

Without question, he bent down over the grill and looked out the pass-through into the restaurant.

"Any one of those men out there butted up to the counter." He wagged his spatula at me.

"Thanks." I headed down the hall, my stomach growling. I put my hand on it and decided I did need to eat something. It was going to be a long night.

I headed straight to the barstools and approached the first man.

"Sheriff Kenni Lowry." I flashed my badge.

He pulled back and stared at me from underneath the bill of his cap.

"I need a cigarette, and I understand from Mr. Fry you may have one that I can have." My eyes drew past him to the next few men down the row who were now staring at me. "Please."

"Yeah. Um. Sure." He leaned back on his hip and pulled out a crunched-up pack of cigarettes. Hard box. He handed it to me. "Take it."

"I just need one." I opened it and took one out. "Thank you so much. The town of Cottonwood appreciates your donation."

I smiled and gave a nod to the other gentleman before I headed back to the department.

When I opened the door, Betty had turned her chair to the cell and stared straight ahead at Bartleby.

"She didn't take her eyes off me at all." Bradley snickered and jerked forward, trying to get Betty to flinch. "Nothing. She's like steel."

"Thank you, Betty." I held the cigarette up in the air. "You want this, right?"

"Yes." He put his arm through the bars.

"There's no smoking in public government buildings." I carefully laid the smoke on top of my desk. "But if you answer me a few questions, I'm more than happy to take you outside and let you puff away."

"Nah," he snarled. "I think I'll wait for my lawyer."

Betty held up the piece of paper with the lawyer's name and number on it.

I took the piece of paper from Betty and sat down at my desk. I picked up the phone and dialed the lawyer's number. When he answered, I said, "Good evening, Mr. Pennington. Matt Pennington?"

I moved the receiver from my chin and gave Bradley a smile.

"Good." I noted when he confirmed who he was. "I'm Sheriff Kenni Lowry from Cottonwood, Kentucky, and we've got a client of yours, a Mr. Bradley Ines, here in custody for questioning related to a murder investigation."

The lawyer mumbled some words.

"Yes. A murder in-vest-igation." I made sure he heard me correctly. "I'm sure he is a good man, but we have reason to hold him, and he's asked for your assistance. We are located behind Cowboy's Catfish in downtown Cottonwood, Kentucky. We will be awaiting your arrival, and according to him, it's going to be a few hours."

Betty grabbed another hush puppy out of the food container and stuffed it in her mouth.

"I'm telling you that you better stop eating like that, Betty." Poppa had appeared over Betty's shoulder. "You're gonna end up like me." He held his chest and pretended to be stumbling backwards. "Ain't that right, Kenni bug?"

"Betty, are you okay?" I asked, taking my poppa's not-so-subtle cue to say something to Betty.

"Mmhmmm." She hummed through a mouthful of the doughy, delicious, fried goodness.

"You can go home if you want. I can miss euchre night and stay here with him until the attorney gets here." I wanted to make sure she knew she didn't have to stay, especially since I knew her bedtime was around eight o'clock.

"Y'all still having euchre, even after the wedding?" She cocked her head and looked up at me.

"You're serious. This isn't a prank, is it?" Bradley's emotions were on a roller coaster.

"This boy thinks the sun comes up just to hear him crow." Poppa stood at the bars of the cell, looking at a very fidgety Bradley. "Let him squirm a while. He'll get the hint."

It was interesting, because I couldn't decide if he was honestly shocked he was here and didn't do it or trying to play a really good part. Generally I was great at reading body language, but Bradley was one of those types who appeared to always be a little shady, but also one of those types who could manipulate the situation to get anything he wanted.

"I see you thinking, Kenni bug." Poppa swept his way across the floor to my desk. He looked down at the initial paperwork I'd started for the murder investigation.

"Since the wedding was at noon and the reception to follow, Tibbie said there wasn't any reason not to have it, and well, there's no reason for me and you to both be here." I knew there wasn't enough evidence to hold Bradley, and I didn't expect his lawyer to offer anything but to get him out of here, which meant literally he'd go free as soon as the lawyer walked through the door.

My eyes slid across the room to the door as though his release was playing out.

There'd not be any sort of initial autopsy from Max Bogus unless he worked through the night, and even at that I wouldn't get a fax until morning.

"You gonna behave if the sheriff leaves?" Betty pulled up her reader glasses and looked overtop them.

"If this isn't a joke, then I have no other option, do I?" Bradley's response made Betty's nose curl as though she'd smelled a polecat.

"Kenni, you go on. I'll be just fine." She nodded. "But next week the

Women's Club has a meeting during the afternoon, and I'd like to take off for that."

"Of course you can. You don't have to work tonight to take off. You know that." I flipped the case's envelope up and put it on Scott's desk. "Besides, Scott should be back with some evidence bags, and he can stay."

"We'll see," she said and went back to eating.

I walked over to her, leaned down, and whispered into her ear so Bradley didn't hear. After all, I didn't want him to think I was really a good guy in this particular instance.

"See if Bradley wants something to eat, and get Bartleby to fix him up something." Even though Bradley was a suspect and at this time my only suspect, he was still human and needed to be treated as such.

"What was that?" Bradley asked when I grabbed my belongings and started to the door. "Did you whisper for her to come clean about this prank when you walk out?" He had a big smile on his face, looking back and forth between me and Betty.

I let go of a long sigh before I walked out into the dreary, dusky night, thinking to myself that this was going to be one long case to solve.

CHAPTER SIX

"Hello," I called into Tibbie's house when I walked in the front door. The chatter I'd first heard when I walked in had stopped. I took a couple of steps into the entry and looked into the room on the right.

On euchre nights Tibbie turned the sitting room into the eating room. And I'd never seen this entire group of women stop eating and talking before, even when I'd previously walked into a room.

I was met with an eerie silence. Other than while drinking a good glass of sweet iced tea, I'd never seen half of these women's lips stop flapping.

Ever.

"I guess that's one way to make an entrance." Mama's dissatisfied sigh dripped out of her mouth as she set down the plate of goodies she'd brought for the game on the table. "Honey, we didn't expect to see you here since you've insisted on being the sheriff in Cottonwood."

Mama wore the sweet smile on her face as she hurried across the room to greet me.

"I mean, I guess the killer is safe and sound at the jail." Mama curled her arm in mine, giving it a little squeeze I knew very well.

I wasn't too old for the squeeze. She'd done it all my life when she wanted me not to embarrass her.

"It's all good." I looked at her as she snapped her eyes at me. I whispered, "I guess you've not taken to the bed."

"Now." She was good at ignoring, not just today but every day, when it came to what I wanted to do. She pulled out a tube of lipstick nestled in the front pocket of her pants and slipped it into my hands like no one was looking.

Joke was on her. All eyes were still on me.

"Why don't you go freshen up and wash your hands." She patted me on the arm. "I'm sure all that police stuff you've been doing has left you famished."

"I'll get the tables all set up." Tibbie Bell finally took the initiative to come save me. "Can we talk?" she asked when she passed by.

"Sure." I put the lipstick in my pocket, since Mama's hot-pink color wasn't something I wanted on my lips just when I was going to go get a big square of Lulu's lemon bars. I didn't see them on the table in the other room, but I could smell those suckers from a mile away.

Tibbie and I left everyone to mingle around the food tables to go into the room just across the hall where she'd already set up the card tables with four chairs, a deck of cards, and a notepad and pen to keep score.

"Did you get that murderer off to jail?" Tibbie had gone from long, luscious hair down her back to a pulled-up ponytail. It swung side to side as her head bobbled and her eyes grew. "Because if you didn't, I'd love one minute alone with him."

She curled her hand into a fist, and her long nails dug into the palm of her hand, making even me cringe.

"And why is that?" I asked.

"Because he ruined my chances at being in *Barnwood Brides*." The tears resting on her eyelids must've been stinging at her nose, as it flared, and she sucked back a full-on cry.

"Oh, Tibbie. I'm so sorry." I gave her a hug.

"All those women in there had taken photos and posted it all on social media." She was talking about all the ladies gathered around the food table in the other room.

"I wouldn't worry about the magazine. We can fix this with the next big wedding you're doing, and I bet Edna would do a big spread in the *Cotton-*

wood Chronicle." The idea of all the people at the wedding taking photos had really started to swirl around.

"*Cottonwood Chronicle?*" The tone in her voice didn't match my excitement. "Aren't you trying to sell Edna Easterly a little too hard? I know you want me to feel better and all, but Kenni."

"Actually you gave me a good tip for the investigation for the murder." Her face lit up a little. "If everyone was taking pictures, I can get a subpoena for the phones at the wedding."

"Please don't give me credit for that." She didn't show the same amount of joy I'd gotten from the idea. "This whole mess has already gotten all over town. And if you do that, then I'll never get another job again." She leaned a little to the right and glanced over my shoulder.

"Social media," Poppa said behind me. "Photos."

I looked back to see exactly where he was. He was standing right next to Toots Buford with his nose stuck into Viola White's tomato pie. Another treat I would have tonight.

"I sure do miss all this good food." He tapped his nose. "Nothing's wrong with my smeller."

"Social media." I turned back and smiled at Tibbie. "You're brilliant."

"I am?" She drew a hand up to her chest.

"Yes. There were so many cameras there tonight, including *Barnwood Brides*, right?" I wanted to make sure what Poppa had mentioned and what I was thinking was right.

"Yes. One really good one of the dead body underneath the tablecloth." She put her hand up to her head. "What are you going to do to help me save my business?" She put her hand on her hips, her hazel eyes bearing down on me.

"First and foremost, I need to worry about this murder and getting it solved. With that will come out how you had nothing to do with it. I'll make sure it's in my statement." I wasn't sure, but somehow I'd help her.

"The caterer too?" She was pushing it. "She's had clients drop too. Thinking it's the food that was poisoned."

"Clearly the umbrella sticking out of him was the cause of death." It didn't take an autopsy report from Max Bogus to tell me that did have something to do with the man's demise. "I guess he could've been poisoned then stabbed."

There was a real need for clarification because I didn't need Tibbie going around Cottonwood saving her business by telling people that I said it was the umbrella that stopped Gary's heart.

Tibbie had a funny look on her face before she gave a slight shrug.

"Do you know something about the murder? Did you see anything?" I asked.

She looked baffled. Unable to answer my question.

"Let's just wait for the autopsy to confirm, and then we can make a plan." I told her and as I tried to keep my personal life out of my sheriff's business, but in a small town like Cottonwood, it was hard to do.

"Fine. But I want to know the minute you hear," she demanded.

"About those umbrellas," I asked just as the ladies came into the room with their plates so we could get our card game started.

"Kenni, you never made mention about my hair." Ruby fluffed her bright-red hair with the edges of her fingers. "I got a different shade of red tucked into the roots a little."

"Nice. Is that a new technique Tina is using these days?" I asked about Tina Bowers, the owner of Tiny Tina's, the local hair salon in Cottonwood.

There was more than hair being twisted in Tiny Tina's. Gossip swirled around in there, and over half wasn't even true. I'd always thought whoever made and produced hair products put some sort of scent in the liquids that made women want to spill their guts.

Euchre night was no different. Literally I could sit here all night, play my hand, and just listen. Somewhere between all the chatter would be truth that I would use to sift through to get a lead here and there. Tonight wasn't any different. I was going to listen in for any sorts of arguments that might've taken place with Gary or even with Bradley.

"Well." Ruby's lips pursed. She'd definitely not changed her signature orange lipstick to match that hair of hers. "If you'd like to get your hair done, I've got an appointment on Monday that I'd scheduled just in case I didn't like this new look, but now that I've gotten so many compliments, I don't need it."

Her eyes drew up and around my honey-blond hair. My golden high-lights weren't too golden, since I was much overdue for a color and a cut.

"Maybe." I shrugged, not committing, since I wanted to see what I could gather here before I let Tina get her hands into my hair, which she was always dying to do. "I'll let you know."

It was then I noticed Ruby shift her eyes to look at Mama, who was standing a few feet away, looking pleased. No doubt she'd put Ruby up to getting me to the salon.

"Thank you, Mama. I'm an adult now. I think I know when I need to go get my hair done. It's finding the time." I shook my head and headed over to the table where my partner was sitting.

"You have to make time for upkeep. Kenni, you aren't getting any younger. Finn is a good-looking man. He won't be on the market for long." Mama was so old-school. She wanted to have grandchildren so bad, and the first step was to make me a bride.

"That he is." There was no need to ruin anyone's night by fussing with Mama.

My relationship with my dad was so much easier. He didn't try to force me to try out for cheerleading when I was in high school or run for any silly office. He accepted me for the tomboy I truly was and had taken me to hunt with him and his friends. He even took me to his hunting club meetings and his little Saturday trips to the local diner, where he met up with these friends.

Today that was Ben's Diner located downtown. I swear Dad has name etched in one of the stools at the counter, where he spent most of his mornings these days.

I looked around and saw euchre partners Mama and Viola ready to play against Gina Kim and Katy Lee Hart. They were about to start their first hand. Mama was shuffling the cards like nobody's business like it was her business.

"Cut your luck." Mama arched a sly brow and dared poor Gina to cut the deck of cards. Gina gave a low grunt before she shook her hand to gesture "no."

With that, Mama wasted no time as she started to pass the cards out in her usual way. She rounded the table, giving each player two cards, then made another round where she distributed three cards before she flipped over the top card of the cards left in the deck, which might be the would-be trump if someone called it up.

"Hey. Sorry I'm late." Jolee Fischer, my euchre partner, had finally gotten there. "It's been a crazy day."

Jolee was dressed in a pair of overalls with a light dusting of flour down the front pocket. Her blond hair was braided on each side.

"Yeah. I missed you at the wedding." I wanted to jump in to ask her why she hadn't been there.

"I heard the big news. Sorry I missed it." Her green eyes danced with a sparkle as the freckles along the bridge of her nose grew along with the smile.

"Yes!" The bangles on Viola's wrist jingled as she cheered on Mama for taking a trick. "I got the next one!"

"Who's our opponent?" Jolee looked around at the tables and noticed the two empty chairs at our table.

"I think it's Tibbie and Myrna Savage." I nodded toward the two of them coming toward us.

"I have no idea what I'm going to do with all of those flowers. Looks like the sheriff has ruined both of our businesses." Myrna and Tibbie had to be talking about the wedding reception. "Oh, Kenni."

Myrna hadn't noticed me sitting there.

"I'm sorry, Myrna. I have to do my job." I was kinda sick and tired of everyone blaming Gary's death on me. "I'm sorry this has ruined everyone's expectation of what *Barnwood Brides Magazine* was going to do for everyone's business, but I assure you that I'll do everything I can within the arm of the law to make it right."

"I'd never hurt your feelings in the world." Myrna took the chair to my left and Tibbie took the chair to my right, opposite her partner. "I voted for you to get in office, and I'd do it again, but sometimes it's best to…"

"Best to roll the body out and let the party continue?" My brows winged up. "Let everyone walk all over any evidence that will lead to an arrest so Gary's family can have some sort of peace with his passing? No. I can't do that."

From across the room, I heard Mama clearing her throat. Her not-so-subtle way of telling me to put a lid on it.

"And I'm not here to talk about business. I'm here to have some down-time while I wait on a lawyer to show up for his client at the department." I picked up the cards Tibbie had dealt in front of me.

Something was going right for me tonight. My hand included the left and right of the suit Tibbie had flipped over, along with the ace, king, and nine.

"Pick it up," I told Tibbie as Jolee gasped across from me—her way of saying she had zero of the trump I'd called. I arranged my hand with the two trump cards, ace, and king with the nine on the far right. "I'm going alone."

"Thank you, Jesus!" Jolee hollered, throwing her cards on the table before she got up. "I'm going to get some food."

"Here you go, ladies." I laid down all four cards while they threw down any trump cards they might have, then I laid down the nine since I knew they were out of any trump cards, which meant I took all the hands played, giving me and Jolee the win.

"Maybe my night will get better after all." I had some high hopes.

As the night went on, the talk of the wedding and very little talk about the murder had died down. Poppa had ghosted off somewhere, and I'd not seen him in a while.

Within a few hours, I'd started to feel somewhat normal again. Food, chatter, and some laughs were exactly what I needed before the next forty-eight hours of my life. I knew I would be digging deep into the life of Gary Futch and images of Jasmine and Dickie Dee's wedding.

"Kenni, I'm so glad to see you here," Lulu said when we met in front of the dessert table. "I want you to take that handsome young man of yours some of my chess bars."

Finn fell head over heels in love with all things Southern when he first moved to Cottonwood. That included Lulu's chess bars.

She brought them to everything. Weddings, funerals, wakes, baby showers, farmer's market, any sort of fundraiser. It was her claim to fame in the Henny Hens circle—not a title to take too lightly.

Food, or more importantly, the unequivocal love from the community for someone's recipe, was a mark of fame around here. Several women have tried to duplicate Lulu's chess bars, and all have miserably failed. She was still the reigning queen of the dessert table.

While she was sweet, Mama was more along the lines of savory with her many in-demand casseroles. And when someone outside of the Henny Hens tried to duplicate one of their recipes, oh Lordy, Mama and them would peck them to the death.

"Don't forget to remind me to give them to you before you leave." Lulu pulled her shoulder up to her ears and winked before she rushed off to talk to a few of the other ladies.

"I'm telling you, I heard him cussing someone." I looked over to see who was talking. It was Stella from Mama's church circle. She was talking to Vita Jones and Tibbie. "I heard him saying that he'd take care of it. I was waiting to see if it was going to be one of those things you see all over social media where they get up and do one of them dances all together."

"A flash mob?" Tibbie questioned.

By this time I'd turned my body away from them and nibbled on the chess bar so I didn't appear to be eavesdropping.

When I did that, I couldn't hear the full conversation. Nonchalantly I took a few steps backwards and casually turned around right before I got into close proximity of them.

I slowly turned and reached my arm out toward the platter of pigs in a blanket.

"Don't you dare." Mama smacked my hand away.

"Where did you come from?" Over the years I'd prided myself on the ability to assess a room and everyone in it, and I had to say that Mama had been nowhere near the food table. "You're like a stealth ninja."

"That's right. I'm keeping my eye on you." Her face crinkled up. "No matter how it happened, you caught that bouquet, and in all of the weddings I've been to, there's the tried-and-true saying about whoever catches the bouquet is the next one down the aisle." Mama reached over the vegetable tray and used the tongs to pluck out a carrot. "Here."

"I've never liked carrots." I snarled at the orange stick.

"That's why you have bad eyes." Mama was now just making stuff up.

"I don't have bad eyes. Twenty-twenty," I noted with pride and decided to take my chances on another shot at grabbing one of the pigs in a blanket.

"Score!" I yelled and popped it into my mouth before Mama could fight me for it. "What is wrong with you?"

"I could ask you the same thing, Kendrick Lowry." Mama's use of my full name was a sure sign she was up in arms about something.

"Are you honestly upset because I'm not married?" I put my hand on my hip and stared at her. My mouth was slightly open because I couldn't believe she'd take it to this length.

"I'm not getting any younger." She tapped the back of her fingers up underneath her chin before she ran them across her forehead where she'd taken to getting Botox, which she claimed was for migraines, but I think you had to go to a real doctor for that type of Botox.

Tiny Tina's was no doctor's office, last time I drove past the salon during my daily safety drives through Cottonwood.

"More importantly, you aren't, either." She dragged her finger to jab me in the arm. "Don't you get it? Finn is a virile young man. There are several young and available women who want to take care of a man such as Finn."

"If he wants to be taken care of"—I snorted, because I knew Finn and what he liked most was the independence our relationship afford him, where we were exclusive but not hovering over each other—"then he's with the wrong Lowry. Last I checked, you're taken."

Mama's mouth dropped, and her eyes widened. She was literally at a loss for words.

I took pleasure in this odd behavior of hers, since it was rare to stump Vivian Lowry.

Her mouth popped up, a grunting noise like she was about to say something, but it didn't come out of her before she gave up and stormed away from me. I enjoyed a couple more pigs in a blanket.

I turned my ears back to the conversation between Stella, Tibbie, and Vita. This time I was slightly closer.

"Was it the groomsman they were calling for to make the toast?" Vita asked with a hint of wonder.

"Ye-yus." Stella's Southern twang came out in agreement. "One of them. But then they started the toasts, so I took a seat. That's when I looked back and noticed he'd taken the phone call outside. It only made sense it was him. You know, the one they were looking for to make a toast."

Was she talking about Bradley? Was he on the phone? And if so, who was he telling he'd take care of it? Did he take care of the waiter?

"Forget it." I popped around and smiled, becoming a fourth in their little circle. "Did you say you saw one of the groomsmen on the phone right before the waiter was found?"

I just decided to ask Stella directly before I lost my opportunity to question any of them.

She was in midmotion with her spray cheese on top of a butter cracker. She closed her mouth and casually reached across me as if none of us noticed and put the cracker back on the silver tray with the other crackers.

"I'm not sure if I should be talking about this here." Stella brushed her hands together, and with shifty eyes, she looked at the other two.

"I would appreciate any information you have that might lead me to a suspect so the victim can have some sort of peace." My phoned chirped. I pulled it from my pocket. "Excuse me, I need to take this."

I headed toward the hall to take the phone in somewhat privacy.

"That was good timing," I heard Stella say with some relief.

Stella was a nice lady, and she never steered away from gossip, but when it came time to turn the gossip into fact, a lot of them didn't want to talk to me. Like Poppa used to tell Daddy about Mama's tales, "Boy, you've got to cut whatever Viv tells you in half. In that half is where you'll find some truth to the tale she was speaking of."

Regardless, it was seared into my head that Stella had seen something, and I would get to the bottom of it.

"Hey, Scott," I answered the phone.

"Hey, Sheriff. I found out the victim's name and some personal things on him from the caterer. I'm down at the department to fill out my report, and the suspect's lawyer is here."

"What's he saying?" I opened the door to walk out on Tibbie's front porch.

"He wants his client to be released unless we are going to charge him with something." Scott and I both knew we didn't have sufficient evidence to keep him for even a few hours. "I can stall a little bit with the proper paperwork. What do you want me to do?"

Poppa's silhouette stood next to the Wagoneer.

"We'll be there in a minute." I knew Poppa had something to say by the way he was standing.

I'd seen it a million times before. It was a little game we liked to play when I was a little girl and even up until he died.

The little game of what-if, where he would bounce off me scenarios of the crime, and I'd start giving theories by answering his questions. Most of the time it didn't solve the crime, but it did give us some great places to start.

"We?" Scott asked.

"Me." I laughed it off, knowing I wasn't doing a good job covering up the fact Poppa was a ghost and no one could see him. "For a second I was thinking Duke was with me." Good excuse, and Scott fell for it, so I let it go.

"Weee-doggy, Kenni bug." Poppa ghosted into the truck. "We've got a hot one on our hands."

The pleasure of a good case always showed on Poppa's face. He loved a good puzzle, and this was turning out to have more pieces than I liked.

I turned the engine, bringing the old Jeep to life. I pulled the old gear shift to Drive and looked back at Tibbie's house. I'd not even told anyone I was leaving.

I pushed down on the gas and gave one more glance to where Mama was standing on the porch, shaking her head. She knew all too well I was going to go to the department for a long night and even longer day tomorrow.

CHAPTER SEVEN

Tibbie's house was located off the town branch, which was just a street over from Main Street. It was probably quicker for me to walk there instead of drive to the department.

Darkness had covered the town, and the glow of the carriage lights that dotted downtown were the only lights besides the Wagoneer's headlights.

For a spring night, there was a chill that hung in the air. A light breeze fluttered through the open windows, leaving a trail of goose bumps along my arm.

The excess water from the rain that'd fallen over the hanging baskets of the carriage lights ran out of the bottom of them like a faucet, giving the spring florals a really good drink of water.

"At least the rain has stopped," I told Poppa as I turned down the alley in back of Cowboy's Catfish. "Why does it always seem to rain when someone dies?"

Poppa didn't say anything.

"Is there anything to that?" I asked him. "You're up there when you're not here, right? Next time do you mind asking the Big Guy?"

"Now, Kenni, you know I can't discuss the afterlife with you." Poppa had made some sort of rule in his ghostly form with the main man in the sky where he couldn't tell me nothing and was only here to assist me so I was to stay safe. "I guess we won't have time to come up with some quick scenarios, but if you're up for it, then I've got an idea once we get in there."

Poppa changed the subject. He had a plan. I could always count on him to have a plan.

"I'm up for anything and any ideas. As long as we can keep someone else safe, you know I'm ready." It was so nice to have him here even if it was my secret to keep. "You and I both know that when the sun comes up, that office is going to be under fire."

There was no doubt in my mind Mayor Ryland, along with Edna Easterly and any other sort of media that wanted to cover a homicide once it got out about Gary Futch, would be standing either on the sidewalk outside or dead in the middle of Cowboy's Catfish to get a chance to even shout out questions.

There was a fancy luxury car practically parked in front of the door of the department.

Since the quick drive didn't give me and Poppa too much time play our little game, I knew we would be sure to do it after everyone left for the night.

"Here we go." I shoved the gear shift to Park.

"Not before you put that on." Poppa's eyes shifted to the back seat, where my sheriff's coat with my badge pinned to the front was laid across. "Always gotta remind them who's in charge."

He was right. Always right.

It was hard being a sheriff, but a woman sheriff came with much greater challenges, and in no uncertain terms Poppa was telling me that I was going to have to play hardball. There was not an opportunity to ask him how he knew because he'd already wisped out of the truck and I assumed was inside.

I reached behind me to grab my coat and tugged it on when I got out. It didn't look all that great with the dress I was still wearing from the wedding, but now that Finn wasn't working with me, I didn't really care too much what I looked like.

"Evening." I was surprised I'd not walked into a bunch of arguing. "Looks like we are having a social supper."

Betty, Scott, Bradley, and a woman who I assumed was the lawyer all sat inside of Bradley's cell, eating a big plate of Bartleby's fried chicken breasts. Something I rarely was able to score because it was so high in demand.

"Order up!" Bartleby's voice boomed through the door before he even entered the department. "Order going back," he yelled and did a quick one-hundred-eighty turn when he saw I was now there.

"You must be Sheriff Lowry." The attorney got to her feet and waited for Scott to unlock the door and let her out.

Shortly thereafter, Scott and Betty joined us on the outside of the cell while Scott locked Bradley inside.

"You don't need to do that." The attorney wagged her finger at Scott. "Now that the sheriff is here, we can clear up this entire misunderstanding, and we will be leaving. If not, we will be filing a suit against you, you, and the sheriff that will go in conjunction with the suit already filed by Jasmine Dee's father, Evan Burch."

"You've got to be kidding me!" Poppa spat in disbelief.

"Sheriff." The lawyer's steely gaze assessed me.

"Sheriff Lowry." I walked over to her with my arm outstretched to gesture her to take a seat in front of my desk.

"Can I interest you in a piece of fried chicken?" She was one of those lawyers who so loved to play a cat-and-mouse game. I could smell them a mile away. "If not, we'd love to get Mr. Fry to get us a to-go sack, along with that plate of cornbread he hurried out of here with. It seems like everyone around here is scared of you." She leaned in a little and whispered, "I'm not. Now let my client go, or I'll for sure be filing a suit first thing in the morning."

"Tomorrow is—" I was about to say Sunday.

"I know where the judge lives." She wasn't about to be let me think she was anything less than serious on her word.

"Did she say somethin' about a lawsuit with that bride?" Poppa's lips turned in, his wide nose flared with anger. "That just burns me up," he griped.

"I want him to answer a few questions for me before you take him." No way was I going to let the two of them waltz right out of this department without a few questions. I needed answers to satisfy me.

The lawyer swiveled her head to look back at the cell, where Bradley gave her a slight nod.

"Janice Gallo." She whipped out a business card and tossed it on my desk.

"Are her kinfolk Reggie and Caroline Gallo?" Poppa got really close to Janice. "I do see a smidgen of resemblance. Ask her, Kenni bug."

"Are you related to Reggie or Caroline Gallo?" I asked and noticed a tiny gesture of softening in her eyes.

"They were my parents." She eased back into the chair. There was bit of curiosity dancing in her eyes.

"Lordy be, I go way back with her people." Poppa smacked his leg in delight. "Tell her that."

I hesitated.

"Go on, Kenni, tell her." Poppa sat his ghost tushy on the edge of my desk, between me and Janice, with his arms folded across his chest.

"My grandfather knew your people. I spent a lot of time with him. He was sheriff, and he used to talk about your parents." I was always uneasy to tell anything Poppa told me, but in this case I needed to find a common thread with her to get her to break just enough to see my side of why I was holding Bradley.

Plus the fact she mentioned a lawsuit involving Jasmine Dee was not news I wanted to hear. Surely if the facts came to light, she'd be able to talk that crazy bride down.

"That's nice, but it's not going to take away the fact you are holding my client for no reason. Now, I'm asking as nice as I can for you to let him go. Now that I've had time to sit here and think, we would like to make an appointment to come back and give a statement." She put her arms on each arm of the chair and pushed herself to stand. "Deputy, you can let him out now."

"Kenni?" Scott looked at me for the answer.

"You changed your mind in the thirty seconds?" I was curious how we'd gone from exchanging business cards to Poppa knowing her family to abruptly leaving.

"It took me that long to realize you're the granddaughter who put my parents in jail for life and put me in an orphanage."

CHAPTER EIGHT

"That went well." I tapped the steering wheel with my hand as I talked to an empty car on my way down Main Street. "You could've told me you arrested her family for illegal moonshining back in the day. It was the least you could've done!"

I screamed into the air.

"Of course," I whispered.

Ghost Poppa had gotten good at disappearing when he got into hot water—A luxury I didn't have and couldn't afford at this point.

After Janice had threatened me a second, then third time with the lawsuits, I let Betty Murphy make an appointment with Janice and Bradley for tomorrow. At least they were going to come in on a Sunday.

Scott and I had decided to just call it a night and come back an hour before Janice was bringing Bradley so we could discuss all of Gary Futch's particulars. Even try to come up with some other possible suspects by digging into his life.

It'd been a full day, and I was too tired to give the case the necessary attention it was going to need. With Janice holding a lawsuit over my head, there was no room for errors. Not that I ever did have any of those issues, but this time there couldn't even be the possibility.

I turned down Broadway Street, where I owned a little cottage on the south side of Cottonwood known as "Free Row."

Living on "Free Row" wasn't exactly everyone's cup of tea in Cottonwood. And by everyone, I mostly meant Mama. She had tried everything in the world to sell the cottage house after Poppa had willed it to me.

That's what I loved most about living on "Free Row." Him and the memories we shared there.

Yeah, there were cars in the front yard propped up on cement blocks, ripped-up couches on porches, and maybe an unruly teenager or two—who didn't think I knew they were unruly—but I gave them the stare-down if I saw them outside to put a little fear in them. No one on Free Row ever bothered me, or they knew I'd be loading more than my washer and dryer.

I pulled into the driveway and noticed I'd not left a light on for Duke. Poor guy. I hadn't even thought to ask my neighbor, Mrs. Brown. Duke loved her, and he did keep her company since she was elderly and lived alone.

Too late now.

Duke wasn't in the front window with his nose pressed against it, and the blinds were still hanging. Something was strange.

Quietly I got out and opened the back door so I could get out my twelve-gauge from underneath the bench seat. Call me paranoid. When Duke was home alone, and he wasn't waiting at the window, and the blinds were still hanging, there was something off.

Slowly I walked up the drive, staying close in the shadows outside of the moon's glow.

The loud and low hound-dog bark echoed from my backyard before I'd even gotten to the gate.

"Kenni?" A sigh of relief settled in my gut when I heard Finn call my name.

"Yeah! I'll be right there!" I called and hurried back to the truck to put the shotgun back in and grab the flower bouquet I'd been whacked on the head with.

When I made it back to the gate, Finn and Duke were patiently waiting, one with a huge smile and the other with his tongue sticking out of his mouth.

"Look at my two big boys," I joked and tossed the bouquet on the ground so I could give both of them a scratch on the head overtop the fence. That was enough for Duke. He pushed his front paws off the fence and took off into the darkness.

Finn looked at the bouquet and snickered.

"I hate to tell you, but there's some videos on the Cottonwood Community social media page where that bride is whacking you with that bouquet."

"Great," I groaned and swiped the bouquet off of the ground.

"I got you a beer." Finn opened the gate and took me into his arms. "I thought you could use it. So I used my key to let Duke out, and I fed him."

I held the bouquet up to my nose. It actually smelled pretty good.

"Thanks. You are too good to me." I gave that I'm-going-to-be-fine grin and looked up into his big brown eyes. I tapped the flowers on his chest. "Too good to me."

"I love you. I'd do anything for you." He ran a finger along my cheek.

"Where's the suit? You looked so good today." I changed the subject. All that mumbo-jumbo marriage talk from Mama made my stomach hurt.

"I couldn't wait to get that thing off." He cradled my chin with his finger and thumb before he gave me a soft kiss on the lips. "Want to talk? Or you need to hit the sack?"

"I can stay up for a little bit. This homicide is going to be a pain in my you-know-what." We walked over to my back patio, where Finn had his little cooler of beer he'd brought down from his house.

He'd bought a house on Free Row a few houses down and also inherited a cat, Cosmo, who he ended up taking in after we arrested someone for murder and the cat had no place to go.

He had a sensitive side to go with those good looks. The entire package. All six foot of him.

"You want to talk about it?" He sat down and opened the cooler. He took out two beers and used the bottle opener to pop off the lids, then handed me one.

I took it and sat down in the chair next to him, tossing the flowers on the table.

"There's a lot of things that bug me about Bradley. And I'm not sure if it's the fact he's so smug, and he thinks he's so great, that makes it seem like he'd be one to kill the waiter, or the fact I overheard him talking about the groom getting his sloppy seconds that makes me think he's a jerk." I took a swig of the beer.

"Those things don't point to him as the killer." Finn glanced over at me with duck lips.

"Right, but Gary Futch, my victim, was stabbed with one of those umbrellas, and Bradley was the only one who was seen outside without an umbrella right before Gary was murdered." I knew it didn't make a lot of sense when I said it out loud, but in my head I felt like these pieces fit together somehow.

In time, I told myself. Time was the hard part, and everyone in law enforcement knew the first forty-eight hours were the most precious in any investigation.

"Where are you going with this?" Finn asked.

"I don't know. I really want to know what he meant by sloppy seconds. I want to know what he did with the umbrella. I want to know if he had any fights with Gary. Anything that would tie him to the murder." It was so early in the investigation, I knew I wasn't going to be able to solve it while sitting here drinking a beer. "I'm just going to sit here and enjoy the silence with you and Duke."

I reached over and took Finn's hand.

"How was your night?" I asked him.

Finn had recently taken the sheriff's job in the neighboring town of Clay's Ferry. Their department was in an actual building of their own with a lot more deputies and dispatch compared to my one Scott and one Betty. Finn could go into work at nine a.m. and get home by five p.m. That's how much help he had. He even his own forensic department, where I had to use a lab on the border of Clay's Ferry and Cottonwood.

"You know. Cosmo wanted a bunch of treats." He continued to talk about his night, but it was only background noise to all the rattling going on in my head.

I had so many more questions. I didn't even know if the umbrella stuck through Gary was in fact the one Tibbie had given to Bradley.

"Kenni. Earth to Kenni." Finn's hand waved in front of my face. "I'm not sure if you heard a thing I said, but Duke has been pawing at you for attention for the last minute, and you were nowhere near recognizing it." He stood up. "Which I know this activity all too well." He leaned down and gave me a kiss on my cheek. "Good night. Try to not sit up and solve the case tonight. Get some sleep."

"I'm sorry." I reached in front of me and ran my hands down Duke's fur. "Pick me up for church?"

"We are going to church?"

"Mmhmmm. Mama will be so happy." I smirked, but truthfully I wanted to get in front of Preacher Bing and a few of the auxiliary women to pick their brain on what they'd seen.

It was getting late, and Finn was right. I needed to get in bed and start fresh in the morning.

"Let's go to bed, Duke," I hollered, since he'd decided to do another fast lap around the fenced-in yard to tide him over until the morning.

I held the back door for him, and on the run past the table, he'd jumped up and grabbed those darn flowers.

"Good boy!" Poppa called, ghosting himself from the darkness of the yard to the patio. He was laughing so hard.

"You get in here too," I told him and shut the door behind me. "That's not funny," I said and looked down at Duke standing next to the kitchen table with the bouquet in his mouth as he sat so still, looking at Poppa.

He loved Poppa as much as I did. Rightfully so. Poppa had bought Duke for me as a present. The best present ever.

"Give me that." I jerked the flowers out of Duke's mouth and headed over to the kitchen cabinet to retrieve a milk-glass flower vase that'd been there a long time, years before me, from underneath the sink.

I turned on the sink faucet and filled up the vase while I heard Poppa and Duke behind me playing.

"What if Bradley and Jasmine had dated before?" I turned the faucet off and put the vase on the sill of the window. "I heard him say 'sloppy seconds.'" I pushed the bouquet into the vase, satisfied with how it looked.

"And to take it a step further, he and the bride were caught in some sort of situation by the waiter. Bradley didn't want it to come out, so he killed him." Poppa and I started our little back-and-forth.

"What could the waiter have seen that Bradley and Jasmine didn't want to come out and was so bad to kill him for?" I wondered, to add to the theory.

"There were a lot of people there. Going back to the cameras. Did someone catch anything on film? Other than you getting pelted by those flowers." Poppa's gaze passed my shoulder to look at the vase. "That was funny."

"Not too." I gave him a flat look.

"A little." He held his fingers up about an inch apart.

I started to laugh.

"It wasn't at the time, but looking back, I can't believe she came at me like that." I smiled.

"There's my little firecracker." Poppa always knew how to turn my mood around. "Now, what do you say we get some shut-eye and start fresh in the morning. Not only are you going to be busy getting everyone's phones from them, or sweet-talking them into showing you their phones, you're gonna have one crazy bride and her father, plus Viv."

"Mama?" I asked, not following him.

"When you show up in church tomorrow, she just might have a heart attack. Especially if you take that boy." Poppa rolled his eyes.

"Now Poppa. You know I love Finn. There's going to come a time I'm going to have to tell him about you." It was getting harder and harder for me to conceal my conversations with Poppa when Finn was around.

It always seemed like Finn would walk in at the moment Poppa and I had really made some headway in cases.

"I've made the excuse more than enough that I'm talking things out loud."

"You also know that you can't have both of us." Poppa's grim reality washed sadness all over me.

CHAPTER NINE

The Cottonwood First Baptist Church, located downtown, wasn't just any church. It was more of a social few hours than anything. It's where you showed off your best clothes, and as Mama would say, your Sunday go-to-meeting clothes. It's where you fix your hair, put on makeup and jewelry. You mustn't forget the jewelry.

Again, as Mama would say, it's the spit polish to any outfit.

And it was where all the gossip for the week would start. That gossip would trickle down as Sunday dragged on and filter right on into the week. That would be what the talk of the town would be about, and then come next Sunday, they'd find something different to gossip about.

This week I was particularly interested in the gossip sure to be swirling around about the murder of Gary Futch.

Boy, I was counting on hearing what everyone had to say, since pretty much ninety percent of the Cottonwood population had been invited, gone, and taken pictures. But who took snapshots of not only my only current suspect, Bradley Ines, but also any photos of the waiter, any sort of interaction between the waiter and Bradley, or just anyone?

So when I opened my closet door, you bet I was pulling out my finest Sunday go-to-meeting clothes as well as fixing my hair up real nice-like, adding a little more color to my cheeks, and splashing on red lipstick as thick as a brick to finish off the look.

"Okay, Duke." I grabbed the light wrap I'd thrown on the chair in my room after I figured I'd need to cover my exposed shoulders from the current morning chill. I headed down the hall with Duke on my heels. "Let's go out one more time, because you can't go to church, or Mama would forget I did all of this when she noticed you."

I ran my hand down my sleeveless red dress that hit right below my knees and noticed my gams didn't look half bad, since the height of my heels pushed the muscle up a little more than my tennis shoes did.

Duke jumped and bounced over to the door. Just the mere mentioning of the word "out," and excitement spilled out of my deputy canine.

"And I'll be back to pick you up afterwards, since we've got a big interview this afternoon." Bradley and his comment about Jasmine Dee, the bride, hadn't left my mind.

Even while I tried to get a little shut-eye, images of him and the other groomsmen standing there, teasing about something having to do with his sloppy seconds, played over and over.

Duke ran to the back of the yard as fast as he could to get at the squirrel doing his balancing act along the top of the fence.

"You'll get him next time!" I hollered out to him from the screen door and couldn't stop smiling. "Maybe," I whispered and turned to the kitchen when I heard the coffeepot beep Brewed.

The slamming car door echoed from outside. I glanced up at the wall clock and knew it had to be Finn. He was always right on time and never late. Mama loved this part of Finn so much. Said he kept me in line.

I grabbed two mugs from the cabinet and watched out the kitchen window over the sink. Duke's head popped up from the grass, his ears perked up, and he looked at the gate before he bolted off in that direction.

"Good morning, buddy." Finn's voice put a smile on my face. I sure was one lucky gal when it came to him, and I knew it. "Where's your mama?" He spoke in a baby voice.

My smile grew, as did the level of the coffee in the mug I was pouring for him.

"I'm in here," I called with my mouth toward the screen door. "Do we have time for a cup of coffee?"

"I guess we do." Finn stepped inside the door, Duke nearly bowling him over to get to me for a treat. "My goodness." Finn blinked a couple of times. "You look gorgeous."

"Why, thank you, Finn Vincent." I threw a little more of my Southern accent into it. "You clean up mighty good yourself."

"What if I forgo the coffee and get a kiss or two?" He glided over, staring down at me with his big brown eyes, then kissed me.

"I should arrest you, Sheriff, for stealing a kiss and messing up my lipstick." I winked and turned back to the counter to retrieve our mugs. "Here." I pushed his mug between us when he went in for another kiss. "I can't have you messing up an investigation."

"Oh," he snickered and threw his head back. "I should've known you were doing this for the job and not me."

"Are you saying that I don't look this great all the time?" I asked.

"To me I like you best with none of this on, but sometimes it's nice to see you all. . ." He didn't seem to have the word for it as he wiggled the fingers on his left hand in front of my face. "Are you sure your mama is going to survive you coming into the Baptist church looking like this?"

"Sunday go-to-meeting clothes." I adjusted the knot in his tie.

"Your meeting clothes are some fancy duds." Duke wasn't going to stand there any longer waiting for a treat. He shoved his big head between me and Finn, hitting right at Finn's free hand. "Sorry, buddy."

Finn gave him a good scratch, opened the treat jar, and flipped Duke a treat.

"What exactly is your plan, so I know what to do?" Finn asked.

"My plan is to listen to the gossip. Then I want to figure out who took some really great photos of the reception." I took a few sips of coffee as I walked over to the screen door and locked it and then the main door.

"I'm sure there won't be any shortage of that." Finn picked up my wrap and my phone off the counter.

"Thank you." We took a couple quick sips before we headed out the front door to his Dodge Charger parked in my driveway. The windows were rolled down, and the car was still humming where he'd not turned it off.

"Where are you two lovebirds heading out this morning?" Mrs. Brown was pretty much a shut-in and rarely went too many places. She stood at the edge of the property line, giving her azalea bushes a nice drink of water from the garden hose. Her nightcap was still pulled down over her hair, and her night cream was as thick as when she'd put it on.

"Church," I said while Finn hurried around me to open the door.

"Lookin' like that, child?" Her eyes drew up and down me.

"Mrs. Brown, I said the exact same thing." Finn wiggled his eyes. He shut my door and ran around the car to get in on the driver's side.

"I sure hope Preacher Bing doesn't catch you giving her the eyes." Her brows wiggled up and down. "Or anyone else, for that matter." She stuck the end of the hose deep in the bushes with one hand and waved us off in the other.

Finn and I waved bye to her. I would've asked her to join us, but it would take an hour for her to get ready, so I made a mental note to ask her on Saturday nights if she wanted to go.

The Cottonwood First Baptist Church was on the south end of town, and we took our time driving through town, going in and out of streets to get there. There was no way I wanted to get there before Polly.

The church stood off the road with about an acre between Main Street and the building itself. There was a large staircase that led up to a huge concrete-covered porch with five large pillars holding it up. Four large doors were evenly spaced along the porch that opened up into the vestibule of the church.

"Don't forget. Prayer circle is tomorrow night in the undercroft." Viola White flailed her arms, looking like a bird about to take flight right there in the vestibule with her feather boa wrapped around her neck, feathers flying everywhere.

Viola was standing in the middle of most of the auxiliary women and a few who I recognized as being in the bell choir.

"My goodness, Kenni Lowry." She rushed over. "Are you trying to show me up? Or is there some news?" Her eyes moved past my face and straight to my hand, where she was searching for a ring.

An engagement ring.

"I woke up this morning and thought I would show you up." I winked and gave her a quick hug. "I just heard you're gearing up for this week's prayer meeting."

"That's right. There's a lot to be praying for around here." She pulled me closer, but she faced the doors and gave a little smile and wave when she recognized someone. "Did you hear about Darby Gray?"

"No. What happened?" I loved going to see Darby, the owner of the inn. It was one of few places to stay when folks came to visit Cottonwood. It was located in the country, and it had a large wraparound porch that was good for sittin' and sippin' sweet tea.

"I heard at the wedding she'd fallen and broken her leg. We've got to get her to the top of the prayer list." Viola nodded a few times with her eyes all bugged open. She patted my hand. "Don't you worry. I've got you second."

"Me?" I asked. By this time, Finn had gone over to talk to some of the other members of the congregation.

The organ music filtered out of the nave, letting everyone know service was about to start.

"With all this murdering and stuff happening underneath your nose yesterday, the talk around town is maybe there needs to be some fresh blood in the sheriff's department."

"Fresh blood?" This was not the gossip I wanted to hear, and I certainly didn't want to be the talk of the town when I needed it to be about the murder.

Not me.

"Ahem." Preacher Bing cleared his throat from the doors to enter the nave. He pinched a closed-mouth grin and gave a nod through the doors.

"We will talk later. You go first so I can make my grand entrance." She gestured me ahead of her with her finger.

Now I was mad. I couldn't believe how this had gotten turned around on me.

"Uh-oh, what's wrong?" Finn was waiting inside the doors to walk down the aisle so we could take a seat in the front pew, where Mama was so proudly leaning past the side of the pew with a huge grin on her face.

"I'll tell you later," I muttered as my eyes narrowed, taking in all the whispers filtering behind me and Finn as we walked down the aisle.

"Scoot down, Ruby," Mama whispered, knocking her hips for Ruby to scoot over to make room for us. "Look at you." Mama's chin jutted forward to look at the altar with pride written all over her face. "Cottonwood got a glimpse just now. You two are going to make me real proud when you walk down the aisle in my wedding dress."

"Your dress?" I laughed.

"I've been saving it for you." She gave a long, satisfied sigh that matched the hum of the organ.

CHAPTER TEN

"You two made a very grand entrance." Preacher Bing stood in the undercroft next to the punch bowl. "I couldn't hardly keep everyone's attention for the sermon, for all the people staring at you two."

"Goodness, if something was to happen, Preacher, you'd be the first one to know, since you make everyone take premarital classes." I sipped on the delicious ice cream punch. I picked up the ladle and put it into the glass bowl, making sure I got a little bit of the ice cream.

It was a Southern staple to serve a big glass bowl of ice cream punch, even though the Presbyterians called it Presbyterian punch. I wasn't sure who came up with the combination of using 7UP, pineapple juice, frozen limeade, frozen orange juice, and a full gallon of rainbow sherbet to make up the delicious drink, but I was mighty happy to see it here today.

"Speaking of premarital classes and weddings." I looked at the preacher.

He'd been the preacher since I was a little girl. He was as scary back then as he was now. He stood well over six feet tall. His hair was plastered to his head, and his bangs hung down on his forehead. He was a lanky man who reminded me of Lurch from the Addams Family. See how I meant he was scary?

Plus he had a direct line to God, and right now I needed that since I'd yet to see Poppa anywhere around.

"When you counseled Jasmine and Dickie Dee, did you see anything unusual about the two?" I asked.

"What do you mean by unusual? Every couple is different." He stared down at me with his dark eyes, circles underneath to match.

"Any sort of arguments? Disagreements?" I asked.

"Do you think they had something to do with the waiter's death?" Preacher Bing asked.

"I'm not sure."

"Or are you upset and trying to find something to blame for the possible lawsuit they want to file against you." He shot me a glance before he lifted the glass to take another sip of the punch. His eyes glazed over the brim.

My brows knotted, and my jaw dropped.

"No. They have no grounds to sue me. She's the one who assaulted me." My nostrils flared. I downed the little punch left in my paper cup before I squeezed it tight in my hands and tossed it into the trash can.

"Oh, I saw the entire fight on social media." He smiled. "I wish people didn't put everything on there. It can be entertaining, though."

"Whose social media did you see?" If someone filmed me, it was a good possibility they got more than one fight. The waiter and his killer, for one.

"If you use hashtag-the-couple's-name, you'll find all sorts of things." Why on earth had I not thought about that? "Other than that, I'm not really allowed to tell you about the sessions I had with the young couple."

"Not without a warrant," I warned and made darn sure to remember to make good on the threat I'd just given him.

"We can't be having that." Preacher Bing knew I'd make good on my promise to get a warrant now, since I'd done it before.

"There was an issue." He paused as if he were trying to choose his words.

"Issue? Like argument? Disagreement?" I helped him along.

"Umm"—his head bobbled—"argument. Definitely an argument."

"Do you know what the argument was about?" I asked.

"Something about the bachelor party, and I didn't get into specifics. I only dealt with how they were going to handle it as a couple and if it did arise after they were married." Preacher Bing blushed.

"Are you saying he might've gone to, like, a strip club or something to that effect?" I asked, wondering if that's what Bradley had been talking about when he was in custody—calling the entire time in jail a prank and asking if they were getting back at him for what had happened.

The question lingered before I pushed it aside to make sure I used the time I did have with Preacher Bing.

"During these premarital sessions," I started to say, before I noticed the wandering eye of Mama upon me. She jerked around to talk to Ruby as if she didn't see me. "What types of things do you cover in them?"

"Are you asking for the investigation or for personal reasons?" His right brow shot up.

"You never know." I shrugged. "For now, it's for the purpose of knowing what was covered."

"First and foremost, we talk about where each of them stand in accordance with religious beliefs. We also cover things like finances. . ." His voice trailed off, the wrinkles on his forehead deepening as though he'd realized something.

"Something with finances?" I asked.

"Finances create a big stir in marriages. When we covered that part of the class, Dickie had very different ideas of how he would run the family company," Preacher Bing recalled.

"Family company?" It was the first time I'd heard anything about a family company, which would explain the huge wedding and inviting all the government officials if they were going to do something very local.

It was a whole mindset around Cottonwood business owners—you scratch my back, I scratch your back. It was the oldest trick in the book to have me over for supper or even a wedding, only to call in the time they'd invited me when they needed me to look the other way or turn the other cheek.

"Jasmine's family business, where her father has been grooming Dickie for a few years." Preacher Bing shrugged like it was no big deal. "Dickie has an idea for the company where Jasmine said it was, and I quote, stupid. That's when they got into an argument about her calling him names."

"There was already trouble in paradise." I couldn't help but think this would create some motives to not get married, but to kill a waiter to stop the wedding was a little too far-fetched for me.

"That and little white lies. Children." He said "children" in a deeper voice when he went back to rattling off what issues come up in the premarital classes. "I think the issues surrounding children take up a lot of time. And how people try to bring in how they were raised to combine with how their partner was parented. It's a tricky subject."

"Other than the bachelor party incident and the family business, you felt pretty confident they were meant to get married?" I asked, making sure there were no other reasons that might spark either to hurt the waiter. "Nothing like wedding disagreements? Or any sort of family coming together? Friends?"

"You know a bride." He pulled his lips tight. "Actually, you don't." He caught himself. "I've been around a lot of them. They never like any of the groomsmen or things they do. She did want to know the best man's speech before he was to give it, but as you noticed, he didn't even show up for the toast, and they didn't even get to finish them before—" Preacher Bing made the motion of a stab to his stomach.

"Back up." Poppa decided to join us. "Did he say she wanted to know the speech?"

"Jasmine wanted to know the speech of the best man or everyone?" I asked.

"Just the best man." Preacher Bing scratched his temple. "His name escapes me."

"Bradley Ines."

"Yes. Bradley. That's right." He nodded.

"Other than the premarital counseling, did you see anything out of the ordinary at the reception? I know you've been to so many." I reiterated how he'd mentioned he knew a lot of brides.

"I can't say there was. The music was fun. The food was delightful, and Tibbie did a fantastic job coordinating everyone, down to the little umbrellas. Nice touch." He snorted. "Always the little party planner in Sunday school when she was little. Remember that?"

My brows knotted.

"That's right. You were always down at the drugstore, trying to get a cherry soda-fountain drink. You were never on time." There was a hint of scolding in his voice. "I've got to mingle. The duty calls."

"If I have any more questions, I'll stop by." I didn't see a reason to get his statement on file, since he really didn't seem to tell me anything of great importance. The only thing I wanted to check out was the bachelor party and if anything happened there.

That was mainly for my curiosity, since the waiter was dead and not the bride or Bradley.

I walked toward Tibbie and Jolee. Both of them were in the soup-beans-and-cornbread line.

"Are you eating?" Jolee asked.

"No. My stomach is in knots. This murder has got me upside down, and knowing that I'm going to be the talk of the town this week isn't setting well."

"Good." Jolee shoved a Styrofoam bowl into my hands. "Can you get a bowl of beans for Mrs. Brown? She called me this morning and told me she didn't want to eat what Meals On Wheels had for tonight and if I'd get her some beans. You know how all these Henny Hens talk if you get seconds."

I listened to her go on.

"'If Jolee keeps eating like that, Ben will never come back to her. She'll be as big as a house. She should wait to eat like that until after she gets her a man,'" Jolee mocked.

"Speaking of Ben." It was a sore subject. Jolee and Ben Harrison had been enemies to lovers in a sense, then gone back to enemies recently. Only because Ben had broken up with her and we'd yet to know why. "Any news on that front?"

This was when I needed to flip the switch from the job to the friend. I'd steered clear of asking her last night at the euchre game because there were just too many ears around.

"I heard he's just as miserable as you." Tibbie put her two cents in. "Maybe you should talk to him."

"There's no more talking." Jolee grabbed two pieces of cornbread and headed off to get us a table.

"She didn't say anything about cornbread for Mrs. Brown." I held up two fingers for the volunteer to give me two pieces.

"Who wants to eat soup beans without cornbread?" Tibbie was right. We loved to crumble up the cornbread and mix it into the soup beans along with some cut-up onion.

Mouthwatering.

"Say, Tibbie, I was wondering about those umbrellas you had gotten for the wedding." I followed her and Jolee to an empty table next to the exit.

It was a perfect spot for me to slip away without being noticed.

"Wedding party," she stated with a mouthful of beans. "Only for the wedding party. I got them last minute down at Lulu's Boutique. After I saw what the weather was going to do, I wanted to make sure we had some on hand for when they walked out of the church."

"That was smart thinking." Jolee nodded and glanced over at the person sitting next to us. "I didn't get any punch." She pulled her shoulders back and looked up over the heads of all the people sitting at the table toward the back of the undercroft where the punch bowl was. "I'm going to get me some punch. Y'all want any?"

Tibbie and I both said we'd take a cup before Jolee scurried off.

"Lulu is pretty amazing. She came up with the wedding monogram because she's got one of those Cricket machines in her shop in the back craft area." Craft night at Lulu's Boutique was fun. She did have everything you needed to craft whatever your little heart desired.

My heart didn't desire crafts at all. I went along just to hang out with my friends. But a lot of the time I went there when Jolee's On The Run food truck was parked there. Lulu and Jolee had an agreement. While the food truck was serving food, the customers could go into the craft area in Lulu's Boutique to sit and eat.

It was a deal Jolee had worked out with a few of the area businesses after she'd gotten the town council to approve the necessary permits to operate a food truck in Cottonwood. That was one of the sore subjects between her and Ben.

"You only got twelve umbrellas, and one went right through the chest of the waiter." I sighed. "What can you tell me about Bradley and the bride?"

"Nothing but they dated back in college. That's how she met Dickie. Bradley and Dickie were best friends."

"Sloppy seconds," I whispered.

"Kenni!" Tibbie jerked up and covered her mouth. "That's terrible to say."

"I didn't say it. Bradley Ines said it."

Did Bradley Ines really believe Dickie had gotten his sloppy seconds, or did he kill the waiter to sabotage the wedding? The wedding he thought he would have with Jasmine.

It was a far-fetched theory, but at least it was a theory I could chew into when Bradley came to the department this afternoon.

About that time, Edna Easterly walked by.

"Ouch, Kenni." She groaned and jerked from my grip on her fishing jacket. "You're rude."

"I wanted to tell you how nice you looked at the wedding yesterday." I offered her Jolee's seat since Jolee had been stopped by another group of women, who didn't seem to care Jolee had her hands full with three punch cups.

"I already know what you want. Scott Lee told me at the reception yesterday you wanted all the photos off my camera." She lifted one of the many pockets on her jacket and pulled out a thumb drive. She wagged it with each word. "The only reason I'm doing this is because you've ruined everyone else's career with that little stunt of shutting down the wedding, and I'm not going down with your ship."

She smacked the thumb drive that I assumed contained all the wedding photos down on the table before she headed off in another direction.

"Why is it that everyone is mad at me for ruining the reception, when they should be mad at the waiter for getting killed or the killer for killing the waiter at the reception?" I looked across the table at Tibbie, who probably wasn't the best one to discuss this with since she was the first one who said I ruined her event-planning business. "Do you happen to have copies of the speeches from the toast?"

"I'm going to get some banana pudding." Tibbie planted her hands on top of the table and pushed herself up. "I'll see you later."

"Let's get out of here." Poppa saved me from beating myself up. "We've got wedding photos to look at."

I put my hand up on the table and got the thumb drive off before I started my search for Finn. When I glanced around the undercroft and didn't see him, I headed outside to where he was standing with most of the men discussing their favorite Kentucky Derby contender, maybe thinking about placing a wager or two.

It was spring in Kentucky, and that meant one thing. Horse racing. Soon the gossip for the women would turn to what hat they'd be wearing to the Derby while the men would discuss betting odds.

I had to strike the auxiliary women while they were hot, or I would lose my window of opportunity.

"Daddy, when is Mama's next auxiliary meeting?" I pulled Daddy aside from the men for a few minutes.

"Tomorrow night over at Vita and Luke Jones's before the town council meeting."

"Good. Two birds with one stone, Kenni bug." Poppa rubbed his hands together. "Do you think you could go back in there and get a banana puddin' to go?" Poppa watched Vernon Bishop, the president of the Cottonwood First National Bank, walk past with a big bowl of the delicious sweet.

"Kenni!" Tibbie called out to me when Finn and I were walking to his Charger. "Here."

She handed me a white binder with a slip of paper in the clear pocket on the front with "Jasmine and Dickie's Wedding" scrolled in fancy writing.

"That's their entire wedding planner. Speeches and all." Her lips drew into a thin, bird-like smile. "I'm sorry. You didn't ruin my career, but I want you to catch the SOB who did."

"Thank you." I hugged her tight.

CHAPTER ELEVEN

"What did you mean when you said sloppy seconds?" I asked Bradley once he got settled into the one of the chairs in front of my desk.

Bradley shifted. His lawyer next to him gave him the nod to answer the question. Bradley turned his chin over his right shoulder to look at Finn. Finn was sitting at Betty's desk, eating the bowl of the banana pudding I'd gotten, and Poppa was hovering over him, licking his chops.

Finn looked up and noticed us all staring at him.

"I'll be over at Cowboy's Catfish if you need me." Finn got up and took the bowl of pudding with him.

"Back to the question." I shifted my eyes from Finn to Scott and back to Bradley. "Did you date Jasmine back in college?"

"I did," he confirmed.

"What does this have to do with the murder of the waiter?" Janice Gallo asked.

Her black hair parted down the middle and was cut to her shoulders, with both sides neatly tucked behind her ears. It lay slick against her head with not one flyaway or stray. She had thick black brows and big round black eyes that didn't miss a beat.

When she talked, I tried not to stare at the small mole just above her upper lip on the right side. Mama would call that a beauty mark. Janice probably woke up like this.

I ran my hand down my hair, feeling a bit self-conscious since I'd gotten to the office right before they'd gotten there and grabbed one of the extra sheriff uniforms from the supply closet so I could change out of my Sunday go-to-meeting clothes.

"I'm just gathering facts." I gave her a flat look.

"Fine. You can answer." She jerked her chin toward him.

"Yeah. We dated, and that's how she met Dickie. It wasn't like we dated a while. Really it was like two dates, and that was it. Nothing else. She was decent enough to tell me she was going out with Dickie. I moved on to the next girl." He snickered.

I wanted to smack the grin off of his face, but then I'd not be able to slap the cuffs around his wrists when it came time.

"Did you plan the bachelor party?" I asked.

He shifted uncomfortably in the wooden chair. The chair groaned from the movement of his weight he put on the arm as his elbow leaned heavily on it.

"Sure. I was the best man." His bottom teeth raked his top lip a couple of times before he sucked in a big inhale. "That's the duty. Send the groom out of his single life with a bang."

"What did you do to send him off with a bang?" I used his own words against him.

"Again, what does this have to do with a murder investigation?" Janice asked.

Scott motioned behind their backs that he had seen something in the photos from Edna. He'd downloaded them to his computer after I got back to the office.

"I am trying to establish the frame of mind of all the people in the wedding. From what I could see even before Mr. Futch's death, there was some tension between the bride and Mr. Ines here." I sighed and flipped a page in the file. There was nothing there, but they didn't see that.

"According to the photos on this device." I picked up the thumb drive Edna had given me and showed it to them. I'd yet to have time to look through them, so I was going out on a big limb.

However, Scott had gone through a few of them and was currently printing some off.

"There were a few moments when the bride and Mr. Ines were in a heated discussion. I am wondering if it had anything to do with the night of the bachelor party or the fact that your client is still holding a flame for the one who got away and would do anything to ruin her wedding." I jerked my head to face Bradley straight on. Scott walked over and handed me the two photos. "Where Mr. Bradley"—I took the photos and just on a hope and a prayer laid them out in front of Janice and Bradley—"and the bride are in what looks like a heated discussion. Here you can clearly see the waiter standing next to them. So either your client knows Mr. Futch, or Mr. Futch heard something he didn't need to hear, and your client killed him."

I smacked the top of my desk with a flat palm.

"Which is it, Mr. Ines?" I stood up over my desk and poked my finger down on the photos. "What is going on in these photos? It sure doesn't look like the toast you was supposed to give to a happy couple."

I reached down by my feet where I'd put my purse and the wedding binder Tibbie had given me. I opened up the binder and flipped to the tab labeled Speeches. Thank God Tibbie was really good at organizing.

"Here's your speech to the happy couple. It says. . ." I picked up the paper and read straight from it, not leaving a single word out. "Ladies and gentlemen, thank you all for coming out tonight to celebrate the wedding of two people we all love, Jasmine & Dickie!

"When I first met Jasmine, I knew that she was the woman Dickie would end up marrying. Even if it hadn't dawned on him quite yet, it was obvious to everyone around just how smitten he was with her. They talk about a bride's glow, but this man was shining since the moment he met her. He changed for the better without realizing it. And we all could see it."

The more I read the speech, the more shifting he did in the chair. I didn't look at him. I just kept reading with Poppa cheering me on in the background.

"You've got him now, girl! Keep going!" Poppa was doing some uppercuts and jabs like he was training for a ghost boxing league.

"Dickie couldn't stop talking about her. We'd go out with the boys, and Jasmine's name would be brought up every two minutes. So when he came to me to tell me that he would be proposing, my only response was, 'Well, it's about time!'"

I used my best theatrical voice to play up how I thought the speech would sound if it really were heartfelt.

"Look at that smug face. Knock him in that pretty jaw, Kenni bug." Poppa had moved next to Bradley. He bent down close to Bradley so he could blow a steady stream of air toward Bradley's nose.

Bradley reached up and grabbed around it, like there was a hair hanging or something tickling it, before he rubbed it a few times.

I went on reading aloud. "There's something special about these two. They go together without forcing it. They love each other without fighting it. And they care about each other without thinking about it. She was the one from the very beginning, Dickie, and we're all so happy to be able to take part in your big day. Cheers!"

I smacked the piece of paper down in front of Janice. Scott took the papers shuffling off the fax machine. There was really only one person who ever faxed the department on a late Sunday afternoon. Max Bogus.

Poppa had ghosted behind Scott. Now both of them were reading the report.

Poppa slid his eyes across the room. There was something in them. Something telling. Something he'd seen in the report.

"Does this sound like a speech you'd give someone who was taking your sloppy seconds?" I emphasized. "This is an entire speech of lies. You know it. The groom knows it. And the bride knows it. What else could you be lying about, Mr. Ines? Did you or did you not kill Mr. Futch to ruin Jasmine and Dickie Dee's wedding because they made you look like a fool years ago, bruising that big ego of yours in front of all of those men in the wedding party? Who, by the way, have known you as long as you've known Dickie."

"This is ridiculous. There's not one single piece of evidence that my client laid a hand on Mr. Futch."

"Maybe not a hand, but the force of stabbing someone with an umbrella. Because last we checked, everyone in the wedding party had their umbrella except your client, and he was drenched along with Mr. Futch." I leaned back in my chair and folded my arms.

Bradley went to open his mouth.

"I'm sorry. I forgot you were outside vaping in the pouring rain." I reached over and picked up the cigarette I'd gotten him last night. It'd rolled over to the side of the phone. "I thought you said you didn't smoke cigarettes." I snapped a finger toward Scott. "Deputy Lee and I picked up all the cigarette butts on the venue's entire property. They are all in that bag."

Scott scrambled to go through the evidence we'd collected to be tested, and when he got to the bag, he held it up.

"Am I going to need you to give us a DNA sample?" He scoffed at my words. "If you did nothing wrong, then I don't see why you'd have a problem." I looked between him and Janice.

Playing bad cop was exhausting.

"You need to go see Max," Poppa whispered.

"As a matter of fact, Deputy Lee will follow along behind y'all while you head on down to the health department just a couple blocks over to submit." I smiled and cocked my head toward Scott. "Deputy?"

"Fine. I'm fully believing in my client, and I'm going to clear his name." Janice stood up and Bradley followed. "That's why I took this job. I'm tired of the Lowrys putting my people in jail."

"'Scuse me." Mama pushed past Janice on her way into the department. "Hello there. I am so glad I ran into you. Thank you so much for letting me borrow your umbrella at the wedding reception. I hate to say it, but I think I lost it. I put it on the table when I came in, and someone must've picked it up."

The air left my lungs.

"Looks like you have a new suspect, Sheriff." The look on Janice's face said a million words.

CHAPTER TWELVE

"That's ridiculous." Mama scoffed on our way out the door as I walked her to her car. "The only thing I said to the waiter that might be off-color was about how he was slow, and when the sheriff gets married, we will make sure that caterer won't hire him."

"You didn't." My shoulders slumped.

"You've got all the tongues wagging about a big wedding announcement," Mama cackled, her hand dug down into her pocketbook where she searched around. "Where are those keys?"

"I'm not talking about me and Finn. I'm talking about the waiter. You didn't have an argument with him, right?" I questioned her.

"I most certainly wouldn't call it an argument, Kenni." She played it off. "Ask Viola and Ruby—they were right there. And maybe Tibbie. Or that caterer. She's the one who told him the customer is always right."

"I just overheard the fancy lawyer saying she was coming to the town council meeting tomorrow night." Poppa shifted to Mama's car. A worried look settled on his face, and I knew this wasn't going to turn out good.

"What would you call it, Mama?" I asked and bent down to get her to look at me.

"I know I threw those keys in here." She lifted the purse up to her eyes, tilting it one way and then the other to get a good look inside.

"They are on the car." Poppa pointed. "And the car is locked."

"How on earth did you do that?" I shook my head and covered my eyes, resting the sides of my hands on the driver's side window to look in.

"Do what?" Mama continued to rummage through her purse.

"Lock the keys inside." I tapped the window.

"You've got to be kidding me." She gasped and shook her head. "I have a terrible habit of hitting the lock when I get out when I come to see you. Especially when I come to the house on Free Row. I know you love that house and Finn loves living a few doors down from you, but Kenni, Poppa would want the best for you. I know." She placed her silky hand on her chest. "He was my daddy."

"Viv, there's nothing wrong with my house." Poppa's nose flared.

"If that was the case, he wouldn't've left it for me." I walked around the car and lifted up the handles to see if just one would open.

No chance.

"He left it for you to sell and have money." Her assessing eyes looked me up and down.

"Listen, you better go inside and give me a statement about the interaction between you and Gary Futch, because I have reason to believe you've now become a suspect. If not on my list, then Janice's list." I gestured to the passing car with Janice and Bradley inside.

Janice had a look of satisfaction on her face. She had something up her sleeve.

"Don't you worry yourself about that." Mama giggled. "It looks like he had more than one argument by the way it ended up."

"Mama, you're the only one who had a public disagreement with him."

"I wouldn't call it that, honey." Her brows knitted. "I guess we better call your father. He's going to have to bring me the spare key. He's not going to be happy. He wanted to go to the afternoon races. I told him that you're not supposed to gamble on the sabbath, and I swear Preacher Bing overheard him and all those men in the parking lot planning their little rendezvous."

"Mama. Stop!" I yelled to get her attention.

"Kenni. You're screaming like a child. What is wrong with you?" She looked around as if there was someone who could have heard us.

No one was in the alley, unless you counted the mice scurrying around in the dumpster, feasting on the Cowboy Catfish's garbage.

"Do you understand no one on record had an argument with the waiter who is now dead? Stabbed with what appears to be Bradley's umbrella? No one but you." I gave her a hard look.

"But it was his umbrella. . ." Her voice fell away. She put her hand to her mouth. "Oh dear." She looked at me with the worry on her face that matched my insides. "Oh." She hooted a few times. "This doesn't look good, does it?"

"No, Mama." I took her by the elbow. "I'm going to have you go inside and give a statement to Deputy Lee because I can't take my own mama's statement." She shuffled along beside me, probably not hearing what I was saying because the worry had settled on her brows and she was looking down, gnawing on her lip. "While he is doing that, I'm going to go to the funeral home and see Max. I'll call Daddy from my car on the way over there."

I opened the door.

Scott was thumbing through all the paperwork and appeared to be getting the file for the case in order.

He watched silently while I sat Mama in the chair next to his desk. She put her little pocketbook in her lap. She sat still, looking forward but with no real focus.

I gave my head a quick tilt, gesturing for Scott to follow me.

"What are we going to do about the umbrella now?" he asked as I turned my body away from Mama so she'd not hear me, even though the department was so small it made it hard not to.

"Mama and Gary had a disagreement of sorts." I looked at Scott. The worry on his face said it all. "Right. I want Mama to give you a statement of everything. From brushing her teeth in the morning to her daily constitution."

Scott's face softened, letting me know he wasn't going to ask Mama when the last time was she went to the bathroom.

"You know what I mean. I need to know exactly when and how she got the umbrella from Bradley and hopefully get some clear answers on just how hard someone stabbed Gary with that umbrella, because Mama isn't that strong. That's the only thing we have to hang our hat on." I looked around Scott and peered at Mama. "I need to go see Viola White, Ruby Smith, and Tibbie Bell. Mama said they all heard it."

Now I knew why they were all acting so suspicious when I asked them if they'd seen anything. They had, and they didn't want to rat out Mama.

This was the longest I'd ever seen her go without talking.

"You think you can do this?" I asked.

"Yeah." He sighed.

My mind fluttered back to the church, when Viola had asked me if I had a minute right before Preacher Bing had interrupted us, and right after she'd told me there were rumors of needing fresh blood in the sheriff's department.

I couldn't help but wonder if she was going to tell me about the disagreement Mama and Gary had. I'd sure find out tomorrow when I stopped by the jewelry store to pay her a little visit. Then I wondered what time Ruby Smith's appointment was at Tiny Tina's tomorrow. Maybe I did need a little trim on the edges of my hair.

I lifted my hands up to feel the edges.

"What are you thinking?" Scott asked.

"Not sure just yet, but once you get Mama's statement, you can let her go. I'll call my dad to bring her extra car key to her." I sighed. "You and I will do a workup on the whiteboard when I get back."

I gave Mama a kiss on the forehead before I headed into Cowboy's Catfish to tell Finn my plans.

"I'll walk home." He was sitting at the bar, shooting the breeze with Bartleby. "It's a nice afternoon."

"Are you sure?" I asked.

"Don't let him fool you." Bartleby's smile held a secret.

"What?" I looked between the two men.

"I've got an apple pie coming out of the oven in a few." Bartleby told on Finn.

"Finn Vincent," I gasped. "You just ate a big bunch of banana pudding."

"I've got that sweet tooth today." He pouted in a very cute and charming way.

"Fine. I'll see you later this afternoon." I kissed him goodbye. "Send Finn home with an extra slice for me." I winked at Bartleby on my way out the front door of the diner.

I didn't want to go back through the department because Mama was in there and I didn't want to disturb her or even hear what she was telling Scott during her statement. If there was any way Janice could turn Mama's recollection of her tiff with Gary—and I was calling it a tiff—it would be how I had somehow manipulated Mama's words.

I wasn't going to let that happen, but I sure was going to go to the town council meeting and make sure I put in my two cents.

Unlike Mama, I did keep my keys in my old Wagoneer. Cottonwood residents were still able to keep their doors unlocked and keys in their cars. It wasn't like we had a high crime rate when it came to things like break-ins, and I hoped they'd felt safe enough to keep to the simple ways of life. Those were the things they needed to remember when it came to election time, not things like Gary's murder that were out of my control

When I got into the Jeep, I tuned into WCKK, the local radio station, so I could get some music in my head and Mama out of it. I needed to be as impartial as I could be, and when Max Bogus gave me details on Gary's autopsy, I needed Mama out of my head. Music did that for me.

Before I knew it, I'd pulled right on up in front of the Cottonwood Funeral Home, where the morgue was located. It was the only funeral home in Cottonwood, and since they already did have the facility in the basement to fix everyone up for their eternal slumber, it only made sense for the town to also rent the space and equipment for times such as this.

Plus there was no one better than Max Bogus to be elected as the county coroner. He had the experience as the funeral home director. Though you didn't need a medical degree to be the coroner, Max had one, so it all just came together.

It never got any easier, standing in the door of the cold, institutional-looking room, staring at the dead body lying on the stainless-steel table. My eyes took in the scene before I put on the blue gown and gloves Max had left for me at the door.

"Good afternoon." Max's voice echoed off the cold walls when I walked in. The first smell of death really did knock me for a loop as soon as I walked in. "Hairnet on the counter."

"I'm curious as to what you found out." I pulled the net over my hair, giving the top of my head a few scratches from the itchy fabric. I also plucked a paper mask from the box and kept my hand up to my nose to hold it in place to ward off the stench.

"You okay?" he asked, glancing up.

"Yeah. Fine," I said and looked around to see where Gary was. "Where's the body?"

I was expecting to see Gary lying on the surgical table with the Y cut, but the stainless table was empty and shiny.

"That's why I wanted you to come down here. I didn't want to proceed with opening him until you got a look at the X-rays you told me to make sure I took, and I'm glad I did." He waved me over to the window into the X-ray room.

When I looked in, there was Gary with the machine overtop of his lifeless body.

"It appears there was a blow to the side of his head that killed him. Pretty hard too. He was hit so hard it blew out his right pupil." He'd pulled up the X-ray to show me Gary's skull and facial features. "That wasn't the only hit. He also sustained a blow to the back of the body, which I believe caused him to go down. As for the umbrella, I think that it was outside and the killer used it on him after he was dead." He held up a finger when I opened my mouth to ask a question. "Stick with me."

If that was the case, maybe Mama had left the umbrella outside and not taken it in. Which was plausible because Mama never took an umbrella inside in fear it caused bad luck, especially not a wet one in fear it'd make a mess. Mama's house was always visitor ready from the tidiness and the coffee cake in the freezer that could never be touched because it was only there to be enjoyed by drop-in guests.

"I found some residue from the pavement on the party patio." He scanned down images slowly. "Now, these other wounds came afterwards."

"Afterwards?" I asked, knowing if someone had killed him then beat up the body postmortem, it was what I'd consider a hate crime.

Then we had a whole different amount of charges for the killer.

"Cracked ribs, right arm is broken in two places, along with a shattered femur. That's when the umbrella was shoved into him."

"Postmortem?" I made sure I was clearly understanding him.

"I wanted you to see this first, before I opened him and the DA or that snoopy lawyer tried to come back in here saying I cracked the ribs or broke any bones to perform the autopsy." He shoved a few of the photos he'd taken in my face. "I made sure I documented everything."

"We're looking for evidence of a hate crime." I glanced through the photos

"Yeah. I believe so." He confirmed my suspicions. "And I don't think there was any sort of motive like robbery, because his watch and ring are still on. He's got a lot of cash in his wallet."

"A lot of cash?" I asked.

"At least a few thousand." Max caught me off guard. "I took photos of each one and sent them to your email."

"Thanks." My mind went into overdrive. "Wonder why he had so much cash?" I really wondered why Gary was working as a wedding waiter with thousands of dollars in his wallet. Seemed like something was off.

Max tucked his blue button-down shirt into his khaki pants before he turned to go back to his office. I followed him.

"Have a seat, and we can go over the preliminary again before I get started on the internal autopsy."

I sat down and looked around his pretty simple office.

He had a desk full of paper piled high, which I'd gotten used to seeing. On the wall were his medical license, business license, and coroner's license. He only had up the necessary items to prove who he was in case he was audited.

Max lived a simple life. He went to work, did his job, and enjoyed his home in the country. There wasn't any romance or social life that I knew of, but then again, I didn't stay in the gossip groups. He was able to keep his mouth completely zipped when it came to murder victims.

"The wife already called this morning to come identify the body." He looked at me as if he wanted me to clear it.

"That's fine. I need to talk to her. Maybe I'll wait around to question her." There was a buzz that rang on Max's computer.

He tapped the keyboard and looked at the screen.

"She's here now." He swiveled the monitor around to show me the video

274

footage of her walking into the funeral home. He kept this system on his computer so when he was working alone, he knew when someone was coming in, since he couldn't hear anything from down in the basement.

She stood in the front room of the funeral home with her hands down to her sides and looked around.

"I'll go with you and leave after I ask her a few questions." I also wanted to understand why she'd not called Deputy Lee back.

Max and I didn't have much time to talk about anything else with Gary's X-ray, and I would wait until the internal autopsy was performed to ask any further questions.

For now, the X-ray told me enough about how Gary had died and that this was not just a little squabble. Someone had planned this. And it was my job to shift gears to see exactly what was in Mr. Futch's past to garner such an end to his life.

"Mrs. Futch." Max walked straight across the floor at the entrance of the funeral home. "I'm Max Bogus, the coroner, and this is Sheriff Lowry."

"I'm sorry to meet you under such circumstances." She didn't look at me when I addressed her.

"Why haven't you called Deputy Lee back?"

"After his initial visit to tell me about Gary, I needed a few hours to myself. It took everything I had to drag myself out of the house this afternoon to come here and…" Her voice fell away. Her eyes filled with tears.

Max stepped aside and plucked a few of the tissues from the box sitting on the credenza next to the wall, where there were flower arrangements and a few framed photos along with a condolence book for the corpse in the next room.

"You do know this is a murder investigation? And I'm going to need to ask you a few questions in order to find the person who did this to your husband and you." I wanted her to tell me that she'd answer some questions now, but she only continued to nod her head and look down at her feet.

"Mrs. Futch, do you understand what I'm asking of you?" I needed the confirmation.

"Brenda. Yes. I just can't think clearly right now." She swallowed, bringing her chin up. She had on a full face of makeup. Complete with lip liner and lipstick.

I'd never seen a woman who had just lost her husband in a tragedy with a full face of makeup on that hadn't run down her face. This was a concern and set off all sorts of alarms.

"Gary and I have been together for fifteen years. I can't imagine living life without him."

"Your husband had a large amount of cash on him. Do you know how he got that money?" I asked.

"No." She was quick to answer. A little too quick in my opinion.

"You have no idea why Gary would have thousands of dollars on him?" I tried to restate the question but was met with silence. "It's my understanding he was only making two hundred dollars for the entire night, and I'm not sure why Mr. Futch would want to do a job for such a little payout when he had the money in his pocket." I sucked in a deep breath when I noticed Poppa had joined us.

"Unless he was there for other reasons," Poppa said. "Follow the money."

For a split second I looked at Poppa then quickly followed up. "Unless he was there for other reasons," I repeated.

Both of us paused.

"Maybe he wanted to see someone from the wedding? Or someone invited to the wedding? There were a lot of government officials there. Did Gary have any dealings with anyone in the government?" I went on to theorize.

"No." She shook her head. "Not that I know of."

"What about anyone in the wedding party?" I asked. "Or the That's A Toast catering company he was working for."

"Working for?" The shock on her face told me she didn't have a clue where he was last night. "I don't know all the people Gary knows. He knows a lot of folks. He helps out a lot of people."

"Venetta Stenner, the owner of the company that employs your husband, said he'd been working for her for the past few months." I kept a close eye on her to gauge the response from her body. "Did you know that?"

She put her hand up. "I can't do this now."

"When can you do this?" I asked. "You see, I can't do my job and bring your husband's killer to justice until you give me some names of some people who might've wanted to do this to him."

"Maybe tomorrow." She turned to Max. "Can I please go see my husband now?"

Max glanced over at me.

I pinched a thin smile and nodded.

"I'm sorry for your loss," I told her as she walked past me to follow Max to the basement.

Poppa and I stood there in silence until we were alone.

"She's hiding something." Poppa took the words right out of my mouth.

"She sure is, but what?" I wondered.

CHAPTER THIRTEEN

"She had no idea her husband was doing the side gig." Poppa sat up in the front of the Wagoneer. "GGR513," Poppa repeated a few times.

"GGR513?" I asked as I pulled out of the parking lot of the funeral home.

"The license of the car Brenda was driving. I made sure I watched for her to come in so you could run the plates." Poppa was always so quick with all the details. "We need to run the plates and see if there's any stops."

"Great point." I picked up the phone to call Scott, since I didn't have my usual uniform with my walkie-talkie on it.

"Hey, Sheriff." Scott was always so professional.

"Can you run some plates for me and let me know if you come up with anything?" I asked him.

"Sure. Go ahead." I could hear some papers shuffling in the background.

I rattled off the license plate and told him to get back to me when he knew something before we hung up the phone.

"I have no idea. None of it makes sense. There was no employment history in his file Scott had pulled, so I wonder where their income comes from." I knew the little he was getting from the catering jobs wasn't enough for two people to live on. "I need to look into his wife. When I mentioned his job, she had a strange look on her face."

"Are you thinking she killed him?" Poppa took the words right out of my head.

"You and I both know we are to look at the spouse as the first person of interest, but when she wasn't at the wedding, I really thought it was Bradley." I knew it was all preliminary stuff, and weeding out suspects took time, but I wasn't one to dillydally. I liked to get things wrapped up pretty quickly. "Now we know Gary was hit in the head with something before someone did a number on his corpse."

"It would make sense if he was outside smoking and she was lurking in the darkness. When he was alone, she hit him from behind, grabbed the umbrella, and stabbed him with it." Poppa's theory could've easily been what had happened.

"And with little cooperation from her, or biding time, I. . ." I sighed and took a right on Broadway so I could go home and let Duke out. "I think I need to watch her for a little bit. Get a feel for what she's up to."

"I think you're right." Poppa rubbed his hands together in delight. "We are going on a stakeout."

"I reckon we are." I looked at him and smiled. "Even though we only get to see each other during these investigations, I do love being with you."

"What about that boy?" He referred to Finn.

"I love him, Poppa. I do, but. . ." My heart sank, taking my breath away.

"You can't have us both." Poppa told me something that made things so much more difficult for me.

"I don't want to be alone all of my life." I gripped the wheel. "Do you not like him because if I do spend the rest of my life with him, then you know you can't be here like you are now, or do you really not like him?"

There was a difference, and I needed to know why from Poppa.

"I don't want to leave you without protection. I don't know him well, and I know I can protect you. I can make sure you're okay in this job." He had such a strong voice and spoke with such conviction. "Being sheriff isn't the safest job in the world. You could be killed."

"Isn't that the risk you took all those years?" I asked and pulled into the driveway, shoving the gear shift into Park.

A horn beeped two quick times. Jolee's On the Run food truck pulled up to the curb in front of Mrs. Brown's house.

Poppa ghosted off. He left me with more questions than answers. My future with Finn wasn't what was most important right now. It was solving Gary's murder, and if I was going to get any answers about how elusive his wife had seemed, the only way was to do a little stakeout.

Duke was at the front window of the house. His nose prints had made smear marks all over the glass, and the window blinds were cockeyed.

"Hey, Jolee!" I called and waved. "I need to talk to you! Don't leave."

"Sounds good!" she called with the Styrofoam bowl of soup beans I'd gotten for her at church earlier today. She was doing her Sunday rounds for Meals on Wheels.

Jolee had a heart of gold. When she decided to open her food truck business, she had a mission to also give back. Meals on Wheels was a perfect volunteer job for her, and she had the perfect vehicle for it.

I heard Mrs. Brown greet Jolee when I walked around the side of my house so I could let Duke out into the backyard to burn off some energy.

"I'm sorry, buddy." I was greeted with the dancing dog at the back door. He jumped up a couple of times to say hello before he took off in a dead sprint, circling the yard a few times until he found the perfect scent, where he finally used the bathroom.

He darted back and forth a few times then dropped his ball at my feet. I threw it for him. Then he sauntered back up with his tongue hanging out of the side of his mouth.

"You're a good boy." I scratched his head a few times.

The gate rattled open.

"What's up?" Jolee came in the gate. Duke ran to the very back corner of the yard and quickly returned, dropping the ball he'd retrieved at Jolee's feet.

"Go get it!" She gave the ball a hard throw, sending it back to the corner.

"How many more deliveries do you have?" I asked.

"Mrs. Brown was the last one." Duke once again dropped the ball at her feet, and they started the fetch and throw game, doing this a few more times as we talked.

"Are you busy?" I asked.

"I was going to go home and sit outside, since it's so nice, with one of those masks I got at the Dixon's Foodtown while I read on my book-club book." She grinned. "You'd love it. It's a cozy mystery about a campground, and it's set in Kentucky."

Any books set in Kentucky were always enjoyable to read, since we lived here.

"It's a hoot. There's this group of ladies called the Laundry Club Ladies, and they solve crimes." The way she described it didn't sound like it was too different from life here in Cottonwood.

"I'll have to read it." It sounded interesting and fun. "I wonder if I can solve the murder in them?"

"I challenge you to read them. But other than that, I'm not doing much." She shrugged. "Not that Ben matters, but if we were dating, we'd be grilling out and going over the menus for the diner and my truck."

"I can do that while we stake out the victim's house."

"You mean like a real-life Laundry Club Ladies moment in the mystery I'm reading?" She lit up. A huge grin crossed her face.

"I guess, if that's something they do." I clicked my tongue a few times for Duke to come. "I think your food truck would be a good disguise."

"Sure. I'm all in. Now?" she asked and gave Duke a few pats down his back since he'd dropped himself on her feet.

"Now." I walked over to the door. "Come on, Duke. I'll give you some treats."

He jumped to his feet and darted into the open door.

"I'll be in the truck," Jolee called on her way out of the backyard. I heard the click of the gate, so I knew I didn't have to go out the back door to make sure it was locked.

"I promise we will go for a walk when I get home." Duke had followed me to the front door. He looked at me with sad hound-dog eyes that made my heart melt. "I said, I promise."

He sat down. There was a little hope in his eyes that I'd change my mind and take him, but I didn't. I grabbed my purse, phone, and keys and locked the front door behind me.

Jolee had already started the food truck.

"Where to?" she asked.

"They live on Liberty." I remembered reading Scott's report and trying to recall their house, but I'd not.

The food truck headed down Broadway toward Main Street, then Jolee took a left on Main. The way she gripped the wheel when we passed Ben's Diner made me decide to start talking because I could tell she was trying not to look.

Ben sure did break her heart, and that made me mad, but he was really a nice guy.

"What did you think of church today?" I asked.

"Really, Kenni, you don't need to save my feelings. You've never asked about church, and I know you're only trying to keep me from thinking about Ben." Jolee was one of the smartest people I knew.

"I don't like seeing you hurt. That's all." I looked out the window and watched us pass by the shops, making a plan in my head to go see Ruby and Viola tomorrow, now that I needed to make sure Mama didn't become the next suspect. "Are you going to the town council meeting tomorrow night?" We passed Cemetery Lane. It made me wonder where Poppa was.

"You know I am. I have to make sure no one tries to keep me from getting my monthly permits." She was talking about Ben yet again.

When she first started her food truck, she had to file permits in order to pull up and park to sell her food. Ben gave her one hell of a time. Anyone could protest her parking somewhere, but hopefully no one would.

"I'll be there. I think Bradley Ines is going to be there with his lawyer. She has a vendetta against me and my family because years ago, Poppa put her parents in jail, making her an orphan." I held on as she turned down Lake Street.

Soon we'd be on Liberty.

"She basically told me she had it in for me and would do anything to make sure I paid for putting her client in lockup without proper counsel." I knew it wouldn't fly in court if she did try to do something, but I always had to cover my back. "Now Mama has confessed just by opening her mouth that she'd borrowed the only piece of evidence I had tied to Bradley."

"The umbrella?" Jolee asked.

"How did you. . ." I started to say, but she didn't let me finish.

"Tibbie told me. She said that she didn't know how to tell you because your mom really did get on the waiter when he brought her a Long Island iced tea and not a sweet tea like she'd ordered. Then he told her she needed the Long Island because she was too wound up."

"He did?" Not that he wasn't right about Mama needing a little relaxation, but that he'd say something was out of character from what his wife and Venetta Stenner had said about his quiet and shy personality.

"That's what Tibbie said. She also said that your mama was outside the church waiting on Viola or somebody to go to the reception, and Bradley was walking out after the photos. He handed her the umbrella after Edna Easterly had gotten a wedding party photo of them in front of the church using the umbrellas." Again, something I wished Mama would've told me before I had gone all hog wild on Bradley.

I'd given her ample time to do such a thing when she was begging me to come back into the barn so I wouldn't get sick.

"Not that I think she did kill him, but it would explain why Bradley's umbrella was missing." Jolee slowly drove past the house. The car in the driveway looked like the same car I'd noticed in the funeral home parking lot, and it had the same plate I'd asked Scott to run for me.

"Go down and turn around. Park a few houses back." When I did a stakeout, I liked to be facing the main road so I could exit quickly. In this case, we'd be facing out toward Main Street.

"I'm sure you'll figure this out in no time. What's up with the wife?" Jolee put the truck in Park and climbed into the back of the truck.

I could hear her opening the refrigerator door, but I kept my eyes on the house.

"I'm not sure. She didn't really want to talk, but she did seem surprised when I told her he was working for the catering company. That's why I want to see what's going on over here." I sat up a little when I noticed a car had pulled up. A couple girls got out of the car before it zoomed off, but I couldn't get the license plate of that car.

Jolee got back up into the driver's seat with a couple of cans of Diet Coke for us and a bag of popcorn.

"We might as well snack on something." She set everything in the console attached to the front of the dashboard. She flipped on the radio. "Do you have any other suspects?"

It wasn't too long after that, maybe ten minutes, that I noticed another car had pulled up, and the same two girls ran out of the house and got into it before it zoomed off. This time I did get the license plate and texted it to Scott.

"The spouse, of course. Honestly, she wasn't even on my radar until the way she acted at the funeral home." Normally I didn't discuss cases with my friends, but Jolee was a good ear to lean on, and right now I was in an emotional turmoil with not only being threatened with being sued by the bride, but also by Bradley.

Add on the fact that Mama was pushing me down the aisle when I wasn't even engaged, plus trying to figure out what to do about Poppa and the dynamics of marrying Finn, if it ever did happen, was weighing heavily on me. Those issues made this whole murder thing seem like a cakewalk.

"She was very shocked, like I said, about her husband working for the catering service. And it is odd because we did find some money on him where it did raise a red flag about why he'd be doing the wedding. Why was he at this wedding?" I asked and saw Brenda walk out of the house. "There's the wife."

"She doesn't look too upset to me," Jolee noticed.

"She sure doesn't, does she," I agreed. "Follow her," I instructed Jolee after Brenda had gotten into her car and pulled out.

Brenda didn't seem to notice us as she drove down to Main Street and hooked a left then an immediate right into the bank parking lot.

Jolee pulled the food truck up along the curb like she would on any given day, making it less obvious we were following Brenda in case she did notice us.

We watched as Brenda got out of the car and made a cash deposit in the ATM.

"Now what?" Jolee asked.

"Now I put going to bank to see Vernon Bishop with a warrant to see the finances of the Futches on my list." There was something tied to this money. I could feel it in my bones.

"Do you want me to keep following her?" Jolee asked.

"Nah." I needed to get back to the department so Scott and I could go over the clues we'd already collected as well as the game plan for the week. "Do you mind dropping me off at the department?"

"Not a bit." Jolee was able to drive the road parallel behind Main Street to avoid going back by the diner in fear of seeing Ben. She didn't say that, but I knew her well enough to know exactly how she would do anything to avoid seeing him.

"Let me know if you need something else." She smiled after she pulled up to the top of the alley, where she let me out.

"I know I don't have to say it, but I'm going to anyways." I held the door open and looked at her. "Don't tell anyone what we did today."

"I won't." She made a crisscross with her finger over her chest. "I'll call you tomorrow."

"Call me if you need me before that." By her reaction, I knew she was aware I was talking about Ben or just an ear. I shut the door and walked down the alley, eager to tell Scott what I'd just witnessed.

CHAPTER FOURTEEN

W e used a big whiteboard on wheels with dry-erase markers. We could easily turn it around if someone came into the department. If we had a bigger department, I would've loved to have a room for investigating.

Scott had gotten a photo of Gary taped up on the board. There was one of Bradley and now Mama, both listed as suspects.

"I got all the photos from Edna's thumb drive." He stood at the whiteboard with the black marker in his hand as he scribbled names under them. He also had made bullet points under their names with the facts. Only the facts. "I also gave the guests at the wedding our email here to send in their photos. We already have a few, but I'm expecting a lot more."

"Make sure you get Polly Ryland's." I remembered her snapping a lot at the wedding when she wanted me to move my big head out of the way, plus I'd seen her gushing over all the decorations at the reception, the phone never leaving her hand.

I stood back and watched while he finished writing what we knew. At some point during the investigation, all of this would make sense.

"I have a list of guests printed out in the file." Scott was so good at taking his instructions and following through without me even having to ask him a second time.

"We need to add Brenda Futch to the list." I gave Scott a brief rundown about what Jolee and I had witnessed, before I called the judge to ask for a warrant for the financial records for the Futches.

Judge agreed I had enough evidence with the money alone to get the warrant, and he'd fax it over to me by morning.

"Where did you put the thumb drive from Edna?" I asked him.

"I downloaded them onto our hard drive, so you should be able to pull them up." He looked at his watch.

"Great." I walked over to my desk and sat down, wiggling the keyboard mouse so my computer monitor would come to life. "I'm going to take my time this afternoon to go through them. All of them. Wow."

There were more than a thousand photos.

"There's a lot of them too." Edna Easterly must've taken a photo of every single detail of this wedding. "You go on home. You've worked way too much this weekend, and I'm sure you've got something or someone to go home to."

"Are you sure?" he asked, eluding my hopes of him divulging any information about the mention of someone.

"Of course. Get out of here." I waved to the door. "You need to take some time before we really hit it hard this week. I'm hoping to find some photos in here of anyone near Mama when she was having her little tizzy. As well as all the movements of the waiter."

The good thing about Edna's photos and being so many, I could tell from the initial few I'd looked at so far that there was almost an exact timeline of events.

Scott headed out, leaving me alone with the photos and the whiteboard. There had to be something in them, and really I didn't have much to do over the next couple of hours. Duke would be fine at home.

Edna had gotten Jasmine before the wedding, sitting with the bridesmaids, to a private moment with Jasmine and her father. If I clicked fast enough through them, it was like a reel in a movie.

Click, click, click.

The movement of my finger pushing down the mouse button was the only sound piercing my ears.

One after the other was white tulle, bright teeth, and huge smiles all around.

Until.

Edna's photos of the groomsmen in their room where they were getting ready.

They appeared to be pretty normal—pats on the back for Dickie, the passing of the bourbon bottle where they were all either taking a gulp or filling up a flask, to the endearing one of Bradley handing the ring box to Dickie, and the usual one where they were all posing.

Nothing here that caught my eye as I clicked on through.

Click, click, click.

One after the other, the photos scrolled. Each time Bradley caught my eye, I'd pause for a moment and search the surroundings to see if anything jumped out.

Then it did.

Jasmine and Dickie had gotten their wedding photos taken before the bride walked down the aisle. From an arm's length, one of the photos appeared as the rest. Everyone facing forward, the bride and groom in the middle while the wedding party stood on each side. Groomsmen on one side, bridesmaids on the other.

Until.

I clicked the mouse to zoom in, and in one particular photo, Bradley's eyes were shifted to the right as though he were focusing on Jasmine.

The pose changed to where the groomsmen were surrounding Jasmine, and there was an ever-so-slight touch from Bradley that would've gone unnoticed by anyone else. Edna had used a rapid-fire shutter speed during the event, and unless someone had their eye on Bradley, you'd never have seen his subtle and quick gentle touch on her arm, where she slowly eased it away and glared at him.

"Do you think they were having an affair?" Poppa had ghosted himself over my shoulder.

"I don't know. I do know Bradley is certainly not over her after all of these years. What is that song with Garth Brooks about showing up at the wedding to toast the bride and groom?" I asked, trying to recall how it went exactly, though it didn't matter. "For some reason it's escaping me."

"I don't listen to all that new country stuff." Poppa snarled. "Give me some Hank Williams and some Patsy Cline, then we can compare."

Poppa drifted off into some twangy, sad song while I clicked and clicked rapidly to when the bridal party had come to the reception.

"They played the song." Thank goodness Edna was click happy with the camera, because she got the sequence of photos that I recalled from when the bridal party came into the reception and he sang the song so loud before the waiter walked by with the shot glasses.

"He took two." I had thought I'd seen him just do one shot. "Look at the waiter."

"What?" Poppa stopped belting out the music. He gave his attention to the screen.

"The song was playing when the bridal party had come to the reception. Bradley didn't miss a note. He waltzed in and started singing just as the waiter passed, like it was rehearsed this way. It was flawless." I clicked through the sequence of photos to show Poppa a few times before I zoomed in on Gary's face, where there was really more of an amused look.

It was Bradley's face that stopped me in my tracks.

"Have you ever stood at the intersection of a crosswalk and thought the coast was clear to walk. You take the first step off the curve, and a car zooms by, sending you into a heart attack?" I asked Poppa and blew up Bradley's face when he really took a moment to look at the waiter. "That initial wave of shock and feeling when you almost got hit and killed?"

"Yeah." Poppa was trying to figure out where I was going with this.

"That's the look on Bradley's face when he did finally look into Gary's eyes." I pointed to Bradley. "But not Gary. He has a very satisfied look on his face. As if taking pleasure in Bradley noticing him."

"They know each other." Poppa slid his ghostly glance to me. "Good work, Kenni bug. Good work."

When I printed the photos off, I made sure I did it one at time, processing them in order by writing the order on the back of the photo. I'd even blown them up so you could clearly see the facial expressions on both. Once I had what I felt was some sort of interaction that warranted another conversation with Bradley, I taped them up on the whiteboard and took a couple of steps back to gain some perspective.

As clear as day, there was true recognition of the other.

I picked up the file and opened it, laying it flat on my desk. I used my finger to scan down the page until I found Janice's phone number. Right next to it was Bradley's.

"Bradley." I was a bit shocked he'd answered. I'd decided to call him first and if he hesitated then call Janice. "I have a few photos at the station that I would like you to look at. Do you think you could call Janice and see if the two of you could come down here really fast so we can get this cleared up and your name out of it?"

"If that's the case, I don't need her." He was giving up his right to counsel. I had to make it very clear he was doing so.

"You are being recorded," I quickly murmured and hit the record button. "It's my understanding that you are giving up your right to have counsel present while you are going to come down here and look at photos taken from the wedding reception of Jasmine and Dickie Dee?"

"Yes. If it's just photos I need to ID. Do you know how much Janice is costing me?" He laughed.

"I'm sorry. I do not, but I'm here, so if you'd like to come down here and take a look, or you can call Janice to meet you here as your counsel." I stated it again for the record.

"Nah." He played it off, not realizing what I was about to hit him with. "I can come on down. I was about to leave town, anyways. I can do it on my way out."

"Leave town?" I asked.

"Yeah. The wedding party is continuing the fun by going on a group honeymoon."

My heart stopped.

I was not sure if he said goodbye first or I did, because he threw me for a big loop.

"Judge, it's Sheriff Lowry." I knew I had to talk fast. "It's my understanding the bride and groom from the murder investigation are taking the entire wedding party on their honeymoon, and they are leaving tonight. I can't let that happen. We've yet to have time to interview the participants as well as the guests."

"Yes. Yes, sir." I listened to the judge clarify what I was asking him to do as he talked from the other end of the line. "Yes. I need you to make sure they stay in Cottonwood until I can get all of their statements."

"Well, sir, we are a bit shorthanded tonight. Seeing how it's just me and a Sunday." He was trying to talk me into having the twelve come down tonight to give their statements. "Yes, sir. Yes, sir. Fine."

I eased the phone back down on the cradle.

"You didn't win that one, did you?" Poppa asked.

"Nope. He is going to call the district attorney and have her call Jasmine and Dickie to let them know they can't leave town until they give their statements. Which will be tonight." I hesitated even though I knew I needed to call Betty Murphy and Scott Lee to come in.

Neither of them protested too much, but there was a lot of hemming and hawing on Betty's part.

Before too long, the door of the department flew open.

Jasmine Dee had her hands fisted at her sides with the look of the devil on her face as she glared at me, gritted her teeth, and bolted into the department with her daddy and Janice by her side.

CHAPTER FIFTEEN

"This is ridiculous." Jasmine started to throw down before Janice stepped in front of her.

Jasmine's head bobbled to and fro trying to get a look at me.

"Here we go again." Scott sighed and gestured for one of the bridesmaids to come sit down at his desk.

"I will be filing a lawsuit against you and the city of Cottonwood tomorrow while my clients are on their way to their honeymoon. Now you've ruined this for them. We will be seeking damages for not only the cost of the reception venue since they weren't able to get back their money from the caterer or the venue." Her lung capacity was amazing. She didn't stop to take a breath. "This lawsuit will also be introduced at the town council meeting tomorrow night so they are well aware of the taxpayer dollars their sheriff is using up over some ridiculous theory in her head that is based on her own mind instead of evidence. Or how she's trying to cover up her own mother's wrongdoing."

"You get her, Kenni!" Poppa danced on his feet. "Don't you let her talk about your mama like that."

"The quicker you stop talking, the faster we can get these people out of here." I didn't show any emotion as I stared back into Janice's eyes. There was no fear where I stood. "I am the sheriff. This is how I run an investigation in my town, and if I let any one of these witnesses leave town before I can get a statement, it would be negligent of my duties the citizens have elected me to do." I pushed past her, grabbed some statement sheets off the edge of Scott's desk, and called my biggest concern. "Bradley Ines."

"Oh no. I think we've already talked to Bradley," Janice protested, coming between me and Bradley.

"Bradley and I have already discussed the reason I need to talk to him again." I picked up the file and opened it, taking out the extra photos I'd run off before he'd gotten there since I'd already turned the whiteboard around so no one could see the timeline I'd created with them.

After I handed the photos to her, she quickly thumbed through them.

"I'm going to need time to talk to my client before I let him answer any questions you have to say regarding photos." Janice looked at Bradley and gave a slow shake of her head. "I'm sorry, but you may not talk to him at this time."

"So what?" Bradley scoffed and shrugged at her. "I don't get to go on the trip?"

"I'm sorry. No. I can't take care of you and all of them before the flight leaves in the morning. You're going to have to go later in the week." There was a little more discussion between the two of them, and I excused myself for a brief moment when the door opened and Mama was standing there, gawking in.

"Mama." I took her outside. "What are you doing here?" I asked.

"What are all of them doing here?" she questioned me back.

"You shouldn't be here," I told her and ushered her back to her car. "Is that Viola?" I glanced up when I noticed Viola walking around the alley.

"Mmhmm." Mama's brows pinched. "She told me something was going on, and I was left a little uneasy after I felt like that woman in there accused me of killing the waiter, so I decided to come on back down here, because I've been thinking about this."

"We've been thinking about this." Viola pointed between the two of them.

Oh boy. It was awful when Mama got to thinking about something, but with the two of them thinking, it was a travesty. Nothing good.

"What are you two up to?" I asked before I plugged my fingers in my ears. "Don't tell me. I don't want to know." I burrowed my fingers deeper. "Lallallaaa," I sang out when I noticed Mama and Viola's lips were moving at the same time.

Mama grabbed my forearm and tugged it down.

"Fine. Me and Viola will do our own snooping," Mama warned. "Come on, Viola. Let's go get a sweet tea from Ben's Diner."

A few hours later, I was sitting in the chair on my back porch. I was exhausted from all of the statements and just the entire day's activities. There was nothing more discovered about the murder than when I had woken up.

Poppa had disappeared, and Duke was pouting because I'd left him alone all day even though I'd given him almost an entire box of treats.

"Knock, knock." Finn had come through the gate, and I'd not even heard him. "Goodness, you must be tired if you didn't hear me come in."

"I'm mentally spent from Mama and Janice," I told him and took my feet out of the seat of the empty chair. It scooted a little away from me when I gave it a little shove so Finn could sit down with me. "Mama and Viola are up to something, but it'll die down, because they were so excited to tell me about their grand plan but then gave up literally one minute into trying to get me to listen."

"Do you want to talk it out?" he asked.

"You have your own crimes to deal with." I sat up and rested my elbows on my thighs, leaning forward into him. "Unless you want to come back and work at the sheriff's department. I'm happy to make room."

"You are doing great. Don't let that lawyer get to you. Her parents must've been pretty bad if they were both convicted." Finn kissed the tip of my nose. "What do you have so far?"

He really did know all the facts already, but going over everything—how Gary was knocked in the head, giving him the fatal blow, and the umbrella made it a hate crime—once more with him did start to make a picture in my head.

"I have these photos from Edna's camera, and you can see Gary and Bradley recognize each other. There's a connection, but I'm not sure what." I sighed and stood up, since I knew it was getting close to bedtime and I needed some sleep. "I think I'm going to go back to visit Gary's wife tomorrow and show her the photo. Maybe she'll recognize Bradley."

"Good idea." He got up and stood in front of me, holding both of my hands down to his side. "You keep doing you. You are a wonderful sheriff, and you're smart. You have a great sense of intuition, and if you feel this is the lead you need to take, then that's the lead."

"I sure do miss you in the department. Seeing you every day and getting these little pep talks are nice." I rolled up on my toes and kissed him.

"You know I'm here for you." There was a tone in Finn's voice that I'd never heard from him, but I sure had heard that same tone with my daddy when he talked Mama down from something.

My gut clenched.

Was Finn thinking about proposing? Was Mama's dream finally going to come true?

He was right about one thing. I had a very good intuition.

CHAPTER SIXTEEN

"Kenni, Kenni." I heard my mama calling me. My eyes opened. It was five a.m.

I groaned and pulled the covers over my head, knowing I'd been dreaming or having a nightmare about Mama.

"Kendrick Lowry, you get out of that bed right now!"

My eyes popped open. I threw back the sheet and bolted to an upright position.

"Mama." I grasped the edges of the covers when I saw her standing at the bedroom door and pulled them up to my chin as Viola White's eyeballs looked over Mama's shoulder into my bedroom. "I guess it wasn't a dream."

"We have no time to talk about your dreams. Now get up and get your clothes on," she insisted. "Me and Viola have got some news about this here murder. It proves I didn't kill no one."

"Slow down, Mama," I told her. "Why don't you and Viola go get a pot of coffee on while I get some appropriate clothing on. Then we can talk about what it is you're all in a tizzy about at five a.m."

My voice did stress the time so she'd get the point.

"I already let Duke out and fed him." She turned. "Come on, Viola. Let Kenni have her privacy."

Privacy.

That was one word Mama didn't understand the meaning of. Especially when it came to me. Daddy told me not to give Mama the extra key to my house after I'd moved in and had the locks changed. He said she'd be over here all the time, letting herself in. She sure did.

But so did Daddy. If he knew Duke was home all by himself, Daddy would come over and get Duke, take him to their house, and let him be spoiled all day.

Now, I couldn't entirely believe it was Daddy's idea because every time Duke did visit, Mama always had something delicious on the table and insisted she had no idea Daddy was bringing Duke home. Which meant I had to pick Duke up, in turn making me stop by their house. Then have supper, which was always a four-course, Southern-style meal accompanied by an after-supper drink.

"Must be nice to still be able to sleep in while we are out there solving the murder," Viola's under-breath grumble was really meant for me to hear her.

"Ohhhhhh." I gave myself one of those long sighs to prepare myself for whatever it was they'd decided to look into. "At least they aren't dead," I told myself as I peeled back the warm covers and put my feet on the floor.

Instead of throwing something on just to go see what they'd stirred up, I decided to get dressed. Viola was right about one thing—there was still a murder to be solved.

There was no way I was going to go back to bed, so I went straight to my closet and grabbed one of my clean sheriff uniforms. The brown outfit did nothing for my looks, but at least it was something I didn't have to think too hard about putting on, like most people when they went to work. That part of it didn't make me mind wearing the same outfit day in and day out.

I strapped on my utility belt because I knew if I carried it out into the kitchen, Mama would've been all touchy-feely over it, and then one of us might've been dead.

I padded down the hall and heard whispering between them, as much as two older women can whisper.

"I think she'll be fine." Mama was confident in her words.

"I don't. She ain't gonna like us lying to her." Viola really got my attention, but they stopped talking when they heard me, so I took a left into my only bathroom.

"I'm going to brush my teeth and wash my face," I called down to them and barely shut the door once I was inside. I kept my ear open.

"Do you reckon they saw us?" Viola asked.

"If they did, they don't know me or you." Mama again was adamant about something to where Viola was not convinced.

"That's a lie, Vivian Lowry, if I ever heard one," Viola protested. "You told me you thanked him for the umbrella, and trust me, his lawyer, that woman, has probably learned everything about you she can because she's gonna be at the town council meeting tonight. They are going to announce the lawsuit against the sheriff's department, Kenni, and the county."

"That only means Kenni has today to look into things to prove I'm innocent, and me and you just got the evidence we needed."

"Lordy be." I jerked open the bathroom door and bolted down the hallway. "What on earth did you two do?"

"We, um. . . we, um. . ." Viola shuddered, pushing her fingers in her gray hair. A sure sign of nervousness.

"Go on, tell her." Mama's hand whacked Viola's arm. "You're the reason we are here, and you've been dying to tell her."

"You tell her. You said she would be upset." Viola's eyes dropped to my gun. "And with that gun on her, she looks a little scary."

"Viola, you've seen me with my belt on a million times." I sucked in a deep breath, my eyes shifting between the two. "What is it you two did?"

"Don't you need to fix your hair?" Mama's brows furrowed.

"What. Did. You. Two." I wagged my finger between them. Duke was scratching at the door. "Do?"

"Duke wants in." Mama was trying to waste time.

"He can wait."

"Fine. Last night when you caught us in the alley behind the department. . ." Mama gulped.

"Go on." I gave a hard head nod.

"We put a tracker on Bradley Ines's car."

My jaw dropped. That was the last thing I'd ever think Mama would do.

"Viola saw it on a television show, and we ordered one. Did you know you can get packages next day from the internet?" Mama looked as pleased as a dog with two tails.

"You did what?" I still hadn't gotten past the initial shock of the two of them buying a tracker.

"It was really easy like." Viola nodded, shaking the large turquoise beads that lay in three strands around her neck. She looked like she was about to have a fancy photo shoot with all her makeup on, hair styled, and full of jewelry. "You have to sync it to your phone, which Toots Buford knew exactly how to do when I took it down to Tiny Tina's."

"Yep. You just pull the sticky thing off and pop it up underneath the car, anywhere." Mama talked like they were experts. "And you pull up that little app thingy Toots put on my phone, and it showed this little car going on the road."

"Show her, Viv," Viola encouraged Mama.

"No." I put my hand up. "I don't want to have any more information. Do you understand what Viola just said about Janice suing me? Now you are an accomplice to a suspect." I pointed directly at Viola.

"No. I don't. No. I. . ." Viola had lost her words. "I was being a friend to Viv. If that's a crime"—she threw her wrists out in front of her, making the bangles jingle-jangle—"arrest me."

I unclipped my cuffs off my utility belt.

"If you insist." I walked over.

"Kendrick Lowry!" Mama hollered. "I'd be ashamed. You don't even know what we found out when we tracked him."

"I don't want to know."

"You would if you knew it was the victim's house. Where he was in there for at least an hour." Mama did have some interesting information.

"Go on." I put my cuffs back on my utility belt.

Duke had given up on the door. He was either running around the yard or had decided to lie by the door.

"That's right. We tracked him straight over to Gary Futch's house." Viola crossed her arms. "I think we got us a connection. I said Bradley and Mrs. Futch are having an affair, and they got rid of the husband. I saw the same thing on my crime show."

Not half bad, though I didn't tell them that.

"Did they see you?" My mind came up with a few ways I was going to need to spin this so Mama didn't go to jail for obstruction of justice, not to mention how I wasn't able to keep my own mother in check.

"No." Viola shook her head. "We made sure they didn't, but I can't tell you how shocked we were."

Mama nodded her head slowly.

"They were more than a suspect who might've killed that woman's husband. They were in there for a while. Do you understand what I'm saying?" Mama asked, eyes wide open.

"They didn't see you?" I needed to ask one more time.

"Not me." Mama's chin slid to the right, her eyes looked up toward the ceiling, and her lips pursed. She tried hard not to look at me.

"You?" I turned to Viola.

"I was only trying to make sure the tracker stayed in place because he was driving like a bat out of hell and hit the curb." Viola had me for a loss of words. "What? He hit the curb, and it could've fallen off."

"Did he see you?" I asked again since it was clearly the only answer I cared about.

"It's hard tellin'." She sighed. The coffeepot beeped. "Oh good. Coffee."

"Did anyone see her?" I asked Mama. "You better tell me now, because if you don't and someone springs it on me, I won't be able to protect you or me. Do you realize you've not only put yourself in jeopardy, but also Viola and me?"

"It was Viola's idea." Mama was quick to call her out.

"I mentioned how I saw someone on the television," Viola spoke up.

"It's the semantics." Mama used her favorite word to get herself out of a sticky situation and used the task of getting us all a coffee to avoid looking at me.

"I don't need to know any more." I put my hands up. "The less I know, the better."

"This can't be all bad, Kenni bug." I looked up at the door and saw Poppa standing on the other side.

I walked over to the screen door and popped it open.

"What on earth is wrong with that dog?" Viola had leaned over from the kitchen chair far enough to see out.

Mama grabbed a tea towel out the drawer and swiped the countertop on her way over to take a gander at Duke. Poppa must've been keeping Duke quiet and content while I was inside questioning Mama and Viola.

"Viola, you forget he's a very important poo-leece dog. My granddog." Mama clicked her tongue.

"Go," Poppa demanded with a snap of his finger.

Woof! Duke barked and darted into the house.

"See?" Mama grinned like a possum. "He loves his granny."

"Mmhhhmmm," I hummed and stepped out of the way of the door so Poppa could enter as a living being would, but he didn't. I sighed and shut the door. "Back to this little tracker situation."

I wanted to bring Poppa into the conversation because I knew he was able to think a little clearer than me, since I was trying to weed through all the hemming and hawing Mama and Viola had going on between them. Each was pointing the finger at the other.

"Let's go back to the theory of the affair." Poppa's ghost stood in the corner.

"You mentioned Brenda and Bradley might be an item." I picked up the cup of coffee, walked over to the table, and sat down.

Mama was digging through the refrigerator freezer.

"Where is your coffee cake?" Mama asked, her head stuck all the way in.

"I don't keep coffee cake, Mama." I knew this was going to open a can of worms—I just didn't realize it was going to be a bucket of them.

Viola White let out a gasp. Mama's face contorted.

"This is why you aren't married. Don't you understand people want to feel welcome when they pop over?"

"Mama! I'm not married because I don't want to be married!" There was a knock on the screen door. "I don't want to get married. Do you under-stand?" I said on the way over to the door.

"I understand." Finn stood on the other side of the screen.

CHAPTER SEVENTEEN

"They are infuriating," I seethed on the phone with Finn after I got Mama and Viola out of the house, so I could go back to Brenda Futch's to check out exactly why Bradley Ines had gone there this morning.

I rubbed my neck. There was a sudden pain. I couldn't help but wonder if I'd gotten whiplash from watching Finn dart out so fast. Had he heard me say I wasn't getting married?

"You scared that boy off." Poppa's voice carried from the back seat because Duke was standing on the passenger side seat of the Wagoneer with his head stuck out of the window. His ears flapped back from the wind, his tongue was out, and his tail beat a rhythm on the seat back, showing his heart's happiness.

"I had no intentions of doing so." I tried not to think too much about why Finn had run off so fast, but it didn't take a big college degree to figure it out. "I only wanted Mama to see what her and Viola had done to compromise the investigation."

"Kenni bug, your mama and I only want what's best for you." Poppa was playing both sides of the fence.

"You and Mama are on opposite teams." I glanced in the rearview mirror so I could look at Poppa's ghost. "She wants me to marry Finn. You want me to break up with Finn. Either way I'm losing." I gripped the wheel at the stop sign at the end of Free Row and took a left on Main Street.

It was too early to go check out Mama's story at Brenda's house and too late in the morning to sneak over to the Tattered Cover Books and Inn, where Bradley was staying while in town, to get the tracker, which I had planned on doing.

It was best to go to the department and check in with Betty and Scott before I got started on the full day of investigating.

I had to find something to take to the town council meeting. I wasn't sure what, but going to Tiny Tina's was definitely in the schedule, as well as going to Dixon's Foodtown to talk to Toots Buford.

"If I don't get married, Mama is going to die because she thinks I'll be labeled an old spinster. If I do get married, I can't have you." My eyes stung. My nose flared as I tried to keep the emotional feeling of never seeing Poppa again deep inside, buried where it'd been for years before his ghost appeared. "I've lived without you before, and it wasn't easy. But I love Finn too. I can't deny him a life where he could be happily married and with children."

"Are you telling me you've got that mothering instinct?" Poppa smiled.

"Goodness, I don't know, but I do know Finn is really good with kids." Memories of Finn and me working as a team here in the sheriff's department for a few years before he became sheriff in Clay's Ferry flooded my mind. "Life in Cottonwood isn't murder all the time. We did some fun things together, like hand out the cute sticker sheriff's badges to the kids at all the events. Finn was really good with the kids. So much better than me."

"You would be a fine mother." Poppa's thick and wiry brows knotted. "I guess it's not fair of me to continue to ask you not to be with him. He is a good man, Kenni bug. I know he'd protect and care for you. Provide a good life."

"What are you saying?" I asked and looked in the rearview mirror. He wasn't there. I twisted around to see in the back seat. He was gone.

Beep, beep.

A horn called out from behind the Jeep.

My eyes shifted to the side mirror where someone had stopped at the stop sign behind me, signaling me to go.

I threw my hand in the air and hit the gas, pulling out on Main Street, but not without the feeling Poppa had something drastic he was going to do. Not with me. Not with my relationship with Finn.

But him.

"What's wrong with you?" Betty Murphy sat at her desk across from me with narrowed eyes. "You ain't right today."

"I'm thinking about this case." I had settled down in front of my computer once Duke and I got to the station. Duke was content with the treat Betty had given him and he'd lain down in the dog bed next to my desk, on his back, legs in the air.

"That's not thinking about a case." Betty was quick to point out. "I've sat here looking at you for years now, and that's not a look I've ever seen during an investigation. You go from this." She made a very still face. "To this." She grinned. "Then to this." She frowned.

She nailed every single emotion I was feeling with the thoughts of Mama, Finn, and Poppa in my head that traveled to my heart. I loved each of them so dearly, I couldn't disappoint one of them without affecting the other.

"You can tell me what's wrong." Betty's eyes softened. She was so mothering, and I loved that about her, even though we were in a working environment.

Scott had yet to get to the department, which left plenty of room for me to talk to Betty, but there was nothing she could really do since, well... Poppa.

Could you imagine the look on Betty's face when I told her my poppa was a ghost, not to mention a ghost deputy who only appeared when there was a murder in Cottonwood? Or the fact that I had to choose a life with him in it and Finn not? Why, she'd report me to the loony bin in a split second.

I decided to keep my mouth shut and lie.

"I am thinking about Jasmine and Dickie Dee. When Gary's body appeared, I immediately went into sheriff mode." Technically this wasn't a lie. It was the truth, but not what she was asking about. "I didn't take into consideration their feelings about me ruining their big day."

"No, you didn't!" Mayor Chance Ryland stood at the door between Cowboy's Catfish and the department.

Mayor Ryland was debonair and fit for a man in his sixties. His black hair was slicked back, his strong jaw tensed. He'd started running, dying his hair black, and growing the goatee along with doing a lot of manscaping after he'd started dating Polly Parker, who was now the First Lady of Cottonwood.

"Do we have to do this now?" Polly had walked in behind him. "I'm going to be late for my nail appointment."

Polly looked at her petite hands. The diamond rings on her fingers clicked against each other as she picked her cuticles.

She looked up at me with her big puppy-dog eyes. Her perfectly lined pink pouty mouth contorted, her nose snarled, and she spat between the veneers I was sure were stuck in her small mouth.

"He's been throwing a dying duck fit to come in here and talk to you, but I told him to let it be." She moved her hands down to her belly. Slowly she rubbed it counterclockwise. "I told him to watch his stress at his age. After all, we've got a little bundle of joy coming into this world who needs her daddy."

"You're pregnant?" That was the last news I'd expected to hear. Especially after I'd thought men of a certain age weren't able to have children, much less one of Mayor Ryland's age. The age of Polly's own daddy.

"Yes." Polly squealed like a pig. All of her five-foot-two-inch, one-hundred-pound frame bounced on her toes with delight. "We are going to be parents."

"What, are you going to be, like, ninety when that kid graduates from preschool?" Betty Murphy slammed her lips together. Obviously she hadn't kept in her private thoughts as she'd hoped.

"Betty Murphy!" Polly shrieked in horror. "I told you. I told you we'd be made fun of."

Polly twirled around and darted back into the restaurant.

"We are going to have a talk about this lawsuit later today." He gave me and Betty a hard look before he turned to go after his wife. "Honey. She's an old woman. Old women have no filter," we heard him saying.

"Am I wrong?" Betty asked me with a straight face, before we both started to laugh so hard we didn't even hear Scott come in the department door.

"I must've missed something really good." He dropped a piece of paper on my desk.

I picked it up and looked at it.

"The warrant for the bank." I smiled. "Good work, Deputy Lee." I had my first stop of the day. "Before I go, we need to talk about something I found out today."

"What's that?" he asked.

"I can't tell you how or who told me yet." I knew I had to keep Mama and Viola's little stakeout under wraps. "I've got two witnesses who aren't ready yet to come forward with information, but they swear they saw Bradley Ines visiting Brenda Futch's house."

I stood up and walked over to the whiteboard. I gripped one side and pushed it back to face the room.

I picked up the dry-erase marker and popped the lid off so I could write. I drew an arrow from Brenda's photo to Bradley's photo.

"These two know each other." I dotted the end of the marker on the board next to each one of their names. "I'm not sure in what capacity. I only know their visit wasn't just a friendly one. It just so happens he was there for a while, and let's just say they didn't end the visit by screaming."

"Do you mean they were more than friendly?" Betty asked.

"There wasn't any physical activity, if that's what you mean, seen by the two witnesses."

"Two witnesses?" Scott asked.

"Alright. It was Mama and Viola. Viola had come up with this big, grand scheme she's seen on one of those crime shows."

"Those shows are going to be the death of law enforcement." Betty shook her head. "People just think they can do what they show on television."

Who was Betty trying to kid? She was the biggest gossip in all of Cottonwood, and normally she was the one who broadcast what was going on with cases better than any news station.

"Anyways, they put a tracker on his car when he was here yesterday with Janice. They tracked him, and he went to the Futches' house. After I go to the bank to see exactly what was going on with all the money in Gary's pocket and his finances, I'm going to go straight over to see Bradley and find out why he went over to the victim's house." I had a solid plan and hoped for some good answers to present to the town council tonight.

Not that what the town council said or thought mattered. It didn't. They couldn't fire me, and I wasn't quitting, but the townsfolk sure could fire me at the next election if I didn't have some sort of news to report in my defense, since I knew Janice was going to present her case tonight as if we were in a court of law. She'd use the townsfolk as the jury, and I wasn't ready to be tried for a case I'd yet to solve or even gotten a good handle on the suspects.

Plus if I didn't come up with something for Mama, because I knew it was where Janice would go, she'd present at the council meeting that I was going after her client so Mama wouldn't be a suspect, and that was not true.

"Now that I have the warrant for the bank and the Futches' accounts, I'll be able to see if there's some sort of money trail tied to Gary and why he'd have so much cash in his possession at the time of death."

Something deep in my bones told me to follow the money, besides Poppa's whispers here and there.

"I'm telling you to follow the money." Poppa appeared next to the whiteboard.

"Do you want me to go to the bank so you can pay a visit to Bradley?" Scott asked. "Or I can go see Bradley."

"No." I went back to my computer and hit a few keys to bring up my email. "I want you to go through some of these photographs sent in by some of the wedding guests. I hope we can see some action shots with something in the background with any sort of evidence."

"Sounds good." Scott came over to my desk and sat down. "I'll let you know if I see something."

"What can I do?" Betty asked.

"Just man the phones and make sure everyone else in Cottonwood is all good." I didn't anticipate any sorts of calls coming in that she and Scott couldn't take care of. "I'll let you two know if I find out anything at the bank."

I gave a couple of clicks to my tongue.

Duke jumped to his feet and trotted to the door with me.

Cottonwood First National Bank was literally a block down the road. Since I wasn't really sure what we were about to find out with the warrant, I'd decided to drive. If I did find something out that had to do with driving somewhere, I didn't want to waste what daylight hours I had left before the town council meeting by walking to the department to fetch the Jeep.

It was easiest to drive.

The parking lot was empty, which was to be expected since I arrived right as they'd opened. The teller line was along the back wall, and the offices were in the front behind glass walls. There was literally no privacy for Vernon Bishop, so when our eyes caught, he couldn't run from me.

He waved me in and stood up.

He wore a nice three-piece black pinstripe suit. His hair, which was prematurely gray, was neatly combed to the side with the perfect amount of gel. His cologne was a nice touch. He was much younger than he looked— fifteen years older than me, to be exact.

"Sheriff, it's awfully early for you to do some banking business," he greeted me. His eyes shifted to the piece of paper in my hand. "I'm guessing this is about Gary Futch?"

"It sure is." I put the warrant on his desk and slid it across.

"Have a seat." He gestured, sitting himself, and picked up the paper. "This is for Mr. Futch."

"It sure is. We found thousands of dollars in his pocket at the scene of the crime. He was working for two hundred dollars, and well, I just can't seem to wrap my head around why he'd want to cater an event for two hundred dollars when he had thousands. Which makes me think he was either in debt and trying to make as much money as he could to pay something off, or he was at the wedding for some other reason. There's no better place to start than his banking needs."

"I'd love to help you, but Mr. Futch doesn't have an account here."

"What about Brenda Futch?" I asked.

"This warrant is for a Gary Futch." Vernon had me, and he wasn't budging. He put the piece of paper back on the desk and slid it back across to me. "Now, if you had a different warrant, I might be able to help you."

"Vernon." My head tilted. "You and I both know that I'm going to come back here with another warrant, so you might as well save us time and just give the sheriff's department what I need."

"I'm sorry. I can't do that without a warrant, because I'm not a mind reader. I can't tell what you're thinking or who you need what for." Vernon wasn't stupid. He knew good and well what I was there for.

"Fine. Then can you tell me if there's anything illegal going on?" I asked in case there wasn't any need to get a warrant for Brenda. "Anything that might be of help to the investigation into the death of Gary Futch?"

"Brenda is a businesswoman. She's got a good business for one of the oldest professions for women." He shrugged.

"Is she a Mary Kay consultant?" I wondered, recalling all the makeup on her face.

"I can't answer that, but she does make good money for women." He was talking in signals.

"I'll be back." I didn't have time for charades and decided to just call in the warrant to the judge in hopes it'd be sent into the department by the time I got back from my little visit with Bradley Ines.

This time I didn't bother driving the Jeep. Instead, Duke and I walked down to the inn, since it was located in the block between the department and the bank. Plus it was next to Ben's Diner. Not that I needed more on my plate, but Jolee was my best friend, and stopping in to get a biscuit and gravy along with a cup of coffee was the icebreaker I needed to pick Ben's brain about why he was being a jerk to Jolee.

Duke followed alongside of me. I texted Finn as we walked on the sidewalk down Main Street.

Want to meet me at Ben's for a quick breakfast? I texted.

It didn't take him too long to text back, telling me he'd already gotten to Clay's Ferry, and he'd see me tonight at the town council meeting.

The thought of the meeting made my stomach curl. The fact I was going to have to defend myself wasn't something I had planned on worrying with.

The Tattered Cover Book and Inn was the only place to stay in downtown Cottonwood. The inn outside of town was the other. Both filled up pretty quickly, and from what I'd heard from the rumblings at the wedding, both places were completely booked.

"You stay right here," I told Duke and gave him a good scratch on his head. He sat down in front of the hotel before he dropped down to lie on the concrete already warmed up from the sun.

Nanette, the owner and operator of the hotel, who took great pride in offering refreshments and cold iced tea to her inn guests, was in what I called the refreshment room. It was a room located to the right as soon as you walked through the front door of the inn.

She was busying herself at the bar where she had small breakfast offerings for her guests. Food like hard-boiled eggs, fruit, bagels, toast, and all sorts of juices and coffee.

"Good morning, Kenni." She turned around with a large smile on her face. "I thought I was going to be spending the rest of this week cleaning up from the wedding guests. I understand a few of them are staying because you aren't letting them leave."

"I'm sure you've heard all sorts of things, Nanette." I smiled. "How are you doing?"

"Fine. My sciatica has been hurting, going up and down the steps. It's been hard to find any good help these days." She put her hand on the small of her back and pressed on it. "Are you here to question some of the guests? I can clean up real fast and let you use this room."

"That's a generous offer, but I'm here to see Bradley Ines." I pointed to the steps that led up to the rooms. "Do you recall his room number off the top of your head?"

"Five." She held up her hand. "I know because he had the bachelor party after-party here, and I had many complaints that night." She snorted. "That morning."

The front desk phone rang.

"I've got to get that." She hurried out of the room without me able to ask her what she was talking about.

Instead of waiting on her and asking her about that night, I decided to make a stop to see her before I left to get the details in case they were important. I went ahead and walked up the steps to where the rooms were located. I made my way down to room five and gave the already cracked-open door a little knock.

"Bradley," I called into the crack. "It's Sheriff Lowry. Can we have a quick talk?"

I took a step back and stared at the door with my hands resting on my utility belt.

Nothing.

I reached out again and knocked a couple of swift times with my knuckle. I pulled my hand in and rested it on the utility belt again.

Nothing.

I looked down the hall both ways before I decided to take a step forward and give one last knock, this time hard enough to open the door enough to see inside.

This time there was something.

"He's heard his last crow." Poppa appeared over my shoulder.

Bradley Ines was lying on the floor, blood pouring out of his head.

CHAPTER EIGHTEEN

"Anything?" I asked Max Bogus when he walked out of the room after he declared Bradley Ines was in fact... dead.

"Blow to the head. Didn't see it coming." He shook his head. "I'll send over a final once I get a better look at the body."

"Thanks." I nodded and looked over at Nanette. She was crying uncontrollably at the top of the stairs.

After I'd found Bradley, I'd called in backup, which was Scott, before I made a phone call downstairs to the Tattered Cover Book and Inn desk from my phone. When I'd asked Nanette to come up, she immediately bolted up the steps. I told her what had happened in room number five, and she'd not stopped crying since.

It wasn't until after she'd watched Max Bogus and one of his employees carry Bradley's body out that she started hyperventilating.

Since I didn't have my Jeep parked right outside of the hotel, I had to tell Scott to bring a camera and his deputy bag so we could collect evidence and process the scene.

"I just can't believe this." She used a piece of torn-up tissue paper to wipe her seeping nose and wet eyes. "He seemed like such a nice boy too. He was the life of the party. Even last night when they were—" She clamped her lips to stop whatever it was she was about to say.

"They were? Who were? What were?" I asked.

"It was all in good fun. Really, Kenni." Nanette was preparing me for something. I gave her a tight smile. "I mean, he had you down pat."

"He was mocking me?" I didn't mind good fun. I could take it. "He was pretending to be me? To whom?" I asked to her nod.

"The wedding party. They were all in the refreshment room having some pizza, and I thought they were play charades." Her hand fluttered. "You know that game where—"

"I know the game." I interrupted her.

"You should've heard—" She stopped talking. Her brows pinched. "I mean he sounded just like—" She stopped again. "What happened to him?"

"The wedding party is here?" I didn't realize they were staying in this one particular place since they'd already come down to the station to give their statements. I figured they were all gone by now.

"Yes. They are leaving tomorrow. They told me last night they couldn't get a flight out today and they were hoping Bradley was cleared." Nanette knew more than she'd initially let on when I first walked into the inn.

"You know. I overhear things." She gave a quick shake to her head.

"I'm going to need to keep room five locked tight until we can get all the evidence collected we need. You do understand, don't you?" I noticed Scott pop his head out of the door.

"Yes." Nanette's face grew solemn. "Can I do anything?"

"I'd appreciate it if you didn't give any statements to anyone or tell anyone about this." Nanette was also a part of the gossip circle in Cotton-wood. "We don't want the killer to know our next move. Or what we know."

She nodded with a determined look on her face before she headed back down the steps.

I took a deep breath in order to clear my head from one conversation to the one I was about to have with Deputy Lee.

"Did you find anything?" I asked Scott after I walked into the room.

"Cash. Lots of it." He pulled open the small wooden desk drawer. The desk was sitting in front of a window facing Main Street.

"I think we need to print," I told Scott. He pointed to his bag on the bed. I walked over and pulled out a pair of gloves and the dusting powder inside.

Dusting for prints was a tedious and messy job.

"The money. Check the sequence of bills." Poppa made a good point. "Then we need to go back to the bank to see if those came from there."

"Or I need to talk to the wedding party again." I nibbled on my lip as more theories popped into my head.

"What?" Scott asked.

"I was just thinking out loud." My brows pinched. "When you talked to Jasmine and Dickie, did they say anything to you about Bradley?"

"No. They've been friends since college. You knew that. Are you thinking it was one of them?" Scott asked.

"I'm thinking it's got to be someone in the wedding party, unless Brenda had come here last night." My mind twirled with reasons Brenda had a motive to not only kill her husband, but now Bradley. "Have you gotten any word on the warrant for the bank?"

"Not that I've seen." He looked at his watch. "It could be there now."

I gave Scott the powder to continue to dust for prints while I made a walkie-talkie call to the department.

I reached up to the walkie-talkie strapped onto my shoulder and clicked the button. "Hey, Betty." I looked out the front window of the room and down to the sidewalk. Duke was still sitting there like a good boy.

"Sheriff." Her voice screeched over the intercom.

"Did you see a warrant come over the fax for the Cottonwood First National Bank?" I clicked off.

"I heard the fax go off, but I'd not checked it yet. Hold on." She clicked off. I waited in the hall while she got up to look, knowing it would take her a minute to get her footing, grab her glasses, and go check the fax.

There'd been a small gathering down the hall. All of the guests were facing toward room five. I didn't recognize any of them as the wedding party. But I still wanted to talk to the bride and groom.

The walkie-talkie beeped to life. "Yes. It's right here."

"Thanks, Betty. I'll be right over to get it and drop Duke off." I clicked off the walkie-talkie and headed down the steps. "Nanette." I tapped the counter to grab her attention. "Can you tell me what room the Dees are in?"

"The honeymoon suite on the third floor." She caught me off guard. "What? They are on their honeymoon, even though their best friend is. . ." Her voice fluttered off, as did her gaze.

"I didn't realize you had a honeymoon suite." I pointed. "Top of the stairs then what?"

"Oh no." She plucked a tissue from the box sitting on the counter. She dabbed her eyes. "You have to go around the back to the alley. There's an old elevator car to take you up there. Very romantic."

"Okay." I walked out the door. Duke jumped to his feet, and we walked down the street, taking the road leading to the alley of the department so I could grab the warrant.

"Kenni." Polly Parker Ryland ran out of White's Jewelry. "Kenni, I was wanting to speak with you for a minute." She rubbed her belly.

"I'm sorry, Polly, can I come back later?" I asked but thought "later" as in "much later, like a year."

Polly worked for Viola at the jewelry store, which was right up Polly's alley. She loved and wore anything that sparkled and had her initials engraved on it. Much like Viola, Polly's fingers were lined with the best of stones.

"It'll take just a second." She swung the jewelry store door open.

The gray awning above the double doors of the shop flapped in the light breeze. White's Jewelry was written in calligraphy across the front windows of the shop with two solitaire diamond outlines on each side.

"Really, Polly, I am." I was walking and talking at the same time to hurry past her.

"I'll tell Chance to lay off harassing you about the—" She slid her head right and then left before she put her hand up to the side of her mouth and whispered, "Murders."

"Murderssss?" I made the plural very obvious.

"Mmhmmm." Her perfectly lined pinky lips hummed. "Nanette told me about the best man. You scratch my back, I scratch yours. Or at least keep Chance off of your back."

She pushed the door open a little wider, holding the bottom with her foot.

"Fine." How long could whatever she had to say take? "Stay," I told Duke.

He let out a low grumble before he dropped to his belly, letting the late-morning sun give him a little sunbath.

"What's going on?" I stood right inside of the jewelry store. The glass counters around the perimeter of the inside glistened with all sorts of sparkly baubles.

"Do you like any of these?" She gushed over one of the counters that had a sign on top of it that read Here Comes the Bride. "What about a pear shape?" She swung her hands overtop of the display as if she were on that show, *The Price Is Right*.

"Polly, I'm sorry. What is it that you wanted?" I asked. "Not that I don't like visiting with you, but I'm a little busy."

"I know, the murders and all, but I was just thinking." She had a nervous look on her face I'd not recognized. It was as if she were trying to come up with something on the spot.

"Spit it out." God knew she has those fancy veneers in her mouth to spit anything out, I thought to myself.

"Will you have a baby shower for me?" she blurted.

"I, um. . ." I stuttered for the words, trying to figure out why of all people in her life she'd ask me.

I started sweatin' like a pig who knew he was for supper.

She shifted her weight back and forth on her feet.

"Of course." I had to get out of there. She was making me nervous now. "Yes. I'd love to. I'll have it at the church. The auxiliary women will be delighted to help."

"Thank you." The Southern dripped out of her mouth like thick honey. "You're the best, Kenni! I'll repay you when you have a bridal shower," she called out to me on my way out the door.

"Oh!" I turned around. "I'm not into fancy diamonds." I shrugged. "I think I want my grandmother's ring to wear when I get married."

I pushed out the door into the sunlight. Duke jumped to his feet. I glanced back right before the jewelry store door slowly closed. Polly's petite nose was curled, as was the edge of her top lip.

"Last stop." I scratched and led the charge down the street. "Who cares about a ring?" I said to Duke.

"I'll tell you this, that boy ain't getting your granny's ring," Poppa protested. "I'll never tell them where it is."

"Come to think about it," I talked to Duke so no one would think I'd lost my marbles.

Heck, maybe I had. Maybe Poppa wasn't there and the loss of him even after all of these years still had an effect on me.

Maybe.

I shrugged and went on anyways.

"I have never thought about the ring since I moved into your house." My mind circled back to some years ago, and how I'd found it in Poppa's bedside table. A table I'd opened many times since then.

Daily, to be exact.

I kept my gun in there, when in reality I should've immediately put it in the gun safe, but you never knew about Free Row. At any given moment, a gunshot in the air was exactly what the rebels living on Free Row needed when they got a little rowdy at night and hopped up on too much juice.

If you knew what I meant.

"Don't you worry about it. When the time is right, I'll present the ring in a place where the right man can find it." Poppa was making my decision to get married or not to Finn easier than I could've hoped.

"I'm sure it'll all work out fine." I turned the corner of the building and headed down the alley. "Marriage is not on Finn's radar, anyways."

There was no way I was going to bring up this morning, when Finn had stopped by and heard me yelling at Mama and Viola about me and marriage.

Something I didn't want to think about, nor had time or the head space.

"Any news from Max?" I asked Betty as soon as I walked in the department door.

"Hello to you too, Duke." Betty took the lid off the treat jar. She took one out and gave it to Duke. She rubbed his back while he ate it. "Good boy for using good manners."

"Okay. Hello, Betty." I got the hint loud and clear.

"Oh, hi, Sheriff." Betty's beady eyes snapped at me. "Just because you're the big cheese around here, still doesn't mean you can't use manners. And no. Nothing from Max, but your mama called. She heard about Bradley and insists you call her."

"She did." I looked at the fax from the judge on my desk to make sure it was the exact warrant I needed for the bank.

"Mmhmmm." Betty hummed.

"I mean she heard about Bradley?" Betty didn't look up at me. "Or someone here told her about Bradley?"

"Kenni, you know that I'm part of the prayer chain for the church, and when I heard the call come through, I had to start praying for him. Regardless if he killed Gary or not, he still needs praying for." Betty typed away on the computer.

It appeared she was typing in the report from the witness statements.

"Did you come across the statement from Jasmine and Dickie Dee yet?" I asked and folded the warrant then put it in my jacket pocket.

"I just finished typing it." She peered at me from overtop her reading glasses.

"And nothing stuck out to you?" I would pore over them later this afternoon when I got back from the bank and my little visit with Brenda Futch.

"There was one event that stood out from the groomsmen."

"Yeah? What was that?" I asked.

"They said the bachelor party got a little out of hand, and they all smiled fondly." Betty had my attention. "When Scott asked Dickie about it, he put a note on the report that Dickie didn't want to discuss it now that he was married."

"Did anyone say when the bachelor party was?" I wondered. "Preacher Bing mentioned something about a bachelor party when I questioned him about the premarital counseling sessions."

I flipped through Gary's file and looked at the photos we'd taken of the cash from his pocket.

"No, but I can find out." Betty grabbed the phone and waved me off. She moved the receiver down past her chin and said, "I'll let you know."

"Duke is staying here." I gestured and mouthed the words because she started talking to the person on the other end of the phone.

She nodded two quick times and waved me out with her free hand.

Since my Jeep was already down at the Cottonwood First National Bank and I needed some thinking time, I took my time walking down the alley which would bring me to West Oak. I went ahead and jogged my way across the street, where I took a right to walk down the sidewalk and left into the bank parking lot.

It was like Vernon Bishop was waiting on me when I walked in.

He waved me on into his office.

"I got a call from the judge. I figured you'd be here soon." Vernon pulled some papers off the printer behind him. "Here is Brenda's account. Here is a sum of money she deposited as soon as the bank opened. I'm guessing you wanted those serial numbers too."

"How did you know?" I asked and looked to where he was pointing his finger.

Oddly familiar. I pulled my phone out of my pocket and thumbed through to my email where Max had mentioned he'd emailed photos of the cash in Gary's pocket. Though I knew the cash Brenda had deposited wasn't the same since Gary's cash was in an evidence bag in lockup, it would be interesting if there were some similar numbers.

"My goodness." I couldn't contain the shock. "These are in the same serial number family. Which tells me whoever gave Gary the money in his pocket came from the same place."

"How do you know it wasn't Brenda?" Vernon asked. "I guess she got it from someone since we don't have that serial sequence here before her deposit. Maybe she gave Gary some?"

"Could've." My eyes scanned down Brenda's bank statements. "She makes large deposits every other day."

Vernon's chair creaked when he sat back. His fingers folded, and his elbows tented out and rested on the arms of his chair.

"I don't see a business on here." I thumbed through the papers.

"That's her only account. It's a personal one."

"You mentioned her business. I'm assuming a woman would run one like Mary Kay or Tupperware." I was fishing for some answers.

"Yes. She's a businesswoman." Vernon shrugged. "She does that whole quarterly tax thing, I guess."

"Have you ever seen her come in here with anyone else?" I asked.

"Maybe one or two of the girls that work under her." He didn't seem like he was too concerned or worried about it.

"Thanks, Vernon." I had no idea why I was thanking him since I had to get a warrant, but like I had with Betty earlier, I guessed it was best to play nice. Especially since I knew Vernon would be at the council meeting tonight.

"Kenni, um, Sheriff Lowry," Betty's voice cracked over the walkie-talkie.

"Excuse me." I took the papers, folded them up, and stuck them in my back pocket as I headed out the door to talk back to answer Betty's dispatch. "I'm here."

"So is Janice Gallo. She's ranting and raving about her client, Bradley Ines, and demanding to talk to you." Betty's voice twitched with nervousness.

"You can tell her I'm out of the office doing my job, and we can talk at the town council meeting." I clicked off and scrolled the volume button down.

There was no way I was going to let Janice Gallo run my investigation now that her client was dead. I was the sheriff, and this was my town.

She was going to have to deal with me tonight at the town council meeting.

CHAPTER NINETEEN

With Brenda Futch in mind, I got back into my Wagoneer and pulled out left on Main Street from West Oak, headed back to Liberty Street where the Futches lived.

I wasn't sure what I was going to say to her, other than what was her job and where did she get all this money.

There were some answers that needed to be heard, and I knew she was a missing link, if not the link.

I pushed the walkie-talkie button and scrolled up the volume. "Deputy Lee."

"Go ahead, Sheriff."

"I am heading over to Liberty Street to talk to Brenda Futch. Are you in the vicinity?" Not that he would be far. We could reach each side of town in ten minutes going at a snail's pace.

"I can be. On my way." He clicked off.

The On The Run food truck was pulled up tight to the curb in front of Lulu's Boutique. Which made me think of Lulu McClain, which made me think of Mama and Viola getting tracker information from Tiny Tina's.

I glanced at the arms on the old clock on the Wagoneer dashboard and knew Tiny Tina's was open, but the gossip didn't get started until well into the afternoon. That was when everyone was fully caffeinated, with their lips flapping a million miles a minute.

It was something I had to mentally prepare myself for. It was the weeding through all the gossip to find bits and pieces of the truth that exhausted me.

But first I had to deal with Brenda. More importantly, how she was connected to Bradley.

"What are you doing here?" Brenda's voice carried past me, as did her gaze. "I have already given my statement to Deputy Scott Lee, just like you said. Now what do you want?"

"We can either talk about this out here." I looked behind me. There was a group of neighbors who'd gathered on the lawn across the street. They didn't even try to cover up their stares. "Or we can go inside where there's a little more privacy, so we can discuss your banking business and the large deposits you've been making at the Cottonwood First National Bank."

I grabbed the warrant from my back pocket and with a good flick of my wrist unfolded the paper.

She leaned in and took a look.

"It's a warrant I used to get your bank records." I pulled the bank records I'd gotten from Vernon out of my other back pocket and handed them to her, leaving it to her to open them.

"I have reason to believe you and your husband knew my new victim. And what you and your husband had to do with the Dees' wedding." I stood there waiting for the invite to go inside.

I had no reason not to conduct my business on her front porch, so I continued, because apparently she didn't care who heard our business. The hedges between her house and the next-door neighbor's shook to life. I glanced over and realized we now had an audience listening in from all sides.

"It's been brought to my attention your husband was stabbed with Bradley's umbrella. Plus eyewitnesses had identified Bradley Ines walking in and out of your house before he was killed." She still didn't budge. Brenda looked at me with a blank face. I got louder. "I have reason to believe you and Bradley are in some sort of tangled-up web, and well, I'm going to find out exactly what that is."

There was a glimmer of anger in her eyes, giving me a little hope she was going to take this inside.

"I can keep going, and much louder, for everyone here on Liberty Street to hear me if you'd like." I gave Brenda a second to think about it before I opened my mouth.

"Fine." She closed her eyes in frustration before she sucked in a deep breath, letting it out as she used the toe of her shoe to hold the storm door open. "You can come in."

I took the first step inside and walked into a family room with a couple of couches, chairs, and a television that was on the local station. There were two women sitting on the couch, and they quickly got up to go into the other room.

"Family? Friends?" I asked.

"Employees," she said with a flat tone.

"Oh."

I heard the ghost of my poppa before I saw him sprinkle himself in ghost form on the other side of the room. "I know where I recognize Gary from."

I'd forgotten all about how Poppa had made mention of recognizing him when he saw Gary lying there at the reception.

"It's the oldest business around." Poppa shook his head. "I arrested them a few times down on the town branch."

"Oldest business?" I asked out loud. "That's what Vernon said."

Brenda slowly looked over her shoulder to where Poppa was standing and turned back to me with big eyes.

"Who are you talking to?" She shivered.

"I never arrested them, just tried to get them off the street. Didn't look good for Cottonwood, and Gary insisted it was an up-and-up business. Sex will never be banished." Poppa had a way.

"Here I thought you sold cosmetics." I scoffed at my naivety. "What exactly is your business, before I jump to any conclusions?"

"I own a sorta dating service." Brenda sat down on the edge of the couch and gestured me to sit.

"Is that what we are calling it these days?" I asked.

"I run a legitimate escort business. All my employees are offered health insurance and other benefits." She tugged on a footstool next to the couch and opened a secret file cabinet. "You can look through any of the files. No warrant necessary."

"Why didn't you disclose any of this information to Deputy Lee?" I wondered, sitting back on the couch and pulling out my notebook and my phone from the front pocket of my shirt.

"He didn't ask what my occupation or business is." She was a sneaky one.

"Sheriff Kendrick Lowry interviewing Brenda Futch." I had hit the record button on the memo app of my phone and set it on the arm of the couch closest to Brenda. "Why don't you start from the beginning to when you were first contacted by Bradley Ines."

It had become increasingly clear this had to do with Bradley and the escort service. This was the tie between the two victims I'd been trying to get at for the last forty-eight hours, almost.

"Would you like something to drink?" she asked, as if we were here for story hour.

I declined. "Just start at the beginning," I encouraged her. Since I'd learned of what she was loosely calling an escort service, my suspect pool just got a little bigger.

I had no idea what was going to come out of Brenda's mouth. What if one of her girls killed Gary and then Bradley? This was going to shake down and shake down now.

Poppa had ghosted himself next to me. He was ready to listen.

"Time sure hasn't been kind to her." Poppa eyeballed Brenda. "They were young when they started out this business, and many times I had to arrest them. Put him in the clink for a night or two."

I shifted, so Poppa would get the hint to hush so I could listen.

"My business is no different than any dating app three-fourths of Cottonwood has downloaded on their phone." Brenda had taken the defensive side right off. "About two months ago, one of my employees got into a little trouble. We needed a lawyer, so Gary and I spent a lot of what we had in fees to help her out. Gary had taken a part-time job at That's a Toast catering service with Venetta Stenner to help pay some of the bills."

Brenda looked at me from up underneath her brows.

"A couple of months ago." I restarted her tale for her.

"Yes. We were sitting right here. That's when I got a call from Bradley

Ines. He said he was the best man in a wedding taking place locally, and they were coming to town for a bachelor party. He also said he'd dropped the ball, and this was a last-minute booking for a little fun. Now, for the right price, we were able to offer him a package that suited his needs. Since Gary and I were in a bit of a pinch, as was Bradley with his timing, we didn't find it unnecessary to charge him a little more, seeing how we had to pull some of our best employees for the job."

I was so glad she'd left out what skills her best employees had.

"Bradley's group was the handsy type. If you know what I mean." She crossed one leg over the other, dangling her foot in the air. "Nothing illegal. Just immoral, if you catch my drift, and it was my employees' fault too. So I can't blame Bradley and that crew."

She paused and looked out into the room.

"One of my girls fell head over heels in love with the groom, Dickie. So much so they'd even started a little fling over the past couple of months. He thought it was a fling, but my employee did not. Unfortunately with cell phones these days, one of my employees took photos of the bachelor party and started to blackmail Dickie after he'd tried to call if off with my girl."

I could see this playing out since I knew a couple of the characters involved.

"I don't see it as blackmail as much as him paying her for her escort services, so when Bradley Ines called Gary about the blackmail, Gary told him such."

"He told him to think of the blackmail as paying for her services?" I wanted to be very clear because this was something I was going to have to go talk to Dickie Dee about, and that was a whole nother can of worms to open.

"We don't think of it as blackmail. He used her for services, and we saw it as services rendered. We also told Bradley and Dickie they needed to hire That's a Toast for the reception, so we could get the last payment in exchange for the photos."

"That's why Gary worked for Venetta." I shook my head. "And that's why he had all the cash on him. I'd like to see the photos."

"Gary handed them off to Bradley when they were at the wedding reception," she said. "Our business with those two were done."

"I don't recall seeing any photos at Bradley's hotel." Scott and I had combed the place. There weren't any photos.

"Then Dickie has them. That's not my problem. Bradley came over here to let me know our business was done and that he didn't kill my husband." She was talking about the time Mama and Viola had tracked him here.

"What about your employees who had to do with all this?" I asked. "Are they available to talk to Deputy Lee, and do they have an alibi for the nights in question for both of my victims?"

"Yes. I have all their on-duty records as well as cell phone pings. I told you, I keep a close eye on my escort business. I am more than happy to have them talk to him." She was so confident in her delivery of her story, I truly found myself believing every word as she told it.

"What about you? It seems like the killer is plucking off victims one at a time in fear they might tell the secret of Dickie's affair. Aren't you worried you're next?" I asked.

"I never thought of it." Her brows pinched, as though the realization she could be the next victim was a real possibility.

"Didn't Preacher Bing mention something about Dickie taking over Jasmine's father's business and an argument there?" Poppa reminded me of what I'd considered a silly argument, but it turned out it wasn't so silly, after all.

"Yes, but not if those photos get out or a whisper of what he's done to Jasmine gets out." I knew firsthand what type of poppa bear Jasmine's dad was. It was him leading the charge to sue me and the city of Cottonwood because I ruined the wedding reception.

"Looks like we got one on the line, Kenni bug." Poppa rubbed his hands vigorously together.

"What?" Brenda uncurled her legs and inched up to the edge of the couch.

"I'm talking to myself." My eyes narrowed. I stood up. "I have to go, but I'll call Deputy Lee to come here and take the statements of your employees. We will need to do a check on them, but I also want him to sit out front. Make sure no one comes to pay you any unwanted visits while I'm buttoning up who killed your husband."

"I don't think it would do too good for business if you planted a Cottonwood deputy's car out front of my business." What she was saying was loud and clear.

"What if it was a few houses down?" I offered.

"That would be fine." She blinked a few times, and a sadness fell upon her face. "I do hope you find out who killed Gary and Bradley."

"I think I'm on the right track." I let myself out of the house and got in the Jeep.

Instead of calling Scott on the walkie-talkie and letting the dispatch, Betty, hear what I'd found out, since I needed to make sure it was kept under wraps and not let out to the entire prayer chain, I called him.

After I dialed Scott's number, I put the phone up to my ear and stared out the windshield down Liberty Street. With my free hand, I cranked the manual window down to let in some fresh air. It was a gorgeous spring day, and fresh air was always good for the brain. Right now my brain was reeling with ideas on how I was going to get in front of Dickie without Jasmine and her father hammering down on me.

"Hey, Scott. I wanted to call you instead of going over dispatch." I was about to tell him everything I'd found out about Brenda and Gary's business when I looked at the car driving slowly past.

As if in slow motion, the driver of the other vehicle turned their head as they were passing me. The eyes blinked open, and we stared at each other, lingering for a moment too long as we realized who each other was.

Then time sped up and fast. The engine of his car roared to life when he punched the gas and zoomed down the street.

"Dickie Dee," I gasped. "He's driving past the Futches'. I need you to get to the Futches'." I jammed the phone between my ear and shoulder, pulling the gear shift into Drive and making a U-turn in the middle of the road, barely missing the car parked across the street.

"Dickie Dee was being blackmailed by Gary Futch." I gave Scott just enough information to make it dire for him to drop everything and get over there now. "My fear is Dickie is trying to silence anyone who knows what is going on. And I can't help but to think if Jasmine's father knew, Dickie would be out of the family business for good."

Scott and I hung up the phone as soon as I rounded the corner of Liberty where it met Cemetery Road. I threw the phone on the passenger seat. With one hand on the wheel and eyes on Dickie's taillights, I reached under my seat and pulled out the old beacon police siren.

I brought the siren's suction cup up to my mouth and licked it before I put it out the window and stuck it up on the roof of my Jeep. My finger slid down the side of the light and flipped the switch on, bringing the loud siren to life and making the light flash.

With both hands on the wheel, I maneuvered the old Wagoneer through the winding, single-lane road in the cemetery, hot on Dickie's bumper.

His car was a little four-door, which made it easier for him to get around the cars parked along the edge of the tombstones where their owners were visiting with their loved ones.

"Whoa!" Even Poppa's ghost was hanging on tight to the arm of the door. "Don't be hitting no one or no stones."

"I'm not." I had to slow down a smidgen when we got to an active grave-side service.

"This is a send-off." Poppa's sick sense of humor about me barreling through, practically ruining the service for whoever was being laid to rest, wasn't sitting well with me.

"I don't like this at all." I kept the wheel steady even though my heart rapidly beat to the small breaths I was taking in. "We are coming to the front and then on Main Street."

It was like I had a premonition of what was going to happen.

"If someone doesn't let him out of the cemetery, I'm afraid he'll just pull out in front of them." I didn't have to finish my thought about him hitting someone's car in the process because just as I said it, Dickie jerked a right out of the cemetery, barely missing getting hit by a car going northbound on Main Street.

By the time I got to the entrance of the cemetery and the oncoming traffic heard the siren and had stopped, Dickie had already zoomed past Ruby's Antiques and turned left off Main onto Richmond Avenue, where I knew he'd be heading for the country. Not a risk I was going to take to lose him there. He could easily slip onto a small gravel country road, hide in the brush, and wait me out all day.

"Dang." I beat the stirring wheel with the palm of my hand and pulled over at the rear of Cottonwood Cleaners.

"You'll get him. He can't hide forever, especially with the lawyer coming tonight to the town council meeting. I know Jasmine's dad is going to be there about the lawsuit. Then you can spring it on them." Poppa had always been able to play it really cool when it came to hauling in suspects, but in the case of Dickie, he ran from me, and that itself was criminal enough for me to bring his heinie in and make him sit in jail.

"Tonight." One by one I peeled my fingers off the stirring wheel, keeping my palms on it. I looked at each one of my fingernails. I moved my gaze to the rearview mirror and took in the woolly worms sitting above my eyes, better known as my thick eyebrows. "I could stand a good manicure and brow wax."

"And some good homespun gossip." Poppa reminded me just how much I could learn from my little break at the local salon, where I was guaranteed to hear something I'd not yet heard. "And Ruby did give you her time slot if you needed it."

"Then Tiny Tina's it is." I put the Jeep in Drive and took a left out of the Cottonwood Cleaners parking lot to get back on Main Street.

Tiny Tina's was located in the strip mall along with the dentist's office, The Pawn, Cottonwood Federal Savings, Hart's insurance office, and a Subway. A few of the rockers that lined the front of the strip mall shops were already occupied by customers' spouses. When I pulled up, it was hard not to notice all of their eyes on me, wondering what on earth the sheriff was doing there.

I'd called Scott back on my way there to let him know exactly what had happened and why I was headed to the salon.

"I want to talk to the bride," I told Poppa. "I'm not sure why they aren't on their honeymoon, and I'm not sure why Dickie ran from me, other than guilt."

"We need to think about it. What if he told Bradley Ines to take care of everything? Bradley was still in love with Jasmine. Maybe Bradley was doing his own sort of blackmailing with all the information."

"What a tangled web they weave." I sighed and turned the engine off. "Let's go see what we can find out in here."

I grabbed the door handle and swept the door open. The hum of hairdryers, hissing of aerosol sprays, and smell of astringent cleaners and chemical hair dyes, mixed in with chatter, told me Tiny Tina's was full of life.

"Hey, Kenni!" Tina Bowers, the owner of Tiny Tina's, was all the way in the back of the salon, sitting on a low-to-the-ground stool in front of Polly Parker Ryland.

Tina's hands were rubbing Polly's shins, slathering on her specialty rub. Really it was lotion she'd gotten down at Dixon's Foodtown. She fancied it with drops of vanilla extract before she put it in small bottles she'd bought off the internet and slapped on some labels she'd printed off herself, making it her own brand of spa lotion.

I waved my hand in front of my face after a big spray of something made its way into my mouth.

"Pftt, pftt." I spit and rubbed my nose.

"Ruby told me you might be in," Tina called out with a big smile.

Tina loved getting her fingers all tangled up in my hair, which happened about twice a year at most. Honestly, my hair was pretty much always worn up in a ponytail, and fixing it wasn't high on my list. This was why Mama used it as a good example for losing Finn.

She claimed in order to keep a good man like Finn, I had to keep up my appearance. That wasn't how I felt, and it certainly wasn't how Finn had made me feel, but for the sake of the murders, I was willing to let Tina Bowers shampoo, blow-dry, and snip—whatever needed to be done to find the killer.

"Ladies," I greeted everyone when I walked around the counter and past the group of ladies under the pink hair dryers with their curlers snugged tight to their heads.

The sound of scissors snipping and a dry broom sweeping across the floor mixed in with laughs and stories.

"Sheriff." Each one of them stopped telling their tales and nodded with pinched smiles as I passed.

"Polly. Just the woman I wanted to see. I'm glad you're here." I sat down in the pedicure chair next to her, allowing my body to sink into the pleather chair.

"You have? What on earth do you want with me?" Polly lifted her petite hand to her chest.

"I'm going to need your help with getting your husband off my back." I knew if anyone could talk to the mayor, it was his own wife.

I planted my forearm on the arm of the spa chair and leaned over a little closer to Polly.

"I'm going to need a little more time to get the case solved, and with Chance breathing down my neck, I'm afraid he's making it a little more difficult for all the people who I need to have cooperate." I had no idea what Chance had been telling people, but I knew he could make tonight's town council meeting go smoother if he wanted to.

"Now, Kenni, you and I both know Chance is his own man." Polly shook her head. Her freshly cut short blond bob waved back and forth, not a hair out of place. No doubt Tina had plastered the strands with high-hold hair spray.

"We both know you wear the pants and Chance would do anything for you." I'd been a witness to this courtship and marriage. She knew what I was saying was true.

My brows rose when I took a look at the phone in her hand.

She slid it to the side of her leg, slipping it underneath as if I didn't see her.

"I had asked for your photos from your phone from the wedding, but when I got back to the office and looked through Deputy Lee's list of wedding guests who sent in their photos, you weren't checked off." I sighed. "That's not cooperating with the sheriff, and as the first lady of Cottonwood, you do want to make sure everyone knows that you are cooperating with me to keep Cottonwood safe."

She pushed her back into the pleather just enough for it to let out a little squeak.

"I don't mind you looking at my photos right now." She jerked the phone up from underneath her leg and used her shiny, newly painted red fingernail to tap it to life.

Tina glanced up from in between Polly's feet and smiled with a wink. She had her hair pulled up in a topknot, and it shook back and forth as she ground the pumice stone on the heels of Polly's feet. The dry skin sprinkled all over the black towel in Tina's lap like falling snow.

She batted the pad of her finger on the screen until she was satisfied she had found what she was looking for and then shoved the phone into my face.

"Here you go." Polly handed me the phone. "Swipe right."

Tina put Polly's feet back into the foot spa. The water bubbled to life after Tina flipped on the switch.

"Oh Tina." Polly laid the back of her head on the pillow attached to the back of the chair. "This is heaven."

I could hear Polly's feet moving around the rocks Tina had put into the foot spa tubs like Tiny Tina's was some fancy, high-dollar salon with their little marbles and crystals. The only person who knew those rocks were dug out from the town branch was me, her, and the woman who'd called dispatch to tell me Tina was trespassing and stealing rocks from the creek.

I told Tina we wouldn't press charges if she stopped stealing rocks and telling everyone the rocks she used at the spa were fancy. I'd not heard a word since.

"How many photos did you take?" I asked, my eyes glazing over when all the photos started to look the same.

One after the other of Jasmine, a few of the entire bridal party, but none of the waiter or Bradley Ines that I could see. Even when I used my fingers to pinch the photo bigger, there was nothing.

"You can never take too many because if you don't, then you might miss something." Polly used her finger to suggest me to flip forward. "If you look at those centerpieces, those will be perfect for the Winter Jam."

"Winter Jam?" Tina got a little excited. Her voice went up an octave. "What is that?" Tina patted Polly's leg and stood up, gesturing for me to follow her.

"Something extra special for Cottonwood that I'm personally overseeing." Polly loved being part of every single club in Cottonwood. That was really her full-time job. Her little part-time gig at White's Jewelry was just a hobby for her.

"I'm going to text myself a few of these." I quickly tapped on Select and hit a few of the reception where I'd noticed Mama's table and the umbrella sitting on it. It looked as though Mama didn't leave the umbrella outside like I thought she would've.

If the umbrella was still inside, how did it get into Gary's dead body?

That would mean Max Bogus's assessment of the umbrella being left outside was not right.

"Come on, Kenni, I've got a full day." Tina's patience was being tested. "We've got to get some of those golden highlights touched up, and those brows." She tsk-tsked. "It's a shame too. You've got such pretty green eyes. You cover them up with those brows."

"I like her brows." Polly looked up, batting her long fake lashes. "Thick brows are coming back in style."

"See there, Tina," I teased and sent myself a few more photos before I got up. "If I wait long enough, I'll be in total style."

"Heaven help us." Tina's words weren't ones of flattery.

CHAPTER TWENTY

I barely had enough time to make it to the town council meeting before it started. By the time Tina let loose of my hair, it'd been a few hours. My scalp hurt from all the chemicals, hair brushing, curling iron, and products she'd used on it. I was sure my hair was in its own kinda shock.

The skin between my eyes and underneath my eyebrows was bright red. It was as if each eyebrow had its own heartbeat, because they thumped in pain.

Just a little more here and here was what Tina had said as she applied the hot wax and ripped it right off. I knew I should've been worried when she didn't have any sort of instrument to apply the melted liquid and made me eat a Popsicle that looked like it'd been in the freezer for years so she could use the stick to apply the wax.

My stomach ached, and I was sure it was from the old Popsicle that Tina proclaimed had what was called protective covering. It was freezer rot to me.

Still, I let her do it for the sake of the investigation and to keep Polly entertained so she'd get Chance to lay off my back.

When I finally walked into Luke and Vita Joneses' basement, I barely made it just as Chance Ryland was bringing the meeting to order.

"This session is in order!" Mayor Ryland stood behind the podium in the front of Luke's basement. He banged the wooden gavel. "Let's get this meeting started."

He glanced over at Toots Buford, who had found her a new part-time job taking the minutes of the weekly meetings. I tried to attend most of them, but some days it was just easier than others. Today it seemed as if the entire town had come out to see what the word was on the murders.

Chance slid his eyes up to the back where I was standing.

"We'd like to call Sheriff Lowry to the podium so she can give us an update on the double homicide. I'm sure she'll give us some peace." I followed his eyes as they moved to the front row where Polly was smiling, her big veneers boldly glowing as she smiled at her husband.

Obviously she'd talked to him after she left the salon.

All the folding metal chairs were filled, and as I wove my way around them, I noticed practically everyone I knew was there.

Camille, Ben, Viola, and Ruby were seated in the second row. The Kims, along with their daughter and my friend Gina, were sitting in the first row with Mama and Daddy, who were seated next to Polly.

Mama gave me a little silent clap. My dad sat proud next to her, smiling.

"Go get 'em, Kenni bug." Poppa gave me a double thumbs-up and a toothy grin.

I stepped up in front of everyone and noticed Jasmine Dee, her daddy, and Janice sitting in the third row.

Edna Easterly wasn't hard to spot. She knelt down in the front. The feathered fedora choice for tonight's meeting was a lime-green number. The feather was a foot taller than any head in the crowd. The darn thing waved in the air as her head bobbled back and forth as she tried to get her hand-held tape recorder as close to me as possible.

Luke Jones was busy trying to get the pull-down movie screen in the rolled-up position as he jerked on the bottom of it a couple of times. It was being moody.

"It's fine," Chance told Luke and shook his hand for Luke to forget it.

"Okay," Luke whispered and hurried back into the crowd. He walked to the front of the basement where there was now standing room only.

"Thank you, Mayor." I bent over and spoke into the microphone. The door opened, and what was left of the day's sun fluttered in, making the figure walking in shadowy. I squinted in hopes it was Dickie Dee so I could arrest him right now on the spot. "Thank you, Luke and Vita, for allowing us this space to come together as a community to discuss not only how amazing Cottonwood is, but to also be updated on the current crime spree."

The door completely closed, and the figure stepped inside.

It was Finn.

Our eyes caught. The edges of his lips ticked up, as did my heart. I gave him a slow blink like Cosmo gave him to let him know how grateful I was for being here to support me.

"What are you going to do about this rash of murders?" someone blurted out.

"I understand y'all are very concerned." I had learned at the academy how to deal with the public by making sure they felt as if everything was about them. "Deputy Lee and I have some promising leads. He's not here because he's following up on one now."

I shot a look at Jasmine and her father. Neither looked impressed.

"What are you going to do about my clients?" Janice stood up. She crossed her arms on her chest. "Not only have you single-handedly ruined their reception as well as their honeymoon, Mrs. Dee needs to have some counseling due to the PTSD the sheriff's department has caused."

"Where is Mr. Dee?" I asked. "If we are going to discuss this here, I would like to know where Mr. Dee is located, because we need to talk to him."

It wasn't the right place for this type of chatter if I were in a big city, but around these parts, we needed every citizen on alert.

Jasmine's face dropped. She blurted out a cry before her father wrapped his arms around her, cradling his little girl to him.

"I'm sorry, Sheriff, but this is not the time and place to discuss the whereabouts of my client. But this is the time to let the good citizens of Cottonwood know we intend to sue the town and you for the damages caused to my clients." Janice was going to go in for the kill.

The chatter was above a whisper as the news fluttered over the room.

Janice was giving a little pause to let the effect of her speech settle in, giving me a glimpse of what was to come if she got me in a courtroom.

Jasmine's dad pulled on Janice's shirt. She bent down to let him whisper something in her ear.

She gave him a nod. He took Jasmine by the hand, and they got up. He cuddled her the entire way to the back of the room, where Jasmine yelled out in tears.

"I believe you will see it differently once the murderer is brought to justice," I assured not only the citizens, but Mayor Ryland. I couldn't help but notice Jasmine was on her cell phone in the back of the room next to Finn.

Finn's face was still. Stern. Serious. He gave me a slow blink letting me know he was listening to the conversation Jasmine was having with whoever was on the other end of the phone.

"If you'll just let me say a few words," Mayor Ryland interrupted and took the microphone. "I understand everyone is on edge, and we are too. We have to let the sheriff do her job in order to apprehend the killer, and if that means stopping a wedding reception or even a honeymoon, then so be it. These two men were someone's sons."

I checked out who Mayor Ryland was looking at, thinking he was giving Janice the what, when, and how, but it was Polly. She was rubbing her belly in the subtle Southern way a mama gives the daddy the what-if-it-were-your-baby look.

Then and there, I knew I was going to have to throw Polly Parker Ryland the baby shower.

"Psst, psst." My head jerked to the sound of someone trying to get my attention.

It was Mama.

Viola had made her way over to Mama, and they were looking at Viola's phone. Ruby was holding her phone up in the air with the screen pointed outward, and Mama was jutting her finger at it like she wanted me to see it.

I squinted.

"Car." Mama made the air motions with her hands of driving a car. Then she pointed to her phone. "On the move."

"Bradley's car," Poppa said as the freight fell over on me.

"Excuse me for a minute." I didn't bother giving Mayor Ryland any sort of explanation and darted through the crowd.

Edna called out a question. It didn't even register with me—it was her voice that I recognized.

"Mama, what are you doing?" I asked her when she and Viola followed me and Finn out of the town council meeting.

All four of us stood in Luke's side yard.

"What do you mean?" Mama poked herself in the chest then poked Viola's arm. "Me and Viola are the ones who tracked him, and me and Viola are going to go find him."

"Ouch." Viola groaned, running her hand over the area where Mama kept poking her.

"You tracked someone?" Finn's eyes grew.

"We are going to lose him." Mama took the first step toward the Wagoneer.

"Mama, you cannot go. This is official business." I held out my hand for Viola's phone. "I need the phone, Viola."

"Give her the phone." Finn didn't mince words. They were stern and hard.

"Fine." Viola slapped her phone on the palm of my hand. "1-2-3-4 is my code to unlock the phone."

The basement door opened.

"Where do you think you're going?" Mayor Ryland stood there, pointing back to the door. "You've got a whole lot of explaining to do to people in there. You've got to give them something. I've stuck my neck out for you tonight."

"You didn't stick your neck out for me," I told him. "You did this for your wife. But I can't stand here because I've got a very important lead."

"Yeah. One me and Viola came up with." Mama's voice had something I'd never heard her have since I was sheriff.

Pride.

"Come on, Kenni!" Poppa hollered from the Wagoneer.

"If you'll excuse me." I took off.

"Kenni, wait!" Finn ran behind me. "You can't just follow a car when you know the owner has been killed. I will come along."

"No." I stopped shy of the Jeep. "You make sure Mama leaves and let me do my job. You don't work here. Remember?"

"I don't like you going after a car when we don't know who is driving."

"I don't have time to tell you everything I found out today, but I have reason, good reason, to believe it's Dickie Dee, since he led me on a car chase." The words fell on Finn. There was a fright in his eyes, telling me he knew he couldn't go with me, but the idea of me, his girlfriend, going alone scared the hell out of him.

"I'll be fine." I gave him a kiss on the cheek and turned to get into the Jeep.

"Kenni, I overheard Jasmine talking to him on the phone. She was begging him to meet her at her parents'. She said something about how her dad would let him do what he wanted for the business and they would work all of this out. She forgives him for the affair." He crossed his arms. "I'm guessing you know all about this?"

"Yes. And now I have to go track a killer." I wagged Viola's phone in the air and jumped in the Jeep.

CHAPTER TWENTY-ONE

The tracker app on Viola's phone was similar to the map app on my phone I used for directions. The little car icon moved as Dickie drove it.

There was no way I was going to use the siren. He'd gotten away from me once. It was not going to happen again.

Everything had to go as smoothly as possible. The car appeared to have stopped in the downtown area, and the closer I drove toward the spot on the map, I realized he'd gone to the inn.

Slowly I passed the car parked exactly where the tracker app reported. No one was in the car, and it was in front of where the wedding party was staying.

"What's going on up in that head of yours?" Poppa asked.

"It would make sense for Dickie to dump his car, since he knows I'm looking for it. And it would be easy for him to have gotten Bradley's keys when he killed Bradley."

"Which would explain why we couldn't find the keys." Poppa snapped his thick fingers. "Now you're thinkin'."

"Jasmine and Dickie didn't go on their honeymoon because he's been hiding out. So from what Finn reported about what she said, it's clear there's something going on that Jasmine is trying to figure out. Plus she knew about the affair." I drove the Jeep a few more feet before I parked in a vacant spot with Bradley's car in sight from my rearview mirror.

"I say you get on in there and confront him before you have to do something on the street." Poppa was revising our plan.

I got out of the Jeep and pushed the button on the walkie-talkie to Betty Murphy at dispatch.

"Go ahead," Betty answered.

"Betty, it's Kenni." I didn't give her any time to greet me. I kept the button pushed down. "I need you to get Deputy Lee down to the Tattered Covered Books and Inn. I want him to be waiting at the back of the building. I found Dickie Dee driving Bradley's car, and I've got him in the inn. I'm not sure if he'll make a run for it, but I want to make sure Scott is out back if he does."

"Got it." Betty clicked off.

My utility belt rattled as I hurried up the sidewalk toward the car. I kept the palm of my hand on the handle of the gun, with my trigger finger on the holster snap. It would be a quick flick of the finger if I needed to arm myself.

With my back to the car, I stood at the door and glanced inside. Poppa had ghosted into the back seat and looked around.

"Kenni bug, there's a manila envelope back here," Poppa pointed out.

"I need to see if that's the photos of Dickie and the blackmailing." I just named it what it was and not how Brenda Futch had gently put the scheme they were dealing Dickie Dee.

With one eye on the door of the inn, I slowly took my hand off the gun and reached to the door handle, only to find the car was locked.

"And here we go." Poppa somehow used his ghostly self to unlock the door.

"I love having you here." I smiled and reached into the back seat to grab the large envelope.

I peeled back the flap and took out the stack of photos that were not very becoming of a man about to get married.

Instead of taking them with me as evidence since I didn't have the warrant I needed to break into the car, I pulled my phone out to snap some shots. I didn't have anything but circumstantial evidence to arrest Dickie on for murder, but I could certainly take him in for questioning and then get the warrant for not only the cars, but his room.

"Everything has to be done by the book," I told Poppa. "You and I both know Janice will be looking for any loopholes, and we can't have that."

I opened my camera app, and as soon as I did, the pictures I'd gotten off Polly's phone opened automatically.

There were two of Mama talking to Jasmine. Normally I wouldn't even think of it as different, but in one of them Jasmine was a foot taller than Mama.

"This is odd." I used my fingers to blow up the photo and noticed Jasmine had heels on in the taller photo. I swiped to the next photo and noticed she was shorter and the heels were replaced by tennis shoes.

"And look there." Poppa was looking at the picture. "The hem of her dress looks stained."

"Stained," I whispered. "We've got the wrong killer."

"Jasmine Dee." Poppa and I both knew at that instant Jasmine Dee was the killer.

I took a few quick snapshots of the photos of her husband with Brenda's employee before I darted into the inn.

"My stars, Kenni." Nadine jerked up from the front desk when I bolted past her.

"Jasmine Dee?" I stood at the bottom of the steps leading up to the second floor and pointed up.

"Yes." She nodded with big eyes. "She hurried past a few minutes ago, saying they were checking out."

"She might be checking out of here, but she'll be checking into the Cottonwood Sheriff's Department cell." Poppa snickered in delight.

"Dickie?" I asked.

"I've not seen him." She kept her eyes on my gun.

"Do not let anyone leave this inn. Lock the door," I instructed her and flipped the snap off my gun, slowly walking out of the inn so I could hurry to the alley where the steps leading up to the honeymoon suite were located.

Luckily I didn't encounter anyone along the way and felt somewhat better once I climbed the steps and noticed the door to the suite was cracked open. I glanced into the room before I made the decision to wait her out.

"You have made a mess of things." I jerked back and put my back against the outside of the door so I could listen in after I heard Jasmine.

From the sound of things, she was opening drawers and zipping up what sounded like a suitcase, as if she were packing.

"I should've stayed with Bradley Ines when I had the chance. But no, I had to trust you would be the one to take over Daddy's business. And then you go and get caught cheating on me with a hooker? One that you ended up having an affair with? Which was fine until they blackmailed you." Jasmine's footsteps moved away from the door as her voice carried from another room. "Do you think I was just going to let you ruin everything I have worked for? Being Daddy's little girl so I could have the money the company would bring us as soon as I got married and sold it?" A bitter and hard voice poured out of her.

She busted out in a cold laughter.

"Good job at screwing this up. Bradley told me a long time ago how you had a habit of sleeping around. That would've been fine as long as we weren't getting blackmailed." The more she talked, the more I waited. I knew I needed to hear her admit to at least one death.

I curled a shoulder back around the door and twisted my head just enough to see with my eye what was going on.

Jasmine had the suitcase on the floor and was too busy throwing stuff in to have even noticed me or the fact she'd not closed the door all the way. Her back was to the door, so I slid over a little more to get a bigger picture of the room, and that's when I saw Dickie tied up to a chair, with his mouth stuffed with something and her garter belt from the wedding holding it in place around his head.

Dickie's eyes grew big when he saw my shadow cast from the crack. He slid them up to meet mine. I put my finger up to my mouth for him not to say something.

Did he listen to me? No.

Dickie jerked his untied legs, making the chair legs jump up and in the air a few times.

"Now what do you want?" Jasmine asked him through her gritted teeth.

Dickie mumbled through his stuffed mouth and wiggled his head. Jasmine let go of a long sigh and threw the hairdryer on the floor next to the suitcase before she darted over to him and jerked the stuffing out of his mouth.

I moved back around the door and held my gun in position for when Dickie spilled the beans about me being out there.

"I have to go to the bathroom," he said. I closed my eyes as relief settled into my shoulders after he kept me a secret.

"He's going to help you," Poppa had ghosted into the room.

"Fine." Jasmine walked over and grabbed her umbrella from the wedding. "You make any funny moves, and I'll knock you upside your head."

Though I would've loved that to be some sort of admission as to what she'd done with the other umbrella to Gary, it wasn't enough.

Dickie shot me a look, thinking it was enough for me to bolt in and save him. I shook my head and mouthed *more*, rolling my wrist in gesture.

"I agreed to marry you, and after I get the company, to turn it over to you." Dickie started to plead with her. "Please, Jasmine. Let me have this. Let me go, and let me be with Vicky. You don't even love me. You just want the company."

Jasmine jerked on the knots around his wrist as she stood behind the chair, listening to Dickie plead for his freedom.

"You're right, but now that I have to go on the run due to your affair, you should suffer with me." There wasn't a confession from her.

"You don't have to run." Dickie rolled his wrists in circles after they were free. He got up and turned to face her. She shoved the umbrella point in his side.

"You're right." She jabbed him toward the bathroom. "You do. I just gave that sheriff's boyfriend a little show of my own at the town council meeting. Thankfully, you told me about running from her this afternoon. She'd mentioned they had a lead on the killer, and well, I'm so smart I knew it had to be you." She pouted and rubbed her eyes like a baby. "I pretended to cry, boo-hoo, in the meeting, and Daddy took me out. I made it a point to pretend to have gotten a call from you that clearly made you the killer."

"Why? Why didn't we just stick with the plan?" he questioned. "Me and you get married. I take the company. I give you the company, and we get divorced."

"Don't you get it?" she scoffed. "Wait. I thought you had to go to the bathroom. Why all the questions?"

"I just want to know, are you going to kill me like you did Gary and Bradley?" Here was the answer I needed to hear.

"I want you to suffer just like you've made me suffer." She snarled. "Do you think I took pleasure in killing Gary because he was blackmailing you? Then Bradley because he knew?"

"So what's next? Are you going to kill everyone who knows?" he asked, catching her off guard.

"I've had enough of you!" she screamed. She lifted her arm in the air to give him a good whack with the umbrella just as I raised my leg and kicked the door as hard as I could, sending splintered pieces of wood across the room.

"Hold it right there!" I yelled with my gun pointed right at her head. "Put down the umbrella now!"

Jasmine's eyes rounded in shock.

"Clearly she wasn't privy to what an awesome sheriff Kenni Lowry is." Poppa stood next to them, smiling.

"Jasmine Dee, you are under arrest for the murder of Gary Futch." I took a step closer to her as she dropped the umbrella on the floor. With one hand on my gun and the other snapping my cuffs off my utility belt and my eyes on her, I said, "And the murder of Bradley Ines, along with whatever other charges I can get to make sure you never see the light of day again."

CHAPTER TWENTY-TWO

Mama had insisted on throwing a little party for me at Luke and Vita Joneses' movie theater since me, Tibbie Bell, and Jolee Fischer loved to have a girls' movie night. This month's movie was *My Best Friend's Wedding*, and though we'd seen it a million times together already, we knew it would still be fun to watch it again. Only this time Mama wanted all the euchre ladies there too.

Even Polly Parker Ryland had showed up, looking even bigger than she had last week when I saw her at the town council meeting.

It was great to see every one of my friends enjoying a night to celebrate. It'd been a long week, getting Jasmine Dee transported to the state penitentiary, not to even mention the lengthy meetings with Janice Gallo. She knew she didn't stand a chance to win the lawsuit with a killer's motives leading her case. Jasmine's father had also walked away, still in charge of his company. Though Dickie Dee couldn't be charged with anything that would stick, I knew he was going to go straight to Vicky, the woman he'd met through the escort service.

I'd also gone to pay Brenda a visit to let her know I was watching her and her escort business. It was what Poppa had done years ago. When and if I found out there was some sort of illegal gig going on, I'd be at her door quicker than a jackrabbit.

"I'll take another one," I told Vita. My mouth watered just watching her scoop the buttery goodness into a bag. "Thank you."

The popcorn smelled so good and so fresh. I would be back to get another one before the movie started, along with some chocolaty candies to sprinkle down into the bag.

"No, thank you for keeping us safe." Vita handed the bags of warm popcorn to me.

"Just doing my job." I smiled and did that awful thing where I ate a piece of popcorn right off the top of the bag using my mouth instead of my fingers.

"We will all remember that come time for reelection too." Vita winked and moved on to help Viola.

I walked over to Polly and held out one of the bags of popcorn.

"I want to thank you for what you did last week with your husband. You know, getting him on my side at the town council meeting." I wanted to make sure to give credit where credit was due.

"It was the right thing, you know." She batted those big eyes and picked up some of the kernels, tossing them into her mouth. "I told him that I wanted to continue to be the first lady and he needed to support his sheriff."

"That's not a bad idea, to have the same ticket for the election." I did like the idea.

"I told him when he was sitting at the table, gobbling up a pot roast, potatoes, and carrots I'd spent all day in the kitchen preparing. Laundry was piled high on the laundry room floor and bills were stacked on the kitchen counter." Polly painted a not-so-rosy picture of married life. "If he thinks he's going to retire and not afford me the benefits of getting out of that house as the first lady and all the duties that come along with that, he's got another thing coming to him." She rubbed her ever-growing baby belly. "I'm going to get me a nanny, a housekeeper, and a cook when this stinker comes."

Suddenly she gasped.

"What?" I looked down at her stomach and then up to her eyes. "Is the baby okay? You aren't going into labor, are you? Do we need to get you to the hospital? I can put my siren on." The words rushed out of my mouth.

Polly looked up at me and blinked several times. Her mouth was wide open. She pointed behind me.

Oh Lord, was Mama right? Was there going to be a fall wedding? I looked down at Finn Vincent and suddenly my future passed before my eyes.

"Well? I'm waiting." Finn broke into my thoughts.

Though I appeared to be looking down at him while he was on one knee, I was just seeing through him.

Everyone I knew and loved was standing behind Finn, all of them waiting for my answer.

"I know it's not your grandmother's ring. We couldn't find it, but we will continue to look." He held the box even higher. "Kendrick Lowry," he nervously asked, "will you marry me?"

I blinked a few times, recalling how this was exactly what I'd thought I wanted. I certainly didn't want the scenario playing in my head.

I gulped.

"Kenni, um, everyone is waiting on your answer." Finn smiled. His lips quivered on the edges just enough for me to notice the nervousness from me not answering. "I'm kinda feeling like a fool," he said ventriloquist style. "I thought this was what we've been heading toward."

I put a fake smile on my face and looked up behind him where everyone was also waiting. I grazed their heads and noticed Poppa had appeared.

He had his arms folded across his chest. He wasn't as vibrant as when we had a case, and I knew this was the moment.

How was I ever going to choose between the two? A life with Finn by my side in the living? Or the man I respected most in the world in ghost form?

"Kenni?" Finn asked again.

I stood there, not sure what my answer was going to be.

-Will Kenni say yes to Finn? What is going to happen next in Cottonwood?

HEAVENS TO BRIBERY

A KENNI LOWRY MYSTERY BOOK 9

Holding my breath, I pointed the flashlight toward the body, preparing myself for what was to come next. Regardless of who the victim was, this night was clearly taking a turn that none of us had expected.

Though I was all too familiar with this part of my job, the sight of a life so brutally snuffed out still caused my stomach to twist uneasily. Yet I couldn't let emotion sway me. I had a crime scene to survey, a growing crowd to manage, and a murder to solve.

"Who is it, Kenni?" Mama's voice cut through the silent night, her curiosity echoing in the hushed crowd. As I hesitated, she added, more to her friends than me, "Kenni will tell us."

Her confidence in me was comforting, but in this moment, it felt misplaced. I had no answer to give her, no name to assign to the lifeless body before me. Despite the shock of the situation, I was surprisingly calm, my mind beginning to fall into the familiar rhythm of deductive reasoning.

The man was a stranger to me, a face I had never seen in the tightly knit community of Cottonwood. His dark hair was matted with blood, and his clothes were nondescript, the kind that wouldn't draw attention in any crowd. I felt a pang of sadness at the sight of a life extinguished under the cover of darkness, far from home.

Mama had been right about something, though. There hadn't been a train. Cottonwood was a town molded by routine and rhythm, and the chugging of the trains passing through was as regular as the sunrise. A long, drawn-out whistle usually announced their arrival, breaking the silence of the night with a mechanical howl that could be heard all the way to the Jones's basement. The sound had woven itself into the fabric of our lives, an auditory reminder of the outside world.

There was no such sound tonight. No whistle, no rumbling of wheels against the tracks, no rhythmic clacking of the cargo. The silence was a stark contradiction to the chaotic scene that had unfolded. And it wasn't just the silence. Looking more closely, I could see the lack of typical gruesome injuries that one would associate with a train accident.

The moonlight glinted off the rails, unblemished and smooth. There was no sign that a train had rushed over this body. My gut twisted with unease as the implications of my observations sank in. This was not an accident. This was something much darker.

I slowly stood up, tucking away my phone and turning to face the anxious crowd.

"I need everyone to stay back," I said, trying to keep my voice steady. "This is a crime scene. We need to preserve it until help arrives. So why don't you all go on home, and we will have some details in the morning. We won't have anything here tonight."

I locked eyes with Finn, giving him a curt nod. He understood, moving quickly to usher Patty and her dogs away from the tracks and back toward the crowd. As a murmur of confusion and fear rippled through the townsfolk, I took a deep breath, preparing myself for the tumultuous investigation that lay ahead. This night was far from over.

CHAPTER ONE

Mama always used to say that a woman's life was a series of surprises, but nothing had prepared me for this.

Here I was, the sheriff of Cottonwood, Kentucky, with a murder case half solved, and a man was kneeling before me, proposing in front of my whole family, a couple of townsfolk who'd been drawn by the commotion, and Edna Easterly, the one and only employee of the *Cottonwood Chronicles*. I was sure Mama had hired her for such an occasion as this.

After all, Mama wanted everything on film, and the camera stuck up in my face was certainly going to capture it all.

And I mean all. Including the look on my face.

Finn Vincent, my handsome boyfriend, was looking up at me, his brown eyes filled with hope. I'd seen that look in the eyes of people I'd helped before, but it was never directed at me in this way.

A deafening silence surrounded us, as though all the air had been sucked out of the summer evening. A few steps away, my spectral poppa, the ghost of the former town sheriff in our small town of Cottonwood, Kentucky, had shown up. Only I could see him.

I was on the precipice of answering, my eyes flitting between Finn's hopeful brown gaze and Poppa's ethereal, patient presence. I could feel the weight of Finn's anticipation, a current of electricity humming between us.

Poppa, in contrast, emanated calm, a steady beacon in the chaos of this moment.

His phantasmal shoulders lifted in a noncommittal shrug. This decision, he seemed to say, was entirely mine. Thoughts of the murder case that remained unresolved gnawed at my mind, a persistent reminder of my duties as Cottonwood's sheriff, but also the wild unpredictability that life here presented

"Kenni," Finn whispered, his eyes darting to the left and the right. His chest filled with air before he looked back up at me, waiting for my answer.

"I..." I began, the word an unfinished symphony hanging in the warm summer air. Finn's gaze was locked on mine, but his attention wavered as my eyes darted past his shoulder in a brief, bewildered glance toward the place where Poppa stood. Of course, Finn could see nothing but empty space.

Abruptly, a scream pierced the quiet evening, like the piercing whistle of a tea kettle reaching the boiling point.

The hair on the back of my neck stood on end, and everyone's focus shifted in unison towards the alarming sound. It was a harsh intrusion, a reminder that stark danger often punctuated Cottonwood's tranquility.

Without a second thought, I found myself moving, an almost automatic reaction, reaching for the trusty weapon holstered around my ankle.

Finn, always quick on his feet, was right behind me. His unanswered proposal hung between us, another silent specter adding to the charged atmosphere.

"Oh Lord!" Mama's voice drifted to us from behind, her tone a cocktail of exasperation and concern. "Can't a woman get proposed to in peace in this town anymore?"

Adrenaline coursed through my veins as we ran out of the makeshift basement movie theater and rounded the corner, heading toward the screaming.

My heart pounded against my ribs like a wild drum. An unexpected sense of relief washed over me—the crisis had provided me a momentary reprieve from answering Finn. But that relief quickly gave way to a sense of dread, a familiar taste of anxiety on my tongue as I imagined the sight we were about to encounter.

In the larger scheme of my life, I knew this incident was merely the start of a new chapter. Another twist in the winding tale of love, duty, and death that defined my existence in Cottonwood. And Finn's proposal, as yet unanswered, would undoubtedly change everything forever.

The frantic cries for help were now louder, echoing through the still night. The voice was unmistakably Patty Dunaway's.

"There!" A long, thin shadow in the moonlight pointed toward the railroad tracks.

Those tracks ran like a metallic scar through the heart of the town, right behind Luke and Vita Jones's house. The stark light of the full moon painted Patty's lanky silhouette against the inky night, forming a tableau of fear and urgency.

Three dog leashes were wrapped around one of her hands as she tried to reel in the dogs attached to them.

With the echoes of Patty's panicked cries still ringing in my ears, I turned to Finn, my voice carrying the firm authority I'd honed as Cottonwood's sheriff. My sheriff mode was like a switch that automatically flipped on and off.

It was completely off when Finn was on one knee, but now that I was standing here with a body lying across the train tracks, the sheriff switch had flipped.

"Finn, I need you to get Patty and the dogs back. And keep the crowd at a distance," I said, motioning to the gathering knot of curious townsfolk who'd begun to drift over from Luke and Vita's.

Although he was no longer part of my department, Finn was someone I trusted implicitly, especially in situations like these. His broad shoulders tensed in understanding, and he nodded, his dark eyes lingering on me for a moment as if he was trying to process how he went from one knee to standing over a body in seconds. He turned toward Patty.

In the soft moonlight, Patty looked even more disheveled than usual. Her frizzy hair was a wild halo around her head, her usually cheerful face pale and stricken with terror. The three dogs she had been walking—a spirited spaniel, a large brindled mutt, and a tiny terrier—whimpered and tugged at their leashes, their sensitive noses detecting that something was wrong.

Finn gently but firmly guided Patty and the canines away from the railway tracks, his calming presence seeming to soothe them slightly.

Meanwhile, the inquisitive onlookers who'd followed us from the movie theater were held at bay by Finn's commanding stature, their speculative whispers and concerned glances creating a subdued background buzz.

From the edges of the curious crowd, Mama's voice rang out. Her distinctive southern twang was a comforting soundtrack to most of my life, but right now it rang through the night with an edge of anxiety.

"Finn Vincent, what in heaven's name is going on?" Mama demanded. Her slightly accusatory tone betrayed her concern, an emotion she was quick to share. "Don't y'all worry. Kenni will get to the bottom of this, and we will be back to Finn's proposal in no time."

Finn looked flustered, glancing back at me before turning to Mama. "Kenni is doing her job. We should let her—"

"There's someone on the tracks," Patty said in a shaky voice.

"But I didn't hear no train, did y'all?" Mama cut him off, turning to her companions with a challenging look on her face.

Her question was aimed at her small posse of friends, three formidable ladies who were among the most influential business owners in Cottonwood.

Viola White, the owner of White's Jewelry, was a petite woman who stood just five feet, four inches. Her gray hair was styled immaculately.

Beside her, Ruby Smith, the owner of Ruby's Antiques, was a stark contrast. Her short red hair was as fiery as her personality, and her vibrant orange lipstick only added to her overall vivid personality.

Then there was Lulu McClain, who owned Lulu's Boutique. Her very short black hair and pronounced southern accent made her a distinctive character. She had a motherly quality that put people at ease and a sense of style that made her boutique the talk of the town.

With the crowd momentarily placated, I turned my attention back to the body. My heart pounded in my chest as I crouched down beside the figure, and the sharp smell of iron filled my nostrils. I fumbled for my phone and turned the screen's brightness up to its maximum, providing the only other source of illumination against the moonlit darkness.

Holding my breath, I pointed the flashlight toward the body, preparing myself for what was to come next. Regardless of who the victim was, this night was clearly taking a turn that none of us had expected.

Though I was all too familiar with this part of my job, the sight of a life so brutally snuffed out still caused my stomach to twist uneasily. Yet I couldn't let emotion sway me. I had a crime scene to survey, a growing crowd to manage, and a murder to solve.

"Who is it, Kenni?" Mama's voice cut through the silent night, her curiosity echoing in the hushed crowd. As I hesitated, she added, more to her friends than me, "Kenni will tell us."

Her confidence in me was comforting, but in this moment, it felt misplaced. I had no answer to give her, no name to assign to the lifeless body before me. Despite the shock of the situation, I was surprisingly calm, my mind beginning to fall into the familiar rhythm of deductive reasoning.

The man was a stranger to me, a face I had never seen in the tightly knit community of Cottonwood. His dark hair was matted with blood, and his clothes were nondescript, the kind that wouldn't draw attention in any crowd. I felt a pang of sadness at the sight of a life extinguished under the cover of darkness, far from home.

Mama had been right about something, though. There hadn't been a train. Cottonwood was a town molded by routine and rhythm, and the chugging of the trains passing through was as regular as the sunrise. A long, drawn-out whistle usually announced their arrival, breaking the silence of the night with a mechanical howl that could be heard all the way to the Jones's basement. The sound had woven itself into the fabric of our lives, an auditory reminder of the outside world.

There was no such sound tonight. No whistle, no rumbling of wheels against the tracks, no rhythmic clacking of the cargo. The silence was a stark contradiction to the chaotic scene that had unfolded. And it wasn't just the silence. Looking more closely, I could see the lack of typical gruesome injuries that one would associate with a train accident.

The moonlight glinted off the rails, unblemished and smooth. There was no sign that a train had rushed over this body. My gut twisted with unease as the implications of my observations sank in. This was not an accident. This was something much darker.

I slowly stood up, tucking away my phone and turning to face the anxious crowd.

"I need everyone to stay back," I said, trying to keep my voice steady. "This is a crime scene. We need to preserve it until help arrives. So why don't you all go on home, and we will have some details in the morning. We won't have anything here tonight."

I locked eyes with Finn, giving him a curt nod. He understood, moving quickly to usher Patty and her dogs away from the tracks and back toward the crowd. As a murmur of confusion and fear rippled through the townsfolk, I took a deep breath, preparing myself for the tumultuous investigation that lay ahead. This night was far from over.

CHAPTER TWO

F inn, recognizing the gravity of the situation, moved away from the crowd, pulling out his phone as he went. I could see his brow furrowed in concentration as he dialed the numbers. First, he spoke to Deputy Scott Hill, explaining the situation and urging him to get here quickly. Next, he dialed Coroner Max Bogus and spoke in a low, controlled voice as he relayed the grim discovery we'd made.

As Finn took charge of the initial calls, the crowd began to disperse. I stood over the body and watched as they left.

Ruby's high-heeled boots click-clacked against the cobblestones as she led the way, her fiery-red hair a stark contrast against the moonlit night. Lulu, always the quintessential southern lady, followed closely behind, whispering something to Viola, whose diamond earrings glinted in the dim light. The friends, still in shock, departed arm in arm with Mama in the mix, their laughter from earlier now a distant memory.

Left alone with the haunting scene, I suddenly noticed a chill running down my spine. I turned to find Poppa, his spectral form shimmering in the cool night air.

"Shoo-wee, that was a close one, huh, kiddo?" he said, his ghostly eyes twinkling with amusement.

Ignoring the remark about Finn's proposal, I returned my attention to the lifeless body on the tracks. The silence that now enveloped the scene felt eerily oppressive, punctuated only by the distant hoot of an owl and the soft rustling of the wind through the trees.

Poppa wasn't one to be ignored, though. "Now ain't the time to dwell on matters of the heart, kiddo," he continued, his spectral figure floating closer to me. "We've got a murder on our hands, and it looks like a complicated one at that."

With a deep breath, I focused on the scene again.

"We need to look for any possible clues," I said, as though I were talking to myself rather than Poppa.

It'd gotten around town a few times that I'd been caught talking to myself and even visiting Poppa's resting place in the Maple Grove Cemetery. In reality, I was playing our little game of what-if.

As a child, I spent a lot of time with my poppa and in his house, which was where I lived now. When he was working a case, he loved to play the what-if game. What if this happened? What if that happened?

In truth, he was teaching me, training me to be the sheriff and one day take his spot, which I did. Now that didn't keep Mama from having a hissy fit. Oh, she did.

It was of gigantic proportions, and she cried all the way through my graduation at the police academy, nearly going through eight of the ten handkerchiefs she'd brought to mourn the occasion. Mama would never be caught dead using a piece of tissue.

Not ladylike, she'd say.

"And we need to get the Federal Railroad Administration to stop all trains on this route. The last thing we need is more chaos," I mentioned, knowing we'd have to bring the rail system to a halt.

At least until we got some daylight hours.

Finn returned then, pocketing his phone. "Scott and Max are on their way," he confirmed, his eyes meeting mine.

My stomach started to turn. It was a combination of the excitement of the proposal, the idea of never seeing Poppa again if I'd said yes, and now a dead body that caused me to heave.

"Here." Immediately, Finn reached into his pocket and pulled out a handkerchief with his initials on it, something Mama had gotten him for Christmas last year and insisted he carry.

"Thank you." I held it over my mouth and nose.

My breath hitched as the strong smells of iron, sweat, and dirt hit my senses. The rough texture of the handkerchief against my skin and the faint scent of Finn's cologne still lingering on it offered a small semblance of comfort amidst the chaos.

"Deep breaths, Kenni," Finn said softly, concern etched into his handsome features. His presence was a pillar of strength in the face of crisis, a trait I had always admired.

"Thank you." I shook my head as the thought that I needed to say something about his proposal lingered on my mind.

"You're welcome." He watched me with a mixture of understanding and worry, one hand on my shoulder, grounding me.

Regaining my composure, I straightened up, tucking the handkerchief into my pocket. I gave him a nod of gratitude and gazed back at the daunting task at hand. The adrenaline was kicking in again, staving off the nausea and rekindling my focus.

"All right," I said, the sheriff in me taking over once more. "We need to secure the scene and wait for Scott and Max." I gestured to the dimly lit crime scene where the poor soul's life had been abruptly and mercilessly cut short. "About tonight," I was about to say, my eyes flickering between Finn and Poppa's spectral figure.

I drew a deep breath, the words hovering on the tip of my tongue. But before I could voice them, Finn raised a hand to halt me.

"Not now, Kenni," he said, his eyes locking onto mine. His jaw had a determined set, his voice firm yet filled with a tenderness that always managed to catch me off guard. "This isn't the time or the place."

The faint flicker of streetlamps reflected in his gaze, casting shadows across his chiseled features. His hand moved from my shoulder and gently squeezed my own hand, offering silent support. His touch was warm, grounding, a stark contrast to the chill permeating the night air.

"We've had a long night, and it's not over yet," he continued, the corners of his lips tilting up into a wistful smile. "I want your answer, Kenni. But I want it to come from a place of peace, not in the midst of a crime scene."

His sincerity was as unexpected as his proposal. A soft sigh escaped my lips as I nodded in acknowledgment of his words. The tension in the air eased a fraction, replaced by a silent understanding.

"Just... promise me you'll think about it," he added, releasing my hand to step back, the distance suddenly feeling much farther than it was. "Besides, it might give me time to find your granny's ring."

A shared glance with Poppa confirmed what I already knew. Finn had a point. Now wasn't the time for personal dilemmas. We had a job to do. My answer and whatever changes it would bring could wait until Cottonwood was safe once more.

Poppa floated over to us, his phantasmal brows furrowed. "Remember, kiddo," he chimed in, his voice a comforting echo from the past. "Every detail matters. The tiniest bit could be the key to unlocking this puzzle."

I nodded at Finn. "Every detail matters. The tiniest bit could be a key to unlocking this man's death."

I'd gotten good at listening to Poppa and taking his ghostly leads on some of the crimes I'd had to deal with over the last few years. After two crimes had happened at once and Poppa's ghost couldn't scare them off, he'd revealed himself to me.

Yeah. I thought I'd gone cuckoo. Mama had insisted the job had finally gotten to me, but in truth, I'd accepted that Poppa was really here in ghost form and had helped out with a lot of crimes.

A gentle blush warmed my cheeks, bringing me out of my thoughts.

I started a methodical scan of the area. I noticed the scuffle marks in the dirt near the tracks, the discarded cigarette butt, and a tarnished pocket watch near the edge of the scene. Each detail could be a clue, a piece of the puzzle that would explain how and why this man ended up dead on the tracks.

As the coroner's van pulled up, bathing the scene in stark white light, I looked up to see Finn walking back towards me, his cell phone pressed to his ear. The words "Yes, we need to halt all trains on this route immediately" escaped his lips.

I was happy to see he'd made the call to the Federal Railroad Administration, FRA for short.

That was the first step.

"You can go ahead and go on home," I told Finn, since he really didn't need to be here. I knew he had to work in the morning, and the drive to Clay's Ferry wasn't the shortest. Plus, he wasn't here as an officer of the law. He was here only to support me. "I'll be fine now."

"Are you sure?" he asked as Max Bogus walked up to us with his little black bag in his grip.

"Positive." I nodded.

He nodded back and disappeared into the night, which had certainly not turned out like he thought it would.

I watched as Finn reluctantly turned and left, his silhouette fading into the night. The weight of the investigation was now solely on my shoulders, and I needed to focus on the task at hand. As Max Bogus, the county coroner, approached with his black bag in hand, I braced myself for the grim details that awaited.

"Evening, Kenni," Max said to me, his round face mirroring the weariness that clung to the night. He had been a constant presence in Cottonwood, not only as the coroner but also as the owner of the town's sole funeral home. With his expertise, he could shed light on the mysteries hidden inside the lifeless body on the tracks.

"Evening, Max," I replied, my voice steady despite the unease stirring within me. "What can you tell me so far?"

Max knelt next to the body, his gloved hands carefully examining the lifeless form. Behind thick spectacles, his eyes darted across the scene as his mind pieced together the puzzle of death.

Scott Hill, my one and only deputy, had arrived, his deputy truck's spotlight illuminating the area, casting harsh shadows against the gravel.

"Well, Kenni," Max began, his voice low and measured, "rigor mortis has already set in. Based on that and the lividity, I'd estimate the time of death to be approximately four to six hours ago."

I listened intently, trying to absorb every detail that Max provided. The significance of the time frame meant that the man had been deceased before he was placed on the tracks, confirming my initial suspicions.

Max continued his examination, noting the injuries on the body while I continued to look around it for any sort of clues.

"There are signs of blunt force trauma to the head and torso," he explained. "It appears he was already dead before being placed here. There are no train marks."

As Max spoke, I retrieved a pair of gloves from him and slipped them on.

"This man was murdered." Max's words were exactly what I expected to hear.

Carefully, I began searching the pockets of the victim's clothing for any form of identification, but my efforts proved futile. No wallet, no ID, nothing that would give us a lead on his identity.

Max's brow furrowed, mirroring my own frustration.

"Seems our victim didn't carry any identification with him," I said. "Or it was taken by his killer. We'll have to rely on other means to discover who he was."

"Who found him?" Max asked.

I stood up, the weight of the investigation pressing down on me. The absence of identification only added another layer of complexity to the case. It meant that finding the truth, unraveling the motives and the mystery surrounding this man's death, would be that much harder.

"Patty Dunaway," I replied to Max's question, my mind shifting gears to focus on the person who had discovered the body.

She was a local dog walker who owned Patty's Pet Pantry. Her business had been booming lately.

She was a familiar face in Cottonwood, always bustling around with a group of dogs in tow. Her love for animals showed in the way she cared for her clients' pets, treating them as if they were her own. It was common to see her strolling down Main Street, a fistful of leashes in one hand and a cheerful smile on her face.

"I'm guessing these dogs were under her care," I continued, removing the gloves and tucking them back into Max's outstretched hand. "Patty has a loyal following, and I can't imagine what she went through stumbling upon this. She was so upset I just sent her home."

Max nodded, his gaze shifting toward the distant silhouette of Patty, who was now speaking with Scott.

"We'll need to speak with her, get her account of what happened. She might have seen or heard something that could help us piece this together," I said.

I contemplated the significance of Patty's presence at the scene. Was it a mere coincidence, or did she and the victim have a deeper connection? The possibilities swirled in my mind, yet I knew that jumping to conclusions would only lead us astray.

Not that I thought Patty could or did do it, but Poppa's words always haunted me.

"No stone unturned," I said loudly enough for Poppa to smack his leg.

"That's right, Kenni bug." Poppa skittered over the body as he addressed me by the nickname he'd given me as a child.

"We'll have to be thorough in our questioning," I said, my voice resolute.

Max nodded, his professional demeanor unwavering.

As Max concluded his preliminary examination, I took a step closer.

"Anything of note?" I inquired, my voice low to avoid disturbing the somber atmosphere.

Max straightened up, his spectacles glinting under the bright lights.

"Well, Sheriff," he began, his tone measured, "apart from the lack of identification, I found this tucked inside the victim's jacket pocket." He held up a folded piece of paper, its edges slightly frayed.

I grabbed another glove from Max's bag and carefully took the paper.

I unfolded the paper, revealing a handwritten note. My eyes scanned the words. The note was a cryptic message, a puzzle in itself, suggesting that this murder was not simply a random act of violence.

Beware the tracks of fate, for they hold the secrets of the fallen. Seek the signs where iron meets the earth, and the truth shall be revealed but not by you.

As I read the words over and over, my mind raced to decipher their meaning. What did they imply? Was this message a warning, a clue, or something more sinister?

The mention of the "tracks of fate" and the "secrets of the fallen" hinted at a deeper connection to the victim and the circumstances surrounding his death.

I shared a perplexed glance with Max, his brow furrowed again in contemplation. The message was not something we could easily dismiss.

I reread it out loud.

As we stood there, enveloped in the crime scene's eerie silence, I couldn't shake the feeling that we were just scratching the surface of a much larger web of intrigue.

"Let's check it for fingerprints," I said, which urged Max to grab an evidence bag from his coroner's kit. My own bag was back in my Jeep Wagoneer parked in front of Luke's house.

Max opened the mouth of the bag, allowing me to drop the note in. Scott took the bag from Max, wrote on the front of it, and stuck it alongside other items he'd collected, like the cigarette butts and the old pocket watch.

"What about this?" I bent down when I saw an inhaler. Then I picked up the inhaler, which had seen much better days. "I can't read the prescription label well, but I can make out Camille's name," I said, referring to Dr. Camille Shively.

"I'm sure a lot of folks around here have an inhaler for something or another." Scott made a great point. "And I bet her patient list is long."

"Then we will have to do the task of getting the list and calling each patient to see if they are still alive." I dropped the inhaler into the bag Scott had opened for me.

I left him to seal it and tag it while I continued to look around.

"What about the note?" I asked, shining my flashlight underneath the rails in case something, anything stood out. "'The truth will come out but not by him,' which tells me someone did shut him up. But where? Where is the other crime scene?"

There were so many questions that had no answers in sight. The night was far from over, and the path ahead was treacherous, but we were undeterred.

As Poppa floated nearby, his ghostly form lending an ethereal presence, I couldn't help but feel a surge of determination. The note had given us a purpose, a tangible lead to pursue. And as the investigation unfolded, I knew we would unravel the truth, no matter how tangled it might be.

CHAPTER THREE

As the first rays of dawn painted the sky in shades of orange, I made my way down Broadway Street—or Free Row, as the townsfolk referred to it—toward my little cottage. The chirping birds filled the air. The neighborhood was humble, often overlooked by those who sought comfort in Cottonwood's more polished corners.

Free Row had its own unique charm, though. It was a place where hardships were shared, where neighbors looked out for one another amidst their own struggles.

On this street, cars sat on cement blocks, worn-out couches adorned front porches, and unruly teenagers tested the boundaries. But they knew better than to cross paths with the sheriff, for my reputation preceded me.

My little house, a modest abode that Poppa had passed down to me, stood proudly among its surroundings. The house held the memories of his presence, his guidance, and the love he had showered upon me throughout my life. In this small space, I found solace and a sense of belonging.

I pulled the old Wagoneer into the small driveway and got out. I couldn't help but look down a few houses to see if Finn had already gone for the day.

He had.

It would've been much easier if Finn had kept his job as my deputy sheriff, but he was right. If he wanted to move up, either he had to run against me or I had to step down and find a different job.

Neither was about to happen. At least he'd better not run against me. That wouldn't make a happy household.

A smile crossed my lips at just the thought of a household. In my mind, that meant I would take Finn up on his proposal and need to deal with Poppa somehow. Or at least come to grips with the knowledge that Poppa would become dead again.

The idea of it made me feel sad all over.

"You know it's cruel," I said out loud, in case Poppa's ghost was hanging around his old house when I got out of the Wagoneer. "If I went on to have a family of my own, that means I'd have to grieve you all over again."

I stopped shy of the gate of the chain-length fence that surrounded my backyard.

I pulled my phone out of my pocket to see if I'd missed any calls from Finn. I'd put it on Do Not Disturb mode because Mama had called me several times last night after she'd left what I now believed was a crime scene. When I didn't answer her, she'd resorted to texting.

She wore me out.

It was one of those situations in which she felt she had the authority to know what was going on because I was her daughter, though I'd reminded her several times that I was the sheriff and she'd have to wait for some things like the rest of the public.

That didn't suit Mama.

I filled the old coffeepot with water, the sound of it gurgling as I poured it into the machine. Duke's tail wagged enthusiastically outside the kitchen window, his hound instincts in full swing as if someone were out there playing with him.

I knew it was Poppa, even though he hadn't revealed himself to me. His mischievous spirit always found a way to make its presence known. Duke loved him.

Just as I reached for the coffee grounds, my phone erupted with a jingle, signaling an incoming call. Mama's name flashed on the screen, and I couldn't help but smile. She had an uncanny way of always calling at the most unexpected times.

"Hey, Mama," I said to her, holding the phone between my ear and shoulder as I continued to prepare the coffee.

"Oh, thank goodness you finally answered." Mama's voice crackled with urgency. "I've been trying to reach you all night. Why didn't you call me back or send a text? You know I worry, especially when there's a body found on the train tracks."

I chuckled softly, knowing Mama's penchant for worry or at least acting worried was her way of getting information.

Yep. Gossip.

"Sorry, Mama, it was a hectic night. I didn't want to disturb you." I had to make it sound as though I weren't on to her. Viv Lowry's angry side was something I didn't want to deal with this morning.

Especially if I hadn't had my coffee or, more importantly, sleep this morning.

"Well, I heard that train whistle in town this morning, so I figured the tracks were clear and I could call you," she replied, sounding slightly breathless. "Now, spill the beans. What happened? Who was it? Do you have any leads?"

Mama's rapid-fire questioning didn't leave me a moment to breathe. She had a way of getting straight to the point, but she also had a heart of gold, always caring for our town's well-being, even in the midst of her own busy life.

"Mama, I wish I could tell you everything, but it's an ongoing investigation," I said, stirring the coffee grounds into the pot. "I can't share all the details just yet. You know how it goes."

She let out an exasperated sigh.

"Now, Kenni, you and your secrets. The girls at bell choir practice are going to ask me what happened. I've got to give them some details if we want to pray for his soul and his family. At least give me a little something, a morsel of information to satisfy everyone. After all, what good is it if my daughter is the sheriff and I don't have any details?"

I couldn't help but smile at Mama's persistence. She could balance her genuine concern with the curious nature of small-town life.

"All right, Mama, just a little something," I conceded, pouring myself a cup of coffee. "The victim was a man, still unidentified. Max Bogus, the coroner, believes foul play was involved. We're digging deep to uncover the truth."

Those weren't exactly the details Mama wanted, but telling her there was more to look into was enough to feed her appetite for being in the know—or at least appearing to be in the know.

My walkie-talkie, sitting next to my coffee pot on the counter, chirped.

"Kenni Sheriff?" Betty Murphy, my dispatcher, was calling on the other end. "Sheriff Lowry?"

"Mama," I said in a rush after Betty continued to call out my name. Her voice was laced with concern.

"Was that your walkie-talkie?" Mama asked. Just a little ounce more of information she could tell the rest of the bell choir. "Is that Betty?"

"Mama, I'll call you later," I said in a hurry, clicking off the call before she could ask any further questions.

I picked up the walkie-talkie and clicked the button. I had a distinct feeling my day had started before I could even have that first cup of coffee. With the pad of my thumb, I slid the volume dial up so I could let Duke inside and grab my to-go mug.

"Go ahead," I called, nestling the device in my hand while popping the screen door open with the other. Duke rushed inside and over to his empty bowl.

Our morning routine consisted of me letting him out while the coffee brewed, so it was unusual for him to see his kibble piled up to the top of his dish when he came back inside.

"Oh, Kenni. Oh, Kenni," Betts cried out.

I wasn't alarmed yet. Betty was part of Mama's crowd, but she was also my elderly dispatcher who knew that she had to keep information close to the cuff. There was no distinction between Betty's *there's a cat in the tree* call and her *there's a dead body* call.

That meant my heart hadn't started to palpitate quite yet.

Until it did.

"We've got us a missing person case," she called. "And I hate to say this because I know you've just gotten home from the situation at the Town Branch…" She was referring to an area of downtown Cottonwood that was actually Second Street if you looked on a map.

It was a small creek bed, sometimes wet but mostly dry, which ran right through the entire length of town. Second Street had a lot of old Victorian-style homes that were built in the twenties. Back then, people buried family members on their property. And this was the exact location where we'd found our John Doe last night on the tracks.

"And the description I took from his wife sounds a lot like your John Doe," she finished.

My hand gripped the handle of the coffee pot even tighter.

"Kenni. Sheriff?" she said, waffling between the two.

I sucked in a deep breath and filled up the to-go mug, trying to collect my thoughts and consider what I needed to do first about our John Doe or this missing person case.

"I'd be careful, Kenni bug." Poppa appeared behind me, sitting at the old kitchen table I'd seen him sit at many times in his human body. "Was this someone reporting a missing person because they killed him and got to having some guilty feelings about leaving him on the tracks where the train could've torn him so bad he was unrecognizable?"

I picked up the walkie-talkie and clicked it to life.

"Who called in the missing person case?" I asked, thinking of Poppa's good theory, knowing in this instance, he would say to leave no stone unturned.

"The man's wife. She said he went to work yesterday morning and never came home. Didn't even return any of her phone calls. She also said he calls her every night on his way home and asks if she needs anything from the store," Betty reported.

"Innocent enough," I shrugged and said to Poppa before I clicked back to Betty. "Did you ask her to come down to the department?"

"I did. She said she'd be down here directly. I'd barely got my pocketbook hung up and the lights barely on when the call came through. As I talking to her, Scott came in and was lookin' over my shoulder at what I was writing." She paused. Her voice cracked as she said, "That's when he told me about the body on the tracks over on the Town Branch. The missing man doesn't live too far from there. I mean, how did she not hear about the body?"

"You didn't know about the body until this morning," I told her while opening the cabinet door behind the sink where I kept Duke's kibble. "We

371

didn't have to call dispatch, since I heard the scream, so anyone in with a scanner didn't get the alert."

In Cottonwood, the police scanner was an unofficial soundtrack that played in the background of everyday life. Whether it was a sweltering summer day or a bitter winter night, the residents of our small town were always tuned in to the scanner, their ears pricked for the sound of a call. It didn't matter if they were in the middle of a family dinner or tending to their own business—when the scanner crackled with an incident, the people of Cottonwood showed up, eager to be a part of the community's collective watchful eye. Even the most mundane reports, like a raccoon in a trash can, drew a crowd of concerned citizens ready to lend a helping hand or simply be present in the face of any challenge. This was the essence of Cottonwood —a tight-knit community united by a shared sense of duty and a commitment to keeping one another safe.

"Let me get my uniform on and I'll be right down," I told her, clicking off one last time and walking down the small hallway and into my bathroom.

"Kenni, wait, are you engaged now?" Betty asked before she clicked right back on. "Everyone knew he was going to ask you last night, and I'm sorry I wasn't there."

I flipped the switch to the bathroom light on and rolled the volume down on the walkie-talkie, ignoring Betty's question.

With the hot and cold handles of the bathroom sink's faucet turned on, I stood in front of the mirror, my weary reflection staring back at me. Honey-blond locks kissed by golden highlights cascaded around my face, framing my tired features. My green eyes, usually vibrant and full of life, now bore dark circles underneath, evidence of sleepless nights and the relentless demands of my role as sheriff.

I had never been one to fuss over my appearance, and today was no exception. The standard-issue brown sheriff's uniform did little to flatter my figure, but practicality always took precedence over style. There was no time for elaborate makeup or perfectly styled hair when you had investigations to pursue and justice to be served.

This was also something Mama didn't like. She said if I had to be the sheriff and fulfill some sort of guilt I had surrounding Poppa, I should do it presentably. If it were up to Mama, she would have already had pearls sewn along the collar of my uniform and gotten some sort of scarf to go around my neck. Possibly even a monogram above the pocket where I pinned my sheriff's badge.

The dark circles under my eyes were as prominent as the cloud of murder that hung over our small southern town. Perhaps a bit of concealer could temporarily disguise the toll that this ongoing battle had taken on me.

It wasn't about how perfectly put together I appeared on the outside. Rather, the exertion came from my burning determination and unwavering commitment to solving the puzzle of the man on the railroad tracks and now this missing person.

A puzzle. That was exactly what my job was about. Of course, I maintained law and order, handling the everyday incidents and disturbances, but the cases involving death were what truly stimulated my inner puzzle solver. Maybe I looked at it this way because it was the game Poppa played with me.

These cases were intricate mysteries, filled with hidden clues, tangled webs of motives, and secrets waiting to be unraveled.

I stared at my reflection and saw a flicker of determination igniting in my eyes. The exhaustion and weariness melted away, replaced by a fierce resolve.

I was the sheriff of Cottonwood, and it was my duty to bring justice to those whose lives had been unjustly taken. It wasn't just a job. It was a personal mission.

With a final glance in the mirror, I straightened my shoulders, giving myself my own little pep talk. I might not be perfectly dolled up or devoid of the weariness that came with sleepless nights, but none of that mattered.

With a sigh, I lifted my hand to turn the light switch off behind me, getting a glance at my left hand—in particular, my ring finger.

If things hadn't gone as they had last night, with Patty screaming and the dead body, I imagined what my finger would've looked like with the sparkler Finn had gotten for his proposal to me.

I hadn't gotten a good look at it, and it certainly wasn't my granny's ring, which Poppa gave me and which I was sure I'd wear as my engagement ring, but it was a ring Finn thought I would like.

I was sure it was perfect.

"I guess we will have to wait and see," I said and patted Duke on the head.

He followed me to our bedroom, where I opened my closet and pulled out one of the many clean brown uniforms to don. That was one part of the job I loved. I didn't have to fuss over what outfits to wear to work.

"You ready?" I asked my deputy dog, who was waiting patiently by the bedroom door. He knew the drill. "We've got a missing person to check into and a murder to solve."

Duke darted down the hall, galloping like a small pony and beating me to the back door.

My utility belt was sitting on the bench seating on the far side of the kitchen table. I clipped it around my waist before I grabbed my coffee.

As soon as I opened the screen door, Duke ran out and circled the yard one last time as I locked the door behind us and met him at the gate.

"Mornin', Sheriff!" a neighbor yelled out while walking his dog. "You're up bright and early."

"The safety of Cottonwood never stops," I said and opened the door to the old Wagoneer, cringing because I sounded like a politician.

Something I stood against. I never once ran a campaign to get elected to office.

Poppa always said the job was about caring for the community and loving the people in it as if I were related to all of them. All the other stuff just didn't matter. Let the people in suits duke it out, embarrassing themselves in public.

But this year was an election year, and times had changed. My competition was a man fresh out of the academy with little to no experience, but he had the governor backing him, who just so happened to be his father's college roommate.

Not that I thought the governor's opinion mattered in our small town, but they sure did have a bunch of ads running on TV encouraging the prejudice that it was better for the town to have a man in office. It had taken me the better part of the four-year term to get the local citizens to drop that stigma from their minds.

Still, my answer, though it tasted sour on my tongue, seemed to satisfy my neighbor.

Duke situated himself in the passenger seat while I took a sip of the steaming coffee. Then I put the beverage in the beanbag cup holder that lay over the hump on the floorboard. It was one of those old cup holders that could only be found in places like Ruby's Antiques, and it had been left there since Poppa put it in the Wagoneer.

Two other things I'd inherited from him—the Wagoneer and the cup holder.

I leaned over the seat and across Duke and gripped the handle of the crank for the manual window. With each rotation, I could feel someone staring at me from the corner of my eye.

"Hello, Poppa," I greeted Poppa, who Duke happened to be ignoring because the window was rolled down, and he was going to hang out of it.

I eased myself into the driver's seat and adjusted the rearview mirror so I could catch the glimpse of Poppa.

"You know, Kenni, we have a knack for seeing connections where others might miss 'em," Poppa mused, a hint of mischief in his voice. "I've got a hunch that this missing person and the John Doe from the railroad tracks might just be one and the same."

"Betty said that too," I said, making sure I reached over and patted Duke before I turned over the ignition as if I were talking to my hound dog.

I couldn't risk someone seeing me talking to myself. I'd been caught before, and being caught again wouldn't be good during an election year.

But I couldn't shake off Poppa's comment.

Poppa's instincts had guided me before, and more often than not, he was right.

I turned the key in the ignition and drove the Jeep down Second Street where it met Main Street.

Little did I know, as I pulled a left out of Free Row, that I was about to embark on a journey on which the lines between truth and deception would blur, and the cost of seeking justice would be higher than I could ever imagine.

CHAPTER FOUR

I turned into the alley behind Cowboy's Catfish. I parked the Wagoneer behind the dumpster in my normal parking spot, sandwiched between Betty's car and Scott's deputy truck.

"Here's the sheriff now." Betty pointed me out before I could get the toes of my boots inside the door.

She looked at the client, a woman, and gestured to the chair in front of my desk for her to have a seat before. Then Betty patted over her short grey hair. Her blue eyes held concern that I couldn't ask her about at the moment.

"Sheriff," the woman started, ignoring Duke's sniffing around her shoes.

He was as much a part of this department as Scott, Betty, and I were. Duke's sniffing her shoes told me a few things because it was the kind of sniffing he did when animals were involved. Then he moved up her leg, and the woman finally patted his head as if she did this all day long.

When Duke got the final whiff, he settled himself down on the big dog bed next to the desk.

"I need to file a missing persons report," she said, her voice tinged with a mixture of hope and fear.

Nodding, I motioned for Betty to hand me the report she'd started before I'd arrived.

"Of course. Betty has already started some of the paperwork, but I'm going to need to ask you some more questions." I took the file from Betty and scanned it. "What's the name of the missing person?"

She took a deep breath, composing herself before answering. "His name is Dilbert Thistle. He's my husband."

"I'm so sorry to hear that, Mrs. Thistle," I replied, my voice filled with genuine concern. "Can you provide me with some details about Dilbert? When did you last see him? Did he have any plans or reasons to be away?"

She hesitated as her eyes welled with tears. "I saw him yesterday morning before he left for work. He didn't mention any plans or give any indication that something was wrong. Dilbert is usually punctual and would never disappear without letting me know."

I jotted down the information. My pen danced across the paper, noting down every detail she shared.

"Does Dilbert have any distinguishing features or personal belongings that could aid in his identification?" I asked, wondering if Max Bogus had started his initial autopsy and found any sort of birthmarks, tattoos, or identifying features.

She rummaged through her handbag and produced a worn photograph. As I looked at it, my heart sank. Dilbert Thistle, as captured in the picture, had a warm smile and a twinkle in his eyes.

I couldn't recall the details of our John Doe, since we'd discovered him at night and were just working around the body to collect as much evidence as possible so we didn't have to keep the trains from coming through all night long.

"I've tried the hospital over in Clay's Ferry, and they don't have him there. I even tried to call his work, but since it's Saturday, I'm sure they won't be there at all today," she said, her voice quivering with anxiety.

"How tall is he?" I asked. When she replied, I jotted down six foot seven. "Do you know what he weighs?"

"Oh dear." Mrs. Thistle's brows knotted. "You know, he just had a physical, his annual physical for work from Dr. Shively. I guess I can get his records."

"That'd be great." I noted in Dilbert's file that she was going to get us his medical records, which would be great to have to compare against whatever

Max pulled from our John Doe. "I'm going to need a list of Dilbert's friends. Anyone who he hung around as well as family members. All family members. Anyone who might have had an argument with him."

"Argument?" She jerked up, and her mouth dropped open as her eyes widened. "Do you think he's dead?"

"Mrs. Thistle, these are just standard questions the sheriff has to ask. They do not mean anything has happened to your husband," Scott chimed in.

"We all have someone who doesn't like us." Her accent took a heavier southern twang. "I can't think of anyone who would want to kill him." She let go of a long sigh. "Or harm him."

"Where does he work?" I asked.

"Over yonder at the drywall plant."

"Does your husband drink?" I asked.

"Are you accusing my husband of being a drunk?" She seemed even more appalled at this question than the one I'd asked.

"Anything to help find him," I said, reiterating what Scott was trying to say.

"He's nipped at the bottle a time or two." She blinked. "Only after they win."

"Win?" I asked for clarification.

"He's on the softball team for Dee's Dairy Bar. He and the guys like to go have a beer after a good win—or loss." She shrugged with a smile as if reliving fond memories. Her emotions must have taken a swift turn then because sadness replaced the smile. "It's Saturday. I bet they are wondering where he is at."

"Dairy Bar softball team has a game today?" Scott threw me a look.

"Yes. It's going to start down at the fairground about noon-ish. The reason I say '-ish' is that a lot of the time, the men like to get together the night before and knock a few back while they talk about game strategy. And, well, it takes them a lot longer to recuperate from a night of drinking than it did when they were younger," she mumbled, fidgeting with her jewelry.

"That would've been last night, right?" I circled back to the timeframe she'd just given me. Scott was busy behind me, writing down details on the

378

whiteboard we used for noting things like timelines and clues so we could see where they might connect and follow up on them.

"Yes, but Dilbert always calls me." She blinked rapidly, the fear of where he might be reflected in her eyes.

"Did you call any of his team members?" I asked in hopes she'd give me a few names.

"No." She shook her head.

"Surely if your husband was on this team, as you say"—I looked down at the notes I'd just written—"in his younger days—and by his photo, he doesn't look like he's been younger for a while—you must have gotten to know the partners of some of the other team members."

"I don't go to the games." She sat back and crossed her legs and arms. "I don't like sitting in the hot sun unless my toes are in the sand and I'm holding a fruity alcoholic drink with an umbrella sticking out of a piece of fruit."

That would explain the tan on Mrs. Thistle's skin. She might not have been going to the Tan-O-Rama down in Edgewood, another part of town. The salon remained busy this time of the year.

"Sheriff?" Betty interrupted us from her desk. She held the old rotary phone up to her ear, her hand covering the mouthpiece. "Max is on the phone."

I lifted my finger in the air, signaling for her to tell him to hold on.

"I think I've got all I need to file the report and put out some feelers, but I'm going to need you to go home and compile me a list of the people I asked about," I said. "Family, friends, co-workers, and even softball team members. Anyone who might've had a little falling-out with your husband."

She nodded and got up.

Scott stood up next to her and walked her out.

As soon as she was out of earshot, I grabbed the phone on my desk and punched the blinking light to connect with Max.

"Hey, Max, anything on our John Doe?" I asked.

"Yeah. I got some fingerprints as soon as we got back last night and put them in the database before I went home." There was some clicking noise in the background of his end of the conversation as he talked. "I got in the office a few minutes ago and pulled up the report to see if we got a hit, and our John Doe's name is Dilbert Thistle."

Max's voice crackled through the phone as he relayed the information I had been anxiously waiting for. The revelation sent a jolt of surprise and confirmation through my veins.

Dilbert Thistle, I thought to myself and gulped when I saw Georgina walk back over near my desk.

"Hold on," I told Max and covered the receiver with my hand. "Did your husband have an inhaler?" I asked.

"No." She shook her head.

"Are you sure it's him?" I questioned Max with a whisper.

"I might not be sure, but the DNA is." In no uncertain terms, Max let me know he didn't appreciate me questioning his competency.

"I'm sorry. I know you're the expert, but I have a missing persons case here with the same man missing, and, well, it's not just a missing person now." My mind circled back to the lack of evidence we'd collected at the crime scene or at least at the last part of it, which made me question where the first part of the crime scene was located.

The missing person and the unidentified body were indeed one and the same. The puzzle pieces were fitting together, but the image they revealed was far from comforting. If Dilbert was in our database, that meant Dilbert was on the wrong side of the law at one time. It also told me he did have a few enemies, but who were they?

I hung up with Max and went back to Georgina.

"Did your husband have any enemies?" I asked.

"Why, no." She shook her head and ran the back of her hand along the bottom of her nose as if she were wiping away some dripping snot that wasn't there.

"Did your husband run off with someone else?" I asked.

Her body contorted at the thought of that slight possibility.

"What are you saying?" She scooted up on the edge of her chair. "We had our squabbles, but we also had our routine, and Dilbert never strayed from our routine."

My mind curled back to the note.

"Did your husband have any secrets about anyone or anything that someone wouldn't want him to tell?" I questioned.

"Is someone else in here capable of just filing a missing person's report for me?" Georgina popped up and looked between Betty and Scott.

Both pointed at me.

Before I could respond, Poppa's ghostly presence materialized beside me, his eyes twinkling mischievously.

"Well, looks like our John Doe's name is no longer a thistle in the wind but a real-life Dilbert Thistle. Death sure knows how to make a point, don't it?" He rubbed his hands together and danced a little jig. "Looks like we got ourselves another case."

CHAPTER FIVE

The small town of Cottonwood greeted Duke and me with its familiar charm as I made the left turn on Main Street to drive a couple of blocks over to the Funeral Home, our one-stop shop for death of any kind.

The southern town seemed at peace today despite what had taken place just a couple of blocks down on the railroad tracks. That tranquility would disappear once the town woke up and people started calling one another.

For now, though, I couldn't help but look at the warm glow of carriage lights as they illuminated the sidewalks. Those lamps would still be on until the sun fully rose.

It was still early, and a slight breeze was coming in from a cold front. At least, that was just reported on WCKK, our very own radio station.

"It looks like it's going to be a great week for the county fair. Y'all be sure to head on out tonight for the baby beauty pageant. There's going to be some music over at the pavilion, and don't forget to bring extra money for those awesome carnival rides or try your luck at winning your sweetie a big ol' teddy bear at the ring toss. But for now, let's take a listen to Lin-elle Richie."

"Lionel," I repeated to the DJ as if he could hear me correct him. I brought the Wagoneer to a halt when the light stopped me at the intersection of Main Street and West Oak Street, where I needed to turn left.

Duke's head was flung out the window, as was half of his body. His ears perked every time one of the colorful banners heralding the county fair whipped around on a light dowel rod. Every few seconds, the crisp breeze mingled with the sweet fragrance of the vibrant flowers in the large ceramic pots on both sidewalks of Main Street. Myrna Savage from Petal Pushers had donated those blossoms.

As soon as the light turned, I hooked a left and passed the Cottonwood First National Bank on the right. Next to that were the funeral home and its parking lot, where I parked the Jeep right behind Max's hearse.

"You stay," I instructed Duke, though I knew there was a good chance he wouldn't. And that was all right.

Everyone in town knew Duke, and he knew all of them. If the Run Food Truck drove past, an event that had a favorable chance by my calculations, he'd jump out and run after it until my best friend and the truck's owner, Jolee Fischer, saw him in the rearview mirror and stopped to let him go with her for the morning.

Still, I patted him on the head and left him in the car.

The awning over the steps of the funeral home was already fully extended. That told me without even reading the obituary section of the *Cottonwood Chronicles* that someone had died and today was either the layout or the funeral, so I was going to have limited access to Max.

That was only one issue in a small town. Most people had two jobs, and since Max was both the coroner and the undertaker, well, he had to do both in order to make his living.

When I let myself inside, the smell hit me, turning my stomach and summoning memories that were hard to banish.

Poppa's funeral.

My heart sank as I entered the front room of the funeral home, my eyes drawn to the beautifully arranged flowers adorning the movable platform shelves. Myrna Savage had meticulously crafted the display, arranging the blooms based on size rather than their monetary value. That detail was small, but it spoke volumes about the unspoken hierarchy that existed within our community.

The most extravagant floral arrangements were strategically posi-tioned near the casket, in the room off to the right. Myrna had a reputation for showcasing the most opulent displays in that prime spot. It was a subtle status symbol, a silent competition among the mourners. The size and grandeur of the floral tributes reflected not only the deceased's importance but also the generosity and social standing of those who sent them.

But it wasn't just about the flowers.

The South had a code of hospitality and community support that extended beyond the funeral service. The repast, the gathering held after the funeral, was a time for fellowship and solace, when people came together to find comfort in shared memories and stories. And, of course, the food played a central role.

The repast was a celebration of southern traditions, in which homemade casseroles, delectable desserts, and refreshing teas were lovingly prepared by friends, neighbors, and church members. It was a demonstration of care and compassion, a way of offering comfort to the grieving family. The repast was more than just a meal; it was a symbol of unity and support during a time of profound loss.

As I took in the scene and the delicate fragrance of the flowers mingling with the anticipation of the upcoming gathering, I couldn't help but reflect on the unique dynamics of our southern community. In the face of tragedy, we rallied together, each playing a part in the intricate dance of tradition, comfort, and unwavering support, wondering what on earth Dilbert Thistle did to someone that ended his life.

I found my way downstairs and stood in front of the door where the chilly morgue was located. I looked in one of the small portal windows and saw a covered body on a steel table.

My head must've cast a shadow because Max Bogus looked up from the eyehole of his digital camera and waved me in.

Seeing a dead body first thing in the morning wasn't always on my to-do list, but it came with the job. I sucked in a deep breath and prepared myself for what I was about to see.

It never got any easier, no matter how many times my professors in school told us it would. Not the empathy part but how I'd become almost numb to seeing dead people.

At least not for me.

"You got here awfully early." I slipped through the swinging metal doors and immediately walked over to the clipboard, on which I signed my name.

Max kept meticulous notes on who came in and out of the morgue.

When I entered the morgue, the air grew cooler, tinged with a sterile scent that sent a chill down my spine. Stainless steel tables stood in orderly rows, each one a silent witness to the mysteries of death.

Max stood at the table where Dilbert Thistle lay, his features serene in the pale glow of the overhead lights.

"I figured we needed to get our John Doe here ID'd." He brought the digital camera back up to his face. After placing his hands on the lens, he rotated it left and then right as he used his trigger finger to click away. "I'm glad I did too. Now that we have an ID."

He pulled his eyes away from the camera just enough to glance at me and give a quick nod.

"The fingerprints and paperwork are over there." He threw a chin toward the table just outside of his office.

"I'll let you finish up while I take them in the office and read over them." I walked over, ignoring the body for now, and grabbed the appropriate folder. John Doe, the previous name written on the front, was crossed out, and Dilbert Thistle was written below.

Ghost Poppa materialized beside me, his ethereal form fading in and out as he watched me. I couldn't help but feel the weight of his presence, his guidance and protection always by my side. My mind wandered to Finn and the unanswered proposal. My decision hinged on having Poppa's protection, but I had enough confidence in my ability as sheriff to know I could protect myself.

In this life, I couldn't take comfort in knowing my Poppa's ghost was here.

"As you can see, our victim has a history." Max Bogus entered the office, taking me out of my thoughts and causing Poppa to disappear.

Max's room was nearly bare. Two chairs were in front of his desk, neither of them matching, which made me think they came from Ruby's Antiques on Main Street. Behind the desk was a bookshelf wall, only it didn't hold a single book. It was filled with files upon files.

"I've not gotten a chance to open it." I sat down in one of the chairs, crossed my leg over my knee, and opened the file. "I'm more interested in his history on the wrong side of the law."

If Dilbert had been doing something illegal, someone had had a good motive to kill him. And it would give me a great place to start an investigation.

"He's not some hard criminal, just a few EPO violations." Max referred to what was called an Ex Parte Order of Protection, filed against Dilbert by none other than his ex-wife, Georgina Thistle.

Ex.

"Interesting." I read the file again. "Georgina Thistle came into the department before I even got to the office, wanting to file a missing person's report on her husband, Dilbert."

In the meantime, Max busied himself by pouring a cup of coffee and taking out a doughnut from the Pump and Munch gas station on the corner.

Now, as I glanced at Max, his lips smudged with remnants of a sugary doughnut, I couldn't help but cringe inwardly. The juxtaposition of his indulgence and the somber atmosphere of the morgue felt almost surreal.

How could anyone find the appetite to enjoy a doughnut while surrounded by dead bodies?

I gulped and tried to concentrate on the file.

"That's interesting." Max licked his fingers and picked up the mug, which was stained brown on the outside. "Ex, huh?"

"Yeah. That means there's more to her story than she was willing to share." My brows rose. I put Georgina on my list of people to visit today, possibly right after this little visit with her ex-husband's dead body.

"Did she appear to be strong enough to put a body on the tracks?" Max asked, grabbing my attention.

I leaned against Max's cluttered desk, studying his face for some answers to the context of his question.

Max adjusted his glasses, his expression turning serious.

"Well, Kenni, the initial findings indicate that the gash on Dilbert's head is postmortem. It appears someone killed him using a different method. I'm not entirely sure what that is, but I'm guessing and running tests on poison in the samples of tissues and blood."

"So someone wanted to make it look like Dilbert was hit by a train to cover up the poisoning?" I wanted to make sure I understood the exact gravity of a killer's mind.

It wasn't like I could just go arrest someone for Dilbert's murder. I had to know all the details so I had a solid case to present to the local prosecutor when I did bring the killer in on charges of murder.

Max nodded, taking a sip of his coffee.

"That seems to be the case. The poison is still being analyzed, so we should have more information soon. But, Kenni, I must say, this is a peculiar and elaborate method for concealing a murder." He gazed over the rim of the mug and took another sip.

I furrowed my brow, deep in thought.

"It makes me wonder who would go to such lengths and why. And what connection does Georgina, Dilbert's ex-wife, have to all of this? She conveniently left out that they were divorced when she came to file the missing person report, which only makes me think I need to go pay her a little visit."

Max leaned back in his chair, a contemplative expression on his face. "Ah, the tangled webs we weave. It's not uncommon for murder cases to involve someone close to the victim, someone they know intimately. Could Georgina be hiding something? Or was it just a simple oversight?"

"She seemed pretty passionate about him missing." My voice fell flat, but my mind was reeling. "Did you send this to the office?" I wagged the file in case I needed to get some copies before I left.

"I did. And I hope to have the blood and tissue results back this afternoon, if not in the morning," Max noted.

"I know I don't have to tell you, but if there's a way to rush it without compromising the results, please do so." I stood up, satisfied that I'd gotten some excellent information to start asking the right questions for the investigation.

That meant going straight to see Georgina Thistle.

CHAPTER SIX

M y thumb tapped on the steering wheel as I pondered Georgina Thistle's behavior this morning.

"Hey, buddy," I said to Duke, who continued to jump back and forth between the front seat, where I sat, and the back seat, where Poppa floated. "I'm glad you listened and stayed."

"What's with the chitchat?" Poppa asked.

"Just making sure if someone sees me talking, they think it's to Duke," I said and slightly turned in my seat to look back at Duke. He was sitting right next to Poppa.

A series of questions raced through my mind, each one probing deeper into what Georgina's motive was for deceiving me.

I scratched behind Duke's ear, lost in thought. "Well, Duke, what do you make of all this?" I asked aloud, my voice carrying my uncertainty.

"Seems mighty suspicious, doesn't it, Kenni bug? There's more to this story, I reckon." Poppa raised his head between the seats.

Nodding, I mulled over the puzzling situation. "You're right, Poppa. Something doesn't add up with Georgina's actions. Filing a missing person report while keeping their divorce a secret? It's all too fishy."

"Why would Georgina file a missing person report on Dilbert if she had a history of filing Emergency Protective Orders against him?" I asked. "What prompted her sudden concern for his well-being?"

"Did Georgina conveniently leave out the fact that she and Dilbert were divorced?" Poppa asked that even more important question. "What's she tryin' to hide?"

"We are going to find out." I gave Poppa the side-eye as I reached up to my shoulder and clicked the button that brought the walkie-talkie to life.

"Go ahead," Betty chirped back.

"Our John Doe is Dilbert Thistle, and he has a record," I said, my finger holding the button down. "There's a restraining order against him from Georgina, his ex-wife."

"Ex-wife?" Betty cried out. "I've never seen no ex-wife with an EPO against her ex-husband file a missing person report."

I squinted, figuring I should've known to roll the volume down.

"Me either, which means I need you to bring up the EPO and also look at the missing person report she filled out. It has her address on it. I'm going to pay her a little visit," I said.

The EPO would've been filed in the system the sheriff's department had access to, and I needed all the order's particulars as well as the address.

"I'll text them over." Betty clicked off, knowing I would request that she send the items I'd asked her for through text messaging.

Scott Lee had been trying to bring us up to date on technology. No one, not even Finn, had gotten me to even think about upgrading the walkie-talkies or the old siren beacon I used to slap atop the Wagoneer's roof when I had to hightail it to an emergency.

Even the way we processed evidence was considered the old way of doing things. Today I'd drive to the lab on the outskirts of Clay's Ferry to drop off the inhaler. There, I would see if it had any DNA evidence that could link its owner to Dilbert or anything in the note we'd found in Dilbert's pocket.

Now, I pulled back out on Main Street and headed north, right behind the On the Run food truck. In the truck's side mirror, I saw Jolee at the wheel.

"You know I love you, but I think it would be better if I go see Georgina alone," I told Duke in hopes his already droopy eyes would at least droop a little more.

He wasn't.

His tail was thumping against the back of the passenger seat. His front paws were on the door rest, pushing his whole torso out of the window. His ears perked as the food truck accelerated, a sound he'd become very familiar with after going with Jolee a few times.

He let out a loud, extended howl with his nose up to the morning sky, causing Jolee to slow down.

With two fingers peeled off the steering wheel, I gave her a slight wave when I saw her look to her side mirror.

She smiled widely when she saw who we were.

Still right behind the food truck, I pulled up to the curb in front of Lulu's Boutique.

I threw the Jeep in park but didn't bother turning it off because I was just going to get right back in it.

Every morning, Jolee would park her food truck in front of Lulu's Boutique. The spot was perfect for people going to and from town this time of the morning on their way to work. Also, there were plenty of spots to park and grab something on the go.

Lulu McClain, one of Mama's friends, owned an old clapboard house that she'd turned into a cute shop. She had local items, knickknacks, candles, some clothing, and other accessories for the home. She had even worked out a deal with Jolee to use the craft room in the back of the shop, where Lulu held various crafty classes, as a small dining area for people who didn't need to take the delicious food on the go.

Jolee pushed open the order window on the side of the food truck and popped her head out of it. "To what do I owe this pleasure?"

Her blond hair was neatly braided in pigtails that framed her face. The freckles along the bridge of her nose grew when she noticed Duke bolt around to see where she was.

"There's my buddy." She giggled, her green eyes lighting up. "I've got a special treat for you."

She reached into her flour-covered apron's pocket and tossed him a homemade treat.

"There's plenty more where that came from." She tossed another one. Then she shifted to me. "Did you get an ID on the—you know," she whispered, knowing that when she'd left the scene last night, we had had to tag Dilbert as John Doe. "Choo-choo?" she followed up as though I didn't get what she was asking.

"Yeah." I nodded. "Dilbert Thistle. Do you know him?"

Jolee was such a good secret keeper, and her truck was very popular. Even though I was the sheriff, I didn't know half the people in Cottonwood that she did, which made her a great person to question. Furthermore, Poppa had offered me no help, and that meant I needed to tell someone who I could trust so I could hear myself talking it out.

"I don't." She shook her head. "Wait." She looked off into the distance. "I might. I think he plays on the Dairy Bar's softball team, right?"

"He does. How did you know that?" I asked because I knew Jolee wasn't on any softball team.

"Last year, when the team won, he had a strikeout game or something. I was one of the sponsors for the championship, and he bought a round of hot bowl sammies for the entire team afterwards." She smiled. "He tipped pretty good too. Shame he fell on the tracks but not surprising."

Jolee fiddled around in the food truck, getting ready for the opening crowd that would soon form a line at the window. I put my elbows on the steel counter and leaned in a little, watching her fry the eggs before she slid a sheet of homemade biscuits into the oven.

"Why would you not be surprised?" I wondered, not telling her that he didn't fall on the tracks and was instead thrown on them.

"The way he was knocking back the brews, that's how. That's how I got the big tip." She stopped in the middle of cracking eggshells and looked at me. "He came to the truck the next day, asking for his tip back. Said he couldn't pay off some debts, and he was in a bit of a legal pickle."

Was the debt to Georgina? Was the legal pickle his court fees from the EPO Georgina had filed?

"What happened?" I asked.

"I gave it back to him, but it wasn't but maybe three days until he showed up again with the tip." She shrugged, wiped her hands on her apron, and picked up the spatula. She pointed it at me. "Only this time, it was more money. He said he came into some money and didn't want me to go without my tip."

"Really," I said in more of a shocked tone than anything. This anecdote gave a personal, endearing side to Dilbert, whereas previously I had questioned his integrity.

That was the horrible aspect of working on my side of the law. It wasn't that I'd misjudged him. It was the fact of the matter that when a judge granted an EPO on someone, it was because the person, in this case Dilbert, did something to warrant such a harsh penalty.

"Yeah. I've not seen him again…" Jolee's words fell off as if she realized the severity of last night. "Until last night." She frowned and moved to the pancake griddle.

"You never had any sort of personal conversation with him?" I dug deeper. "Like if he was married? Or anyone who would want to kill him?"

Jolee's face jerked up while she was flipping the pancake.

"You never know." I grinned when I saw her put one of the pancakes in a paper bowl and top the flapjack with a runny egg and some syrup.

"He didn't. But I'm guessing you're asking because this wasn't some random drunken fall on the train tracks." She stuck a fork in the top of her concoction and slid it out the window to me.

She turned and made me a cup of coffee. I gladly accepted because I'd long since drunk my cup from home while taking Georgina's missing person report.

"Georgina Thistle came in before the department was even open, and she claimed her husband had been missing since yesterday. He just so happens to be our John Doe, which I've not told her." I told Jolee this little bit of information so she knew not to say a word to anyone, even if they asked her about the body on the train tracks.

The sole reason it hadn't gotten around the telephone gossip chain was that the only people who knew about it were my loved ones who'd gathered at the Luke Jones movie night that Mama had put on for me to cover up the proposal.

They and Patty Dunaway, who I needed to go see today as well. I had questions for her too.

But once Patty Dunaway got her wits about her this morning, the flood-

392

gates of gossip would open, and everyone would either gather at Ben's Diner to exchange information or show up here at Jolee's food truck because they knew she was my best friend.

I wanted to get in front of Georgina before all of that happened, not only to tell her we'd ID'd the victim but also to ask her why she'd left out that she'd put an EPO out on Dilbert.

"Oh my. That's terrible," Jolee said, her voice cracking at the thought of poor Georgina. "Let me get you a doughnut to take to her, since I bet that's where you're going."

"I don't want to butter her up. She left out the little-known fact she had put an EPO out on him." I almost snorted out a mouthful of the coffee when Jolee's face contorted into the recognizable expression she pulled when she knew someone had become a suspect in one of my investigations.

"Shut up!" She smacked the counter. "She must've killed him."

"Don't be jumping to no conclusions." I used my left hand to pick up the breakfast treat.

Jolee looked down. I could see questions about the proposal were on the tip of her tongue.

"Don't even ask," I warned.

"My lips are zipped until euchre." Her brows bounced up and down. She and I both knew all bets were off the table during our weekly euchre game, which was tomorrow night. There, we'd be surrounded by people we loved, and they would all expect answers to their questions.

I didn't have time to think about how that would play out, and I didn't mean the euchre cards.

"You leave Duke with Auntie Jolee," she told him in a baby-talk voice as she flipped him another treat. "We will have a great day."

"Are you going to the fairgrounds this afternoon?" I asked.

"I have a permit but wasn't planning on going until tonight. But I can," she offered.

"Today the Dairy Bar and Lulu's Boutique are playing for the softball title. I figured I'd go out there and question some of the team members." I looked over my shoulder when I heard a few doors slamming.

People were starting to arrive, which told me it was probably between eight and eight thirty a.m., late enough to pay Georgina Thistle that visit.

"I'll meet up with you at some point today, or you can drop Duke off at the house. Thanks for the food." I gave a slight smile to the people in the line that had formed behind me when I turned around to leave.

Duke didn't even bother trying to follow me. He wasn't about to leave Jolee now that he was here. He'd already made himself at home underneath the steel counter, where a piece of food just might drop. He was better than any street sweep, and Jolee didn't even have to clean up a mess when he was there.

They made a great team.

Just like Poppa and me.

"I noticed Jolee was going to ask about the questions." Poppa had shifted himself into the passenger seat.

I got out my phone, pulled up the text Betty had sent with Georgina's address in it, and hit the hyperlink to send it to the Maps app. I recognized the subdivision and knew where it was located but not the street name.

"Yes, Poppa. I guess I'm in a little bit of a pickle." I smiled at him and put the Wagoneer in drive. I made a U-turn back out to the stop sign, and that put me right back on Main Street, where I hung a left.

The old Jeep rattled north as I set my sights on heading up to what was called the Orchard Subdivision. It was behind the Wal-Mart and other various chain restaurants and shops like the Dollar Store.

"You know I love you and only want the best for you." Poppa had refused to accept that I was in love with Finn, but my love for him ran so deep, he knew this wasn't fair to me. "But I also know that I can keep you safe."

"You've not given him a chance to do so. Since I've dated him, you've made it abundantly clear you don't want me to get married." I took a left on Orchard Drive and drove the length close to the intersected with Union Mill Road.

I checked the directions twice on my phone. I didn't know this area well. There weren't many calls to dispatch despite the numerous houses that'd gone up in the past few years.

"It has nothing to do with that boy. It has everything to do with me taking care of you, and you are the most important thing to me." Poppa sighed, giving a huge huff out of his large nose before crossing his arms.

Who knew ghosts could have such emotions?

"I have to say that I'm terribly shocked Granny's ring is missing." I hadn't talked to him about the ring he'd given me that I'd been waiting to put on my own finger.

Finn knew that too. So when he went to get the ring, my parents couldn't find it. To me, that meant only one thing.

Poppa did something with it.

"You don't have proof." Poppa looked out the window. "I can't believe they took all of this farmland for rows and rows of houses. What on earth has Cottonwood done? It's that mayor!"

"You can't ignore the fact you've taken the ring. What if..." I started down the little road of the little game Poppa and I were used to playing.

"I leave," he protested before his body faded away.

"You can't run from this forever!" I called out into the air because I knew he was still there. Not only did the goosebumps all over my body tell me so, but there was no way he'd let me go to Georgina's house without some protection.

And I didn't mean my own gun.

Georgina's house blended seamlessly with the other cookie-cutter houses that lined the suburban street. It was a two-story structure with a generic design that prioritized efficiency and speed of construction. The exterior showcased a symmetrical facade devoid of any unique architectural details or flourishes.

I'd call them bologna on white.

Plain.

The house was painted beige. The front yard consisted of a small patch of grass, neatly trimmed and with very little landscaping.

A solitary tree stood near the edge of the property, offering little shade.

Approaching the front door, I noticed the standard-issue porch, just wide enough to accommodate a couple of the plastic chairs and the lone glass ashtray sitting on the concrete between them.

The entrance lacked any distinct features, its plain white door blending in with the monotonous uniformity of the neighborhood.

I gave a hard knock on the door.

The curtain in the window shifted slightly before Georgina opened the door.

"Sheriff," Georgina said to me. "Come in."

"Thank you," I said and looked back to see what her eyes had settled on.

"Don't bother with him. He's a nosy neighbor, and he'll be telling everyone the sheriff stopped by." She glared at him before she shut the door behind her.

After stepping inside, I followed her through the house and noticed a living room to the left, a dining area to the right, and a generic kitchen straight ahead, which was where she offered me a cup of coffee.

"No thank you," I declined.

"Sit. Please." She pointed at the kitchen table, where the *Cottonwood Chronicles* was laid out, along with a pack of cigarettes and a coffee cup. "I came home and started to read the paper." She sat down, and her fingers went directly into her mouth.

By the way the fingernails on her other hand looked, I could tell she was a biter.

Her body language screamed discomfort, her crossed arms and fidgeting fingers betraying her unease.

I took a deep breath, preparing to delve into the delicate matter at hand.

"Georgina, I have some questions for you," I began, my voice steady but firm. "Why didn't you mention that you had filed an EPO against Dilbert? And why didn't you tell me you were divorced?"

Georgina's eyes darted around the kitchen, avoiding direct contact with mine. She seemed uneasy, as if grappling with her own internal turmoil. Finally, she sighed, her shoulders slumping slightly.

"I... I didn't think it was relevant," she stammered, her voice wavering. "The EPO, well... It was a precaution. We had our issues, but it didn't mean I wanted anything bad to happen to him."

I observed her closely, noticing the subtle signs of guilt that flickered across her face. The slight downturn of her lips and her avoidance of eye contact spoke volumes. There was more to this story, something she was holding back.

"Georgina, I need you to be honest with me," I pressed, my tone gentle but insistent. "Did you and Dilbert have any recent conflicts? Any reason to believe that someone might want to harm him?"

Georgina hesitated for a moment, her gaze fixed on the floor.

Finally, she said in a hushed tone, almost a whisper, "We... we had arguments, like any couple does. But nothing that would lead to something like this. Dilbert wasn't perfect, but he was a good man."

"Then why did you put out an EPO on him?" I asked. I kept a close eye on her because if she did kill him, she was great at disguising it.

"He owed me money. He pays the mortgage, and that's what the judge ordered." She got up and walked over to the counter, where she pulled a stack of papers out of a drawer. "He was late this month. The bank called to let me know they hadn't received his payment. I knew he got paid this week, so I called him. When he didn't answer, I knew something was wrong because he always answers."

"Why would he always answer? That'd be in violation of his EPO," I said.

"Because he said he'd always answer, since he was holding out hope I'd take him back." She produced their divorce papers, which showed he was to pay her mortgage instead of her getting any of his 401K from the drywall plant.

As I contemplated her response, a sudden realization struck me. It was time for me to tell her about Dilbert and where he was now, even though I still considered her a suspect—currently my only suspect.

"Georgina, I'm sorry to have to tell you this, but Dilbert was found dead on the railroad tracks," I said, my voice heavy with the weight of the truth.

Georgina's eyes widened in shock, her hand instinctively rising to her mouth. The color drained from her face, and her body went limp.

Before I could react, she slumped back against the couch, losing consciousness.

My heart raced as I hurried to her side.

"11-41, 11-41!" I screamed the code for an ambulance into the walkie-talkie with one hand on the button and Georgina in my other arm. "Georgina's home. 11-41!"

"Copy 11-41," Betty said, quickly clicking back. "On the way."

"Georgina, Georgina," I continued to call, though Georgina wasn't one bit conscious.

As the distant sound of sirens grew louder, I focused on Georgina, checking her pulse with a gentle touch. Relief washed over me as I felt the faint throb of her heartbeat. She was still with us, but her condition was precarious.

The front door swung open, and in walked a woman with a glass of sweet tea in hand.

"Well, I'll be hornswoggled," she exclaimed, her eyes widening as she took in the scene. "I just knew something wasn't right when Rance told me the sheriff's car pulled up. Had a hunch I should turn on the ol' scanner, and wouldn't you know it, here I am."

"Please, ma'am," I said, about to tell her to leave.

"Claudia Forhordt, Georgina's neighbor," she replied, taking the situation as if it were the right time for introductions. "Is she all right? Did she have some sort of diabetic episode?"

"Well, I'm not sure what is going on with her. She fainted. I've called for an ambulance. It's on the way to take her to the county hospital. She's alive, so if you don't mind"—I nodded to the door—"I need to do my job."

Claudia's eyebrows shot up in surprise. "Fainted, you say? Mercy me! I hope that ambulance is on the double, sugah. They are the slowest group of EMTs around."

Claudia took it upon herself to give commentary as I tried to position Georgina so her head didn't fall back.

"Here, you need Rance's help. He's a strong man." Claudia tried to position herself behind me with her arms outstretched. "Rance! Rance Forhordt, you get over here right now!"

My eyes squinted shut as she screamed right into my ear.

"Please leave. I've got it," I told her.

"I don't think you do. Georgina ain't the skinniest." Claudia began yelling for Rance. "I said get over here! I know you hear me!" She sighed and stuck her body to me like glue, her arms around me and up under Georgina's armpits. "He is normally glued to the fence out there, trying to hear what's going on around here, so he ain't foolin' me none by not hurrying up over here."

"Did you say something about Georgina and diabetes?" I asked, thinking she was having some sort of heart episode, since I noticed the pack of cigarettes.

"Oh yeah. Sticks herself with them needles," Claudia said.

The sound of sirens drew closer.

"Honestly, you can move. I have her," I told Claudia one more time before I demanded it.

"Fine." She stood up and tugged on the edges of her shirt. "I guess what Taven Tidwell is tootin' about you hurting our sweet little town by not receiving any help is ringin' true."

"Keep it together, Kenni bug." Poppa's voice was faint, but I heard it. I couldn't see him, but I could hear him. "Don't you worry about Taven Tidwell," he said, referring to the man who was rumored to run against me in the election.

"Excuse me, ma'am." A young EMT rushed into the house, asking Claudia to step out of the way.

"Sheriff, you okay?" I heard Scott call from behind me.

"Deputy Lee, get that woman out of here," I demanded and happily let the EMT take Georgina out of my arms. "She may have passed out from shock after I told her that her husband had died."

"Ex, Sheriff," Scott corrected me.

I shot him a look.

"Sorry." He threw his hands up.

"Or she could be having some sort of diabetic thing." I craned my neck to crack it back in line with my spine, since it went all cockeyed while I was holding Georgina.

I let the EMTs do their thing while I went looking for Scott. He'd gone outside and was talking to Claudia and someone I assumed was Rance.

"It wasn't like they weren't in love, but he drank most of their money, and he got dried out. That's when he started coming around again, saying he was making all sorts of money at the drywall plant." Claudia smacked Rance with the back of her hand. "Ain't that right, Rance?"

"I reckon. Whatever you say, honey."

Rance and I exchanged glances.

As I stood outside Georgina's house, waiting for the paramedics to finish attending to her, I took notice of Rance. He was a sturdy man with a salt-and-pepper beard, leaning against the railing while Claudia clutched her empty glass of sweet tea.

"Sheriff," Claudia began, her voice tinged with concern. "We've known

Georgina and Dilbert for a good eight years now. Seen 'em through their ups and downs, just like any married couple. Well, until they got divorced, that is."

Rance nodded. "Yep, it's true. Those two had their fair share of arguments and disagreements. Never did see eye to eye on much, but what couple does?"

I raised an eyebrow, curious to know more.

"Did you ever notice anything peculiar about their relationship, anything that might shed light on them?" I asked.

Claudia pursed her lips thoughtfully. "Well, I can't say for certain, but Dilbert always had a temper on him. He'd get riled up over the smallest things. I remember a few times when we could hear him shoutin' through them thin walls of theirs."

In a gruff voice, Rance chimed in, "Yeah, he had a reputation for being a hothead. Folks 'round here knew to steer clear when he was in a mood. Can't say I blame Georgina for puttin' that EPO on him."

I nodded, taking in their observations. The picture they painted of Dilbert matched my suspicions. However, there was still much to uncover.

"Did either of you hear about any recent conflicts between Georgina and Dilbert?"

Claudia sighed, her gaze distant. "Well, it's hard to say for sure. But I do remember Georgina mentionin' that they were still havin' some legal disputes even after the divorce. Property, finances, you know how messy those things can get."

Rance scratched his beard and added his own input. "And there was talk 'round town that Georgina was demandin' more from him, claimin' he owed her for all those years of marriage. Could be that it pushed Dilbert over the edge, ya know?"

With a mischievous twinkle in her eye, Claudia leaned in closer. "So, Kenni, spill the beans. What's got you all up in arms? Why did you come running over here?"

"Dilbert Thistle was found dead on the railroad tracks. And when I told Georgina, his ex-wife, she fainted."

Their gasps filled the air as the weight of the revelation settled upon us. Claudia's hand flew to her mouth, and Rance's eyes widened.

Claudia's eyes widened, too, and she nearly choked on her tea. "Well, bless my grits! That's some serious business. Ain't every day a body turns up on them tracks. You reckon she had somethin' to do with it?"

I paused, my mind working through the possibilities. "Hard to say, Claudia. But it sure seems mighty suspicious, don't it?" I slid my eyes to Rance.

"M-Murdered?" Rance stammered, his voice trembling. "But who would do such a thing?"

"That's what I aim to find out," I replied firmly. "But I need your help, Claudia, Rance. If you remember anything else, no matter how insignificant it may seem, please let me know. We have to bring justice to Dilbert."

Just as Claudia was about to respond, the EMTs brought Georgina out on a stretcher and put her in the back of the ambulance.

They must've thought it best to take her in for observation, even though she appeared to be awake. She was sitting up on the stretcher with an oxygen mask over her face and a wet cloth on her forehead.

"He knows something." Poppa made his presence known to me. He stood about one inch from Rance's face. "Ask him about why he and Georgina had that weird stare."

Poppa was right. I'd not forgotten about Rance walking past Georgina's house when I first got there. Their exchange of glares and Rance's peculiar behavior stood out to me and held a great deal of tension.

Having Poppa as my ghost deputy was a benefit. He picked up on things I couldn't, and sometimes those things included items in a house or even the movement of a hand.

"Rance, I couldn't help but notice a bit of tension between you and Georgina when I arrived earlier," I said, raising an eyebrow in a playful manner. "Is everything all right between you two?"

Rance's discomfort grew more apparent as he waved his hand frantically in front of his face, as if shooing away an unwanted pest. I stifled a chuckle, glancing at Poppa, who seemed rather pleased with himself.

"What's the sheriff talkin' about?" Claudia turned and asked her husband. The tone in her voice made me believe there was more to the story.

Rance scratched his head, trying to find the right words. "Well, you see, Claudia... It's a long story.

"Well, I reckon we had a little tiff this morning. Nothing major, just one of those silly disagreements about the branches over her shed in the back. When Dilbert lived here, he took care of the lawn and all the trimming. Now that he's gone..." He gulped. "I guess really gone, I'm gonna have to make good on my threat."

"Your threat?" I jumped at the word.

"Not a threat like hurting someone," Rance quickly clarified. "I told Claudia this morning that if she didn't get someone over here to cut back her branches, I'd get my saw myself and do it."

I couldn't help but wonder if more lay beneath the surface, but for now, I had to focus on the murder investigation.

"Well, Rance, thank you for sharing. If you remember anything else related to Dilbert or anything that could be relevant to the case, please don't hesitate to reach out." I plucked a sheriff's card from the pocket of my shirt.

With the card planted between my pointer and middle finger, I held it out for Rance to take, but he nodded to it as if he wanted Claudia to get it. She did.

He nodded, a mix of relief and concern in his eyes. "Will do, Sheriff. We just want to see justice served." He put his arm around his wife and cuddled her to him. "Right, honey?"

"Mm-hmmm, that's right, sweetie." She nodded.

The two of them shuffled back over to the house, leaving me there with Deputy Lee as the ambulance drove away.

Poppa was nowhere to be seen.

"I had Betty run a check on the Forhordts." Scott showed me the screen of his phone. "It appears they've never been too neighborly. They've filed several complaints against each other, and Finn was the deputy who took the calls."

He scrolled up and showed me the actual forms that had to be filled out. They had blanks for the officer who came, the date, the time, the complaint. All the things.

I nodded, knowing I would ask Finn about these two because he'd totally remember them. When he first came to Kentucky as a reserve officer, he wasn't used to rural life. He'd come from Chicago then become a reserve officer, but he really served in the larger Kentucky cities. Getting used to people like the Forhordts and even someone as forceful as Mama did take him some time.

"Kenni bug," Poppa called out to me from the door of Georgina's house. "I've got something to show you." He waved me into the house and then disappeared.

"Do you want me to go back over there and ask them about these?" Scott asked.

"No." I shook my head. "I want you to go follow the ambulance and hang around there to get a statement from Georgina. I'm not convinced she and Dilbert were adhering to the EPO."

"I'll find out." Scott turned and went to his car.

After I could no longer see his car, I used my better judgement and went back inside Georgina's home. I was very aware of the Forhordts' four eyeballs on me, which made me take the extra step to place a pretend phone call.

"Betty, it's Sheriff Lowry," I said loudly to make sure they heard me. "I'm going to go into Georgina's home to lock up. I'll be back directly."

Lies, lies, and more lies.

It was true that I was going to lock up Georgina's home but not without looking at what Poppa had found. Nor would I go back to the department when I was done here.

It was almost time for the softball game to get underway, and I was determined to talk to Dilbert's teammates.

When I hung up my pretend phone call, I walked back into the front door, where I suddenly felt the eerie silence that enveloped the house.

The dim light filtering through the curtains cast long shadows on the worn-out furniture and faded wallpaper, adding to the unsettling atmosphere. The air felt heavy with anticipation, as if the house itself held secrets waiting to be revealed.

Poppa led me to the kitchen, his spectral finger pointing at the cluttered junk drawer. Its contents spilled out haphazardly, revealing an assortment of old receipts, loose change, and faded photographs. But among the mess, my eyes locked onto something that sent a shiver down my spine—several physical maps, each one marked with intricate routes in red ink.

"What do we have here?" I asked Poppa.

We both looked at each other.

I got the maps out of the drawer and laid them out on the kitchen table.

"All those look like routes down to the river to me." Poppa made a good observation.

"And they are all surrounding the drywall plant." I tapped the exact location of the plant, and all the squiggly red routes nearly touched the pad of my finger.

"Was sweet and innocent Georgina mapping out a sinister plan?" Poppa asked.

"Was one of these the first scene of the crime where Dilbert's actual murder took place?" I asked, my eyes fixed on the routes.

"What does that say?" Poppa's head turned as he pointed out some scribble at the top of the map.

"'Beneath the bridge lies the key to the truth.' Bridge," I said, trying to picture the areas along that part of the river near Dilbert's place of employment.

"Not that it's particularly close to the plant, but High Bridge." Poppa shrugged.

"Poppa! You're a genius!" I squealed and folded up the map, knowing I had other places to go before I could take the trip to the very popular Kentucky attraction.

As I headed out the door, about to call Scott to make sure he questioned Georgina about this map, Poppa yelled, "And that's why you can't get married! I'm a genius, and you need me."

CHAPTER SEVEN

W hen I turned off Bone Road into the fairgrounds, I saw the parking volunteers were waving their little orange sticks to the overflow parking lot.

The grass.

The attendant put his wand up, signaling for me to stop.

After making his way over to my window, he said, "Sheriff, we have official spaces up near the pageant stage if you want to go on up there and park. I'll wave you through."

"That's great. Thank you," I said and turned the Jeep as he waved me through. With a slight wave of two fingers, I passed by and found a spot in the front line. There, orange cones with homemade signs stapled to sticks protruded from the hole. The word Official was written in black marker on each sign.

The lively atmosphere echoed through the window of my car, and the familiar scents of cotton candy and funnel cakes mingling with the savory aromas of corn dogs and grilled burgers wafted through the air.

My stomach grumbled to life. I'd not eaten at all today, and suddenly I had a hankering for some greasy and horrible-for-me carny food.

When I got out of the Jeep, the laughter of the folks enjoying our annual summer carnival made me smile for a moment.

Only for a moment as I scanned the grounds with my sight on the ball field, which reminded me of why I was here in the first place.

A sudden scream piercing the cheerful melodies of carousel music made me jump. I tossed my hand on the butt of my gun, which was strapped into my utility belt.

My eyes darted to the source of the scream and zeroed in on the kids who'd had their hands way up in the air on the Scrambler. Their mouths opened wide with huge smiles as they screamed in delight.

As a sheriff, I got a lot of stares from people who wondered if something sinister was going on.

I made eye contact and gave a solid nod as I passed them.

The fair was in full swing, and the sight before me was a kaleidoscope of colors and sounds. People strolled around with their faces beaming with joy and triumph, carrying oversized stuffed animals won at the game booths.

The beauty pageant on the stage captivated the audience as a voice boomed through the speakers, announcing the contestants and their achievements. The crowd erupted into applause and cheers, adding to the festive atmosphere.

This was the epitome of a summer in Cottonwood. Walking through the carnival rides to get to the softball field brought up a lot of memories, not only of being a teenager and running through the house of mirrors or seeing the bearded lady but ones as recent as riding the Ferris wheel with Finn the first week he'd spent in Cottonwood.

That was the first time he'd asked me to go on a date. My hunger pangs were now replaced by the butterflies I'd felt that very night.

The crack of the bat, the cheers from the crowd, and the shouts of encouragement filled the air, taking me out of the first romantic moment I'd had with Finn.

I tucked my left thumb on my ring finger and wondered if I would feel different today if I'd said yes to him last night.

Even though I was hungry, I was great at eating my feelings, and right now, with the murder and proposal lingering, I thought the cartoon poster of a pretzel I saw when I approached the hot pretzel stand looked delicious.

"I'll have a salty pretzel with a cup of cheese and jalapeños," I ordered when it was my turn. "And a large Diet Coke."

It didn't take but a second for the worker to wrap up a pretzel with all the fixings and my Diet Coke.

I made my way toward the softball field stands, balancing a warm pretzel in one hand and a large Diet Coke in the other, and stopped at the fence near second base.

I took a bite of the warm, salty pretzel, sipped my cold soda, and scanned the field to try to figure out what inning they were in so I could gauge how long I might be there before I could talk to Dilbert's teammates.

"Oh my Lordy." Poppa ghosted next to me.

I put the pretzel up to my mouth to disguise that I was talking to him.

"It's so good too. I wish you could taste it," I told him, taking another bite.

"Not that." He snorted, and his ghostly hand pointed at the pitcher's mound.

My pretzel went from shielding my conversation with a ghost to shielding my eyes from the sun so I could clearly see what I thought I was seeing.

Mama.

She wore a vibrant pink tutu and knee-high socks, representing Lulu's Boutique.

"Swaaaa-innng, batter, batter. Swaaaa-ing!" The chants from her teammates only made her competitive spirit shine through as she prepared to deliver a pitch with precision.

"I had no idea." I shook my head, not fazed at all by the sight.

Mama was never one to shy away from a good challenge, and this would be no different.

I looked at the stands, the chatter of the spectators surrounding me. Friends and neighbors caught up with one another. When I saw a couple pointing at me, there was no doubt in my mind they were discussing the latest town gossip.

Dilbert Thistle's murder.

With the next batter up, I knew it was at least one strike down. There was no scoreboard to tell me what inning we were in or where we stood on outs, so I had to kind of just hang around until I could find a good opening to go over to the dugout to see what Dilbert's teammates had to say.

As Mama's teammates heckled the next batter on the Dairy Bar's team, I stayed near the first-base fence, savoring each bite of my warm pretzel. For a few moments, I was lost in the lively atmosphere of the softball game.

The sound of the bat hitting the ball and the cheers of the crowd filled the air, creating a sense of camaraderie and community, giving me hope that someone had seen something to do with Dilbert's murder and loved our town enough to come forward.

Someone knew something.

But my respite was abruptly interrupted when I heard a familiar voice calling my name.

"Hey there, Sheriff Kenni," Taven Tidwell cried, his phone thrust in my direction. "Care to share your plans for tackling the crime wave in Cottonwood? The good folks are dying to know!"

Taven Tidwell was a tall and imposing figure, standing at around six feet with a strong, athletic build. His dark hair was meticulously styled, perfectly coiffed to project an image of confidence and charisma. His piercing blue eyes seemed to hold an intensity that matched his ambitious demeanor. Taven's sharp jawline accentuated his self-assuredness, and he always wore a neatly trimmed beard that added a touch of ruggedness to his overall appearance.

He wore a well-tailored short-sleeved button-down with the town logo on the pocket. I'd never seen that before, which made me think he'd gotten the suit made down at Lulu's Boutique.

At closer inspection, the stitches sure did look like ones her monogram machine would make. I'd know. Everything Mama bought me was monogrammed, even a sheriff's shirt she'd had Lulu make that I never wore.

Still, Taven exuded an air of professionalism and ambition, as though ready to take on any challenge that came his way.

Confusion clouded my face as I looked at Taven, trying to comprehend what he was doing. "Taven, now's not the time or place for this," I replied, gesturing toward the ongoing game. I pushed off the fence and walked down to the stands, hoping to lose him.

But Taven seemed relentless, following me toward the stands, his phone still recording. The crowd, now aware of the unfolding situation, turned their attention to us, their phones held high to capture the moment for Taven's Facebook Live.

With a self-assured grin, Taven adjusted the camera on his phone and pointed it back at himself.

"Folks, you're looking at the future sheriff of Cottonwood," he proclaimed, his voice amplified by the phone. "I'm here to bring real change, to make this town safe and secure. Unlike our current sheriff, I have a concrete plan!"

My internal turmoil grew as I listened to Taven's grandiose promises.

I was well aware all eyes were on me when I took a seat next to Tibbie Bell, one of my best friends, in the first row. She snuggled up to me and put her arm in mine. We were elbow to elbow with her chin slightly up in the air as her eyes were focused on the game.

"Ouch!" the batter cried out before he bent down and held his shin. "What was that!" It was more of an exclamation than a question as he threw his bat and stalked out to Mama.

Apparently, Mama's throw made unexpected contact with the batter's shin.

Another high-pitched yelp escaped his lips as he continued to hobble out to the pitcher's mound. A string of colorful words followed.

The crowd gasped in surprise, and all eyes turned to the commotion at home plate. There stood Mama, her face a mix of panic and guilt as she jumped around on one foot, her pink tutu bouncing with each hop.

"Lord have mercy!" Mama exclaimed, dramatically throwing down her glove and putting her fists up, ready to engage in a mock fight. "I didn't mean to hit you!"

The batter spat on the ground, missing Mama's shoe.

Barely.

Laughter erupted from the stands as the absurdity of the situation sank in. Mama, in her pink tutu and exaggerated defensive stance, had unintentionally added an unexpected twist to the game. The spectators couldn't help but chuckle at the sight. Some even spouted playful jeers and calls for a rematch.

Meanwhile, Taven Tidwell stood at the edge of the stands, his phone still in hand, capturing the whole scene on his live stream.

The corners of his mouth twitched. He was trying to suppress a smile as he realized the humorous turn of events.

He shifted the camera back on himself, chuckling and saying, "Well, folks, the sheriff ain't even trying to break up a fight. It looks like even the sheriff's family brings some excitement to the softball game!"

I knew that the role of sheriff went beyond mere words and campaign slogans. It required dedication, experience, and a deep understanding of the community's needs.

As Taven rambled on, I couldn't help but feel a mix of frustration, anger, and determination.

My gaze shifted from Taven's self-assured expression to the faces in the crowd, some nodding, others watching with skeptical eyes. I knew I had to respond, to defend the hard work and sacrifices I had made as the sheriff of Cottonwood.

"Kenni, you have to do something." Tibbie pushed a strand of her long brown hair behind her shoulder. Her hazel eyes blinked as if they were begging me. "You have to stand up for this office."

Taking a deep breath, I stood up and walked closer to Taven, my eyes locked on his.

"Taven, being the sheriff is more than just making promises on Facebook Live. It's about building trust, working with the community, and being there for them every step of the way," I said, my voice filled with conviction. "I may not have all the answers, but I can assure you that I will continue to give my all to keep Cottonwood safe."

Taven's confident façade wavered for a moment, but he quickly regained his composure, dismissing my words with a wave of his hand.

"Actions speak louder than words, Sheriff Kenni," he retorted, turning the camera back on himself. "And I'll prove to the good people of Cottonwood that I'm the leader they need!"

As Taven continued his grandiose monologue, I couldn't help but feel a surge of determination welling up within me. I knew that my track record and commitment to the town spoke for themselves. This conflict was not a matter of proving myself to Taven or anyone else but of staying true to my values and fulfilling my duty to Cottonwood.

"That was good," Tibbie said when I went back over to sit by her. "But we've got to get a social media strategy if you're going to continue being the sheriff."

I sucked in a deep breath and looked back out at the ball field, where the team had called a quick timeout to check out the batter.

I got up once again, thinking this was the time I needed to walk over to the dugout. I'd spent too much time at the fair and the ball field while the killer was still out there.

"We can talk about it at euchre tomorrow night," Tibbie called out to me, relentless in reminding me that I had to do some sort of campaigning if I were to keep my job.

Every week, a bunch of us got together for a card game called euchre. We played in teams, and Jolee was on mine. Dilbert's murder had taken up all the room in my brain, so I'd forgotten that our get-together was tomorrow.

Looking over my shoulder as I proceeded to the Dairy Bar dugout, I saw Taven still yammering at his phone. I rolled my eyes and shook my head. Right now wasn't the time to worry about him. It was time to talk to his team members.

"Sheriff, you've caused quite a stir today," a man with a clipboard told me. He had a wad of chew in the pocket of his cheek. "Come out to see your mama get a whoopin'?"

Though he was teasing, the joke was on him.

"Sir, you don't know my mama if you think that," I said and placed both my hands on the outside of the dugout fence, wrapping my fingers around the steel. "Kenni Lowry," I introduced myself just as the game resumed.

"Bill Johnson," he replied. He had a burly physique and a stern expression that hinted at his no-nonsense approach to the game.

"All right, next up to bat, we've got Jake and then Sarah!" Bill called out, his voice carrying across the field.

I glanced out onto the field where Viola White, adorned with a pink tutu and oversized green-rimmed sunglasses, now stood on the pitcher's mound. Her bright-yellow shirt contrasted with the vibrant colors of the field.

Jake, a husky man with a beard, stepped forward, adjusting his grip on the bat. Sarah, a petite woman with a determined expression, stood by the on-deck circle, awaiting her turn.

The game continued with a renewed energy as the players focused on their swings and the crowd cheered them on.

With a determined expression, Viola wound up her arm, her diamond necklace sparkling under the sun's rays. The crowd fell silent, anticipation hanging in the air.

In one swift motion, Viola sent the ball hurtling toward Jake at lightning speed. The ball zipped through the air, leaving a trail of blurred movement in its wake. Jake swung his bat with all his might, but his timing was off.

"Strike one!" Bill's voice boomed across the field, his disappointment evident in his tone. Viola's pitch was a force to be reckoned with, and Jake had barely had a chance to react. "Come on, Jake!"

"Are you the team manager?" I asked, knowing Bill was trying to watch the game. "This is official business. Not me watching my mama wear a tutu and beat y'all."

Bill turned his gaze toward me and sized me up before nodding. "That's right. What can I do for you, Sheriff?"

Bill glanced at me, a mix of amusement and frustration on his face. He handed the clipboard to the batboy and stepped out of the dugout, signaling that he was ready to talk.

"All right, Sheriff, what's on your mind?" he asked, his voice laced with curiosity.

I took a moment to gather my thoughts before diving into the questions that had been swirling in my brain.

"I want to know more about Dilbert. How well did you know him outside of the team? Did he have any notable characteristics or habits that stood out to you? And did you notice anything unusual about his behavior in the days leading up to his disappearance?" I peppered him with questions.

Bill leaned against the fence, his arms crossed, as he pondered my queries.

"Dilbert... He was a dedicated player, always showed up to practice on time and gave his all during the games. As for his character, well, he was a bit of a jokester. Always trying to lighten the mood with his witty remarks." Bill spit some chew liquid out of his mouth, slightly away from me.

I took out my notebook from my pocket and jotted down some of his comments.

"And how did he interact with the other players on the team? Any conflicts or disputes?" I continued.

Bill shook his head, a hint of sadness in his eyes. "No, nothing like that. Dilbert got along with everyone, always had a smile on his face. He was a good teammate."

"Did Dilbert ever mention anything unusual happening in his personal life? Any enemies, threats, or concerns?"

Bill sighed. His gaze drifted toward the field, where the game was in full swing.

"Honestly, Sheriff, Dilbert kept his personal life separate from the team. We were just a group of guys playing softball, having a good time. I can't say I knew much about what was going on outside of that. But I can say he was slightly upset last night when I told him he was being replaced today by..." He pointed at Jake.

The man who'd just struck out slammed his batting hard hat on the ground.

"One down, one to go!" Viola hollered just as Sarah took her stance behind home plate with her back slightly swaying under her right shoulder.

Bill let out a sigh and turned back to me, his expression filled with frustration.

"Why did you do that?" I asked.

"When we get together the night before a game to talk strategy, we usually go to a bar." Bill shrugged. "I'm not saying it's the best place to go, but we like it, and sometimes Dilbert can drink a little too much, even though he's supposed to be dried out. He's not."

"You told him last night he was being replaced?" The message wasn't clear.

"I could tell by the way he was throwing them back that he wasn't going to be of any account today on the field. This is the championship, and I need someone who is going to be in tip-top shape." He glanced into the dugout and then turned back to me. "Apparently I was wrong about Jake being his replacement, but it is what it is."

"Did he and Jake have words?" I asked.

"Why all these questions? Go ask Dilbert." He acted as if he'd not heard what'd happened to Dilbert.

"I'm sorry to tell you, but Dilbert Thistle was murdered." My words fell on a cool and steady face, but the eyes were windows to his soul, and the fear in them ran deep.

"I did not know that." His words were static as Dilbert's fate started to sink into his mind. "I did not hear that. Who did it?"

"That's where I was hoping you could help me. We don't have anyone in custody at this time, but we are checking out anyone who knew him or was involved with him." I flipped the notepad shut, stuffed it back into my pocket, and pulled out a card, which I handed to him.

"Dilbert Thistle, one of our star players," he said.

"If you think of anything that could help find Dilbert's killer, call me," I told him, giving him some space to digest what I'd told him before I decided to pay him another potential visit later. "By the way…" I hesitated, leaving a dramatic pause. "Where were you last night between the hours of midnight and one o'clock a.m.?"

"At home with my wife," he said in a way that left no room for me to believe otherwise. "She's right over there in the stands. First row, pink sleeveless dress. You can go right over there and ask her."

"I just might do that," I said, giving him back a little bit of the attitude he'd taken with me.

As I walked away from the dugout, the sounds of laughter and cama-raderie filled the air. I couldn't help but smile as I heard the Lulu's Boutique teammates chanting in unison, their voices a playful melody:

"Lulu's, Lulu's, we're here to play.

We'll hit those balls, all the way!

With tutus on and socks pulled high,

We'll win this game, oh my, oh my!

Lulu's, Lulu's, fierce and strong,

We'll keep playing all day long!

In tutus and with bats in hand,

We'll show them all we're the winning band!"

Poppa floated near me as I continued walking away amused by the lively atmosphere and the chants of the Lulu's Boutique teammates.

"It's mighty funny, ain't it?" Poppa chimed in, his ghostly voice carrying a hint of mischief. "Just a moment ago, Bill was grumbling about Dilbert,

414

and now he's proclaiming him as the star player? Talk about a change of tune."

"Yep, I saw that," I whispered. I glanced up when I heard a car door slam in the overflow grassy parking lot, followed by someone yelling.

I furrowed my brow in confusion as the door swung open and a disheveled, frantic Georgina emerged in her hospital gown and night-clothes.

Without a moment's hesitation, she dashed toward the dugout, her bare feet slapping against the grass, her hospital gown billowing in the wind.

I quickened my pace, trying to catch up to her, but her fury seemed to propel her forward faster than I could move. I was on the opposite side of her receiving end, which meant I had to do double time to even get back to the dugout before she did.

"Georgina, wait!" I called out, my voice filled with urgency. "Please, let's talk this through!"

But Georgina was in no mood to listen. As she reached the dugout, she confronted Bill, rage and accusation in her voice. Her body language was tense, her arms flailing in the air as she unleashed a torrent of words.

"You! You did this! You killed Dilbert!" Georgina shouted, her eyes ablaze with anger. "I know you had something to do with it!"

Bill's expression shifted from surprise to disbelief as he raised his hands defensively. "Georgina, calm down! You're not making any sense!"

But Georgina was relentless, fueled by her suspicions and grief.

She continued to hurl accusations at Bill, her voice quivering. Her pain and confusion had reached a breaking point, and I had to intervene before the situation escalated further.

I rushed forward, placing myself between Georgina and Bill, my hands outstretched in a calming gesture.

"Georgina, please, take a deep breath and let's talk. Accusing Bill won't solve anything," I said, trying to talk her down.

"Accusing Bill of what?" The woman in the pink sleeveless dress Bill had pointed at had gotten all up in it.

"Murder! He murdered my Dilbert!" Georgina yelled through her gritted teeth.

Tears streamed down Georgina's face as she glared at Bill, her body trembling with a mix of anger and sorrow. "I loved Dilbert, and now he's gone! Someone has to pay!"

"Ma'am, where was your husband between the hours of midnight and one o'clock a.m. last night?" I asked, maintaining a firm but gentle grip on Georgina's shoulders, trying to steady her.

"He was at home with me. I picked him up from the bar over there about ten thirty." Her eyes softened when she realized the pain Georgina was in. "I remember seeing Dilbert there. In fact, I offered him a ride, and he was mad at Bill. Something about kicking him off the team, but Bill told me in the car he didn't. He said he just replaced him for this game."

"Thank you, ma'am," I said politely and turned to take Georgina away. "I understand your pain, Georgina. We're investigating Dilbert's death, and we will find out the truth. But accusing someone without evidence won't bring him back," I said, trying to ignore the crowd who'd gathered around.

Cell phones pointed at us. Now was not the time for me to ask her why she felt this way.

Her shoulders heaved with each heavy breath, and slowly her anger subsided into exhaustion and despair. She sank to her knees, sobbing uncontrollably, as I knelt beside her, offering comfort and support.

"You know, I don't think Sheriff Lowry knows what end is up these days," someone said from behind me. I couldn't see who it was due to the fact that they were shielded by the group of people gathered around. "I heard she left that cute ex-deputy waiting on bended knee last night when he poured his heart out asking her to marry him."

I gulped, closed my eyes, and tried to calm Georgina.

"Yep. She can't make up her mind on things. No wonder he's an ex-deputy. I bet he's now an ex-boyfriend because I don't see no ring," someone commented.

I'd just about had enough when I glanced up and saw Taven Tidwell had that phone camera stuck up in the air, taking video.

"I'm only giving people what a day in the life of our elected sheriff is like," he snorted underneath his words. "There ya have it, folks. That's your sheriff." He took a step back and turned the phone around. "If you're tired of the hemming and hawing around Sheriff Kendrick Lowry has given you over the past four years, vote for me, Taven Tidwell. Strong Convictions, Clear Solutions!"

Amidst the chaos of the ball game and the accusations flying, I realized that beneath everything was a woman consumed by grief and desperate for answers. My duty as sheriff went beyond solving crimes—it also encompassed providing support and understanding to those in need.

And no Taven Tidwell could do that.

CHAPTER EIGHT

F rustrated and angry with Taven Tidwell, I felt a surge of irritation erupting deep in my gut. I might've mentioned his name in a string of curse words as I drove back to the department.

The scent of greasy, mouthwatering food from Cowboy's Catfish filled the air as I walked into the department located in the back of the building. Conversations and the clinking of cutlery from the bustling restaurant up front added to the background symphony.

While I wanted to address him or even bite back, I knew now was not the time to do it. There would be a time or place, and I'd know it. Until then, I got angry with him using my own words against me.

Actions speak louder than words.

Those words never rang truer to me than in this moment. There were many matters I needed to take action on.

One of those was Finn and where we stood in the engagement. Though no one asked me about it, the gossip was still all over town.

"Strong Convictions, Clear Solutions!" I mimicked Taven Tidwell and turned the Jeep down the alley behind the department as I curled my nose and rolled my eyes.

Ignoring Betty, who was on the phone, I strolled past her desk.

She quickly whispered into the phone, "Oh, I'll have to call you back. She's here." Her false teeth clacked as she closed the conversation, unable to conceal her gossiping tendencies. Although I would have loved to believe that the conversation was about Dilbert's murder, it was more likely centered around Taven Tidwell and his infamous Facebook Live.

"Anything new?" Betty asked, her voice holding a tinge of southern empathy, as if she could sense my frustration.

"I've got a few leads," I replied, walking around my desk and taking a seat.

Betty smiled and got up.

When she opened the door between the department and Cowboy's Catfish, the aroma of delicious southern cuisine wafted through the air, tempting my growling stomach. I resisted Betty's offer to fetch me some food from Bartlby and pretended I wasn't hungry, though Bartlby's famous greasy cornbread was calling my name.

Truthfully, my stomach churned with a mix of emotions.

Taven's accusations, my indecision regarding Finn's proposal, the realization that I might have to bid farewell to Poppa—each factor added to my inner turmoil. I felt sick to my stomach, unsure of the precise cause—whether it was the weight of Taven's accusations, the need to choose between Finn and Poppa, or the overwhelming responsibility of solving Dilbert's murder.

In moments like these, I couldn't help but think back to that pivotal summer before heading off to college, when the weight of expectations clashed with the desires of my own heart. I had to confront my own mother's dreams and find my own path. And now, in the midst of this murder investigation, I found myself facing a similar situation.

Determined to tackle the easiest problem on my list, I focused my attention on Dilbert's murder. I knew finding the killer wouldn't be easy, but I had some clues to add to the whiteboard. The murder board, adorned with photos of suspects and evidence, stood as a visual representation of the investigation.

"Did we get any results back from Max concerning the toxicology?" I asked Deputy Scott Lee.

"Not yet," Scott reported and looked over to the board, where he'd put some photos of Georgina and Dilbert up along with some of the basic stats.

Facts like Georgina's address, her place of employment, a copy of the divorce decree and EPO all hung from her photo.

The space underneath Dilbert's picture seemed a little bare.

"Bill Johnson has an alibi." I told Scott and Betty the story Bill's wife seemed to back up. "I want you to run by the fairgrounds and ask the volunteers working the beer bar booth that night if they noticed anything. Did they see Bill's wife in fact pick him up? Talk to Dilbert? Anything you can find out."

"Yes, ma'am." Scott nodded respectfully.

"Let's see what Max has." I picked up the phone and dialed Max.

The phone rang a few times before Max's voice came through the line, his tone filled with professional yet weary determination.

"Max, it's Kenni. Any news on the autopsy or the toxicology reports?" I asked, anticipation lacing my voice.

"Not yet, Kenni," Max replied. "We're still waiting for the results to come in. But don't worry. I'll keep you posted as soon as we have something."

I let out a sigh of disappointment, but I understood that these things took time. Murder investigations were intricate puzzles, and each piece of evidence had to be examined thoroughly.

I looked up at Scott and shook my head.

As I hung up the phone, Deputy Scott Lee picked up a file and walked straight over to the murder board. His boots resounded on the worn linoleum floor. With a stack of papers in hand, he began updating the board with new information.

I watched Scott as he meticulously pinned up more witness statements, photographs we'd taken of the tracks, and other pertinent details. His focused expression and efficient movements revealed his dedication to his work. I couldn't have asked for a better deputy.

"Any new leads, Scott?" I asked, stepping closer to the murder board.

Scott glanced over his shoulder, scanning the board as if he were double-checking the information. "Not yet, Sheriff," he replied. "But I've been following up on Dilbert's acquaintances, digging into his work and personal life. Hopefully, we'll uncover something soon."

Betty handed me her phone, showing me Dilbert Thistle's Facebook profile.

"You sit here and eat your cornbread while you scroll through Dilbert's Facebook posts," she said. "You might see something that sparks a clue."

I glanced up at her, my eyes wide.

"Just 'cause I'm old don't mean I'm not able to have my own Facebook." She snickered and moseyed back over to her desk. "Just don't get butter on my phone." Betty tsked and looked at my fingers.

I'd already bitten into a piece of the cornbread, and the butter oozed down the side of my finger.

"I won't," I told her. I opened the drawer of my desk and grabbed one of the many Cowboy's Catfish takeout napkins that'd accumulated there.

After one more big bite of cornbread, I wiped off my fingers and began to go down the rabbit hole of social media research to see what Dilbert Thistle had posted.

"Betty," I called when the phone screen went black. "I've timed out."

"Why don't you get on the Cottonwood Sheriff's Facebook on the desktop?" Scott asked. "I set it up a year ago. Remember?"

"Oh yeah," I said with a sigh. "Plus I don't have to worry about eating my cornbread and getting butter all over the keyboard," I teased. Another big bite later, I shook the computer mouse and brought the screen to life.

"Suit yourself." Betty came back over and got her phone. "But I'm warning you."

"Warning about what?" I asked. I clicked on the icon for the internet browser, and when the window opened, I typed Facebook.com into the address bar.

"That." She nodded at the screen. "I gave you my phone to bypass all that junk."

The first post that came up on the sheriff's department feed was the live video Taven Tidwell had done at the fairgrounds.

"Oh my gosh," I gasped, shaking my head and watching a little of it in horror.

"It don't look bad, Kenni bug." Poppa stood behind me, looking over my shoulder. "Just make no big deal of it. Say something about how you wished he'd gotten your good side or something. You can't be worrying about Taven Tidwell. He wants to get your goat."

He ghosted in front of my desk, right behind the screen. Betty was rattling on about something involving the video, but I wasn't listening to her. She was more background noise than anything.

"You are the sheriff. He is not. Use that to your advantage," Poppa encouraged me.

"Did you hear me?" Betty asked, forcing Poppa to disappear. "I said you need to rebut him."

"I don't." I shook my head and scrolled down the page, noticing there were several shares of his video that tagged the department.

"You gasped when you saw it." Betty's teeth clacked. She jutted her hip out and stuck her hand on her waist.

"You're gonna break a hip if you keep thrusting it out there," I teased. "I gasped because he could've at least gotten my good side."

Although I didn't move an inch, my eyes slid up over the monitor. Scott's eyes caught mine, and we both grinned.

"Now, we can't be getting all upset about a video or two. We have a job to do, and that means we do our job," he said.

I gave a hard nod and moved the cursor up to the search bar, in which I typed Dilbert's name to bring up his profile.

Without another word, Betty meandered back over to her desk and sat down. By the way she was shuffling the papers, filing items, and huffing, she wasn't satisfied with my answer.

But Poppa was right. Taven wanted me to respond. He wanted me to come unhinged, but I wasn't going to do that.

Without giving it any more thought, I picked up my coffee and started to drink it as I scrolled through Dilbert's virtual scrapbook. His page showed pictures of him with friends, snapshots of his softball team, and some shots from their victory celebrations.

There were even a few from what looked to be happier days with Georgina.

My eyes widened as I stumbled upon a photo of Dilbert and Bill Johnson, side by side, both wearing their work uniforms in what seemed to be the drywall plant.

"What do we have here?" I asked. A rush of surprise coursed through me.

How had I missed this connection before? Dilbert and Bill were coworkers, and yet I had been oblivious that they shared a workplace.

I opened a new search engine tab. My fingers danced across the keyboard as I delved into the realm of toxicology. I browsed the results that appeared on the screen, my eyes quickly scanning through the information.

"Common toxins in drywall plants," I muttered under my breath as my search yielded a plethora of results.

Scott and Betty heard me and rushed over.

"What are you thinking?" Scott asked.

"Well, Bill Johnson and Dilbert Thistle worked together. When I talked to Bill at the softball game, he left out that little detail about him and Dilbert. He mentioned a few things about Dilbert drinking and how he'd replaced him. He was with Dilbert last night, and that's when he said he knew by the way Dilbert was acting he needed to be replaced today for the championship." I rambled about everything, probably not making much sense to Betty and Scott, even though I was making perfect sense to myself. "And could this poison be something administered in small doses? Did Bill slowly poison Dilbert?"

"Dilbert and Bill could've gotten into an argument," Poppa pointed out.

"We know Dilbert went drinking last night at a bar at the fairgrounds," I said to Poppa, but Scott apparently thought I was talking to him.

He immediately walked over to the board, flipped off the cap off the marker, and started to write down the bullet points of the theory I shared with Poppa, though it looked like mine exclusively.

"Or possibly they didn't get along well at work and Bill poisoned him slowly?" Poppa spat out what I'd said just a few seconds ago and pointed at the board for me to write down the idea.

"Bill is strong enough to have carried Dilbert, transported him to the tracks." The words came to life as Scott wrote them down. "And there are poisons at the drywall plant."

I skimmed down the list, noting substances like formaldehyde, silica, and various chemical compounds used in the production of drywall.

As I named them out loud, Scott wrote them.

My mind raced as I contemplated the possibilities.

"Could one of these substances have been used as a deadly weapon?" Poppa asked.

I knew I had to dig deeper, gather more evidence, and consult with Max to narrow down the list of potential poisons.

"Are we looking at one of those as the weapon that killed Dilbert?" I asked Poppa's question so Scott and Betty could hear me.

"It's a start." Scott snapped the lid back on the marker and took a step back. He crossed his arms and looked at the board.

"And was there any sort of connection between Bill Johnson and Georgina?" I wondered if they'd had some sort of affair. "Not that I have any reason to believe so, but Georgina sure was laying into Bill at the ball field."

"I'll look these up and see what I can come up with," Scott said about the chemicals I'd found during my internet search for what drywall plants contained.

"We don't even know if any of those are at the plant, which means I need to go down there on Monday and check it out," I said without any urgency.

There was no need to say that Dilbert was definitely poisoned until the toxicology report came back from Max. But we could certainly get some leads started. The weekends were slow, and places of business weren't open, so it would be futile for me to try to find someone down at the plant who would open it for me unless Dilbert's autopsy came back with some sort of poison that could be connected to the drywall plant.

After I finished going through Dilbert's photos, I scrolled down his Facebook posts. He really didn't post much other than images of tools, funny memes, or a few reposts from the drywall plant's page. When I saw he'd shared the softball team photo from the plant's page, I clicked on it and decided to see what the plant posted.

They kept their page up with minimal postings about such things as celebrating the national holidays and a few photos thanking various employees for their dedication to the plant. There were also a few photos from Christmas parties and one about a recent retirement.

Nothing screamed that the workers were disgruntled, which could've been another motive.

However, I wasn't ignorant enough to believe that behind all the smiles and good cheer shown by some of the people in the photos, no one was unhappy.

"It's a puzzle, Kenni bug. The slightest little pieces will make the biggest difference," Poppa said, reappearing at the door between Cowboy's Catfish and the department. "Man, oh man, I wish I could have some of that fried catfish."

"Here is what we know." I got bored with looking at all the Facebook stuff and stood up. "Our victim is Dilbert Thistle."

I approached the whiteboard where Scott had pinned up the suspects' photos, each accompanied by their names and potential motives.

Taking a deep breath, I picked up the marker and started to go through each suspect, analyzing their possible involvement in Dilbert's murder.

"Claudia and Rance Forhordt," I said, adding their names to the suspect list. "Georgina's neighbors. Their motive could be linked to a past disagreement with Dilbert, potentially fueled by long-standing animosity. Perhaps there was a hidden grudge that had simmered beneath the surface for years."

"I'll look them up and see if they've called in a report or something," Betty offered. She started to type on her computer to bring up anything on the Forhordts.

"Bill Johnson, the manager of the Dairy Bar softball team," I said and circled his name. "He is someone I really want to check into first thing Monday morning."

"His motive could be connected to Dilbert's performance on the team. There might have been a rivalry or jealousy that led to a deadly act," Scott suggested. "Could they have had any conflicts or tensions during their time together at the drywall plant?"

"Then there's Georgina herself," I moved on. "She has to be considered a suspect, despite her emotional outburst at the game. They had a troubled relationship, and she had a restraining order filed against Dilbert. All of this screams motive."

It was crucial to delve deeper into their past to uncover any hidden secrets or resentments she might've had.

"And she said Bill had motive. I didn't get it from her because she was so distraught at the game, I felt it was best to get her home," I said.

I could've pressed Georgina harder and brought her down to the station, but I didn't want to have a situation on my hands in which she passed out again, so giving her a few hours to either get herself together or mess up was best.

The latter, messing up, wasn't unusual in a case like this. It was a known fact that most murder victims were killed by someone in their life. In Georgina's case, she was acting very irrationally. For someone who loathed Dilbert so much she'd taken out restraining orders against him, acting like she had when he died was a huge red flag.

If I let her simmer for a while, stew in the thought that I wasn't arresting her, she might just leave her house and lead us right to the reason why she'd killed him.

"Scott." I jerked around and got his attention. "Do you mind going and sitting in front of Georgina's house? Following her? See what she's got going on tonight?"

"Don't mind at all." He got up and grabbed his iPad and keys. "I can still do some research on some of the toxins."

"What about the guy who replaced Dilbert on the team?" Betty asked. "Wouldn't that give Dilbert a reason to be mad?"

"Jake," I said.

"Looking through Dilbert's social media, he sure was proud of being on the team," Betty said. "Most men around here I know have big egos and pride. Jake would be someone Dilbert would agree with, give some lip to, and get beaten up by."

She had my attention.

"Dilbert could obviously push the right buttons," she said, referring to the EPO against him. "But instead of filing a complaint, did Jake do the unthinkable? And if they worked together, what if Dilbert knew this was coming down the line and it really didn't happen like Bill Johnson said it did?"

"Are you saying Bill Johnson had told Dilbert he was being replaced on the team with Jake? Jake and Dilbert had some sort of words over the last days, and Jake poisoned him?" I asked.

"I don't know what I'm saying. I'm just thinking out loud here, like you do all the time," Betty told me in no uncertain terms, even though she didn't know it, that I talked to myself and it didn't go unnoticed.

"I know, I know it's how your Poppa did it, and I think it's smart, but I can't help but see all these people tagging the department, saying that you talk to yourself. It makes you look a little crazy." Betty circled her finger around her ear. "It's just my two cents, so take it for what it's worth, but maybe you should not talk to yourself until the election is over."

"That's months away," I told her and decided to focus on the whiteboard.

As I scribbled notes and connected the dots on the board, I felt the weight of responsibility on my shoulders as sheriff. I glanced down at my ring finger and then over to Poppa. He still had his nose up to the crack in the door so he could continue to inhale all the food smells.

The only way I knew I would avoid talking to myself was to say yes to Finn's proposal.

Finding the truth and bringing justice to Dilbert's killer was my duty as the sheriff of Cottonwood. I knew that one wrong move or oversight could jeopardize the entire investigation. That also meant the integrity of the office, which meant that the sheriff couldn't look crazy.

I couldn't look crazy.

I sighed, put the marker down, and picked up my cell phone.

I knew what I had to do. It was best for everyone.

Solve this murder!

"Betty?"

She looked my way.

I stopped at her desk with my keys in hand. "What is Patty Dunaway's address?"

"You ain't gonna find her there." Betty pointed at the to-go box she'd brought me. "Are you gonna finish the cornbread?"

"No, you can have it. Where is she?" I asked.

"Patty?" Betty acted as if I should've known Patty's schedule. "I heard she's taken to bed. Cancelled all her doggy walks."

I glanced up at the clock on the wall. It was probably too late to just drop in on Patty, but I still had to talk to her, whether she'd taken to bed or not. It was getting up into the late afternoon, and I'd already kept Betty here long enough. Scott, he was different. He was a lot like me when it came to work.

I didn't wear that as a badge of honor. This job seeped into your blood, and it would take up your entire life if you let it.

"Betty, why don't you go on and switch the lines over to Clay's Ferry," I told her.

Our sheriff's department was so small, we didn't have the funds to maintain a full-time dispatch service like larger towns in our area. Clay's Ferry wasn't too far away, and they had a much larger population—and a very cute sheriff, if I said so myself.

But they were also able to provide us with dispatch at night and on the weekends. They didn't send their officers or anything like that. They'd dispatch the EMTs or to me as needed, and the calls for our department were forwarded to their call center. It was something I didn't really want to do, but Mayor Ryland had decided that any extra tax dollars would go to small-business owners, which was fine.

It didn't take me twice to tell Betty to go on. She was out of there in a flash.

"I'm going to stop by the church on my way home to see if Patty is still there." I gathered up Dilbert's file so I could sit at home and stare at it. Something might come to me. "We still need to get her statement, and it's more important than ever now that Max has put in the initial report that it looks suspicious."

When Scott didn't respond, I glanced over at him.

"Scott," I called. "Scott," I repeated, a little more loudly.

"Oh." He looked surprised and popped his head up. "Sorry, Sheriff. I just found Dilbert's new address."

"New address?" I asked and dropped the file back on my desk. I walked over and stood behind Scott.

"Yeah. No wonder we couldn't find where he lived." He pointed at the monitor screen. "I thought I recognized the apartments in his Facebook photos. They are short-term housing for people who come out of a program. I put a call in to the appointed attorney who was on his EPO. The attorney said Dilbert had gone to a rehab and when he got out, he went to the residential program home because he was waiting for the divorce money Georgina owed him for the house."

"I'm listening." I was impressed with the research Scott had done.

"I searched the database for new home buyers in the area, and this house popped up with Dilbert's name on it." He clicked and scrolled until he brought up a small home near the water treatment plant that wasn't too far from my house.

It was on the southern side of town and in what would probably be considered a lower-income area, but it was safe and clean.

"Who was the agent?" I asked.

Scott typed away.

"Also, get me a warrant," I said.

Patty would have to wait.

Though it was important to get into Dilbert's house, it wasn't siren-on-top-of-the-old-Wagoneer important. However, it was enough for me to drive a little above the twenty-five-mile-an-hour speed limit.

"Hi," I said when the realtor answered the phone. "Is this Michelle Wright?"

I thought I'd call her on my way over to Dilbert's house and see if she'd be available to come chat.

When she confirmed, I proceeded.

"This is Sheriff Lowry, and I'm calling to see if you have time to meet me over at 529 Courtmead Drive?"

After a bit of hesitation on her end, she asked me what this was about.

"Unfortunately, Dilbert Thistle, the man who purchased the property from you, has been murdered," I said.

"Oh no." Her gasp told me she'd not heard about it. "Murdered?"

"Yes, ma'am. I'm heading over to his house right now, and I wondered if you could meet me there?" I asked.

"I'm sorry, but I'm showing a house right now. They are looking around, so I might have a couple of minutes to answer any questions you have for me," she said.

"That'd be great." I knew it was a crapshoot trying to get someone to meet me on the spot, but it was worth the attempt. I always liked to see people's body language when I questioned them. "How did Dilbert get in contact with you?"

"His lawyer had gotten in touch with me. He said Dilbert had gotten an FHA loan out from the bank and was ready to purchase. He also mentioned something about waiting on money from an ex-wife or something. It was pretty seamless." She chuckled. "Honestly, I thought the deal was never going to come through."

"Why would you think that?" I asked.

"Let's just say working with the Cottonwood First National Bank on any FHA loan is a nightmare, so when Dilbert's loan got approved, I was pretty impressed," she said.

"Did he ever say anything to you about his personal life?"

"Oh no," she quickly added. "He never really said anything. I showed him and Mr. Deaton the house once. Then he signed on the dotted line. No inspection. No nothing."

"Mr. Deaton, the lawyer." I recognized the name from my work as the sheriff but never had any dealings with him.

"Yes. He's the court-appointed attorney Dilbert got. He really takes good care of his clients. Oh, I've got to go, but did you want me to call you back?" she asked.

"No. I'm going to go take a look around Dilbert's home, but if you can remember anything Dilbert might've said or you overheard anything he might've talked about with Mr. Deaton, I'd greatly appreciate you letting me know."

We said our goodbyes.

"Little by little, you'll get this," Poppa said from the passenger seat.

"We will." I glanced over at him and smiled. "Are you sure you won't be part of my life if I were to get married?"

"It's what I hear." He shrugged. "Kenni, I know you love Finn. I've been doin' a lot of thinking."

Poppa brought his chunky finger up and patted his temple. I grinned, recalling seeing him doing that when he was sheriff. He'd tell his deputy he knew something was brewing, and when something did brew, he'd tap his temple and tell them how he knew it.

"There was no greater feeling than watching your children grow. Then you get grandchildren, and that I can't even explain. But I want you to know that I've come to realize I want you to experience those things..." His voice trailed off.

"What are you saying?" I asked, my brows knotted. My hands moved one over the other as I turned the steering wheel to move down Dilbert's street.

"I'm saying I want you to be happy. And if we keep doing what we are doing, you'll end up resenting me, and I can't do that to you." He ghosted away just as I pulled up to the house and threw the old Wagoneer in park.

"Poppa?" My heart pounded as I frantically looked behind me into the Jeep for any sign of him. "Poppa? What does that mean?"

The knock on my driver's-side window caused me to jump.

It was Scott. For a brief moment, I saw his gaze shift from the ring to my eyes as he waved the signed search warrant in his hand.

CHAPTER NINE

With one more quick glance into the back of the Jeep and no sign of Poppa, I got out.

"The warrant?" I asked.

He nodded.

"That was fast."

"He said he was waiting to get a call regarding anything you needed." Scott shrugged. "Let's go."

"I called the realtor on the way over, and she didn't have much information, only that Dilbert had gotten an FHA loan. I'll go down to see Vernon on Monday," I said, meaning Vernon Bishop, the bank president.

"You've got a lot to do on Monday." Scott snorted as we approached the front door. He gripped the handle, and after we confirmed it was locked, he jiggled it again, a little more firmly.

Nothing.

"Darn," I said and peeked into the window, where there were just a few pieces of furniture. "Looks like you're going to have to break in."

"I'll go grab my bag," he said and hurried back toward his car while I started to walk around to the side of the house. "And I'll go take a look inside," he called.

Despite its humble exterior, the house was impeccably maintained.

There didn't need to be any tuck-pointing on the brick, and the lawn was trimmed. Some summer flowers bloomed along the side of the house.

Nothing looked like it had been disturbed, so I didn't think there was a break-in, which would have possibly been the first crime scene involved in this investigation. I figured there had to be at least two crime scenes, but where was the first?

My curiosity was piqued as I ventured around the side of the house, my footsteps accompanied by the gentle crunch of gravel beneath my shoes. The path led me to the backyard, where a well-maintained shed stood nestled in the corner. Its weathered wooden panels told a story of years gone by, yet its sturdy frame spoke of resilience.

My phone rang out in Max Bogus's ring tone.

"Sheriff," I answered, even though I knew it was him.

"Sheriff, I've gotten back the toxicology report. In addition to some alcohol in his system, there was calcium hydroxide, which would be consistent with poisoning." His words confirmed the murder weapon.

My heart skipped a beat as I listened to Max's words.

Calcium hydroxide? That was a dangerous substance, not something you'd expect to find in someone's system. I quickly gathered my thoughts and responded to Max in a calm yet determined voice.

I walked toward the shed, taking in the surrounding sights and sounds. The warm breeze rustled the leaves of nearby trees, carrying with it a faint scent of freshly cut grass. The chirping of birds filled the air, giving my exploration a melodious backdrop that did not mesh with what I was hearing from Max.

"Max, are you saying that Dilbert was poisoned with calcium hydroxide? How is that even possible? And more importantly, how could someone ingest it?" I asked, my mind racing with questions.

Once I reached the shed, I ran my free hand along its rough surface, feeling the texture of the worn wood beneath my fingertips. A small window adorned with delicate lace curtains offered a glimpse into the hidden treasures within.

With a sense of intrigue, I opened the door, revealing a space filled with tools and gardening equipment. The shelves were lined with neatly arranged pots, and gardening gloves and a watering can hung from hooks on the wall. The scent of soil and fertilizer lingered in the air, a reminder of the care and attention poured into nurturing the plants that flourished in the yard.

For a brief moment, I felt like I could sense Dilbert in there with me. When I looked back over my shoulder, I realized that presence was Poppa. He'd not left me yet.

Max's big sigh on the other end of the line brought me back to the phone conversation, his weariness evident in his voice. "Sheriff, calcium hydroxide, also known as slaked lime, is commonly used in various industries, including construction, agriculture, and even food processing. It's possible that Dilbert came into contact with it unknowingly, perhaps through contaminated food or drink. But from the amounts in his system, I have to conclude it's more likely due to someone deliberately poisoning him."

I frowned, trying to wrap my head around the idea. "But how could it be poisonous? Isn't calcium hydroxide used in certain food products like pickles and as a dietary supplement?"

"Yes, you're right," Max confirmed. "In small amounts, calcium hydroxide is considered safe for consumption. However, when ingested in larger quantities or in concentrated form, it can cause severe damage to the digestive system. It's crucial that we determine the source and concentration of the calcium hydroxide in Dilbert's case."

Poppa appeared in the back of the shed, behind the push lawnmower, trying to get my attention. He pointed urgently at something on the ground.

"Did anyone tell you that Dilbert had been coughing?" I asked. "What about the inhaler? Georgina said Dilbert didn't use one."

I definitely needed to get the inhaler to the lab and go see Camille. The one problem with a murder happening on the weekend was that offices were closed. The chances that I could get in touch with Camille without a warrant were slim, so that was something else I needed Scott to get a warrant for.

"If Dilbert was being slowly poisoned, he might've been diagnosed and given an inhaler. The symptoms of calcium hydroxide poisoning can emulate some upper respiratory issues," Max said.

"Max, hold on a moment," I interjected, keeping my eyes fixed on the shed. "I think there's something important here. Let me check it out, and I'll get back to you."

Without waiting for Max's response, I hung the phone up and stuck it in my pocket. Then I hurried toward the shed, where Poppa had found something he definitely wanted me to check out.

As I entered the shed, a sense of anticipation filled the air. Poppa's eyes were fixed on a particular spot on the ground. I followed his gaze, my heart pounding with a mixture of apprehension and curiosity. He was looking at fresh dirt that'd been placed there.

"Hhmm," I hummed and looked at the mound. "This looks pretty fresh."

With trembling hands, I grabbed one of the shovels from a hook on the wall of the shed and began to dig.

The truth slowly emerged with each shovelful of dirt I removed. Beneath the soil was a small box the size of a shoebox.

"What do you think's in there?" Poppa questioned.

"Only one way to find out." I put the shovel on the ground and used my hand to clean off the top of the box before I started digging around.

I didn't want to use the shovel in case some sort of evidence was here. In a case that involved a murder, I had to make sure there were no missteps along the way, especially now that Taven Tidwell was on my ass. He was looking for anything to add to his little smear campaign against me. I'd be damned if I let Dilbert Thistle be the reason I wasn't re-elected.

"Woooweee." Poppa hopped around. "I ain't seen nothing like that since before I got married. Your grandma sure wouldn't do something like that. Talk about a reason for someone to get a thing about not revealing secrets."

I could hardly believe my eyes.

There were photographs in the box, and I didn't mean just any photographs. They depicted a naked woman lying on a couch, her eyes filled with lust, almost as if she were excited to be nude. One photo after another showed her in various positions and on different pieces of furniture or scenery.

"Who on earth is this?" I questioned. "Do you recognize her, Poppa?" I asked as his shadow hovered over me.

The images sent a chill down my spine. I couldn't help but wonder what they meant and how they were connected to Dilbert's murder.

"Poppa?"

I looked up and found Scott had come in.

"Poppa?" He jerked back, and his eyes caught mine for a second. "I mean, sorry, Sheriff. I should've announced my arrival."

His eyes moved over my shoulder and to the photos.

"I didn't see anything in the house. Like literally nothing but a High Bridge water distributor." Scott was talking about the industrial type of water bottles seen in offices and some people's homes.

High Bridge was a local railroad bridge located on the Kentucky River. It was a spot tourists liked to see and the highest railroad bridge over navigable waters in the entire United States. The drywall plant where Dilbert worked wasn't too far from there. The caves down there also had a water company that boasted of selling the best water that poured off the limestone. People around Cottonwood swore by it, so it wouldn't be unusual for Dilbert to have a High Bridge system in his house.

Heck, I had several sixteen-ounce bottles of that water in my refrigerator.

"I found something freshly buried, and I can't help but think they might have something to do with the note we found in Dilbert's pocket," I said, noting that it seemed odd that Dilbert had nothing in his house. But maybe that wasn't too odd for someone who just moved there.

I carefully wiped the remaining dirt off the box, which I handed to Scott so I could claw back into the dirt hole to see if anything else was there.

I knew that this discovery was significant. It was a clue, a piece of the puzzle that would lead us closer to unraveling the mystery surrounding Dilbert's death.

"What about the maps?" Scott asked. "Do you think Dilbert used them as a guide to where he could've buried something else?"

"I don't know. I think we have to follow every lead, which means I have to get the evidence we collected from the scene to the lab. I was hoping to talk to Tom Geary instead of dropping it off in the box, but I guess I can just call him because come Monday morning, we have to go see Dr. Shively. Get a warrant to get her list of patients. I need to go back and question Georgina on why she never revealed she was divorced and ask her about why she really wanted to find him."

Tom owned the lab where I took all of my crime scene evidence for processing. He was not only efficient but thorough.

"I think we will get a lot of information out of her now." Scott raised a brow. "I'll get the warrants we need."

My nerves settled a little more now that it seemed he hadn't heard me talking to Poppa or at least had decided not to acknowledge it. I was lucky to have Scott Lee as a deputy if I couldn't have Finn.

With the photograph in my possession, I walked out of the shed, my mind still reeling from the shocking revelation. As I closed the door behind me, I knew that both Max's findings and this unexpected piece of evidence would play a crucial role in our investigation.

Taking a deep breath, I pulled out my phone so I could call Max back and left Scott to bag the photos and mark them as evidence.

"Max, I've made a significant discovery here. But first, we need to focus on finding out where someone could obtain calcium hydroxide. It may hold the key to unraveling this case. I'll keep you updated with any new leads," I said into his answering machine. "I'm sure you're doing the funeral, but keep me posted if you find anything else from the tox report."

Once I hung up the phone, I glanced back at the shed. As the pieces of the puzzle were starting to reveal themselves, I couldn't help but try to force them into places they didn't yet fit.

Like the note we found on Dilbert's body. Where did that fit into his life? Were these photos part of that secret someone didn't want Dilbert to expose? Was Dilbert blackmailing someone? Why did he or someone else bury this box recently?

"Everything all right over there, Sheriff?" the neighbor called out, her voice carrying a hint of concern.

I recognized her.

Mrs. Evelyn Reynolds was a petite and sprightly woman in her late sixties. Her silver hair peeked out from beneath her wide-brimmed straw hat, complementing her kind, wrinkled face. Her eyes, a vibrant shade of blue, sparkled with a youthful energy, and her warm smile showcased her genuine friendliness.

As I walked over to Evelyn's house, the sun beat down on the quiet suburban street, casting long shadows across the neatly trimmed lawns and colorful flower beds. The scent of freshly cut grass mingled with the blooms' fragrances, creating a soothing atmosphere in the neighborhood.

She lowered the watering can, and droplets of water sparkled in the air before gently landing on the ferns' emerald leaves. I gave her a warm smile and a slight wave, acknowledging her presence.

"Hi, Mrs. Reynolds," I said to her as I approached her deck and pulled out my card, ready to gather any information she might have. "I wanted to know if you'd seen anything odd going on next door? Anything unusual?"

She shifted her weight, holding the watering can with both hands, and her gaze turned thoughtful. She cocked her head slightly, as if searching her memory for any unusual occurrences.

"Nah," she finally replied, shaking her head gently. Her lips twisted in contemplation, and she accidentally dropped the watering can to her side, causing a sprinkle of water to wet my shoe.

"I'm so sorry," she exclaimed, her eyes widening with guilt.

I noticed her eyes occasionally wandered toward the flowerbeds, ensuring that each bloom received its fair share of water. Her love for gardening was evident in the way she nurtured her plants, the verdant foliage serving as a testament to her green thumb.

"It's fine," I reassured her, lifting my foot and shaking off the excess water. "Accidents happen." I gave her a friendly smile, hoping to put her at ease. "Your flowers are beautiful."

"Thank you. I make sure we spend time together every day." She exhibited graceful movements as she adjusted the watering can and tended to her beloved ferns. Mrs. Reynolds embodied the spirit of the neighborhood, a caring and observant individual who took pride in her surroundings.

Meanwhile, Dilbert's flower beds looked like they'd not been tended to at all.

My curiosity piqued again, I continued the conversation, eager to gather any relevant information about Dilbert's recent activities. I handed her my card, inviting her to share any details she could recall.

"How long has Dilbert lived here?" I asked, my voice gentle and inquisitive.

Her face wrinkled with a mixture of uncertainty and remembrance.

"Not long," she replied, her voice tinged with hesitation. "I mean, I don't pay too much attention to the comings and goings of my neighbors." She paused for a moment, as if trying to recollect specific details. "Although... now that you mention it, I did see Georgina, Dilbert's wife, over there a while ago."

My interest rose at the mention of Georgina. I leaned in slightly, eager to hear more, my eyes fixed on the neighbor.

"You remember when that was?" I asked, my voice gentle but filled with curiosity. By the way Mrs. Reynolds hung out in her yard, I knew she saw Dilbert and anything going on at his place.

It was just the nature of a neighbor in a small town.

She furrowed her brow, staring off into the distance as she tried to recall the memory. After a moment of thoughtful silence, her face brightened as the memory came back to her.

"Yes, it was a few days back. They had a bit of a heated argument," she revealed, her tone low and confidential. "I couldn't hear everything they were saying, but I caught snippets of their conversation. I mean, I was really busy making sure my plants were happy."

"Yes. Of course. But if you can remember anything, I'd really appreciate it." I hated to tell her why I needed to know, since I'd yet to do a press conference. "Dilbert Thistle was murdered last night, and we are trying to gather any information we can."

"I think Georgina mentioned something about needing money within a certain time frame."

I nodded, absorbing the information and mentally connecting the dots. Georgina's presence at Dilbert's house during a heated argument and the mention of money added another layer of complexity to the investigation. It seemed like there might be more to the story than met the eye, especially since there was an active EPO against him.

"Thank you for sharing that with me," I said sincerely, appreciating Mrs. Reynolds's willingness to help. "If you happen to remember anything else or notice any other unusual activity, please don't hesitate to reach out."

"Of course, Sheriff. I'll keep an eye out and let you know if anything comes up." She nodded.

As I turned to walk away from Mrs. Reynolds, she called out to me, her voice filled with a mix of concern and excitement.

"Sheriff, before you go, I have to tell you something," she said, her eyes sparkling with anticipation. "You know, after that whole incident at the ball field, there's been quite a buzz going around town about you."

I raised an eyebrow, wanting to hear what gossip had been circulating. "Oh really? What are people saying?"

Mrs. Reynolds leaned in closer, as if about to divulge a well-kept secret. "Well, you know that live video Taven Tidwell filmed of you? The one where he was going on and on about his campaign and caught you in the background?"

I nodded, remembering the incident. "Yes, I'm aware of it."

She continued, her voice containing both amusement and disbelief, "Well, let me tell you, everyone's been talking about it. I overheard Martha and Tom from across the street discussing it earlier while we were getting our mail from our mailboxes."

Feeling even more curious, I urged her to share the juicy details. "What did Martha and Tom have to say?"

Mrs. Reynolds put her hand on her chest dramatically and said, imitating Martha's voice, "Did you see that? Taven's got nerve, filming the sheriff like that. I can't believe she didn't knock his lights out!"

We both chuckled at Martha's bold statement.

Mrs. Reynolds then shifted to a voice like Tom's, adding, "I heard he did it on purpose to get under her skin. Trying to rattle her before the election. But you know what? Kenni has my vote, no matter what. She's a tough cookie, that one. Just like her poppa, and I like that."

I smiled, grateful for the support.

"Thank you, Mrs. Reynolds. I appreciate your kind words and your vote. It means a lot to me," I said with a smile.

She patted my arm affectionately. "You're a good sheriff, Kenni. Don't let anyone's antics shake your confidence. We know you're the one to keep this town safe."

"I appreciate that. Now you have a good day." I gave her a wave.

As I left Mrs. Reynolds's yard and met Scott on the property boundary, a sudden shiver ran down my spine. I could feel the weight of Poppa's presence lingering in the air, his voice echoing in my mind.

"Remember, darlin', when the breeze carries a hint of deception, it's time to dig deeper," he whispered in my ear with his southern drawl.

The hairs on the back of my neck stood on end, and I knew there was more to this case than I thought initially. If Poppa sensed someone was lying, especially someone like Georgina, then I had no time to waste. I needed answers, and I needed them now.

With an urgency burning in my chest, I turned to Scott. "Scott, I have to go back to Georgina's place. There's something important I need to find out. Meet me there as soon as you can."

His eyes widened with concern, mirroring my own unease. "All right, Sheriff. I'll be right behind you."

As I hurried toward my Jeep, a mix of determination and that uneasiness flooded my veins. The pieces of the puzzle were slowly falling into place, and I knew that stepping back into Georgina's world would lead me one step closer to the truth.

Little did I know, the answers I sought would bring me face-to-face with a darkness more sinister than I could ever have imagined.

CHAPTER TEN

When I got into the Jeep, I took a quick look at my phone to see if Max or Finn or even Jolee had texted or called. There wasn't anything, so I was free to go right on over to pay Georgina a visit.

Not many people were downtown as I drove north on Main Street. Even Ben's Diner was pretty desolate. It wasn't uncommon for the town to be a little deserted while the county fair was going on. From the looks of it when I went there this morning, it was packed.

Tonight was the tractor pull, so most everyone I knew was going to be there. Finn and I had planned to go, but since I'd not heard from him, I wasn't sure what he had going on over in Clay's Ferry.

But I sure was looking forward to talking to him about this case and what his thoughts were. That was the one thing I loved about our relationship. We were able to bounce scenarios off each other like I used to do with Poppa but with more modern technologies at our disposal as we dug deeper into cases. I could also argue that it was Poppa's good old tried-and-true investigating techniques that helped solve the cases. No fancy stuff needed.

I put all that in the back of my head as I drove up and parked in front of Georgina's house. She was sitting in one chair on the small front porch. Claudia, her neighbor, sat in the other chair. Claudia popped out of it, and Georgina stayed still. Both watched me as I got out of the Wagoneer.

"I'll see you later, hon," Claudia told Georgina after I'd walked up. "Sheriff."

"Claudia, have a nice evening," I told her and turned to watch her walk away before returning to Georgina. "Do you mind if I sit?"

"I reckon not, now that you are sitting." She pointed out that I'd just taken the liberty of making myself comfortable. "Why is he here?" She threw her chin at Scott's sheriff's truck when he pulled up behind my Jeep.

Then she folded her arms, crossed one leg over the other, and bounced her foot in the air. "Are you arresting me for Dilbert's murder? Because I didn't do it."

Scott walked up, and they gave each other what we called the Baptist nod around here. Just a friendly greeting of sorts without all the chatter. Most times, you saw it from people who didn't really care for one another but were doing the right thing of acknowledging that they were in each other's presence. Mainly in social situations.

"No. Nothing like that," I said. "But we have some questions that we need clarified. I was going to do that this morning, but you passed out when you heard Dilbert had been murdered." As my words landed on her, I could see they were still just as raw as the news that had hit her this morning. "I'm sorry to have to talk to you about this, but I'm thinking you probably knew him best."

"When you came in to file the missing person report, you failed to mention you and Dilbert were divorced," Scott said to start the conversation. He sat down on the step of the small porch, and he twisted his body around to talk to her. "Why is that?"

"Because if I came in there saying my ex-husband is missing, it wouldn't've gotten anywhere because we were exes." She was probably right.

In any other circumstance such as this, we would have followed up, but I couldn't help but think if she'd started this morning off by telling us they were divorced, I'd have told her that he probably wasn't taking her call—or missing.

As we all knew, that wasn't how it happened.

"What about the EPO you have against him?" I asked, not a bit shocked she'd not responded to the reminder that she'd filed a legal document that clearly defined and spelled out that there was to be no interaction between them. "It seems to me that if you didn't want to be around Dilbert, wouldn't you have known he was missing?"

"And we know you went to his house a couple of days ago, asking about some money," Scott added.

"Elizabeth Reynolds is nosy," she spat. "I told Dilbert moving next door to her was the worst thing he could do. His business would be all over town."

"Take the EPO out of it and tell me what money you were talking about?" I asked, not thinking Georgina gave two iotas about any EPO.

"I found out down at the bank he was trying to get a loan. In fact, they called me because he was trying to withdraw money from my savings for the down payment on the house. Thank God Vernon Baxter called me because I never look at the savings, since I never touch it," she said. "Instead of getting my lawyer to contact Dilbert about it because it costs me a pretty penny each time I get the lawyer to do something, I took it upon myself to contact Dilbert."

"This was obviously before he got the house." I was trying to put together a timeline of events.

"Mm-hmmm, that's right," she hummed. "And I said, 'Now, Dilbert, you can't be withdrawing my money. That's my money.' And I also told him that if he were any account of a husband, we'd still be married, and he'd be living right here with me."

I let out a long sigh. We could do without all the extra information, but it was her way of telling the story, which I could see fell on Scott and got him all wrapped up in it.

"What did he say?" I asked about Dilbert's response.

"He said that he'd done everything he needed to do to get back at me and was now moving on." She sparked yet another question I had.

"Not to move on yet, but I do want you to tell me about Dilbert's drinking problem," I said.

She shifted uncomfortably.

"You did get a bit offended this morning when I questioned you about his drinking."

She shifted again as I reminded her of all the lies she'd told us when filing the missing person report.

444

"It seems like you gave us false statements, and it's illegal to file reports with misinformation." My brow rose.

"Jail time," Scott added.

"I'll let you off the hook for the charges I could arrest you on if you will cooperate and answer the questions we have honestly as we move forward with our investigation." I had decided to use the information I could charge her with for my good.

"Don't you want to bring Dilbert's killer to justice?" Scott asked, giving me the side-eye.

Scott and I were a good team. We were able to read one another and practically finish each other's thoughts as we interrogated people. This connection was definitely hard to find in any deputy, much less in my only one.

"You aren't going to charge me with nothin'?" Georgina asked as she pondered our deal.

"Nothing having to do with false information," Scott said. "And we will need to check out your alibi for the entire day before Dilbert's body was found."

"That's easy. I was over in Clay's Ferry, doing some antiquing with my sister." Georgina rambled on about the pieces she'd found, and I recognized a few of the antique stores' names. "Not only did we stay there all day, but after that, we ate at that really good Mexican place over there." She snickered as she appeared to remember something from the trip. "Me and Sis had one too many margaritas. We had to get a hotel room. I have all those receipts and my sis's phone number if you want to get her side of the story."

"We will need to see all the receipts, and I'd love to call her," Scott said as he took a small notebook out of another pocket.

"Now that we feel like you are telling us the truth, why didn't you tell us about Dilbert's just getting out of rehab for drinking?" I asked, noticing Scott had started to take notes.

"Because it wouldn't've mattered. Once that lawyer got him the house, Dilbert was comfortable. He started nippin' at the bottle again. I knew he was no-account, and it was all going to go downhill from there." She frowned. "I was a fool to believe him when he told me he was going to rehab and asked me for the money."

"Is that the money Mrs. Reynolds was talking about overhearing you discuss with him?" I needed all the details of any conversation they'd had.

"Yes. He worked at the drywall plant, which don't pay a thing." She huffed. "And rehab is expensive. So I went on down to the Cottonwood First National and got out enough money to cover his drying out."

"Ask about them maps." The word wisped past my ears in Poppa's voice.

"Why did you go to his house and ask for the money?" I wasn't satisfied with the topic of the money, so I wasn't going to move on to the maps. I would, just not now.

"Because he was able to get a loan from the bank, so I knew he had money stuffed somewhere, and I wanted my money. He promised, and if you know Dilbert Thistle like I know Dilbert Thistle, you know he don't keep promises sober, much less drunk." She uncurled her arms and looked at her fingernails before she stuck one in her mouth and gnawed it down.

"Did he give you the money back?" I asked.

"Now, why do you think I wanted y'all to find him? No." Her face pinched, then she spit out some of the chewed-off fingernail into the grass. "That's why I went there. He said something about a payday he was getting soon."

"Payday?" That was something I'd not heard about, and I wanted to explore it. "What kind of payday?"

"I do not know," she said flatly. "Dilbert Thistle was always trying to come into a payday. And I didn't care as long as I got my money back."

"You never borrow money from family," Poppa said behind me.

I cleared my throat. Then my phone vibrated in my pocket. I pulled it out to see who it was, wanting to make sure it had nothing to do with Dilbert's case.

It was Finn. He'd sent a text, but I decided to wait to read it until I was done with questioning Georgina.

"Yep, he can wait," Poppa said from over my shoulder. Such a snooper.

I shoved my phone back into my pocket.

"That's when he gave me some maps to hold on to." Georgina stood up. "I'll go get them."

"You don't need to do that," I told her and pointed for her to sit back

446

down. "When you were taken to the hospital, we got a warrant to search your house."

I gave Scott a glance from the side of my eye.

He stood up and fished for the documents in the deep shirt pocket. He shuffled through all the warrants he was carrying before handing me the one that pertained to her property.

"We took the maps," I told her as I watched her eyes read left to right. "I found them, and without going through why we took them, I need to ask you if he told you anything about them."

"He didn't. He told me to keep them for him. When I asked him about them, he said it was part of his big payday," she said without hesitation, making me believe her. "Now, I also wondered if he was making all this stuff up because he was nippin' again, and sometimes he comes up with some outrageous tales. He could've been making all this up so he was holding off on paying me." She shook the finger with the chewed-off nail at me. "And that's something Dilbert Thistle would do."

"The maps could be nothing," Scott said.

"Or they could be something," I added, knowing I needed to follow every single lead. I turned my attention back to Georgina. "I'll worry about it. What can you tell me about his job at the plant?"

"It was fairly new. He's way overqualified to be on the line, and I told him he needed to apply for every single internal position available." She frowned. "The fact of the matter is that I knew he was back on the wagon because that's when I made sure I held up the EPO in his face."

"When he wasn't drinking, you didn't enforce the EPO?" I questioned, loving how she thought she could just be her own law and toss the order around whenever she wanted to.

"I know that's not how it works in your world, but sometimes the world isn't so black and white. Me and Dilbert"—she jutted her finger against her chest—"we had history. Lots of history, and he was ah-mazin' when he was sober. But the devil would get in him when he was drinking. We had some knockdowns, and I won every time."

She laughed like she was recalling a fond memory, but the volatile relationship sure didn't seem so great to me.

"If he was like this with you, he had to be like this with others," Scott said as he continued to take notes. "Say, in the workplace?"

"He loved working. He was an after-work drinker. He would sober up for work, and he did a fine job. And I told him that he needed to think more of himself than he did and apply for some of those higher-up positions like line manager," she said and threw her hand up at a passing car as it slowed down. "Go on! Ain't nothin' to see here!"

The driver hit the gas and zoomed by.

"That's what you need to be doing around here." She tossed a finger at the car. "Be on pee-trol for yahoos like that. Zooming past over the speed limit. Instead, you're here bugging me."

"Tell me about your little trip to the ball field from the hospital this afternoon." I hated to even bring it up because I didn't want to make her reexperience those feelings, but as the sheriff, I had to know.

"After I come to myself and remembered you telling me about Dilbert..." Her voice cracked.

I leaned over and touched her knee, giving her a hand of support.

"I knew he had a softball game today," she said. "One of the last messages he left on my recorder was telling me he was getting close to a new position at work. If he'd only gotten the position, he wouldn't have done whatever it was for this so-called payday that got him killed because he'd have been paid what he deserved by that darn Bill Johnson."

My phone chirped again. I pulled it out and saw one text message from Max and another from Mama, which I'd not heard.

Max: The tox is definitely calcium hydroxide, and it can be found in drywall plants.

I gulped and slipped the phone back into my pocket.

Scott looked at me.

Our eyes caught.

"Well, Georgina," Scott said, "thank you for your time. But remember, you're working with us now, and if we have any questions, we will need you to answer them."

"Before we go, can you play me the voicemail Dilbert sent you?" I asked.

Georgina fumbled with her phone. Once she found the message, she played it. Dilbert had said exactly what she'd told us.

"We are going to need that. Scott, do you mind forwarding the message to me? I'm going to get out of your hair." I said my goodbyes to Georgina and waited for Scott by my Jeep.

"Bill Johnson called him a drunk. He was with Bill Johnson last night," I said to Scott underneath my breath so no one heard me but him.

"He is strong, which means he could've thrown Dilbert's body on the tracks," Scott pointed out.

"He could've gotten into an argument at work with Dilbert about not giving him a promotion because of Dilbert's drinking." I knew we were tossing out theories we could try to get a lead on.

"I need to get to the fairgrounds to ask those questions and see what others might've seen." Scott was referring to my request that he check out the last known place where Dilbert and Bill were seen together.

Someone saw something. I knew it. The issue was trying to get them to talk.

As Scott and I stood by my Jeep, discussing the possible motives behind Dilbert's murder, a chilling thought sent shivers down my spine.

"What if there's something more to this, Scott?" I whispered, my voice filled with both concern and anticipation. "What if there's a deeper conspiracy at the drywall plant? Something that goes beyond just a workplace rivalry?"

Scott's eyes widened, mirroring my growing realization. "You think there's more to it? Like someone intentionally sabotaging Dilbert's chances for a promotion?"

I nodded, my mind racing with speculations. "It's possible. Maybe there's someone within the plant who didn't want Dilbert to succeed, who had a hidden agenda. And if Bill Johnson was involved, it raises even more questions."

"Perhaps Bill saw Dilbert as a threat, a potential obstacle to his own ambitions," Scott mused. "Or maybe there's something else going on, something we haven't even considered."

More pieces of the puzzle were starting to come together, but there were still missing elements, questions that needed answering. We needed to dig deeper, uncover the truth lurking beneath the surface of the drywall plant.

449

CHAPTER ELEVEN

Before I put the Jeep in drive, I knew I needed to check in with everyone. That meant Mama.

"Mama," I said when she answered. "Did you call?"

"Why yes. I was wanting to tell you that I bought Polly Parker's baby shower gift for us. You owe me fifty dollars," she said.

"Fifty dollars?" I asked. "You mean twenty-five, right? Halfsies?"

"Yes. Fifty dollars is halfsies, Kendrick," Mama retorted. "See, that's the thing with you."

Mama rambled on and on about how I didn't know the cost of things because I never thought about that part of life, and I sort of zoned out when she started talking about the proposal she'd spent so much time and effort on when Finn dropped down on one knee.

"Mm-hmm," I replied several times throughout Mama's monologue so she'd think I was listening to her. My gaze shifted out the window to where Georgina's neighbor had joined her on the porch again.

All six eyeballs were on me, so I decided to hit the speaker on my phone and drive off.

"Did you hear what I said?" Mama asked in a tone that caught my attention. "The cost of monogrammed baby clothes is not cheap, and I had to get three pieces that Polly's baby will grow into. A baby. Can you imagine? Do you think it'll have her teeth? Oh, good Gawd," Mama yammered. "I sure hope it don't have her teeth."

"Mama," I gasped and tried not to smile. "She does have some big bright-white teeth, don't she?"

I snickered, giving in to Mama's gossip. Polly Parker was beautiful. Don't get me wrong. She was probably the prettiest woman in town. So when she and Chase Ryland were sneaking around and necking in the back seat of his car down off the country roads, it sent more shivers up my spine than did any murder case I'd ever worked.

Mayor Ryland was her daddy's age, and when what Polly and Chase were doing came out in the open, her mama about had to be admitted to the psych ward at the big hospital in Clay's Ferry. It wasn't pretty, from what I understood, and though we were called out to the Parker mansion after a big fight over it, I tried to stick to the facts and not listen to any of the gossip.

I really shouldn't've made any comments about Polly's teeth to Mama. They were pretty teeth, but it sure did look like Polly got her some veneers, and they didn't look natural. They didn't make her ugly, though. She was beautiful.

"I reckon it was all those years her mama put her in them pageants and brushed on that teeth-whitening paste that did it. Poor girl," Mama croaked.

"Oh, Mama," I laughed and brought the Jeep to a complete stop once I got to the stop sign that intersected Main Street. "But fifty dollars apiece?"

"If you had a two-person income, fifty dollars wouldn't seem like so much, and yes, I want my money." Mama was trying to prove a point, and I didn't have time to prove her wrong by avoiding buying Polly Parker a gift that would require me to pay fifty dollars.

It really wasn't about the money. It was that it was Polly. What was wrong with a box of wipes and a pack of diapers? That would be something Polly would expect from me. Not some fancy-shmancy monogrammed outfit that, as Mama said, would grow with the baby.

"You need to stop by Dixon's and grab your own card," Mama said just as I turned left on Main Street.

"Mama, I've got to go," I told her after Finn beeped in. "Finn is calling."

"I hope you two didn't forget that I'm in the bell choir, and we're performing tomorrow morning at church. I'm expecting you and him right in the front pew," Mama quickly spat out before I clicked over.

"You are a lifesaver," I said, answering Finn's call.

"Let me guess," he teased. "You were on the phone with Viv."

"How did you know?" I laughed and drove down the mostly deserted Main Street. "Downtown is a ghost town."

"Good one," Poppa called from the passenger seat. "If you only knew," he teased as if there were many other ghosts floating around town.

Maybe there were, and I just couldn't see them.

"Are we going on our Ferris wheel ride tonight? I'm on my way to Dixon's Foodtown to get a card for Polly's baby gift," I rambled before Finn hollered into the phone to stop me just as I got downtown.

"Kenni," he said as I took a breath. "I can't tonight. I have to work. We've had a few deputies call in sick."

"Oh." Instead of feeling down, I turned the situation around. "Then you can look in on something I need for the case. Dilbert's murder."

As I drove through downtown, the heart of Cottonwood, the familiar sights of small-town life unfolded before me. The vibrant shops lined the streets, each with its own unique charm. The local radio station, situated at the fairgrounds during the county fair festival, buzzed with live broadcasts and music that added a lively atmosphere to the town.

"Sure. What is it?" Finn asked.

"Georgina Thistle, his wife—ex-wife—claimed she was over in Clay's Ferry and spent the night, making Clay's Ferry her alibi. I'll have Scott send you her receipts if that's okay, and you can possibly go to the hotel, see if there's any footage that means she was there that night," I said. I passed by the carriage lights, which adorned the sidewalks one by one, their gentle glow illuminating the path for the few passersby.

The sight of the Cottonwood First National Bank caught my attention, a reminder that I needed to visit Vernon Bishop, the bank's president, on Monday to inquire about Dilbert's loan and gather any relevant information.

"I will be more than happy to do that. But I'll call Scott to get them. I don't want you on the phone and driving," he said. Then he added, "It's an election year, and, well, you can't be doing anything you'd pull people over and ticket them for."

I passed by White's Jewelry, its display windows shimmering with an array of sparkling gems and delicate trinkets. I gripped the wheel and looked at my ring finger. Once again, I wondered if the ring Finn had bought because we couldn't find my granny's had come from Viola White's jewelry store.

"I will have you know that you are on speaker. I wouldn't do anything illegal," I stated matter-of-factly.

Farther down the street, I passed Ruby's Antiques and Ben's Diner. Both were weathered with charm and showed just how old Cottonwood really was.

The inn, with its quaint facade, beckoned to travelers and tourists. It was a cute little boutique hotel in the middle of town. It didn't take but another minute until I was well past Broadway, my street, as the Wagoneer rattled down toward what was known as Edgewood, where Dixon's Foodtown was located.

"Also, Mama reminded me about her—" I was about to say.

"Bell choir performance. I already got the text." He chuckled. "Then I have to—what she said—skedaddle afterward because 'the baby shower is only for the women of the church.'" He did his best impression of Mama's southern accent, which wasn't too good, but it was still cute. "I better get off here and call Scott so I can work on those before anything happens around here and I get busy."

"Sounds good. I'm about to pull into Dixon's." I glanced over at Poppa. His words about the hidden ghosts of Cottonwood made it hard for me to shake the feeling that there was more to uncover. "Do you need anything?"

"Nah. I'm good. I'll pick you up for church in the morning." His voice trailed off as we said our goodbyes.

"That boy sure does have you roped up like a calf."

Poppa's choice of words cracked me up.

"As hard as I try to not see it," he said, "you two do make a nice couple. Shame he's not from around here."

Poppa ghosted away as I pulled into Dixon's parking lot and parked right next to Toots Buford's pink 1965 VW Bug. It was the cutest car, and it sure did clash with the bright-red hair she'd gotten from the #R42 L'Oréal box of hair dye.

I put the Jeep in park and turned off the ignition to prepare myself for seeing Toots. She was bold and brash. There was no way I would get out of the grocery store without her stopping me to talk about the you-know-what.

And I didn't mean the murder.

I meant the proposal that wasn't.

Before I got out, a glimmer of light caught my eye. There, nestled in the crease of the passenger seat, was a small, shiny object. My heart skipped a beat as I reached over and picked it up.

It was Granny's ring, the one I had been searching for, the one I had hoped would be my engagement ring from Finn.

The ring glistened with a radiant beauty. The gold band reflected the last little bit of sunlight in dazzling splendor, holding memories of Granny's love and wisdom, a symbol of family and tradition. But it also held the weight of my mixed emotions, of the unspoken understanding between ghost Poppa and me.

His fate.

Tears welled up in my eyes as I stared at the ring, feeling the bittersweet ache in my chest. Poppa, my guardian and confidant, had taken the ring before, not wanting me to move on with my life, fearing that Finn's presence would replace his own. But now, seeing the ring before me, I sensed a shift in his stance.

In that moment, it felt as if Poppa had come to terms with my decision, with the knowledge that I would marry Finn.

The realization washed over me, filling me with a complex blend of gratitude, sadness, and a twinge of guilt. It was as if Poppa, in his own way, had given his blessing, acknowledging that my happiness mattered above all else.

With trembling hands, I slipped the ring onto my finger, feeling its cool metal against my skin. The ring fit perfectly, as if it had been waiting for this moment all along. I glanced at the empty seat beside me, half expecting to see Poppa's ghostly figure, but he remained unseen.

"It's on my finger now. You can't take it back," I called out in case he was listening.

There was zero chance I was leaving it in the car. I sure didn't want to find the ring gone when I got back in if he changed his mind.

I pushed open the car door, stepped out, and walked toward the store. I couldn't help but smile.

Was this really going to happen?

I glanced down at the ring one more time before I walked through the mechanical sliding doors of the grocery store, wondering what it would feel like when Finn asked me again to marry him as he slipped the ring on my finger.

I swore it felt wrong to smile my way down the card aisle when there was a murder to be solved. A few of the shoppers stared, and I couldn't help but think they'd seen the video Taven had put on his Facebook.

It was something I would have to deal with but not over the weekend. I would host a live news conference on Monday after talking to a few more people from Dilbert's life and give an update on where we stood with the case.

It was too early in my investigation to even think about giving any sort of detail, and it would be premature to do it for the sake of getting something out there to beat Taven to the punch.

Not my style.

I should've taken more time to look for a card for Polly. One with meaning and celebration about the bundle of joy, but heck, her stepkids were her age—our age. It felt so weird she was even pregnant, so I just plucked off the first card I saw and headed up to the counter.

"Well, hey, Kenni," Toots Buford said to me from the other side of the Dixon's Foodtown checkout line. "I reckon I'll be seeing you at the shower I'm giving Polly after church tomorrow."

"Yes." I nodded and stuck my hands in my pants pockets while I waited for her to ring me up.

"I understand you've been a little busy with the murder and all." Toots winked. "I did see the video. I mean"—she pushed her fingers up in her hair —"really, you might want to start wearing makeup and fixing your hair." She shrugged and tapped the screen to make my total come up, then she reached for a plastic bag to put my card in.

"I don't need a bag," I told her. I was about to say something about the video when I held my hand out to take the card.

My left hand.

The one with Granny's ring.

"Oh my! Heavens to Betsy!" Toots Buford squealed and reached across the conveyor belt to grab my hand. "That ring is a real sparkler! Where'd you get it? You didn't mention nothin' 'bout an engagement!" Her eyes widened with curiosity and excitement, her gossipy nature taking over. "Oh Lordy. I can't believe I've not heard the news. I mean, I did hear 'bout you leaving him down on his knee for a while, and then I thought, 'Well, lucky Kenni,' when someone said that's when Patty screamed. I was guessing you just didn't know if you wanted to get married, leaving him down like that. But that's a real sparkler, it is."

I pulled back a little to try to reclaim my hand, but when she didn't let go, I yanked it out of her grip.

"Toots, I'd appreciate it if you didn't mention this to anyone." I picked up the card. "Finn and I haven't told a soul yet because we don't want to take the shine off of Polly."

I lied. But I couldn't tell her that Finn didn't even know about the ring or that we might be engaged.

For that matter, I wasn't even sure what this ring meant. It was my only way of making sure it stayed in my possession so Poppa couldn't take it again.

Toots leaned in conspiratorially, her eyes twinkling with mischief. "Oh, you can count on me, Kenni. I'm the keeper of secrets 'round these parts. Polly may be my best friend, but you and me, we're almost like sisters now, sharin' this special bond. Our little secret, tucked away in our hearts."

She winked.

I chuckled, appreciating Toots's enthusiasm and dramatic flair. "Well, Toots, I appreciate your discretion. I better be on my way now, but I'll see you at the baby shower tomorrow."

As I turned to leave, Toots couldn't resist sharing the news, as she did with anyone who would listen. "Y'all see that? That's the sheriff right there, and we're practically best friends now! Ain't that a hoot?"

I couldn't help but blush as I hurried out of the store, the sound of Toots's exaggerated proclamation echoing behind me. She seemed to have a way of turning the simplest of interactions into something larger than life, just like she did to all the stories she'd heard in her cashier line.

That was just Toots Buford for you, a master storyteller and gossip extraordinaire.

CHAPTER TWELVE

The next morning, I woke up so energized and alive. I'd had the best night's sleep that I'd had in days and didn't once wake up thinking about Dilbert's case.

"I guess I really needed that." I yawned, and my hand fell on Duke's belly.

Jolee had dropped him off at some point yesterday during all my travels investigating Dilbert's murder.

"But now we have to get up, drink the coffee, and get ready for church," I told him, giving him another good pat before I peeled the covers off me and got out of bed. "And I better take a shower or your granny is going to kill me."

Duke jumped off the bed and beat me to the kitchen door. I let him out to go run around the back yard and do his business, and then he darted back in to eat the kibble I'd thrown in his bowl after I'd poured myself a hot cup of coffee.

"I'm going to get my shower while you eat," I called to him over my shoulder while sauntering down the hall where my tiny bathroom was located.

With my left hand, I reached into the shower and turned on the water.

"Hello there," I said to the sparkling ring on my left hand. "I forgot all about you."

I pulled my hand back and held it out in front of my face to get another look.

"It feels no different," I said, referring to how natural it felt for the ring to be there like it had been on my finger all along. "But you will not be going with me today."

I made the mental note to take the ring off before I went to church. I wasn't sure how to tell Finn about finding it. During my entire shower, I was focused on how to slip the subject into the conversation.

"Hey, Finn." I started to rehearse what I might say to him when I stepped out of the shower. "I found my granny's engagement ring." I held my hand out to Duke like he was Finn.

My dog was sitting outside of the shower curtain, waiting for me to get out, like he always did. Duke jumped to his feet and wagged his tail.

I put my robe on and started to towel dry my hair.

"You can ask me now," I told Duke right as my phone rang. "To marry you," I said and walked down the hall back to the kitchen, where I'd plugged in my phone to charge before I'd gone to bed last night.

"Good morning," I told Finn when I answered his call.

"Good morning." He sounded like he knew something was wrong. "I checked on Georgina's alibi, and it does fit. The manager of the bed-and-breakfast did confirm she and her sister were there. He remembered them because they requested banana pancakes for breakfast."

"I can cross her off," I said and walked back to the bedroom, where I was going to slip on a dress that would make Mama so happy to see me in. "Are you on your way over?"

"That's what I was really calling about," he said. "I've not been home all night. I'm on my way now, so I'm going to have to meet you at church. I don't want both of us to be late."

"No problem. But you're going to have to apologize to Mama for being late," I told him.

"I'll come up with some good excuse." He laughed. "I'll see you in a little while."

I hung up the phone and hurried now that I had to drive myself. Getting ready never really took me too long. But today I would have to put on at least some lipstick to appease Mama. The baby shower card was still in the Jeep, so the process was pretty much brushing my hair, slapping on some lipstick, and taking another swig of coffee before I was out the door.

The challenge would be finding a parking spot. I glanced around the lot to see if I could detect any openings and realized just how easy it would be for someone to rob anyone's home or business in Cottonwood on Sunday morning.

Everyone and their brother attended church, whether they believed or not. In the South, it was beaten into your brain that you better go to church on the off chance God was real, and you'd have a fighting chance if you could honestly say you went instead of the alternative.

I counted numerous people as I looked around from the front-row pew Mama had saved for Finn and me. She'd done that by laying out all the church bulletins across the long padded bench, which had my name written in big black letters across the day's printed hymnal readings.

"Reserved for the sheriff," they read.

The crowd hushed when the first sound of the pipe organ came to life.

Preacher Bing walked down the center aisle as the bell choir filed out of the back room, left of the stage. I recognized all of Mama's friends and prayer circle, all in their maroon robes and white gloves, each person holding one bell.

They had a choreographed walk as they made a V formation, their shoulders all tugged back as if they were playing for the New York Symphony Orchestra.

The bell choir was truly fascinating. Mama's bell was a different tone from Viola's, whose bell was different from Polly's. Speaking of Polly…

She made sure her free hand was propped up underneath her protruding belly, like she wanted everyone to make sure the robe didn't make her look fat and that the next heir to the Ryland fortune was cooking underneath it.

I followed her gaze and then smiled to see Chance Ryland in the front-row pew on the other side of the aisle. Quickly, I turned away.

He was the last person I wanted to notice me, if he hadn't already. No doubt he'd be on me about Dilbert's case and why I hadn't let him know the details.

Though the murder was still not solved, I was looking forward to having a little time off from it, even if that time was for celebrating Chance's soon-to-be-born child.

There was another new addition to the bell choir besides Polly.

Edna Easterly.

Though I knew she wasn't pregnant, there was definitely something under her choir robe. I'd bet money on it that she had her journalist vest on underneath.

A sudden movement to my left caught my attention. It was Finn trying to slip in next to me just before the first ring of the bell started the performance.

"You look nice," Finn whispered in my ear as he bent over and sat down to my left.

"You do too," I told him and patted his leg.

I glanced back up to the bell choir.

Mama's face had started to contort with anger at Finn's lateness. I could almost feel the heat coming off of her.

Poppa ghosted behind her and was mouthing something I couldn't hear over the bells now that the performance had started.

I shifted in my seat to focus on Polly, crossing my legs and laying my hands on top so Mama didn't keep sending me the death stare right there in church.

Polly dropped her hand from her baby bulge and picked up another bell. She held one in each hand as she began her solo.

The glee coming off Chance glowed as he watched his young wife taking center stage as she played the part of the first wife of Cottonwood to a hilt. Polly had her neatly and perfectly polished fingernails in everything and every club of Cottonwood. And now they were in the bell choir.

A sudden burst of ringing that seemed out of place echoed throughout the church.

"Thank you, Lord!" Mama's familiar voice screamed out. She had lifted the bell above her head and was giving it a good go, wielding it back and forth. "You are so good!"

She hiked up the maroon robe with her free gloved hand and gathered the garment around her waist as she hightailed it out of the choir, rushing down the few steps as she darted at me.

"We are having us a wedding!" She threw her arms around Finn and me as my heart sank, and I realized I'd forgotten to take off the ring.

I honestly couldn't have described the look on Finn's face. It was like nothing I'd ever seen. The look was a combination of fear, confusion, and trepidation, not excitement or happiness. But then again, he hadn't asked me a second time, and in his mind, the ring on my finger had been missing, misplaced, or gone. Take your pick.

"Where did you get that?" Finn whispered in my ear, disguising the question in a kiss to my temple. "And what is happening?"

The entire congregation was silent until Polly Parker let out a howl, which gave Edna Easterly the signal that this moment would be great to document. Within seconds, she'd ripped the robe off over her head and, sure enough, exposed the old fishing vest with all the pockets filled with anything she'd need if she came across a newsworthy story.

Including her camera.

"Oh my God!" she screamed and threw the bell on the floor. "Why can't I ever have my day? Chance! She ruined it again!"

"Now, honey," Chance Ryland said. His voice was dripping with concern for his wife as he shot his death-arrow stare at me on his way up the steps to help Polly down and console her. "You're still going to have your day."

He turned and looked at Edna, and he grinned as Edna snapped away.

Always the politician.

"No, I'm not. She knew my baby shower was right after church, and now she's going to get all the attention. Not me. Or your baby." She smacked his chest. The ring on her finger was ten times as big as my little precious stone, which she was so up in arms over.

"Honestly, I wasn't," I stammered, searching for a way to say I never intended to take attention from her. That would be the truth, but the truth wasn't going to help Mama none.

The click of the camera made me turn and look at Edna. For a moment, she pulled her eye away from the lens and smirked.

Mama was so overjoyed she'd started crying.

"Mama, now's not the time." I shook my head and put my finger to my lips.

"You're telling me." Finn kept the fake smile planted on his face. It was like he was a ventriloquist. "We should just go."

"Yes. Great idea." My eyes shot up to his. "We are just going to leave. Great solo," I told Polly.

"What? Engaged?" Jolee Fischer found her way down the aisle, dragging Ben behind her. Seeing the shocked look on Jolee's face made my mouth go dry. I wasn't going to get out of this one.

"Yep. I was trying to tell you about the ring, but you ignored me," Poppa said with a shrug. "Can't this boy ever dress up?" He turned his attention to Ben Harrison.

Ben was rarely seen without his backwards baseball cap, but we were in church, and out of respect he'd stuffed it in the back pocket of his jeans, letting his shaggy brown hair lie every which way.

"God doesn't care how you dress," I said.

"What?" Jolee looked at me. "I'm not talking about your dress. I'm talking about the ring." She looked down.

"I'd love everyone to join me in congratulating Sheriff Kenni Lowry and Sheriff Finn Vincent on their engagement. We are so blessed in our community to have such quality folks." Preacher Bing had stepped up to the pedestal and taken it upon himself to bring order to the church.

"I didn't say a word, Kenni," Toots Buford hollered out from the third pew across the aisle, making a finger gesture between herself and me. "We are besties now." She nudged Viola White, who was sitting next to her. "She told me last night at Dixon's Foodtown."

"You told Toots Buford last night and didn't bother to tell me?" Jolee's jaw tensed, and her nose flared. "I can't believe this."

My eyes narrowed, and I glared at Poppa.

"What? I didn't tell you to put it on your finger. I just put it on the seat of the car because you wanted all of this." He motioned around us and then disappeared.

"Thank you." I turned to the congregation and waved as Preacher Bing's words brought applause all around. "We are leaving."

I opened my purse and took out Polly's card.

"I hope you love your gift," I told Polly as I handed the card to her.

"A card?" She rolled her eyes. "I'm so glad my husband is backing Taven Tidwell. He's a professional and a man."

The words hit me like a punch to the gut, sending a surge of shock and disbelief through my veins.

How could Mayor Ryland turn his support against me? The man I had known for years, the man who had claimed to believe in me as sheriff, was now throwing his weight behind my opponent.

A whirlwind of emotions swept through my mind. Betrayal, confusion, and a nagging sense of insecurity swirled together, threatening to consume me. I kept my composure, putting on a brave face for Polly and the others, but inside, I felt a mixture of anger and hurt.

How could he do this to me?

As I handed Polly the card with a forced smile, my grip tightened on the edges of the paper. I wanted to scream, to lash out at the injustice of it all. But instead, I swallowed my pride and mustered a response.

"Thank you, Polly," I said, my voice strained but steady. "I hope you enjoy your gift," I said again, this time forcing her to take the card and also very aware that Edna Easterly was pushing the little button on the camera as she snapped up all the photos she could.

Deep down, I knew this setback would only fuel my determination.

I couldn't let Mayor Ryland's betrayal derail my campaign or shake my belief in myself. I would fight harder than ever to prove that I was the right person for the job, regardless of who backed my opponent.

And that meant no days off until I solved Dilbert Thistle's murder.

CHAPTER THIRTEEN

"What is going on?" Finn sped ahead of me and busted out the front door of the church.

Luckily, Preacher Bing had gotten the service back on track, and the bell choir had restarted their performance from the beginning.

Mama was giving the bell hell when I turned to look back before I followed Finn out. She was glowing with excitement.

"I found the ring," I said, squinting from the bright early-afternoon sun beating down on the front steps of the church.

"Found it and put it on?" Finn shook his head. "You saw the ring and said, 'Well, he proposed. I might'swell stick it on my finger and get engaged without telling him'?" He threw his hands up in the air before he ran one through his black hair, his brown eyes boring into me. "You certainly don't do things like they are supposed to be done."

"I guess that's what you get with me. I don't do things like they are supposed to be done. Is there really a right way to everything, Finn?" I asked. "Do you have to get down on one knee and ask me to marry you? Is that the man's job? Is it the man's job to be a sheriff? I mean, I had that obstacle to overcome when I was running, and now it seems like the entire town or at least the mayor wants a man sheriff."

"Don't make this about that." His voice softened. "You know how girls have a dream of their big proposal, their wedding day?"

I gave him a flat look.

"I know, you aren't one of those girls, but you know my sister, and you have friends." His brows furrowed. "Which, by the way—you told Toots Buford we were engaged?"

The look of confusion on his face was so funny that I couldn't stop myself from bursting out laughing.

Finn caught it too.

"It's so off-the-chart strange how this happened that I don't even think you'd believe me if I told you." I shook my head and slipped the ring off my finger.

Poppa had come out from behind one of the large columns that held up the porch-style roof of the front of the church. He was shaking his head as if he didn't want me to tell Finn about him.

Oh, I wasn't. I wasn't telling anyone about ghost Poppa.

"I know we searched the Jeep, the house, the office, and my parents' house for this ring. I guess we didn't search the Jeep good enough. Or it was so jammed between the seat cushion and back of the passenger seat that it wiggled its way up. I saw a glimpse of glistening when I pulled into Dixon's Foodtown last night." I smiled at my handsome boyfriend as he struggled to understand how this ring got on my finger.

I continued to tell him the story, only my telling was slightly different from reality.

"You couldn't imagine my surprise when I picked it up. I wasn't about to leave it in the Jeep, so I put it on my finger, not figuring anyone would pay attention to it." I snorted. "I didn't even think about Toots Buford's big eyeballs. I should've known when I saw her car."

Some noises came from the side of the church, but I didn't bother glancing over. I only wanted Finn to see I was solely focused on him and this ring.

I handed it to him.

He inspected it while I told him that I'd not wanted to lose it and that it felt so natural that I'd forgotten it was even on my finger.

"I'm glad you found it," he said with the loving look I was used to seeing on his face when we were together. "Kenni, I..." he began, about to apologize for his behavior.

At least, that was what I thought was happening until he bent down on one knee.

"Finn," I gasped just as Poppa's ghost rushed so fast to Finn's side it made the edge of my dress blow.

Finn looked around as if he noticed the gust of wind and was trying to see if the weather had suddenly changed.

"I know this isn't how your mama wanted it. She wanted the photos, the friends, the family, but I know you really wanted this ring. No matter what happened in there"—he gestured back to the church—"with the mayor and Polly. What is happening in here"—he used the ring to tap his chest—"this feels right, right now."

I licked my lips. Out of the corner of my eye, I saw Jolee had walked up where Poppa had been standing with Ben behind her. That must have been who I'd heard walking from the side of the church.

"Will you marry me?" Finn asked.

"Kenni bug?" Poppa called my name as if he wanted to get my attention.

"Yes!" I blurted out so I didn't have time to look at Poppa or try to avoid feeling guilty for loving Finn and wanting a life with him. "Yes. I'll marry you."

My eyes welled up with tears. I felt as though I were losing Poppa again, like the day he did die—and I could feel myself stepping into the opportunity to spend the rest of my living days with Finn.

Finn slipped the ring on my finger and stood up. He took me in his arms and snuggled his face in my neck as he twirled around with me in his arms.

When he finally put me down, I looked over his shoulder and saw Jolee was crying tears of happiness and had caught the entire real proposal on her phone.

CHAPTER FOURTEEN

Thank goodness Jolee knew me well enough to know I would never tell Toots Buford I was engaged, and she'd taken the side door of the church to follow me to my Jeep. That was when she found Finn and me talking it out on the steps of the church, where she ultimately realized Finn had no idea we were engaged.

But she was keen enough to know what was about to happen when she pulled her phone out to start filming the real proposal.

It was exactly how I was supposed to get engaged.

Instead of taking her and Ben up on their offer to go back to Ben's Diner, where Ben and she were going to use their amazing culinary skills to fix us an engagement breakfast, Finn and I had decided to drive ourselves home. There, he could feed his cat, and I could get Dilbert Thistle's maps and Duke so we could take a Sunday drive down to the Kentucky River.

I agreed to let Jolee handle a few things for the euchre game tonight and told her we could celebrate there, which not only made her happy but would keep her busy for the day.

Even after my engagement, Dilbert was still dead, and the threat of Mayor Chance Ryland giving Taven his endorsement loomed. Finn knew how much weight that could pull in Cottonwood, and that was why we decided to work on the case.

"We will get this solved in no time." Finn was driving the Jeep down the windy roads that would eventually take us down to the river where Dilbert's map ended. The area depicted on that part of the map stopped shy of the drywall plant, but I wasn't sure exactly where that location was.

I had rolled down the back window for Duke to stick his body out and feel the wind. I glanced down at my hand and smiled before I looked into the back seat. Poppa's absence made itself felt in my soul.

I knew he wasn't there. I turned back around and looked in the side mirror at Duke. His big floppy ears were pinned back by the wind, and his tongue stuck out of the side of his mouth.

"Are you okay?" Finn asked. "That was a big sigh."

"I didn't even realize I sighed. It must be a sigh of love and happiness," I gushed in hopes it covered up that my heart had been broken yet again by Poppa's death.

I'd hear people say how time healed, but it didn't. That was a lie. Today my heart felt the exact same loneliness and emptiness it had the day Poppa had died.

The only difference was that now, I was able to pick up and move on as I learned to live comfortably with that hole in my heart. I'd been spoiled over the last few years with ghost Poppa and started to wonder if he was ever really here as a ghost or if I'd made it all up this entire time.

No matter how much I tried to reason, he wasn't here now. It was a risk I took to let go of my past. When I looked back over at Finn, I knew I was looking into my future.

My phone rang.

"I bet it's Mama," I said, looking out the window at the limestone walls that flanked each side of the old country road as I tugged my phone out of my pocket. "I don't know who it is."

Out of the corner of my eye, I could see Finn glance over as I answered it.

"Sheriff Lowry," I said.

"Sheriff, it's Evelyn Reynolds, Dilbert's neighbor. You said to call if I saw anything, and, well, today I wasn't able to make it to church, though I heard I missed a good one," she said and coughed. Her voice was a melody against the lazy buzz of the cicadas in the background.

The air was thick and heavy, carrying with it the sweet scent of honeysuckle blooming somewhere nearby.

"I'm not feeling all that well," she said, "and when I was standing at the sink to fix me a glass of water to take my pills, I saw the shed out back of Dilbert's house was wide open, and some stuff seemed to be flung out."

Her words hung in the air like a question, waiting to be answered. I glanced over at Finn, his face a mask of concentration. His hand was gripping the steering wheel so tightly his knuckles turned white.

"Are you saying you think someone broke into the shed?" I asked.

The trees lining the road rustled softly in the summer breeze, a whispered counterpoint to the tension mounting inside the car.

"Yes. They must've come in the middle of the night because I didn't hear a thing." Her words echoed eerily in the quiet afternoon.

"Okay. Don't go over there. I'll be right there."

I didn't even have to tell Finn to turn the Jeep around. His hand moved swiftly, pulling the old beacon siren from underneath my seat and passing it to me. I could feel the heat emanating from the old metal; years of dust and dirt were rubbed away from frequent use.

Like always, I put a little spit on the suction cup of the bottom of the siren, stuck it out the window, and slapped it on top of the roof as I ran my finger down to switch on the siren. When the siren came to life, the sun overhead cast a blinding glare on it, its red hue seeming to ignite in the golden rays.

"529 Courtmead Drive," I said, easing back into the seat as the adrenaline coursed through my veins. The warm, cushioned vinyl enveloped me, a familiar comfort in the face of unexpected danger. The sound of the siren and the roll of the red light across the limestone walls filled the previously hollow space Poppa had left. I could almost feel his ghost in the worn-out seat beside me.

Duke added his mournful howls to the cacophony, and the Jeep's engine purred like a gigantic cat beneath us.

Before long, the picturesque silhouette of Dilbert's house materialized in front of us. The quaint structure stood like a lonely relic amid the manicured lawns, the golden hues of the summer afternoon casting long, reaching shadows around it.

"I heard y'all coming down the road, so I figured it was okay to come out," Evelyn said, appearing from behind the bright-green shrubbery lining the yard. The midday sun draped a gentle halo around her, making her seem ethereal. "I heard about the big engagement. Congratulations. If I'd known you were engaged yesterday, I would've said something then."

"Thank you, Mrs. Reynolds," Finn said. He'd come so far with his southern manners since the first day he'd arrived in Cottonwood as a Kentucky State Reserve officer. "Kenni, I'll take Duke for a walk."

I was about to protest and tell him to come, but he shook his head, letting me know that I had to do this—if not because I was the sheriff and he didn't work here anymore then because I had to prove to every single citizen that I was worth their vote.

"You didn't hear anything?" I asked and started to walk in between her house and Dilbert's.

"No. Sugar, I have to take out my hearing aids or I don't get a wink of sleep." She pointed at her ears.

I didn't even see anything in them.

"They sure do make them smaller now," I replied. "You didn't see anything or anyone either?"

"Sure didn't. Like I said, I was standing at my kitchen window, minding my own business, when I just so happened to look across the yard over here, and that's what I found." She pointed ahead of us and revealed that what she'd described on the phone was real.

The doors of the shed were wide open, and inside were a few pieces of the equipment I'd seen in there yesterday, but they weren't hanging up like I'd left them. They were tossed out of the shed like someone had made a way for themselves, as if they were looking for something.

"You stay right here," I told her and reached down to pull out the gun strapped around my ankle. I might not have had my utility belt on, but I was always packing.

I could clearly see inside the shed as I walked closer, the empty void a stark reminder of the stolen photos. The absence resounded more loudly than any physical evidence. Swallowing the lump in my throat, I slid my gun back into my ankle holster and fished my phone out of my pocket.

"What's up?" Scott answered in an unhurried tone, the sound of him

471

shuffling papers in the background meeting my ears. "I heard at breakfast this morning that someone got engaged."

"Yeah. But I'm calling because someone has broken into Dilbert's shed. Evelyn called me when I was driving down to the river to check out one of the maps Dilbert had given Georgina. She says it must've happened in the middle of the night.

"Apparently, they are looking for those photos we dug up because there's an even bigger hole dug in the exact same spot. I'm guessing whoever is in those photos is looking for them, and that person could be our killer," I suggested.

"I'm on my way. I'll scour the scene and dust for prints." His casual demeanor changed in an instant as he struggled to keep his surprise from seeping into his voice. "I went by the fairgrounds last night. I figured Saturday night was as good as any, and it was packed. Bill and Dilbert were there, according to a few of the bartending volunteers. They said they would come down to the department and give a statement. Both of them confirmed they saw Bill's wife come get him. One of them also confirmed that she asked Dilbert if he wanted a ride, but he declined. The volunteer told Dilbert he should probably take her up on the offer because they weren't serving him anymore, and he told the volunteer to mind his own business and got up."

"Did you get their names and numbers?" I asked so we could get all the information in the report.

"Yes, ma'am. I've already written up the reports and put them in Dilbert's file. Sittin' on your desk for you." His hurried words about checking for prints and his swift goodbye were an unspoken testament to his shared concern.

Scott was a gem. He was very organized and just did the job.

Exiting the shed, I spotted Finn and Duke lounging in Mrs. Reynold's back yard, Finn sipping a glass of tea in a leisurely way.

When I walked over, Evelyn offered me a glass, too, her overly steady hand and forced smile revealing her attempt at maintaining normalcy in the face of uncertainty.

"Kenni, let me get you a glass of tea." She got to her feet without waiting for an answer, and her figure disappeared behind the screen door before I could refuse.

"Anything?" Finn's eyebrows rose in curiosity as I mentioned our discovery from the shed, his hand tightening unconsciously around his tea glass.

"I've not been able to tell you, but we found something in the shed yesterday," I said.

His chin lifted in the air as he got a curious look on his face.

"Something really odd and, well, it would fit with a motive, but I'm not sure who," I said.

We exchanged our suspicions before Evelyn returned, her warm smile slightly strained as she handed me a glass of her sweet tea. The clinking ice served as a momentary distraction, the sound underscoring the unsettling events.

"Thank you, Mrs. Reynolds," I said and took the glass.

"Evelyn, honey," she corrected me. "We've had enough interactions in the last twenty-four hours that we should be on a first-name basis. Unless you want me to address you as Sheriff."

"No, ma'am." I took a drink. "Don't tell Mama, but you make really good sweet tea."

"It's our little secret." She winked and sat down, pointing for me to sit.

"I'm having Deputy Lee come over to see if there's any evidence the intruder left behind," I said.

"May I ask you a question?" Finn interjected, addressing Evelyn. When she nodded, he asked, "Did you and Dilbert ever have any conversations?"

"We did about the water treatment facility." She pointed off in the distance behind their houses to the Cottonwood water treatment plant's location. It'd been there for years.

Our conversation veered toward Dilbert, and I could see a flicker of something cross Evelyn's eyes when she mentioned their conversations about the water treatment facility. Finn and I shared a knowing look, silently asking the same question—was that facility somehow linked to Dilbert's murder?

"What was the conversation?" I asked.

"I don't recall all of it, but I remember him saying how he didn't think it was good-quality water, and he'd gotten one of them water bottles from the High Bridge Limestone Water Company."

Her mention of the water reminded me of what was in Dilbert's house.

"You know, he doesn't have anything in the house but a High Bridge Limestone water cooler," I said and took a last drink of the tea.

"I never saw the man move anything in there, but I figured it was because Georgina didn't give him nothing to take with him." Evelyn made a good point.

"Thank you for calling and the tea," I said and looked at Finn. "We've taken up enough of your Sunday. I think I hear Scott pulling up front."

I didn't really hear him, but I heard a car door slam, which was a good excuse for Finn and me to get out of there.

"Thank you again," I told her as Finn and I walked back toward the Jeep in the front of the houses, where I saw I was right.

Scott had met us halfway.

"I'll let you know if I find anything," he said.

"Thanks. In the meantime, we are going to drive down to the river using Dilbert's maps." I clicked my tongue for Duke to come. Just before now, he'd jumped out of the Jeep and run around the yard, sniffing all the good smells.

"Nothing you found, though?" Scott asked.

"Not a thing, but someone was looking for the items we found." I shifted my eyes to the Jeep. I'd put the box of photos and the other evidence I'd gathered in the back of the vehicle so I could drop those items off with Tom Geary. "I've just not had a lot of time to get them to the lab. Every time I think I'm headed that way, something else comes up that takes my attention."

"We can head over there now before we go to the river," Finn suggested.

A wave of tension washed over Scott as we discussed dropping off the evidence at the lab. His posture stiffened, and a slight grimace tugged at the corners of his mouth. The lines around his eyes tightened in an attempt to hide his discomfort, a silent objection to Finn's involvement. Finn caught on quickly and averted his gaze, the muscles in his jaw twitching as he excused himself and called for Duke.

"What do you think, Scott?" I threw Finn's suggestion to Scott so he didn't feel like he was playing second fiddle to the old deputy whose place he'd taken.

"Yeah. Sure, whatever Sheriff Vincent says." Scott's face said what his words didn't. And the little bit of bite in his tone made me pause.

"I think that's all fine and dandy, but Sheriff Vincent doesn't have jurisdiction on our cases," I reminded Scott, though he didn't need reminding. The point was to imply that his opinion mattered more than Finn's.

Did it really?

"Sheriff Lowry is right," Finn said. "I'm sorry. I shouldn't've even said anything. Duke and I will be in the Jeep."

Finn walked away, patting his leg for Duke to follow.

"Are you okay?" I asked, knowing if Scott wasn't okay, then we were going to have a problem. He was the only one I could really rely on to help me solve this murder.

His half-hearted nod and forced smile revealed his gratitude but also his lingering unease.

"I'm good. Sorry about that. I shouldn't've made it seem like I didn't want Finn's, um, Sheriff Vincent's opinion. I mean, he is a veteran and has a lot of knowledge." Scott just about changed his tune.

"It's all good," I said, letting him off the hook. The last thing I needed was a diva in the office. "Your thoughts on this case trump whatever Finn says. We are in the trenches together."

I nodded at him several times, hoping he would nod back.

He didn't.

"I'll go look around, and you go do whatever it was you were doing. I'll keep you posted," he said.

I couldn't help the worry that gnawed at me as I watched him walk away, his steps slightly heavier than usual. He obviously had other things on his mind. It wasn't like we knew each other's personal life outside of work. Yeah, he knew Mama and how she rambled on about things only because she came to the department a lot and told us everything.

Because of the crime we were investigating, this case was also one of those instances in which the job weighed much more today than during the weeks we didn't have a murder on our hands. This job was tough, and when the sheriff's department consisted of only two people besides the dispatch operator—in our case, the elderly Betty Murphy—then the job could play havoc in your head.

Unfortunately, it was another instance of the mayor taking any extra money and throwing it at various things that really didn't matter or keep Cottonwood safe. I'd begged for the mayor to either let me hire a new deputy or at least get an office somewhere other than the back of Cowboy's Catfish.

Neither one was given to me. My jaw tensed as I sucked in a deep breath, glancing one more time over my shoulder, thinking I would say something else to Scott, but he was already out of view.

The weight of the situation pressed upon me as I slid into the Jeep and next to Finn.

"Are you good?" Finn asked as soon as I got in the Jeep. He'd moved to the passenger seat. "I can't be having my fiancée all stressed out."

His concern was evident in his soft gaze and the way he lightly touched my arm, a silent offer of comfort.

He caught me off guard. I pinched a smile.

"I'm good." I winked and turned the keys stuck in the ignition, starting the Wagoneer. "I think we need to drop off the evidence before we head on down to the river if we have time."

"Time?" Finn's elbow was resting on the sill of the open window.

After I took off, he reached down and cranked the window until it was halfway closed.

"I have euchre tonight." I gripped the wheel, the and sparkler on my finger twinkled. "I'm going to have to face the music tonight with my friends, and I'm not going to miss it."

"I thought you wanted to check out the map," he said.

"I do, and I will. I think the evidence needs to get out of my car and into Tom's hands so I can see what we get back." I wasn't sure why I had a lingering feeling that something more was going on with Scott. That was how I decided I needed to make sure everything that was solid about the case—the evidence, in other words—had to be put into the lab.

And all the other stuff, like chasing down a red line on a map from

Dilbert or anything to do with water in the back of my head, was not solid evidence. They were just theories that more often than not led to dead ends and lost time.

I was having a nigglin' feeling, and it had everything to do with time.

Getting this case solved would probably determine whether or not I was reelected.

CHAPTER FIFTEEN

The brick structure of the lab, aged by time, served as a solemn reminder of the many visits I'd made here with Poppa, back when he was the sheriff. Those memories swirled around in my mind as I disembarked from the Jeep's front seat and reached into the back to collect the evidence bags.

Finn remained stationary, his grip on the Jeep's handle betraying a tension that his casual stance tried to hide.

"I'll wait out here," he stated, each word clipped and definitive. It wasn't a request but a quiet declaration of boundaries.

Tom Geary's car was parked off to the side of the building—an unusual sight for the weekend. Typically, on days like these, I'd place evidence bags in the impersonal drop box Tom had set up. The sight of his car, however, suggested that today would be different.

"Don't be silly. Come on in." I snorted.

"I think it's best we keep our professional life professional." Finn made it very clear he was setting a boundary in our life.

"Suit yourself." The retort slipped past my lips before I could restrain it, sounding more acidic than I'd intended. The finality in Finn's declaration had sparked a prickling annoyance in me. We'd built our romance around our professional lives, woven together through the very threads of our work. The sudden wall he seemed determined to erect felt jarringly out of place.

His noncommittal shrug in response only stoked the embers of my irritation. But, biting back the wave of questions I wanted to ask, I closed the Jeep door a little more forcefully than necessary and turned my attention to the task at hand. Underneath my actions, a pang of hurt pulsed, mingling with a rush of frustration. But there was work to do, and I had no time for this silent war of sentiments.

"Sheriff Lowry," Tom Geary said to me as soon as I walked into the waiting room and made the bell above the door ding. The gray-haired man looked me over. His brows narrowed.

"Sunday?" he asked. "Must be important."

"I could say the same for you. I don't know if I've ever seen you work on a Sunday." I held the bags up and walked over to him.

"Come on in." He waved me over to the door leading into the lab.

The lab's sterile scent immediately filled my nostrils as Tom led the way through the heavy steel door. Fluorescent lights hummed overhead, casting a cold, eerie glow over the rows of stainless steel counters that gleamed in the artificial light. Lab instruments were meticulously organized, and various types of high-tech machinery, both large and small, adorned the workspaces. There were microscopes, DNA sequencers, and spectrometers for analyzing samples, each piece of equipment in its own dedicated space. Several corkboards filled with pinned photographs and papers were mounted on the wall, a testament to the many cases that passed through these doors.

As I followed Tom, he moved with a methodical, unhurried gait. His shoulders were slightly stooped from the countless hours he'd spent hunched over microscopes, the wrinkles on his forehead a permanent feature etched by years of concentration. He didn't look back, his trust in my familiarity with the place evident.

I took a deep breath, adjusting to the scent of antiseptic that was unique to places like this. The atmosphere was sterile and far removed from the human chaos that instigated the need for such facilities. However, it was necessary to step into this realm of cold objectivity to seek out the truth that lay hidden in the evidence.

Feeling the weight of the evidence bags in my hand, I noticed my palms were slightly sweaty, a common reaction I had in these situations. It was the anticipation, the knowledge that these bags could potentially hold answers. I glanced at Tom's back, noticing how the lab coat hung loose on his frame. His movements were automatic, almost mechanical, bespeaking a man so absorbed in his work that his physical presence seemed secondary to his mental engagement.

Although our exchange had been brief and practical, an undercurrent of mutual respect was palpable in the air. We were two professionals in our respective fields, striving to piece together narratives from fragments of truth, our roles intertwined in the pursuit of justice.

"What do we have?" he asked, getting out one of the clipboards he used when logging new evidence that needed testing.

"I have an inhaler without a name, which I'll get tomorrow when Dr. Shively opens, but I wanted to go ahead and get it tested to see if it matched the DNA of a murder victim." I handed him the bag. "Dilbert Thistle," I said, knowing Tom was about to ask me the victim's name.

We'd done this song and dance a few times already.

He wrote down and checked off items before he looked at me for the next piece of evidence.

"These," I said in almost a whisper as I felt my face blush, "are, um, photos I found at the victim's house." My voice caught, and then I cleared my throat. "I'm not sure what these have to do with the investigation."

I tried not to look at Tom's face when I handed him the box of nudes.

"Oh my." The words jumped out of his mouth. I could tell he was also trying not to look at me.

"They were buried in his shed, which someone broke into overnight. When I checked it out, I saw the hole where I'd found these had been dug even deeper this morning, which makes me think the killer knew these were there and didn't figure I would find them." I sighed and handed him the other evidence bag. "This note I found on the victim's person makes me believe he was killed over some sort of secret."

"I'm not sure if I'll be able to find out who the people in the photos are, but I sure can tell you the year these were taken, and from the looks of them, I'd say it's the late seventies into the eighties." He was talking about the years between 1970 and 1980-something. "If there are any prints other than the victim's…" He looked at me.

I handed him the copy of Max's report with all of Dilbert's collected DNA so when the evidence was run through the lab, Tom could eliminate Dilbert's DNA or fingerprints.

"I'll be able to get those off and run through the database, but…" The dreaded word came from his mouth. "I hate to tell you this, but I'm here because I'm swamped. There's a lot of cases in front of you, so I hope you're not in any big hurry."

"I am, kinda." My lips drew in together. "But it'll be fine," I finished when I saw how tense he became when I told him I was in fact in a hurry.

"I know you want to get the murder solved, but I'm working my hardest," he confided. "If I get a break between two of the other cases, this one should be pretty easy to squeeze in."

"I appreciate it." I felt a bit relieved to know he would actually at least try to get me some initial information for the case.

"What's that?" His eyes drew down to my hand. "Is that what I think it is?"

I smiled and nodded.

"It's about time Sheriff Vincent asked you," he said, returning the smile. "I could tell he was smitten with you the first time you brought him here."

"The feeling was and is mutual." I looked back at the evidence. "This is all I have right now, but it's a start."

I wanted to put the spotlight back on the case. From the interactions I'd had today, it was evident the proposal was going to have to be a side chat until everyone got used to the idea that I was engaged.

This proposal couldn't have come at a worse time. Dilbert's murder. The election. Taven Tidwell.

Everything together was starting to make my head swim.

"Well, I'll see what I can do, but I'm not promising anything," he reiterated when he walked me out of the lab and back down the hall to the waiting room where we first started.

"It's all I can ask. If you weren't so darn good, you wouldn't have this problem," I said, knowing a little bit of buttering up couldn't hurt.

After all, I was my poppa's granddaughter.

That also meant that I was going to have a spotless, perfect record. And I wouldn't stop at anything to keep it that way.

CHAPTER SIXTEEN

Dilbert Thistle had taken a secret to his grave. That was exactly how the killer wanted and had planned it. I was more convinced than ever that the note I'd found on Dilbert's person was in fact from the killer.

The killer underestimated the power of gossip.

Specifically, gossip from the euchre women. They had a way of getting others to do what needed to be done, and I was confident I would have some sort of new clues to go on. Now, we all knew most or at least half of what was said was fabricated. That was when I had to weed out the tidbits that held some merit and check on them.

Most women loved to go to the salon for a good cut, curl, and gossip session. Here in Cottonwood, all the women were in one room of Tibbie Bell's house, playing cards, eating, and drinking, which was the perfect storm for the loose lips to let out all the town's weekly secrets.

Trust me.

Dilbert's murder was on everyone's lips in my inner circle. I could only imagine what was circulating town.

Everyone else had already arrived at Tibbie's for the euchre game, and I wasn't late. I was right on time, which told me they were there early so they didn't miss a word of what I had to say—or avoid saying—about Dilbert.

Finn and I didn't make it to the river, but we did have a quick bite to eat on my back porch, where we decided not to talk about the murder or the impromptu proposal.

I thought we were both still so shocked by the way the events had happened that we were trying to process them.

The regulars were at euchre—Katy Lee, Jolee, who was my partner, Mama, Viola, Ruby, Darby Gray, Lulu McClain, Myrna Savage, Marcy Carver, and Malina Woody, just to name a few. Or at least the few who'd gathered in the room on the right, just inside the front door. In that room, Tibbie had moved back all the furniture and made a U shape with all the folding tables for the food line.

I went straight to the desserts section.

"Kenni, I'm so glad to see you," Lulu said. She was peeling the Saran Wrap off the glass plate of chess bars. "I've got an extra plate of chess bars in my car for your handsome fiancé." She winked. "Don't forget to remind me to give them to you."

"He asked me if you were going to bring him some and warned me not to steal any on the way home," I said as she grabbed my hand and looked at the ring.

Once she did that, it was open season for everyone in the room to rush over and surround me to get a look.

"Who on earth did Toots Buford think she was kidding when she said she and Kenni were best friends?" I overheard Jolee asking someone in the hallway. "Kenni and I have been playing together since we were knee-high to a June bug."

"You better watch out for Jolee," Myrna Savage said. "She might come over here and pee on you. Marking her territory." She laughed, and her black hair swayed. "Remember me for all of your flower needs. Petal Pushers would love to get in on the big day."

"We are getting together this week to discuss all the particulars." Mama had rushed over in between Myrna and me, obviously stopping me from making any sort of promise to the only florist in Cottonwood.

"Who else would do the flowers?" Myrna jerked back. "Unless you go all the way to Clay's Ferry."

"We don't know what we are doing yet, Myrna." Mama tugged her shoulders back and stood firm.

Myrna glared at Mama before turning on the balls of her feet and darting out of the room and across the hall. She stopped at Viola and Ruby's euchre table, where everyone else was seated and ready to get started.

"Mama..." I gasped at her ill manners.

"What? I've got one daughter. And one shot at a wedding. Let me have my day in the sunlight." In no uncertain terms, she told me she was going to run the show.

For now, I'd pacify her and let her think that. Finn and I had no idea what we were going to do, when we were going to do it, or how. As far as that was concerned, heck, maybe we'd elope.

That would kill Mama.

Speaking of killing, I glanced around the room to see if Poppa had appeared. Sadly, there was not even a wisp to be seen. I'd not seen him since this morning's spectacle at church, and I wasn't sure if the rule was that he would never come back once I got married or once I got engaged.

Neither would've been my choice, but sometimes in life, you had to do hard things that no one wanted to do.

"I have to say Polly Parker did end up loving the baby clothes. She gushed and gushed over them, never once thanking you, though." Mama's brows pinched. "Oh well. She was still spittin' mad about you taking her thunder away. And when I say spittin', I mean out of them teeth of hers."

"Mama," I gasped again. "Stop that. It's one thing to talk about her to me privately but not here. Not now." I reached for the spoon stuck deep in the banana pudding. "I'm already tuckered out. When I get a big helping of this 'nanner puddin', I'll be ready to go to bed," I said loudly enough for Marcy Carver to hear me.

She was the local librarian and knew the articles in every little periodical the archive had about the history of Cottonwood, marriages, deeds, and gossip—like an EPO against Dilbert Thistle. It was always important to stay on her good side.

"Kenni, you sure do know how to make a woman blush." Marcy's cheeks puffed up when she smiled.

"I bet your grandkids and Wade love your pudding." I always made sure to comment on family members, which told them I cared and gave them a little more incentive to vote for me.

Even though I figured everyone in here would vote for me, it was always good manners to ask about family.

"They do. Every time I make one to bring somewhere, I make two." She handed me a plate. "Get you two helpings. You're gonna need some brain-power to plan that big wedding."

Just as I was about to scoop me a big helping, Darby Gray, the owner of the inn located on Main Street, had come up to me.

"There's something weighing on my heart I need to discuss with you," she told me as she pulled me away from the dessert table.

This better be good, I thought, following her out of the room and to Tibbie's front porch.

Her tone struck me as an example of a Southerner sprinkling sugar on something she wanted to say so she didn't seem to be or get labeled as a gossip.

"I've been praying on it, thinking about it." The edges of her almond eyes dipped, and she fiddled with the edges of her brown hair that wrapped around her ear.

"My goodness," I said in sympathy, not sure what Darby had heard, but as the owner of the inn on Main Street, she saw all sorts of people and was privy to what they said.

"Kenni, don't take this lightly. The Lord has placed it on my heart to talk to you." She gave a slow nod.

My eyes narrowed. Why on earth would she put such a thing on me?

"Then if the Lord did it, we must go find a spot to talk." I was going to find out exactly what she knew about Dilbert Thistle's murder.

"I'm worried." The lines between her eyes deepened as her look took on an appearance that better reflected her words. "I think Taven Tidwell is running on a good platform, and if he keeps it up, I'm not sure I can honestly vote for you." She gave me a pursed lip and peered at me.

Lord help me, and Lord help Darby. I was about to lose my ever-lovin' mind right here on Tibbie's porch situated on the town branch.

"I'm so sorry you feel that way," I said and tried to offer a sympathetic smile to her comment.

"That's all you've got to say to me?" Darby asked. "No way you want to talk me into otherwise?"

"Mrs. Gray," I said, calling her by her formal name, taking her a bit by surprise, "I cannot and will not try to change your mind about how you feel. Your feelings are valid, and I want you to be true to them."

I walked back into the house.

I had so much more to say, but I was afraid if I said another word, it would solidify her vote for Taven because the cuss words were on the tip of my tongue, and I was just waiting to unleash on her.

"I'm about to fly off the handle," I told Jolee under my breath as I passed by her to sit across from her at the table where the euchre hand had been dealt.

I picked up the five cards, fanned them out in my hand, and stared at them.

"I dealt, so it's your call." Tibbie Bell nudged me. She and Katy Lee, two of my best friends, were partners. "What's wrong?" Tibbie asked.

I knocked my knuckle on the table in the gesture to pass on calling the suit for this round of the game.

"Spades," Jolee called as it passed by Katy. "And I'll go alone so you can tell us what's going on," she said, telling me she had all the cards in her hand and that I didn't have to play that round.

"Good because I've got all red," I said, referring to the diamonds and hearts in my hand, meaning I wouldn't have been able to help her out in any way because I didn't have a single black card in my hand, much less a spade. "And I'm not talking my face."

"This sounds serious." Tibbie glanced across the table at Katy. Her long brown hair, which she parted down the middle, framed her face as she tried to cover her hazel eyes, giving Katy some sort of telepathic message that she needed help with this hand.

"I've got nothing." Katy dropped all her cards on the table after Jolee put down the top four cards in the trump suit, which forced Katy and Tibbie to lay their cards down and give us the full points for the round. "What's going on?"

"Darby just told me that she felt like she needed to vote for Taven," I said after I leaned in so only the four of us could hear.

Naturally I wouldn't be telling just anyone that, but these three were my closest friends, and I was having a crisis.

"The nerve of her. And on your engagement day." Tibbie's eyes darted around her family room, where she'd set up all the card tables for the various teams. "And in my house."

"Don't say anything. I told her she had to do what she felt she needed to. But in all honesty, I helped her out so many times as sheriff when she was low on the pole for that day's list of complaints. I bet Taven Tidwell wouldn't do that."

"I'm telling you we need to hit back. Play his game." Tibbie had been dying for me to agree to a social media campaign. "I'm telling you, social media is what drives traffic to my business, and if you aren't on there, you might'swell join Dilbert Thistle down at the funeral home."

"Tibbie, that's awful." Jolee gasped and shoved all the cards on the table in my direction.

"The social media thing or the Dilbert funeral home thing?" I asked in a joking tone and swept all the cards up into a nice tidy little pile. I shuffled them what felt like a million times.

"You know what I mean." Jolee shook her head and gathered the cards one by one as I shuffled the five out.

"Pass," they all said as they looked at the hand I'd dealt each of them, bringing to me the decision of what suit to call for the next hand to be played.

"Hearts," I said and laid down the highest trump so I could pull out any of the trump cards they might be holding.

"I'm telling you we can say things like the time you went to Darby's when the guest lost their pet lizard," Tibbie said, reminding me of how I spent hours looking for the tiny thing and finally found it in the guest room's air-conditioning duct.

"Or all the times you stop driving when you see kids on the street playing and you get out and play or hand them a sheriff sticker." Katy Lee put her two cents in. "You can stop by Shabby Trends, and I can outfit you into something very appropriate, something that screams you're the right choice for the job still and forever."

She tucked a loose blond curl behind her ear, pulled the ten of hearts out of her hand, and tossed the card in the middle of the table.

Winning the next three hands, I was thinking more and more about doing some sort of promotion that focused on the good I did for the community seventy percent of the time rather than the murder-related thirty percent. Even though I had a one hundred percent crime-solving percentage.

"It doesn't help how people see you talking to yourself all the time either," Jolee mentioned, glancing at me over the tops of her cards.

"I'm talking to Du—" I started to protest when they all yelled out his name before I could spit it out.

"We know. We know." Katy shuffled the cards, since it was her turn to deal. "Now isn't the time to talk." Without turning her head, her eyes shifted left and then right.

The air in the room shifted, and the chatter had stopped. Without even looking, I could sense that all eyes were on me. No doubt they'd heard us talking and maybe even knew how the Lord had placed something on Darby's heart.

My best friends and I had made a date later in the week to get together at Luke and Vita Jones's basement for the weekly movie. This week, they were showing *A League of Their Own*, the women's baseball movie. Not that we were very interested in baseball, but we could chat, hang out, and eat popcorn with M&M's on top, not to mention wash it all down with a very large Diet Coke.

"The Lord did no such thing." Mama sidled up to me as we were leaving for the night. "I heard Darby mention something about the Lord, and, well, let me tell you, Taven's family owns the building of the inn. I can only imagine they got to her, and maybe told her they'd raise the rent."

"They can't do that," I told Mama and hugged the pan of chess bars to my stomach as we stood out on the street in front of the Wagoneer.

"They can do whatever they want. They think they are so high and mighty." Mama shivered. "Don't you worry about no Taven Tidwell. You hear me?"

"Yes, Mama." I gave her a one-armed hug before she hurried off toward her car.

Just as I put the chess bars safely in the passenger seat and got in the Jeep, Gina Kim and her mom stopped me.

"Go on, Mom. Tell her." Gina, who was also a good friend of mine and worked at her family's restaurant, Kim's Buffet, encouraged her mom to tell me something.

"I wasn't going to put my nose in it, but Gina told me about that man who died on the tracks." Mrs. Kim nodded. Her short black hair bounced up and down. "I told Gina how I wanted to stay out of it, but she insisted I tell you."

"Yes. Please. If it has anything to do with Dilbert Thistle, I'd love to know." This was what I'd come here to endure all night to get—the one little piece that might give me something to go on.

"I do not know who he was, but he was in the restaurant with Dilbert Thistle the morning of the day the man died. They were arguing over water or something. The man even bought the lunch special, but he was a bad tipper. I would bet money on it that he killed Dilbert." Mrs. Kim had somehow assumed a bad tipper was a murderer.

"You didn't get his name?" I asked.

"No. No." Mrs. Kim shook her head. "Not a good tipper. Not even on the credit card."

"Credit card?" I asked. "He paid with a credit card?"

"Yes." She gave a solid nod.

"Then you have his name, Mom," Gina huffed. "I'll go through all the credit cards tomorrow and text you his name," she said to me.

"That'd be great," I told her and then looked back down at Mrs. Kim, who was very tiny. "You don't recall anything about the conversation and water?"

"No. Just talked about water." She shrugged.

The water plant was behind his house, and I couldn't help but wonder if Dilbert had some sort of issue with the water plant's proximity or perhaps something I had no idea about. Either way, he was seen at the restaurant, having what Mrs. Kim believed to be an argument.

That was a clue and a solid public fight that just might lead me to Dilbert's killer.

CHAPTER SEVENTEEN

"There's just not enough time in the day," I told Finn after he'd surprised me by making it home at an early enough hour to at least have one beer on the back patio.

"I know it makes it more difficult, but at least you know Georgina didn't do it." Finn held the bottle by the neck, tipping it up to take a swig. "What's wrong with Duke?"

He gave a slight nod towards Duke.

Now that I've accidentally gotten engaged to you and Poppa has ghosted back to the great beyond like he told me he was going to do, he's missing Poppa. And if it weren't for this beer I might be drowning my sadness and troubles in, I might be moping, too, I thought.

I didn't say it, but I knew Duke was moping around the backyard, looking for Poppa.

"What do you mean?" I asked, making sure there was an upward inflection in my tone.

"He doesn't seem right. Over the past few years, he's galloped around, tossing the ball to himself in the air to catch it. I've never seen him just lie back there like he's waiting for someone." Finn got up and stood at the edge of the concrete patio to get a closer look at the sad-eyed dog.

"Duke!" I called.

He raised his chin.

"You okay?" I hollered out to him. "You want a treat?"

Not even the magic word helped. He simply put his little fur chin down on top of the ball.

"I think you need to take him to the vet." Finn was like anyone else who didn't know what was actually wrong with Duke. "I think he's got something really wrong."

"I don't know. Maybe he's having an off day." I shrugged and took a drink of my beer, swallowing the sadness that I'd brought on both of us.

It would be easy to take back the proposal, but in my heart, even through the ache it felt, I knew Finn was my future. He was my happiness. It was okay to be sad, even if Duke and I were the only ones who really knew why we were sad.

"I've been around a couple years, and I've never seen him this way." Finn continued yammering on, and I took a deep breath to stop myself from spilling the beans just so we didn't have to talk about this anymore.

The only problem with telling Finn the actual truth was that I would no longer be able to prove that as long as he'd been haunting Cottonwood, my ghost deputy had helped me out more than Finn had. I also risked him leaving me because, well, I figured when you wanted to spend the rest of your life with someone and they told you they'd been running an entire sheriff's department with a ghost deputy, it would make them think you were all sorts of crazy.

And that was something we tried to hide around here.

Then I'd lose him forever. The risk-versus-reward ratio was too much, and sometimes the juice wasn't worth the squeeze.

So I sat there and replied with a lot of mm-hmmms, nods, yeps, and agreeing to take Duke to the vet in the morning, though that would be pretty low on my to-do list.

"I do have to make a lot of stops tomorrow," I finally said, "but I guess I could squeeze in an appointment with the vet."

"Why not ask Viv?" Finn meant Mama. Had he lost his mind? Maybe I could tell him about Poppa because Finn and I both knew Mama wasn't about to take Duke to the vet.

"What?" he said. "You're asking as if it were the most absurd thing."

"Finn, in case you haven't noticed, Duke is a dog, not a grandchild." I snickered, knowing Mama liked Duke and appreciated that he kept me safe, but at the end of the day, he would come in her house, mess up her floors with paw prints, and sit his butthole on her couch, and she wasn't down with all that.

Of course, when I visited, Mama took it on the chin. She even gave Duke treats. According to Dad, it took Mama the better part of the rest of the day to disinfect the entire house and scrub the couch cushions.

"She is dying to be a part of our life, and I told her you had a big case right now." Finn's eyes grew as though he'd let something slip out.

"She called you?" I asked.

"Yeah, I wasn't supposed to say anything." He gnawed on his lip and walked back over to me. Then he bent down and positioned himself between my legs, setting his beer on the patio and taking my hands into his. "She wants you to pick out a dress, go eat cake or something. She called me to talk to me."

"There's more." I jerked a brow. "I see it in your eyes."

He looked away, took a deep breath, and puffed out his cheeks and sighed.

"You're not going to like what she asked me to do, and I probably shouldn't tell you because I flat-out told her no." He took an even deeper breath before he told me something that really shouldn't have shocked me but did. "She wants me to run against you and Tavin."

"Run against me?" I pulled my hands out.

"See, this is why I shouldn't've told you. I said I wasn't going to do it." He tilted his head sideways. "You're the best sheriff. She only wants you to have a life outside of the job."

"She wants me to be like her and be in the bell choir, women's league, and whatever other club she's in. Barefoot and pregnant." Aggravated, I put the bottle up to my lips and tossed back the rest of the beer. "I don't want that."

"Me either. So let's just drop it. I tried, and I can say I tried when I told her that if I could be the one barefoot and pregnant, I would," he said with a smile. "Look there. I got you to smile."

"Stop it." I shoved his pointed finger from my face. "It would be funny if you could, though."

"If I could, I would," he said in a way that made me really believe him. "I told her there were plenty of women sheriffs who raised very strong children and kept their town safe."

"Who?" I asked.

"She asked me the same thing, and I told her I got an emergency call, which I can't do with you." He leaned in. "But I can do this."

His lips touched mine. The wild sensation of his kiss made me recall just how crazy attracted I was to him, sealing the deal against my ever having another inkling of a thought of taking off my ring.

"You know how to make my head swim," I whispered as he pulled away. "I love you."

"I love you. You are going to win this election. You are going to be my companion for life, and you are going to be a great mother if you choose to be." He remained squatting between my legs and tucked a loose strand of my long hair behind my ear. "If you're happy, I'm happy. If Duke's happy, I'm happy."

"Duke is fine, but if you think it'll keep Mama off our backs while we figure out when we want to get married, I'll call her to take Duke to the vet." I gulped back the idea of a vet bill that just wasn't in my budget.

Being sheriff in Cottonwood was actually a job I did more for desire and passion than for the income. It was pretty low on the scale of paying government gigs around here, but I loved it. I was good at it. I was the sheriff.

"And it'll let me follow up on some leads."

My shop talk made Finn stand up and go sit in the chair again.

"I'm guessing that killed the mood?"

"Well, we have a hard time turning it off, don't we?" He winked and grinned. His smile sent my heart and stomach spiraling into circles, and I had to catch my breath.

"If there's anything I can do," he said, "you know I'm here."

"You can help me play a little game." I shrugged.

"You mean the game you like to play with Duke?" he asked, referring to how I played the what-if game with ghost Poppa, but Duke just so happened to be around, wagging his tail like he knew what I was talking about.

What Finn couldn't see was Poppa playing with Duke, making it appear as though Duke were listening and responding.

"Yeah. I just throw out theories and see which one sticks in my gut." I wasn't sure what my goal was here, but I had a feeling I was trying to replace the idea that Finn could come play along just like Poppa had taught me.

"Game on." Finn rested his forearms on the top of his thighs and vigorously rubbed his hands together.

"I found some old photos in a shoebox buried in Dilbert's shed. When I went back to Dilbert's after Elizabeth told me someone had broken into his shed, the hole where the photos were was dug up again, only it went deeper, like someone knew they were there. And I'm sure they weren't photos that were meant to be shared," I said.

He gave me a questioning look.

"Nudes. And I'm saying older-woman-on-a-bearskin-rug nudes."

"You said there was a note in Dilbert's pocket about uncovering something. Maybe the owner of the photos knew they were there. Is it possible Dilbert found them after he bought the house and knew who they belonged to? Possibly could've been bribing them for money?" he asked.

"Yeah, but who is in the photos? That's the question. I gave them to Tom so he could run some tests to find out the approximate year because they are actually photographs. Not digitally taken and printed but actual take-them-to-the-photo-shop-to-get-them-printed. Film." I just wasn't sure Dilbert Thistle would know anything about photographs, and if I didn't recognize the woman, I wasn't so sure Dilbert had either.

But then again, Cottonwood had grown so much that I didn't know everyone. I knew a lot of people from the past, though.

"With the photos out of the picture"—Finn snickered at the little pun—"let's go through the other suspects," he coaxed me.

"We have Bill Johnson. He has an alibi. His wife came to pick him up at the fairground bar," I said, using the word "bar" loosely.

It wasn't so much a bar as it was a tent sponsored by a local restaurant at the fairgrounds during the county fair. "Scott checked the alibi for me about that night. He confirmed from the volunteers working the tent that night that they'd seen Bill leave with his wife. And one of them did say they heard Bill's wife ask Dilbert if she could give him a ride home."

"There wouldn't be enough evidence from eyewitnesses to charge Bill." Finn frowned. He could tell I was in a bit of a pickle with this case. "Anyone else?"

"Yeah. Jake, the young kid that Bill put in to play Dilbert's part," I said.

Finn's forehead wrinkled as he waited for me to tell him what Jake was all about.

"I don't know much, but I plan on stopping at the drywall plant tomorrow after I talk to Patty."

I hadn't yet been able to talk to Patty about what she might remember hearing or seeing. The only thing I'd gotten from her was her initial statement, which barely qualified as a statement. Just a lot of muttering, crying, and yelling at the dogs she'd been walking.

"Mrs. Kim told me Dilbert and another man were at the restaurant, arguing over water. Now, I don't know what that means, but I guess I'll find out when I ask Bill to pull him from work," I said, making a solid plan for my Monday pretty much putting two and two together being it had to be Jake. "You know, it's difficult to do anything on a case during the weekend."

"Yeah. No one or nothing is open, and people are out having fun at the fair." Finn acknowledged that this case was a rough one. "And you still haven't found the first crime scene."

"Yeah. I can't even take the warrant Scott got for Camille Shively's list of patients who use an inhaler." I sighed and finally stood up. "I've got to add her to my list. I am going to try to get a good night's sleep and see if anything comes to me in my dreams," I said loudly just in case ghost Poppa, who had really ghosted me, was lingering around and listening.

Judging by the way Duke was sauntering across the backyard to the porch, I knew that was only wishful thinking. If Poppa was around, Duke would've told me.

CHAPTER EIGHTEEN

"Have you thought about what I said?" Tibbie Bell had called me right as I was walking out the door the next morning.

"Tibbie, I have a million and one stops today. I don't have time to worry about any social media live appearances or whatever it is you are wanting me to do. My only focus right now is to find out who killed Dilbert." I didn't have time for all of this nonsense.

Of course, Tibbie replied with a long sigh before she finally said, "All right. Don't say we didn't try to help you."

"And I appreciate that. I know you are only looking out for me. Honestly, I think the best way to be reelected is to emphasize my record as sheriff." I gripped the wheel on the way over to the bank.

It was literally a two-minute drive from Free Row and just yonder past the department. I knew Vernon got there first, and they opened at eight a.m., which meant I would get there as he put the key in the bank door.

Sure as shinola, he was doing exactly that when I hung up on Tibbie.

"You stay," I told Duke, who wasn't about to let me leave him at the house for the day. "Hey, Vernon!" I called out when he didn't pay a bit of attention to me while he turned the key.

"Kenni," he called and smiled. He wore a nice three-piece pinstriped suit. His grey hair was neatly combed to the side.

Vernon also wore the perfect amounts of hair gel and cologne. He was about fifteen years older than me, much younger than he looked. His wife, Lynn, was a nice woman. She stayed home and cared for their three children, who were distant in ages.

"What can I do you for?" he asked with a smile.

"I need to talk to you about Dilbert Thistle." I cut straight to the chase. My plate was full, and I had much more important people than Vernon to visit.

"Let me get in here and turn off all the alarms, and I'll be right with you," he said and pointed at me to stay put. "We've got opening procedures, so if you don't mind, I'll be right back."

I nodded, knowing some of the tellers were parked across the street at the Pump and Munch, the local gas station Luke Jones owned and operated. They waited over there until Vernon went into the bank to make sure there were no robbers, then he'd come out and signal to the tellers that it was A-OK to come on in.

He did just that and waved me in, too, but he took me straight into his fancy office with glass walls. I couldn't keep from helping myself to one of the suckers in a container sitting on his desk. I took a sucker and a seat.

"I hear big congratulations are in order," he said, looking at my ring. "I'm so happy for you and Finn."

"Thank you. How's Lynn and the girls?" I asked as my eyes shifted to the framed photos lined up on the credenza behind him.

"They are good. We are actually getting ready to go on vacation." He folded his hands and placed them on his desk. "I have to come in for a morning meeting, but after that, we are on vacation."

"I'd love a vacation," I groaned. "I think I'll have to wait until the honeymoon to go on one. Where are y'all headed?"

"We are going to the Virgin Islands." He took me by surprise. "I can see by the look on your face that you're shocked. It took a lot of convincing by Lynn for me to take the girls on a vacation that far away."

"I bet." I smiled, knowing it was Lynn who loved the beach. Vernon not so much. "I remember the time y'all went to Florida, and you came back a lobster."

"Burnt to a crisp, but Lynn bought me a swim shirt with long sleeves. Have you ever seen one of them?" He laughed.

"I have but never used one." I snapped my fingers. "I think I might look into them for my honeymoon with Finn."

"Are you going to the beach?" Vernon asked.

"No, no. I don't know. We haven't planned that far ahead because we are both busy." I plucked the wrapper off the sucker.

Like a father, Vernon unclasped his hands and held one out for my trash.

"I'm actually here to ask you about Dilbert Thistle's mortgage loan."

"I heard about what happened to him." Vernon dropped the wrapper in the trash can behind his desk. "I also heard it was murder, but you didn't do a press conference, and, well, you can't really tell what's real and what's not on social media or what someone will say when they want to take away your life."

"Huh?" I asked with knotted brows.

"Taven…" His voice trailed off. He didn't finish saying Taven's full name when he saw the anger flash across my face. "We are Sheriff Kenni Lowry voters all the way."

"Thank you, but Taven doesn't have me rattled." I gulped back the lie. Taven was starting to really rattle me.

I didn't like that Tibbie called me this morning about it and that Vernon had mentioned him now, which meant they had both heard Taven's rants and raves.

"The ad he took out in the paper is ridiculous too. Edna Easterly shouldn't have let that happen." Vernon tapped the copy of the neatly folded *Cottonwood Chronicles* sticking out of the briefcase on his desk.

"Thank you. I will always take the support, and I think running on merit and record is what will keep me the sheriff," I told him with bold confidence but more for myself than for him. "Which is, again, why I'm here about Dilbert."

I had to turn the conversation off me and get back to the matter at hand. I was on borrowed time and, again, had a very full schedule of people to see and talk to today.

"I understand he came in here to get a loan. Is that right?" I already knew it was right, but I wanted to hear Vernon's side of things without tainting any possible evidence by coaxing him to say something that the defense would claim indicated I manipulated him.

"Yes." He nodded but didn't elaborate.

"Can you tell me how all of that took place?" I asked.

"Sure." He turned on his computer's monitor. "Do you have a warrant for it?"

"I don't, but I'm not here to see the documents. I believe those were in some of the papers at his house. I was curious to see what he said and how he qualified." I spoke while Vernon busied himself with starting up the computer.

"He came in and said he was going to buy a house. He had the purchase agreement, and we sat here and filled out the application. I didn't expect it to come back as approved, but he had the down payment in his account, and really, that's all I'm sure they looked at. I called him when it came back approved, and he signed the papers as soon as they were ready after the process of inspection, appraisal, and the rest. It was fairly quick." He shrugged, took a piece of paper from the notepad, and scribbled down Dilbert's name and some numbers. "That's his account. If you can get a warrant, you can just bring that back in here, since I'll be on vacation. It'll make it easier for you."

"Nothing stuck out to you?" I asked only to receive head shakes as I took the piece of paper, folded it, and stuck it into my sheriff's shirt pocket, where I kept a little notebook.

"Not a thing. Trust me, when he came in here asking for a mortgage loan, I didn't want to waste my time. I was just as shocked as you." His lips went flat. "Honestly, you wouldn't believe the folks who you think are broke who have more money than all of us."

He laughed before he went into a coughing fit.

"You just never know, do you?" I asked and helped myself to another sucker before I stood up.

He raised his fist to his mouth, covered it, and choked out, "I swallowed the wrong way."

"I hate when that happens," I said. "But if you think of anything, you know where to find me."

He nodded and put his hand up to signify he heard and understood me before I let the man be.

When I got back to the Jeep, downtown Cottonwood had started to come alive. The sun was shining, and the birds were chirping. A light breeze blew, feeling good along the back of my neck, giving me a little more energy now that I'd walked out of the bank with no more news than I had before.

I pulled the notebook out of my pocket and stuck it in the sheriff's bag I kept at all times in the back seat of my Jeep. It was what we called a typical police bag, holding items like flashlights, evidence bags, pens, gloves, shoe covers—anything I'd need to go into a crime scene or transport out of a crime scene.

Just as I turned the engine over, Taven Tidwell's voice came out of the speakers in an ad on WCKK radio station. With a hard push, I turned the radio off.

"We don't need any bad juju today, Duke," I told my deputy dog, who was just sitting in the seat. His eyes looked even droopier than they already naturally were. His ears weren't perked up. He didn't give even an inkling of wanting to stick his head out the window when I pulled out of the bank parking lot.

"Listen, you're going to have to get over Poppa," I told him, making his ears rise. Just as he gave out a little howl, we passed Maple Grove Cemetery, where I could see Poppa's grave standing to the right side of the cemetery near the entrance. "I sure don't think he's coming back," I said in almost a warning tone just in case Poppa was lingering around listening.

I kept an eye on the back seat, where Poppa loved to appear when Duke was up front. Nothing. Not even a wisp.

"You be a good boy," I said to Duke and pulled up to the emergency lane at Dr. Camille Shively's office. After I parked, I grabbed the warrant from where I'd stuck it up behind the visor.

For a split second, I thought about moving the Jeep to a spot in fear Taven Tidwell was watching me and would take a video of me parking in the emergency lane, but this was an emergency. I had a warrant to serve to Camille to get her patient records and solve a murder.

The waiting room was typical of a doctor's office. The walls were painted grey, and the equally grey carpet had small white diamond shapes scattered about. Chairs lined the walls. A television hanging on the wall played one of those twenty-four-hour news stations. Underneath the television stood a rack filled with all sorts of magazines and the latest copy of the *Cottonwood Chronicles*, which just tempted me to pick it up and read it.

I refused.

"Kenni, come on back." Camille stuck her head out the receptionist window and pointed at a door. "Betty called this morning to tell me you'd be by."

When I opened it, she was on the other side, waiting for me. I followed her down a couple of halls until we made it to her office.

"I hated missing euchre the other night, but I was told you are getting married." She ushered me into the office.

"I am." I nodded and saw a look on her face that told me she thought I was there because of the wedding. "But I'm not here for that."

"Oh." She pulled back, and her face stilled as she watched me hand her the warrant.

"I'm sure you heard about Dilbert Thistle."

Based on her expression, I knew she had.

"I found an inhaler at the scene, and there's not much left on the label but your name. I'm going to need a list of patients who you prescribed that exact inhaler to," I said as she scanned over the place on the warrant where the judge specifically added the brand name.

"I will tell you that I pretty much always prescribe the same brand but can't always get it filled by the pharmacy. Some patients opt to get the cheaper brand." She moved around her desk and picked up her phone. "Do you mind coming in here?" she asked whoever she called. Then she hung up.

"I'm only looking for someone who might be associated with Dilbert," I said. "What can you tell me about calcium hydroxide?"

"Calcium hydroxide?" A puzzled look crossed over her face. "I don't use it, but I know dentists do."

"How so?" I asked.

"They use them to make compounds for fractured teeth. Not a permanent solution, of course, because it can be…" Her jaw dropped, and her eyes widened. "Was Dilbert Thistle poisoned? And by calcium hydroxide?"

"I'm not able to give any particulars about any evidence." I couldn't tell her. I would never want to compromise evidence.

"What a horrible way to die." She blinked a few times as though clearing an image from her mind.

Camille pushed her chair back from her desk, eased her head back, and looked up at the ceiling.

"I didn't know Dilbert, but this is awful," she said. "Just awful."

Her office door opened, and Suzie, her nurse, peeped inside.

"Suzie, I'm going to need you to start working on files for Sheriff Lowry." She handed Suzie the warrant and pointed out the exact patient files they would have to pull. "We are switching over systems, so it might take a couple of days."

"Just as long as we get them as soon as you can give them to us." I smiled at Camille and Suzie.

"I'll start right now," Suzie noted and walked out of the office.

"Listen, Kenni, if there's anything else I can do, please let me know." Camille stood up but didn't come from behind her desk to walk me out. "You know your way out."

"Thanks, Camille." I waved her off and headed out of the office, wondering what the cold reception she'd given me was all about.

Just as I headed out of the office toward my Wagoneer, my phone rang.

"Good morning, Tom," I said to Tom Geary from the Clay's Ferry evidence lab, where I'd dropped off any evidence that needed testing. I noted that it was still early morning. "Please tell me you have something."

"I do."

I was never so happy to hear "I do" from a man in my life. Now I might change my mind when I heard the words come out of Finn's mouth, but hearing them coming from Tom was glorious. "Calcium hydroxide is definitely the killer. And that's not all."

I held my breath so the blow I knew was coming wouldn't show on my face as I walked past a few citizens on the way to my Jeep. There, I found a note from Jolee taped to the steering wheel, saying she drove past and saw Duke with a frowny face, so she took him.

"I called Max Bogus, and he found a very small needle hole in between

Dilbert's ring finger and middle finger. He was injected with it." Tom's tone told me that was unusual.

"I wonder if he had any recently fixed teeth fractures or anything else dental. Did you?" I questioned.

"I asked Tom, and he looked at Dilbert's teeth because both of us know the compound is used at the dentist. From with Max said about the looks of Dilbert's teeth, he didn't ever go to the dentist." That was Tom's way of telling me Dilbert could not have been accidentally poisoned by tooth work. "He was deliberately poisoned, and Max said he was going to put on my final report that this was a homicide. Dilbert Thistle was purposely poisoned."

CHAPTER NINETEEN

With a quick search on my phone about calcium hydroxide, I came up with a lot of things, like Dr. Google. The answers that couldn't be truly trusted. One thing, though, stuck out to me.

Calcium hydroxide was found in limestone deposits.

Limestone deposits, albeit probably small ones, were put in drywall. But were those deposits too small to kill someone?

"Betty," I called into the walkie-talkie, "I'm heading over to Patty's house, and then I'll be going down to the drywall plant. Call Scott if something comes up and I'm not in town."

The walkie-talkie beeped when it clicked off.

"Got it, Kenni—um, Sheriff," she crackled back over the old Wagoneer's rattling as I made my way over the Cottonwood bypass on Keene Road, which would lead me to Route 68.

Route 68, also known as Harrodsburg Road, was another way to get to the Kentucky River, where I also needed to go today. The drywall plant.

It just so happened there were many horse farms down that way, and Patty Dunaway's business, Patty's Pet Pantry, was located there.

This was one of those two-birds-with-one-stone kinds of deals. I was expecting answers to some very important questions about Dilbert Thistle.

The early morning's rosy hue was giving way to a bright-baby-blue sky.

Not a cloud in sight. I navigated the meandering stretch of Harrodsburg Road in my trusty old Wagoneer.

Wilmore, Kentucky, sprawled out ahead, a quiet hamlet tucked away amid the endless roll of countryside. I'd traveled this road more times than I could count, but today, a hint of foreboding lingered, as if the surrounding pastoral beauty hid a secret.

The familiar hum of my car mingled with the WCKK radio tunes floating through the open windows. The radio announcer's voice cut in, cheerfully promising a sunny day in the Bluegrass State, but it did little to distract me from the task at hand. The summer wind, warm and languid, slipped in carrying a bouquet of scents—fresh-cut grass, blooming wild-flowers, and the faintly earthy tang of the houses that flanked each side of the tiny town I had to drive through to get to Patty's and the drywall plant.

I rolled through Wilmore in my trusty old Wagoneer, the town unfolding around me like a well-worn, cozy quilt. Back in 1882, this town was just a flag stop called Scott's Station, after John D. Scott, who owned the land. Soon enough, it got a fresh name—Wilmore—and boy, did it grow from there.

In the blink of an eye, Wilmore transformed into a bustling little spot of about six hundred folks. You name it, and we had it—blacksmiths, drug stores, shops of all shapes and sizes, schools, churches, and even a grain mill. Asbury College, now Asbury University, opened its doors in 1890, inviting an influx of eager young minds each year.

Today, driving down Main Street was like flipping through a photo album of memories. Folks cradled their morning coffee and waved from their porch swings. Neighbors' chatter sprinkled the air. The IGA grocery, a long-standing fixture of Wilmore, was just opening for the day, the scent of freshly baked goods wafting out the doors. As I passed by the quaint shops, their windows filled with knickknacks and homemade goods, the sense of tight-knit community was unmistakable.

Asbury sat on my right, its students out for the summer. The usually vibrant campus rested under the warm sun. Past the college, modern subdivisions dotted the landscape, creating a sweet contrast with the town's historical charm.

Leaving the town proper behind, I found myself on a winding road that led me to Patty's farm. The air changed, tasting fresher, carrying the scent of fields and wildflowers. And yet, even in the quiet countryside, the warm, steady, unchanging heartbeat of Wilmore resonated around me.

That was how we liked it around here, and I planned on keeping it that way. It was a promise I made when I ran for sheriff and one I intended to keep. No games. Which meant no slandering on live streams or social media.

The river sliced through the landscape like a liquid silver ribbon, its calm surface a stark contrast to the imposing silhouette of the High Bridge that loomed overhead. My stomach tightened as my mind flicked back to this exact spot on Dilbert's redlined map. Those maps were in my bag, and if I had time after visiting the drywall plant, I just might pull one out and see what I could find.

As soon as I took a hairpin curve, Patty's came into view. A gravel path veered off the main road and led right up to her farm.

Her place wasn't a typical Kentucky horse farm. Instead, the paddocks were filled with dogs of all breeds and various sizes, all happily scampering under Patty's attentive gaze.

The grounds were impeccable, lush meadows surrounding a collection of charming buildings that wore their age with dignified grace. At the heart of it all, an elegant antebellum-style farmhouse sat proudly, its whitewashed facade gleaming in the morning light, the ornate gables and inviting porch brimming with southern allure.

Over to the side, a repurposed old school bus burst with color, emblazoned with the name Mutt Bus. The sight triggered a smile, despite the seriousness of my visit.

Patty, herding her canine troupe onto the bus, barely gave the old Wagoneer a second glance. She didn't even pay attention when I put the Jeep in park and got out.

I climbed into the bus and was hit with a wave of barks, yaps, and the undeniable scent of dog.

"Morning, Patty," I said, catching sight of the woman amidst a sea of wagging tails.

"Well, if it isn't Sheriff Lowry," Patty responded, not looking up from her task of fastening a French bulldog into its seatbelt. "Welcome to the Mutt Bus."

Patty's rhythm was uncanny, her attention shared equally between the dogs, from the smallest terrier to the largest mastiff. She pulled out a bag from her apron pocket and started distributing treats. "That's for you, Jordan. And you, Patrick. Susie, here's your favorite. Buster, you gave Tippy a tough time, but I'll let you off with a warning... and a treat."

Despite the bus full of dogs, Patty's world had order. I admired how she had everything under control.

A chorus of barks and yips greeted me, and Patty left the bus, beckoning me to join her. "I hope you're not here about Dilbert, Sheriff. I've already told the others. I can't remember anything."

I took a deep breath. "Patty, any small detail could help. Did you notice anything odd that night?"

Patty paused, her brow furrowed in thought. "No, it was pretty typical. Dogs were excited, as always."

"And the route?" I prodded.

"Same as always, down to the town branch," she responded, seemingly puzzled. "We cross over the tracks..." Her voice fell off because we both knew what happened after that.

"How about the dogs? Any of them act out of character?" I continued, hopeful.

Patty thought for a moment. "Well, Buster was a bit more antagonistic toward Tippy, but they squabble now and then."

"And the trip back?" I asked. "Before you found Dilbert."

"Uneventful," Patty confirmed. "Just dropped off the dogs who live on the way back."

"Do you do this every night in Cottonwood?" I asked.

"I do. I have clients who like to give their dogs long walks before bed, and those are in Cottonwood. I don't do it around here because Wilmore isn't that big, and, well, it's just dark," she said. "At least Cottonwood has streetlights."

I hesitated then decided to ask one last question. "Did you notice any unusual cars or people that night?"

Her eyes flickered. "Well, there was this sedan. It was going fast, heading out of town, away from the tracks. But it was dark, and I was busy with the dogs. I did have to jerk my leashes back because the car was going so fast I wasn't sure if the driver noticed all the blinking lights on the dog collars."

My heart pounded in my chest. It was a small detail, but in cases like these, small details were everything.

"I forgot all about that." She gave me a shocked look. "It just came to me as we were talking."

"That's not unusual." I was so happy to hear she was starting to remember some details. "When someone has a traumatic experience, their mind has a way of protecting them so their body doesn't truly absorb what they just witnessed. I wouldn't be surprised if you started recalling other things, like maybe someone you'd seen outside during your walk right before the car flew past you. If you did recall something like that, I could interview that person."

I was giving her scenarios so she'd understand exactly what it was I wanted.

No stone unturned. I repeated Poppa's mantra and took a quick look around to see if he'd showed up to help.

Nothing.

He loved dogs too. This would be the place for him to finally wisp around.

"I will call you or Scott." Patty took the step back up on the bus. She sat down in the seat and snapped on her seat belt as she said, "I've got to go. These dogs aren't going to walk themselves."

"Thanks!" I raised my hand in the air to wave her off when she closed the door, and the Mutt Bus took off.

I sucked in a deep breath and, with a blank stare, thought about Bill Johnson. Though he had an alibi and now a witness from the fairground bar, I was still very curious about the poison, a substance that was put in drywalls. But did Bill drive a sedan?

"Let's go find out," I muttered and headed back to the Jeep.

Patty's place wasn't too far from the river, and many little side roads lay nearby to take you there. Instead of taking off too quickly, I reached into the back seat of the Jeep and took out the map. Laying my eyes on it, I studied the area and saw where each little red line Dilbert had drawn led. All of them dumped out near the drywall plant.

There was also High Bridge, which was a railroad bridge famous in its own right. The High Bridge area had its own little community with a fire department, churches, and a small park you could rent to host events. It did have spectacular views.

For a second, the idea of having my own wedding popped into my head. Just a second.

"If he threw something in the river, I'll never find it." I tried to find a common denominator to Dilbert's little treasure hunt, and it was just the river. "I guess I won't know until I go look."

I folded the map up the best I could. It was damn near impossible to fold it back the way it was. At least for me. Obviously, Dilbert had done it. My excuse was that I was in a hurry.

Lunchtime was coming up, and I knew it because my stomach was growling.

I had to drive underneath High Bridge just to get to the road where the drywall plant was.

The river held so many secrets, and I was afraid whatever Dilbert was hiding would die with him. It wouldn't if I could help it.

The drywall plant was huge, consisting of four large buildings covered in cream siding with a large swath of green siding around the top of each one. Each building was connected to some sort of conveyor that took the piece of drywall through the plant and to its final destination, which was either one of the large eighteen-wheeler trucks lined up on the far end of the plant or one of the few barges waiting out in the river.

"Sedan, sedan," I repeated when I pulled into the parking lot and noticed all the cars must have belonged to the plant's employees.

I circled the parking lot before I got to the line of cars parked in front of the entrance. The word Office appeared in white vinyl letters above the glass door and in the parking spot.

Bill Johnson's space had a truck, not a sedan, parked in it.

"Can I help you, Sheriff?" the woman behind the desk inquired, her eyes taking in the badge proudly pinned to my shirt.

"I'm here to see Bill Johnson," I responded, letting my gaze wander around the office. The room was a flurry of organized chaos, stacked paper-work, blueprints, and gypsum samples, a testament to the drywall business that thrived here. The faint scent of coffee fought a losing battle with the more pungent aroma of gypsum dust.

The woman, a matronly figure in her late forties with a meticulously coiled perm and worn-out business suit, picked up the phone. I could see her efficient manner in the way she held herself—straight, composed, stern.

"Bill," she announced into the receiver, her eyes never leaving mine. "Sheriff Lowry is here to see you." As she waited for a response, I found my curiosity piqued by a model house that sat on a nearby table. It had been cut away to reveal the layers of drywall within.

I gestured to it. "Calcium hydroxide," I began. "How much do you use in your drywall production?"

The woman blinked at my question, surprise flickering across her face. She set the phone down and gave me her full attention. "Well, Sheriff, it's a key component. It helps with the hardening process, makes the drywall sturdy. Why do you ask?"

"Just gathering information," I replied nonchalantly. "Have there been any issues with it recently? Shortages, tampering, anything out of the ordinary?"

She considered my question, her lips pressing into a thin line. "Not that I'm aware of, Sheriff. Everything's been business as usual."

"And the employees?" I pressed on. "Anyone acting out of the ordinary? Anyone that maybe knew Dilbert Thistle?"

Just as she opened her mouth, the door behind her swung open, effec-tively cutting off her response.

"Sheriff Lowry." A deep voice resonated through the room.

Bill Johnson had arrived.

"Thank you, Marjorie," he said, offering a warm nod to the woman before gesturing for me to follow him.

His 6'2" frame dwarfed my own as we made our way down a carpeted corridor to a large, empty conference room.

Stepping into the room felt like stepping into the heart of the plant. One entire wall was glass, affording a panoramic view of the factory floor below. Conveyor belts moved like relentless rivers, carrying heaps of raw materials and finished drywall. Though muffled, the clatter of machinery formed a persistent hum in the background.

We took a seat on opposite sides of the room's long, glossy table, on which an assortment of architectural plans and project timelines lay spread before us. The harsh fluorescent lights above threw long, cold shadows over everything, creating a stark contrast against the bustling factory scene outside the glass.

"Why didn't you tell me you were Dilbert's boss, Bill?" I asked, the question hanging heavy in the room.

He seemed taken aback. "I didn't think it was relevant, Kenni. You asked about the softball game, not work."

"But it is relevant," I insisted. "It adds context. Dilbert's job, his coworkers... It all paints a picture."

"I see that now," Bill confessed, running a hand through his thinning hair. His brows knitted together in worry. "Dilbert was a good worker, despite his personal troubles. In fact, he'd recently been promoted to line manager."

"Promoted?" I echoed, raising an eyebrow. "Was Jake overlooked for the position?"

Bill furrowed his brows. "Jake? Jake who?"

"Jake who took Dilbert's place on the softball team," I clarified, leaning in slightly.

His expression softened, confusion giving way to understanding. "Oh, Kenni, our softball team is a mixed lot, not just drywall plant folks. Jake works for High Bridge Limestone Water Co."

The conversation halted abruptly as the revelation hit me like a runaway train. Limestone. Calcium hydroxide. The connections were falling into place likes pieces of a sinister puzzle that I couldn't yet fully grasp.

"Like I already told you and my wife confirmed my alibi, I had nothing to do with Dilbert's death." He looked out over the plant, his back to me.

"I'd like a list of Dilbert's co-workers and anyone that might've been overlooked for the job he was given." I had to walk out of here with something to take back and gnaw on even if I knew I would make a pit stop to see Jake at the High Bridge Limestone Water first.

"No one knew Dilbert had gotten the job. He was going to be announced today, in fact." Bill turned and shrugged. "I guess it's possible Dilbert told someone, but no one was in line for the job. We didn't have a second shift manager because we didn't have that shift. We had day shift and night shift, but since the building boom, we couldn't keep up with demand, so we decided to add a second shift. We will be announcing it on the evening news and open the hiring process."

Instead of Bill Johnson being a criminal to our community, he was actually growing it by bringing more jobs to the area. From his speech and his body language, Bill Johnson had moved down on my list of suspects.

Maybe even off it.

CHAPTER TWENTY

I stood outside the drywall plant, on the sidewalk overlooking the Kentucky River, a coiled blue-green ribbon winding its way along the edge of the property. Its gentle currents swirled in lazy patterns, as though taking their time to greet the day.

Barges, enormous flat-bottomed behemoths, lined up obediently, waited their turn to dock and receive their cargo of drywall sheets. They looked almost peaceful in the afternoon sunlight, like giant steel water lilies. A silhouetted figure in a fluorescent safety vest guided them from the tugboat, his directions echoing over the quiet lapping of the river against the bank.

Above, the sky was a watercolor masterpiece, blushing shades of blue. Faint echoes of cicadas broke the silence. Fluffy clouds, fringed with golden light, floated lazily overhead.

In the distance, a small motorboat hummed along the river's surface, breaking the serene tableau with its frothy white wake. The boat's engine was a distant purr, a minor disruption to the tranquil symphony of the river and its inhabitants. Two herons took flight at the boat's approach, their large wings flapping slowly as they ascended to the safety of the sky.

The scent of the river, a mix of fresh water and earthy undertones, filled my senses. I took a moment to close my eyes and absorb the sounds and smells of the riverfront. I was but a small dot in the grand scheme of this bustling hub of industry nestled in nature's splendor, but I was big enough to know Dilbert's secret needed to come to the surface and that I was the one to bring it up.

The river whispered stories to those who listened, murmuring secrets with every ripple. And as I stood there, I couldn't help but look at High Bridge and feel like there was something to this whole limestone-and-calcium-hydroxide connection.

I glanced around.

"Poppa," I whispered, "why does it have to be one or the other? I need you."

My heart had a void since he'd been absent. Over the past few years, I'd not realized how it might look like I was alone when I went out on calls or dispatch runs but I wasn't.

This was a feeling I didn't like.

The walkie-talkie beeped, taking me out of my thoughts. When I brought my hand up to push in the side button to talk, the sunlight caught my ring and made it glisten, reminding me what I was giving up to get.

A life. A lifetime. A love.

"Go ahead," I said into the walkie-talkie.

"Sheriff, Dilbert's lawyer came into the office and he said he'd not heard anything from Dilbert about a letter or anyone who wanted to harm his client. He did mention Georgina but didn't say anything about her that would make me put her back on the list of suspects despite her having an alibi." Scott knew I was busy, so he kept talking, "He said Dilbert had been promoted at work and was buying the house to get his life back in order and show Georgina he could be the husband she wanted."

"I just left the drywall plant." I didn't bother asking any more questions because the lawyer didn't sound like he knew much more than we did. "I'm going to go see Jake at High Bridge Limestone Water. Calcium hydroxide is found in limestone, which is how they make their water. Jake was seen at Kim's restaurant, arguing with Dilbert, the day Dilbert was murdered."

All of the evidence was mounting up against Jake, and I couldn't shake it. The facts were the facts. They would not only get a conviction but also me reelected.

"And Dilbert had one of the jugs of High Bridge Limestone Water at his house, which could've contained more of the calcium hydroxide in a liquid form that wasn't combined with water. Slowly killing him..." Scott trailed off as though he had a thought before he said, "I will run over to Dilbert's house and get the water. Then I'll run on by Tom Geary's lab to drop it off. He left a message today saying the photos and the note were ready to be picked up."

"Did he say anything else?" I'd started the Wagoneer and pulled out of the parking lot to head to High Bridge Limestone Water Company, which was just about a mile as the crow flew.

"He said the photos were dated back to the fifties or sixties. So I imagine whoever was in the photo is probably dead now." By Scott's tone, I could tell he didn't think the photos had anything to do with Dilbert's murder.

I'd tried to teach Scott the way Poppa had taught me to think—leave no stone unturned.

"What if the woman in the photo is somehow related to Jake?" I asked, knowing I would have to show Jake the photo. "I know we took photos of the evidence, and I want you to text me the copy of the photo."

"You are going to show Jake a photo of a nude woman?" Scott asked.

"Yes. I'm going to exhaust all possibilities that the woman is not in any way related to him. And if she is, then we have a motive." My hands gripped the wheel as I took a right turn down into what initially looked like a rock quarry.

I pulled my cruiser slowly down the gravel road, the crunch of stones beneath the tires a steady rhythm against the quiet. Dust rose around me like a tan fog, and my gaze flitted to the imposing silhouettes of the two mountains that cradled the landscape. Their sheer cliffs cast long shadows, swaddling the area in a twilight gloom even at this midday hour.

At the road's end, a parking lot crammed with tour buses and cars sprawled out before me. This was the face of the High Bridge Limestone Water Company, tucked away inside the mouth of a sprawling cave. The cavernous entrance loomed like an open maw, inviting and intimidating all at once.

A gust of chilled air hit me as I stepped out of the car, wrapping around me like a cool shroud. The cave's mouth beckoned me forward, its internal temperature always steady at 58 degrees, no matter the weather outside. I steeled myself and moved toward the darkness, the crisp air nipping at my skin.

Inside, my eyes needed a moment to adjust to the dim light, but as they did, the water plant's sprawling infrastructure unfolded before me. A group was gathering for a tour, and I slipped in, blending with the assortment of tourists.

A bright-eyed tour guide started to talk, gesturing enthusiastically to the towering stalactites and stalagmites. "There are thirty-two open acres in this cave," she began, her voice echoing off the rock walls. "The High Bridge spring water is produced right here, in the 5.3 miles of drivable corridors spread through this facility, a network of veins one hundred thirty feet underground."

An awed murmur ran through the group, punctuated by a raised hand. "How tall are the ceilings?" a tourist asked.

"Thirty feet," the guide replied, a proud smile tugging at her lips. She proceeded to point at the gushing streams. "Every day, about sixty thousand gallons of water flow through here. We only bottle about a third of that, but due to the size of our aquifer, the supply never stops."

"Is that why the water tastes so different?" another tourist inquired.

"Indeed." The guide nodded. "It's the limestone! It naturally filters the water, giving it its unique taste."

With the explanation still ringing in my ears, I followed the group into the bottling line. Amid the orchestrated chaos of the production line, a familiar figure stood out. There he was, Jake, wearing a hard hat and carrying a clipboard in his hand. He was inspecting the line of water bottles with a studious furrow to his brow, oblivious to the tour group watching him.

As I watched him work, my mind started to churn with questions, thoughts, and theories. The scent of damp earth filled the cavernous facility, a stark contrast to the chilled sterility of the bottling line. This was the start, a new trail to follow, and I knew it led me to a deeper place than just the recesses of this cave.

The whirring hum of machinery filled the cavern, punctuated by the conveyor belt rhythmically moving along. Amid this industrial symphony, my eyes never left Jake. Eventually, his gaze rose from his clipboard and swept over the group of tourists. His own eyes momentarily passed over me before they snapped back, recognition flickering within them.

The overhead lighting bathed him in an ethereal glow, highlighting the dust particles dancing around his hard hat. A small frown tugged at his features, crinkling the space between his eyebrows as he squinted, trying to place me.

Then his expression cleared, and I watched as the corners of his mouth curved into a slight smile. Of course, he recognized me as Sheriff Lowry from the softball field.

Slowly, he began to proceed toward me. With each stride, his hard hat bobbed lightly. His steel-toed boots crunched on the cave floor, the sound barely audible over the constant hum of the machinery. His dark-blue coveralls, marked with the company logo, were smeared with limestone dust, bearing the evidence of a hard day's work.

As he approached, I noticed the subtle changes in his demeanor. The familiar stoop of his shoulders straightened, and that furrow in his brow relaxed. His eyes, a curious mix of green and gold like the landscape outside, were brighter, more alive.

"Sheriff?" he called, his voice blending with the mechanical drone of the bottling line. The sound echoed off the damp cave walls, bouncing back to us. The smile on his face broadened as he reached me, extending a gloved hand in greeting.

In that moment, I was acutely aware of the chill of the cave, the constant rush of the underground spring, and the pulsating hum of the machinery. This unexpected encounter, amidst the unique blend of nature and industry, marked the beginning of what felt like a significant chapter in my investigation.

"Jake," I began, my smile receding into a more serious expression. "I need to talk to you about something."

His brow furrowed again slightly at my tone, but his welcoming smile remained in place. "Sure, Sheriff. What's up?"

"It's about Dilbert Thistle." I glanced around at the group of tourists, their eyes wide with fascination as they observed the bustling operations of the bottling line. "It's... not a conversation for here."

Now that smile faded, replaced by a puzzled look. "Dilbert?" he asked, his voice dropping a few notches. "The man from the drywall plant? The guy whose position I took on the softball team?"

"Yes." I nodded, my gaze steady on him. "I'd rather discuss it privately, if you don't mind."

For a moment, he was silent, his forehead creasing as he digested the information. Then, with a brisk nod, he led me away from the production line and the tourists' curious gazes.

We navigated through a maze of drivable corridors, the sound of machinery slowly dimming until a hushed whisper replaced it. The cool, damp air of the cave gradually yielded to the slightly warmer and drier air of a nearby passage.

Jake stopped in front of a nondescript metal door marked with a simple placard: Employee Room. He swiped a card through the reader, and the door clicked open.

Inside, the room was sparsely furnished. A wooden table sat in the middle, surrounded by a couple of chairs. Fluorescent lights flickered on the ceiling, casting a harsh white light that contrasted with the warm ambient glow of the cave.

As we stepped in, he removed his hard hat, revealing his tousled hair, and set his clipboard on the table. "I... I have no idea what this is about, Sheriff," he admitted, concern etching lines into his forehead. "But please, sit. Let's talk."

With that invitation, I knew I was on the precipice of something significant. The chill from the cave hadn't quite left my skin, but a different kind of chill was now setting in— one brought on by the serious conversation we were about to have.

"We have reason to believe Dilbert was murdered by injected calcium hydroxide."

I watched Jake's body language. It appeared as though the wind went right on out of his body as his shoulders slumped. "I also have witnesses that said you and Dilbert were seen at Kim's Restaurant in what looked like an argument."

"Hold up one second." He held his hands in front of him. "He came to me. He came in here to get the large bottle of water for his house, and out of fairness, I told him about how the softball team was looking to put me on.

He asked me to lunch because he said he needed something to be stored and wanted me to bring whatever that was here. I told him at the restaurant I couldn't just store things here. It's not a storage unit, and I told him that. He got mad and said that no one could ever find it. I guess a big cave like this is good for hiding something you never want to see the light of day, but I wanted no part of that, and he got mad."

"Do you know what he wanted to store?" I asked as my phone chirped with the text that I knew was the photo.

"I have no clue, but he didn't want to take no for an answer, so I flat-out told him no, and that was it." He eyeballed me as I brought up the text of the photo of the woman.

"Do you know this woman?" I asked and used my fingers to blow up the photo only to show her face.

He looked at it and immediately denied knowing who she was.

"Should I?" he asked.

"I'm asking the questions here." I knew by how he reacted that he was telling the truth. But I continued, "Were you at the fairgrounds bar the night before the game where Bill Johnson told Dilbert he was replacing him in his position with you?"

"I was there but not when that conversation took place," he said. "Are you asking for an alibi? Do I need to call a lawyer?"

"You only need a lawyer if you are guilty of something," I told him and put the phone back in my pocket. "Are you guilty of something?"

"Guilty of being a damn good softball player. That's it. As for where I was, I took my daughters on the carnival rides, and we went home. That's that," he said right as the door opened.

He looked up, and I turned to see who stood there.

After all, this was the employee room.

"Anja has started the Monday morning meeting. She's looking for your report." The woman took in my uniform and gave a half-hearted smile. I could only imagine what she was thinking about why I was there.

"I've got to go." He popped his hard hat back on his head. "I have no way of knowing what Dilbert wanted stored here or who that lady is. But I do know one thing—I didn't have anything to do with his murder. Can I go to my meeting now?"

"Here's my card." I pulled it out of my pocket. "If you remember anything, and I mean the slightest bit of information that brings up Dilbert, no matter how small, I want you to call me."

He took the card and stuck it underneath the clipboard's clip, though I figured he wouldn't use it. For now, I had to wait for the toxicology report on the water jug Scott was taking to the lab to see if it had high levels of calcium hydroxide before I questioned Jake again.

CHAPTER TWENTY-ONE

The winding road back to Cottonwood and the sheriff's department seemed to stretch on forever as I navigated my Jeep away from the limestone plant. The surrounding trees stood silent and immovable, towering guardians cloaked in emerald, bearing silent witness to the riddles swirling in my mind.

The back of my brain held a relentless itch, like the echo of a song with lyrics you couldn't remember. That itch came from Jake, Dilbert, and the unknown woman in the photo, their images tangling together in a confounding puzzle.

The Wagoneer's hum under me made for a comforting and familiar presence as I threaded the needle between thought and reality. My fingers drummed on the steering wheel, my mind going a hundred miles an hour while the world outside moved in its usual languid southern rhythm.

Jake's denial that he knew the woman was convincing, yet his public altercation with Dilbert in Kim's Restaurant kept him squarely in my sights. Then there were Bill and Georgina, both with solid alibis but deeply woven into the fabric of this mystery.

The situation was as layered and complex as the water plant's limestone caverns—the very place where Jake worked and where a lethal dose of calcium hydroxide, potentially originating from there, had claimed Dilbert's life. My gut twisted at the thought. If the toxicology report confirmed my suspicions, my path would lead me back to Jake.

But it was the unknown woman that nagged at me. Her face was a cipher, a tantalizing piece of this puzzle that I was determined to slot into place. And what of the mysterious object Dilbert wanted to hide in the labyrinthine cave?

I cast a glance at the road through the Jeep's dusty windshield.

This was Cottonwood, my town, my responsibility. The unspoken implications of a murder unsolved hung heavy in the air. This case was not only about justice for Dilbert but also my own position. The clock was ticking, the grains of sand were slipping through the hourglass, and the urgency wasn't lost on me.

I tightened my grip on the steering wheel, feeling a determined set to my jaw. Time was of the essence, and I had a murder to solve. The peace of the drive contrasted sharply with the storm brewing in my mind. This brief tranquility was a perfect prelude to the upcoming tempest. This mystery had sunk its claws into me, and I wasn't about to let it go. One thing was certain—I was going to find Dilbert's killer, no matter where the path led.

My stomach rumbled to life as soon as I got out of the Jeep. The aroma of fried food smelled so good that I decided to walk around the building and into Cowboy's Catfish to get lunch before I went into the office.

The diner was packed. When I opened the door, all eyes were on me.

The chairs groaned when I didn't make eye contact with anyone and instead made a beeline to the counter, since everyone shifted in their seats to watch me walk.

"Now that you've got everyone's attention," Bartlby Fry said with a smirk, "would you like the Monday special?"

He didn't have to tell me the special. Every Monday, it was the fried catfish dinner with hush puppies.

"I'd love to have that," I confirmed just before I felt someone come up behind me. "I wondered how long it was going to take until you showed up."

I turned around and found Edna Easterly so close that the feather in her fedora tickled the tip of my nose.

"How did you know it was me?" she asked, her notebook and pen at the ready.

"I saw you out of the corner of my eye when I came in, and I knew you wouldn't let this opportunity just go on by, Edna." I sighed and took a step back from her.

"Do you want to give a statement about Dilbert Thistle?" she asked with a curious look. "I have a statement from Taven Tidwell I'm going to post in tomorrow's paper, and I would like to offer you an opportunity for a rebuttal. It's fair journalism."

I turned to fully face Edna, a small smile pulling at my lips. "Sure, Edna. I'd like to make a statement." I took a deep breath, pausing a moment for effect. Every eye in the diner was on me, every ear tuned in to what I was about to say.

"Dilbert Thistle's death is a tragedy that has affected all of us in Cottonwood. His untimely departure is a painful reminder of the fragility of life and the need for justice. I want to assure everyone that my team and I are working diligently and tirelessly to uncover the truth behind Dilbert's demise. And we will leave no stone unturned until we do." I scanned the room as I spoke, meeting the eyes of the townsfolk. It was important to reassure them that I was in control, that I was on their side.

"As for Taven Tidwell's statement," I continued, my voice steady and firm, "I'm focused on my job, which is serving the people of Cottonwood, ensuring your safety, and upholding the law. Every moment I spend serving this town is a moment I dedicate to preserving the peace we so dearly value and solving the mysteries that threaten it. Every citizen deserves nothing less than my complete commitment, and that's what I pledge."

I took a pause, letting my words sink in. "These challenging times demand focus and resilience, not distractions or petty politics. So let's not lose sight of what truly matters—justice for Dilbert and the continued peace and security of Cottonwood. I'm here to do my job, to serve and protect, and that's exactly what I'll continue to do, no matter what anyone says or does to undermine that. Because at the end of the day, actions speak louder than words."

As I finished, a profound silence fell over the diner. I met Edna's wide-eyed gaze then turned back to Bartlby. "Now, how about that catfish dinner?"

The diner's normal hum of conversation resumed, but I knew my words had made an impact, just as I intended.

"Here you go," he said with a huge smile, handing me a Styrofoam box. "I even added a few extra hush puppies." He winked.

Without bothering to look behind me, I took the box and headed straight back into the office.

The scent of fried catfish clung to my uniform as I stepped into the Cottonwood Sheriff's Department. The single-room office was the pulse point of our quiet town—a hub of information, order, and peacekeeping. One open cell, its bars cold and unyielding, sat vacant in the corner, a stern reminder of the order we upheld.

The room was modest, a bit worn around the edges, but it was ours, complete with creaking wooden floorboards, a large oak desk strewn with case files and coffee mugs, and a board wall showcasing our town map and ongoing cases.

Scott, my deputy, was standing in front of that board, studying the pieces of information pinned haphazardly across its surface. The most prominent among them was the unidentified woman's photograph from the 1950s or 60s. She was haunting in her anonymity.

"What do we have?" I asked, setting my hat on the rack and moving to join him. The smell of the catfish from my lunch wafted off me, creating an oddly comforting aura in the stark seriousness of the office.

Scott sighed, rubbing the back of his neck as he looked at the evidence. "No hits on the photo. Google couldn't find anything." His voice was tinged with frustration. The anonymity of the woman in the picture was a road-block we hadn't anticipated.

We stood there for a moment, silently taking in the assortment of infor-mation, photos, and notes. Each piece felt like a jigsaw that wouldn't fit, a cipher we couldn't crack. Calcium hydroxide as the murder weapon, the public argument at Kim's Restaurant, the mysterious woman in the photo—it all seemed disparate, random.

"We're missing something," I said. It was more a statement than a question.

Scott nodded, the crease between his brows deepening. "Everything just falls flat, Kenni."

The weight of the unsolved case hung in the air, the unspoken challenge echoing off the four walls of our little department. Dilbert's face seemed to stare back at us from the board in a silent plea for justice. As the minutes ticked by, they reminded me of how each moment mattered, bringing us closer to answers or to a dead end. All we could do was keep digging, keep pushing, until the truth unveiled itself.

"Nothing back from the jug of water you took to the lab?" I asked, hoping we'd at least have that back soon.

"No." He shook his head. "Even Dilbert's realtor said he never once mentioned where he got the down payment for the house, but it was all cash."

"Cash is so hard to trace too," I noted.

My phone chirped with a text. It was from Mama. She'd gone to get Duke from Jolee and taken him to the vet, where they found nothing wrong with him.

I knew exactly what was wrong.

Poppa.

Right now, I could use Poppa too. His ability to find out more clues than I could had proven to be invaluable. He was able to ghost himself into places and learn information, which helped me with many cases over the past few years. And now that he wasn't here, well...

The timing couldn't be worse. Dilbert's murder really had me stumped. That wasn't easy to do.

"Scott, Bernice Asrenner's dog is on the loose," Betty said, giving him the order to leave the office and help Bernice get her dog.

"You good?" he asked.

"I'm fine. You go. You can do the daily rounds then go home for the day. If I think of something or hear anything, I'll give you a holler," I said to him. Then I stopped him right before he went out the door. "Scott, thank you. You're doing great work."

He didn't say a word. He only nodded, and that was enough for me.

"Kenni bug," Betty called out, breaking the silence in the room.

I looked over at her.

She was peering at me over the top of her silver-rimmed glasses, a hint of mischief twinkling in her pale-blue eyes.

"What did you say?" I asked. Hearing her use Poppa's nickname for me was new.

"Why don't you go home and get some rest?" she suggested, her voice as soothing as a lullaby. "Call your girlfriends over, order some pizzas, let your hair down a bit."

I blinked at her, slightly taken aback by the unexpected advice. It sounded just like my Poppa, only it came from Betty. But as she held my gaze, her expression shifted to one of pure sincerity.

"You've been running on empty, Kenni," she continued, her eyes flicking to the now-quiet dispatch radio and then back to me. "Distance can offer a clearer perspective. You might just stumble upon something you overlooked before."

I considered her words, my gaze drifting back to the neatly organized files on my desk. Was I really that transparent? But when I looked at the photo and the note and packed them up in my police bag, I had to admit she had a point. I had been cooped up in my thoughts for too long, spinning my wheels on a case that refused to give up its secrets.

I let out a long sigh and nodded, acquiescing to her wisdom. "You know, that doesn't sound half-bad, Betty. Maybe a change of scenery will do me some good."

Her lips curled into a knowing smile. "Good. I took the liberty of calling Tibbie and Jolee. They're already at your place, ready for a girls' night."

I stood there too stunned to react, mouth slightly open. That woman was full of surprises. "Betty…" I began, not entirely sure what to say.

Betty waved me off, her eyes returning to her paperwork. "Go on, Kenni bug. Your friends are waiting, and so are the answers you've been looking for. Don't come in early. It's Scott's day to get here in the morning. Take your time. It'll all be here when you come in."

I hesitated for a moment when she repeated my nickname.

"Thanks, Betty." I grabbed my bag. "You know where to find me."

By the time I arrived home, the hot afternoon sun was still casting long shadows around the yard. Duke was thrilled to see me, his tail wagging a mile a minute.

He was a bit peppier than when I'd seen him last.

After a quick change into more comfortable clothes and a refreshing glass of sweet iced tea, I decided to take Duke out for an afternoon walk before Tibbie and Jolee came over.

We strolled along the familiar streets of Cottonwood, greeting the occasional neighbor with a wave or a quick hello. Our path eventually took us to the railroad tracks. The place was quieter now, different from the chaotic scene when Patty found Dilbert's body.

I gazed around, trying to see something we might've missed earlier, a clue that could shed light on the mystery, but nothing appeared out of the ordinary.

As Duke and I trudged back home, I felt an unsettled sensation in the pit of my stomach. The murder case was no longer just a professional responsibility; it had encroached into my personal space, disrupting the peace of my little town.

Once back home, I busied myself with some light housekeeping, my mind a whirlwind of wedding plans and murder theories. By the time the sun began its descent, casting an orange hue over Cottonwood, I felt the fatigue of the day seeping into my bones.

It wasn't long until Jolee and Tibbie arrived, pizzas in hand, that my day took a turn from the somber thoughts of murder investigations to the more delightful issue of wedding plans.

They were comfortably settled on the back porch by the time I joined them with napkins and drinks, their faces illuminated by the soft twinkling lights strung haphazardly above us, creating an enchanting starlight effect.

The aromas of melting cheese and tangy tomato sauce wafted through the night air. The comforting scent of pizza combining with the woodsy perfume of burning logs in the firepit was welcome, as was the experience of washing it down with a beer.

The summer evening had veered into a surprising chill, making the fire all the more appreciated, its warmth radiating outward and lending a comforting, cozy atmosphere to our little gathering.

Jolee, her laughter bubbling up like a brook, teasingly offered the overly spoiled Duke another piece of pizza crust. "Duke, you're turning into quite the little moocher," she said, her tone affectionate. The flickering firelight glowed in her eyes, mirroring her spirited demeanor.

"Kenni, you have so much to plan," Tibbie started, leaning forward with a look of earnest concern. "There's the wedding dress to choose—and I know you have your heart set on that boutique in Louisville. Then there's the cake tasting. Oh, and we need to finalize the photographer! And we haven't even touched upon the venue and the seating arrangements!"

A smile spread across my face as I listened to my friends. Their enthusiasm was not just for the wedding but also the love that Finn and I shared. Their excitement was infectious, sparking joy and a heightened sense of anticipation of the fun times ahead of me. Discussions, laughter, and friendly debates about the wedding details filled the night, each conversation thread knitting us closer together.

Yet even amidst the lively chatter and my friends' soothing presence, Dilbert Thistle's unsolved case loomed at the back of my mind. Despite the delightful diversion, I knew I couldn't fully immerse myself in the wedding plans until justice had been served.

Jolee seemed to sense my shift in mood, and she reached over to give my hand a comforting squeeze.

Time seemed to dance alongside the flames in our firepit, hours slipping away into the canvas of the star-studded night. Eventually, the girls departed, their echoing laughter and whispered promises to "help with everything" adding a beautiful undertone to the crisp evening air.

Alone, except for the reassuring presence of Duke curled at my feet, I found myself staring into the dwindling embers of the fire. The hush of the night seemed to mirror my quiet introspection. I absentmindedly scratched behind Duke's ears, and he leaned into my touch as my thoughts circling back to Dilbert's case.

I held onto the hope that the morning would bring fresh insights, a clear path to justice.

"Are you ready for bed?" I asked Duke.

He jumped to his feet and went straight to the screen door.

In a few short minutes, I'd washed my face, brushed my teeth, and slipped into my pajamas. Duke and I snuggled until I fell asleep, but I tossed and turned and awoke with thoughts of Dilbert Thistle all night long.

CHAPTER TWENTY-TWO

I glanced at the time on my phone, realizing that I had barely slept in my pursuit of justice. The investigation weighed heavily on my mind, the enigmatic note and absence of real answers on the photos fueling my determination to uncover the truth.

It seemed like my suspects—Georgina, Bill, and Jake—all had solid alibis that wouldn't crack even slightly, so the prosecutor couldn't move forward in arresting any of them.

The sun would rise soon, casting its warm light upon Cottonwood, where once again I would have to defend myself and the actions I'd taken in handling Dilbert's case to Taven Tidwell.

I lay in bed, knowing Duke was curled up at the foot. I closed my eyes, finding comfort in the familiar surroundings. The events of last night swirled in my mind, intertwining with memories of Poppa's wisdom and the love that filled my heart. In this small cottage on Free Row, I found solace, purpose, and the strength to face whatever challenges lay ahead.

Duke's ears popped up. He could hear anything going on outside that seemed unusual.

I reached across his body, slowly opened the small drawer in the bedside table, and took out my pistol and suppressor. Carefully, I lined up the silencer and screwed it on.

If someone was going to break into my house, knowing I was the sheriff, it was never a good thing. Everyone in Cottonwood knew where I lived, and Free Row wasn't without its fair share of gunshots going off in the night or, in this case, early morning.

I was in no mood for a show if I had to shoot someone, so I engaged my silencer.

With a subtle rattle, someone's keys slid into the lock of the kitchen door, and the noise resounded down the hall. I knew who it was before she opened the door.

"Kendrick Lowry! Are you still in the bed?" Mama called out from the kitchen. "Where's my Duke? Granny brought you some special treats!"

Duke's head shot up. This time, the word "treat" worked. He slid off the bed front legs first and used his back legs to push himself into a running start as he bolted out the bedroom door.

"You are going to be such a cute flower fur baby," I heard Mama gush as I put the gun back in the drawer. "Lordy be, Kendrick. What on earth are you doing?"

"I'm coming," I said, projecting my voice down the hall as I sat up on the edge of the bed.

I was not looking forward to today. The mayor had called me into his office and was going to ask me about all the details of the case. I knew Chance really well, and if I didn't have sufficient evidence for him to think I was moving the case along, he'd bring in the Kentucky Reserves to help out and then the Federal Bureau of Investigation, which was what Taven Tidwell had been suggesting on his social media streams.

"Damn Taven," I groaned and stepped into my sheriff's pants, spitting out even more curse words as I got my shirt over my head and used the rubber band to pull all my hair back into a ponytail.

"Honey," Mama said to me at the door, "do you have any Preparation H? You need a little dab. It'll take the puff right on out from underneath your eyes. Imagine what it does to the undercarriage region. It'll do that to your eyes."

Mama got really close to me, and her beady little eyes zeroed in on my dark bags.

"I'm fine, Mama." I shook my head and pushed past her. "Thank you for taking Duke to the vet yesterday. He seems a lot better."

"She said nothing was wrong with him, as far as she could tell. I went home and found me some recipes online for dog treats. This one here is guaranteed to perk up any doggy," Mama said, following me down the hall. "And I've also got some lipstick the girl down at the beauty counter said would perk up any face. I'm thinking you need a little perkin'."

Mama unsnapped the top of the bag dangling from her elbow and dug down deep.

"That poor girl probably could've taken her own advice because she'd been hit a time or two with the ugly stick, but she was real nice." Mama's eyes held concern for the beauty consultant as she stuck the tube of lipstick in my face. "Bless her heart. I buy makeup from her just to make her feel good."

"I'm sure she feels just fine, Mama," I said, knowing she had a hard time understanding that most people didn't share her feelings. "But I'll take your word for it."

Mama helped herself to a cup of freshly brewed coffee that'd been brewed on the timer while I opened the lipstick. Without looking, I applied it across my bottom lip, pressed my lips together, and gave them a good roll between my teeth. The quicker I could get this over with, the faster she'd leave, at which point I could wipe this junk off.

"What on earth?" Mama's eyes grew, and she nearly spat out the sip of hot coffee she'd taken before she'd turned around. "Oh my goodness. I gave you the stick I picked up for Ruby."

Letting go of a low growl, I ran into the family room, where a mirror hung on the wall just above the table where I stuck my keys and sheriff's bag so I could grab them on my way out the door.

"My gosh, Mama." I used the back of my hand to wipe the lipstick clear across my face and along my arm. "This stuff is thick as cement, and I look like a clown."

"Taven might call you Sheriff Clown Kenni." Mama snickered and stood behind me. "I know it's not funny, but it is. Here."

"You aren't going to do this to me a second time," I said. This time, I looked at the rolled-up lipstick before applying a very faint shade of pink that didn't look half bad.

"What's this?" Mama stuck her big nosy hand into my bag and pulled out those old photos Tom had me pick up last night.

"Mama, that's all evidence." I shook my head and grabbed the edge of the photo to get her grubby hands off of it.

"Evidence?" Mama was very interested in the photo and didn't let go, even when I tugged a little harder to get it back. "What on earth does Cybil Childress have to do with your investigation?"

"Who?" I should've known Mama knew who was in the photo.

"Well, I'll be corn-swoggled!" Poppa's familiar voice caught my ear, as did a dancing Duke.

"Look at that. That internet was right about them treats." Mama smacked my arm, and we both looked in astonishment. She was looking at Duke, and I was looking at Poppa, wondering where he'd been. "Kenni, do you think I should open up a dog bakery and make some of them biscuits?"

"No, Mama. Who is Cybil Childress?" I asked.

"I knew I recognized that woman, but she was always so busy doing the books down at the bank that I rarely saw her. The only time she crawled out of the basement of the bank was when she snuck into Junior Burton's car." Poppa and Mama were talking at the same time.

"Focus on me, Kenni." Mama meant for me to look at her and not past her to where Poppa was standing.

They both continued to talk, confusing me.

"It was no secret she and Junior were having that affair for all of them years. There were rumors about photos and Vernon catching them in the act…" Poppa trailed off.

"And?" I asked him.

"Poor Vernon. I don't think he ever got over it, but no one talked about it. When his mama got ill, he stuck her in a nursing home and never went to see her." Mama sighed. "You aren't going to put in me that old nursing home, are you?"

"Are you cheating on Daddy and lying on a bear skin rug?" I asked Mama.

"Don't I wish I were that exciting," she teased. "Now, what does this photo of Cybil Childress have to do with your investigation? She's been dead for years."

"Dilbert Thistle couldn't get a loan but only one way. If those photos got leaked and Vernon Bishop never got over his mama's indiscretions, well, I guess that would be somethin'." Poppa smacked his hands together. "Look at the killer's note and compare it to the scribble Vernon gave you."

Mama was yammering on, but it was only background noise as I pulled out the killer's note Tom had given me with the nude photo. I also took out my little notebook. I'd stuck Vernon's scribble, which included Dilbert's account number, in there.

Poppa ghosted over and stood next to me. We both took in each note.

At the same time, we said, "Vernon Bishop."

CHAPTER TWENTY-THREE

I kissed Mama on the cheek and grabbed the bag and keys.

"Mama, can you watch Duke until the doctor calls with the results of those blood tests you had her take?" I said.

She stammered a few moans, but I cut her off.

"Thank you. You're going to be a wonderful granny to my children," I replied.

That perked her right up.

"Yes I am, and I'm a good fur grammy too," I heard her say when I got out the door.

"Where have you been?" I asked my ghost poppa. "I'm not married yet."

"I was giving you some thinking time and wondering how you would do without me around." He'd already wisped into the truck before I could get the driver's-side door open.

As I eased the old Jeep Wagoneer onto Free Row, the sun beamed overhead, casting a vibrant glow across the small, joyful town of Cottonwood. Cottonwood was the kind of town where everyone knew one another and their business; it thrummed with a neighborly charm that was both frustrating and endearing. Ghost Poppa sat in the passenger seat, a wisp of his former self, his gaze intent on the road ahead.

I reached underneath my seat and grabbed the old beacon siren. I glanced over at Poppa, who gave me a slight nod before I licked the suction cup and slapped it on top of the roof. Then I pushed the gas pedal with my foot and slid my finger down the beacon to turn on the old siren.

"Kenni," Poppa said, his voice echoing with an ethereal quality. "Remember when we used to drive down this road when you were little? And all those times I told you about the deeds of little boys…"

"Little boys who would do anything to protect their family's legacy, even if it was tainted?" I finished for him, tightening my grip on the steering wheel. His remark made me think about Vernon, about the truth that was coming to light.

Poppa nodded solemnly. "Yes, and how true it is here in the South. More so than anywhere else, I reckon."

As we moved toward North Main Street, the rhythm of Cottonwood thrummed around us. Storefronts, painted in a rainbow of colors, lined the bustling street. The proprietors of Ruby's Antiques, Ben's Diner, White's Jewelry, Cowboy's Catfish, and others were out, waving as I drove by. A gaggle of children ran alongside the road, their high-pitched laughter mingling with the hum of the town. I was proud to be sheriff, and soon I'd have the killer I sought cuffed in the backseat.

The Wagoneer, with its distinctive old beacon siren on the roof, commanded respect, and cars moved to the side as we headed straight for the bank. It was from there that I knew Vernon Bishop would be emerging, his morning meeting ending and a big family vacation waiting.

Poppa's words played in my mind, drawing me back to our conversation about Vernon and Cybil Childress. The images from the past kept burning at the edges of my thoughts. I flashed back to the note from Dilbert that said, "*Beware the tracks of fate, for they hold the secrets of the fallen. Seek the signs where iron meets the earth, and the truth shall be revealed but not by you*"—the time I served Dr. Camille Shively a warrant and saw Vernon in her office— and the maps that led me to the drywall plant where Dilbert had buried photos as he blackmailed and bribed Vernon.

As we pulled up in front of the bank, I spotted Vernon walking to his car.

"Poppa," I whispered, as if he could physically hear me, "I think Dilbert had something on Vernon. Something that forced Vernon to give him that loan."

"Little boys and their secrets, huh?" Poppa chuckled, a deep ghostly sound that was more comforting than it should have been.

With my heart pounding, I pulled the walkie-talkie off my shoulder and called for backup. "Betty, I need you to get Scott Lee over to the bank, ASAP."

"Is there a robbery?" she replied when she clicked back.

"No. Vernon Baxter killed Dilbert Thistle."

The only confirmation my words got was a crackle, and again, I tightened my grip on the steering wheel, my eyes locked on Vernon. I drove my Jeep around the bank's parking lot, cutting off Vernon's escape.

As I skidded to a stop, the tires squealing against the hot tarmac, I threw the gear into park. The dust stirred up by our abrupt halt hung in the air around us like a suspenseful fog, a contrast to the cheeriness of the sunny day.

Vernon looked up, startled, his face pale as he recognized me. Just then, I knew we were on the precipice of revealing a secret that had long been buried in the heart of Cottonwood.

"Vernon Bishop," I murmured, taking a deep breath, "it's time to pay for what you've done."

A flicker of fear danced across Vernon's face as he stared at the beacon atop my old Wagoneer. The wailing siren blared through the sunbaked streets of Cottonwood, casting a heavy silence over the usually bustling town. Store owners paused, peeking out from their businesses, their faces twisted with a mix of curiosity and concern.

"Stay in the car, Vernon," I ordered as I stepped out of the Jeep, my voice loud and clear, slicing through the silence that had descended. I squinted under the blinding sun, my sheriff badge glinting and my heart pounding against my rib cage. Ghost Poppa's form remained seated in the car, his gaze riveted to Vernon.

"Kenni, take care," Poppa said, his concern clear despite his spectral condition.

But I didn't have time to respond.

Ignoring the nerves prickling at the base of my spine, I walked toward Vernon, pulling the brim of my hat down to shield my eyes. His face had turned an odd shade of white, contrasting with the warm hues of the rustic town that served as our backdrop.

Within moments, I heard the familiar growl of Deputy Scott Lee's cruiser. It slid to a halt next to my Jeep, kicking up a swirl of dust that danced under the bright sunrays, much like the local kids at the annual county fair.

He joined me, his boots crunching on the gravel, echoing the tension in the air.

"What's the situation, Sheriff?" he asked, his deep voice bouncing around the now-silent street.

I glanced at Vernon, his eyes darting between Scott and me then back to the Jeep. The afternoon sun turned his car's windows into mirrors, reflecting the image of the silent, watchful town.

"We're about to find out," I replied. I approached Vernon's Jeep, my shadow stretching over him and forming a silhouette against the brightness of the day.

My walkie-talkie crackled to life, and Betty's voice broke the intense silence. "Scott, Sheriff, be advised that additional backup is en route."

As the reality of the situation closed in on Vernon, I noticed him subtly reaching for something beneath his seat. My heart pounded in my ears, the dull throb matching Cottonwood's heartbeat. The town seemed to hold its breath as the story was about to take a crucial turn.

"Vernon," I warned, my hand inching toward the holster at my hip, "don't do anything you'd regret."

Poppa's spectral form appeared beside me, his transparent hand reaching out in a protective gesture. "Kenni, remember, little boys in the South will do anything to protect their legacy."

Vernon's gaze flickered to where Poppa stood, his eyes filled with a strange confusion. He couldn't see Poppa, of course, but it was as if he sensed the spectral presence. The words hung heavy between us, a bridge connecting the past with the unraveling present.

And just like that, the sunny day in Cottonwood seemed clouded by secrets threatening to explode under the summer sun. The charming streets of our town were poised on the brink of a revelation that could change everything. As the silence of the standoff stretched between us, the town continued to hold its breath, waiting for the secrets to be unearthed.

I watched as Vernon slowly withdrew his hand from beneath his seat. He was holding not a weapon but a weathered photograph. It was an image of his wife, Lynn, her sun-kissed hair cascading down her shoulders, and his three children, their eyes full of youthful innocence. A perfect portrait of a family unaware of the turmoil brewing beneath the surface.

As he looked at the picture, his gaze held a softness, contrasting with the harsh truth he was about to unveil. "Dilbert... he figured it out," he said in a trembling voice , breaking the eerie silence that hung in the air.

I felt a tug at my heart, but I had to maintain my professionalism.

"Figured what out, Vernon?" I asked, my voice steady despite the emotions swirling within me.

"The woman in the photo, the one you found... It was my mother, Cybil Childress." His voice barely rose above a whisper, yet it echoed loudly in the stillness, sending shock waves through my system. But I didn't let my surprise show.

"And then?" I pushed, my tone clinical, matching Scott's stoic demeanor as he stood beside me.

"When I told Dilbert he didn't qualify for a loan, he threatened me... with those photographs." His grip on the family picture tightened. "He wouldn't give them back, even after I pulled some strings, even after I gave him the down payment. He wouldn't stop."

I took a step closer, and the gravel crunched under my boots. "And then you took matters into your own hands?"

Vernon nodded, a single tear slipping down his cheek. "I waited by the fairgrounds... offered him a ride home. That's when I injected him with the poison I'd stolen from Camille's office." The confession hung heavy in the air.

"And the tracks?" Scott's voice echoed the question in my mind. "The inhaler we found at the tracks was yours, too, right?"

The coughing fit Vernon had when he told me he'd swallowed wrong was a lie. He'd needed his inhaler. My heart sank for not only Lynn but the three girls.

Vernon nodded and then frowned.

"I left him there... hoping a train would come by. Make it look like he stumbled..." Vernon trailed off. The echo of his confession continued to hang in the atmosphere, seeping into the very fabric of our sunny small town. "I had to take a few puffs of my inhaler because he was so heavy it knocked the wind out of me. I didn't realize I'd dropped it until it was too late."

I took a deep breath, wrestling with the wave of emotions threatening to break my professional demeanor. This was a man I'd known, a man whose children I watched grow up. A man who let fear and the weight of a hidden past drive him to the unthinkable.

The moment was profound, steeped in raw emotion and marred by a tragedy that reached far beyond Dilbert's demise. Cottonwood would never be the same. Our bright, charming town had been doused with a dark reality, a secret that had remained buried for far too long.

But this profession had no room for personal feelings. And as the sheriff, I had a duty to perform. Looking into the teary eyes of a shattered man, I reached for my handcuffs. It was time to uphold the law, no matter how painful the truth.

"Vernon Bishop, you're under arrest for the murder of Dilbert Thistle," I declared, my voice resolute, echoing through the silent street of our once-blissful town.

Scott ran past me and, quicker than a whip, got Vernon's hands behind his back and in cuffs before I could sputter off the rest of his rights.

"And there you have it, folks," I heard Taven say from the sidewalk. "Taven Tidwell and Deputy Scott Lee will bring this town to justice."

"Scott Lee?" I gasped and, without thinking, looked at Taven.

"Oh, he hasn't told you yet?" Taven smiled and went back to looking into the camera on his phone. "You heard it here first, folks. Scott Lee is going to run as my deputy. He, too, is tired of what's going on in the Cottonwood sheriff's office. It's time for a change. A Tidwell change."

I felt the words crash into me like a wave. Scott Lee? My deputy, my confidant, the only other pair of hands I had in maintaining law and order in this quaint town, was about to stand against me?

Taven's taunting voice trailed off in my mind, but his words had left a searing imprint. I was frozen, staring at Taven's smug face then at Scott. His gaze was at the ground, his silence confirming the validity of Taven's claim.

In an instant, it was as if Cottonwood, with its sunlit streets and bustling downtown, had shrunk. The warmth of the sun seemed colder, the light harsher. But I had to maintain my composure. No matter how I felt inside, I was still Sheriff Kenni Lowry, and I had a duty to perform.

Gritting my teeth, I straightened up, pushing the whirlwind of emotions into the furthest corner of my mind. "Scott, please take Vernon to the station. I'll meet you there."

Scott merely nodded, his eyes never meeting mine, as he led Vernon away.

I watched them walk away, Scott's betrayal seeping into me, stinging more than Vernon's confession. But more was at stake here, and I couldn't afford to let personal emotions get in the way of justice.

I took a deep breath, smoothing down the imaginary wrinkles on my uniform. Then I turned and proceeded back to the jeep. I paused before I climbed in, glancing back at the town I had sworn to protect. It wasn't just about Vernon or Scott or even Taven. It was about Cottonwood and the people who called it home.

As the engine roared to life, I took one last look at the lively town, a kaleidoscope of colors under the sun. But now, shadows of doubt were creeping into its corners. The coming days would be a test for all of us. And I, Kenni Lowry, was at the helm of it.

Gripping the steering wheel tighter, I pulled out of the parking lot, leaving behind a storm of uncertainty. There was much to do, much to uncover, and the future of Cottonwood hung in the balance. As the dust rose in my wake, I couldn't shake off a gnawing feeling: the storm was just beginning. And as I drove off into the distance, the siren's wail rang through the air, a grim herald of the tumult that lay ahead.

I did know one thing. I still had Poppa and Finn by my side.

"I guess you've got to get hitched before you get rid of me." Poppa's voice was just a whisper, but the comfort in it lay over me like a warm protective blanket that I knew I wouldn't take for granted while I had it.

For the next few months, everything in my world would be easy. With

Poppa beside me, I was ready to take on Taven Tidwell, and I wouldn't go down without a fight.

THE END

IF YOU ENJOYED READING this book as much as I enjoyed writing it then be sure to return to the Amazon page and leave a review.

Go to Tonyakappes.com for a full reading order of my novels and while there join my newsletter. You can also find links to Facebook, Instagram and Goodreads.

BOOKS BY TONYA
SOUTHERN HOSPITALITY WITH A SMIDGEN OF HOMICIDE

Camper & Criminals Cozy Mystery Series

All is good in the camper-hood until a dead body shows up in the woods.

BEACHES, BUNGALOWS, AND BURGLARIES
DESERTS, DRIVING, & DERELICTS
FORESTS, FISHING, & FORGERY
CHRISTMAS, CRIMINALS, AND CAMPERS
MOTORHOMES, MAPS, & MURDER
CANYONS, CARAVANS, & CADAVERS
HITCHES, HIDEOUTS, & HOMICIDES
ASSAILANTS, ASPHALT & ALIBIS
VALLEYS, VEHICLES & VICTIMS
SUNSETS, SABBATICAL AND SCANDAL
TENTS, TRAILS AND TURMOIL
KICKBACKS, KAYAKS, AND KIDNAPPING
GEAR, GRILLS & GUNS
EGGNOG, EXTORTION, AND EVERGREEN
ROPES, RIDDLES, & ROBBERIES
PADDLERS, PROMISES & POISON
INSECTS, IVY, & INVESTIGATIONS
OUTDOORS, OARS, & OATH
WILDLIFE, WARRANTS, & WEAPONS
BLOSSOMS, BBQ, & BLACKMAIL
LANTERNS, LAKES, & LARCENY
JACKETS, JACK-O-LANTERN, & JUSTICE
SANTA, SUNRISES, & SUSPICIONS
VISTAS, VICES, & VALENTINES
ADVENTURE, ABDUCTION, & ARREST
RANGERS, RVS, & REVENGE

CAMPFIRES, COURAGE & CONVICTS
TRAPPING, TURKEY & THANKSGIVING
GIFTS, GLAMPING & GLOCKS
ZONING, ZEALOTS, & ZIPLINES
HAMMOCKS, HANDGUNS, & HEARSAY
QUESTIONS, QUARRELS, & QUANDARY
WITNESS, WOODS, & WEDDING
ELVES, EVERGREENS, & EVIDENCE
MOONLIGHT, MARSHMALLOWS, & MANSLAUGHTER
BONFIRE, BACKPACKS, & BRAWLS
FIREWORKS, FREEDOM, & FELONIES
AUTUMNS, AWINGS, & ARSON
SNOWCAPS, SKIING, & SABOTAGE

Killer Coffee Cozy Mystery Series

Welcome to the Bean Hive Coffee Shop where the gossip is just as hot as the coffee.

SCENE OF THE GRIND
MOCHA AND MURDER
FRESHLY GROUND MURDER
COLD BLOODED BREW
DECAFFEINATED SCANDAL
A KILLER LATTE
HOLIDAY ROAST MORTEM
DEAD TO THE LAST DROP
A CHARMING BLEND NOVELLA (CROSSOVER WITH MAGICAL
CURES MYSTERY)
FROTHY FOUL PLAY
SPOONFUL OF MURDER
BARISTA BUMP-OFF
CAPPUCCINO CRIMINAL
MACCHIATO MURDER
POUR-OVER PREDICAMENT

ICE COFFEE CORRUPTION
STEAMED SECRETS

Holiday Cozy Mystery Series

CELEBRATE GOOD CRIMES!

FOUR LEAF FELONY
MOTHER'S DAY MURDER
A HALLOWEEN HOMICIDE
NEW YEAR NUISANCE
CHOCOLATE BUNNY BETRAYAL
FOURTH OF JULY FORGERY
SANTA CLAUSE SURPRISE
APRIL FOOL'S ALIBI
COLUMBUS DAY CONUNDRUM
HOLLY HOMICIDE

Kenni Lowry Mystery Series

Mysteries so delicious it'll make your mouth water and leave you hankerin' for more.

FIXIN' TO DIE
SOUTHERN FRIED
AX TO GRIND
SIX FEET UNDER
DEAD AS A DOORNAIL
TANGLED UP IN TINSEL
DIGGIN' UP DIRT
BLOWIN' UP A MURDER
HEAVENS TO BRIBERY
GRAVE AS ALL GET-OUT
THICK AS THIEVES

About Tonya

Tonya has written over 100 novels, all of which have graced numerous bestseller lists, including the USA Today. *Best known for stories charged with emotion and humor and filled with flawed characters, her novels have garnered reader praise and glowing critical reviews. She lives with her husband and a very spoiled rescue cat named Ro. Tonya grew up in the small southern Kentucky town of Nicholasville. Now that her four boys are grown men, Tonya writes full-time in her camper she calls her SHAMPER (she-camper).*

Learn more about her be sure to check out her website tonyakappes.com. Find her on Facebook, Twitter, BookBub, and Instagram

Sign up to receive her newsletter, where you'll get free books, exclusive bonus content, and news of her releases and sales.

If you liked this book, please take a few minutes to leave a review now! Authors (Tonya included) really appreciate this, and it helps draw more readers to books they might like. Thanks!

Cover artist: Mariah Sinclair: The Cover Vault

Made in United States
Orlando, FL
18 March 2025

59602593R10305